Pearl River Mansion

www.mascotbooks.com

Pearl River Mansion

©2020 Richard Schwartz. All Rights Reserved. No part of this publication may
be reproduced, stored in a retrieval system or transmitted in any form by any
means electronic, mechanical, or photocopying, recording or otherwise without the
permission of the author.

This is a work of fiction. Names, characters, businesses, places, events, and
incidents are either the products of the author's imagination or used in a fictitious
manner. Any resemblance to actual persons, living or dead, or actual events is
purely coincidental.

For more information, please contact:
Mascot Books
620 Herndon Parkway #320
Herndon, VA 20170
info@mascotbooks.com

CPSIA Code: PRV0520A
Library of Congress Control Number: 2018913647
ISBN-13: 978-1-64307-158-9

Printed in the United States of America

PEARL
RIVER
MANSION

RICHARD SCHWARTZ

Books by Richard Schwartz in the
Underdog Detective Series

Two Dead and Counting...

Pearl River Mansion

CAST OF CHARACTERS

Jack Kendall .... *Private Investigator*

Stacy Young .... *Jack's Assistant*

Kevin Thomas .... *Jackson Police Captain*

Tyler Chandler .... *Joan Chandler's Son*

Sarah Chandler .... *Tyler Chandler's Wife*

Cody Chandler .... *Rachael's Twin Brother*

Rachael Chandler .... *Cody's Twin Sister*

Pamela Clarkston .... *Tyler's Supervisor*

Jacob Clarkston .... *Pamela's Son*

Joan Chandler .... *Tyler Chandler's Mother*

Mr. Gibbs .... *Caretaker: Pearl River Mansion*

Regina (Mr. Gibbs' sister) .... *Supervisor: Pearl River Mansion*

Dillia (Mr. Gibbs' Daughter) .... *Maid: Pearl River Mansion*

Jayden (Dillia's son) .... *Mr. Gibbs' Grandson*

Billy Ray Richards .... *Sarah Chandler's Father*

Leeann Richards .... *Sarah Chandler's Mother*

Tommy Lee Richards .... *Sarah Chandler's Uncle*

Emily Richards .... *Sarah Chandler's Sister*

A NOTE FROM THE AUTHOR

The most rewarding part of writing is hearing from my readers. After *Two Dead and Counting...* came out, the first novel in the Underdog Detective Series, people were eager to share their thoughts and feelings. I received all kinds of constructive and encouraging comments, but when people tell me that they took a sick day from work or that they ate lunch in their car just to keep reading, it humbles me and lets me know that I'm on the right track. We writers appreciate passionate readers! Thank you for reading my books.

Here's to books and quiet, stolen moments when we may escape, explore, learn, and be entertained.

Enjoy,

Richard Schwartz

CHAPTER ONE

As the sun slipped behind the trees along the overgrown banks of the Pearl River, Mr. Gibbs, known simply as "Mr. G" to most folks, kicked back in his chair to rest his tired, seventy-four-year-old bones and cast his fishing line one last time. It was a rare afternoon away from his duties, time special and cherished.

He yawned wide, lulled by the gently rolling current beneath his bare feet. Of course, he'd never own a houseboat like this, but he could pretend for a while—he and Jayden, his five-year-old grandson, who sat with his legs dangling over the side of the anchored pontoon boat.

"Papa!" Jayden cried, his eyes springing wide with surprise. "I think I hooked something!"

"Well, hang on to it, and let me see what you got."

Mr. Gibbs secured his pole and reached down to give Jayden's line a firm tug. "You got somethin' all right, but that ain't no fish." He reeled the line in as far as he could and yanked. Out from the water burst a black, badly decayed arm, ragged skin draping from its severed end, fingers dangling limp and grotesque.

"Papa!" Jayden gasped as it landed about five feet from the boat and bobbed in the water.

"I see it. Now you hold the line while I get my clippers."

"But Papa, what about the rest of him?"

Mr. Gibbs gripped the railing to steady himself as a dizzy spell washed over him. "Whatever happened here ain't none of our business. Mrs. Chandler would have herself a fit if we report it, and you know it."

"But shouldn't we give his arm a funeral?"

Mr. Gibbs wiped his brow with a red bandanna and retrieved the line clippers from his tackle box. "You're right. We'll bury the arm and pray for his soul." As he reached for Jayden's rod, the jaws of a huge gator surged out of the water, swallowing the arm and the tip of the fishing pole, yanking Jayden from the boat.

"Let go!" Mr. Gibbs yelled as the alligator pulled Jayden beneath the surface of the water. He made a desperate grab, but the boy was gone. "Jayden!" He rushed to the other side of the boat, but the river was calm. "Jayden!" He clutched at his chest and fell to his knees. "Oh, please, God, don't take the boy." A splash towards the stern brought him round.

"Papa! Help me back into the boat."

Tears rolled from his eyes as he grasped the back of Jayden's shirt and plucked him from the river.

Jayden collapsed on the deck, coughing murky water from his lungs. "Did you see that, Papa? That gator swallowed the arm."

Mr. Gibbs gathered him close and wept.

"Don't cry, Papa. We'll pray for him just like you said."

Mr. Gibbs allowed the boy to pull away. He didn't want him to know how close he'd come to—

He couldn't even think it.

He wiped his eyes. "We will, Jayden. We'll pray for his soul."

A large flock of thrashers suddenly took flight.

Mr. Gibbs shielded his eyes from the setting sun and scanned the bushes along the bank. "Let's clean up, now, Jayden, and get on out of here."

"But we didn't catch any fish. We still have your pole."

"We's done fishin' today, and we ain't comin' back here again neither."

Jayden leaned out over the side and peered into the murky water. "Papa? Do you think the rest of him is down there?"

Remembering how the hook resisted before the arm tore free, he grimaced and said, "I reckon so, whatever them gators didn't eat. Now, come away. Them gators rule this part of the river. We best leave them to it."

"How do you think he got there, Papa?"

"I ain't gonna think about that, and neither should you."

"But what if he ain't alone down there? What if he has a family somewhere? How we gonna pray for 'im if we don't think about it?"

Scowling, Mr. Gibbs wagged his finger in Jayden's face. "Don't you talk like me! You mind your language and use yer education."

Jayden lowered his gaze. "I'm sorry, Papa, but that arm…"

"Now, you listen to me. We's gonna pray for that man once, then we gonna forget about what we saw here today. It's best for everyone concerned. Ya hear me, boy?"

"Yes, sir, but I doubt I'll ever forget it. That arm was mighty gruesome."

"Not a word to anyone, especially Mrs. Chandler. Now, bow your head while I pray for his soul—and yers and mine, too, while I'm at it."

"Then you'd best pray for Mama, too. She needs it more than all of us put together."

A heavy sigh escaped Mr. Gibbs's lips. "That she do, boy. That she do."

CHAPTER TWO

*O*ne year later...

Sarah Chandler took another quick draw on her cigarette, climbed onto the bathtub rim, and blew the smoke out the small window in the master bathroom. Crushing the butt against the metal window frame, she waved the residual smoke away from her face. She closed her eyes and sighed while little fists banged on the bathroom door.

"Momma, Momma, Rachael took my cookie."

"It's *my* cookie," Rachael cried.

"Go away! I'll be out in a minute." Sarah stepped down from the tub. As she washed her hands, she looked at her tired face in the mirror. Life used to be fun. Now all she did was cook, clean, and do laundry while her husband stayed out till all hours of the night, drinking and carousing with his friends. This wasn't what she had bargained for.

"Momma, let me in," Cody cried.

She turned off the water and rubbed her eyes. "I'm comin'. Just give me a damn minute."

Heaving a deep sigh, she opened the door and looked down at her four-year-old son. Chocolate stained his face and hands, as well as the door and doorframe. Grabbing his wrist before he could touch anything else, she hauled him up to the sink and stretched his hand towards the faucet. Ignoring his bloodcurdling screams, she grabbed a washcloth from the rack above the toilet and washed his face, which only made him cry louder.

"Quit yer fussin', Cody. I'm almost done." A moment later, she set him free, scrubbed chocolate smears off the door, and went in search of his twin sister. She didn't want Tyler finding chocolate stains all over the house. The last time that happened, he had thought it was something else and backhanded her across the face.

"Rachael? Where are you? Come out here this minute!" After checking the living room, she made her way down the narrow hallway of their singlewide trailer and into the smaller of the two bedrooms.

Rachael looked up from where she sat on the floor and held up her cookie. "My cookie, but I'll share with *you*, Mommy."

Sarah snatched the cookie and gave it to Cody, who had followed her into the room. "Let me wipe your hands, Rachael."

Rachael held them up, but they were clean, as was her face. Her big brown eyes filled with tears as she watched her brother eat her cookie. "*My* cookie."

Cody laughed and ran towards the living room.

"Stay in your room until I call you." Sarah slammed the door and went in search of Cody, yet again.

* * *

At the very moment Sarah was searching for Cody, Tyler Chandler's eyes were following the rounded curves beneath his new boss's suit as she paced in front of the whiteboard and addressed the sales staff at the end of a long day. He was sick of hearing about budgets and numbers. He and his group were doing well this quarter. He performed best when he ignored the sales goals and concentrated on his customers, most of whom were women. As far as he was concerned, this corporate mumbo-jumbo crap didn't work well in Mississippi. Nevertheless, he pretended to listen. When he finally caught her eye, he smiled.

When she smiled back, he slid off his wedding ring and stuffed it into his pocket.

"Okay, y'all, let's push hard the rest of the month. That new auto plant brought all kinds of support business to this state. We have the potential to set records. Let's do it!"

Tyler hung back as the advertising staff of the local newspaper filed out of the room. "Motivating speech, Ms. Clarkston," he said, admiring the jiggle of her skirt and the sway of her long auburn hair as she erased the whiteboard.

"Call me Pamela, please. And thanks. I hope it pays off. Pressure comes from the top down in this business."

"Everybody's got pressure. Where did you move from?"

"Atlanta. I have a feeling that things move a little slower here."

He chuckled. "You think? How about a drink before we head home? I'll take you to our most happening bar and break you in right proper."

Turning from the whiteboard, she gathered up her files. "No, thanks. I still have some boxes to unpack. Besides, it's against company policy to fraternize with employees. You do work for me, you know."

"Ouch," he said with a lazy smile. "I was just bein' friendly. Good night then, *Ms. Clarkston*." As Tyler sauntered through the door, it took everything in him not to look back. He knew she was watching him, but he refused to give her the satisfaction of looking over his shoulder. The next time there was an invitation, it would come from her, and assuming he had read her right, it wouldn't take long.

* * *

By the time Sarah had the plates on the table and the kids buckled into their booster seats, she was a nervous wreck. Taking care of twins was harder than she had ever imagined. The only peace she found in the daytime was in the rare few minutes when they were both asleep.

Cody banged both hands on the table. "Juice, Momma. I want juice."

A truck door slammed.

"Just a minute, baby. Daddy's home."

"Daddy!" Cody banged harder.

Sarah turned down the butter beans, pulled the biscuits from the oven, and ran to the front door, which opened before she could get there. "Hey, honey. Dinner's ready." She wrapped her arms around her husband's neck and kissed him a good one.

Tyler reached down and squeezed her bottom. "Now that's what I call a welcome."

"Daddy!" Cody cried.

"The kids are waitin'. Are you hungry?"

"For *you*." He headed for the kitchen and took a beer out of the fridge. "What's with all the racket in here?" Releasing the buckle on Cody's booster seat, he swung his son up into his arms. "Hey, Cody. How's my little man?"

"Daddy," Rachael mumbled softly as she watched him toss her brother into the air and catch him on the way down.

"I made yer favorite: pot roast, potatoes, butter beans, and biscuits. Wanna grab the honey while I put everything on the table?"

"Daddy," Rachael said a bit louder.

Sarah poured the beans into a bowl and set it on the table. "How was yer day?"

"We got a new advertising manager this week." He squeezed some honey onto his finger. Cody grabbed his hand and sucked it from his fingertip. "She's from Atlanta. I get the impression she thinks she's hot stuff. We'll see." He squeezed more honey on his finger and offered it to Rachael. Just as she reached for it, he smeared some on her nose, which made her cry, and then he gave the rest to Cody.

Sarah, having seen what he did, set the potatoes on the table and wiped Rachael's nose as she turned back for the roast. "Put Cody in his seat so we can eat."

Tyler dropped his son back into place and latched the buckle, which made him cry, too. "Shut up!" Tyler yelled. "I didn't come home just to hear you two fuss."

The children immediately stopped crying, but Sarah put biscuits on the table in front of them, just in case. She filled Tyler's plate first, and then fixed plates for the children.

"Let's hurry up and eat so you can put them to bed," he said before she could even sit down. "I'm in need of some female companionship tonight if you know what I mean."

"Tyler, honey, maybe you could play with the kids while I clean up the dishes. Then we could put 'em down."

"You can clean up afterwards. I'm going out with my friends tonight."

Sarah turned back to the stove and reminded herself that she was lucky he had come home at all. "Cody's been waitin' all day to see you. Don't you wanna spend a few minutes with him before you go out?" She placed the basket of biscuits on the table and sat down.

"If I can't get what I want here, I'll get it someplace else."

"Fine," she said, ignoring the searing pain she felt in her chest. "I'll put 'em down right away. Whatever you want is fine with me."

"That's more like it." He winked at her and reached for a biscuit.

"Where's your wedding ring?" she said, her heart still stinging from his threat.

Tyler yanked his hand back, and then reached for the biscuits again. "Thanks for reminding me. It's right here in my pocket. I was doing some work with ink copy today, and I didn't want to get it stained." He returned the ring to his finger.

"You could lose it doing that. What if I had thrown your pants into the wash?"

"Don't start on me, Sarah."

She glanced at the children. Cody shoved the biscuit into his mouth, but Rachael's eyes met hers. The sadness there made her wonder how much of their conversation she understood.

"The biscuits are cold."

"I'm sorry. I took 'em straight from the oven when you got home. Want me to heat 'em in the microwave right quick?"

"No. You're a damn good cook, Sarah. I'm glad I came home."

She looked up at him and beamed. He could be so darn sweet when he wanted to be, and he was ten kinds of handsome. Everywhere they went, women noticed Tyler. It wasn't just that he wore his soft brown hair on the longer side, layered and stylish. Tyler was a snappy dresser. She, on the other hand, had plain brown hair and was as country as country could get. His family was cultured, but her people were rednecks, more comfortable in hunting gear than Sunday clothes, which Tyler's mother seemed to wear every day of the week. If Tyler hadn't gotten her pregnant, he wouldn't have given her a second look, not after he got what he wanted that night at the county fair.

As these thoughts ran through her mind, whatever anger she had felt towards him melted. He was so darn handsome. She'd never do better for herself than Tyler Chandler.

* * *

Friday's sales meeting was anything but boring as Tyler took in every move Pamela Clarkston made. She'd taken off her suit jacket, which left her tight-fitting skirt and sheer, cream-colored blouse to feed his imagination. She was sexy in a way he hadn't pursued before. She was exceedingly bright and professional, yet feminine underneath. He wanted to see what she looked like sitting on a blanket by the lake in a pair of blue jean shorts and a tank top.

He was the last one to leave the room again, and he waited to see if she'd say something to make him stay.

"You put up some good numbers again this week. Your team's way out in front."

"That's how I like it. How's the unpacking coming?"

"Done. I'm ready to explore. Any suggestions?"

He chuckled. "I'm full of suggestions."

"Any of them legal?"

A network of windows formed the greater part of the conference room walls, so he maintained a respectful distance. "Sure, if you quit your job or promise not to tell. Are you good at keeping secrets?"

"I love secrets. Especially when they're juicy."

"The offer stands," he heard himself say.

"I can't tonight; I have plans. I'm entertaining my four-year-old son."

"Wow, am I ever an idiot? I didn't realize you were married."

"Oh, I'm not. It's just Jacob and me, and I've been thinking about your offer. It sounds quite tempting."

Tyler looked over his shoulder to see if anyone was listening. "I'd be happy to show you and Jacob around. I love little kids, especially boys."

Her face lit with pleasure. "Can I get your number then? Maybe we can do something tomorrow, but we'll have to keep it secret."

"Top secret," he said. "You have my word."

* * *

After the nightly battle of putting the twins to bed, Sarah dropped a sexy nightgown over her head, tugged it past her sagging breasts and belly, and scowled at herself in the mirror. Birthing twins had certainly changed her figure. She was no special beauty before, but now, well, the nightgown helped—especially from the back, she decided, as she turned to evaluate. Tyler had always liked her backside, and he never complained about her weight. He still wanted as much sex as she would give him, but with comments like he made the other night, it was hard for her to feel confident of his fidelity.

She turned out the bathroom light and crawled into bed. "Hey, baby. You want to?"

"Don't I always?" Tyler rolled on top of her and looked down into her face. "Have I thanked you lately for my son?"

She gave him a dazzling smile. "You can thank me now if you like."

He kissed her and nuzzled her neck. "You sure smell good." As he raised himself into position, he whispered, "I love you, Sarah."

"I love you, too." She heaved a happy sigh as their bodies merged into one. As Tyler sought his pleasure, she closed her eyes and surrendered heart, body, and soul. This, she told herself, was when she felt safe and secure. In these intimate moments, she knew that Tyler Chandler was hers.

It never took very long, and when Tyler rolled to the side, she rolled with him. When he had caught his breath, she said, "Your Momma called today. She wants us to stay at her place tomorrow night. I told her I'd talk to you and call her in the mornin'. Do you want to go? It makes me nervous just thinkin' about it. You know the way Cody runs wild. I'm afraid he'll break somethin'."

"I might have to work tomorrow, but you and the kids should go. I'll join you after work."

Sarah's brow wrinkled with resentment. "Why do you have to work on Saturday? They get enough of your time."

"It happens sometimes," he said.

"I'll go to your mother's if you want me to, but I'm stayin' with you until you have to go to work. I don't get to see you near enough, and you know how much Cody loves to spend time with his daddy."

Tyler brushed the hair from her face. "I guess I can't avoid Mother forever. We'll all go out together tomorrow morning, and I'll stay until they call me in."

She snuggled close and laid her head on his chest.

It was the best deal she was going to get.

CHAPTER THREE

Sarah bit her fingernails, one by one, and dropped them out the window. She glanced over at Tyler, but he seemed focused on the road. The children were asleep in the back seat, and it was quiet for once. She sighed and tried to prepare herself for a weekend with Tyler's mother. It was hard to be herself around Joan Chandler. She worried that she might say or do something wrong. This was only the second time that Joan had invited her out to her house. *House*—Sarah scoffed inwardly; Tyler's mother lived in a mansion.

The first time she saw Pearl River Mansion, she was amazed to see such a fancy place tucked away in the woods. Tyler never talked about his family's wealth, and he refused to accept any help from his mother, which Sarah didn't understand at all—especially after seeing Pearl River Mansion.

The mansion sat upon a ridge at the end of one of the many fingers of the Pearl River above the Ross Barnett Reservoir. It was the grandest house she had ever seen, like the ones over in Natchez, the antebellum kind. According to Tyler's mother, the acres of beautifully manicured gardens that now surrounded the mansion used to be cotton fields. Supposedly, back when the plantation was operational, the owners shipped cotton down the Pearl River before hauling it overland to Vicksburg, where it was loaded onto barges, sent down the Mississippi River to New Orleans, and then sold to the highest bidder.

She had no reason to doubt her, of course, and it wasn't in her general nature to be suspicious, but she sometimes felt like Tyler's mother said things just to test her. She always seemed to be watching and measuring. She'd never tell Tyler this, but she wasn't the least bit fond of his mother.

On their first visit, Tyler had explained that the property was fenced, even along the riverfront, which kept out all but the baby alligators—once they had woven the chicken wire through it. Still, she didn't want the children anywhere near the river without Tyler. She'd heard too many stories of alligators snatching dogs off the riverbank. There were plenty of other places for the children to play.

To her credit, Tyler's mother had been reasonably gracious during her first visit, in a stiff sort of way, though she'd made it clear that she wasn't at all what she had hoped for in a wife for her son. It still hurt when she thought about it. While she could understand that Mrs. Chandler resented not being informed about the wedding until after it had taken place, she and Tyler had thought she'd be more accepting by now. Since that hadn't happened, she was hoping this weekend might be the beginning of a better relationship between them. Unlike Tyler, Joan doted on Rachael, or at least she had the few times she'd come by their trailer to visit. This was the first time that the twins would visit the mansion.

Once they had entered into the interior forty-acre gardens, Sarah rolled down her window and let the wind blow through her hair.

Tyler glanced over. "What are you doing?"

"Tryin' to catch the flowers in the breeze. It must smell amazin' out there. I've never seen so many roses. Will you take me walkin' tomorrow? I'd love to explore."

"You'd like it by the creek. There are lots of flowers up there. Mr. Gibbs built two gazebos, one on either side of the stream."

"Oh, could we?" She clasped her hands as if in prayer. "We could take a picnic lunch up there. It's been forever since we've had a picnic, and you know the kids would love it."

Tyler chuckled. "We'll see."

As they approached the house, they entered beneath a canopy created by the live oak trees that lined both sides of the narrow lane.

"I would never get tired of this. It reminds me of that movie, *Gone with the Wind*."

"I think that's what the owners had in mind," Tyler said. "They fashioned portions of the gardens after Bellingrath, but the entrance reminds me of Rosedown."

"Where?"

"Never mind."

A gate and a garden fence blocked the circular driveway, which led to the grand entrance, an addition Tyler's mother had installed to keep vehicles from blocking her view from the front of the house. The driveway now led to a parking area ensconced in the trees. It was a short walk to the front door for guests, and it provided easy access for the family through the butler's pantry.

Tyler parked in front of the gate and phoned his mother. "We're here," he said and hung up. "Sarah, you get the kids. I'll get the bags."

"We're here, babies. We're gonna visit Grandma today." She still couldn't get used to calling Joan "Grandma." She called *her* grandmother Mammaw. Smiling at her son, she released his buckle and set him on his feet.

"Good morning, Cody." Joan walked through the gate and stood by as Sarah helped Rachael from the car.

"Gramma!" Rachael cried, reaching out for her as soon as her feet touched the ground.

"How is my precious girl?" Joan said as she picked her up. "Grandma is so happy to see you. Hello, Sarah. Thank you for coming."

"I stay with you, Gramma."

"Yes, and I have the perfect bedroom for you to sleep in. It's fit for a princess. Would you like to see it?"

Rachael smiled and nodded with excitement.

Sarah saw her expression and realized how rare it was to see her smile.

"Hello, Tyler. Nice to see you. Pull into the parking area, won't you?" she called over her shoulder as she headed for the house.

Sarah glanced around and spotted Cody as he took off running. "Tyler! Don't let him get into the woods."

Tyler easily overtook his giggling son and scooped him off his feet. "Go on into the house with your momma. I've got to get our bags out of the car, and then I'll take you down to the river."

"I wanna see the croc-a-gators!"

"Oh, you'll see them, but it's easier to see them at night when their eyes shine in the dark."

Sarah grabbed his hand and followed Joan. "There's no such thing as a croc-a-gator, Cody. They're called alligators."

Cody pulled away. "I want my daddy."

Tyler grabbed their bags and caught up. "Hold onto Momma or no croc-a-gators."

Cody stopped tugging. "See, Momma? Croc-a-gators."

Sarah glowered at Tyler, but he just winked and gave her the roguish grin she loved. Biting back a smile, she said, "They're alligators, Cody."

Her heart beat faster as she climbed the porch steps and glanced longingly at the wooden rocking chairs and hanging porch swing. The wrap-around-porch and soaring marble columns were her favorite part of the house. She'd been after Tyler to build a covered deck outside their trailer ever since her first visit.

She followed Joan into the foyer and paused. She felt unworthy to enter. Her family was poor white trash compared to Tyler's family. She doubted she'd ever feel comfortable here. She was afraid to touch anything.

"Come into the kitchen, Sarah. We'll fix the children a snack."

"Cookies!" Cody said.

"We like cookies," Rachael agreed.

"Then cookies it shall be."

Sarah glanced into the living room and formal dining room, both on her right, as she followed Joan down the central hallway, which ran beside the grand staircase and through an archway that led to the kitchen. She'd never understand why one person needed such a big house all to themselves, lovely though it was. When she entered the kitchen, she was surprised to see two new booster seats sitting upon chairs at the breakfast table. "You bought booster seats?"

"Certainly. I want my grandchildren to feel at home here. Will you get them seated for me?"

Sarah put Cody in first, but he began to fuss. "I want Daddy!"

"Hold on, son. Grandma's got cookies. Remember?"

"And some milk." Joan set a small plate and cup in front of him.

"I want cookies, too," Rachael said.

"May I?" Sarah stepped back as Joan picked Rachael up and settled her into her seat. "I've got them right here, sweetheart."

"Thank you, Gramma."

"You're welcome, sweetie. Would you like something to drink, Sarah?"

"Just some water, thanks, and maybe a cookie." Sarah saw Joan's eyes drop to her stomach and immediately pulled her shirt down. "Um, forget the cookie. Just some water, please."

"Good call," Joan said as she reached for a glass.

Sarah looked out the window, which made up one whole wall of the breakfast room. "You sure have a pretty view from here. I like all them flowery bushes. Does the river ever come up into the yard?"

"Heavens, no. This house is nearly a hundred-and-fifty years old. It's situated well above the river. You'll see that when we take the children out to the boat dock."

"You've got a boat, too?" She sighed. "It must be nice to have so much money. When I was comin' up, all I wanted was my own bedroom. I had to share with my sister."

"It's not polite to talk about money, Sarah."

"Oh, I'm sorry. I didn't mean nothin' by it. It's just that your world is so different from mine."

"Yes, well, since you brought it up. I've been wondering what to do about my grandchildren. I don't want to interfere, of course, but I want them to have a better life than the one you had. I want them to wear fine clothes, go to the best schools, and enjoy annual vacations. I want my grandchildren to see the world. You want that for them, too, don't you?"

"What are you sayin'?"

"Obviously, you and Tyler can't give them the quality of life that I can. I want to help your family, but Tyler is so damn stubborn, he'd rather keep you poor."

"Are you sayin' that Tyler won't take your money?"

"Are you saying that you will? I would tell you how to use it, of course, but there'd be plenty of extra for you to spend as you please. Wouldn't you like to have some new clothes? From what I've seen, Tyler spends most of his money on himself."

Sarah looked into Joan's cold blue eyes and turned away. She was right; Tyler gave her very little spending money, but she wasn't going to say so.

"I'd like to keep the children here for the summer," Joan said. "I plan to hire a private tutor to help prepare them for kindergarten. My guess is, though they speak surprisingly well, they're behind in their development. It's critically important that they learn to speak proper English instead of the atrocious slang that's so common around here. Preparing them now will make all the difference in how well they do from their first day of school forward."

"Whatever you may think of us, Mrs. Chandler, we give 'em what matters most."

Tyler appeared in the doorway. "Here you are. How's my little man?"

"Hi, Daddy. Let's go see the croc-a-gators."

"Daddy," Rachael mumbled.

As Tyler unlatched Cody's lap-belt, Joan stepped forward with a damp cloth. "Let me wipe Cody's hands before you go."

"Let's go, Daddy." Cody started to climb down, but Joan stopped him. He allowed her to wipe the crumbs from his hands, but when she reached for his face, he twisted away.

"Let me wipe your face, young man."

"No!"

"Cody, let me wipe your face!" When she tried to turn his head, he squealed and started to cry. "Tell him, Tyler."

"I'll do it," Tyler said.

Joan scowled as he took the cloth. "That only teaches him that he can get his way by being a brat."

"He's not a brat. He just likes having a dirty face. Don't you, Cody?"

Cody nodded.

"You can wash *me*, Gramma," Rachael said with her hands held high.

Tyler tossed the cloth onto the table. "You heard her; clean up that mess. Come on, Cody. Let's go find some croc-a-gators."

Joan gently wiped Rachael's hands and face and took her out of her seat. "That's my good girl. You have your hands full with Cody, I see."

Sarah smiled. "He's all boy, that's for sure. Tyler wouldn't have married me if at least one of our babies wasn't a boy. Cody means everything to Tyler."

Joan flinched. "You shouldn't say things like that in front of Rachael."

"It ain't no secret, and it ain't no worse than you callin' Cody a brat." Fearing she'd say something she'd regret, Sarah strode through the back hallway, past the laundry room and maids' quarters, and onto the back porch, which was almost as grand as the front. She trotted down the steps and found three pathways leading into the garden. She didn't know which one to take, but she didn't want to go back inside. They had been here less than thirty minutes and, already, she was angry enough to leave.

Who did Joan think she was, telling her that the life they gave their children wasn't good enough? She wondered what Tyler would say when he heard that his mother was trying to get her to take money behind his back, and she meant to tell him too. She may have been raised poor, but that didn't mean she was for sale. She wiped the sweat from her brow, chose the center path, and set out in search of Tyler and her son.

* * *

"Is that right? If I drive all that way, are you going to cook me dinner?" Tyler covered the receiver. "Cody, get back from there! You're gonna fall in." Grabbing his son by the hand, he pulled him back from the edge of the dock. "No, I'm here. What did you say?"

Cody squirmed free and crouched down to look into the water.

"Now *that* sounds delicious. Where'd you learn to cook like that? Paris? No way. What are you doing working at the newspaper then?" He watched as Cody ran to the left side of the dock, picked up a handful of stones, and came running back to set them in a pile at his feet.

"Watch, Daddy. I'm gonna throw 'em."

Tyler covered the receiver again. "I'm watching. Who? Oh, that's my son, Cody. I have a four-year-old also. Maybe our boys could meet sometime. Uh, I don't know about today, but soon maybe. What time should I come by?" He chuckled at her answer. "You sure you don't wanna quit your job?"

"Cody, get back from there!" Sarah cried.

Tyler glanced over his shoulder. "Uh…I've gotta go. See you soon." He slipped the phone into his pocket and smiled at his wife. "He's all right. I've got an eye on him. Come here," he said and opened his arms.

Sarah rushed into them and wrapped her arms around his waist. Rising on tiptoe, she gave him a quick kiss. "I want to go home, Tyler. Can we?"

"Very funny. Unfortunately, the office just called. I have to go to work. I'll be back later though."

"I don't want to stay here," she said, wrinkling her nose. "Your mother's making me very uncomfortable."

"Give her a chance; she'll warm up. You'll see."

"Look, Daddy, a fish! I just saw a huge fish!"

Tyler lifted her chin and looked into her eyes. "You'll stay?" She gave him a half smile and nodded. Releasing her, he said, "Way to go, Cody. Let's go find your Grandma. I've gotta go to work now."

"I don't wanna go inside," he whined.

"I'll stay with him," Sarah said. "Hurry back."

He kissed her forehead. "Goodbye, Cody."

"When you come back, you can show me the crock-a-gators."

"I will, Son. You mind your momma, now." As he took the left path, he turned back at hearing his son's voice.

"Watch, Momma. I'm gonna hit the fish with these rocks."

"It's not nice to throw rocks at the fish, Cody. Just throw 'em into the water."

"You're no fun. I wish Daddy could stay."

"So do I, but you're stuck with me. Don't hit the fish with those rocks, or I'll take you back inside to your grandmother."

"I won't hit no fish, Momma. I'll just hit the water."

"Good boy."

Tyler chuckled to himself. There was nothing in the world that he loved more than his son.

* * *

"Hello?" Sarah called as she and Cody entered the kitchen. "Where is everybody?" She set Cody down but kept hold of his hand as she led him back through the hallway, past the dining room and living room, and onto the front porch. "They must be upstairs, Cody."

"Let's go up, Momma. Let's go up!"

She stayed close behind him as he climbed the wide staircase. She wondered what it must be like to live in such a fine house and climb these stairs every night to go to bed. "Mrs. Chandler?" she called from the top of the landing, which opened into a wide sitting area that looked down over the lower floor. Sarah's eyebrows rose as she saw huge portraits of people dressed in fancy clothes lining the gallery wall. She recognized Tyler's mother standing in the garden with a very handsome gentleman, whom she assumed was Tyler's father. It was a fabulous painting, and the frame was thicker than any she had ever seen.

"Where are we going, Momma?"

Two hallways extended from this room, forming a U shape that led to two separate wings of the house, one to the left, and one to the right. She suddenly felt like she was trespassing where she didn't belong.

"Come, Cody. Let's go back downstairs and wait until someone shows up."

"Okay! Watch me, Momma! I'll go down first."

Just as she took her first step, she heard Rachael laugh. It surprised her. She hardly ever heard Rachael laugh.

"Come back, Cody. They're up here." She grabbed his hand and walked down the west hallway, past two closed doors, and stopped at the room at the end of the hall. As she peered inside the open doorway, her eyes widened with surprise. "Oh my," she gasped.

Joan and Rachael turned. "Look at my room, Mommy. Isn't it pretty?"

Sarah let go of Cody's hand and gazed around the room. The walls were a soft shade of pink, and a large rose-shaped rug served as the centerpiece on the polished hardwood floor. A miniature staircase sat beside a queen-size bed with a white bedspread embroidered with delicate pink roses. Four bedposts rose from an elaborate white bed frame in the form of castle turrets. Crystal lamps glistened on matching end tables on either side of the bed. Even the dresser was white with sparkling crystal drawer knobs. A white rocking chair with a pink cushion sat next to a bookshelf stacked with children's books, and a cedar chest filled with toys sat against the opposite wall. Beyond beckoned a lovely bay window with a wrap-around window seat lined with colorful pillows. Tears filled her eyes. This room was a fairytale dream come true. It was perfect.

"Oh, Rachael, it's beautiful."

"Gramma gave it to me."

"I see."

"Cody, don't touch that!" Joan snapped as he reached for a miniature glass carousel, which sat on the dresser. "Sarah, why don't you stay here with Rachael while I take Cody to see his new room? We have surprises for him today also. Would you like that, Cody?"

"I wanna see my new room."

"Come on, then." Taking his hand, she led him to the door. Pausing, she said, "Sarah?"

"Yes?"

"No matter how much you love them, you could never give them anything like this."

She looked down at her dirty feet and felt ashamed.

"I want you to think about what I said earlier. Tyler might not be willing to accept what I can offer, but you can change his mind. After all, you want your children to have nice things, don't you?"

She nodded.

"Tyler had nice things when he was growing up. Why should his stupid, stubborn pride cause his children to do without? Enjoy your daughter. We'll talk later."

"Joan?"

"Yes?"

"Can I take Cody to his new room?"

Their eyes met, and the corner of Joan's mouth twitched with what Sarah thought was amusement. "Excellent idea. His room is two doors down on the left. The nursery is in the middle. That's where their tutors will instruct them in their lessons. In addition to science, math, geography, and reading, they'll learn language, art, and music. Feel free to explore it if you like. I'll take you to your room whenever you're ready."

"Come on, Momma. I wanna see my room!"

Sarah felt Joan's eyes on her back as she stepped out into the hall. She didn't know how to act. She wanted to run down the stairs and out of the house. There were lots of things more important than money, but she was having a difficult time remembering what they were just now. She opened the door to Cody's room.

"Whoa!" Cody ran forward and climbed the ladder of the tree house-style bunk bed. A painted mural covered all four walls, making it look and feel like a happy jungle filled with colorful birds, plants, flowers, and trees. White puffy clouds and glow-in-the-dark stars decorated the light-blue ceiling. The lower part of the L-shaped bed structure had walls that had been formed, sculpted, and painted like a cave, and vines draped the entrance, creating the perfect hideout for an adventurous little boy. A sturdy oak dresser matched the small table and chairs, which sat in the opposite corner of the room, giving him plenty of space to draw, play, and work puzzles. He also had a handsome bookshelf loaded with books.

Sarah suppressed a smile; Rachael was much more likely to explore her books than Cody was his. It could be months before he even noticed them.

Cody climbed down from the bed and ducked inside the cave. "Look Momma! There's a bed in here, too! I wanna sleep in the cave!"

She smiled through her tears. Their rooms at home were woefully inadequate compared to these.

He ran to what appeared to be a treasure chest and threw it open. "Look, Momma!" He immediately began tossing toys behind his back as fast as he could pull them out.

"Stop, Cody! Don't take everything out at once." She knelt beside him and began putting toys back into the trunk.

Cody snatched a dump truck from her hands. "That's my truck."

"Let's put some of these away."

Cody ran the truck along the floor and onto the bamboo rug. "Vroom, vroom!"

She smiled. He was so cute. How could he not be excited? She opened the closet and found dozens of little outfits including a coat, a light jacket, and several sweaters. A shoe rack stood against the back wall containing tennis shoes, loafers, boots, house slippers, and a pair of leather dress shoes. He didn't have nearly this many clothes at home.

For a moment, she envied her children. She hardly ever bought new clothes for herself. Everything Tyler made paid for their bills, the children, his work wardrobe, and drinking with his friends. She was tired of scrimping and doing without. She picked up a truck and crawled across the floor to be near her son. "Vroom, vroom."

* * *

Tyler dropped his wedding ring into the cup holder, checked his hair in the rearview mirror, and stepped out of his truck. His heart was racing. He had always been a flirt, but he had more on his mind than a one-night stand with this girl. She had class. She was his equal, but she didn't yet know that he was hers. He walked to the front door of the Southern colonial-style tract home. It was a charming two-story house with dormer windows, built of brick and accented with cream-colored siding and hunter-green shutters. It had a pleasant front porch and a yard full of mature trees. It wasn't Pearl River Mansion, but it was certainly more impressive than his trailer.

He rang the bell.

He sighed at the thought of what he'd left behind, but everything had changed after his father died. The mansion no longer felt like home, and his mother, well she—

Pamela opened the door and greeted him with a warm smile. "Hey, Tyler. Glad you could make it."

She stepped aside as Tyler walked past her into the foyer. "Fine place you have here."

"Thanks. Would you like some tea?"

"Sure." He followed her into the kitchen, taking note of the newly decorated living room and formal dining room as they walked by. "You have excellent taste."

"And I taste good, too," she teased as she reached into the refrigerator for the pitcher of tea.

He raised a brow. Perhaps this was going to be easier than he thought.

"I'm ready, Momma. Let's go swimming!"

Pamela opened her arms to welcome her son as he came running into the room wearing floaties around his upper arms. His deep green eyes, when he turned towards him, appeared to be identical to hers, but his curly blond hair favored someone else. Tyler felt an irrational jealousy surge through his body, which he both recognized and banished within moments.

"Tyler, this is my son, Jacob."

Tyler leaned over and lifted his hand. "Hey, buddy. Give me five."

Jacob smiled and struck his hand. "Want to swim with us?

I can jump off the side of the pool."

Tyler was impressed by the clarity of his speech and the intelligence in his eyes. "How old are you, Jacob?"

"I'll be five in thirty-nine days. Come on, Momma. Let's go swimming!"

Pamela gave him a sideways smile. "I did promise. I might have some trunks around here. Care to go for a dip?"

"That depends. Whose swimming trunks are they?"

She took a bag from the counter and tossed it to him. "I bought them at Dillard's this morning. See you in the pool. Come on, Jacob. Let's go."

"Yay!" Jacob cheered.

Tyler watched as Pamela followed her son out the French doors and onto the patio. Her back was to him as she peeled off her shirt and tossed it onto the lounge chair. When she sat down to wriggle out of her jeans, he turned to find the nearest bathroom. He was very much looking forward to seeing her in a bikini.

* * *

"Sarah?" Joan said as she peered into Cody's room.

"Yes, ma'am?"

"I just put Rachael down for a nap. Why don't you put Cody down, too, and I'll show you to your room? You can rest up a bit before dinner."

Cody wrinkled his brow and puffed out his lip. "I don't wanna take a nap."

"Do you like your new room?" He nodded. "Then climb up to your bed and take a nap like a good boy. When you wake up, you can play some more."

"Do it, Cody," Sarah said.

Cody got up and walked over to the ladder. "But I have doo-doo."

"Oh, let me run down and get his bag. This still happens sometimes." Sarah raced out the door and down the steps. The last thing she wanted was for Cody to soil his new sheets. She found their bags near the front door and raced back up the stairs, clutching her side and gasping for breath by the time she reached the top. "Got it," she said, but Cody's room was empty. "Cody?"

"We're in here, Sarah."

Sarah hadn't noticed the door to the right, which was hidden from view when Cody's door stood open. The bedroom included its own bathroom. When she stepped inside, she saw Cody sitting on the toilet atop a child's potty seat with Joan standing guard beside him.

"I told him he's not getting up from there until he puts something into that toilet, even if it's only a drop. He's way past the age when he should be toilet trained."

Cody started to cry. "Momma, I don't wanna go potty."

"Well, *we* don't want to keep changing your stinky pants. Now go to the bathroom like a good little boy, so we can all leave this room."

"Mrs. Chandler, it doesn't happen very often. It's probably all the excitement."

"Don't sass me, Sarah. The way you coddle this child, he'll never grow up. If I have anything to say about it, this will be the last pair of stinky pants you ever have to change. Now hurry up, young man. By the way, did I mention that I have chocolate ice cream downstairs for dessert?"

Sarah was shocked to hear a trickle hit the water in the toilet.

"Look, Grandma, I did it!"

"Of course, you did. Good boy. Your mother's going to clean you up and put you down for a nap while I see about dinner. When you wake up, you'll use the toilet again. Then we'll have something good to eat. As long as you don't dirty your britches, you can have ice cream for dessert."

"Oh boy!"

Sarah caught Joan's eye. "Thank you. It sure would be nice if this was the last...well, you know. I was beginning to think this day would never come."

"We can help each other, Sarah. I'll be back in a few minutes to take you to your room."

* * *

Tyler dropped his clothes on top of Pamela's and stepped into the pool. She increased the distance between them and smiled from beneath her sunglasses.

"Jacob, show Tyler how you can jump."

Jacob, who was holding onto the side of the pool, kicked his feet until he got back to the stairs, where he climbed out and rushed around to the side of the pool. "Ready, set, go!" He landed with a splash and a squeal of joy.

"That's it. Do it again!"

"Good job, buddy." Tyler couldn't imagine Cody doing that. "How long has he been swimming?"

Pamela swam within reach. "About a week. He's a fast learner."

His eyes traveled through the water, taking in her average sized breasts and firm, flat stomach. "I like you in a bathing suit. Care to get out so I can see the bottom half?"

She smiled and turned towards her son. "We're watching, Jacob. Do it again!" Jacob got into position and jumped. "Very good, Son. Swim to us!"

Jacob kicked his feet. When he got close enough, Tyler held out his hand, and Jacob giggled as he pulled him quickly through the water.

"This is great," Tyler said. "I could get used to this."

"Jacob, honey, Mommy forgot her towel. Would you go into the house and get it for me?"

"Sure, Momma."

"Thank you. Swim to the stairs. We're watching."

After Jacob climbed out, he wrapped up in his towel and ran into the house.

"He's an amazing little boy."

Pamela chuckled. "He's a mess, but he makes me happy. I'm just missing one thing in my life."

"What's that?"

She took his hand and led him towards the stairs. "Someone special. Someone I can trust and confide in."

Tyler's heart pounded as she straddled his leg, which he had unwittingly propped on one of the stairs.

She wrapped her arms around his neck and looked into his eyes. "Know anyone like that?"

Her slightest movement against his leg sent desire raging through his body. "Do I know what?"

She laughed and swam away. "Like that, do you? You have no idea how happy I could make you."

He missed her immediately. "If it weren't for Jacob, I'd swim over there and show you how happy I can make *you*."

"It takes more than a good lover to make me happy, Tyler.

I'm telling you these things because I've been watching you. I like the way you treat your customers and handle your sales team. I like the way you think. You're honest and fair, and you're reasonable when there's a conflict. I think we could be good together."

"I've been thinking the same thing," he said, flattered that she'd been paying such close attention.

"I'm not interested in a one-night stand. I'm looking for a man who's interested in more than my body. I want someone who wants to discover who I am on the inside. If we pursue this, we place both of our jobs at risk. That's why I'm being so forward about what I want. We don't have time for games. There's too much at stake."

He closed the distance between them and pulled her into his arms. As she looked into his eyes, he felt her breath against his lips. "Give me the chance, Pamela. I'm interested in discovering your secrets."

"Prove it." She dropped into the water and pushed off the side, out of reach. When she resurfaced at the far end of the pool, she was short of breath.

"You hear that?" he said.

"What?"

"Your breathing. That's how I'll leave you the first time we kiss."

She laughed. "I hope so, Tyler. I truly hope so."

* * *

Sarah followed Joan through the upstairs sitting area and down the other hallway to the first door on the left.

"This is Tyler's room," Joan said. "The master suite is at the far end of the hall. I'd appreciate it if you respect my privacy and refrain from coming beyond this point. You'll find fresh towels in the bathroom. I'll have Mr. Gibbs bring up your bags."

"Who?"

"Mr. Gibbs is my groundskeeper. He rarely works inside the house, but I'll make an exception and ask him to set your bags in the hallway. You can retrieve them after your bath. We have about two hours before dinner. Perhaps Tyler will be back by then. Rest well."

Sarah smiled as she closed the door and glanced around the room, which was about the size of her living room at home. This cozy space held a sofa, two end tables, a coffee table, lamps, a fireplace, and a window seat that managed to look inviting and lonely at the same time. She cocked her head and wondered why it wasn't as welcoming as the one in Rachael's room.

Shrugging it off, she turned towards the mantle and picked up a photograph of Tyler standing with an older man whom she recognized from the portrait in the sitting room above the stairs. Their relaxed posture and genuine smiles made it seem as though they were close.

She wondered why Tyler never talked about his parents. She didn't even know how his father died.

The gold, brown, green, and burgundy that decorated the room created a rich and luxurious setting, so different from the country blue and rust shades she had used inside their trailer. If she accepted some of Joan's money, maybe she could decorate more like Tyler was accustomed to.

She wandered into the bedroom and ran her hand over the beautiful paisley bedspread. Golden tassels bordered the hunter-green throw pillows. She crawled onto the bed and lay against them. The elegant dresser was clear of objects, unlike their dusty dresser top at home, which housed her perfume bottles, knickknacks, and cheap jewelry box. She'd never seen a dresser with nothing on it before. The wood was beautiful. Hers was made of particleboard and had several dents and scratches in it. She'd never realized how shabby it was until now.

The warm afternoon sun shone through the window. She hopped off the bed to find a stunning view of the courtyard fountain below, the centerpiece of which was a bronzed Roman warrior gripping the reigns of his powerful horses as they reared before his mighty chariot. It was so detailed and lifelike that she imagined how terrifying it would be to have an army of such men marching from town to town, taking whatever they wanted, while she and her family sheltered within the mansion, awaiting their fate. Her heart beat faster as she gazed at the warrior again. How many families had faced such armies over the centuries? She laughed at herself; she rarely had time for daydreaming, but the statue *was* nearly naked, after all.

A pair of cardinals drew her attention to the countless birds that fluttered among an army of trees and bushes rather than a company of soldiers. They were safe here, but threats came in all shapes and sizes. She was a mother, and she'd do anything to protect her children.

She stepped away from the window and entered the bathroom, which was three times the size of hers at home. She saw the large

Jacuzzi bathtub and smiled in anticipation; she'd never taken a Jacuzzi bath before. Staying here was like staying in a fancy hotel. How could Tyler possibly be happy living in their trailer? It was old and worn out, not to mention it was a singlewide. If he didn't resent her now, he might after staying here this weekend. Would he remember what it's like to live with money and regret getting her pregnant?

She turned on the water.

Next to the tub sat a bottle of sea breeze-scented bubble bath. She added nearly half the contents to the steamy water and stepped out of her clothes. Too impatient to wait, she settled into the tub, giggling like a schoolgirl as the bubbles formed and grew into a billowing cloud-like layer. Lying back against the tub, she found it pleasant, sensual even, to feel the water rise gradually over her body, which she artfully covered with glistening, crackling, bubbles. She wished that Tyler would walk in; she'd never done it in a bathtub before.

Her thoughts drifted to several things, but they kept returning to Joan Chandler. What did she have in mind for the children? She had always liked to draw. Were they really going to learn about art and music? Would she take them to see the world? Would she get to go with them? It was intimidating and exhilarating all at the same time.

Closing her eyes, she sank deeper into the warm churning bubbles. After this weekend, she had several questions for Tyler.

* * *

Pamela took the towel from her son and rose from the water. "Thank you, Jacob. Are you ready for a snack?"

Tyler caught the briefest glance of her backside before she wrapped the towel around her waist. She was exceptionally well built and an outrageous flirt. She had surprised him by how sensual and playful she seemed to be, not to mention direct.

"What about you, Tyler. Are you hungry?"

Her eyes danced with mischief, but he was game. "Starved."

"How about something juicy?"

"What do you have in mind?"

"Grapes, for now. I'll be right back."

Turning his attention to Jacob, he said. "Wanna jump off the side again?"

"Then I'll swim to you," Jacob said. "Are you ready?"

Tyler glanced back to Pamela. "Oh, I'm definitely ready."

* * *

Sarah reluctantly left the Jacuzzi and wrapped herself in a plush, gold-colored towel. It felt nothing like her threadbare towels at home. She took a matching hand towel and dried her hair. Hoping to find a comb, she opened a drawer and was surprised to see not only a hairbrush but makeup, too. It was brand new makeup: eyeliner, mascara, eye shadow, blush, and a lovely shade of rose-colored lipstick. In the bottom of the drawer was a note with her name on it. She smiled; she felt like a princess in someone else's fairytale.

Sarah, help yourself to whatever you find. There are clothes in the closet for you and some other items in the dresser. We dress up for dinner. I'll see to the children myself. Dinner is served in the dining room at seven.

—Joan

She dropped the note and ran to the closet. Inside were more clothes than she had in her entire closet at home. Everything was neat and well arranged, and the dresses were gorgeous. She counted eight dresses, some soft and silky, others made of lace. She held up a cream-colored gown so lovely that she could've worn it at her wedding. In addition to the dresses, she found blouses and frilly skirts, too.

She had wanted to take a nap, but now she was far too excited to sleep. It had been a long time since Tyler had seen her dressed up, and never in anything as fine as these. She wanted him to look into her eyes and tell her she was the most beautiful woman in the world, just as he did the first night they met, when he talked her into giving up her virginity. She gazed into the mirror and smiled. Maybe the girl she used to be was still in there somewhere, after all.

* * *

Tyler watched Pamela tease the seeds out of the grape she was eating. He couldn't remember ever feeling this turned on, especially when he couldn't act on it. She knew it, too. He could tell by the way her eyes danced with laughter.

He looked at his watch. His mother would be putting dinner on the table in another thirty minutes. He really should be leaving. Besides, with Jacob here, they weren't going to have any alone time until after he fell asleep, and he definitely couldn't stay that long.

"It's been fun, you two, but I have to go. Perhaps we can pick up where we left off one of these days soon."

Pamela raised a brow. "What about dessert?"

"Dessert comes after dinner, and unfortunately, I have other plans. I'll take a rain check though. You've given me an assignment, and I intend to take it seriously." He had already changed into his clothes, so he headed for the door. "You'll grant me that rain check, won't you?"

"Mommy will be right back, Jacob. I'm going to walk Tyler out."

"Okay, Momma. I know you want to kiss him."

"Jacob!"

"Well, you do. I'm not stupid, you know."

Tyler ruffled Jacob's hair and held up his hand for a high-five.

Jacob gave it. "I hope you come back. I had fun today."

"Me, too. Take care of your momma for me."

Jacob nodded and popped another grape into his mouth. His

method of extracting the seeds was to spit them out.

Pamela followed Tyler out to his truck. "Too bad you couldn't bring Cody today. Maybe next time."

"Maybe."

She leaned against his chest and looked up into his eyes. "What's the assignment you'll be working on?"

"You and your heart. If you're gonna steal mine, I damn sure wanna steal yours."

She smiled one of the sweetest smiles he'd ever seen. "Well, you'd best get busy then."

He looked at her soft full lips and whispered, "I want to kiss you, but I'm not. Good night, Miss Pamela. Dream about my kisses because once you've had one, you won't want to live without them. And that's a fact."

She laughed and stepped away. "I'm looking forward to seeing if you're a man of your word, Tyler Chandler. If you can kiss me breathless, you'll have found one of the keys to my heart, but that's only one. Good night."

He watched her until she had entered the house and closed the door. As he backed down the driveway, he asked himself one simple question: What the hell was he doing?

* * *

Tyler was a wreck by the time he parked near the garden gate at Pearl River Mansion. All he could think about was Pamela. When would he see her again? When could he hold her? When could he kiss her? How could he work with her and pretend nothing was between them? Facing his family, especially Sarah, was the last thing he wanted to do right now. What's more, hiding his preoccupation from his mother would be difficult. She watched him like a hawk. He opened the cup holder and slid his wedding ring back onto his finger.

He stepped into the foyer just as Sarah made her way down the stairs. He did a double take. "Sarah?" She smiled shyly and met him at the landing where he kissed her cheek. "You look beautiful, Sarah." Her eyes sparkled as she gazed up at him. He'd forgotten how pretty she was. It had been a long time since she'd worn any makeup. "Sorry it took so long, but at least I'm back in time for dinner." Taking her hand, he led her into the dining room and was surprised to see his children, also dressed in formal clothes, sitting quietly in their booster seats on the opposite side of the table. Joan sat at the head of the table, of course, while Dillia, his mother's housemaid, set water on the table.

"Perfect timing, Tyler," Joan said. "Doesn't your family look lovely?"

Both children looked up. "Daddy!" they cried.

"Cody, Rachael, remember what Grandma told you. Children are quiet at the dinner table."

"Because we want chocolate ice cream!" Rachael said with a clap of her hands.

"That's right, you smart girl."

Tyler pulled out a chair for Sarah and then walked around the table and kissed his son.

"Daddy," Rachael said, but he just thumped her on the head and went back to his seat. He caught his mother's glower as he sat down. Perhaps he should have kissed her cheek as well.

Dillia placed their plates before them one at a time.

"Sarah, I trust you found everything to your liking?"

"Yes, ma'am. I can't tell you how much I enjoyed my bath, and the clothes are beautiful. I don't know how to thank you."

"I'll think of something," she said with a tight smile. "So, Tyler, tell us about your day."

He looked up but avoided making eye contact. "We had a budget meeting. Seems like we talk more about making money than actually doing the work of it. Makes no sense to me."

"Did *everyone* have to work today?" she pressed.

"Just the advertising department. What did you do all day, Sarah?"

"Wait until you see the kids' rooms, Tyler. They're amazing. Cody's room looks like a jungle, and Rachael's room was made for a princess."

"I'm a princess, Daddy."

"I wanna see the croc-a-gators."

"Children," Joan said.

"Mother, they aren't used to your rules. They're normal little kids. I'd like to keep it that way if you don't mind."

"Normal? Is that what you call it? Is it normal to throw tantrums and act like a spoiled brat? Because that's what Cody is. With some time, I can straighten him out, but only if you stop interfering."

"Interfering? They're my children. You're the one who's interfering."

"Tyler—" Sarah said as she placed her hand on his thigh.

"Don't tell me she's already gotten to you with her grand promises. Has she offered you money yet? Because she will. That's how it works around here. She pays people to do and say what she wants them to. Isn't that right, Dillia?"

The thin black woman, who had just placed the last dinner plate in front of him, nearly knocked over his water glass. Her eyes flew to Joan and then back to him. "I just work here, Mr. Tyler. I'ze supposed to do what I'm told."

"Thank you, Dillia. You may leave us now. I'll ring the bell if we need you," Joan said.

Dillia bowed her head and retreated from the room.

"What's this about, Tyler? Bringing a servant into the conversation is unacceptable, and you know it. What did you expect her to say?"

"Dillia isn't a servant, Mother. She's an employee. People don't exist in this world simply to do your bidding, and that includes my wife!"

"You're the one who abandoned them this afternoon. I've done everything possible to make them feel welcome. It's not polite to complain about my hospitality."

He sighed. "I'm sorry, Mother. It's been a long day. I shouldn't be taking it out on you."

Joan dabbed the corners of her mouth with a monogramed napkin. "That is correct. Now that we're back on track, I thought you might like to take your family on a picnic upriver tomorrow."

"Oh, Tyler, could we?" Sarah said, her eyes every bit as big and brown as Rachael's.

Tyler gave his mother a withering look. "If the weather is good, I don't see why not."

"On a boat, Daddy?" Cody said. "I wanna go on a boat."

"We can all go on the boat, and after dinner, we're going to hunt alligators—the kind that live in the river, not in fancy houses." Sarah's eyes widened, and he laughed.

Joan scowled at him. "You think you're clever, Tyler Chandler, but I'd watch myself if I were you. Your father isn't here anymore to intervene on your behalf."

"I can defend myself now."

"You're more interesting now; I'll give you that, though I've had my fill of your lazy English. You know I detest it."

Tyler felt Sarah's hand on his left thigh again and reached down to give it a squeeze. He'd never told her about his relationship with his mother and their continual sparring matches with one another. It was a battle of wills nearly every time they got together, just as it had been between her and his father. Sometimes he thought his mother had just plain worn his father out. At other times, he wondered if something more sinister had happened between them. There was no proof, of course, but she'd had so much to gain by his death, even though she had controlled it all by that point anyway. His father was a weak man. Tyler, however, was determined to be strong. He refused to allow his mother to control him or his family.

He winked at Sarah. She had to be confused. What poor country girl wouldn't be swayed by the lavish gifts his mother was heaping upon her? He should have known it would begin the moment he turned his back. He should've warned her.

"I can't believe how quiet the children are. Can you, Tyler?"

"She probably bribed them. Ring your bell, Mother. I'm ready for dessert."

"Patience, Tyler. If you wouldn't scarf down your food, you wouldn't finish ahead of everyone else."

Pushing from the table, he said, "All right, that's it. Come on, Cody. Let's go huntin'!" He rounded the table, scooped up his son, and headed down the hall.

"But he'll get his new clothes dirty," Sarah called after him.

Tyler slammed the door on his way out.

* * *

Sarah pulled the blanket over her sleeping daughter. She looked so pretty in her new bed. She'd paid so little attention to Rachael during her young life. She was quiet, where Cody was lively and rambunctious. It was easier to love Cody; he looked so much like Tyler. Rachael reminded her of herself when she was a child.

Her parents had desperately wanted a son. After her older sister Emily was born, her mother had miscarried twice, both of them boys. When she got pregnant again and found out it was another girl, her parents considered terminating the pregnancy, but the doctor felt that doing so might make it harder to conceive again in the future. As it turned out, Sarah was their last child. She always felt like they resented her for that. She had wanted to make it up to them by giving them a grandson. Everyone had expected twin boys, but one of them had turned out to be a girl. Tyler was indescribably disappointed, but at least they had Cody.

Sarah swallowed the bitter guilt that rose up in her stomach. She knew she should be better about showing love to Rachael. It wasn't her fault. Still, what good is a daughter when you have a son?

She gently closed the door and hurried back to Tyler's room to await him there. She didn't want another conversation with Joan. Watching what had happened between them was upsetting; she'd never seen Tyler act like that before. Maybe he had a reason for rejecting his mother's money. She intended to demand some answers, but she may as well enjoy herself while she could.

She found a peach-colored nightgown in the dresser and put it on. She refreshed her lipstick, combed her hair, and lounged on the bed. Even if she fell asleep, he'd wake her when he came in. She wanted to make love. She felt beautiful tonight and wanted to share it with Tyler, especially if it was all about to end. She wondered if she'd get to keep her new clothes. She hated herself for wondering, but she did. And what about the children's bedrooms? Surely, Joan wouldn't take everything back to the store!

Well, it did no good to worry about it. She'd do whatever Tyler said. Joan was *his* mother.

Sometime later, she felt Tyler's lips playing softly upon her mouth. "Hey, baby. I tried to wait up for you," she said. "Come to bed."

"I have to take a shower first. I stink."

She watched him take off his clothes and lay them in the chair. She loved the chiseled curves of his muscular frame. "Wanna take a bubble bath instead? I could wash you all over."

He looked at her and smiled. "Now that's the best offer I've had all day."

She got up from the bed and hurried into the bathroom to get the water going. He followed. Turning her towards the mirror, he stood behind her. "You look beautiful, Sarah. If there's one thing I can say about my mother, she has good taste in clothes."

"I'm the one with good taste," she teased. "I chose you." She turned around and sat on the counter.

Tyler stepped between her legs and pushed the gown upwards, bearing her thighs. "You're my kind of girl, Sarah. Don't you ever forget that."

"Don't you forget it, either." She gave him her most sultry smile and wrapped her arms around his neck.

"I mean it, Sarah. Guys get stupid sometimes. No matter what happens, don't forget that I love you."

"Stop talkin', Tyler, and kiss me." She closed her eyes as he crushed her mouth in that dizzying way that made her so happy.

"Into the water with you. Let's take our time tonight. Let's love each other like there's no tomorrow."

She pulled the straps from her shoulders and let the gown fall to the floor. "I love you, Tyler. I always love you like there's no tomorrow."

He climbed into the tub, banished Pamela from his mind, and took Sarah into his arms.

CHAPTER FOUR

"**I** wish I could, but I can't get away today," Tyler said.

"Tell me you don't want to skinny dip with me in my pool," Pamela teased.

Tyler glanced over his shoulder as Sarah struggled to clip a life jacket onto Cody, not twenty feet away. "What about Jacob?"

"He's spending the day with a friend. We'll have all afternoon to explore one another. If you care for me, you'll find a way."

"I care, but—"

"Please, don't disappoint me. I've been dreaming about that kiss you promised me."

He looked at his watch. "I'll find a way."

"See you soon, then."

Cody let out an impatient scream and began to cry.

"Tyler, can you help me with this? It's twisted."

Tyler dropped the phone into his pocket and walked over to where Sarah knelt with Cody at the end of the dock. "Stop crying, Cody. Daddy will fix it." He unhooked everything and started over.

"Thank you," Sarah said. "I'll go find Rachael."

Tyler quickly clipped Cody's jacket into place. "Come on, son. Let's get into the fishing boat so that we can row out to the big boat."

"I don't wanna go in the small boat, Daddy. There's too many croc-a-gators!"

Tyler grimaced. This was the downside of taking Cody out last night. The river had teemed with alligators, their red beady eyes shining in the beam of his powerful flashlight. He was surprised to see how many more there were than when he had lived here. Their outing had upset Cody, which wasn't entirely a bad thing. The last thing he wanted was for him to jump into the river. He might make it out in daylight, but at night, when the gators came out to feed, the chances weren't as good. As it was, people lost pets from the shoreline every year, even in the daytime.

"We'll wait for Momma, and then I'll row out to the boat by myself."

"Then I'll go in the big boat," Cody said.

Sarah came skipping down the flagstone stairway to the dock. "Guess it's just us today. Joan wants to keep Rachael while we go out."

"Stay with Cody while I get the houseboat," Tyler said. "He's afraid to get in the fishing boat because of the alligators."

"I'm surprised he didn't have nightmares."

"Don't start on me, Sarah. It's probably for the best. We don't want him jumping in." He climbed into the boat and untied it from the dock. Taking up the oars, he rowed the one hundred yards or so before maneuvering around a dense outcropping of cypress and sumac trees and over to the boathouse. Why his mother kept the pontoon boat was a mystery. As far as he knew, she hadn't set foot on it since his father died. Nevertheless, Mr. Gibbs took it out on a regular basis and kept it well maintained. A smile tugged at his lips. He had to give it to Ole Gibbs— putting up with his mother all these years couldn't have been easy.

He rowed the fishing boat up to the side of the metal A-frame boathouse and tied it off. He entered beneath the roof and walked along the side deck, admiring the pontoon vessel. He'd had a lot of fun on this boat during his college years when he'd been free to do as he pleased. He certainly hadn't planned to marry when he did, but Sarah had turned up pregnant, and now he was tied down good.

His cell phone rang.

"Hey, Tyler. Are you on your way?"

"Not yet, but I'm working on it."

"Guess what I'm doing."

"Tell me," he said as he made his way to the helm.

"I'm lying in bed thinking about you."

"Oooh. I wish I was there." On a hunch, he stepped into the galley and opened the refrigerator. Inside, he found fresh fruit, bottled water, cookies, and what he had hoped for most—beer.

"Wanna know what else I'm doing?"

"Tell me," he said as he stepped back onto the deck to untie the rope and pull in the mooring buoys. The water rippled gently beneath the pontoons.

"I'm sucking on my middle finger."

"You're killing me, Pamela. Don't say anymore. I promised my boy that I'd take him out on the boat today. Once I do that, I'll leave him with my mother and head over."

"I've waited a long time to be with someone, Tyler. If you're just looking for a good time, tell me now. My career is at stake."

"The no-fraternizing rule goes both ways."

"You didn't answer my question."

Tyler rolled his eyes. Why did girls always do this? He wasn't in the mood for making promises he couldn't keep. "If you're not comfortable with me coming over, maybe we should wait."

"Perhaps you're right," she said. "The last thing I need is a broken heart."

Tyler could have kicked himself. "Look, Pamela, I'm not in a position to make any promises, but I can't wait to see you again. I think about you all the time."

"I just wish I knew what was going to happen. It's hard for me to let anyone close to Jacob and me. I'm the type of girl who knows what she wants and goes after it, but I'm risking everything."

Returning to the helm, Tyler paused. He knew he should end it with Pamela. It couldn't go anywhere, and lots of people were going to get hurt if he continued, but he couldn't find it within himself to say the right words. He *wanted* to see her again. He wanted to see where it would lead. "You and your fingers behave yourselves. I'll call you when I'm on my way."

She laughed. "All right then. I'll be waiting."

"See you soon." Tyler turned the key, and the motor started like a champ. Smoke rose from the back of the boat, floated over the top, and stung his nostrils. He waved the cloud away and pulled the boat forward. Once he was on the river, he took a deep breath and sighed. The greenish-brown water and lush vegetation called to him in a way he couldn't explain. It felt like freedom, a passage from the real world with its demands to an exciting, unknown future. Whatever it was, he savored every moment of it before rounding the bend where the mansion loomed and Sarah and Cody waited.

"Daddy! I want to ride in the big boat!"

Tyler pulled back on the throttle and swung the back end around until it gently bumped against the dock. He stepped onto the deck and reached for his son. "Come on, then. We're goin' upriver! He turned to help Sarah. As she made her way to the bench seat, his gaze lingered on her rounded backside. He couldn't help comparing it to the smaller, firmer curves he was dying to get his hands on. It wasn't fair and he knew it. Sarah had borne twins. Having twins may have changed her body, he reminded himself, but not her willingness to give of herself whenever he wanted. He loved her for that.

He pushed from the dock, and Cody climbed into his lap as he retook the wheel.

"Can I steer?" Cody said.

"You can help."

It was a beautiful morning, sunny, and bright. The birds overhead sang while the boat twisted its way along the overgrown bank.

Wildflowers bloomed everywhere the sun pierced the dense brush.

"Where are the alligators, Daddy?"

"They're sleepin', Cody. We don't have to worry about them as long as we stay in the boat." He was glad to see the wrinkles ease from his son's brow.

Sarah arched her back and sighed. "It's so peaceful out here. Are there any more houses up this way?"

"Not until we get to the main channel. There are many houses scattered along the Pearl, but most of them are hard to see." Holding Cody in one arm, he stood up and pointed upriver. "See where the river gets wide? That's what we call the 'lake,' though it looks more like a swamp right now. That's why you'll sometimes hear us refer to the house as the 'lake house.' Dad and I used to drop anchor there. We'd fish and swim all day. There used to be a dock somewhere to the right. Most of the time, we'd build a fire on the bank and cook our catch out here. I miss those days."

A few minutes later, Sarah jumped to her feet and pointed to the bank. "Look, Tyler. Is that it?"

Squinting into the sun, Tyler saw that the dock still stood. "Well I'll be damned. Mr. Gibbs strikes again. Good for him."

"Can we go swimming, Daddy?" Cody said, squirming until Tyler set him on his feet.

"No!" Sarah snapped.

Tyler shot her a look. "There are more alligators now than when I swam here. Besides, we're goin' upriver."

The channel narrowed again as they left the lake behind.

"There are islands in the main channel where people go to party. I used to put a little motor on the back of the fishing boat and take it out there when I was in high school. The main island is a half mile further up river." He chuckled. "Those parties got pretty wild sometimes, especially on holidays. Lots of skinny dippin' goin' on back then."

"What about the alligators?" Sarah said with surprise.

He shrugged. "I don't remember even thinking about it. Maybe we thought the risk was worth it."

She laughed. "Knowing you, that's probably true!"

"Quiet," he said. "Let's see if we can tell when we're getting close to the main channel."

"How will we know?"

"Sometimes you can hear other boats or people's voices as they carry over the water."

Sarah glanced around. "Where's Cody?"

Tyler watched over his shoulder as she hurried through the kitchen and opened the bathroom door. "Cody? Where are you?" She checked the bedroom. "Tyler, he's not here. Where could he be?"

"Check outside. Check the back deck."

Sarah hurried along the narrow walkway on the side of the boat towards the back deck. "Cody, where are you? Answer me this minute!"

Tyler slowed the boat to a stop, but he couldn't drop anchor, nor could he risk letting the boat drift towards shore because of the submerged trees and undergrowth that could puncture the pontoons. "Sarah, did you find him?"

"Oh my God, Cody! Get down from there!"

The next thing he heard was a splash.

"Tyler! Cody's in the water! He went down the slide!"

He heard another splash as Sarah jumped in after him. "Dammit!" Tyler said. He switched off the motor and rushed around to the back of the boat. Sarah was swimming towards Cody, who was coughing and sputtering for breath. He grabbed the life preserver and tossed it into the water. Out of the corner of his eye, he saw an alligator slide into the water from the shoreline. "Hurry, Sarah!"

Sarah grabbed Cody and pulled him towards the life preserver. "Look, Cody. Daddy's gonna give us a ride." Her attention snapped to the left as she dog paddled to stay afloat. "Grab tight, Cody. Don't let go. Pull him in, Tyler!"

"Grab on, Sarah. I'll pull you both."

"Do it, Tyler. There's no time!"

Tyler began gathering the rope, focusing on Cody as he held on to the life preserver. "Hang on, Cody. I've got you." He didn't dare pull too quickly lest Cody let go. "You're almost here, son. Hang on." A few moments later, he reached over the side and scooped Cody into the boat. Once Cody was on board, he grabbed the life preserver to toss back out to Sarah, but the current had pulled the boat further down river.

"Hang on, Sarah! I've got to back up," he yelled over the cries of his frightened son. The wide-eyed panic on her face sent shock waves coursing through his veins. Why hadn't he insisted that he pull them in together?

"I've got to get out of the water! I saw an alligator," she yelled as she dogpaddled towards the bank. "Pick me up from shore."

He plucked up Cody, who continued to cry, and raced along the side of the boat towards the front.

Sarah's screams stopped him cold.

"Momma!" Cody cried.

Tyler rushed to the controls and fired up the motor. If an alligator had attacked, what could he do without a gun?

Upon turning the boat, he saw Sarah gasping for breath as she climbed through the tall, thick grass in the shallow water.

"Sarah! I'll bring the boat in as close as I can."

"I'm snake bit!" she cried as she struggled to pull herself out of the river and onto the bank. "Moccasins, two of 'em."

"Oh, God," he mumbled as new fears washed over him. "You've got to stop exerting yourself. Stay still. I'm coming for you!"

"Momma!"

Tyler headed straight for the bank, cringing as the bottom scraped submerged trees and other debris. He pressed as far as he dared, but he couldn't get near her.

"Tyler, I feel the poison. I can't breathe."

"Yes, you can! We're gonna get you out of here." Tears blurred his vision as he watched her fall to her knees in the shallow water.

"I'm so tired." She struggled to pull herself onto the bank, wheezing so loudly that he could hear it from the boat.

He thought about swimming to her, but if something happened to him, who would see to Cody? He couldn't leave a four-year-old stranded in the middle of a river. His mind was spinning. "Sarah, say something! Sarah!"

"I'm sorry, Daddy. I'm sorry I went down the slide."

"It's not your fault, Cody. Some snakes bit your mommy." Keeping hold of Cody's hand, he pulled out his cell phone and scrolled through the numbers.

"Ratliff Ferry," a gruff voice said.

"My wife's been snake bit, and she's stranded on the riverbank. I can't get my pontoon boat close enough to reach her, and the gators are reacting to the activity in the water. Can you help me?"

"We got a couple of ski boats out here. Where you at?"

"About a mile and a half upriver from you, just off the main river. Do you know where Pearl River Mansion is?"

"I know it. I'll send some boys up there right away. You need to call 911. There ain't no time to waste. Ya hear?"

"I understand. I've got my four-year-old boy aboard."

"We'll be there as soon as we can."

Tyler stared at the phone and then at Cody, who had finally stopped crying. His eyes appeared vacant and his face pale as he stared across the water. Pulling him into his arms, he held him to his chest and patted his back. "Someone's coming to help your momma." He dialed 911. After repeating the information, he called out to Sarah again, but she didn't respond.

When the ski boats arrived, he took Cody inside. A few minutes later, he heard the voices of two men as they stepped aboard. He put

Cody in the bedroom and closed the door.

"How is she?"

One of the men shook his head, and they both lowered their eyes.

"Are you sure?" Tyler said, his voice cracking. "Maybe she's just unconscious."

"She took a bite to the throat, another on the arm. I doubt she suffered long."

Tyler turned away.

"Where do you want us to take her? We could take her to Ratliff Ferry."

"I—" Tyler swallowed hard. "I told 911 to meet us at the dock at Pearl River Mansion, but maybe Ratliff Ferry is better, easier for the kids. I'll call them back."

He dialed 911 again. "I just called about my wife. Should I take her to Pearl River Mansion, or should we take her to Ratliff Ferry?" He turned to look at the two men. "No. She's not breathing. Where will you take her?" He said as his voice began to quiver. He closed his eyes, but the image of Sarah lying on the bank wouldn't go away. "Yes, that's fine. Our four-year-old boy is with me. I don't want him to see her like that. As it is, he watched her die. He's very upset."

The two men, bearded and tattooed, looked to be about twenty years older than he was. By their pacing, Tyler knew they were uncomfortable, but he was grateful for their presence. "Yes, sir. That's what we'll do."

"They think it's best if we take her back to the house. They're sending the police there to take my statement. I'll anchor the boat in the center of the lake, which is about a quarter mile farther in, then my boy and I can ride in one of the ski boats back to the house. I'll take him inside and wait for the paramedics. The second boat can follow with Sarah. I'll direct the paramedics once they arrive. That way, Cody won't have to see her."

"We're real sorry this happened," the older of the two said. "There ain't no words for somethin' like this."

Tyler nodded. He didn't trust himself to respond. If he was still in shock, he couldn't imagine how Cody must be feeling. "Is Sarah out of sight? I don't want Cody to see her."

"Give me a minute to back up my boat," the same man said.

"When I anchor this one, please stay back while we get into the other boat."

"Got it."

The two men stepped into their boats, removed the buoys, and pushed off. Tyler settled at the controls and headed back to the lake. Tears welled in his eyes. How could this be happening? Was there more he should have done? It had happened so quickly!

He wiped his eyes and stared straight ahead until he entered the wide spot in the river. Slowing the boat, he cruised to the center of the lake. Making his way to the front of the boat, he tossed the anchor overboard and waited for it to hit bottom. He tugged until it caught and he felt certain it would hold. One of the ski boats pulled alongside. "I'll get my boy," he said, raising his voice over the motor. He made his way to the bedroom and opened the door. Cody sat on the bed, but his eyes looked dead. All the fire had gone out of them. "Cody, are you all right?"

"Where's Momma?"

"She's riding in a ski boat. We're gonna ride in a ski boat, too. Are you ready?"

"I wanna ride with Momma."

"Well, you're gonna ride with me. Let's go."

"I want my Momma!" Tyler reached for him, but Cody screamed and kicked his legs. "I want my Momma!"

Tyler scooped him up and carried him down the hall, out through the glass doors and into the ski boat. Cody screamed even louder. Tyler spanked the side of his leg. "Stop it, Cody. Right now! We're goin' riding in the ski boat. Look!"

As the ski boat took off, Cody stopped crying and turned his face into the wind. He looked at his dad with surprise and then smiled.

"See, Cody? This is a ski boat. Pretty fast, huh?"

As the wind blew the hair back from his face, Cody giggled. "I like ski boats. I want a ski boat."

"Okay, Son. We'll get you a ski boat."

* * *

The police were waiting at the landing. Joan stepped forward and took hold of Cody's hand.

"Come on, Cody. I've got fresh cookies in the kitchen."

"No!" He pulled his hand free and ran back to Tyler, wrapping his arms around his right leg. "I don't want to go with Grandma. I want to stay with you!"

Tyler scooped him up and carried him away from the dock and deposited him at the base of the steps where Joan was waiting, hands on her hips and scowl on her face. "You go with your Grandma now. I have to talk to the police."

When Joan took his hand, he screamed. Keeping hold of him, she gave him one sound swat on his bottom. "You straighten up, young man. That's no way to behave. We've got fresh cookies straight from the oven, and we need to go see how they turned out."

"I want my Momma!" he cried.

"Your daddy is going to see to her while we see about the cookies. You don't want Rachael to eat them all, do you?"

He shook his head and wiped his face on the back of his sleeve.

"Then we'd better go check on them before she does."

Tyler gave her a weak smile as they turned to climb the steps up to the house.

When they were out of sight, the second ski boat pulled up to the dock. Tyler gasped as he got his first look at Sarah. Her neck and arm were grotesquely swollen and spotted with ugly patches of black and red.

The paramedics rushed forward and placed her onto a stretcher.

"Wait! I want to say goodbye." He caught a glance between the police officers and paramedics, who then stepped back and let him approach.

He picked up her hand. "Oh, Sarah, baby, I'm so sorry this happened. How can we make it without you?" He dropped his head onto her chest and wept. The vision of Sarah's panicked face as she had looked up at him from the water, Cody's eyes as he watched her pull herself through the grass, the helplessness he had felt, all came rushing back to him. If only he could do it over…he should've pulled her and Cody in at the same time. He should've jumped in after them. Something! His shoulders shook with grief. He loved Sarah. He didn't want to lose her like this. Not like this!

He felt a strong, firm hand upon his shoulder.

"Come on, Son. Let them see to your wife now. There's nothing you can do to change what's happened."

Tyler sniffed and pressed her hand to his cheek. "Sarah, honey, I'm so sorry!"

"Come on, now," the officer said. "We need to talk about what happened."

The police officer stood by while Tyler unwrapped his fingers from her hand and laid it gently at her side. He knew that the next time he saw her, she'd be in a box, and he couldn't stand the thought of it. As the officers led him away, he covered his ears to drown out her screams. If only he could have saved her, but he couldn't, not from the venom of water moccasins when help wasn't readily available.

"Are you all right, Mr. Chandler?"

"I can still hear her screaming. I can't stand it!" He dropped to his knees and wept again.

One of the officers, a heavyset man, patted him on the shoulder. "I'm Officer Richards, but folks around here just call me Charlie. This is Officer Holmes. We need to know what happened out there today. Do you want to go inside?"

Tyler wiped his face and pushed to his feet. "No. My kids are in there. What do you want to know?"

"Tell us what happened."

As he recounted his story, he couldn't stop his voice from shaking as he waited for them to accuse him, to tell him what he should have done and didn't.

"And your son saw all of this?" Officer Holmes said.

"I tried to cover his eyes, but he squirmed free. He heard her screaming, but there was nothing I could do."

"There ain't nothin' anybody can do when something like this happens," Charlie said. "You wanna see a doctor? Maybe they can prescribe somethin' to calm you down and help you sleep, though nothin' but time is gonna make this easier to accept. Awful things happen sometimes, and there ain't no good reason for it."

"I don't want any drugs. I just want my wife back. Can I go check on my son now?"

Charlie scribbled a number on the back of a card. "Call this woman tomorrow. Your son's gonna need help getting over what he saw. She specializes in young children, but she may be able to give you the name of someone who can help you also."

Tyler took the card and headed towards the house. As he approached the porch, he was surprised to see Mr. Gibbs standing by as Rachael played in the grass with another child, a light-skinned black child with dark curly hair. He nodded and went inside.

He found his mother reading a magazine in her favorite chair, next to the sofa where Cody lay sleeping with his thumb in his mouth, something he hadn't done in months. Joan normally wouldn't countenance such behavior, so Tyler knew that getting him to sleep was no easy task. She looked up when he entered.

"Come into the kitchen," she said. "I just brewed some coffee."

He sat at the breakfast table with his back towards the window and rubbed his eyes. He still couldn't believe what had happened.

Joan set a steaming mug on the table and sat in the chair across from him. "The police didn't say much. Will you tell me what happened?"

He sighed. How many times would he have to tell this story? Well, at least with his mother, if he were to blame, she'd say so. "We watched Sarah die." He recounted the incident, and then buried his head into his arms and waited, but instead of condemnation, he felt her hand on his head.

"I'm sorry, Tyler. Who would have guessed that such an awful thing would happen today? It was over quickly for Sarah, but it won't be as easy for you and Cody, I'm afraid."

He raised his head and looked into her eyes. He saw sympathy in the cold blue, perhaps for the first time in his life. "I keep wondering what more I could have done, but I had Cody with me."

"You can't blame yourself. It was a horrible accident, and that's all there is to it. The question is where you go from here."

Tyler closed his eyes. "I haven't thought that far yet. I can't."

"I'll make the funeral arrangements if you like, but you'll have to inform her family. Where do her people live?"

"Arkansas. I doubt they have the money to spend on a hotel. I can let them stay at my place if I can stay here with you."

"Of course. You'll get through this, Tyler, and so will the children, though Cody may need some help."

"That's what the police officer said. He gave me a name to call, but I can't deal with that today. Can you watch the kids this afternoon? I'd like to go to my room."

Joan jumped to her feet. "Good heavens! Where's Rachael? I'm not used to minding after little ones."

"She's fine. I saw her with Mr. Gibbs on the back lawn. She's playing with his grandson. At least, I think that's his grandson. He could have a young girlfriend, I suppose."

"Don't be vulgar. You know I detest it when you act so familiar with those people."

"Mother, I've been around Mr. Gibbs my entire life. It's difficult *not* to act familiar with him. I'm going upstairs. See you at dinner."

Joan scowled and hurried from the room.

He rolled his eyes and started down the hallway just as the back door slammed.

* * *

"How dare you let him touch her?" Joan snapped as she stormed down the back porch steps. "Rachael, come here this instant. You're headed for the bath, young lady."

Startled, Rachael stood up and looked down at her clothes. She brushed fresh dirt from her yellow shirt. "I'm sorry I got dirty, Gramma. I've been playing with Jayden. We've been picking butter beans."

"I'm sorry, Mrs. Chandler," the thin, black, gray-haired man said. "The li'l Miss wandered outside while you was busy with young Mister Cody. With everything going on with Miss Sarah and Mister Tyler, I thought it best to keep her busy. I meant no harm."

Joan swallowed a retort. He was right, of course. She was the one who lost sight of Rachael. In all the confusion, and Cody crying and screaming, she hadn't even noticed that Rachael had slipped away.

"It's good of you to be concerned, Mr. Gibbs, but I can't countenance Dillia's bastard touching my granddaughter. It's not proper, and you know it. Where is Dillia anyway? She didn't show up to work this morning."

"She's done run off again, Miss Chandler."

Joan grabbed Rachael by the arm. "Dillia is a whore; that's what she is. You just wait; she'll turn up pregnant again before you know it."

"Bye, Jayden," Rachael said, tripping over her feet as she looked back over her shoulder.

Joan yanked her arm as she headed towards the house. "Don't speak to him, Rachael. Jayden doesn't concern you."

* * *

Tyler's cell phone rang for the second time. Lifting his head off the bed, he saw that it was Pamela. He'd forgotten about her. "Hey," he said halfheartedly.

"Where are you? If you're going to stand me up, the least you could do is tell me."

"There was an accident today. Cody's mom just died; everything's a mess. We have to arrange the funeral. It was awful."

"Oh, Tyler. I'm so sorry."

"I don't know what to feel," he said. "It happened so quickly."

"Tyler, don't. You don't have to tell me. I just wish I could hold you."

Tyler sighed. "That's what I need. I can't just lie around here. Can I come over? I'm not the best company right now, but I sure could use a hug."

"Yes, of course. Bring Cody, too, if you want."

"Thanks, Pamela. See you soon." He pushed off the bed and looked at himself in the mirror. It seemed wrong to seek comfort in the arms of another woman, but he didn't want to face reality on his own. He couldn't bear to think of what they might be doing to Sarah at this very moment. Sarah was gone, and she wasn't coming back. If Pamela could make that easier to accept, why shouldn't he go? He rushed down the stairs, hoping to avoid a confrontation with his mother.

Cody was fast asleep on the sofa. Without waking him, he laid him over his shoulder and walked out the front door, careful not to let the screen door slam behind him. He crossed the yard and maneuvered quietly through the gate. With a sigh of relief, he climbed into his truck and left Pearl River Mansion and all of its painful memories behind him.

CHAPTER FIVE

"**W**hat do you mean; he's not available? Isn't he at work today?"

"No, ma'am."

"Did he work yesterday?"

"No, ma'am."

Joan felt her blood pressure soar. "I want to talk with his supervisor. Whom might that be?"

"Uh, that would be Pamela Clarkston, ma'am, but she's out of the office right now."

Joan stopped pacing long enough to take a quick sip of water. She set the glass on the kitchen counter and resumed pacing. "And when do you expect her to return?"

"I'm not sure. She called in sick yesterday and today."

"Look, dammit. I've got a funeral to arrange, and I need some answers. Is the publisher in?"

"I'll check for you, Mrs. Chandler. Hold, please."

Joan shook her head. Four days and there was still no word from Tyler. How dare he do this to her, not to mention abandoning little Rachael?

"Mrs. Chandler? I've got the publisher on the line for you."

"Good afternoon, Mrs. Chandler. How may I help you?"

Joan sat down for the first time in hours. "Thank you for taking my call. I need some answers. Has Tyler been to work the past couple of days? I haven't heard from him since the accident."

"I'm very sorry to hear about Sarah's death, Mrs. Chandler."

"Thank you. It is especially tragic for the children, of course."

"Tyler hasn't been to work since last Friday. We've left him several messages, but he hasn't returned our calls. Unfortunately, we have reason to believe that he's staying with his immediate supervisor, a young woman who has recently moved here from Atlanta. One of his workmates reported seeing Tyler's truck parked in her driveway the past few days."

"I see. May I have her address and phone number, please? I need to contact Sarah's family, and Tyler is the only one who has that information. The funeral service is tomorrow evening. Her family *must* be informed."

"Under normal circumstances, I wouldn't divulge an employee's personal information, but I believe an exception is appropriate. Tyler's been with us for several years, Mrs. Chandler. We're all concerned for his welfare. We'll be as understanding as possible in the early stages of this tragic incident."

"Tyler's career is important to him," Joan said. "He'll get his emotions under control and return to work soon. We appreciate your patience. I can see why Tyler speaks so highly of you."

"How nice of you to say. The young woman's name is Pamela Clarkston."

"One moment while I get some paper." After taking down the information, she stared at it and wondered what she should say once she got the woman on the phone. Did she know what had happened? Did she know that Sarah was Tyler's wife? Well, she couldn't be responsible for *that*. She dialed the number.

"Hello?" said a female voice.

"Is this Pamela?"

"Yes. Who's this?"

"My name is Joan Chandler. I'm Tyler's mother. I desperately need to speak with Tyler. Please put him on the phone."

"I've been trying to get him to call you. Hold on."

Joan raised a brow. That went better than expected.

"How did you get this number?" Tyler demanded a moment later.

"The funeral is tomorrow night, Tyler. Sarah's family must be informed. You need to call them."

"Don't tell me what I need to do, Mother."

"All right then, *I'll* call them. Give me her mother's name and number."

"What time is the funeral?"

"It's at the Grandview Funeral Home at seven o'clock. Are you bringing Cody?"

"I don't want him to see her like that."

"The viewing starts at five, but they will close the casket for the service. How is Cody doing?"

"Let me worry about Cody."

"Tyler, I'm on your side. Why are you shutting me out?"

"I'll call you back with Sarah's family information. Don't call me here again."

The dial tone buzzed in her ear causing Joan to scowl at the phone. She didn't understand why he was taking it out on her, and he didn't even ask about Rachael. He was acting as if he didn't even have a daughter. For Rachael, it was as if she had lost her mother, father, and her brother, all in one day. She was withdrawn and cried most of the time, and who could blame her?

For the first time in her life, she didn't know how to handle a situation.

* * *

Joan left Rachael under the watchful eye of Mr. Gibbs, just two doors down from the viewing room. She wasn't happy that Jayden was present, but there was simply no other place for him to be. Straightening her shoulders, she entered the viewing room and was surprised to find it empty. Tyler hadn't arrived yet, and neither had Sarah's family. She scowled at her non-present son and made her way down the center aisle, between approximately ten rows of chairs, to the casket. The flowers she had ordered were lovely. The extravagant array of white lilies sprinkled with miniature red carnations draped over the lower half of the solid oak casket. No other flower arrangements had arrived, not even from Tyler. She shook her head in disgust. What was he thinking?

Steeling herself, she looked down into Sarah's face. They had done an excellent job of preparing her. She looked quite sweet, and so very young. She *was* young. Sarah may not have been what she had wanted as a wife for Tyler, but she never wanted this. Losing a mother, any mother, was difficult for a child, especially on children as young as Rachael and Cody. With Tyler acting out the way he was, she worried that he might take the children away somewhere, and she didn't want to lose contact with Rachael.

"No. I can't do it, Billy Ray. You go."

Joan turned to see two men and two women appear in the doorway.

"It's all right, Leeann. We done talked about this already," a large, bearded man said with an accent so thick that Joan might have laughed had it not been real. "You wait here. I'll go pay our respects and be back directly."

"I'll stay with you till Daddy comes back," the younger woman said as she wrapped an arm around her mother's shoulder.

Joan surmised that she must be Sarah's sister; they looked so much alike. She had never met Sarah's family; she hadn't known about Sarah until after the wedding had already taken place. She made her way to the entrance. "Hello, everyone. I'm Joan Chandler, Tyler's mother." She extended her hand to Sarah's father, which he shook. His rough, dry hand was so large that it completely engulfed hers.

"I'm Sarah's mother, Leeann," said the thin, auburn-haired woman of about forty-five. "We spoke on the phone. Thanks for callin' us. We're still in shock."

"Hi. I'm Emily, Sarah's sister, and this is my uncle, Tommy Lee. Where's Tyler? We can't wait to see them kids."

Joan nodded respectfully to Tommy Lee, a man who looked as round and rough as Billy Ray. "Tyler hasn't arrived yet. He's very upset, as you can imagine. He loved Sarah very much. As for the children, we feel it's best not to let them see Sarah. Rachael is being supervised a few doors down. When you're ready, I'll take you to see her. Cody is with Tyler. I expect them any minute."

Sarah's father nodded. "Ma'am." He and Tommy Lee left the group and approached the casket. Everyone grew silent as they watched the two men. Tommy Lee shook his head and placed his hand on Billy Ray's shoulder. Billy Ray took one look at his daughter and dropped to his knees. "Why, Lord? Why did you take our precious Sarah?" His forehead hit the side of the casket with a thud, and his massive shoulders shook with grief as he cried for his daughter.

Joan was astounded.

"Will you stay with Momma?" Emily whispered.

"Of course."

Emily hurried to the casket and wrapped her arms around her father's neck. "It's okay, Daddy. Sarah's in heaven, now, singin' with Jesus." She turned to look at Sarah and began to cry also.

Billy Ray rose to his feet and drew Emily and Tommy Lee into his arms for a genuine group embrace. Joan had never seen anything more touching. These poor, uneducated, backwards people had something she'd never had. They sought strength and openly took comfort in each other. It was extraordinary. She wrapped an arm around Leeann, who turned into her shoulder and cried even harder. As the trio turned to make their way up the aisle, Emily plucked a carnation from the arrangement and brought it to her mother.

Accepting it with trembling hands, Leeann kissed it and pulled Emily into her arms. "I love you, Emmy. I don't tell you that near enough."

"I love you, too, Momma."

Feeling uncomfortable, Joan took a few steps back. "Would you like some time alone with Sarah, or are you ready to see Rachael now?"

"We're ready," Leeann sniffed. She grabbed some Kleenex from the table beside the door and blew her nose. The others followed as Joan led them down the main concourse to the other room.

"Give me a moment," Joan said as she went inside and closed the door. As she expected, Rachael and Jayden were playing together on the floor. They were looking at children's books, which belonged to the funeral home. "Sarah's family is here, and they want to see her."

"Come, Jayden. You heard Mrs. Chandler."

Jayden closed his book and stood quietly beside his grandfather against the wall.

Rachael glanced up from her book. "I don't need a bath, Gramma."

"I know, Rachael. Now listen to me. There are some people here to see you: your other grandmother and grandfather, your aunt Emily, and your uncle, Tommy Lee. The last time you saw them, you were a tiny baby, so you probably don't remember them, but they remember you. They love you very much, so be nice to them." Rachael nodded, but she looked wary. "Are you ready to meet them?"

Rachael stood and raised both arms. "Hold me, Gramma."

"You are getting too big for Grandma to hold, but let's hold hands." She opened the door and stepped out into the hall.

"My goodness. Look how sweet you are!" Leeann exclaimed as she rushed forward.

Rachael hid her face in the folds of Joan's skirt.

"Give her some time," Joan said. "The last few days have been extremely difficult."

"Look, I brought you a present." Reaching into her pocket, Leeann pulled out a necklace with a heart-shaped locket on it.

Rachael turned to see it.

"Take it. The heart opens up, and there's a picture inside. See if you can guess who it is."

Rachael took the necklace and tried to open the locket, but she couldn't do it.

"She's so pretty, Momma," Emily said. "Hi, Rachael. I'm your Auntie Emily."

Rachael smiled. "Hi, Auntie Emily!"

Emily giggled.

"Let's sit on the sofa," Joan said, waving them towards one of the many parlor rooms set aside for family visitation. "Then Grandma Leeann can help you open the locket."

"She looks just like my Sarah did at her age," Billy Ray said as he swiped a tear from his eye.

Tommy Lee nodded. "Sure 'nuff does. She's a perdy li'l thing."

Once they sat on the sofa, the Richards family gathered around.

Leeann, who sat to Rachael's right, opened the locket and handed it back to her. "Do you know who that is?"

"That's my Mommy!"

"That's right." Leeann swallowed hard. "That's our Sarah."

"That necklace is a very special gift," Joan said. "You must take care never to lose it. Did you thank Grandma Leeann?"

"Thank you, Gramma Leeann."

"You're welcome, Rachael."

"Rachael, I need to call your daddy. May I leave you here for a few minutes?"

"Sure, Gramma. You said they love me."

"Yes, they do, and I'll be right back." Joan walked away from the group and went to check the viewing room. Still no sign of Tyler. She took out her cell phone and dialed, but it went straight to voicemail.

"Tyler, where are you? The funeral is set to begin in fifteen minutes. Call me!" She dialed Pamela's number, too, but it also went to voicemail. Sighing with frustration, she went back to check on Rachael, whom she found enjoying the attention that usually went to Cody. She stayed back and allowed them to visit.

A few minutes later, the funeral director, a tall, plain-looking man in a posh designer suit, approached. "Excuse me, ma'am, but we're getting ready to start. May we close the casket and prepare for the ceremony?"

Pressing her lips into a straight line, she nodded. Surely, Tyler would arrive in time for the funeral.

"I'll let you know when it's time for the guests to be seated," he said. "We'll wait as long as we can."

"Thank you."

"Excuse me for interrupting," Emily Richards said, her cheeks flushed. "Is the minister here? I wanna talk to him about the ceremony."

The funeral director glanced at Joan, and she nodded. "I'll ask him to speak with you directly."

Once he was gone, Emily rubbed her arms. It was cold, Joan thought. Funeral homes were always cold.

"Do you know which scriptures he'll be readin' or which songs will be sung?"

"It never occurred to me to ask," Joan said. She was beginning to wonder if Tyler was coming at all.

"Sarah was raised Baptist. She'd want some Bible verses read durin' the service. Her favorite song is 'Amazin' Grace.' I'd like to sing it for her if you don't mind. I sing right well, some say. I do solos at our church."

"Make whatever changes you like."

Emily reached out and took hold of her hand. "Thank you, Mrs. Chandler. That'll mean the world to my family."

The director and the minister stepped out into the hall and walked towards them.

Joan pulled her hand free. "I'll leave you to discuss the arrangements." She returned to the group, taking care to stand where Rachael could see her. The next thirty minutes went by in a blur. All she could think about was Tyler. There was no excuse for him to miss Sarah's funeral!

She had delayed the service as long as she could, but they'd finally had to start without him.

Emily was in the midst of a truly lovely rendition of "Amazing Grace" when a commotion in the hallway caught everyone's attention. She heard a child crying who sounded very much like Cody. It was all she could do not to get up. A moment later, Tyler staggered into the room holding Cody, who was indeed crying and struggling to get down. Behind Tyler stood a lovely young woman who was leading a young child of her own, a boy about the same age as Cody. Joan felt the blood drain from her face. How on Earth could Tyler do something so tasteless?

Tyler sat down in the back row and none too quietly told Cody to shut up.

Joan snapped her face back towards the front. How could she possibly explain Tyler showing up at his wife's funeral half-drunk, which he obviously was, and with a new girlfriend? She had raised him better than this. It was humiliating.

Billy Ray stood up. "Hey, hold up everybody. Hold up. Tyler, who the hell is that?"

"That's none of your business, Billy Ray."

As Billy Ray headed up the center aisle, the young woman grabbed her child and hurried out the door.

"That's right, girlie. You'd better run. How dare you come up in here, to my daughter's funeral, with my daughter's husband? Stand up, Tyler. I'm gonna whoop yer ass."

"Rachael, stay with Grandma Leeann," Joan said as she went to the outside aisle, along the wall, towards the back row. "Come here, Cody. Come see Grandma."

"No," Tyler said. "Cody's staying right here with me."

"Let him go, Tyler. He doesn't belong in the middle of this."

"Listen to yer momma, boy," Billy Ray said, his voice booming through the small room like a war drum. "Face me like a man, and don't be hiding behind my grandson."

"Security!" the minister cried. "Security!"

Tyler pushed Cody towards Joan and stood up. "There's no reason to make a big deal out of this. I miss Sarah more than anyone, but that doesn't mean I don't have needs."

"Needs? My daughter ain't even in the ground yet, and you're satisfyin' yer needs?"

Fear and adrenaline kept Joan's knees from buckling when she imagined what an angry Billy Ray could do to her impudent, disrespectful son. "Tyler, you've disgraced yourself and this entire gathering!" She slapped the side of Cody's leg as he struggled to get away. "Stop it, Cody! Mr. Richards, I don't blame you for being outraged. Tyler's bad judgment and lack of sensitivity is shocking. I apologize in his stead, and ask for your forgiveness, but please—for Sarah's sake—let's finish the service and deal with this unfortunate business afterwards."

"You don't have the right to apologize for me, Mother. I'm of age."

"And, apparently, that hasn't made you any smarter. Sit down, Tyler, and for once in your life, keep your mouth shut."

Leeann came up behind Billy Ray and placed her hand on his back. "Come on, Billy Ray. We owe it to Sarah."

Billy Ray glared at Tyler and pointed his finger at him. "Don't think this is over, boy. How dare you insult my daughter's memory at her funeral?"

Two security guards arrived and stationed themselves at either side of the door.

Billy Ray took his seat, and Leeann nodded to Emily, who began singing where she left off. Joan picked up Cody and carried him back to her seat. "Come on Cody, let's go see Rachael."

"I don't wanna see Rachael. I want my daddy!"

When she and Cody sat down, Rachael's eyes brightened. "Hi, Cody!"

"I've been staying with Daddy," he said.

"I've been sleeping in my princess bed. Wanna come play with our toys?"

"Hush! You two can play after the service," Joan said, her heart still beating wildly.

"Okay, Gramma." Rachael reached for Cody's hand, but he kicked her viciously, which made her cry.

Joan and Leeann looked at each other with surprise. Joan picked Rachael up and held her against her chest, while Leeann pulled Cody closer to her.

As the service concluded, the minister said a prayer that included the need to be forgiving and merciful towards one another as grief expressed itself in many ways. After everyone had filed out of the room, Tyler made his way to the front. He slid the flower arrangement towards the bottom of the casket and opened it.

Joan lingered at the door, gently bouncing Rachael, who had fallen asleep. A few moments later, Leeann and Billy Ray joined her. Leeann was struggling to hold on to Cody, who was fussing and trying to get away.

Billy Ray reached down and scooped him up. "I'm your papaw, boy. You stop that fussin', or I'll spank you a good one."

Cody looked up at him with big brown eyes, and to Joan's surprise, he stuck his thumb into his mouth and laid his head against Billy Ray's massive chest.

Everyone turned to watch Tyler.

"Sarah, honey, I miss you so much. No matter what anyone says, I loved you more than you'll ever know. Don't you forget that." His voice broke as it projected throughout the empty room. He plucked several carnations and laid them around Sarah's body, gently, one at a time.

Joan glanced over at Sarah's family. Leeann and Emily were crying. They turned and walked into the hallway together. Billy Ray followed. She took one last look at Tyler and stepped out into the hall. As angry as she was with him, he deserved the privacy to say goodbye.

"Want me to take her for you?" Leeann said as she lightly stroked Rachael's cheek.

"Sure," she said, but Rachael woke up and wanted to stand on her own.

Billy Ray hauled Cody higher onto his shoulder; he was fast asleep.

"This has been very hard on them," Joan said.

Rachael tugged on her skirt. "I want to see Cody sleep."

Leeann picked her up so that she could look into Cody's face. "You can talk to him when he wakes up."

Rachael stared at him intently.

"Are you all right, sweetheart?" Joan asked, wondering what she was thinking.

"I don't want Daddy and Cody to leave me again."

"What's she talking about?" Billy Ray said. "Is Tyler livin' with that girl?"

"Don't worry, sweetie. It'll all work out. You'll see."

Rachael held out her arms. "Hold me, Gramma. You hold me."

Leeann quickly set her down. "Thank you for letting me hold you, Rachael. We'll just take our time gettin' to know each other."

Turning to Billy Ray, Joan said, "Maybe we should talk about this once the children are down for their naps." As if on cue, Rachael yawned.

Leeann smiled as she peered into Cody's face. "He's as cute as he can be. I always wanted me a boy, but God gave us two beautiful girls instead. Now we just have one, and we'd give anything to have our Sarah back again. Is there some place we can talk? We're plannin' to camp on the outskirts of town and drive back tomorrow. I can't see you goin' out there, but maybe we could meet at Tyler and Sarah's place in the mornin' and visit there a spell?"

Joan glanced down the hall and saw Pamela waiting at the far end. "Excellent idea. Let's meet at the trailer tomorrow at nine o'clock." She opened her purse and dug into her wallet for three one-hundred-dollar bills. "Here, take this. This will pay for your hotel rooms tonight. You can leave Cody in the care of Mr. Gibbs. He's in the room two doors down on the left. Now, if you'll excuse us, I need to speak to Ms. Clarkston." She hefted Rachael up onto her hip and headed down the hall.

When she approached, Pamela rose to her feet, though she was careful not to jostle her child, who slept peacefully on the sofa beside her. "You must be Pamela Clarkston. Thank you for taking my call yesterday."

"I'm sorry about causing a scene in there," Pamela said. "I told Tyler it wasn't a good idea. The only reason I came was to keep him from driving. He's been drinking all afternoon."

"I appreciate that. Did you know Tyler was married?"

"Not until Sarah died. We haven't slept together if that's what everyone's worried about. I don't intend to be a rebound relationship, Mrs. Chandler. My son and I deserve better than that. That being said, I'm falling in love with your son."

"Tyler is a great catch, though he's certainly not acting like it these days. You're wise to wait. Not only did he love Sarah, he also watched her die. It will take time for him to heal."

"I know, but I lost my job because I allowed Tyler to stay with me. He was technically my employee, and that goes against company policy. I tried to explain, but they wouldn't listen. I don't know what to do now. Tyler says he may want to move to Atlanta with me. Our two boys are already quite close, almost like brothers."

"I see," Joan said, hearing her worst fears confirmed.

"Speaking of babies, who is *that* precious one. She's beautiful."

"This is Rachael. She's Cody's twin sister."

"Oh my gosh. Tyler never told me he had twins." Her brow wrinkled with bewilderment. "Why wouldn't he tell me he had a daughter?"

Scowling, Joan said, "Tyler has no use for Rachael. His affections lie solely with Cody. Rachael is the apple of my eye, though, so don't you worry about Rachael. I'll take good care of her."

"I've always wanted a daughter," Pamela said as she reached out to stroke Rachael's cheek. "Hey, sweetie."

Rachael turned away. "I want my Mommy."

"Excuse me," Joan said as she walked back down the hallway, cursing herself for allowing Pamela to see Rachael. What if she persuaded Tyler to take Rachael and Cody to Atlanta? She couldn't let that happen! "Your Mommy went to heaven, Rachael. It will be a long time before you see her again, but until then, I'll take good care of you. I promise."

Rachael yawned again. "You take care of me, Gramma."

* * *

Joan sighed when she finally pulled the blankets up around Rachael and tiptoed from her room. She intended to contact her attorney first thing in the morning to see about drawing up the paperwork for legally adopting Rachael. She had little doubt that Tyler would give her up, so long as Pamela didn't interfere, and she was prepared with options if she did. As for the Richards family…she rolled her eyes. That's what happens when you're not selective about whom you sleep with. At least Pamela came from a wealthy family. She might not object to the match if it weren't for the threat to her plans for Rachael.

Her eyes narrowed as she remembered Pamela's words, "I've always wanted a daughter." Well, by God, so had she, and she intended to have the adoption papers signed and implemented before anyone could interfere.

* * *

"Cody!" Rachael cried when they arrived at Tyler's trailer. She threw her arms around her brother, but he crinkled his nose and shoved her away.

"I'm going to play in my room," he said.

"I'll come with you."

"I don't want you in my room! I don't want you here at all!" Cody yelled as he ran towards his room.

"Come on, Rachael," Tyler said as he took her by the upper arm and led her down the hallway. "You two stay in here until I come to get you."

"Yes, Daddy," she said.

Joan couldn't help noticing that Tyler had no other words for his daughter, whom he hadn't seen in five days. At this point, it was to her advantage, but it was sad for little Rachael.

"Go see to the young'uns, Emily," Billy Ray said when Tyler returned.

"But I want to hear—"

"You heard me, girl."

"Yes, Daddy," Emily said as her gaze fell to the floor. She walked down the hallway and into Cody's room.

Since the children didn't fuss, Joan assumed that they welcomed their new playmate.

Billy Ray and Leeann sat on the sofa, which sagged under Billy Ray's considerable weight, and Tommy Lee sat in the recliner, leaving Joan and Tyler to pull up chairs from the dining table. The atmosphere couldn't have been more tense.

"Would anyone care for coffee?" Joan said.

"No. We'd like to get right to the point if you don't mind," Billy Ray said as he eyed Tyler. "How long you been seein' that woman? Is that young'un yers?"

Tyler shot to his feet. "I don't have to listen to this!"

"Answer the question," Joan said. "You brought the girl to Sarah's funeral. You had to know there'd be questions."

Dragging a hand through his already mussed hair, he sat down and pressed his lips together. It took a few moments for him to answer. "Pamela and I met about a month ago. She was my supervisor at work until they fired her for being my friend through all of this. We aren't sleeping together, though she gets the credit for that."

"That's what Pamela told me as well," Joan added.

"How are you plannin' to take care of them kids without Sarah to look after 'em in the daytime?" Leeann said.

"What do you mean?" Tyler said. "Daycare, I guess. I'll do what any single parent does."

"Sarah told Emily that you spend a lot of nights out drinkin' with yer friends," Billy Ray said. "That's gotta stop. You got responsibilities now."

"All right, that's it! You can't tell me what I can and can not do! So, I drank the day of Sarah's funeral. Who can blame me? My wife just died. I think I'm entitled to have a drink if it helps me face her funeral, don't you?"

"Not if you have a drinkin' problem, and not if it interferes with how you intend to raise my grandbabies," Billy Ray said.

"Look, Mr. and Mrs. Richards," Joan said, "I know you're concerned, but Tyler is a very good father. As for the children, there won't be any need for daycare or even babysitters. I am more than capable of providing supervision. Not only that, I intend to hire private tutors to help them prepare for kindergarten. In addition to the basics, they'll study art and music and have every imaginable advantage. There's no need for you to worry."

Tyler raised a brow in her direction. "There, you see? It's all worked out. I'll continue to work at my career, and Mother will assist me with the children."

"We want the kids to spend part of the summer with us in Arkansas," Leeann said.

"When they're older, maybe. Until then, you're welcome to visit them any time you like." Tyler rose to his feet. "Now, if we're finished here—"

Billy Ray stood also, as did the rest of the Richards family. "There's one more thing," he said. "We talked to yer young lady friend, who you left sitting by herself down yonder end of the hall. According to her, your momma says you ain't got no use for Rachael. That bein' the case, Leeann and me done talked about it, and we want to adopt her. We'll raise her as one of our own."

Joan gasped, and Tyler pinned her with a hateful glare. "Well, my mother is wrong. I'm not givin' Rachael up to you or anybody else. And now that I think about it, after what Sarah told me about how you raised *her*, there's no way in hell I'd let you anywhere near my kids, so you can forget about summer visits."

"What the hell are you talkin' about?" Billy Ray yelled.

"I'm talking about how you whipped her half to death with your belt buckle one night when you were drunk on moonshine, and how you beat your wife when she does things you don't like, like when she spends too much at the grocery store. So don't go judgin' me about my conduct. You need to be more concerned about your own. Now, get out of my house before I call the police!"

Billy Ray rolled up his shirtsleeves. "I oughta knock you clear to next Sunday for tellin' such lies."

"Are you calling Sarah a liar? Swear on the Bible, Leeann. Has Billy

Ray ever hit you?"

"Come on, Billy Ray. Let's go home," Tommy Lee said. "This ain't gettin' us *nowhere*."

Billy Ray glared at Tyler, but he followed his wife out the door.

"I'll get Emily." Joan hurried down the hall and tapped on the door before she opened it. "Emily, there's been an argument. Your family is waiting outside for you."

"Oh. Goodbye, you two. I love you!"

"Bye, Auntie Emily," Rachael said, but Cody ignored them and continued to play with his toy truck.

Joan followed Emily outside and stood by as she climbed into the back seat of their rusted station wagon. "I'm sorry it turned out this way," she said to Billy Ray through the open window. "Despite his behavior the past few days, Tyler is a very good father. I meant what I said about helping him with the children. I'll see to it that they have every advantage. You have my word on it. Please, drive safely."

"You seem like a real nice lady, Mrs. Chandler, but I meant what I said, too. We're gonna adopt li'l Rachael and give her a home where she feels wanted. We seen how he treats her. He acts like she ain't even there."

"He's terribly upset by Sarah's death. It isn't fair to judge him by what you're seeing now."

"You can talk till yer blue in the face, but it's obvious he don't care nothin' for her. You said so yerself. I done called my cousin. He's a highfalutin attorney over in Little Rock, and he thinks we got a darn good chance of provin' that Tyler's an unfit parent."

"But he's not! He's—"

"Don't try to stand in our way. No offense, Mrs. Chandler, but we're a lot younger than you. Rachael will be better off with us."

Joan's heart was pounding so loudly that she could barely hear his words. "How dare you speak to me like that? You're not getting your hands on Rachael. I'll spend my entire fortune to see that you don't! Whoever your cousin is, he can't hold a candle to the *fleet* of attorneys I'll retain. Now, get out of here, and don't ever come back!"

Billy Ray stomped on the accelerator, spun around, and sped down the long gravel driveway.

Joan was so angry that she was having difficulty catching her breath. Feeling light headed, she made her way to the porch steps and clung to the railing to steady herself. Forcing herself up the stairs, she opened the door and stepped inside.

Tyler was waiting.

"Thanks a lot, Mother! Now my in-laws are going to sue me. Why on earth would you say something stupid like that?"

Her eyes fluttered, and everything went dark.

CHAPTER SIX

"**D**on't take her. Please, don't take her," Joan moaned.

Startled, Tyler leaned forward in his chair. "Mother, can you hear me?"

"Rachael."

Tyler went out into the hall and waved down a nurse. "She's awake."

Returning to her side, he picked up his mother's hand, careful to avoid the tubes and monitors. "Don't worry, Mother. No one's going to take Rachael. She'll be here when you get well. She'll be right here."

"Pretty little Rachael."

Tyler hadn't realized how much she adored his daughter, nor had he realized how much he'd neglected her. It was true; he hardly knew Rachael. He had tried to figure out what was behind his aversion to her, but the best he could come up with was his childhood memories that his mother had desperately wanted a daughter, and her continual verbalized disappointment that she had only borne a son. Perhaps that was why he'd been so close to his father. They had bonded in the same way he and Cody were bonded. They were buddies. They did things together, activities that excluded his mother, and now Rachael. It wasn't right. He could see that, but he didn't know how to relate to a daughter.

He'd spent the past twenty something hours sitting at his mother's side, thanks to Pamela, who was taking care of the kids. She was staying at his trailer because they had agreed it would be easier on Cody and

Rachael than for them to stay at her place. It was awkward, but there didn't seem to be a better solution.

There was a lot to think about when it came to Pamela. She'd lost her job because of him. If she didn't find a new job soon, she'd have to move out of her house. She'd already mentioned the possibility of moving back to Atlanta, which would end their chances of building a relationship unless he went with her. The other option was for her to move in with him on a more permanent basis, which would give her time to look for employment. He didn't know how that would work out; he only knew he wanted her to stay in Mississippi. He didn't want to lose her.

When the nurse came in, he stepped out of the way.

"Mrs. Chandler, can you hear me?" The nurse, a male in his early forties, took hold of her wrist and checked her pulse.

"Rachael. Where's Rachael?" she mumbled.

Making note of the numbers, the nurse said, "Who's Rachael?"

Tyler cleared his throat. "She's my daughter."

"Mrs. Chandler, can you open your eyes for me?" He gently tapped her hand. "Come on, Mrs. Chandler, open your eyes."

Her eyes opened briefly and then shut against the light. A moment later, they opened again. "Stop calling me Mrs. Chandler. My name's Joan."

Tyler chuckled. "Hello, Mother."

"What happened? Why am I here?" She lifted her right hand and scowled at the I.V. "I hate these things. I want to go home."

The nurse made several notes on the chart. "Glad to see you're feeling better. Can you tell me the last thing you remember?"

"I was outside arguing with Billy Ray. He said his attorney was going to prove Tyler an unfit parent so they can adopt Rachael." She reached out for Tyler's hand. "You can't let him take her, Tyler. You can't."

"Your blood pressure's going up, Mrs. Chandler," the nurse said.

"We need to change the subject."

"Don't worry, Mother. Rachael's not going anywhere. In fact, when you get out of the hospital, I thought you might enjoy having her come to stay with you for a few days."

"I'd like that very much." To the nurse, she said, "When can I go home?"

"You've suffered a nasty concussion. Do you remember what happened?"

"I remember feeling upset and light-headed. I climbed the steps to the trailer and went inside. I don't recall anything after that."

"According to your son, you fainted and hit your head on the coffee table when you fell. You've been in and out of consciousness for the last twenty-four hours. We've done several tests, which indicate that you may have suffered a mild stroke. We don't believe there's any permanent damage, but we want to keep you here for another twenty-four hours just to be sure."

"I appreciate everyone's concern, but I'd like to go home now. I'm a very busy woman. I don't have time for this nonsense." She swung her legs out of the bed and proceeded to sit up.

The nurse gently swung her legs back onto the bed. "I'm sorry, Mrs. Cha—, uh, Joan, but I can't let you leave just yet. Your doctor will have to release you first. I'll tell him you're ready to leave though, and we'll see what he says."

She puckered her lips. "How long will that take?"

"I can't say, but I'll tell him you're in a hurry. In the meantime, why don't you lie back and get some rest? I'll bring something to help you relax until it's time for you to leave."

"I'm thirsty. Am I allowed to have anything to drink?"

"Not just yet. We want to hear from the doctor first."

"I thought you'd say that." Turning to Tyler, she said, "See why I want out of here? Don't you call 911 on me again. You hear me, Tyler?"

"How can you ask me that after what I've just been through? No,

Mother. If I need to call them a hundred times, I will. Now do as he says, or we'll have to stay here even longer. Isn't that right, nurse?"

"I'm afraid so."

"Well?" she said. "Go tell the doctor I'm ready."

"Yes, ma'am." The nurse nodded towards Tyler and left the room.

* * *

Mr. Gibbs opened the passenger door of Tyler's truck. "Can I help you down, Mrs. Chandler?"

"No, thank you. Tyler will come around."

Tyler rushed to help her down. She was steady on her feet. As soon as she realized that, she let go of his arm and walked up the porch steps on her own.

"Mr. Gibbs, has Dillia returned?"

"No, ma'am. She done got married and moved to Chicago."

"Well, thank God for small favors," she said. "Perhaps you can concentrate on your duties now."

"She left Jayden behind, ma'am."

Joan turned around. "I see. Well, we'll just have to manage then, won't we, Mr. Gibbs?"

"Yes, ma'am. He's a real good boy, Jayden is. You'll see."

Joan turned back towards the house and went inside.

Tyler followed. He tried to help her, but she waved him off and settled on the living room sofa.

"Tyler, would you mind getting me a glass of water? I'm feeling fine, but I need to rest a minute."

He started for the kitchen.

"Once I've rested, we need to talk about the children."

When he returned with the water, she was asleep. He sighed and drank the water himself before making his way outside, down the back steps, and out onto the dock. He dialed Pamela and could hear the kids screaming in the background.

"Hey, Tyler. How's your mom?" she said. "No, Cody! Don't you dare hit your sister with that! Put it down. Thank you."

"I just brought her home. She's napping. How are you? It sounds like World War III over there."

"You have no idea how much commotion a pack of preschoolers can make. I can't keep up with them. Rachael's no problem, but the other two? Oh my goodness! They play. They fight. They chase each other around. Half the time, they make me laugh. The rest of the time, I'm afraid they'll kill each other."

"Don't say that."

"Oh, I'm sorry, Tyler. It's just an expression. Three is so much more work than one."

"Mom and I are going to talk about the kids when she wakes up. Have you had any time to think about what you want to do? *I* think we have tremendous potential. I want to court you, romance you, and fall in love for all the right reasons."

She sighed into the phone. "I don't know, Tyler. I—Hey! Put that down. Don't you throw that book at Jacob. I mean it, Cody. Put that down."

"Hand him the phone," Tyler said.

"Here, Cody. Your daddy wants to talk to you."

Tyler pulled the phone away from his ear as Cody took the phone and banged it on who knows what as he brought it to his ear.

"Hi, Daddy. When are you coming home?"

"I don't know yet, but if you don't mind Miss Pamela, I'll wear you out when I get there."

"Yes, sir."

"It's nice to have Jacob to play with, isn't it?"

"I like Jacob. He's my friend."

"Well, friends don't throw things at each other. So, you play nice."

"Can I throw the book at Rachael? I don't like Rachael."

"No, you can't throw the book at Rachael. She's your sister. Tell Jacob and Miss Pamela you're sorry."

"I'm sorry, Jacob. I'm sorry, Miss…what's her name again?"

"Her name is Pamela. Let me talk to her again."

Tyler heard more rustling as the phone changed hands.

"Hey, that was nice. Thank you," Pamela said.

"I've got one more request before we finish our conversation," Tyler said. "Can I talk to Rachael for a second?"

"Rachael, do you want to talk to your daddy? Ahhh, she looks scared. Come here, Rachael. It's just your daddy."

Rachael took the phone. "I didn't throw it, Daddy."

"I know you didn't. I just wanted to say good night before you go to bed."

"Oh. Good night, Daddy. I wanna sleep in my princess bed."

"You do? Would you like to sleep in your princess bed tomorrow night?"

"Yes, Daddy! I wanna sleep in it every night!"

"You'll have to sleep in your own bed tonight, but I'll talk to your grandma and see what we can work out for tomorrow night."

"Miss Pamela, Daddy said I can sleep in my princess bed tomorrow night!"

He smiled as Rachael's voice got farther from the phone.

"That's so good!" Pamela laughed as she took the phone. "Go play with the boys now."

"I can't," Tyler heard Rachael say in the background. "Cody only plays with Jacob."

"Hey," Tyler said. "Is that true?"

"Pretty much," Pamela said. "She's quiet and withdrawn most of the time. Talking about her bed just now is the first time I've seen her get excited about anything. Come to think of it, it's the first time I've ever seen her smile. When are you coming home, Tyler?"

"Do you miss me?"

"I don't know what to think about you. You have a lot more going on in your life than I first thought."

Tyler knew his next words were important, and he desperately wanted to say the right thing. "Do you remember when you told me that you were looking for someone to unlock the secrets of your heart?"

"Yes," she said softly.

"Well, I'm looking for the same thing. The only difference is that you're learning first-hand about *my* most painful secrets. I know how special you are, Pamela. I'm willing to go as slow as you need to go. Adjusting to a larger family will take time for all of us, including the kids, so let's not make each other promises we can't possibly know if we can keep right now. Let's just live and see where life takes us. No matter what, I'll always be grateful to you for making these difficult days more bearable."

"Do you have any *more* secrets, Tyler Chandler?" she said with attitude he could see as clearly as if she were standing there.

He chuckled. "I do. Besides, if you leave before you've experienced my kisses, you'll wonder for the rest of your life what you've missed. A man knows when he's good, Pamela."

"Ummm, and you're modest, too. Hurry home. I miss you."

"Just what I wanted to hear. I'll see you tomorrow."

"Good night," she said and hung up the phone.

Tyler took his time walking back to the house. Instead of taking the direct route, he wandered through the gardens, noting how the setting sun danced across the flower petals. He wondered if it was possible to love two women at the same time because he did. He loved Sarah even though she wasn't as educated or sophisticated as he had always imagined his wife would be. She was loving and giving, and she'd do absolutely anything for him. It wasn't right that she had to die.

As for Pamela, she was everything he'd dreamed of in a wife; at least she seemed to be. His heart raced at the briefest thought of her. How quickly life could turn upside down and then turn again. He stopped at the top of the flagstone stairs and let his eyes skip downward towards the river until his gaze fixed upon the fractured light beams teetering at the water's edge.

When he entered the kitchen, Joan had hot tea waiting. He joined her at the table as she poured two cups.

"When do you plan to return to work?"

He scowled. "Monday, I guess, unless they fire me like they did Pamela. I'll find out tomorrow. It'll make a difference as to whether or not I stay in Jackson."

"What do you mean?"

"If I lose my job, I might move to Atlanta with Pamela."

"What about the children?"

"What about them? I'll take them with me."

"It makes more sense for you to stay in Jackson. You're going to need help taking care of the children. I'm available, and I'm free. There's also your trailer and property to consider."

Tyler felt tired all of the sudden. "I'll know more after I call the office tomorrow."

She nodded. "One last thing. I'm sorry for saying what I did to Pamela. I was repeating what Sarah told me. I had no idea that she would tell Sarah's family what I said. The point is I want to keep Rachael with me. I'm her grandmother. I love her, and I want to give her the type of future she deserves. I'll take care of Cody, too, of course, but I really want Rachael."

"Our family isn't shy about picking favorites, is it, Mother?" He drank down his tea, which was painfully hot, and stood up from the table.

"Good night."

"Good night, Son."

He wrinkled his brow and kept walking. That was the first time she had ever called him son.

* * *

It was nearly dark the following evening when Tyler pulled to the side of the road to take a call from the publisher of the newspaper. Finally, a good piece of news; he was still employed. As irresponsible as he'd been since Sarah's death, he deserved to lose his job, but they were willing to show compassion because of his loss. "People do irrational things when they grieve," the publisher had said, though he was quick to point out that his tolerance had reached its limit. Tyler agreed to report to work on Monday.

He sighed with relief and drove the last few miles to the trailer, which was located off of Lakeland Drive, about halfway down Holly Bush Road. His reasons for buying this lot seemed ridiculous now. He had wanted to be independent. He had wanted to prove to his mother that he could make it on his own; he didn't need her money. He had wanted a place to call home, a piece of land he could build a cabin on one day. Now, he didn't even know if he wanted to stay in Mississippi, let alone on his property.

The front door opened as soon as he slammed the door of his truck.

"Daddy! Come and see what me and Jacob made."

Tyler thought about correcting his English, but he didn't. He used to hate it when his mother did that to him. "Give me a hug first." He gave him a squeeze and then hoisted him up onto his shoulders. "Duck when we go through the door."

When they stepped into the living room, Tyler set his son on his feet and allowed himself to be tugged into Cody's bedroom where he and Jacob had built a log cabin out of Lincoln Logs. It was quite impressive. "Did Pamela help you build this?"

"Just Jacob."

Jacob looked up from the corner where he was looking through a book. "Tomorrow we're going to build a castle. See?" He turned the book around to show Tyler a picture of a beautiful castle in the forest.

"Very nice. You did a great job on the cabin. I can't wait to see the castle. I'm gonna go say hello to Pamela now. I'll see you boys in a few minutes." He found Pamela in the kitchen cooking, singing, and dancing to music he couldn't hear. He noticed the earbud wires and smiled. He waited until she turned in his direction.

Startled, she shrieked, and then laughed. "Self-defense," she said, and pulled out the earphones. "If all you heard was screaming twenty-four-seven, you'd understand. Give me a hug, you handsome dog."

"Hey, why are you calling me a dog?"

"Because you get to keep your job, and I don't. That's not fair, you know."

"Agreed," he said, "but at least one of us still has an income, which means you don't have to worry as much. How did you know about that anyway? I just found out ten minutes ago."

"I got a phone call, too. If we didn't work in the same department, they might have given me another chance, but since we do, and since you've worked there for several years, they're keeping you and letting me go. They say it's not personal. They have to enforce company policy."

He took a beer from the fridge. "I don't know what to say, so I'm going to change the subject. What's for dinner? It smells absolutely wonderful."

"Chicken parmesan with homemade spaghetti sauce, Caesar salad, and garlic bread."

"Now that sounds amazing. I forgot that you can cook."

"One of my many talents. And when you're *really* good at something, you know it. Right, Tyler?" she teased.

"How good are you?"

She gave him a saucy look. "Better than you can imagine."

His eyes darkened as he pulled her into his arms, but she

pushed back.

"Did you say hello to Rachael yet?" She pointed to a chair, not three feet away, where Rachael sat quietly.

Seeing her, he knelt in front of the chair. "Hi, Rachael. Did you have a good day?"

"Hi, Daddy! Will you make me tall like you did Cody?"

"What do you mean?"

She grabbed hold of his shirt and stood in the chair. Patting his shoulders, she said, "Can I sit up here like Cody does?"

He realized that of the hundreds of times he'd hoisted Cody onto his shoulders, he had never once done that with Rachael. In fact, he couldn't remember the last time he'd held or even hugged her. "Turn around, and I'll pick you up."

"Don't hurt me, Daddy," she said as she turned and held onto the back of the chair.

A lump formed in his throat. How many times had he purposely reached out to make her cry? A pinch, a push, a slap; what was wrong with him? He gently picked her up and sat her on his shoulders. She squealed and grabbed his head. "Take my hands, Rachael. I won't let go."

"I'm scared, Daddy. This is too tall!"

Pamela stroked her leg. "Don't worry, sweetie. Daddy won't let you fall. Let's go look in the mirror."

"Don't let me fall, Daddy!"

"I won't, Rachael. I've never let Cody fall, and I won't let you fall either. Come on! We're goin' on a pony ride." He walked slowly. "See? You're safe."

She laughed. "I'm riding on a tall pony. Right, Daddy?"

"That's right. Now let's go see your pony in the mirror." Pamela went ahead of them and turned on the bathroom light. He walked slowly down the hallway, more careful than he'd ever been with Cody. When they entered the bathroom, he ducked so that she could see herself in the mirror.

"I'm riding a Daddy Pony!"

He couldn't remember the last time he'd seen her smile, or if he'd ever heard her laugh. "Now we're going into the bedroom to plop you on the bed. Ready?"

"Ready, Daddy!"

He bounced her a little bit, making her giggle with excitement. When they got to her room, he carefully lifted her from his neck and dropped her on the bed. She shrieked with laughter. "Again, Daddy. Do it again!"

He picked her up and dumped her on the bed again. She continued to laugh, which made him smile, too.

Pamela hooked her arm in his. "She's precious. Isn't she?"

He had to admit, she really was.

* * *

"Rachael, where are you? This is no time for you to be roaming about outside. Where are you, child?" Joan wrapped her robe tighter around her waist and turned down yet another gravel path. She wasn't concerned about getting lost. If she were gone too long, Mr. Gibbs would come looking. "Rachael? Come out. Grandma needs to go to bed." She heard footsteps in the gravel and rushed forward.

"Mrs. Chandler, ma'am," Mr. Gibbs said, lowering his eyes to the ground. "Miss Rachael ain't out here. Mr. Tyler done took her home to *his* house. Remember?"

Startled and embarrassed, she said, "Oh, yes. Thank you, Mr. Gibbs. Would you be so kind as to accompany me back to the house? You never know when an alligator might venture up from the dock. I should've brought my pistol along, just in case."

"There ain't never been no alligators in the garden, Mrs. Chandler. They stay near the water where there's food, so don't go worryin' yerself about that. There ain't no need for you to carry no pistol around neither. I watch for gators. That's my job."

She nodded and turned back towards the house. "Good, Mr. Gibbs. You keep an eye out for me. I don't want them hurting my Rachael."

"Yes, ma'am. I don't want 'em hurtin' my grandson neither, but they can't get past the fence, Mrs. Chandler. We's safe up in here. Don't go worrin' yerself about no alligators, ma'am."

"Yes, thank God for the fence. Roger thought I was being overly protective when I demanded that fence, but he wouldn't think that now if he saw how many there are. Somebody needs to start shooting those things! It's criminal the way they're allowed to breed like they do. I think I'll write my congressman tomorrow."

Once they passed through the front lawn, Joan stopped at the bottom of the porch steps. "How am I supposed to run my household without Dillia to do my housework? It was damn inconsiderate of her to run off like she did."

"Yes, ma'am, but I have a sister in Chicago whose husband just passed. She's lookin' for work. A mean cook, Regina is. She worked in the governor's mansion nearly twenty-five years afore she got married. Talks right well, too. Not like me, though we both growed up here. She's more citified than I am. I could ask her to come if you like. Otherwise, I'm right handy around the house. Whatever you need, just let me know."

"Thank you, Mr. Gibbs. A fine breakfast might be in order while I consider the matter of your sister, if you think you're up to the task."

"Just name the time, ma'am, and you can judge for yerself."

"Seven o'clock ought to do. Good night, Mr. Gibbs."

"Good night, ma'am."

* * *

Tyler reveled in the warmth of Pamela's body as she wrapped an arm around his waist. How long he'd been staring down at Rachael as she slept, he didn't know. She looked so much like Sarah it was astonishing.

Pamela smiled up at him and then turned her attention to Rachael. Tyler could imagine them doing this together every night, checking on the children before going to bed. He'd never done it with Sarah. In fact, this was the first time he'd come into Rachael's room to check on her at all. He gently drew Pamela towards the door and into Cody's room where the boys were asleep in Cody's bed. Cody had stolen most of the blankets.

As he looked down at his son, he felt his heart stir.

Cody was his son, his flesh and blood. He'd do absolutely anything for him, even if it meant giving up his life. Why didn't he feel that way about Rachael? She was pretty to look at, but he couldn't honestly say he felt more than that. The why of it bothered him immensely. It was as if there were something fundamentally wrong with him.

"They're so cute," Pamela said as she leaned forward to adjust the blankets evenly over the boys.

Being with Pamela felt natural in a way that being with Sarah never had. He couldn't explain it, but it went beyond physical attraction. It felt like belonging, which seemed ridiculous considering the untried status of their relationship. They settled onto the couch together, tired from the day. He had thought he wanted to talk, but he didn't. Instead, he turned her back to him, drew her against his chest, and leaned back on the pillows. She sighed and relaxed in his arms.

The next thing he knew, it was three o'clock in the morning, and his right arm was aching. Stirring enough to pull it from around her, he shook it to get the blood flowing again. "Let me up," he whispered. Once he slid out from beneath her, he scooped her up, carried her into the bedroom, and laid her on the bed.

"Aren't you going to lie with me?" she whispered.

"I want to, but I'm going to sleep on the couch. I'll see you in the morning."

"Good night," she murmured.

As he lay on the couch, he thought about the events of the past week and tried to make sense of it. Had Sarah died to make way for Pamela and Jacob in his life? Was he ready to take on the responsibility of another child? Where was Jacob's father? He didn't know anything about Pamela's background, but he knew he was falling in love with her. He couldn't imagine losing her, not after losing Sarah. He couldn't let that happen, no matter what.

CHAPTER
SEVEN

Joan heard noises coming from the kitchen. "Dillia, is that you?"

"No, ma'am."

"Mr. Gibbs, what on earth are you doing?" she said as he flipped an omelet and dropped bread into the toaster.

"I'm making breakfast, ma'am. Just like we agreed last night. May I bring yer coffee into the dining room?"

"We agreed to no such thing." Turning, she saw Jayden sitting at the breakfast table, quiet as a mouse. His big brown eyes reminded him of Rachael's. "What's he doing here?"

"Got no place else to go, ma'am, but don't worry; he won't eat nothin'. We done et afore we come over."

She gave Jayden a dirty look. "What's this about a discussion last night?" She accepted the hot mug he offered and took a whiff of the dark brew. It was nice not to have to make it herself.

"You was outside in the garden lookin' for Miss Rachael."

"I most certainly was not!"

He chuckled. "Whatever you say, ma'am, but you was."

She wrinkled her brow and sat at the table. Jayden slipped off his chair and grabbed hold of his grandfather's pant leg.

"Go stand by the wall while I finish up Mrs. Chandler's breakfast. Ya hear?" He nodded and did as he was told.

"Cody could learn a thing or two from Jayden, I see."

"Thank you, ma'am. He's a real good boy, Jayden is." He set a surprisingly appetizing meal on the table and herded Jayden towards the door. "I'll be back to clean up directly. Enjoy yer mornin', Mrs. Chandler, and while you're tryin' to remember last night, see if you remember us talkin' about my sister Regina. Otherwise, I'll be needin' a raise if I'm gonna do my work and Dillia's, too. I'll be in the garden pickin' vegetables for supper. Holler if you need me, ma'am."

"I don't holler, Mr. Gibbs," she said as she waved him off.

She took a bite of the colorful omelet and raised a brow. The fresh onions, green and red peppers, and mushrooms were delicious.

She vaguely remembered their conversation in the garden, but she wouldn't have, had Mr. Gibbs not mentioned it, nor would she have remembered their discussion about his sister. Maybe she had hit her head harder than she thought. What she *did* remember is that Tyler was bringing Rachael over after lunch, and that was welcome news.

After breakfast, she called her attorney, John Carrington. After explaining the situation, she felt reasonably confident that there was little to worry about in the immediate future regarding Billy Ray's threats, so long as Tyler kept his drinking under control and didn't give them anything to use against him. She intended to press Tyler to let her adopt Rachael. Considering how he felt about her, there was a good chance he might agree. Should his new girlfriend present a challenge, she had several options in mind. Money handled most problems, but if that didn't work, she was prepared to fight dirty.

* * *

When Tyler awoke the following morning, he saw Pamela sitting on the floor in the living room looking through family photographs. Tears fell from her eyes as she flipped through the pictures.

"Good morning," he said.

Startled, she sniffed and wiped her eyes. "Rachael pulled these out. I couldn't resist looking at them. She looks so much like Sarah."

He dropped down from the couch and sat next to her. "She does, doesn't she?"

Pamela nodded. "It was easier when I didn't know what Sarah looked like, when she was just a faceless woman from your past. Seeing these pictures make me realize that you were a family, that you loved her. How can you possibly be ready to care about someone new?"

He cupped her chin and waited for her to look at him. "I can't explain it, Pamela, but I'm ready. I was ready before she died. I was ready the first time I met you. There's something between us that I've never felt before. It's as if I've been waiting for you my entire life."

She pulled back and looked down at her hands. "Rachael must remind you of Sarah every time you look at her. I'm not sure how I feel about that."

"It's no secret that I've never connected with Rachael. My bond is with Cody. Always has been." He reached for her hand, but she pulled away. "What about Jacob's father? Where is he?" He motioned for her to move so that they could lean against the couch.

"He died in Afghanistan. Oh, the country is grateful for his service, of course, but that doesn't help Jacob and me."

"I'm sorry. What happened?"

"Michael flew Black Hawk helicopters. It was his favorite thing to do, and he was one of their best pilots. They chose him for their most dangerous missions because he stayed cool under pressure. The conditions are rugged there, and they often have to land in hazardous locations. One day, during a training exercise, he violated a direct order and landed on a steep hillside, which resembled the terrain surrounding the three outermost military outposts. According to his diary, he figured that if he could land there, the army could resupply the outposts without sending troops through the dangerous mountains and valleys controlled by the Taliban. He did it, too," she scoffed. "He landed a Black Hawk helicopter at a twenty-two-degree angle when the maximum landing angle is supposed to be fifteen degrees. Everybody cheered, but then the ground gave way as he stepped from the chopper. He was crushed as the chopper slid down the hillside." She covered her face and cried.

Tyler gathered her into his arms. "He was a hero, Pamela, a man willing to place his life on the line so that others might live. You can be proud of him."

"But what about Jacob and me? Don't we matter? Did he ever stop to think about who would take care of us?"

"I'm here now. I'll take care of you and Jacob. I want us to become a family. You said yourself that the boys are already acting like brothers, and I know you adore me."

"You think way too highly of yourself, Tyler Chandler."

"Then why are you having trouble keeping a straight face?" he teased.

"I don't know what you're talking about. You're a conceited, arrogant, handsome—" She bit her lip to keep from smiling through her tears.

He pressed his mouth to hers and felt her lips part. As their kiss deepened, he heard himself groan. He was exploring, giving, taking, and claiming all in the same moment. Her arms wrapped around his neck and pulled him closer as she slid to the side and lay back on the floor. He followed, never breaking contact as their tongues sucked, teased, and danced for joy. When he finally pulled away, her chest heaved with longing, and her eyes remained half-closed, cloudy with desire.

"Oh, Tyler, no one has ever kissed me like that."

He wanted nothing more than to carry her into the bedroom and finish what they had started, but he knew it wasn't the time. He smiled. "There's plenty more where that came from. You have my heart, Pamela."

She sat up and wrapped her arms around his neck. "You have my heart, too. I guess that means it's time to make some plans."

"I'm ready if you are. I guess the first question is what to do about Rachael. We could keep the two boys and let my mother raise Rachael. They're very fond of each other, and nothing would make my mother happier."

"Give her up?"

"Yes, as awful as it sounds. Besides, if you and I have our own children, we'll have to have room for them. It seems like the perfect solution, and it would keep Billy Ray Richards off our backs."

"I've always wanted a daughter, but I would prefer to have my own." She smiled and looked into his eyes. "We'd make pretty babies, don't you think?"

"Yes, but not right away, I hope."

She laughed. "I agree. We'll have our hands full with the two boys."

"Where do you want to live?" he said.

"That depends on where I find work."

"I could sell the trailer, and we could move into your house if you like. I only bought this place because I wanted to build a big cabin on the lot one day."

"That would be nice. Maybe we could rent the trailer and live in the house I rented. That way, you'd still own the land."

"Hadn't thought of that. It's a good idea. You can stay home with the boys until they're old enough to go to school if you want to."

"There's a lot to think about, isn't there?" she said.

"Just when I thought my future was dark and uncertain, you've made it bright and exciting. I can't wait to make a new life with you."

She kissed him. "It's amazing how quickly life can change. I just lost my job and was facing the prospect of losing my house. I was worried about where to go and what to do. Now I'm sheltered in your arms and planning a new life with my new family. How does that happen?"

"It happened because we allowed ourselves to let love in. Speaking of that, can we make love tonight?"

"Perhaps," she said. "We'll know when the moment is right."

* * *

Rachael didn't understand everything they said, but she knew she wouldn't be staying with Daddy anymore. Cody would, but not her. When her daddy kissed Miss Pamela again, she turned away and walked back to her room. It sounded like she would be living with Gramma now, which meant she could sleep in her princess bed every night. She liked her new room, and she liked her new friend, Jayden. Jayden was nicer to her than Cody was, and so was Jayden's papa. She didn't know why she wasn't supposed to touch Jayden, or why, if he was dirty, he didn't take a bath, but she didn't care. If she lived with Gramma, she could play with him, and that made her happy.

She climbed onto her bed and reached beneath the pillow. Finding the necklace, she pulled it out and opened the heart-shaped locket. "Hi, Mommy. Daddy doesn't want me anymore, so I'm going to live with Gramma."

She hugged the locket to her heart and cried until she finally found comfort in sleep.

* * *

Joan was surprised to see Tyler pull up in an SUV. Pamela got out from the passenger's side; apparently, their relationship was progressing. Joan greeted Pamela warmly and watched for her reaction as she took in the scope of Pearl River Mansion. If money were behind her interest in Tyler, she'd use it to her advantage.

"It's a pleasure to see you again, Mrs. Chandler. I had no idea you lived in such a fine place. Tyler, why didn't you tell me?"

Tyler reached into the back seat to help Cody out of his car seat.

"It didn't occur to me to mention it. Come here, Cody."

"Well, it's quite lovely," Pamela said. "Excuse me while I help my son."

"Can I play in Cody's room?"

"We'll see," Pamela said as she unbuckled his straps and pulled him out.

Rachael waited patiently in the third-row seat.

Scowling, Joan said, "I see that my granddaughter has been relegated to the back of the class. Get Rachael from the car, Tyler."

"And where do you want the rest of her things?" he said.

"What are you talking about? It's hot outside; get Rachael out of the car."

"I'm asking you where you want the rest of her belongings, Mother. We're not taking her back with us. Rachael is staying here with you."

Joan felt her mouth drop open and immediately closed it. "Get her out, Tyler. Get my precious girl."

Tyler reached in to unhook Rachael. Instead of setting her on her feet, he handed her to Joan.

"Oh, my dear girl! How are you today?"

"Daddy doesn't want me anymore, so I'm going to live with you, Gramma."

Pamela's lips twisted in mortification, and Tyler clearly didn't know what to say.

"Your Daddy loves you, Rachael. He just thinks you'd be happier living with me. Isn't that right, Tyler?"

"That's right, Rachael. You want to stay with Grandma, don't you?"

"So you and Pamela have room for more babies?"

"Tyler! What on earth have you been telling this child?"

"She must have overheard us talking this morning," Pamela said. "I feel absolutely terrible."

"As well you should!" She set Rachael down and led her towards the house. "We are going to have great fun together, you and I. You're going to learn many wonderful things. You're going to study art and music, and we're going to travel the world together. Would you like to go to Disney World to see Cinderella and Princess Jasmine?" She smiled as Rachael's eyes grew large with wonder.

"Really, Gramma? Does Cinderella live at Disney World?"

"I have it on good authority that she visits there quite regularly. We may even see Snow White."

"I wanna stay with *you*, Gramma!"

"Of course, you do."

"Am I a princess, Gramma?" Rachael said as they approached the porch steps.

"Yes, my sweet girl. You're my little princess."

She paused to look up at the two-story mansion. "And this is our castle?"

"Yes, indeed." She could hear Tyler and his crew coming up the path. She watched Pamela's eyes as she entered the foyer, walked down the hallway, past the living room and dining room, and into the kitchen. She also noticed how she doted on her son, who admittedly seemed very well behaved as they settled at the kitchen table for snacks. Oh, she knew the type. She might have feelings for Tyler, but her first loyalty would always be to her son.

Rachael lifted her arms in the air. "I'm ready to sit in my chair, Gramma."

"You're such a good girl." She set her into the pink booster seat. "I'll be right back with some cookies." She was furious with Tyler for allowing Rachael to overhear their conversation. No child should know it is unwanted, even if it's true. Since it had happened, though, she planned to use it to her advantage.

Mr. Gibbs appeared from the butler's pantry with a plate of strawberry scones, a pot of tea, and lidded cups filled with juice for the children.

"Mr. Gibbs, you are a surprise."

"Yes, ma'am, but I ain't nothin' compared to my sister, Regina. I likes workin' outside where I can keep my hands in the dirt."

"Well, I hope you washed your hands before you made those scones," Tyler said.

Mr. Gibbs chuckled. "I reckon Mrs. Chandler would skin me alive if'n I didn't."

"After we enjoy our refreshments, Mr. Gibbs, please take the children out to the garden to play," Joan said.

"No! We want to play in my jungle room," Cody said.

"All right," she said, "but you need to ask politely. Try again, Cody."

"We don't want to play outside. We wanna play in my jungle room."

"That's not quite what I had in mind," Joan said.

"I'll do it," Jacob said. "May we please play in Cody's room?"

"Nicely done, Jacob. Did you hear that, Cody? That's how you should speak to your Grandmother. You may go after you finish your snack. You may not take food out of the kitchen."

"Yippee!" Cody hooted as he crammed his scone into his mouth.

Joan scowled at Tyler, but little good it did; he only had eyes for Pamela. She took a hesitant bite and raised a brow. The scones were quite good. If Mr. Gibbs' sister were half as good as he said she was, she'd be far better off than she was with Dillia, and heaven knew she needed *somebody*.

A few moments later, Cody sucked the remainder of his juice through his straw and made everyone aware of it. "I'm done. Can we go play now?"

She was about to correct him again, but Tyler gave permission before she could.

"May I be excused, too, please?" Jacob said.

"Yes, Jacob," Pamela said.

Cody and Jacob climbed down from their chairs and ran down the hall.

Joan looked over at Rachael. "Do you want to go with

them, sweetie?"

"No, Cody won't let me play with them. Can I go outside and play with Jayden in the garden?"

"Jayden is not your playmate, Rachael. You know the rules about that. Don't you?"

"Yes, ma'am. He's not allowed to touch me."

"That's correct. Mr. Gibbs, please accommodate my granddaughter while we adults have a chat."

Mr. Gibbs, his light black skin glistening in the light, smiled. "Yes, ma'am. Miss Rachael and I do right well together."

"Are you ready, Rachael?" Joan said.

She climbed down from her chair and said, "Let's check on the strawberries. I love strawberries."

"Yes, ma'am. I saw some big ones on the vine this mornin'." He nodded towards the group and followed Rachael through the butler's pantry with a smile on his face.

When she heard the back door close, Joan eyed Tyler. "What were you thinking to let her overhear such talk?"

"Probably the same thing you were thinking when I overheard as much from you when I was young," he snapped.

"What are you talking about?"

"I heard you tell Dad that if you knew you were having a son, you would've never had children."

"Good Lord, has that been bothering you all these years?" His countenance darkened, and he looked away. "Honestly, Tyler, that's ridiculous. Nevertheless, we're talking about Rachael here. What plans are you and Pamela making?"

"All we know is that we want to be together. Giving Rachael to you allows us to raise the boys and keep Billy Ray off our backs."

"May I adopt her legally?"

Tyler glanced at Pamela. "What's the point in that?"

"Because I don't want you changing your mind midstream. You

can't give her away one moment and take her back the next. There are emotional consequences for that kind of behavior. She deserves stability in her life, and I intend to give it to her."

"What's it worth to you?"

"Tyler!" Pamela exclaimed.

"Now we're getting to it," Joan said with narrowed eyes. "I should have expected this. How much will it cost me this time?"

"Tyler, what are you doing? You can't sell your daughter!"

"Ah, you don't understand," he said. "This is how it works with her. Everything has a price."

"She's not the one bringing up money."

"But he won't see that," Joan said. "He never does. How do you think he got that piece of land he's on? How do you think he got the shiny new truck he drives?"

"I may have borrowed the down payments, but I paid you back. I don't owe you anything, now, and you know it."

Pamela stood up. "Tyler, I don't like what's going on here."

"Don't you see? This is all part of her plan. She doesn't want us to be together. She doesn't want me to be happy. She never did. Come on, Pamela; we're leaving!" He rose from the table and took hold of her arm, but Pamela yanked herself free.

"I'm not going anywhere with you!" Turning, she said, "I don't know what just happened here, Mrs. Chandler, but I'm not a party to it. If you'll give me your address, I'll call a cab to take Jacob and me home."

"Come on, Pamela, don't act like this! This is an ongoing feud between my mother and me. It has nothing to do with us or our plans together."

"Like hell, it doesn't. If you think I want anything to do with bartering Rachael's future, you've got another thing coming. Thank God I saw this now instead of down the road."

Tyler pointed at Joan. "This is your fault, Mother. You always do this. Whenever I want something, you always get in the way."

Pamela shook her head and started down the hall. Tyler went after her and grabbed her arm. "Wait a damn minute."

"Take your hands off me, Tyler Chandler. Jacob and I are moving to Atlanta, and there's nothing you can do about it." She trotted up the stairs. "Jacob! Come on, honey. We're going home."

Joan was impressed and more than a little surprised. Nevertheless, dealing with Tyler in the aftermath wouldn't be pleasant. Realizing that she had a lot to lose if his anger remained pointed in her direction, she said, "Pamela, may I speak with you before you call your taxi?"

Pamela glanced at Tyler. He threw up his hands and said, "I'll take a walk." He pushed through the screen door and went out onto the porch. Pamela hesitated but came back down the stairs.

Joan sat on the sofa in the living room and waited for Pamela to join her. When she finally sat down, Joan said, "I'm glad to see you aren't in agreement with Tyler's nonsense, but in all fairness, he's been through a lot of stress the past couple of weeks."

"But that doesn't—"

"I'm not excusing him, Pamela. Tyler spent his entire childhood manipulating his father into giving him money for the things he wanted. When his father passed, he had to deal with me. He's had a difficult time adjusting to the fact that his guilt trips and machinations don't work anymore." She chuckled. "He quite resents the need to change his strategy. Be that as it may, it's no secret that he hasn't bonded properly with Rachael. While I regret that, it would be a great blessing to have her in my household. I'm willing to strike a deal with Tyler in order to see that happen."

"That has nothing to do with me. Frankly, the entire exchange is appalling. Families shouldn't bribe one another."

"I'm going to get to the point here," Joan said. "My son obviously cares for you. I don't want him falling apart, which will happen if you leave him. I'm asking you to give him another chance."

"Tyler and I still haven't slept together. After today, I've changed my mind about getting in any deeper. That he might one day barter my wellbeing or that of my son isn't something I'm willing to overlook in a prospective husband."

"What *are* you looking for, Ms. Clarkston? Forgive me for saying so, but I took the liberty of checking into your background before you arrived."

"Excuse me?" Pamela said with a raised brow.

"You're living in the same household as my son and my grandchildren; it's my duty to know who you are and where you've come from. Investigative services are a privilege of the rich, but your family was wealthy, so you know about privilege. Don't you, Ms. Clarkston?"

Pamela gripped her purse so tightly that her knuckles went white. "What's your point?"

"It's unfortunate that your father chose the attorney he did. He's notorious for leaving heirs in the very position you now find yourself. I'm sure it's been difficult coming to terms with the loss of your family's fortune. Your grandparents did quite well for themselves."

"I'm not here to discuss my financial affairs. If you have something to say, say it."

"I'm prepared to make you an offer. What you ultimately do with your relationship with Tyler is entirely up to you, but if you'll stay with him until the adoption goes through, and I am awarded legal custody of Rachael, then I'll make sure you're able to settle anywhere you choose, with or without Tyler. I recognize intelligence when I see it, Ms. Clarkston. Don't throw away an opportunity to provide a comfortable new beginning for yourself and your son, a beginning that doesn't require you to submit to any man."

Pamela stood. "I see that the bartering is two-sided after all. I'll consider your offer, Mrs. Chandler. I am many things, but shortsighted isn't one of them. What are you prepared to pay?"

"If I get my granddaughter, two hundred and fifty thousand dollars."

Pamela stared at her for several seconds. "Where might I find my son?"

"Left at the top of the stairs, first door on the right. Shall I ask Tyler to take you home?"

Pamela exhaled sharply. "Yes."

Joan nodded. "It's a pleasure doing business with you, Ms. Clarkston."

* * *

Joan found Tyler sitting on the edge of the boat dock, swinging both legs over the water. It wasn't wise to wave one's limbs above the swampy water, but now wasn't the time to fan the embers. "Pamela went upstairs to get Jacob. She's waiting for you to take her home."

He skipped another rock across the surface.

"I reminded her that you've been through a lot lately. She's willing to give you another chance."

Tyler's brooding brown eyes met her steely blue ones. "I didn't want Sarah to die, you know, but I love Pamela. I'm hoping she'll marry me one day. If she does, will you welcome her into the family?"

A fish jumped, and Joan watched the ripples spread. "She's a bright girl; she won't tolerate you going out drinking with your buddies like Sarah did. Besides, if you want to stay out of court, you can't give Billy Ray any reason to challenge you. For all his country boy looks, he's well connected. According to the voicemail I received from my private investigator, his attorney is no slouch. He practices in Mississippi and Arkansas and has Capitol connections, too."

"Humph. Billy Ray doesn't want to be messing with me on my turf."

"It's all well and good to talk tough, Tyler, but in a court of law, it's often whom one knows that decides a matter. Right and wrong have very little to do with it."

"They can't just take my kids."

"Can't they? How did a four-year-old boy end up in alligator infested waters? What kind of parent lets that happen?"

Tyler jumped to his feet. "Are you calling me an unfit parent?"

"Of course not, but that's precisely the type of garbage an attorney will say to a judge in order to steal your children. We have to be smart, Tyler. Come now. Take Pamela home and treat her like the lady she is. I seriously doubt a third chance is in the cards."

They walked back to the house together and climbed the back porch steps. He opened the door and followed her to the front foyer where Pamela waited with the two boys.

"I don't wanna go," Cody said, striking the side of his leg with his fist. "Jacob and I are building a space ship."

"We could stay here tonight, I suppose. It's up to Pamela. Whatever she says is fine with me."

"Can we, Momma? I wanna sleep in Cody's jungle bed. Stars glow on the ceiling when you turn off the lights, and you should see the cave he has under his bunk bed. It has hanging vines and everything!"

Tyler gave her a sheepish smile. "I'm sorry about earlier. I've been overwhelmed lately. I'm not myself. Please forgive me."

Pamela glanced at Joan, who smiled and lightly shrugged her shoulders. "Let me talk to Tyler for a few minutes, then we'll make our plans for the night. May we go out onto the front porch?"

"Certainly," Joan said, sweeping her arm in invitation. "Come on, boys. I've got ice cream in the kitchen."

"Oh, boy! I love ice cream," Cody said as he and Jacob took off at a run.

* * *

Tyler and Pamela settled onto the porch swing. When he took her hand, her fingers didn't wrap around his. He felt nervous in a way he had never felt with Sarah. Sarah always wanted to please. He never had to worry about her leaving him, no matter what he did. With Pamela, it was the other way around. He needed to work at making her stay.

"I had an interesting talk with your mother," she said.

"What did she say?"

"Enough to prove that you were right about her using money to negotiate what she wants. I shouldn't have judged you so quickly."

Tyler laid his head on her shoulder. "I was so afraid I'd lost you."

She shrugged away. "I'm not saying I'm comfortable with all this, but I'm willing to give it more time."

Tyler cupped her chin and kissed her gently. "You won't be sorry. I'm falling in love with you, Pamela. I want us to be a family."

She sighed. "When you look at me like that, I almost believe you. Let's go home. I don't want the first time we make love to be under her roof."

His heart skipped a beat. "Let's go."

* * *

After Tyler, Pamela, Cody, and Jacob had all gone home, Joan went looking for Rachael. She wasn't in the garden, so she walked down the path to the caretaker's cabin. She shivered as the wind picked up and wondered if a storm might blow through. She was glad to have Rachael to herself today. It was the beginning of their new life together, and she had so many exciting plans. She felt younger than she had in years.

Coming to a fork in the garden path, she paused for a moment to remember where she was. A few minutes later, she was relieved to see lights burning in the windows of the small, single-story cabin, telling her that she'd found her missing granddaughter. She knocked on the door.

Mr. Gibbs greeted her with a pleasant smile. "Good afternoon, Mrs. Chandler. Miss Rachael and Jayden are practicin' their letters at the kitchen table."

As he held the door wide, Joan saw lights burning in the back room of the house. Curious, she stepped inside. It had been years since she'd seen the interior of the nineteenth-century cabin. The furnishings were old, but everything was clean and in order. She found Rachael and Jayden sitting at the kitchen table looking at alphabet books and saying their ABC's together. Jayden's eyes widened when he saw her, and he closed the book.

"Hi, Gramma! I'm learning my letters. Jayden already knows his."

Raising a brow, she said, "That's very good, Jayden. Where did you learn your letters?"

His eyes shifted to his grandfather, who stood in the doorway. Mr. Gibbs nodded. "Papa taught me. Papa says if I learn to read, I can learn anything I want to know."

Joan, who had never truly looked into Jayden's face before, saw intelligence in his dark brown eyes. His long, loose curls would be the envy of any little girl's mother. His skin, like his grandfather's, was light brown compared to his mother's deeper, darker tone. She smiled as he looked up at her. He was quite an attractive child. "That's true, Jayden. What do you want to learn?"

"I want to help poor people learn to read."

"But poor people can't pay you a salary. Don't you want to make money for your work?"

"I'll get paid for my regular job and teach poor people to read in my spare time. Right, Papa?"

"Be quiet now, Jayden. Mrs. Chandler didn't come here to see you. She came lookin' for Miss Rachael."

The excitement in Jayden's eyes dimmed, and he looked down.

"Yes, sir."

"I want to read, too, Jayden. You can teach me," Rachael said.

"You'll be well able to read, my dear. You'll learn about science and history, geography, politics, technology, music, art, language, and commerce. You'll be in a position to share knowledge with Jayden, not the other way around."

"Can Jayden learn, too?" Rachael said.

Jayden's head snapped up. "Oh, please, can I?"

Joan's mouth fell open. "Well, I— Come now, Rachael. Let's go back to the house." Taking hold of her hand, she pulled Rachael off the chair and past Mr. Gibbs.

Looking over her shoulder, Rachael said, "Goodbye, Jayden. Goodbye, Mr. G. Thanks for helping me."

"Take care, now, Miss. Rachael. We'll be up real soon to cook up them carrots we picked in the garden today, and I'm makin' some strawberry shortcake for dessert tonight."

"Hear that, Gramma? Mr. G is making a cake with the strawberries we picked in the garden today!"

"That sounds delightful. Mr. Gibbs is just full of surprises."

"Would you like me to walk you home, Mrs. Chandler?" Mr. Gibbs said.

"Thank you, but that won't be necessary." She was glad to step back into the sunshine, away from his world, which was confusing and uncertain. Clearly, Jayden was more advanced in his learning than Rachael was. He was a year older than Rachael, but still, it was disconcerting and something she intended to rectify immediately.

Just before Mr. Gibbs closed the door, she said, "About your sister, have you spoken to her?"

"Yes, ma'am. She done bought herself a plane ticket. She'll stay if'n you two likes each other well enough. If not, she's got another job lined up in Natchez. Either way, Regina's comin' to town tomorrow."

* * *

Rachael was content to play in her room until dinner. She liked being at Gramma's house, but she wondered why Cody and Daddy didn't say goodbye. She pulled out some of the books from her bookcase and concentrated on the letters. She couldn't wait until she could read them. Yawning, she reached for Bo, her beloved, worn-out teddy bear, and climbed the miniature steps up to her bed. One by one, she tossed her decorative pillows onto the floor and crawled beneath the covers. Rolling onto her tummy, she pushed to her knees, reached under the pillow, and then fussed with the clasp of her locket until it opened. "Hi, Mommy. I'm staying at Gramma's house now. Daddy said if I am a good girl, you might come to visit me someday, so I'm being *very* good. Look for me in my princess room because Jacob took my bedroom at home. I love you, Mommy."

She closed the locket and slid it back under her pillow.

Tears began to fall as she thought about what she had heard that morning. Daddy didn't want her because she wasn't a boy. She didn't like to think about it, but Mommy also loved Cody more than she loved her. She heard her tell Gramma that. She cried for several minutes. As her tears gradually ceased, she stared up at the ceiling. "Please, Mommy, come back for me. I'll be very good. I promise!"

CHAPTER EIGHT

J oan had taken a sleeping pill sometime around four in the morning, and it was nearly ten o'clock before she roused herself enough to leave her room. She was irritated because she had far too much to do to allow herself the luxury of sleeping in. She tightened the belt of her robe and headed downstairs. When she reached the hallway, she heard Rachael's laughter coming from the kitchen. Rounding the corner, she found her leaning over the counter, pressing a cookie cutter into a circle of fresh cookie dough.

"Hi, Gramma! I'm helping Regina make cookies."

"I see."

"Good mornin', ma'am. Would you be wantin' a cup of coffee before breakfast?"

"Coffee sounds delightful. What are you cooking? It smells heavenly."

"Chicken and dumplin's, ma'am. I got collard greens acookin' and biscuits in the oven. Would you care for hot biscuits and honey with yer coffee?"

"Indeed," Joan said, taking stock of the jolly, rounded woman before her. Regina's skin was darker than her brother's, and her smile every bit as disarming. She seemed to glow with life, as if she were happy just to be moving. "What time did you arrive?"

"About eight o'clock this mornin'. G needed to mow the lawn today, so he asked me to watch after Miss Rachael. Since we was both hungry, it seemed as good a time as any to acquaint myself with yer kitchen. Want an omelet to go with yer biscuits?"

"Biscuits will do. What kind of cookies are you making, Rachael?"

"I don't know."

"Those are oatmeal cookies, Miss Rachael. You can lay the first batch onto the pan if yer ready," Regina said.

Rachael placed a row of star-shaped cookie dough onto the cookie sheet. "Like this?"

"Spread 'em out a bit, 'cuz they'll sure 'nuff get bigger as they bake. There ya go. That'll do." She poured a cup of coffee, set it in front of Joan, and turned back to mind her pot.

Joan breathed in the rich aroma, which wafted in tempting clouds from the steaming mug. "You multitask well. I'll say that for you."

"Got to. You ready with that tray, Miss Rachael?"

"Almost."

Regina waited for her to lay the last three cookies onto the pan, and then she slid it into the oven. She removed a tray of biscuits and shut the oven door. "These look mighty good, ummm hmmm." Taking three small plates from the cabinet, she placed two biscuits on each plate and set them on the table. Turning back for the honey jar, she said, "You don't mind if I have a biscuit or two, do ya, Mrs. Chandler? I haven't had breakfast myself this mornin'."

Stunned, Joan stared at the third plate and nodded. "I suppose that would be all right, just this once."

"Good, 'cuz I wanna make one thing perfectly clear. You'll be blessed to have me work for you. I'm as honest as the day is long. I'm an excellent cook, a fantastic housekeeper, and I'm a very thrifty shopper. I do what I say I'm gonna do, and I don't mess around. What I ain't, however, is anybody's slave or any man's servant. I'm a business professional, and I demand to be treated as such. Does that work for you, Mrs. Chandler? 'Cuz

I sure would like to work here."

Joan bit into a biscuit to keep from cracking a smile. "We'll have to see how things go, Regina, but judging from these biscuits, I'd say we're off to a good start."

Regina raised her arms and waved her hands. "Hallelujah!"

After finishing off their biscuits, Joan said, "Rachael, you and I need to get dressed. I have a lot to do now that you're here. I'll have to find a tutor for you straight away, and I'll need to make up a new grocery list."

"I'll make groceries for you once a week. If there's anything special you want, just let me know. Otherwise, I'll take an inventory of what's already here and make a suggested list of additional items for us to discuss at yer convenience. We need to formalize my salary and my living accommodations, too."

"Very well. Why don't we meet at noon?"

"I'll have dumplin's on the table," Regina said with a smile.

"Perfect." Joan took Rachael's hand and led her towards the hallway.

"One more moment, if you please," Regina said. "These here cookies are ready to come out. It would be a shame if Miss Rachael didn't try her first batch of cookies fresh from the oven." She grabbed a kitchen mitt, pulled the tray from the oven, and set it on the stove. Using a spatula, she scooped up a cookie and wrapped it in a paper towel. "This is for you to share. Don't want to spoil her lunch, now. Do we, Mrs. Chandler?"

Joan offered some to Rachael, and then tore off a piece for herself. "This is absolutely sinful."

"It's yummy, Gramma. Can I have some more?"

"You certainly may."

"Ummm hmmm," Regina said with a nod. "That's Momma's recipe all right."

"You keep cooking like this, Regina, and I'll have to go on a diet."

"You could use some fattening up if you ask me," Regina said with a discerning eye.

"I didn't," Joan replied. As she headed up the stairs, she heard Regina chuckle. She smiled, too. There was something oddly irreverent about Regina, but she was delightful nonetheless.

* * *

After a delicious lunch and a satisfactory meeting with Regina, Joan spent the entire afternoon on the telephone. She spoke at length with several employment agencies, outlining expectations for a proper tutor for Rachael. Her last call was to her attorney.

"I don't care what you have going on. We need to get this done before Tyler's romance falls apart, or he gets some wild idea about moving to Atlanta. If you value my millions, and I know you do, Mr. Carrington, make certain that I get what I want." She leaned back in her chair and took in his words of assurance.

"No, you have never let me down. Just see that you don't. I want my granddaughter to enjoy the best life money can buy, and I don't want any interference from Tyler. I have always wanted a daughter; I can hardly wait to get started."

She checked her watch. Since Rachael was down for her afternoon nap, she had some time to herself before dinner. She rose from her antique desk, which sat by her north-facing bedroom window, from which she could see her favorite fountain, a fabulous bronze sculpture of a Roman warrior gripping the reigns of his powerful horses as they reared before his fearsome war chariot, a masterpiece with or without running water.

Though she preferred to conduct business in her room, there was a formal study downstairs. It had always served as Roger's study. While she admired its cozy fireplace, she wasn't comfortable even sitting at Roger's desk. She had planned to redecorate it one day, to make it her own, but thus far, even after six years, she hadn't had the heart for it. Perhaps now, with Rachael here, she would consider it.

She could no longer keep that side of the house closed off if Rachael was to receive the type of education she had planned for her. It was time to open the music room and library again. A smile touched her lips as her thoughts settled on Rachael. She was already bringing life to Pearl River Mansion. It felt oddly satisfying to walk down the grand staircase knowing that the kitchen brimmed with activity; Mr. Gibbs cared for the grounds, and a child slept next to the nursery. It reminded her of when Tyler was young, and her husband was alive. Who would have thought, after all this time, that she would have a daughter?

She grabbed a sweater from the coat rack, which stood next to the door, and stepped out onto the porch. The heels of her soft leather shoes clicked upon the wooden deck as she walked along the railing. She loved the view from here. The manicured grounds extended well beyond the lawn and flower gardens surrounding the house. She took a deep breath and sighed as she stared past the circular drive and through the tunnel of live oak trees, which stood on either side of the driveway leading up to the house.

As she considered where to go, she reflected on the numerous trails that crisscrossed the property. Although she hadn't been there lately, one of her favorite hideaways lay at the end of the southeastern path where a rocky outcropping overlooked the river. Unlike the rest of the property, that site remained in its natural state, though chiseled steps now made the climb to the cliff top easier. She had spent many happy hours up there watching the river come to life as she blended into the backdrop. The river teemed with wildlife, creatures one might miss without pausing to observe.

As she thought of the river, she shuddered at the thought of what might have happened if Rachael had accompanied Tyler and Sarah on their trip upriver. Had both children sailed off the slide and into the river, there was no doubt which of the twins they would've saved.

She stepped off the porch and headed into the garden. She looked towards the northwest where a large stand of pines concealed the caretaker's cabin, and a second, smaller cabin, which sat at the edge of the knoll, near a stream that meandered through the property and emptied into the Pearl River. A visit to the creek was just what she needed to refresh her spirits before dinner.

She decided to take the long way around. As she passed the many intersecting pathways, she tried to imagine Rachael's reactions to the greenhouse, rose gardens, nursery, workshop, stables, and barn. She chuckled; she would probably want a pony.

The thought of throwing elaborate parties as Rachael matured set her mind spinning with possibilities. Like Bellingrath, the back of the house faced the river with a flagstone walkway that stair-stepped down to the dock. She hadn't kept the tradition of keeping potted plants and flowers upon the many platforms built for that purpose, but she remembered how it had looked when she and her husband had first visited the property. It was magnificent, especially when the fountains were flowing.

She envisioned tables of delicious food and fabulous pastries stationed along the waterfall as it trickled down to the dock where an outdoor band would play. Rachael, of course, would be the bell of the party. Only the finest would do.

It was time to renew her long-neglected acquaintances, and cultivate new ones so that Rachael might have her pick of handsome, wealthy suitors. Surely some of her friends found themselves burdened with children they intended to pass over in favor of grandchildren.

Her connections had once included the finest families in Mississippi, but after his father's death, Tyler had not been interested in pursuing life within the Southern court. With his good looks, he could've had his pick of the pretty college graduates whose families had groomed them for the sole purpose of making such a match, but Tyler was far too stubborn to play the game. She scoffed as she considered what his arrogance had cost them, but through Rachael, she could still live the dream.

She had wandered down a lesser-used trail and realized that she didn't recognize any of the landmarks, and she was holding an array of flowers that she didn't remember picking. This was happening quite a lot lately, and it was disconcerting.

Squinting towards the afternoon sun, she sat on one of the many iron benches scattered throughout the garden and glanced about. She wasn't concerned about being lost, but that would make her late for dinner, and it was important that she set a proper example.

The sun felt warm and comforting upon her shoulders. She decided to retrace her steps and look for something familiar. Before long, she happened upon the stream. On either side of the wooden bridge stood a white gazebo surrounded by expansive white decks and colorful flowerbeds. She sighed with relief and bent to add a few more flowers to her bouquet.

She entered the first gazebo, leaned on the railing, and closed her eyes. The sound of the rushing water worked wonders for her soul. A cool breeze danced through her silver hair, making her smile as she recalled the many times she had visited this place. It was the perfect time of year.

She didn't permit herself to dally, but she took her time in crossing the bridge.

"Ohhh," she whispered at the sight of a doe with her fawns at the water's edge just before they spooked and trotted off. She thought of the cliff trail again. She had lost her joy when Roger died, but she felt as if Rachael were giving her a second chance, a chance to be happy again.

When she reached the other side of the bridge, she was tempted to take off her shoes and wade a bit, but she decided it could wait and continued up the trail and into the woods.

The path wound its way towards a two-room cabin, which sat due west of the caretaker's cabin. Though it was small, it had been modernized with electricity and running water sometime in the early sixties. It was here that Regina had requested to make her home. Regina's aunt and uncle had lived in it while she, her parents, and a young Mr. Gibbs lived in the caretaker's cabin when they were growing up. She had offered to let Regina live in the maid's quarters within the mansion itself, but she had insisted upon the cabin.

As she approached, she heard singing, deep, soulful, gospel singing. The voice was of such quality it could have easily belonged to a world-famous vocalist. Joan shook her head. To hear such beautiful singing coming from a domestic serv— *employee*, she corrected herself, didn't seem right.

As she passed the cabin, she saw that the door and windows stood open. Rugs straddled the wooden fence. Clean sheets hung on the line, and a broom leaned against the wall on the front porch. She chuckled. It seemed that Regina wasn't wasting any time in making herself at home.

Overall, it had turned into an agreeable afternoon. Her attorney was drafting the adoption papers. She would be back in time to dress for dinner, and freshly picked flowers would once again grace her dining room table.

* * *

After tucking the children into bed, Tyler sat waiting for Pamela to emerge from the bathroom. Had she meant what she said about making love tonight? Sarah wouldn't like him having another woman in their bed, especially so soon. He rose, paced the floor, and wondered again if she could see him.

"Penny for your thoughts," Pamela said as she stepped from the bathroom and switched off the light.

"Lots of different things, I reckon. How about you?"

"I'm thinking about you and me, and little Jacob."

"What about Cody?" he said a bit too quickly.

"Yes, of course, Cody, too."

"What are you thinking?" he said, feeling vulnerable and unsure.

She smiled and lay across the bed, her long legs bare against the soft blue blanket. "I'm thinking I want you to kiss me."

He smiled. "That's easy. I can do that with my eyes closed."

"Prove it."

He joined her on the bed, wrapped his fingers around hers, and kissed her gently on the lips.

"I want fire, Tyler. Set me on fire!"

Her words shot through him like lightning. He kissed her hard and deep, and with a passion that kept them wrapped in each other's arms, reveling in wonder.

"Do something for me," he gasped as he pulled back.

"What?" she said, her eyes half-closed. "What do you want me to do?"

"Tell me you love me."

"Tyler, come here. Kiss me."

"Tell me, Pamela. Say the words."

"My mind tells me it's not a good idea, but my heart *wants* to love you."

"Then love me, Pamela. Love me as I love you." He closed his eyes and kissed her breathless. When their passions soared, he reached for her gown and pushed it up along her thigh.

"Wait, Tyler. I can't."

"What?" he said, failing to grasp her words as he continued to seek bare skin.

She reached for his hand and held it still. "I can't. I can't do this here."

"What's wrong? What do you mean?"

Pamela looked up at him with troubled eyes. "I want to, but not like this. Not in Sarah's bed. I don't want to help you get over her only to have you move on and leave me behind. It's too soon. I need to wait."

"But—"

She held her fingers over his lips. "I can't." A tear fell down her cheek. "I'm sorry."

He cleared his throat. "Don't be sorry. You're right about it not being here. I'll be happy just to have you close."

"Really?"

"I want you in my life, Pamela. I don't want to do anything to mess that up."

She smiled as more tears fell.

He gently brushed them away. "Roll over and let me hold you." After they had settled, he said, "Pamela?"

"Yes?"

"That doesn't mean I might not try again. I am a guy, you know."

"That doesn't mean I won't give in, either. But I want to do what's right."

He tensed, and she laughed. "Good night, Tyler."

* * *

Tyler felt Pamela flinch in her sleep and half-wondered why. As sleep began to overtake him, he heard something familiar and yet out of place. More out of instinct than concern, he rose from the bed, opened the bedroom door, and looked out the living room window. He saw low beams at the far end of the driveway.

Thinking it odd, he went to check on the boys. Cody was fast asleep, curled on his side, clutching his blanket between his knees. He reached down to cover him better. Stepping out into the hall, he slowly turned the knob and opened Jacob's door. The room was exceptionally dark. He stepped over to the bed and carefully reached out to feel for Jacob, but the bed was empty. Wrinkling his brow, he whispered, "Jacob? Are you in here? Jacob?" He stepped back into Cody's room to see if he had missed the fact that he was in there, and then he checked the bathroom.

With growing concern, he switched on the hall light and then the light in Jacob's room. Rushing through the living room, he threw open the front door and rushed out onto the porch. The car at the end of the driveway was still there. He took off at a run. "Pamela, look for Jacob!" As the gravel crunched beneath his feet, he recognized what had awakened him; someone had taken Jacob from his room and was running down the long driveway, carrying him towards the car. When he had run about fifteen yards, two car doors slammed, and the car sped away.

"Jacob! Jacob!" He sped up but then slowed again to a walk. It was no use; he couldn't catch them. He kicked at the gravel with frustration. Who would do such a thing? Who would take Jacob?

The porch light came on. "Tyler, where's Jacob?"

"Call the police!" he yelled as he jogged back to the trailer. If there was anything that could destroy what they had begun tonight, it was this. When he stepped into the living room, Cody was up, and Pamela was crying. "Are the police on the way?"

"Somebody came through Jacob's window," Pamela said. "They took the screen out."

"We'll find him, Pamela. Don't worry." He picked up the phone and dialed 911. "Yes, it's an emergency. My girlfriend just reported a kidnapping on Holly Bush Road. The car is heading towards Highway 25 on Holly Bush Road. You've got to stop them before they reach the highway. They've got the boy in the car. I saw them drive off. No, I couldn't make out what kind of car it was. I saw its low beams at the end of my driveway, and then I heard two car doors slam before it took off."

"Why didn't you go after them?" Pamela cried.

"Because I didn't have my car keys; I couldn't catch them. It's better to have the police cut them off before they hit the highway. It's safer for Jacob. Yes, sir, about three minutes ago. His name is Jacob. He's four years old. For God's sake, hurry!" He gathered Cody in his arms and went to sit by Pamela, who had collapsed on the couch.

She shot to her feet. "Stay away from me! You've cost me my job, my house, and now my son!" She stormed into the bedroom and slammed the door.

"They're going to find him, Pamela. They will!"

Cody started crying. "Will they come back for me, Daddy?"

"No, son. You're safe; I promise." Feeling helpless, he rocked his son and closed his eyes. Why were these terrible things happening? Pamela wasn't the only one whose life was upside down. He had lost his wife and given up his daughter.

Several minutes later, sirens pierced the night. Looking up, he saw red and blue lights flashing through the windows as police cars traveled up the driveway. "Come on, son. Let's go outside." Still holding Cody in his arms, he opened the door and stepped out onto the porch.

The first car stopped and waited for the second to arrive. When it did, two officers stepped out of the first car. The driver, a bald man with small, piercing eyes said, "I'm Officer Jenkins. Are you Tyler Chandler?"

"Yes, sir. This is my son, Cody. Did you set up a road block at Highway 25?"

"We did, but they're not gonna find the boy in any of those cars."

"What do you mean?" Tyler said, tensing.

"Where's the boy's momma?"

"If it's bad news, you'd best tell me first. She's terribly upset."

Officer Jenkins waved towards the second car. Two doors opened.

Tyler swallowed hard. Surely, he wasn't—

The front door opened, and Pamela joined him on the porch. "Where's my son?"

Two officers stepped out of the second car, one of them holding Jacob.

"Momma!"

"Jacob!" She ran forward as the officer carried him towards her and handed him over. "My baby! Oh, my baby! You're safe now. You're safe." Clutching him to her chest, she said, "Thank you. Thank you. I'm taking him inside."

"Take Cody with you," Tyler said.

"Come on, Cody. Jacob's back," Pamela said. "We're all going to camp out on the living room floor tonight, like a big slumber party. What do you think of that?"

"Cool!" Cody said. "Can I use my sleeping bag?"

"That's a great idea. Let's go see if we can find it."

"Just a minute, ma'am," Officer Jenkins said. "Stay out of Jacob's room until the detectives have a chance to clear it. Don't touch anything in there. Nothing. You got me?"

"I understand." She shut the door behind them.

"Where did you find him?" Tyler said.

"Walking along the road. He said they kept calling him Rachael, but when they uncovered him, they opened the car door and pushed him out. He was headed this way when we found him, poor little guy. We've got an ambulance coming to check him out. His feet are scratched up, being that he was barefoot and all."

"Did he say anything else?"

"He heard someone say, 'Dammit, Billy Ray, we got the wrong one.' Does that mean anything to you?"

Tyler rubbed his stomach with a clenched fist. "Billy Ray is my late wife's father. He's been threatening to take my kids."

"Why would he do that?" the officer said, eyeing him with suspicion.

"He's angry about Sarah's death, I reckon. She died from snakebite wounds a short while back."

"Up past Ratliff Ferry?"

Tyler nodded.

"I heard about that. Does your having a new girlfriend

have anything to do with your late wife's father wantin' to take your kids?"

"Your guess is as good as mine, but I'll kill that son of a bitch before I ever let him touch one of my kids again!"

"Watch it, son. I know you're angry, but you can't go around makin' threats against someone's life. Do that and we'll have to take you in."

"I'm pissed! What right does he have to break into my house and steal my kids?"

"I understand, but watch what you say or it can be used against you in a court of law. It's serious business."

"You're right, of course. I didn't mean it the way it sounded, but I'd sure as hell like to see him go to jail. He kidnapped Jacob, but he was trying to kidnap my daughter! Can't you arrest him?"

"If he's guilty, we'll get him. We'll have an expert question Jacob, of course, but don't try to coach him or put words in his mouth. If you do, they'll know it. Believe me. If you pull something stupid like that with Jacob, all you'll end up doing is let a kidnapper walk free. You got me?"

"Yes, sir."

"All right; let's go in."

An ambulance, its red lights flashing, pulled into the driveway. Two paramedics stepped out.

"The boy and his momma are inside," the officer told them. Once the men went in, he nodded for Tyler to follow. "We need to ask you a few more questions, and we'll need to collect your statements. The FBI will examine the scene, so remember, no one goes in Jacob's room until they get a chance to do their work. No exceptions."

"Got it," Tyler said. He sat on the couch next to Pamela, who held Jacob on her lap while the paramedics checked him out. He had a few small scratches on his feet, but he was otherwise physically unharmed.

"He seems to be all right, but we can take him down to Dixie Medical Center, if you like," a paramedic said to Pamela. She looked to Tyler.

"It's up to you," Tyler said.

"Jacob, honey. Do you hurt anywhere?"

"No, Momma. I wanna stay here and camp in the living room with Cody."

The officer turned to Pamela. "What's your name, Miss?"

"I'm Pamela Clarkston. This is my son, Jacob."

"Do you want to have Jacob checked out at the hospital?"

"I don't think that's necessary."

"You're sure?"

"Yes, thank you."

He nodded to the paramedics, and they stepped outside. Once they were gone, he took a chair from the kitchen table and sat down in front of Pamela, Tyler, and Jacob. The second officer, who had remained silent the entire time, continued to stand and observe the group.

"What happened, Son? Do you remember someone coming into your bedroom?"

Jacob turned his face into his mother's shoulder.

"It's all right, Jacob." Pamela stroked the back of his blonde head. "We need to know what happened so that we can find those people and put them in jail. Do you remember what happened?" Keeping his face hidden, he nodded. "Will you tell me?" she coaxed.

"Tell me," Cody said. "I wanna know. I was sleepin'."

Jacob turned towards Cody. "I was sleeping, too, but somebody rolled me in a blanket and shoved me into a car. When they took the blanket off, I saw two fat men. One of them said a bad word and pushed me out of the car. I was trying to find you, Momma, but I didn't know which house you were in."

Tears ran down Pamela's face, and Tyler gathered all three of them into his arms. "I'm sorry that happened, Jacob, but we're gonna find those people and put them in jail. They'll never come back *here* again."

"I wanna ride in a police car," Cody said.

Jacob pulled free. "They have red and blue lights."

"I wanna see."

Turning to Officer Jenkins, Jacob said, "Can we show Cody the lights?"

"I need to ask a few more questions first."

"Okay," Jacob said.

"Good boy," Pamela whispered as she wiped her eyes.

"Ready?" the officer said. Jacob nodded. "I was wondering if there was anyone in the car besides the two fat men."

"Some lady was driving."

"Did you see what she looked like?"

Jacob shook his head. "We were in the back seat."

"Did you hear anybody's name?"

"Billy Ray. I remember seeing him at the church."

"Do you know those men?"

"They were at Sarah's funeral," Tyler said. "Billy Ray is Sarah's father; just like I told you."

"Do you remember the other man? Was he at the church, too?"

Jacob nodded. "I remember him, but I don't know his name."

"Did you hear the name Tommy Lee?" Tyler said.

Jacob shook his head.

"Do you remember anything else?" the officer said as he shot a warning glance at Tyler.

"There were stickers in the grass, and I was afraid of the cars going by. They drive fast!"

The officer patted his shoulder. "You're a brave boy. You done real good." He glanced up as the headlights of another car shone through the window. "Where is that sleeping bag you're gonna use tonight?"

"In my room," Cody said. "Wanna see it?"

"Why don't you, Jacob, and Ms. Clarkston go get it, as long as it's not in Jacob's room?"

"Oh, boy!" Jacob said, squirming away from his mother. He and Cody ran down the hall, and Pamela followed.

"Take your time," he added. Pamela glanced back and nodded. When they were gone, he said, "Who's Rachael?"

"My daughter. She's Cody's twin sister," Tyler said.

"Where is she?"

"She's staying at my mother's house, thank God. She lives past Ratliff Ferry."

"You'll need to tell your mother what happened here tonight."

"I will."

A knock sounded, and the second officer opened the door.

Two men in plain clothes flashed their badges. "FBI. We're here to investigate a kidnapping."

After introductions, the silent officer led them to Jacob's room. A half hour later, the two men emerged and went outside. Tyler stood by as they examined the window, dusted for prints, and measured foot patterns in the gravel beneath the window. From there, based upon his account of what happened, they stopped at the end of the driveway to look for tire tracks. Tyler saw the flash go off multiple times as they took pictures. Eventually, everyone left, and they were alone.

Pamela and the boys came out from Cody's bedroom. The boys immediately set to laying out the sleeping bag, which they unzipped so that they could sleep on it together. As they fussed with the pillows and blankets, Pamela glared at Tyler. "You better call your momma. You can't take a chance on them going over there and taking a second shot at Rachael."

Jolted by her words, Tyler pulled out his cell phone. It was one o'clock in the morning. Knowing his mother, he doubted that she'd hear it ring. He scowled and stepped outside onto the front porch. It rang several times as he walked down the driveway.

"Why the hell are you calling me in the middle of the night?" Joan grumbled into the phone.

"The FBI and the police just left here. Billy Ray broke into Rachael's room and kidnapped Jacob thinking he was Rachael. He might go there next."

"Good Lord! Are you sure? Where's Jacob?"

"When they saw it wasn't Rachael, they pushed him out of the car. He heard Billy Ray's name. It was them."

"Well? Are they going to arrest them?"

Tyler could hear the panic in her voice, but he was having a difficult time finding it within himself to calm her. "They have to find them first. I'm calling so that you can take precautions. Maybe Mr. Gibbs should stay in the house in case Billy Ray tries to break in."

"He wouldn't dare!"

"Yes, Mother, apparently he would. Good night."

Tyler hung up and went back in the house. He still had Pamela to worry about. She had spread their blankets into makeshift beds on the living room floor. Only the table lamp lit the room. He slipped off his jeans and lay next to her, but her body was stiff and unyielding. "Is everybody all right?" he said.

"This is fun," Jacob said. "Nobody can get me now."

"That's right," Tyler said. "We're all safe. Good night, everybody."

It was a full five minutes before Pamela relaxed. Thanks to Billy Ray, there was a mile-high wall between them, and all he could think about was getting even.

* * *

Joan tried to blink away the drowsy effects of the sleeping pill she had taken. Her heart was thumping as she slid from the bed. She pulled on her robe and slippers and stumbled to the door. Throwing it open, she flipped on the hall light and hurried to the center gallery above the staircase and hesitated. Should she go to Mr. Gibbs' cabin by herself, or should she take Rachael with her? What if Billy Ray entered the house while she was gone? What if he caught them together outside?

She hurried down the opposite hallway, into Rachael's room, and gently shook her awake. "Wake up, sweetie. Wake up."

"Gramma, you scared me!" Rachael sat up and wrapped her arms around her neck.

"I'm sorry, sweetie, but we have to hide you for a little while. Do you remember your Grandfather, Billy Ray?"

"Yes."

"He snuck into your Daddy's trailer tonight because he thought you were there. He tried to take you away, but he made a mistake and took Jacob instead. Your daddy thinks he might come here next, so we have to hide you. Do you understand?"

"Why would Grampa take me?"

"He doesn't want you to be a princess anymore, but we won't let him take you. Will we?"

"I don't want to go with Grampa. I wanna stay with you."

"Of course, you do. Now, come with me. I'm going to hide you in a safe place while I retrieve Mr. Gibbs. He can stay in the house tonight so we won't be alone if Billy Ray comes calling. Doesn't that sound smart?"

"Will Jayden come, too?"

She scowled; she had forgotten about Jayden. "We'll see. Hurry, now. Put on your housecoat and slippers. It may be chilly where we're going."

Moving Rachael along, she stopped by the hallway linen closet and grabbed a thick blanket. Once they returned to the gallery, she walked to where an alcove created a cozy sitting area. She pulled the rocking chair away from the oak paneled corner. After feeling along the corner groove, she pushed a lever and slid the panel to the left. A dark gaping hole appeared. She felt along the right-hand wall until she found a light switch and turned it on, illuminating a narrow staircase. "Come along, Rachael. We're going up to the secret attic."

"I don't wanna go up there."

Joan coughed as the musty air reached her lungs. "Don't be silly. It's a secret tower room where only queens and princesses can go. Come on. You'll see."

"No!" Rachael tugged on her hand, nearly pulling her off balance.

"Don't tell me no, young lady. Now, get up those stairs before I spank you." Dropping the blanket, she reached back and picked Rachael up. "Come on, now. Let's go see the attic."

Rachael wrapped her arms around her neck as they climbed the stairs. Joan opened another door at the top of the stairs and stepped into a large dark room. "This is the castle attic. There are many wonderful things up here. Old pictures and paintings, lots of old dresses. You'd like this place in the daytime."

"Turn on the lights, Gramma."

"There aren't any lights up here. Besides, if Billy Ray were outside, he'd be able to see the light. We can't let him know there's an attic up here. You'll have to wait in the dark while I fetch Mr. Gibbs. I won't be long."

"No, Gramma! I don't want to stay here. I wanna go with you!"

"I know you do, but if Billy Ray is outside, he might take you away from me. No, I'm sorry for it, but you have to stay here. I promise to hurry back as fast as I can."

Joan peeled Rachael's arms from around her neck and set her on the floor.

"No, Gramma. Don't leave me!"

It was all she could do to get the door closed without smashing Rachael's fingers. She locked the door and hurried down the stairs, hardening herself to Rachael's screams. She saw the blanket. It was cold up there, but she couldn't put either of them through that again. Rachael was banging on the door and crying. It was awful! She shut the panel and slid the chair back into place. Her hands and legs were shaking, but she continued down the main stairway and out the door to find Mr. Gibbs.

When she stepped off the porch, a cold chill that had nothing to do with the wind froze her for several seconds. She peered around, certain that one of the shadows had moved.

Her heart was pounding. She knew she needed to calm herself. If something happened to her, no one would know where Rachael was. Maybe it wasn't a good idea, leaving her like that. Still, she was committed. She hurried along the north path, jumping at every sound. Finally, the cabin came into view. She tripped on the front porch step and barely saved herself from falling. Righting herself, she banged on the door. "Mr. Gibbs, wake up. Mr. Gibbs!"

A moment later, a light shone through the window, and the door squeaked open. "Lordy, Mrs. Chandler. What's the matter?"

"Tyler called. Rachael's grandfather broke into his trailer tonight and tried to kidnap Rachael. Tyler thinks he might come here next."

"Like hell, he is!" Mr. Gibbs reached for something to the left of the door.

"What in tarnation are you doing with a rifle?" Joan said when she realized what it was.

"I does me some huntin' from time to time. Seems it might come in handy tonight. What do you want me to do?"

"Can you keep watch downstairs in case Billy Ray tries to break in? I don't want him coming inside my house, Mr. Gibbs."

"He ain't steppin' one foot inside yer house. Don't you worry 'bout that. Let me get Jayden down to my sister's place. I'll be right up, unless you wanna wait for me."

"I'll wait. It may not be safe for me to walk by myself, now that I've got to worry about Billy Ray Richards lurking about."

"Jayden, grab yer shoes. Yer gonna stay with Regina tonight."

A moment later, Jayden stepped outside.

"Hello, Jayden," Joan said.

"Hello, ma'am." He looked up at his grandfather.

"Come on, boy. Let's go." They hurried up the path to the two-room cabin where he knocked on the door. "Regina, open up." A few moments later, the door cracked open. "Watch out for Jayden. I gots to go to the big house tonight." Regina opened the door to let Jayden slip through. "See you in the mornin'," Mr. Gibbs said with a nod.

"You better," Regina answered back.

Joan was relieved to be heading back towards the house. She hated to think of Rachael up in the attic, but it was infinitely better than letting Billy Ray get hold of her. When they reached the porch, they paused at the front door. "Come in, Mr. Gibbs. I'd like you to check the house."

"Yes, ma'am."

"You check downstairs while I go check on Rachael. Wait for me downstairs."

"Yes, ma'am."

She hurried up the stairs and was breathing hard by the time she pulled the chair out of the way. Finding the latch, she climbed the attic stairs, careful not to trip over the blanket. "Rachael, can you hear me?"

"Gramma! Let me out of here!"

"I'm coming, baby girl. I'm right here." She unlocked the door and carefully opened it.

Rachael grabbed her legs. "Don't leave me, Gramma!"

She picked her up. "It's all right; I'm here. Grandma is sorry she had to hide you, but it's over, now. Mr. Gibbs can keep us safe tonight. Do you want to sleep with me in my bed?"

Rachael was crying so hard that she could barely catch her breath.

"That's enough, now, stop fussing. You're all right. Let's go downstairs and tell Mr. Gibbs that all is well." She shut the attic door and carried Rachael down the stairs. Once she had stepped back into the gallery, she set Rachael on her feet so that she could close the panel door and put the chair back into place. Turning back to Rachael, she said, "My, but your face is a mess. Let's stop in your room and clean you up a bit."

"I'm cold, Gramma."

"Let's get you into something warm and cozy to sleep in."

"Did you see Billy Ray?" Rachael sniffed.

"No, baby, but Mr. Gibbs is downstairs watching to make sure he doesn't come inside. We're safe. There's no need to worry."

"Where's Jayden?"

"He's with Regina."

"I wanna see Jayden."

"You'll see him tomorrow. Let's get you warmed up. How about a quick bubble bath? Would you like that?"

"I've never had a bubble bath."

"You're four years old, and you've never had a bubble bath? Well, it's high time you did. They're quite wonderful."

"Am I still a princess, Gramma?"

"Of course, you are. I didn't leave you in the attic because you were bad, Rachael. I left you there to keep you safe, to protect you in case Billy Ray came into the house before I got back with Mr. Gibbs. Do you understand?"

Rachael nodded, but it was clear that she didn't understand at all. Taking her hand, Joan led her down the hallway to her bedroom where she gathered pink panties, socks, and pajamas from the dresser. "Into the bathroom with you. Let me wipe your face first."

As Joan pulled off Rachael's nightgown, it became apparent that she had wet herself, but Joan couldn't blame her. It wasn't her fault; poor thing. Hopefully, she was young enough to forgive and forget the whole affair.

She turned on the water and squirted liquid bubble bath into the tub. Leaning forward, she agitated the water until it began to bubble up. "See there! We've got bubbles."

Rachael smiled. "I want lots of bubbles!"

Joan reached into the drawer and took out a hair clip. "Let me pin your hair up, and then you can get into the bath. Can you remember not to get your hair wet?"

Rachael nodded.

"Climb in." She felt herself smile as she watched Rachael climb into the tub.

"Look, Gramma, I'm sitting on the bubbles!" Rachael put her face into the water and blew bubbles, and then giggled with delight.

"Silly girl," Joan chuckled.

About twenty minutes later, she and Rachael paused above the stairs. "Mr. Gibbs? Are you there?"

"Yes, ma'am. I'm right here. I ain't seen nothin' amiss."

"Perhaps you could check upstairs before Rachael and I go to bed."

"Yes, ma'am."

Joan didn't often allow him to come upstairs, and though she didn't like it, neither did she like the idea that Billy Ray might be hiding in one of the upstairs rooms. She and Rachael sat on the gallery sofa while he conducted the search. He went down one hallway and then the other.

"I checked everywhere that a man could hide, Mrs. Chandler, and I locked all the downstairs doors and windows. You and Miss Rachael are safe up here tonight."

"Very good. Do you think you can stay awake until Regina comes up to the house in the morning?"

"Yes, ma'am. Don't you worry 'bout a thing. Sweet dreams, Miss Rachael."

"I took a bubble bath, Mr. G. We made lots of bubbles!"

"Why does she call you Mr. G?" Joan asked.

"Lots of folks call me that. Easier than Gibbs, I expect."

"I see. Very well, then. Good night, Mr. Gibbs. I appreciate your service." As she and Rachael walked down the hallway to her bedroom, she felt the stresses of the day aching in her bones. She was incredibly tired, but she needed a quick rinse before she could crawl into bed.

Damn Billy Ray! Unless she wanted to live like a prisoner in her own home, something had to be done about that man.

* * *

Jacob thrashed around in his sleep. His half-formed whimpers woke Tyler and Pamela.

"Should I wake him?" Pamela whispered.

"See if you can calm him first."

Pamela gently stroked Jacob's back until he lay still and the whimpering stopped.

Tyler sighed and lay back on his pillow.

"I'm moving to Atlanta, Tyler. I'm not taking the chance that this might happen again."

"I'll put the trailer up for rent immediately, and we'll go to Atlanta together."

She pushed up so that she could look into his face. "You mean it?"

"I love you, Pamela. I'll do whatever it takes to keep us together." She rested her head on his shoulder and soon fell asleep, but he lay awake a long time thinking about the logistics of making such a move. It would certainly deepen the distance between him and Rachael, but he couldn't let that stop him. He wanted a life with Pamela. He had to make her and Cody his first priorities.

* * *

Rachael let out a shriek and began to cry.

Startled, Joan shot up in the bed. "What is it, child?"

Rachael kept crying, gasping for breath in between sobs.

Joan tried to turn Rachael towards her, but Rachael covered her face. "What is it? What's wrong?"

"It's dark in here!"

"Hush. Don't be afraid. It's all right. Come here." She pulled Rachael up beside her, wrapped her arms around her waist, and stiffened. "Rachael, did you wet the bed?"

Rachael cried louder.

"Oh, for heaven's sake!" Joan pushed Rachael back, flung off the sheets, and turned on the lamp. She scowled at the wet spot beneath her granddaughter. "That is unacceptable, young lady. Do you have any idea how expensive this mattress is?"

Rachael continued to cry.

"Well, that's just great. I feel like crying myself now. Come on. You're getting back into the tub, and then into your own bed. I'll put some plastic down so you don't ruin that bed, too." She pulled on Rachael's arm, but Rachael pulled away. "Come here, Rachael."

"No! I don't want to be in my room by myself!"

"I don't care what you want. You peed in Grandma's bed. That is not acceptable. Why didn't you get up to use the bathroom?"

Rachael kept crying.

"Tell me. I want an answer."

"I was scared!"

"Then you could have woken me up. Anything is better than peeing in the bed! Now, we've got to wash you off again, and I've got to strip this bed." Joan went around to her side of the bed, picked Rachael up, and carried her into the bathroom. When she began to struggle, she slapped her bottom.

"You stop it right now, young lady. What I say goes. Now take off your clothes and get into that tub again. We're just going to rinse you off." She turned on the water and checked the temperature. Turning to Rachael, she said, "Stop crying, or I'll really spank you. I mean it."

Rachael sniffed her cries to a stop.

"Good girl. Now let's get your clothes off." She helped Rachael into the tub. "Sit down so you don't fall." Taking a tissue, she wiped her face again. "Rinse off. Take some soap and wash your bottom. Wash your legs, too. There you go, I'll help you." Once Rachael was clean, Joan reached for a towel and dried her off. Carrying her into the bedroom, she set her on the edge of the bed. "You stay here while I rinse off. Don't move."

"Yes, Gramma," she whimpered.

"Don't look so pitiful. We'll get through this. We've just had a horrible day, didn't we?"

"It was horrible!"

"Indeed, it was. I'll be out in a minute, so stay right there." She closed herself in the bathroom and took a deep breath. She was exhausted. No wonder old people didn't have babies. She couldn't imagine how Sarah managed twins. She quickly rinsed off and stepped back into the bedroom. "Come, now. I'm taking you to your room. Wouldn't you like to sleep in your princess bed?"

She carried her down both hallways and into her room. "I think we'll put a pull-up on you tonight, just to be safe."

"I don't need a pull-up."

"Just for tonight. If you don't wet it, then you won't have to wear another one. That way, I won't have to put plastic on the bed."

Once Rachael was dressed in clean pajamas, she crawled into bed.

"Sleep well, Rachael. Tomorrow will be a much better day."

"Gramma, will you leave the light on?"

"I'll leave the bathroom light on." Joan leaned over and kissed her forehead. "I love you, little princess. Tomorrow we'll have cookies and ice cream; you'll play with Jayden, and you'll be a happy little girl again."

"I miss my Mommy."

"I know you do. She'll always love you. Don't ever forget that."

"Good night Gramma."

"Good night, sweetheart."

Rachael flopped over on her side. Joan wished she could undo the damage she'd done by locking her in the attic, but only time could do that. Damn Billy Ray Richards!

CHAPTER NINE

A constant knocking slowly infiltrated Joan's consciousness.

"Mrs. Chandler, you gots to get up. You got company."

Opening one eye, Joan glanced around the room and wasn't exactly sure where she was. She blinked hard and sat up in the bed. "Who is it?"

"It's Ms. Clarkston, ma'am. She says it's mighty important."

Realizing that she was in Tyler's room, she slipped off the bed, pulled on her robe, and opened the door. "What does she want?"

"She won't say, only that it's urgent."

Joan yawned. "How did you find me?"

"I saw your bed all torn up and went lookin'. Your sheets is already been washed, and I did my best to work out the spot in your bed. Don't worry, Mrs. Chandler, accidents can happen to anyone."

Joan scowled fiercely. "That wasn't me; it was my granddaughter! She slept with me last night until *that* happened. That's why I put her into a pull-up last night. Can you get the smell out, too, or will I need to buy a new mattress? I'm quite disgusted."

Regina chuckled. "Sorry for the misunderstandin'. The spot came out, and I reckon the smell will come out, too. I done washed it with white vinegar, but it'll take some time to dry. We can check it again this afternoon. Should I tell Ms. Clarkston that you'll come down?"

"Where's Rachael?"

"She and Jayden are helpin' G in the garden."

"I'll be down in a few minutes. I'm starving, so if it's not too late for breakfast. I'd like some biscuits and honey."

"You got it," Regina said. "I'll fix you up some grits, too."

"I don't care for grits."

"You ain't never had my grits."

Rolling her eyes, Joan walked down the hallway, into her room, and closed the door, but not soon enough to escape Regina's chuckle.

* * *

Pausing to peer into the mirror at the top of the landing, Joan pinched her cheeks and scowled at her reflection. Pamela's visit couldn't be good news. In fact, if her suspicions were correct, she was here to say she was leaving Tyler. She descended the stairs with practiced grace and joined her company in the living room.

"Grandma!" Cody cried as he ran forward for a hug.

"Hello, my boy. It's lovely to see you, too." She squeezed him tight and set him aside.

"Daddy says if I'm nice to you, you might give me a present. Do you have a present for me today?"

"Hello, Pamela. This is a surprise."

Pamela smiled tightly. "Is Rachael available to play with Jacob and Cody for a few minutes?"

"I don't want to play with Rachael. I wanna play in my room," Cody whined.

"Regina?" Joan called just over her normal voice.

"Right here, ma'am." Regina set a tray with a steaming teapot on the coffee table. "I was just coming to pour you some tea."

"I'll do it. Take the boys upstairs, please."

"Yes, ma'am. Right this way, boys."

"Come on, Jacob. Let's go play in the jungle cave!"

"I want to play with your building blocks," Jacob said as he skipped out the door after Cody.

Once their voices had faded, Pamela said, "I can't stay in Mississippi and risk another encounter with Billy Ray. I don't belong in this fight."

"So, why come here?"

"Tyler wants to move to Atlanta with me. Are you opposed?"

Joan picked up the teapot and poured hot water over a tea bag. "Do you care?"

"Look, Mrs. Chandler, I'd like to accept your previous offer, but not at the risk of my son's safety. Surely, you can understand that."

"Your son's safety isn't my concern."

Pamela lowered her gaze and swept her hand across her lap as if she were brushing something from her skirt. "We could change the terms."

"Go on."

"If I leave today, without Tyler, and agree to stop all communication with him, will you pay me ten grand a month to stay away?"

"Why on earth would I do that?" Joan scoffed.

"Because I *could* let Tyler move to Atlanta with me and talk him into taking Rachael with us. He'd do that if I asked him to."

Joan's hand froze with the cup halfway to her mouth. "Are you willing to sever your ties with him completely?"

"Will you pay what I ask?"

"How long do you expect to be on the payroll before your breakup becomes permanent?"

"Two years. Long enough to buy a house and get back on my feet. It equates to the same amount you offered me before."

"And what guarantee do I have that you won't take my money and become a couple again?"

"I'll reject him. My income depends on me keeping my word."

"Indeed, it does. Not only will you reject him, you won't

even *think* about interfering with my plans to adopt Rachael. I won't tolerate it, and there's nowhere you can go that my private investigator won't find you and your son."

Pamela gasped. "Are you threatening Jacob?"

"One good threat deserves another. Don't you agree? Keep your word and there'll be no need for conflict."

"Tyler *will* come looking for me," Pamela said raising her chin. "I can't control that."

"What matters is what you do if he finds you."

"I want to be clear about what I'm agreeing to," Pamela said.

"So do I. You are agreeing to sever all ties with my family, including Tyler. You are agreeing to refrain from any and all communications with Tyler. You are agreeing not to speak about, or interfere with, my care or adoption of Rachael Chandler, both now and in the future. Do I make myself perfectly clear?"

Pamela swallowed hard. "I understand."

"I want to hear you say it aloud. If you're going to receive ten thousand dollars a month from me, then you had better keep the words you are speaking today because you won't like the consequences if you break our agreement."

"I'm not comfortable with you threatening Jacob."

"And you thought I'd be comfortable with you threatening Rachael? What you are proposing is extortion, Ms. Clarkston. I could have you thrown into jail! Now speak the words or get out of my house. The choice is yours."

Pamela's hands were shaking. "I promise to permanently sever all ties and communications with Tyler, and not to speak about, or interfere with, your care and adoption of Rachael Chandler. Does that cover it?"

"It does. Keep me informed of your whereabouts so that I can send your checks."

"I want your word that you won't harm Jacob as long as I do what we have agreed."

"I won't harm Jacob as long as you keep the vow you've made."

Pamela nodded and rose to her feet. "Very well, then, if that's all settled, I'll take the first installment with me. I left Tyler a note; I won't be returning to the trailer. I'm leaving Mississippi from here."

"Very well, indeed. Wait while I write you a check."

* * *

Tyler was surprised to see the driveway empty. He pulled out his cell phone and dialed Pamela's number, but it went straight to voicemail. "Hey, baby, I just got home. Where are you? Call me."

He unlocked the front door, went to the refrigerator, and pulled out a beer. He popped the top and took a long, slow drink. Leaning over the sink, he looked out the kitchen window. It was time to mow the grass again. Damn, but it grew fast this time of year. Deciding to take a quick shower, he turned towards the living room and saw a folded piece of paper on the counter. It had his name on it. Snatching it up, he read it once, and then again.

> *Dear Tyler,*
>
> *I left Cody at your mother's house this morning. Jacob and I are starting a new life by ourselves. While I care for you, I have already lost too much in this relationship, and I'm not willing to risk losing anything more.*
>
> *Pamela*

He crumpled the paper in his fist. If he went after her, he'd lose his job. There was no way they'd give him more time off, not after all the time he'd taken already. And what about Cody? After all he'd been through, he didn't want to leave Cody here while he chased after Pamela, but he couldn't stand the thought of letting her go. He slammed his fist on the counter. "Dammit! Why didn't you wait until we could talk this through?" He grabbed his keys and stormed out the door. To hell with work. If he didn't have Pamela in his life, nothing else mattered.

It was a long, stressful drive through rush-hour traffic, and all he could think about was Pamela. He turned the wheel and hit the brakes just outside the gate, sending rocks and gravel flying. Knowing he was quick to blame his mother when something went wrong, he tried to calm himself as he knocked on the front door. A minute later, a well-rounded black woman opened the door.

"Who are you?" he said.

"I'm Regina. Who are you?"

"I'm Tyler. Where's my mother?"

"I don't rightly know. Wait here while I find out."

As she walked away, Tyler opened the screen door. Just that fast, Regina blocked him with her body and pushed him back outside. "Until Mrs. Chandler says you can come in, you ain't comin' up in *this* house."

Surprised by how fast she moved, he stepped back. "Fine. I'll wait out here."

She gave him a doubtful look and latched the screen door. Shaking his head, he turned from the house, looked out over the garden, and tried to gather his thoughts.

A few moments later, Joan opened the door. "It's about time you showed up. Cody's been fussy all day. You need to get that boy under control, or you'll have a miserable time when he's older. Bribing him with presents is bad form."

Tyler plopped down on the sofa. "I didn't know you had a new maid."

"Care for tea?" Joan said.

"Where's Cody?"

"He's outside in the garden with Rachael. Is that a yes or a no on the tea?"

"Did Pamela mention where she and Jacob were going?"

"It's not like we're friends, you know. Why do you ask?"

Tyler shook his head. "She left me, Mother. I can't just let her go."

"Give her time. Maybe she'll change her mind."

"I can't imagine my life without her. Will you keep Cody while I go after her?"

"I most certainly will not! You need to take responsibility for your life, Tyler. Cody needs you. You can't just foist him off whenever he's inconvenient. One child is all I can handle."

He shot her a dirty look. "Fine. I'll take him with me. We'll both be out of your hair."

"Regina?"

"Yes, ma'am?" Regina stepped forward from the hallway.

"Bring Cody in from the garden, please, but leave Rachael with Mr. Gibbs."

"Yes, ma'am."

Rising, Joan said, "I'll have Rachael's adoption papers soon. That will be one more responsibility off your plate."

"Rachael is the least of my concerns."

"Instead of chasing a woman who clearly doesn't want to be with you, you'd be better off settling into a new schedule. Allow the details to work themselves out as they may. You'll find someone to replace Pamela soon enough."

"I don't believe she doesn't want me. She left because of Billy Ray. Besides, I don't want anyone else; I want her."

Joan heaved a heavy sigh. "Look, Tyler, I know it hurts, but give the girl some space. She's only known you a short time, and you've already put her through enough to last a lifetime. If she truly loves you, as you believe, she'll come back. You mark my words."

"Daddy!" Cody cried as his boots echoed down the hall.

Swinging Cody up into his arms, Tyler kissed his neck. "Hey, there, buddy. Did you have a good day?"

"Yep. I helped Rachael and Jayden pick carrots in the garden."

"Is that why I see dirt all over your pants and shirt? Who's Jayden?"

"Jayden is Mr. Gibbs' grandson and Regina's nephew," Joan said. "Come along. I'll walk you out."

"You let Cody play with Jayden?"

"I can't be everywhere at once, can I? Have you had any news of Billy Ray?"

"I haven't heard anything. I guess I should follow up on that. What am I supposed to do with Cody tomorrow?"

"I suggest you call a babysitter. Didn't you and Sarah have one?"

"Yes, but she took care of that. I don't even know who she is."

"It's time to grow up, Tyler. As unpleasant as it is, you must learn to handle your own affairs. Having a woman in your life only delays the inevitable. One way or the other, you have to face losing Sarah. Put your affairs in order. Concentrate on raising Cody, and for God's sake, keep Billy Ray from taking *him*."

Tyler bit the inside of his cheek and opened the door. He didn't want her to see how hurt he was. Right or wrong, come Saturday morning, he and Cody were heading for Atlanta.

* * *

Joan rolled to the far side of her mattress and pulled a pillow to her stomach. Sighing, she closed her eyes. Seconds later, she bolted upright and smelled the pillowcase. Shrugging, she flipped it over and smelled the other side. Relieved, she settled into her exquisite, Egyptian cotton sheets.

A few moments later, she smelled the pillow again.

Regina had flipped the mattress, once it was dry, but that didn't alter the fact that Rachael had peed in her bed. She was still thoroughly annoyed. She rolled to her side and looked at the clock again: 2:30 a.m. Pamela's threats made her even more determined to finish the adoption quickly. She didn't like being vulnerable.

It had taken over an hour to get Rachael settled into bed tonight. She regretted leaving her in the attic. She was terrified of the dark, now, and afraid to be alone. She didn't know how to allay her fears, but allowing her to sleep with her certainly wasn't the solution, as last night had proved. She hoped time would heal what her comforting words could not…

Her eyes widened in response to a loud thud.

Mr. Gibbs was on duty, so she wasn't afraid, but it was unusual enough to make her curious. She rose from the bed, stepped into her house shoes, and grabbed her robe. She let herself out into the hall and headed towards the gallery. As she approached the top of the stairway, she heard scuffling noises coming from the back part of the house. She ran back to her room and grabbed her handgun from the nightstand drawer.

When she returned to the gallery, she paused. The house was quiet again. Had she imagined it? She crept to the top of the stairs, dropped to her knees, and watched from between the banister railings as someone crossed through a shaft of light, which shone from a nightlight. Was it Mr. Gibbs? The stairs creaked.

Mr. Gibbs wouldn't come up the stairs. The gun trembled in her hands as she pulled back on the hammer. Would he hear? She backed off and hid beside a table.

Was it Billy Ray?

The steps creaked again.

* * *

Rachael awoke with a shriek; she'd wet the bed again. She pushed the covers aside and slid off the bed. She ran on tiptoes into the bathroom and pulled off her wet panties; Gramma would be mad at her again.

After using her little girl's toilet, she peeked around the corner into her room and ran to the dresser to find another pair of panties. When she climbed up into the bed, she saw the wet spot. She needed to wake Gramma.

She walked to the door, opened it, and looked down the long, dark hallway. There was just enough light to see the far end. She made a run for it. "Gramma, wake up! You have to get up!"

She reached the gallery and kept running.

"Gramma, Gramma—"

Joan reached out from behind the table and snatched Rachael off her feet. Rachael screamed before she could cover her mouth. "Hide under the table. Billy Ray is here," Joan whispered.

Heavy footsteps tramped up the stairs.

"Come out, Rachael," a deep voice said. "I've come to take you home with me."

Joan lifted the gun and pointed it into the dark empty space.

"Come now, girlie. Where are you? It's your Pawpaw, Billy Ray."

"Go away! I don't wanna go with you!" Rachael said.

Horrified, Joan stood up and faced Billy Ray as he turned in their direction. "You heard her. She doesn't want to go with you. Now get out of my house before I shoot you dead."

Billy Ray snickered. "Put that gun down before you hurt yourself. Between you and yer butler, I don't know who's more ridiculous."

"What did you do with Mr. Gibbs?"

"I gave him a headache he won't soon forget. If you don't want the same, give me the girl."

"Over my dead body," she said.

"And mine," Regina said.

Joan and Billy Ray turned to see Regina standing at the top of the stairs, aiming Mr. Gibbs' hunting rifle at Billy Ray.

"Well, if it ain't another darkie. You must be rollin' in dough."

"Shut yer filthy mouth and put yer hands where I can see 'em," Regina said.

"Give me that thing." Billy Ray lunged, and the rifle went off before Joan could react. Regina and Billy Ray both hit the floor.

"Help me, Mrs. Chandler. Get 'im off me!"

"My God, Regina! Are you all right?"

"Yes, ma'am, but he's bleeding all over yer fancy rug!"

"Gramma!" Rachael screamed.

"It's all right, Rachael. Stay where you are while I help Regina. Please don't look! Promise Grandma that you won't look."

"Grandma, I'm scared!"

"I know you are, but stay right there. Don't move!" She turned on the light but turned it back off again. "It's best if we keep it dark, Regina." She grabbed hold of Billy Ray's arm and pulled while Regina shoved. Once he was off her stomach, Regina shot to her feet. "Wha—what do we do now?" Regina stuttered, as she tugged her cold, bloody dress away from her skin. "Sho—should we call the police?"

"If we do, they might take Rachael, and I refuse to allow that stupid idiot to keep me from adopting my granddaughter."

"We gotta do somethin'! He's makin' a mess all over yer floor."

"Let me think!" Joan snapped. "I know. Where's Mr. Gibbs? He can row him out to the wide spot you people call the lake and dump him there. No one ever need know."

"G's got a lump on his head the size of Texas. I need to see if he's all right. He was passed out cold a few minutes ago."

"You're not going anywhere with all that blood on you. I'll get some sheets and blankets and something for you to clean up with. We need to wrap up Billy Ray."

"I don't know about this, Mrs. Chandler. It don't seem right. I think we should call the police."

"Do you want to go to jail? They'll take Jayden, you know."

"But he done it hisself! Sure as I'm standin' here."

"I'm glad he's dead."

"Gramma!" Rachael cried.

"Stay where you are, Rachael!" She hurried towards Cody's bedroom, soaked three hand towels, and took them back to Regina. "Here, wipe yourself off while I get some sheets and blankets."

"I needs me somethin' to wrap up in," Regina said. "My dress is ruint."

Joan raided the hallway linen closet and brought back a pile of sheets and a heavy quilt. She dropped them near Regina's feet and turned her back. Rachael was crying so loudly that she could hardly think.

"I'm decent now," Regina said.

Joan clenched her jaw at the sight of Regina's bloody dress draped over Billy Ray. "Go down to the laundry room and grab a pile of tarps from the bottom far right cabinet. I'll take Rachael to my room."

"On the way."

Joan crouched beside the table near the gallery railing. "Come here, Rachael. I'm taking you to my room." When Rachael crawled forward, Joan picked her up. "Close your eyes, now. I mean it." She trotted down the hall to her bedroom and plopped her on the bed. "You stay here, no matter what."

"I don't wanna stay by myself! I'm scared!"

"I know you are, but Grandma has to take care of some things. You can't come with me, so you have to stay here. Let me wipe your face." She stepped into the bathroom and grabbed a handful of tissue.

"Don't leave me, Grandma," Rachael cried, new tears spilling down her cheeks.

Joan's hands were shaking as she wiped Rachael's face. "What if I get Jayden to stay with you? Would you like that?"

Rachael's cries softened. "Uh huh."

"Good. You wait here, and I'll go get him. Will you do that

for Grandma?"

Rachael quieted still more. "Yes, Gramma. You go get Jayden."

"Good girl. I'll turn on the TV for you to watch until I get back." She grabbed the remote and turned to a cartoon channel. "Here you go. You stay in my room until I get back."

Rachael's eyes fixed on the TV. "Okay, Gramma," she sniffed.

Joan grabbed more sheets from the bathroom linen closet and hurried back to the gallery. Regina was already mopping up the blood. "Rachael wants Jayden to stay with her. Where is he?"

"He's at G's cabin, but it would be better if Rachael went there."

"How is Mr. Gibbs?"

"He's awake, but that lump on his head sure is nasty. He's been throwing up his innards. It'll be a minute before he can help. Why don't you take Miss Rachael to G's cabin while I do what I can here?"

"I can't tell you how much I appreciate what you've done, Regina."

"There'll be plenty of time for that. Let's get him out of here."

Joan went back to her room. "Rachael, I'm going to take you to Mr. Gibbs' cabin so that you can visit with Jayden there. Would you like that?"

"What if Billy Ray is outside? He might get me."

"No, Rachael. We don't have to worry about Billy Ray anymore. Billy Ray has gone away, and he won't ever come back. It's safe to go outside now, so we're going to visit Jayden. You know what else? We're going to play a little game. I'm going to wrap you up like a present and take you to Jayden. When he unwraps you, you'll say, 'Surprise!' Won't that be grand?"

Rachael nodded. "He'll be surprised. Won't he, Gramma?"

"Yes. Come, now, let me wrap you up." She opened the sheet and wrapped it around Rachael, tickling her to make her laugh. "Isn't this fun?"

"Yes, Gramma. Let's go!"

"And don't forget the rules."

"Jayden never touches me. His Papa tells him the same rule."

"That's very good. Now, here we go!" Joan carried her down the hallway, past Billy Ray, down the stairs, and out the front door. As she started down the path, she came to a stop. "Rachael, I can't carry you any farther. You've got to walk, and I'll pick you up again when we get to the cabin."

"But I don't have my shoes."

"All right, I'll carry you, but let me rest a minute." Joan was grateful for the moonlight and the knowledge that Billy Ray was no longer a threat. "When she'd caught her breath, she picked Rachael up and continued towards the cabin. "Jayden will be so surprised."

Though she tried not to show it, her mind was spinning. Perhaps Regina was right. Maybe they should call the police. Billy Ray had no business breaking into her house. It was a clear case of self-defense. Yet the very thought of them taking Racheal was a risk she wasn't prepared to take.

* * *

When Joan got back to the house, Mr. Gibbs called to her from the kitchen. "We got 'im on the back porch, Mrs. Chandler. Yer sure this is what you wanna do?"

Joan tossed Regina the dress she had grabbed from Regina's closet after she'd dropped Rachael off at Mr. Gibbs' cabin. "There's no going back now."

"Someone's gonna come lookin' for 'im," Mr. Gibbs said. "We gots to have a lie ready."

"He's right, Mrs. Chandler. We need a story, and we need to stick to it. Turn around, G, while I put my clothes on." Regina turned her back, dropped the sheet, and stepped into her dress.

Joan rubbed her temples as she tried to think things through.

"Does anyone know how Billy Ray got here? If he left a car out front, what are we going to do with it?"

"We got a dead man on the back porch," Regina said. "We need to get rid of him before we do anything else."

"Regina says you want me to row him out to the lake," Mr. Gibbs said.

"Those alligators may as well count for something," Joan scoffed.

"Mr. Billy Ray wouldn't be the first to meet such a fate, I reckon," Mr. Gibbs said as he shuffled his feet, "but I ain't happy to be party to it."

"None of us are happy about it," Joan said sharply. "If you have a better suggestion, let's hear it."

"Whatever we do," Regina said, "we gotta burn our bloody clothes and that fancy rug too."

"Can you two carry him out to the dock?"

"No, ma'am," Mr. Gibbs said, "but we can drag 'im."

"All right then. Unless you've got something else to say, let's do it."

"What about Miss Rachael?" Regina said. "What if she tells someone what we done?"

"Let's get rid of him, and then we'll decide what to do about Rachael."

Mr. Gibbs slid his arms through Billy Ray's massive arms and locked his hands. Regina picked up his feet and, together, they dragged him down to the dock.

Though he was breathing hard, Mr. Gibbs lowered himself into the fishing boat and pulled it flush against the dock. "Roll him in, Regina."

Regina pushed and shoved, but Billy Ray barely moved. "I can't do it by myself."

"Here, let me help." Joan leaned her weight into it, but Billy Ray wouldn't budge. "It's no use. We can't do it."

"You hold the boat, Mrs. Chandler, while I help Regina."

Joan scowled as she stepped down into the boat, which immediately started to rock as Mr. Gibbs climbed onto the dock. She grabbed hold of the pier to steady herself.

Mr. Gibbs started to shove but stopped. "We gotta unwrap 'im first. We don't want tarps down there if someone finds 'im."

"Mercy, but this is a bother," Regina grumbled as they unwrapped Billy Ray. Together they rolled him into the boat, which pitched so wildly that it nearly tossed Joan over the side.

"Lordy, Mrs. Chandler! Let's get you out of there," Mr. Gibbs said.

Shaking and scared, Joan grasped his hand and climbed onto the dock. Dropping to her knees, she shuddered. Had she gone into the water…

The boat was listing far to the side when Mr. Gibbs climbed back in. "Don't you worry, Mrs. Chandler, I'll set him straight." Lifting one heavy arm at a time, he tugged on Billy Ray until his torso lay across the center bench and his legs hung over the side. He paused to catch his breath. "That'll have to do. If I put all of 'im in here, I'll never get 'im back out." He sat down and began to row.

Joan and Regina stood by as Mr. Gibbs faded into the darkness.

"Hell and tarnation! I got blood on my dress again."

"How can you tell?" Joan scoffed. "It's so damn dark out here; I can barely see my hand in front of my face."

"I know because it's cold against my skin. I should've waited to put it on. Now, I'll have to burn it. I ain't got very many dresses as it is."

"Your dresses are the least of our worries," Joan said. "I'll replace them."

The sounds of crickets and other nighttime creatures resumed as Joan and Regina stood silently by, listening to the rhythm of Mr. Gibbs' rowing. Joan sighed and turned to climb the steps up to the house. "We may as well start cleaning up. It'll be at least an hour before he returns."

A huge splash and a startled cry broke the silence.

"G, are you all right?" Regina called out.

"A gator took off one of Billy Ray's legs! I gots to get to the boathouse right away!"

"Oh my God! Hurry, Mr. Gibbs. Hurry!"

The rowing grew desperate.

"Oooie, but they's thick out here!" Mr. Gibbs called again.

Soon, they could no longer hear his rowing.

"G?" Regina yelled. "G, can you hear me?"

Joan crossed her arms and bent forward to ease her aching stomach. Surely, nothing would happen to Mr. Gibbs.

Regina fell to her knees. "Please, God, forgive what we done, and spare my brother!"

* * *

Rachael sat on the floor looking at one of Jayden's books.

"You never came out here at night before," Jayden said as he turned the page.

"I know, but it's safe now. Billy Ray can't get me anymore."

"Why not?"

"Because a bad thing happened to him."

"What bad thing?"

Rachael scowled. "Gramma told me not to look, but I saw Billy Ray lying on the floor."

"Was he sleeping?"

Rachael shook her head. "Gramma had a gun, and Billy Ray was bleeding."

Jayden's eyes grew wide. "Did she shoot him?"

"I don't want to talk about Billy Ray. Can I go to bed now?"

"We can sleep on the couch."

Rachael climbed onto the sofa and laid her head down on one of the throw pillows. Jayden walked over to a small wooden chest, took out a soft, blue blanket, and gently covered Rachael. After turning off the lamp, he climbed onto the other end of the couch and slipped under the blanket. "Good night, Rachael."

Rachael giggled. "Our feet touched. Gramma wouldn't like that. I better curl up."

"Me, too. Papa would wear me out."

"Jayden? Can we leave the lights on?"

"Papa says no."

"That's okay. I feel safe with you here."

* * *

"G! Are you all right?" Regina yelled, but no answer came back over the water. "G?"

Joan reached out for Regina's hand but stopped herself. "Mr. Gibbs, can you hear us?"

"Lordy, Mrs. Chandler, I think them gators got him, too. What are we gonna do?" Regina sobbed.

"This is intolerable! We have no way to get out there, even in the daytime. The only way to get to the boathouse is by boat."

"I ain't steppin' foot inside no boat!" Regina said.

"What if they find Billy Ray floating around in my fishing boat tomorrow morning with a bullet hole in his chest? How are we going to explain that?"

"What about my brother? What if he's floatin' out there with him? This is what we get for sinnin' against our maker."

Joan realized that she was wringing her hands and forced herself to hold them at her sides. "Hush up and listen!" The low hum of a motor began to grow louder. They looked at each other with widening eyes. "I wonder if that's the houseboat."

"Is it?" Regina said.

"I'm not sure."

"Surely you know what yer own boat sounds like!"

"Well, I don't! I'm never out here when they fetch it."

Regina leaned forward, straining to hear over the noise of the crickets. "It's gotta be!" A few moments later, she began jumping up and down, her large frame jiggling beneath her loose-fitting dress. "Praise the Lord! He done made it to the boathouse."

Running lights appeared.

Joan shook her head. "Something's wrong. It's heading this way. If it were Mr. Gibbs, he'd be heading towards the lake, wouldn't he? Maybe Billy Ray's accomplices came by boat." Her legs went weak, and her hands began to shake. "Let's get out of sight, just in case." She made her way up the flagstone steps, away from the dock.

"Ouch!" Regina muttered as she followed.

"What is it?"

"It's so blasted dark out here that I stubbed my toe," Regina grumbled. "I'm fine. Keep movin'."

Joan crouched behind a gardenia hedge, and Regina hid somewhere across the way. Several minutes later, the houseboat pulled up to the pier, and someone killed the motor. She held her breath.

Finally, someone stepped from behind the controls and tied the boat to the dock. Rising, he said, "Where's everybody at? Is anybody out here?"

"G! It's me!" Regina cried as she rushed down the steps towards him. "What on earth happened out there? What was all that ruckus?"

"That blood must've smelled somethin' fierce cuz them gators was everywhere. If I hadn't got to that boathouse, they would've et me, too. I climbed one of them pilings while they sank that boat to get at Billy Ray. It were an awful sight to see."

Regina wrapped him in a tight embrace. "I would never forgive myself if somethin' had happened to you, G."

"I'm sorry about messin' up the plan, Mrs. Chandler, but that little boat weren't never gonna make it out to that lake. It weren't gonna make it ten more feet. Once them gators—"

"That's quite enough. I'm glad you're safe, Mr. Gibbs. Let's make some tea and figure out what's next. This won't all go away just because

Billy Ray is gone. We still don't know if there's a car out there."

"I'll go check on the kids," Regina said. "While I'm at it, I'll see if there's a car out front."

"Take the rifle," Joan said. "He might not be alone."

Regina's eyes widened. "Maybe I'll just wait till it gets light."

"She's right, Regina," Mr. Gibbs said. "If he's got a partner out there, he'll come lookin' for Billy Ray. I'll go with you."

"Let's all go," Joan said. "I'm not going back inside that house all by myself."

"Then let's check on the car first," Mr. Gibbs said. "No need to drag them young'uns into it."

The three of them made their way around the side of the house, past the vegetable and herb gardens, and along the fence towards the gate. Joan was content to let Mr. Gibbs take the lead. Her stomach ached with tension. They had been through intense trauma tonight, and she was concerned about the toll it would take, especially on Rachael. Between locking her in the attic and seeing her grandfather murdered, how could anyone expect Rachael to remain the same sweet, innocent child? None of them would ever be the same again.

Mr. Gibbs stopped suddenly and crouched down. Joan and Regina did likewise as something gleamed in the moonlight. It was the beat-up fender of an old station wagon, which sat parallel to the gate, poised for a quick get-away. With an index finger to his lips, he motioned for them to stay put. Carrying the rifle horizontally, he crept towards the gate and quietly let himself out. Staying low to the ground, he moved towards the back of the car, and then alongside, rising to look through the windows. Dropping low again, he returned to where Joan and Regina waited. Motioning for silence, he led them a short distance away. "There's a man and a woman asleep in the front seat. What should we do?"

"I'm surprised they didn't hear the rifle shot," Joan said.

"If'n they had, they wouldn't be asleep right now. What do we do?" Regina whispered.

"Rachael wasn't in there, was she?" Joan said, her blood pressure rising with the thought.

"Just them two. I say we put a bullet in their fender and chase 'em on outta here, then we tell the police that they tried to take Miss Rachael. Let *them* chase 'em down."

"What about Billy Ray?" Regina said. "They gonna say he's missin'."

"She's right," Joan said. "How about this? Regina finds you knocked out, which you were, and she chases after Billy Ray as he kidnaps Rachael. She shoots at the car as they get away."

"How do I get Rachael back?"

"You don't. We keep her hidden from the police."

Regina shook her head. "I don't know—"

"We can't let them question Rachael," Joan said, "so it's best if they think Billy Ray's got her. When they question the other two, they'll say Billy Ray never came back to the car. We'll say he did, and there'll be a bullet hole in their fender to prove it. The police will launch a manhunt, but they'll never find either of them."

"But Mrs. Chandler, how long we gonna hide Miss Rachael? She's here, safe and sound," Mr. Gibbs said as he cast a worried glance towards his sister.

"How sound she is has yet to be determined," Joan scoffed. "At any rate, are either of you willing to take a chance that the police will forgive the fact that Regina killed Billy Ray, and we let the alligators eat him?"

"She's right, Regina. The police will throw us all in jail. What will happen to Miss Rachael and Jayden then?"

Regina stamped her foot. "Damn that Billy Ray! He's the one who done all this; now we gotta lie? Give me that gun. I'll run 'em out of here, but we gotta go over our story again so that I get it straight."

"And we'll have to hide them young'uns tonight because the police will come callin' as soon as they know Billy Ray's gone missin'," Mr. Gibbs said.

"And we gotta burn that rug, them sheets, blankets, tarps, and bloody clothes, too. It's gonna be a long night," Regina said. "Maybe we shouldn't call the police just yet. If we gonna lie, we may as well say he took her in the daytime, after we've had time to clean up."

"We should check on the children," Joan said. "If they're all right, let's leave them where they are." She motioned for Regina to take the gun. "You ready?"

Regina took the rifle and made her way to the gate. Sliding the barrel through one of the gaps, she pointed it at the car. "Lord, help me," she whispered as she pulled the trigger.

Joan covered her ears, but the shot was loud as it ricocheted off the front fender. Regina ducked into the shadows and held her ground.

The headlights came on immediately. The engine started, and the car sped down the driveway, spitting gravel as it raced away.

* * *

Joan closed her eyes and rubbed her lower back as Regina added the last pile of material to the fire.

"That'll do it, Mrs. Chandler. There ain't nothing left to burn. I done scrubbed the floor where that rug was twice. We'll see how it looks in the mornin'."

"We'll need to check all the floors, the stairs, the porch, and the dock to make sure there's no trace of blood," Joan said. "Then we'll clean out the attic. It's the best place to hide Rachael when the police come calling."

"It's been a long night. I need to lay down a spell," Regina said.

Joan nodded. "It's nearly four-thirty. I'll see that this fire cools down before I turn in. Where's Mr. Gibbs?"

"That knot on his head is makin' him dizzy again. I sent him back to the cabin. You want me to stay in the house tonight?"

"Yes, thank you. You can stay in the maid's quarters if you like. You should be quite comfortable there."

"I'm so tired I could sleep in the bathtub," Regina said. "See you at breakfast."

Joan turned back to the fire. How the hell had it come to this?

* * *

When Joan woke up, she was so sore that she could barely move. Groaning, she rolled onto her side and gingerly stepped to the floor. She hobbled to the bathroom and looked in the mirror. Her silver-gray hair, typically styled to perfection, was sticking up in various places. Her eyes were red, and a light coating of soot smudged her face.

The heat of the shower did wonders to revive her spirit, but her muscles remained stiff. Walking down the stairs was particularly painful.

Regina took one look at her and said, "You, too? We's walking like we done rode horses for an entire month. Here's yer coffee. I'll have you an omelet in a few minutes."

"Where are the children?" Joan said.

"They ain't come in yet. I probably need to check on 'em, but I ain't lying when I say I'm dreading the walk."

"I understand," Joan said as she eased herself down at the table. "We're clearly not as young as we used to be."

"We ain't never been young enough to do what we done last night." She took two plates from the cabinet, divided the omelet, and sat down at the table. "Oh, I forgot the biscuits. They's ready to come out."

"I'll get them." Joan pushed to her feet and limped to the oven. "I'll grab the honey, too." When she sat back down, she looked at the food. "Thank you. These biscuits look delicious."

"They do, don't they? I'm so hungry I could eat a horse."

"Preferably, the ones we rode in on."

"Oooie, that's a good one!" Regina chuckled.

Smiling, Joan squeezed the honey onto the warm and flakey biscuit and took a bite. They were halfway through breakfast when they heard the children racing up the back steps.

"Hi, Gramma!" Rachael said as she skipped into the kitchen. "Oh, goodie! I love Regina's biscuits!"

"Would you like a biscuit, Jayden?" Regina said.

Joan saw his eyes get big as he turned towards her. "It's all right, Jayden. Come, have breakfast with us."

He climbed up to the table and waited for Regina to hand him a biscuit.

"I'll make you young'uns some eggs in a minute. Where's your Papa, Jayden?"

"He went out to the gate. He said to tell you he'd be along directly."

Joan and Regina exchanged glances. "Let me start on them eggs," Regina said. She got up from the table and set to cooking.

"How did you sleep, Rachael?" Joan said.

"Good."

"Would you and Jayden like to play in the nursery today?"

"We want to play outside, Gramma."

"Well, I want you to play in the nursery. You can practice your letters, but you can also take some toys from your room in there."

Mr. Gibbs entered through the butler's pantry.

"Good morning, Mr. Gibbs. Any news?"

"Not a thing, 'cept this headache won't go away."

Regina set plates in front of Rachael and Jayden. "Here's your eggs. Eat 'em up."

"After breakfast, would you check to see how the back porch and dock are looking? I want everything in tip-top shape if you know what I mean."

"Yes, ma'am. I done scrubbed down the dock first thing this mornin'."

"Excellent. We need to refinish the wood floors upstairs. You can start with the gallery."

"Yes, ma'am. I got me a wood sander, but it don't always work right. I'll check on it directly."

"If it doesn't work, you'll need to go into town to buy a new one. Regina and I will be working in the attic."

"I didn't know there was an attic," Mr. Gibbs said. Regina placed a plate of scrambled eggs on the counter in front of him. "Oh, no, Regina. I don't eat in the big house."

"Today you do," Joan said. "Today, we're all eating in the kitchen. Take a seat at the table and try some of these biscuits. There's some honey over here, too."

"You sure, Mrs. Chandler? It don't seem fittin'."

"Sit down and eat, G. Here's yer coffee," Regina said. "I wanna feel that lump of yers." After setting a steaming mug on the table, she felt along the top of his closely shaved head and winced. "Lord have mercy! Is that thing gettin' bigger?"

"I can't rightly say. I just know it hurts somethin' awful."

Joan pushed from the table and grimaced as her muscles objected. She maneuvered around behind Mr. Gibbs. "May I?" When he nodded, she felt for the knot. "Oh my word! That's the biggest knot I've ever felt. Maybe you should see a doctor."

"I'll be all right. I just need to go slow, is all."

She didn't argue. The work had to be done, and none of them wanted the police to arrive before they were ready. After breakfast, when the children went upstairs to the nursery, she and Regina went up to the attic.

"I declare, this here attic is bigger than G's whole cabin," Regina said as she stepped inside and glanced around. What's in all these boxes?"

"Heirlooms, history, and various other items. I haven't been through them all myself. Some of it belongs to me and my late husband. Some of it belonged to the previous owner. I think we should have Mr. Gibbs build a separate storage closet for it. The rest of the attic we'll turn into living quarters. We'll bring my mattress up here, and buy rugs, tables, a sofa, whatever is needed. It will take time, of course, but today we'll move the boxes so that we can clean properly. We'll need cleaning supplies, of course. Let's go down together so it won't take two trips. Neither of us is walking well today, and I wouldn't wish all those stairs upon my worst enemy."

"Yer a true lady, Mrs. Chandler. A true lady."

* * *

Joan lay in her bathtub wondering if it was worth it. Had Tyler obeyed her wishes, he wouldn't have gotten involved with a girl like Sarah Richards in the first place, but he had always defied her. She had only wanted what was best for him, and now she was reaping what *he* had sown.

The years since her husband's death had been difficult, despite her efforts to reflect the opposite. Outwardly, she had appeared to lead the family, but behind closed doors, in his quiet way, Roger ruled what was his. Adjusting to life without him had taken time. There were pluses, of course, but she missed his comforting strength and wished he were with her now. He'd know what to do about her current dilemma.

Regina had returned to her cottage for the evening, and for the first time since she'd lived in the house, she was frightened to dwell alone. She worried that Billy Ray's partners would return. What would she do if they did? Surely, they wouldn't ignore the fact that Billy Ray was missing. Had they called the police? She should have backed Regina in a claim for self-defense and let the chips fall where they may, but it was too late for that now. She missed having Regina in the house. She had felt safe with Mr. Gibbs keeping watch, but what was she supposed to do, move them all in? Damn Billy Ray! Maybe she should give Rachael back to Tyler and let *him* deal with it.

Yes, that's what she'd do.

She rose from the tub and gingerly stepped out. After drying off, she put on her nightgown and robe and stepped into her slippers. She padded to the nightstand and took out her pistol. It felt heavy in her hand. The walk to Rachael's room seemed longer than normal, and every shadow was suspect. She was not a jumpy woman by nature, but it was impossible to forget what had happened the night before.

When she opened Rachael's door, she half-expected the bed to be empty, but the light from the bathroom revealed otherwise. She pushed the door wider and walked to the bed.

Rachael gasped and sat up. "Gramma, you scared me!" She opened her arms and wrapped them around her neck. "Did you come to tuck me in? Mommy used to tuck me in."

Swallowing hard, Joan laid the gun on the dresser and said, "Yes, I came to kiss you good night."

"I love you, Gramma. I want to stay with you forever!"

"I love you, too, Rachael. Are you warm?"

"Uh huh."

"Did you have fun playing with Jayden today?"

"I did. I can say all my letters now. Wanna hear me?"

"Yes, sweet girl. Tell me your letters." As Rachael recited the alphabet, the fact that she had learned them from a black child weighed heavily on her mind. She had always remained distant from black people, but she was beginning to see things differently.

"What a good girl you are! We'll have to celebrate tomorrow with some ice cream."

"For me and Jayden?"

Rising, she said, "We'll see. Go to sleep, now. I'll see you in the morning."

"Gramma?"

"Yes, dear?"

"You forgot to kiss me good night."

"How silly of me." She leaned over and kissed her forehead. "Sweet dreams, Rachael."

"You, too, Gramma," she said with a sleepy yawn.

Joan smiled. She was such a pretty child. She picked up the gun and slipped out of the room.

She couldn't send Rachael back to Tyler. How could she subject her to neglect again? She had already suffered more shock and trauma than most adults endured in a lifetime. She didn't want to add to it by abandoning her when she clearly wanted to stay. Sighing, she limped her way back to the gallery and paused at the top of the staircase.

The house was quiet.

She had locked all the doors and windows. Still, the thought of sequestering herself in the back bedroom where she might not hear if someone broke in was frightening. She decided to grab her pillow, a couple of warm blankets, and make a bed on the living room sofa. There, at least, she'd hear if someone entered the house.

For the first time ever, she'd seek sleep with a handgun beneath her pillow.

CHAPTER
TEN

"**M**rs. Chandler, Mrs. Chandler, what are you doing down here?"

Joan had to blink a few times before Regina's face came clearly into view. "Good morning to you, too," she snapped. "I must have fallen asleep down here."

"I'll get some coffee," Regina said.

"No need. I'll join you in the kitchen."

"In that case, I'll just take up these here blankets." Regina paused when she plucked up the pillow and saw the revolver beneath it.

"I better put that away before the children see it," Joan grumbled.

"You didn't fall asleep down here. You was afraid to stay upstairs."

"It's a damn big house. I was afraid I wouldn't hear if someone broke in."

"I was afraid in my little cottage, too. I jumped at every sound, just waitin' for somebody to bust down my door and punish me for what we done. If we's both scaredt, maybe we oughta stay in the same house and make each other feel better. Maybe I should reconsider yer offer and move into the maid's quarters. Either way, I want my own gun."

"There's no debating that you can shoot."

"I can, but you should install a security system anyways. We need warnin' if somebody breaks in."

"You're a smart woman, Regina. I'll arrange for it immediately." She opened a drawer in the credenza and placed the gun inside. "Remind me to move that thing after breakfast."

"Yes, ma'am." As they limped towards the kitchen, Regina chuckled. "Didn't do no good to sleep downstairs, did it?"

"What do you mean?"

"You didn't hear me come in this mornin', did ya?"

"That's annoying," Joan replied, making a face.

Regina chuckled again. "It is, ain't it? You could've slept all night in yer big soft bed."

Joan smiled, despite the stress. "You didn't have to point that out, you know."

Regina poured two cups of coffee and set them on the table. "Gotta laugh when you can, Mrs. Chandler. You gotta laugh when you can."

The sound of little shoes running on the hardwood floor caught their attention.

"Gramma, Gramma! I didn't tee-tee in my bed last night."

Joan's eyes narrowed. "Did you wet your bed the night before?"

Rachael climbed to the table and nodded. "That's what I was coming to tell you when you grabbed me."

Exhaling, Joan told herself that it was partially her fault for putting her in the attic. "I see. Did you tell Regina that you peed your bed?"

"No."

"You mean to tell me you slept in a dirty bed last night?" she said, her voice rising despite her efforts to control it.

"It was dry," Rachael said.

"Lord, help me."

"I'll take care of it, Mrs. Chandler. Don't you worry. With all she's been through, poor thing, it's no wonder she peed the bed. She'll stop once she feels safe and secure again."

"I guess you need to start wearing diapers at night," Joan said.

Rachael reached for a biscuit. "But I didn't tee-tee. I was good."

"Yes, you are, and you said your ABC's last night, too. I'm very proud of you."

"And I get ice cream today. Me and Jayden."

"We'll see," Joan said.

Regina set a steaming bowl of oatmeal in front of her.

"Thank you, Miss Regina. I like oatmeal."

"Yer welcome, child."

Joan took another drink of coffee. "I believe with what we uncovered yesterday, we have enough to furnish the entire living room. I was surprised to see that fireplace when we moved the boxes. It seems someone else must have used it as a living space sometime in the past."

Regina turned from the stove. "Certainly seems so. That little green sofa is right pretty and in perfect condition, too. Once I clean it up, it'll be good as new."

"It needs a floor rug or two, but after that, I think it'll be quite comfortable. The wood floors are in surprisingly good condition, don't you think?"

"Yes, ma'am. I wouldn't mind living up there myself. It's got a good view from that little window. If'n you don't mind lookin' through bars, that is, and it's ever so roomy."

"Indeed." Joan stroked her chin. "You and Mr. Gibbs and I have an important phone call to make, and we need to have our stories straight." As their eyes met and held, coffee overflowed the mug Regina was pouring. "Regina, the coffee!"

* * *

"They gonna search the house," Regina said. "What if they find blood? I watch them detective shows. They can find stuff that's invisible to us."

"We'll say he took her from the garden and eliminate the need for them to search the house at all," Joan said. "Besides, now that the floor has been sanded and refinished, it's not likely any residue remains.

We've scattered the ashes from the fireplace. What's left to find?"

Regina looked doubtful. "What if they test the dock?"

"Mr. Gibbs scoured it. Didn't you?" she said, turning for his confirmation. Receiving a nod, she added, "Besides, they have no reason to look there. We're going to tell them that he jumped in the car, and you shot the fender. Remember?"

"I'm worried about Miss Rachael," Mr. Gibbs said. "Are you sure we have to hide her?"

"Maybe we should see what she remembers," Regina said. "Maybe she don't know enough to cause any trouble."

Joan grimaced. "I'm not willing to risk it. I don't like this any better than you do, but we have to see this through. I wonder if Rachael told Jayden what happened."

"Lord o' mercy!" Regina said. "Surely not."

"Mr. Gibbs, where's your grandson?"

"He's out pickin' butter beans, Mrs. Chandler, but surely he don't know nothin'. He'd a told me if he did." He cast a worried glance towards Regina.

"Well, let's go see what he knows." Pushing from the table, Joan led the way through the butler's pantry and down the side-door steps. The sky was dark with menacing clouds, and a brisk wind whipped through her hair and clothes as she hurried along the gravel trail towards the vegetable garden.

"Hello, Jayden."

Jayden's head snapped up, but he smiled when he saw his papa behind her.

"Stand up, boy. Mrs. Chandler needs to ask you some questions. You tell her the truth, now. Ya hear?"

"Yes, sir." He looked wary as he brushed the dirt from his pants.

"Jayden, did Rachael tell you what happened last night before she came to visit you at the cabin?"

"She said something bad happened to Mr. Billy Ray. She said that you told her not to look, but she saw him lying on the floor."

"Heaven help us," Regina muttered.

"Did she say anything else?" Joan said over the whipping wind.

"She said he was bleeding."

"Did she say why?" Joan pressed.

Jayden shook his head.

Joan pressed her lips together but released when she felt a twitch in the lower right corner. "Don't stay out here too long. It's fixin' to rain."

"I'm pickin' butter beans, Mrs. Chandler. Papa says we're having a big harvest this year."

"You're a good boy, Jayden. You make your papa proud." Joan motioned for the other two to follow her back to the house.

A heavy sigh escaped her as she sat down at the table. "This is getting worse by the moment. Now Jayden knows about it."

Regina sank into a chair, "Maybe I should just turn myself in and get it over with."

"It's too late for that," Joan said. "We'll have to hide them both, and that's all there is to it."

* * *

Lights flashed from half a dozen police cars. It had taken two photo IDs and an escort to get into the house where his mother sat on the couch distraught and shaken. "Mother! I got here as soon as I could. Any news?" Tyler said as he sat beside her.

"Not yet. Oh, Tyler, this is awful!" she cried as she turned into his shoulder.

He wrapped an arm around her. "Tell me what happened."

"Regina saw Billy Ray grab Rachael from the garden. She ran back for Mr. Gibbs' rifle, but by the time she caught up with them, she could only aim for the car. She thinks she hit the fender. She was afraid to try again because of Rachael." She shook her head and bit her knuckle. "I can't stand it! They have to find her!"

"They'll find her, Mother. How far can they get in that old car?"

Two uniformed officers came through the front door. Tyler recognized one of them from the night Billy Ray broke into his trailer. "Did you find anything?"

"The tire tracks by the front gate match the ones left at your place the night Jacob Clarkston was abducted, though they've been washed out by all this rain. We found a matching boot print, too. Billy Ray was here, all right. We've issued an APB and an Amber Alert. If that car travels any of the main roads, we'll find it."

"You knew this house was a target," Tyler accused as he rose to his feet. "They should've been apprehended before they ever set foot on this property!"

"Easy there, Mr. Chandler," the officer said. "We're doing everything possible to recover your daughter. Is there any reason to believe that the girl's grandfather might abuse her?"

"He kidnapped her, for God's sake. Isn't that enough? Where's your maid, Mother? I want to talk to her."

"We're already doing that," Officer Jenkins said. "You need to stay out of this and let us do our job."

"Where's Cody?" Joan said.

"I left him with the babysitter. Do you want me to stay with you? We can move in for a while if you like."

"No, that's not necessary. He got what he came for," Joan said. "Besides, Regina's living in the house now, and I'm scheduled to have an alarm system installed."

Tyler gave her the eye, but she seemed resolved. "All right, but if you change your mind, you let me know. Cody and I can stay as long as you need, but I'll be out of town this weekend."

"Going after Pamela?" she scoffed.

"Don't start on me, Mother."

"I think we're finished here for now," Officer Jenkins said. "We'll keep you informed."

"Please find my granddaughter. She belongs with *me*."

"Yes, ma'am. We'll do our best." He tugged lightly on his cap and walked out the door.

Tyler followed. "Look, man, how long does it usually take to solve these things? They couldn't have gotten far, could they?"

"Who knows? They could've ditched that car and be driving another vehicle. It depends on what they plan to do."

Tyler shook his head. "You'd think with them having a house and family, they wouldn't risk something like this. Surely, they know they can't get away with it. It's not like they can enroll her in school somewhere. It makes no sense!"

"People do strange things when they lose a loved one. They may see Rachael as a replacement for the daughter they lost. One thing's for sure; if they cross state lines, it'll make our job a lot more difficult."

"Is there a number I can call to follow up?"

"I left it with your mother. Don't worry, Mr. Chandler. The authorities in Arkansas are watching their trailer. If they take her back there, we'll nab them."

Tyler didn't like feeling helpless. The thought of Billy Ray holding Rachael made him half-crazy with rage, especially after the stories Sarah told him. "Hey, you asked me if I thought Billy Ray might abuse Rachael. I didn't want to say anything in front of my Mother, but Billy Ray gets mean when he drinks, which, according to my wife, is quite often. We need to find him before he does to Rachael what he did to my wife."

"And what is that, Mr. Chandler?"

"He used to beat her within an inch of her life with his belt buckle, and she had the scars to prove it. Now you warned me about saying what I'd like to do to him, but—" he bit his lip. "He'd best not lay a hand on my daughter."

Officer Jenkins placed a steadying hand on his shoulder. "Let's hope for the best."

Tyler nodded and headed back towards the house. He was about to climb the steps but turned to the right instead. As he walked down the pathway towards the garden, he wondered why Rachael had been playing outside by herself. Leaving her with his mother may have been a mistake. She was too young to wander about unsupervised, with or without the threat of Billy Ray.

Uniformed police officers were in the process of taping off the garden. He walked past them and took the walkway down to the river. He was surprised to see the houseboat tied to the dock. Considering all that was going on, it was an odd time for Mr. Gibbs to be doing maintenance. Tyler glanced over his shoulder and stepped onto the boat. Everything appeared to be in order. He walked through the cabin and then worked his way to the back deck. He shuddered at the memory of pulling Cody from the river. It was a wonder he didn't lose both of them that day. He leaned over the railing and stared into the water. Everything had changed, and it would never be the same again.

He made his way back to the bow and onto the dock. Funny how the houseboat used to represent freedom. Now it represented sorrow and death. He climbed the walkway up to the back porch steps, but he didn't go inside. His mood had turned dark, and he didn't want to project that onto his mother. Instead, he headed for the truck. He'd call her later to explain.

On the way home, he dialed Pamela's number for the hundredth time since she had left him. When it went to voicemail, he said, "Hey, it's me. I'm calling to let you know that Billy Ray kidnapped Rachael from my mother's house this afternoon. My world is falling apart. I can't keep losing the people I love. Hug Jacob for me and know that I'd give anything to have you beside me right now." He wanted to say more, but he didn't. He had said it all before, and she'd ignored him. He didn't have anyone else to turn to. Even if she didn't respond, at least she'd know what happened. He ended the call and laid the phone down. A minute later, it rang. He picked it up and glanced at the caller I.D.; it was a private number. "Hello?"

"Tyler, it's me," Pamela said.

"I'm so glad you called back."

"Tell me about Rachael. What happened?"

He had so many questions, but he knew if he said the wrong thing she'd hang up. He told her what he knew.

"I am so sorry, Tyler. I remember how awful it was to have Jacob missing. That's why I called. You were there for me; you shouldn't have to go through this by yourself."

"The police are watching their trailer, but I doubt he'll take her there. They haven't been home since the attempt they made on Jacob. Are you somewhere safe?"

"We haven't settled anywhere yet."

"Can I see you this weekend? I'll meet you wherever you are."

"Don't press me, Tyler. I haven't changed my mind. Maybe I shouldn't have called."

"I'm so glad you did. I won't say anything else about it. Just talk to me about Rachael. I can't handle it by myself."

"How's your mother holding up? I'm sure she's beside herself with worry."

He forced himself to stay on topic. "She is, but she's holding up better than I expected. I offered to move in, but she said she'd rather I didn't. She doesn't think Billy Ray will be back now that he has Rachael."

"Are you concerned that he'll try to take Cody?"

Tensing, he said, "I doubt it. I've been leaving him with a sitter. I don't have anywhere else to take him."

"Your mom won't watch him?"

"She hasn't offered, and I can't put her through any more stress right now. Maybe I should enroll him in preschool."

"I'm sorry you're going through this, Tyler."

"I'm sorry you're not with me. I miss you terribly."

"You've got more important things on your plate than missing me," Pamela said.

"As horrible as this might sound, there's nothing more important to me than being with you."

"I hope they find Rachael soon. I'll be praying for you. Goodbye, Tyler."

"Wait! Don't go. I love—" He heard the dial tone and immediately tried to call her back, but it was useless; private numbers don't go through. The emptiness he felt was even greater than before she called. It was past time to pick up Cody. Somehow, he had to pretend that everything was normal. He had to prepare dinner, entertain his son, and tuck him into bed, all while his heart ached over Pamela, mourned for Sarah, and feared for Rachael. How much could one man take?

* * *

"What about the children?" Mr. Gibbs said.

Joan set her teacup on the kitchen table and paced back to the window. Sooner or later, the police would come, and she damn well wanted to be prepared. "We'll have to keep them in the house," Joan said. "The police could return at any moment during the investigation."

"But Jayden don't know as much as Miss Rachael," Regina said. "Couldn't he stay with G in his cabin?"

"He knows enough. They'll have to stay in the attic together, but not without supervision. Regina, how would you feel about staying up there with them? You can sleep with Rachael on my mattress until we get more beds up there. Jayden can sleep on the sofa."

"But there's no light up there, Mrs. Chandler," Regina said.

"That's just as well. We can't afford to let anyone know that there *is* an attic up there."

"And what are we supposed to do for a bathroom? I'm sorry, Mrs.

Chandler, but that attic ain't ready to live in," Regina said. "Besides, it's colder than the dickens up there at night. We need a better plan."

"All right. I don't like it, but I guess Jayden can stay in Cody's room until we get the attic ready. That will be your priority, Mr. Gibbs. You'll need to get that fireplace working right away, and then I want you to build out three bedrooms, a bathroom, and a small kitchenette. And don't forget the storage room for all those boxes. Can you do that kind of work, or do I need to bring someone in from out of state?"

"I can do all kinds of construction, Mrs. Chandler. Who you think modernized them cabins? Only—"

"What?" Joan said, brows raised.

Mr. Gibbs shook his head. "It's just that I'll miss having the boy around. He's mighty fine company, Jayden is. The cabin will be right lonely without him."

"Had I kept those two apart as I should have, this wouldn't have happened. As it sits, I don't see any way around it. Do you?" He glanced at Regina, but neither said anything. "Go on into town, then. Buy lumber, drywall, insulation, paint, bathroom fixtures, and plumbing parts, whatever you need. Make a list and don't forget anything. We don't have time for you to be running back and forth into town. I want this finished as soon as possible. Do I make myself clear?"

"Yes, ma'am."

"Regina, you keep watch on things while I go online to order new mattresses, rugs, and a few other things for the attic. If anyone comes to the door, you lock those kids up tight before you answer."

"Yes, ma'am. I'll start dinner, too."

"Very well, and don't forget that we are grieving. If and when the police come calling, we need to act accordingly. Regina, you can let Rachael out of the attic, but keep her in the nursery. Mr. Gibbs, fetch your grandson and tell him he's to stay in the nursery with Rachael. Tell him whatever you like, but his days of running free are over. We've got to protect ourselves until the police put this case on the back burner.

It could be months before it's safe to let them out again. From now on, neither child is to venture downstairs for any reason. Do I make myself clear?"

"Yes, ma'am, Mrs. Chandler. I don't like it none, but I'll see to it," Regina said.

"I don't suppose Billy Ray likes his situation much, either," Joan scoffed. "Neither would you if the police take you away. Nevertheless, we're all in this together."

Regina opened her mouth to respond but closed it.

"You have something to say?"

"Only that it seems to me it's them young'uns who are payin' for what we done," Regina mumbled, her eyes downcast.

"That may be, but it won't help anyone if we stay in the attic ourselves. Besides, if Rachael hadn't wet her bed, maybe she wouldn't be in this situation. She should think about that the next time she has to pee and doesn't want to get up!" She pushed from the table and stormed up the stairs.

CHAPTER ELEVEN

Mr. Gibbs struggled under the weight of the firewood he carried, which was a great deal less than he usually hauled in one load. Sweat popped out on his brow in spite of the cool wind that had whipped through the trees in relentless gusts for the past half hour. It smelled like rain.

His legs began to quiver.

"I can count all the way to a hundred in French, Papa. Wanna hear me?" Jayden said as he led the way back to the cabin, carrying his own load of wood. "I practice with Rachael every day."

Mr. Gibbs' arms gave out.

Hearing the crash, Jayden looked back over his shoulder. "Papa?" He dropped the load he was carrying and ran back to where his grandfather lay amongst the scattered logs and pine needles on the forest floor. "Papa!"

"Go get Regina, boy. Get her quick," Mr. Gibbs said as he tried to stay calm. There were worse things than dying, he supposed, but he'd feel better about it if they hadn't done what they did. He'd spent his whole life trying to do right only to make a mess of it at the end.

He groaned as his chest tightened. He wanted to make amends, but there wasn't any way to do it. Regina had killed Billy Ray in self-defense, but that wasn't an excuse for denying the man a proper burial. Hard as he tried, he couldn't forget the image of that alligator ripping

Billy Ray's leg off his body. It haunted him day and night, and that was only the beginning. Those alligators tore him limb from limb. How was God supposed to forgive something like that?

He heard Jayden and Regina coming in the distance. His eyelids fluttered and everything went dark.

* * *

Rachael fell onto her hands and knees as her grandmother pushed her through the door. "Please! Don't leave me in here!"

She only cried out once because she knew it wouldn't do any good. Besides, the sun was going down. She pushed to her feet and hurried past the fireplace. There was usually a fire burning, thanks to Regina, but not tonight. That's why it was colder than usual. She hurried to her bedroom—the only one of three that was finished—and rummaged through the dresser for her warmest pajamas, then she crouched next to the bookshelf to turn on the nightlight. Her teeth chattered as she tugged off her clothes and wriggled into her pj's. "Bo," she whispered. "Where are you?" She crawled onto the bed, searching for her teddy bear, before dropping to her knees onto the floor. Banishing her fear, she took a big breath and dived under the bed to continue her search. Finally, she grasped a fur-covered leg and tugged.

"Oh, Bo, I'm so glad I found you!" She squeezed the bear tight against her chest. "We've got to build a fire, quick!" Leaving her clothes on the floor, she ran on tiptoes down the hallway, past two closed doors, and into the living room.

She glanced up at the small window beside the fireplace. She wasn't tall enough to see out, but she could see that it was dark outside. "Come on, Bo, I almost forgot." She rushed into the bathroom, felt along the wall for the nightlight, and turned it on. She did the same in the kitchenette, in case she needed a glass of water in the night.

Back in the living room, she switched on the last nightlight and glanced around at the eerie shadows it cast upon the walls, floor, and ceiling. Regina said she should think of them as angels, but they didn't look like angels to her!

She swallowed hard and set the bear on the couch. "Don't worry, Bo. I've seen Regina build lots of fires. It'll be warm in here in no time." She picked up some small pieces of wood, laid them at the bottom of the hearth, and then stacked some larger pieces on top of it. There wasn't any newspaper, so she ran to the bathroom for some toilet paper. Returning to the fireplace, she shoved tissue between the bigger pieces of wood and grabbed the matches. She was afraid to light it, but without a fire, it would only get colder.

Her hand shook as she raked the match along the side of the box. Nothing happened. She tried again, only harder this time. The match head broke off, so she took out another one. This time, it lit. She dropped to her knees and held it to the tissue. All three sections caught fire, but they quickly burned and went out. She lit another match and held it to the small pieces of wood, but the fire got close to her fingers, so she dropped it.

"It's not as easy as I thought, Bo. I'll have to get more toilet paper and try again."

She gasped at the sound of someone climbing the stairs. She grabbed her bear and ducked behind the couch. When the door opened, Jayden stumbled in.

"And don't forget your manners towards my granddaughter."

"Yes, ma'am." The door closed and the lock slid into place. "Rachael? Where are you?" Jayden called.

"I'm here. What are you doing here?"

"Papa fell down. Regina told Mrs. Chandler to call a doctor. Once she called him, she said I had to come up here with you. It's cold in here. Let's start a fire."

"I tried, but I can't make it go."

"I'll do it." Jayden knelt before the fireplace and began rearranging the wood. "You need more space beneath the wood so the air can get to it. These little ones burn up quickly. We need more of these, so they will burn long enough to catch the bigger ones. Like this."

"Here, I'll put some on, too." Rachael began placing the kindling like Jayden showed her.

"That's right. We need some paper."

"I was using toilet paper, but I don't want to use it all up."

"Got anything else?" Jayden said.

"Regina usually brings a newspaper."

"Got an old book you don't like?"

"I've got lots of books." She ran to her room and picked one out. "How about this one? I've read it ten times."

"You don't want it anymore?"

"No. You can burn it, but you'd better burn it all. Gramma will be mad if she finds out."

They tore pages from the book, wadded them into balls, and stuffed them in between the wood.

"We don't need it all. Maybe you can hide the rest, in case you need it again."

"Can I light it?" She felt safer now that Jayden was there.

"Sure."

Rachael lit the match on the first try.

"Just light the bottom ones. They'll catch the upper ones when they're ready."

Rachael held the match to the paper until it caught. She giggled as the wood started to pop and burn. "This is fun."

"I've been making fires since I can remember," Jayden said. "It'll warm up in here in a minute."

"I better get Bo. I'll bet he's cold, too."

The two of them sat close to the fire as it started to grow. Jayden added logs and, gradually, the chill lifted from the room. At one point, the flames grew so high that they had to move back.

"I hope Papa gets well soon."

"I hope so, too," she said.

"You and I are alike, you know."

"What do you mean?" she said.

"Your momma's gone. My daddy's gone. Your daddy doesn't want you. My momma doesn't want me. All I have is my papa. All you have is your gramma, and we both have Regina."

"But Gramma doesn't love me anymore. If she did, she wouldn't make me stay up here."

Tears filled Jayden's eyes.

Rachael had never seen him cry before. "What's wrong, Jayden?"

"I don't want my papa to die."

"Maybe if we sing like we do on Sundays, you'll feel better. Just think of your papa playing his banjo and Regina singing like she does."

"I don't feel like singing; I'm scared. What will happen to me if Papa dies?"

"Won't you stay with Regina?"

"I don't know. She might move back to Chicago. She's always talking about it."

"What's Chicago?" Rachael said.

"I don't know."

"I want you to stay here, Jayden. What will happen to me if you leave? Regina is the one who takes care of me."

"What if my momma comes back and I'm not here?" Jayden said.

"Your papa won't die, Jayden. He can't! We need him too bad."

"I love my papa."

Rachael looked down at Bo and then handed him to Jayden.

Jayden wrapped his arms around Rachael's teddy bear and cried.

* * *

"Come on, G. Wake up now. You needs to eat somethin.'"

He blinked a few times and then Regina's face came into focus. He was inside the cabin on his bed. "How did I—"

"I carried you; that's how. Them paramedics done come and gone. You had a mild heart attack and scaredt me plumb to death. They wanted to take you in, but you refused to go, you stubborn old goat. If'n you had insurance, I reckon they'd a taken you anyway. They gave you somethin' to help you rest. You been out nearly six hours. How do you feel?"

"Like I had me a heart attack. Where's Mrs. Chandler? She's like to throw a fit."

"Oh, she did. She done locked herself up inside the house. Said she had to keep Rachael and Jayden outta sight. I'll bet they's up in that attic with no food and no fire. You know how she is. She never thinks about nobody but herself."

"Poor Miss Rachael. She ain't never gonna get outta that house as long as Mrs. Chandler lives."

"G, what's gonna happen to Jayden and me when you, well, you know."

The worry on her face was so intense that he closed his eyes to shut it out. "We done been over it a thousand times. If we tell the truth, then you and me will go to jail. Jayden's got no place to go. As it is, he's gettin' a world-class education. He'll lose all that if we tell the truth."

"But what about Miss Rachael?" Regina said. "She's sufferin' the most for what we done."

"If you and I went to jail, it would only get worse for Miss Rachael." He groaned and closed his eyes. "Mrs. Chandler ain't the same since Billy Ray died. She don't remember things right, and she gets confused real easy like. What's more, she's turned downright mean. If I didn't know better, I'd swear she blames Miss Rachael for how things turned out."

"She do blame Miss Rachael. She complains all the time that

she feels trapped. Hell, we're all trapped. We're damned if we do and damned if we don't, and twice damned for what we done to Billy Ray," Regina said.

"And there ain't no way out of it, neither," Mr. Gibbs said. "The best way to help Jayden and Miss Rachael is to stay quiet. Otherwise, I'd confess. I don't want to meet my maker with blood on my hands, but I don't see no other way."

Regina twisted her lips and nodded. "I know it. It eats me up inside, but the Good Lord saw what happened. He knows the truth, even if nobody else does."

"She can't keep Miss Rachael locked up forever. It just ain't right. There's gotta be an answer."

"You just wait; God will provide," Regina said, worry etched in the deep lines of her face.

"If he's gonna do it before my heart gives out, he'd best hurry," Mr. Gibbs said with a weak chuckle.

* * *

Joan frowned as she rose from the secretary desk in her bedroom. It was nearly two in the afternoon. The letter she received from her sister only served to remind her of how trapped she had become. No one could visit, and she didn't dare leave, all because of Rachael.

If Rachael ever escaped, there'd be hell to pay. There was no convincing her of some made up story. She knew she was being contained, and she resented it. She shook her head as she thought back on the decision that had led to this atrocity. Oh, she had avoided the adoption proceedings, but she had never imagined what the consequences might be. She crumpled her sister's letter and tossed it into the trashcan.

On a whim, she decided to check on the children. They would be studying mathematics about now. She heard voices as she approached, and she stopped to listen outside the nursery door.

"No, Jayden. Do it like this," Rachael said.

She threw the door open, which caused the children to startle apart. "Turn off the computer, Jayden. Right now."

"But we're in the middle of a lesson with Mrs. Johnson."

"Tell Mrs. Johnson you have to go now."

"Yes, ma'am." He typed on the keyboard and then closed the lid on the laptop computer.

Rachael backed up a few steps.

"Rachael, how many times do I have to tell you not to speak while you're in class? What if they are monitoring you in some way?"

"She was only trying to help," Jayden said.

"Silence! Do you want your studies to end right here and now?"

"No, ma'am," Jayden said.

"I'm sorry, Grandma," Rachael said. "I'll be quiet."

"I wonder how often that happens when I'm not around," she said with a scowl. "Where's Regina? She's supposed to be supervising you."

"She went downstairs to make us a snack. It's almost break time," Jayden said.

"We're going to address this; don't think we won't. Go downstairs, Jayden. School is over for today. Rachael, you're going back to the attic. You need to think about how important it is that you obey me when I tell you something."

"Please, Grandma. Can't we stay here? I'll be good; I promise."

"Do as I say!"

Jayden looked back at Rachael as he walked through the door. Rachael reluctantly followed him. When they reached the gallery, Joan moved the rocking chair and opened the hidden panel.

"Why do I have to stay in the attic? Why can't I go to my princess room? Don't you love me anymore?"

Joan considered her granddaughter's upturned face. She was such a pretty thing, but the sparkle in her eyes had long since dimmed. She was sulky, angry, and confused now, and who could blame her? "Listen to me, Rachael. Everything changed when your mother died. I wanted to adopt you and give you a wonderful life, but I can't do that now. I'm sorry."

"But *why*? I don't pee in my bed anymore."

"Well, that's good to hear," she said with a wry twitch of her lip. "I'd like to explain it to you, really, I would, but you're much too young to understand. When I'm gone, and you're all grown up, you'll understand. I'll see to it. Now, go upstairs like a good little girl. Regina will bring your dinner up later."

"What about my snack?" Rachael said with a pout.

"There will be no snack today. You don't get rewarded for being disobedient." Rachael's forehead wrinkled, and she clenched her fists. "Go on, now. I don't have all day." She urged Rachael up the stairs with a wave of her hands. At least she wouldn't have to look at her for the rest of the day. The girl still tugged at her heartstrings, but she couldn't afford to be soft.

She locked Rachael inside the attic, wincing as Rachael pounded on the door in frustration. "Please, Gramma, don't leave me in here!"

She stared at the door and closed her eyes. She wanted to let her out. She wanted to pretend that nothing had happened, but Billy Ray Richards was dead and Rachael saw him die. And *that* changed everything.

Joan hurried down the stairs and closed the secret panel. She regretted taking her from Tyler, but the dye was cast, and she couldn't allow a five-year-old to ruin her life.

Instead of going downstairs, she went back to her bedroom and sat at her desk. She realized that she could never introduce Rachael back into society. There was no way to justify having kept her in the attic, nor could she stop her from talking about what she had seen that night, which she did from time to time despite being told not to.

Rachael was growing up, and she was becoming angrier and more rebellious as the months went by.

It wasn't easy for *her* either. She was tired of fighting nightmares, visions of Billy Ray lying in an expanding puddle of blood, or worse, his bloody body torn limb by limb by alligators as they overwhelmed and sank her fishing boat near the boathouse. She lived in constant fear of the police finding Rachael, and, of course, Rachael wasn't the only threat. Mr. Gibbs, Regina, Jayden, any of them could leak the truth.

She had seen the way they looked at her, taking Rachael's side rather than hers. What right did they have to judge? All of them needed to go! It was the only way to be safe.

She grabbed her metal stapler and threw it against the wall. "Damn you, Billy Ray! You've ruined everything!" Because of him, she was losing what she had wanted most in this world, a daughter upon whom to lavish her love, money, and attention.

She tapped her nails on the desk. She couldn't manage it herself, but she knew who to call. She had used him once to deal with a man foolish enough to blackmail her. That's what had made her think of dumping Billy Ray in the wide part of the river. "At least he has company down there," she mumbled to herself in the mirror. She gazed into her aging blue eyes, now hardened by loss and framed with wrinkles and puffy skin. "It's their own damn fault. And Pamela better keep up her end of the bargain too."

Accessing a hidden compartment among the small drawers of her secretary desk, she took out a folded piece of paper and scowled at it. It wasn't the type of call she wanted to make, but what choice did she have?

She dialed the number and heard herself making the arrangements. That money could so easily buy the end of four lives was obscene, and yet that is exactly what she purchased. He didn't say how, only that he wouldn't make them suffer.

A blinding headache struck so suddenly that the room began to spin. She felt nauseous, and it was all she could do to find her bed. She wouldn't think about this anymore. She couldn't. Tyler had accepted that Rachael might never come home. Now, it must be true.

CHAPTER TWELVE

*M*onths later...

A black and white cat rose from its place on top of the bookshelf. It yawned and stretched, and then jumped down onto Detective Jack Kendall's desk.

"Hey, Bonnie Bella. I was wondering where you were." Jack stroked his hand along her fluffy black tail. She purred loudly and rolled over onto the file he was reviewing. "Hey, I was reading that. Where's your brother? You two should be off chasing mice somewhere, earning your keep for a change." Seeing that Bonnie had no immediate plans to vacate his desk, he set her on the floor and scratched her chin. "Scoot now. I've got work to do."

The front door opened, and Stacy bustled in with two bags full of groceries. "Hey, Jack," she said as she pushed the door closed with a well-rounded hip. She set the bags on her desk, which sat opposite his in the small two-room office space. "I just got an interesting phone call from Arkansas. Seems we might have a missing persons case in the works."

"Why didn't the call come here? I was working."

"I forwarded the phones before I left. You don't multi-task well, and I knew you were working on the Simmons case."

He made a face. "Just because you're right doesn't mean you should make those kinds of decisions. I am the boss, you know."

"Sure, Jack. You just go ahead and think that." She pulled a bag of kitty treats from a grocery sack and shook it. "All right, Bonnie and Clyde, where are you?"

Clyde rounded the corner and joined Bonnie at her feet.

"What was the call about?" Jack said as Stacy charmed the two cats into sitting on their hindquarters to beg for treats.

"Remember that case about the missing child from up around Ratliff Ferry?"

"There hasn't been any news on that for months."

"Well, this was the alleged kidnapper's daughter. She claims that she got a call from her mother and uncle, who are still on the lam, by the way. They claim that Billy Ray—whatever their last name is—never came back to the car the night they tried to kidnap the Chandler girl. They suspect that something bad happened to him, but they're afraid to turn themselves in. The daughter wants us to investigate her mother's suspicions."

"Sounds like something we should tell the police," Jack said.

He stroked his two-day stubble while running different scenarios through his mind to see if they could justify handling it without going to the authorities.

"I was afraid you'd say that," Stacy said. "Come on, Jack, shouldn't we check it out first? I mean, we're detectives, and she did call us. If we learn anything important, then we can go to the police. As far as I know, they've let the case go cold. The girl's been missing for over a year."

"Just because we haven't heard anything doesn't mean they're not still searching," Jack said. "I can ask Kevin if there's been any progress lately."

Stacy rolled her eyes. "Like the police captain isn't gonna wonder why you're asking? He knows you, remember?"

"What do you suggest?"

She tucked her shoulder-length, honey-blonde hair behind her ear, dropped into the chair beside his desk, and crossed her curvy legs. "I'm meeting with her tomorrow. Maybe she'll give me a hint as to where her mother and uncle are hiding. You never know where this could lead."

"And why should you meet with her and not me?" he said.

"Because we're buddies already. If she still trusts me after we talk, then I'll introduce you. What do you say?"

He didn't like it, but he'd been outmaneuvered. Besides, the girl might not agree to meet with him, though women generally found him approachable and trustworthy. He sighed. Stacy might not be conventional, but she was damn good at getting information out of people. "When does she want to meet?"

"Eleven o'clock at Hal and Mal's."

"Fine. A high-profile case would do wonders for our reputation— and God knows we need the money—but I want to meet her before she leaves. You got that? *Before* she leaves."

"Oooh, this is so exciting! I've been waiting for something big to happen, and this is really, really big!"

"Don't go getting all crazy on me. We have to obey the law. At any point it crosses the line, we turn it over to the police. You understand that, right?"

"Got it." She winked at him and went back to her desk. "I've got research to do."

Jack ran a hand through his thick, unruly mass of blondish-brown curls. How was it that he was working on another infidelity case while she was working on one of the hottest kidnapping cases in recent Mississippi history? "Oh, and Stacy?"

She glanced up from her computer screen. "Yes?"

"Unforward the phones, please. I want the calls to come to me first from now on."

"Sure, Jack. Whatever you say. You're the boss."

* * *

Stacy stepped into the dimly lit foyer of Hal and Mal's pub and took off her sunglasses. Perching them on the top of her head, she glanced into the dining room side of the divided restaurant and spotted a young woman in her mid-twenties, with long light-brown hair, sitting at a table. She looked a lot like the young woman whose picture she found in an online obituary. When the woman looked up with inquisitive eyes, Stacy approached the table.

"Are you Emily?" When the girl nodded, Stacy smiled and took a seat. "Thanks for coming. I'm Stacy. I hope you're hungry. The food here is fantastic."

"I'm starved. It's a long drive from Arkansas, and I drove straight through. I don't like to stop when I'm travelin' by myself."

"Did you come through Memphis or Vicksburg? I can tell you some safe places to stop in either direction."

"What's good here?" Emily said, tucking her hair behind her ears.

Noting her thick Southern drawl, and the fact that she had dodged her question, Stacy said, "Everything, especially the gumbo. Do you like seafood?"

"I like barbecue better. We butcher our own beef and venison back home. It makes for real good eatin'."

Stacy wrinkled her nose. "I like eating it, but I'm definitely not into chopping it up."

Emily laughed. "I'm with you on that. I stay home when they skin the hides, or should I say when they used to skin 'em. I haven't seen my Ma, Pa, or Uncle Tommy Lee for over a year now—as you know."

"Where's home?"

"Arkansas."

Seeing that Emily wasn't ready to open up, Stacy said, "Let's order something, and then we can get down to business. I don't know about you, but I could use a huge glass of sweet tea." She waved down the waitress to take their orders.

Once the server had moved away, Stacy said, "Let's start at the beginning. How did you hear about us?"

"I researched detective agencies in Jackson, and I saw on your website that you help find missin' loved ones. My situation's complicated because of the kidnappin' investigation, so my first question is about client privilege. Am I free to talk to you without worryin' that you'll tell the police everything I say?"

"Good question, Emily. While private investigators don't have the same client privilege that attorneys do, we are protected by something called Work Product Doctrine. You can look it up if you like. Since we're not specifically preparing information for trial, we're good to go. That being said, I'll be careful about what I write down. I'm here because I want to help."

Emily exhaled, and her shoulders relaxed. "Thanks, I sure could use someone to talk to. Our neighbors have been actin' all high and mighty ever since the news came out about Rachael's kidnappin'. They throw rocks at our trailer at night, and I hear 'em whisperin' things behind my back when I go into town. The preacher kept preachin' messages directed at my family, so I quit goin' to church a long time ago. There's nowhere left for me to turn."

"Believe it or not, I've been there myself. At one point, I was on the run. If it wasn't for Jack, my boss, I don't know what would've happened to me. He believed in me when no one else would. Now, my life is good again. We'll help you if you'll let us."

Emily looked up at her from beneath her bare lashes as tears trickled down her cheek. "It was wrong of Ma and Pa to try to take Rachael from Tyler, but somethin' must've gone wrong. Ma swears that Pa never came back to the car that night."

"What do they think happened?" Stacy said, noting that Emily had indicated that whatever happened occurred at night, and not in the afternoon as the news story reported.

Emily shrugged. "She's not sure. They thought maybe he took off upriver, but if he got away, he would've contacted her a long time ago."

"The Chandlers claim that Billy Ray grabbed Rachael from the garden. Are you sayin' they're lying?"

Emily nodded. "They must be."

"I've seen them interview the grandmother and father on the news," Stacy said. "They're mourning for that little girl."

"Two families have been torn apart by this, not just one. If Pa and Rachael are out there somewhere, we need to find 'em."

"I can't imagine how difficult this has been for you."

Emily wiped her eyes and appeared to summon her inner strength. "I've been living in our trailer all by myself. I lost my job, and I can't pay our bills no more. If something don't happen soon, we'll lose our trailers and our land."

Stacy nodded, her mind spinning with ideas. The waitress set their drinks on the table. "Lunch will be right out," she said and moved on.

"We need to talk to Jack," Stacy said. "He's good at figuring out what to do next."

"But I'm not comfortable talkin' to nobody else."

"Jack's not like anybody else. He helped me, remember?"

When the waitress delivered their food, Stacy couldn't help noticing how quickly Emily dived in. "When's the last time you ate, Emily?"

"Yesterday," she said as she took another bite of her BBQ sandwich, sighing as if it were the best thing she'd ever tasted. She stuck a French fry into her mouth before she had even swallowed. "I had to save up gas money to get here, which reminds me, we need to talk about your rates. I'm planning to get a job here and pay you each week so that you can keep workin'." She paused to swallow down some tea. "Do you know where I can rent a room? I don't need much, but after they burnt that cross in my yard, I'm too scared to go home."

"Yikes, Emily. How did you get the fire out?"

"With a hose, but I was cryin' and prayin' the whole time, and lookin' over my shoulder, just waitin' for somebody else to attack. Why were you on the run? You know, when Jack helped you?"

"Oh. I broke into my ex-boss's office. I was snooping around because I suspected that he was involved in something illegal. I thought if I could catch him at it—" Stacy's face went blank. "I don't know what I thought, but his partner caught me snooping and threatened to kill me if I didn't leave town that night. I got stuck in New Orleans after someone robbed me, so I called Jack. I had only met him once, but he came down and got me. A lot of crazy-scary things went down, but we eventually unraveled the whole sordid affair. I work with Jack, now, helping people straighten out their lives when bad things happen. We understand what it means to have your life turned upside-down by something someone else does."

"Wow, Jack sounds wonderful," Emily said.

Stacy laughed. "He's wonderful, but he's not perfect. He's incredibly messy and terribly unorganized. He's got a great sense of humor and the craziest curly hair you ever saw. All you have to do is look at it wrong, and it stands up funny. He likes to wear disguises, and he's extremely smart, though he doesn't always act like it. He's, well, he's Jack. You'll like him a lot. Everybody does, except the bad guys, and that's because he has a way of getting to the bottom of whatever's going on."

"When can I meet him?" Emily said.

"I'll call and see if he's around. Our office isn't too far from here, and Jack is always hungry."

"Is he married?" Emily asked.

"Jack? No." She chuckled at the thought as she placed the call. "Hey, Jack. What's up?" She took a sip of her tea. "I'm meeting with someone down at Hal and Mal's and thought you might like to join us." She winked at Emily. "Cool. See you in a few." She dropped her phone back into her purse. "He's on the way."

* * *

Jack stood at the bathroom sink trying to comb his hair into some semblance of order. Like always, it was futile. He frowned at his reflection and dropped the comb inside the drawer. At least, he could say he tried. Clyde jumped onto the sink and rubbed against his chest.

"Hey, what are you doing up here? Yes, I know. Come on, then." He stepped out into the main office and opened the top drawer of Stacy's desk. Bonnie and Clyde came running. He took out a bag of treats and poured a few onto the floor. "Here you go. Be good till I get back."

Smiling as they scarfed up the treats, he grabbed his note tablet and keys and let himself out the front door. He whistled his way along the sidewalk, down the concrete steps to the street, and into his Silver Toyota Tacoma pickup truck. Work was much more fun with Stacy around. Wouldn't it be something if they could solve this case? It would certainly make the headlines.

He'd done his research. Three members of Emily's family were persons of interest in connection with two kidnapping cases, one involving a boy, Jacob Clarkston, who would be about six years old now. But it was the second kidnapping that had received the media attention. Billy Ray Richards had reportedly kidnapped his granddaughter, four-year-old Rachael Chandler, who would also be nearly six by now. He, the girl, and his two accomplices had all disappeared. According to the remaining Richards family members, there had been no contact from any of them since the child went missing.

If what this young woman claimed was true, and her mother *had* contacted her, it could crack the case wide open, and yet, he was skeptical. If Billy Ray's wife believed something nefarious had happened to her husband, why did she wait all this time to report it? Even if it were true, it didn't explain what had happened to Rachael Chandler.

There was a wide chasm between Joan Chandler's account of what happened and this new allegation. Still, he'd seen some jaw-dropping events occur during his twenty-five years as a private investigator. Unfortunately, people were capable of committing despicable acts while appearing completely innocent to the outside world.

Jack stepped into the restaurant foyer and spotted the girls immediately. "Hey, everybody. Got room for one more?"

Emily looked up and giggled.

"What?" Jack said.

"Have a seat, Jack. What happened to your hair? It looks like you came through an electric storm."

Embarrassed, he patted it down. "I tried to comb it; I should have known better." He offered his hand. "How do you do, Emily. I'm Jack Kendall."

"I've heard a lot about you."

He raised a brow and looked at Stacy. "If she said anything good, it was probably true. If it wasn't, I plead the fifth."

"Come on, Jack. I'd be hard-pressed to say anything negative about you unless we want to talk about the way you keep house," Stacy teased.

"Ouch! Next topic, please."

Emily laughed. "You sound like brother and sister."

"Pretty much," Stacy said.

"Unfortunately, I can't say much negative about her either, except that she gets awfully bossy sometimes."

Stacy laughed. "Guilty as charged, and seeing how that's the case, I ordered you a bowl of gumbo."

"Perfect," he said with a grin.

"Emily, why don't you tell Jack what you told me?"

Emily's eyes flew to Stacy for reassurance, but then she began to speak. "Well, it all started when the news of the first kidnapping broke."

As Jack listened to Emily describe the deplorable treatment she had received at the hands of those who should've supported her, it made him both angry and troubled. He tried to imagine what it was like for her, awakened in the night by a thunderous barrage of rocks striking the metal siding of her trailer, knowing that the police, having been called on numerous previous occasions, were unlikely to come to her aid. An attack like that would unsettle him, how much more a single young woman? And to have someone burn a cross in her front yard? He couldn't imagine how terrifying that was.

No, these were not practiced words. The upset clenching of her hands, the distressed wrinkling of her brow, the flush in her cheeks, and the valiant struggle to hold back tears told him that her words were true.

"Tell him what your momma said," Stacy prompted.

"Momma thinks they made up that whole kidnapping story to hide whatever they done to Pa; only she can't come forward and say so on account of the police are lookin' for her and Tommy Lee. I want you to find Pa and Rachael, and clear Ma and Tommy Lee."

Jack cleared his throat. "I appreciate you being honest about your expectations. There's one thing about this kind of work; you never know what you're going to find. You've got to be prepared for that."

"If my family is guilty, they need to be punished, but if they're innocent, they should have the right to come home."

"They could turn themselves in and let the police sort it out," Jack said.

"Ha! That Chandler woman has more money than God! The police don't care what's true. Look how it's gone so far. Everyone takes Mrs. Chandler's word for everything."

"Don't get me wrong, Emily. I'm not on her side, but there were witnesses. The maid and her groundskeeper said they saw your father get into the car with Rachael."

"Momma says that didn't happen."

"Well, then, we need to learn the truth. I'm willing to give it a shot if you are."

"You see?" Stacy said with a bright smile. "I told you Jack would help."

"We ain't talked money yet," Emily said.

The waitress dropped off Jack's gumbo, which he sniffed. "Ummm, that smells good."

Stacy gave Emily a look, and Emily giggled.

"I'm feeling outnumbered here," Jack said, glancing from one to the other.

"When I'm around, you're always outnumbered," Stacy teased. "Back to the money thing. Emily needs to rent a room somewhere, and she needs a job so that she can pay us as we work. She could stay with me for a couple of weeks and take over the cooking and cleaning I do for you on the side if she wants to. That would give her a few hundred dollars a month right there. If that works out, I'm sure we could help her get a few more clients." Turning to Emily, she said, "Or you're free to look for something else. It's completely up to you."

"How much would it cost me to stay with you?" Emily said.

"Free. You can stay for at least two weeks. We'll see how it goes from there. What do you say?"

"I think that's very generous," Emily said. "It's been so long since anyone's been nice to me, I don't know what to say."

"We can't make any guarantees," Jack said, "but we'll certainly do our best."

"What are your rates?" Emily pressed.

"What can you afford?" Jack said, tilting his head to the side.

She wrinkled her nose. "We better go back to my question."

"Can you cook?"

"No one's ever complained."

"Do you keep a clean house?"

"Did I mention I can cook?" Emily said.

Stacy laughed. "Seems like we'll need to come up with another plan, Jack. What did you do in Arkansas?"

"Filing. I'm super organized when it comes to paperwork. Everything else, not so much, but I can't stand to see papers piled on a desk."

Jack's face lit up. "Well, now, that sounds interesting. I got several piles that could use some filing. In fact, I'll bet you could make a nice little business out of that."

"Really? I don't know how to run a business. I just work for people."

"First things first," Stacy said. "Let's take you to my place and get you settled in."

"Wait," Emily said. She reached into her purse and laid an envelope on the table. "There's two hundred dollars in there. Use it however you want. Groceries, rent, detective work, it's all I got, but it's yours. I'll give you more as soon as I get it."

Jack swallowed hard. He didn't want to take it, but he understood that her dignity was at stake. "Thank you," he said. "This is more than enough to get started. I'll pay you twelve dollars an hour to file my paperwork, which you can do while you're looking for other work."

"Wow. I never made twelve dollars an hour before."

"There's one thing I demand, though, so I'll say it up front. I expect you to keep everything you see and hear strictly confidential, even if it relates to your case. If you violate my trust, I'll drop your case immediately. Do you understand?"

She nodded.

"I have to be able to trust you, Emily. You can't lie to me, and you can't hide things from me either. I can't help you if you do that. Just because I know something doesn't mean I'll tell the police. Do you understand?"

"Yes."

"You must also understand that there are certain things I won't be able to keep from the police if they come to light."

"I understand," she said.

"All right, then. As of this moment, we're working together. We'll do everything possible to learn the truth. You can bet your bottom dollar on that."

Emily sighed. "I just did. I'm so glad I came today. For the first time in over a year, I feel like there might be hope."

* * *

Stacy drove her red Volkswagen Beetle down the long narrow driveway that ran beside a six-foot-high wooden fence. Situated near the back border of the property stood a detached two-story garage. Stacy hit the remote and parked inside. Emily pulled her silver Honda Civic into the vacant spot next to her.

When they had both stepped out of their cars, Stacy said, "Well, here we are. My place is upstairs. It only has one bedroom, but there's plenty of room for a blow-up mattress in the living room. You're my first overnight guest," she said with a sparkle in her eyes. "I've been waiting for a chance to entertain."

Emily grabbed her suitcase, followed her up the concrete stairs, and waited for her to unlock the door. Stacy tossed her keys on the counter and took off her shoes. Emily kicked off her shoes and walked through the kitchen and into the living room. "Wow, this is great. I love how you decorate. It's so girlie-like."

"Thanks. I like pretty things. Pink, brown, ivory, and turquoise are my favorite colors as you can see."

"Everything matches. I ain't never been anywhere where everything matched before. It's real nice, Miss Stacy. No wonder you keep a clean house. If I had somethin' as fine as this, I'd keep it clean, too."

Stacy laughed. "I'll hold you to that. I can't stand it when my place is a mess. You can put your suitcase against this wall. I'll clear off the top of this shelf for you to use, and clear out a drawer in the bathroom."

Emily nodded. "Thanks. That'll be great."

Stacy rushed around, making room for her guest. She wanted Emily to feel comfortable, yet she also felt a bit anxious. She wasn't used to having anyone in her private space.

"I'll go down and get my pillow," Emily said, "but I'll leave everything else in the car."

"Go ahead and settle in. The bathroom is through there. The top drawer will be yours. My bedroom is at the end of the hall. I'm going to change into something more comfortable."

Emily nodded.

Stacy's cell phone rang. "Oh, it's Jack. Hey, Jack… No, we just got here. Let me ask." Covering the phone, she said, "Jack wants to know if we want to come over for dinner. He bought some T-bone steaks and wants me to make my famous twice-baked potatoes. How does that sound?"

"How far away does he live? I'm pretty tired," Emily said.

Stacy chuckled. "He lives in the house in front of us. He built this extra apartment for me when he remodeled his house last year. You can come back whenever you like."

"Wow. Dinner sounds good. It'll give us a chance to get to know each other, I guess."

"That's what he said." Uncovering the phone, she said. "We're in. See you soon." She closed her phone and set it on the counter. "He said to call him whenever we're ready to come over. Do you need a nap or anything? What would you like to do?"

"You know, I really could use a nap. I haven't slept much lately, what with the cross burnin' and all. You can wake me whenever you're ready to go."

"I'll go get the blowup mattress and sheets." She went into her room and reached into the back of the closet to find the mattress. Locating the box, she pulled it out and grabbed the extra set of sheets. Taking off her short black skirt, she stepped into a pair of tight-fitting, hot-pink sweatpants. Grabbing the box, she went back into the living room. "I've got it. Emily?"

Emily was asleep on the couch.

"Emily?" She set the bed and sheets on the floor and went to the linen closet to get a blanket. She pulled it over Emily, careful not to wake her. Emily didn't move. Shrugging, she flipped her hair behind her shoulder and headed for the door. She couldn't wait to hear what Jack thought of Emily.

* * *

"Hey, Jack. It's me."

"Come on in, Stacy. I'm in here," Jack called from the den. He rose from his desk and met her in the kitchen. "Where's Emily?"

"She's out like a light. I tried to wake her, but that poor girl is exhausted. I'll take her a plate, just in case she wakes up later. Sounds like she's been through a lot lately. Have you worked out a plan?"

"I have a few ideas." He reached into the fridge and handed her a beer. "We need to track down the mother of the first little boy they kidnapped and talk to her. I also want to talk to Rachael's father to see if he can give me a feel for the grandmother. I'd like to talk to the maid and groundskeeper, too. I'm assuming they'll cooperate."

"Surely, the police have already done that," Stacy said as she sat on one of the bar stools at his new granite counter top.

"The police didn't have any reason to doubt their story," Jack said. "After all, the Richards trio had kidnapped the Clarkston boy a few nights before. That is a certainty. There were matching tire tracks at the Chandler mansion, so their story appears to check out. What Emily's mom is saying throws an entirely new light on the possibilities. It'll be interesting to see what we can dig up."

"I've been reviewing the media coverage, but I haven't found anything particularly helpful," she said. "The four of them disappeared without a trace. Once those tires hit the highway, that was it."

"What about footprints? Did the police find any footprints around the mansion or in the garden?" Jack said as he prepared marinade for the stakes.

"I haven't seen anything yet. It would be helpful to talk to Kevin, but if you do, he'll know something's up. I'd call him myself, but I think he's about as tired of me interfering in police work as he is you."

Jack chuckled. "Oh, no, I've got way more years on you. I'll go light the grill."

"I'll start the potatoes. I still can't get over how nice your house is since you remodeled. Aren't you glad I caused so much trouble?"

He smiled, but he remembered how close they'd come to being killed by the man who had ransacked and vandalized his house. "You're still a lot of trouble," he said, "but you're worth it."

"Oh, I'm definitely worth it."

As she bent to pull the vegetables out of the crisper, he added, "Especially from this perspective." As she whirled around to scold him, he chuckled and ducked out onto the patio.

* * *

"Ooh, ooh. Hot, hot!" Jack said a short time later as he hurried in from the patio with a hot plate in his hands.

"You could've used pot holders, you know," Stacy said.

"What, and miss out on the burning sensation of being alive? Nah, potholders are for sissies."

"The roasted corn cobs look delicious, and the potatoes are almost ready. I'll go see if I can wake Emily. I'd hate for her to miss seeing you take these potatoes out of the oven without potholders. I'll be right back."

Jack smiled as she flounced out of the kitchen. He adored women. They were so much more interesting than men were—except for his buddy Daniel, of course, whom he still missed terribly. He grabbed a platter from the cabinet and went back outside to take the steaks off the grill. Steam rose in tantalizing clouds, causing him to linger; he loved the smell of barbecued meat. He turned off the gas and piled the steaks onto the plate. When he entered the kitchen, Emily was sitting at the dining room table. "Hey, Emily. Glad you could join us. We've got a nice little feast going on. Want a beer?"

"Stacy already offered, but I don't drink. Thanks anyway."

"Everything's on the table," Stacy said. "Let's eat."

Jack set the steaks on the corner of the table and took his seat. "Dig in, everybody."

As they filled their plates, Jack said, "Hey, Emily, what can you tell us about Jacob Clarkston's mother, Pamela?"

"Not much, but Tyler, my sister's husband, brought her to Sarah's funeral. That's what started this whole thing. She told my ma that according to Mrs. Chandler, Tyler had no use for Rachael, so she was plannin' to adopt her. That got my ma and pa to thinkin' that they should adopt Rachael themselves. What with Sarah gone, they didn't want her kids stayin' with that side of the family. They told me they had talked to one of my uncles about adoptin' Rachael. He's an attorney over in Little Rock, so I thought they were gonna handle it through the courts. They never said nothin' about kidnapping her!"

"Did you ever meet Pamela?"

"I saw her, but we didn't say nothin' to each other."

Jack stepped into the den to grab a legal pad. "What's your uncle's name?"

Emily took a bite of corn. "Mmm, this is delicious. His name is Hugh Richards."

"What is Tyler like?" Stacy said.

"Tyler is a hothead like my pa. Sarah covered for him, but I seen bruises on her. I know he drank sometimes, too, and he stayed out a lot. He's real handsome. Thinks he's God's gift to women, if you know what I mean. Sarah worried that he might cheat on her if she didn't give him sex whenever he wanted, which, according to her, was a lot. The rest of the time, he mostly ignored her, but he adored his boy, Cody. But even with Cody, it was like he was playin' with a cute little puppy dog. He'd pet him for a few minutes, and then go back to doing whatever it was he wanted to do. He was too self-absorbed to bother with any of 'em much. I begged her to leave him, but she wouldn't. She thought she could change him, I guess." She sighed and shook her head. "Sarah thought the sun and the moon hung on

Tyler Chandler."

"Do you know where he works?" Jack said.

"At the newspaper. He's a hotshot advertising manager or something. He wears fancy clothes all the time, but he made Sarah and the kids wear hand-me-downs. He made decent money, but he spent it all on drinkin' with his buddies, and on that big expensive truck he drives." She took a bite of her steak and wiped her mouth with a napkin. "Guess you can tell I don't like him much."

"You're allowed," Stacy said.

"This steak is delicious. Sorry to be talking so much," she said with a blush, "but I haven't had anyone I could talk to. I've been holdin' it in for ages."

"Please, keep going. We're the ones asking questions. What were you saying about Tyler?" Stacy said.

"If Tyler hadn't gotten Sarah pregnant, he wouldn't have married her. I mean, his mother lives in a big fancy mansion up the river some place. Sarah says it's like *Gone with the Wind* or somethin'. She tried to fit in, but Sarah's just like me. We're country girls. We don't know nothin' about all that money business. I hate to say it, but Pamela Clarkston seems more like Tyler's type." Tears filled her eyes, but she wiped them away. "It's still hard to believe that Sarah's gone."

"We can stop for now if you like," Stacy said.

Emily sniffed and waved her hand in front of her face. "I'm fine. Keep askin' questions."

"Are Tyler and Pamela still together?" Stacy said.

Emily shrugged.

"Well," Jack said, "I guess you'll soon find out. Won't you, Miss Scarlett?"

Stacy grinned. "You bet I will. If Tyler thinks he's a ladies' man, he's about to get his head turned plumb around."

Emily looked confused for a moment, but then she smiled. Putting on an even thicker accent, she said, "After all, tomorrow *is* another day."

"You catch on quickly," Jack said, and they all laughed.

"I'd love to see Tyler's face when he sees Stacy," Emily said. "Especially if she wears something like she's got on right now. Pamela's pretty, but she don't have near the curves you do, Miss Stacy."

"What? This old thing? Oh, no, honey. I've got far more tempting things to wear than this. Don't I, Jack?"

Jack shoved a big piece of steak into his mouth and nodded.

CHAPTER THIRTEEN

Stacy glanced around the impressive lobby of *The Clarion-Ledger* office building while she waited for Tyler Chandler to respond to the intercom paging system. Its double marble staircase was surprisingly elegant. It seemed out of place in a newspaper building, not that she'd ever been in one before. She had expected a warehouse environment with messy ink stains and huge printing presses, not this beautiful building with its ultra-high ceilings and windows, and classy reception center. Oh well, what did she know?

A set of two-leaved doors opened, and a handsome young man with stylish brown hair approached the reception desk. "Hey, Ron. You called?" he said.

"There's a young lady here to see you," the desk clerk said, gesturing towards Stacy, who watched for Tyler's reaction when he turned around.

His brows rose slightly as his eyes dropped quickly down her body and then returned to her face. "Well, hello. How may I help you?"

"Let me count the ways," she said sarcastically. "May we talk privately?"

The corner of his mouth twitched as if he were amused. "We have several conference rooms. Would you prefer one with windows or without?"

There was an electric attraction between them, and she was aware that he was communicating on more than one level. "I'd prefer not being in a fishbowl if you don't mind. My interest is of a personal, private nature."

"What wonderful news." He stepped back to the reception desk. "Ron, will you check to see if the Walter Anderson Room is available?"

"Just one sec," Ron said as he handed change to the woman with whom he had been speaking. "It's available until three o'clock. Would you like the key?"

"Thank you." Taking the key, Tyler swept his hand towards the stairway. "After you."

"How convenient for you." She turned to climb the stairs knowing that the swing of her short black dress would tempt him every step of the way. Distracting haughty, egotistical men with her body while they, almost unanimously, underestimated her mental capabilities to their detriment had become a form of entertainment. She felt that such men deserved to be manipulated for treating women as sex objects. When she remembered the countless times she'd been treated disrespectfully because of her good looks, it made her blood boil. She tried to feel angry as she imagined Tyler's eyes upon her, but instead, she felt aroused. She hadn't expected *that* to happen, but Tyler Chandler was unusually attractive. Beyond that, he gave off a sensual energy she rarely encountered. She needed to stay focused. This was, after all, about business.

He followed her up the polished marble stairway to the second floor and into the open gallery. As was true on the first floor, to the left stood a set of two-leaved doors that led to a secured area. Left of the doors was a half-wall that served as a loft-wall above the lobby. The half-wall allowed her to see into the upstairs room, which contained dozens of desks, dividers, and cubicles where people moved about with purpose, yet they were quiet as they worked. In many ways, it reminded her of a library.

"That's the newsroom," he said, "one of ten departments here at the paper." Instead of entering through those doors, he led her to the right, to another door. As she waited for him to unlock it, she looked to the left, down a short hallway, towards another set of two-leaved doors.

"After you."

"Thank you," she said, swinging her hips just a bit more than necessary as she walked past him into the room, which housed a mahogany table that could easily seat ten. "This is lovely. The executive conference room, I presume?"

"Hardly," he scoffed. "That one's down the hall. I try to avoid meetings in that room. Have a seat." He sat on the same side of the table and watched as she crossed her legs.

Men were so predictable she thought with disgust.

"Let's start with introductions. I'm Tyler Chandler, the retail advertising manager here. I assume you know that because you asked for me. The question is who are you, and what's on your mind?"

"I'm Stacy. My roommate told me you were handsome. She was certainly right about that."

"That's nice to hear. Who's your roommate?"

"Well, since I'm not here to talk about her, I guess I should get down to business. If we decide to work together...I'm just sayin', I can think of worse things."

His eyes narrowed, and he gave her a sideways look. "Has anyone ever told you that you're an outrageous flirt?"

"Of course, but I'm ready to get serious now. Are you?"

"You're making it extremely difficult to think about business."

She chuckled. "The sooner we get business out of the way, the sooner we can decide our first course of action."

"And what kind of action are you looking for?" His eyes dropped to the curves above her low-cut dress.

"That depends on how you answer my questions," she said, gaining power as she saw him losing his. She wanted him off guard when she asked about his daughter.

"Ask away."

"All right. I have a promising lead regarding your daughter's kidnapping case. Are you willing to explore a radical path if it means we have a good shot at finding her?"

"What?" Tyler said as his face went pale. He stood up and took a few steps back. "Who are you?"

"I'm a private detective. I have new information about what may have happened the day your daughter went missing. I need to know if you're willing to explore possibilities that weren't considered the first time around."

"What kind of possibilities?" he said sinking back into his chair looking dazed.

"I'm not at liberty to say just yet, but I'm serious about spending some time together. We'll have to trust one another for that to work."

"And you build trust by coming in here all sexy-like?" he said.

"It's not like I can hide it, so we may as well get it out of the way. Besides, I wanted to make sure you'd talk with me in private."

"Do you have any credentials? I'm not in the habit of spilling my guts to complete strangers."

She smiled and reached into her purse. She was as bad as Jack was about loving to display her business card, which carried the title, *Private Investigator*. "You can reach me at this number twenty-four seven."

"Who's paying you?"

"Are you still seeing Pamela Clarkston?"

His countenance darkened. "Why do you ask?"

"Because I want to speak with her."

"So do I. If you're willing to hunt her down, then maybe we can make a deal."

"All right. Tell me about Pamela."

He gave her a dirty look. "You go right for the jugular, don't you?"

"I'll help you find her, but I need to know what happened between you."

Tyler's brows knit together, and Stacy could see the muscles contracting along the side of his jaw.

"After Jacob's kidnapping, Pamela was afraid that Billy Ray might come back. She left just before Rachael went missing. At first, I couldn't believe it. We'd been so close before Billy Ray took Jacob. I've only talked with her once since then. I left her a message after Rachael went missing. She called me back, but she wouldn't tell me where she was. I've tried to find her, but…" He shook his head.

"Do you have any idea where she might be?" she said softly.

He met her gaze with eyes that were deep, sorrowful, and brooding. "She always said she'd move back to Atlanta."

Stacy pulled a pen and notepad from her purse. "What was her last phone number?"

After giving her the information, he added, "I still leave voicemails, and she still ignores them."

"Her phone records should be easy enough to trace. Does she have a middle initial?"

Tyler raised his eyebrows. "I don't know. I never thought to ask."

"Has she ever mentioned any relatives?"

"I think she's alone in the world, except for her son, Jacob, but I don't know that for sure. I really want to find her."

"You're still in love with her; that's clear enough. I'll do my best to find her. I'll try to find them both. I may be a flirt, but I make a very loyal friend. Are you ready for a few more questions?"

"I need to get back to work. Besides, there's a meeting scheduled in this room in a few minutes. Would you be interested in dinner?"

"Why not? We've gotta eat, don't we? Besides, you loving Pamela will help to keep our minds on business."

"I don't know. You look incredible in that dress."

"Yeah? Should I wear it to dinner?"

Tyler chuckled and managed a smile. "Absolutely. How 'bout Bravo at six o'clock?"

"Six it is." Stacy rose from the table and waited for him to open the door.

He took his time, letting his eyes roam freely over her body.

Annoyed, she said, "There's just one thing."

"What's that?"

She waited for him to look her in the face. "If you ever lie to me, I'll drop your case. You got that?"

"I've got a tangle of feelings going on right now, but the bottom line is I need to find my daughter."

"That's right. Finding Rachael is the goal."

He nodded and opened the door. "We can take the elevator down if you like."

"Elevator? Why didn't we take it on the way up?"

He winked at her and slid a passkey through the security scanner, which opened the two-leaved doors and revealed the elevator.

* * *

"Hey, I'm back," Stacy said as she pushed through the doorway.

"Wow," Jack said as he took in her short black dress, black hose, and high-heeled shoes. "Did he survive?"

Fluttering her eyes, she said, "Whatever do you mean?"

"You're dressed to kill."

"The dress got me some alone time with him; that's for sure. We're having dinner tonight at Bravo."

"Why do I doubt that would've been the outcome had I talked to him myself?" Jack said.

"We each have our specialties. Did you dig up anything interesting today?"

"I looked up the articles surrounding Tyler's wife's death. You might want to read them."

"I read as many as I could find. I can't imagine watching someone you love die like that and not be able to help them."

"There's not much you can do in that situation."

"Where was Rachael during all of this?" Stacy asked.

"You'll have to ask Tyler. By the way, have you seen my eraser? I've been looking for it all day."

She chuckled. "If I had to guess, I'd say Clyde probably stole it. Check behind the basket in the conference room."

Pushing from his desk, Jack stretched his arms and legs. "How is it that I'm stuck doing book work while you're out schmoozing with our suspects?" Seeing that she was already concentrating on her computer screen, he walked into the conference room and knelt beside the two-tiered kitty basket, both bunks of which were occupied. "All right, Bonnie and Clyde, I've come to raid your stash. He lifted the basket out of the way and was surprised to find a small pile of ill-gotten gains: rolled up tinfoil, his eraser, string, a toy mouse, and of all things, the bathroom sink stopper. He picked up his eraser and the sink stopper and moved the basket back into place. Neither cat bothered to vacate. "See what I have here? These are off limits. Not for cats!" He reached in and scratched each one, chuckled, and returned to his desk. "Maybe I should hole punch this eraser and tie it to the desk drawer."

"Good idea," Stacy said only half-paying attention. "I'm trying to trace Pamela Clarkston on Facebook, but it seems she hasn't made any entries since all this happened. Think Kevin would run a private phone number for you?"

"He'll recognize her name. Give it to me; I'll see what I can do on my own."

She wrote it on a sticky note and handed it over.

"Well, what did you think of him?"

"He's *very* attractive. I can certainly see how a country girl could be swept off her feet. I saw nothing of the darker side Emily alluded to, so that's something I'll try to provoke if I can. He still loves Pamela. That was evident."

"Are they still in contact?"

"Not for lack of trying on his part. That's one of the reasons he's willing to cooperate; I told him I'd try to find Pamela. I wonder if she's ever seen his darker side."

"Tyler may have a darker side, but there were tire tracks on Joan Chandler's property. Billy Ray's car was definitely on her estate. If Emily's mom is telling the truth, then Mrs. Chandler is lying."

"And there's still the question of Rachael," Stacy said.

Jack wedged the eraser into a hole punch and squeezed. "If Mrs. Chandler is lying, that opens up all kinds of possibilities."

"Yes, it does," Stacy agreed.

Frowning at the partially punched hole, he dug in his desk drawer for an alternate method of finishing the hole. "It would be nice to know if they found Billy Ray's footprints on the grounds."

"In other words, it would be nice to talk to Kevin," Stacy said.

"We have to have some serious evidence before I take this case to Kevin," Jack scoffed.

"I'm planning to ask Tyler about his mother over dinner tonight. Anything, in particular, you want to know?"

Jack withdrew a small mallet from the back of the drawer. "Ah, this might work. Ask about her relationships with Sarah and Pamela."

"What are you going to do?"

"I'm going to see if I can find something sharp enough to finish this hole."

"I mean tonight, while I'm at dinner."

"Oh, I thought I'd see what I can dig up on Tyler Chandler this afternoon, but tonight, I'll work on Emily."

"She's a pretty girl, in the girl-next-door sort of way. Don't you think?"

"She is, indeed, but it's her heart I'm concerned about. She's been through a lot this past year. She could use some people in her life she can trust. I'd like to help her get back on her feet if she'll let me."

"That's what I love about you, Jack. You're always for the underdog."

"Yep, that's me, the Underdog Detective."

Stacy laughed, but it was true.

* * *

"Is it safe?"

"Are you kidding me? I lived in his guest room for months, which is right next to his bedroom, and he never so much as knocked on my door. He's the perfect gentleman. Well, he's not perfect, but he is a gentleman."

"Why would he want to take me out to dinner?" Emily said as she fiddled with her hands and watched in the bathroom mirror as Stacy touched up her makeup.

"Jack is the kind of guy who'd pull over if he saw a sick squirrel beside the road. You're completely safe, I promise. He just wants to get to know you better and help you feel more comfortable about working with him." She leaned into the mirror and blinked several times to check her mascara, and then applied her favorite burgundy lipstick. "Do you ever wear makeup?"

Emily blushed. "I put on lip gloss sometimes, but I don't have anything else."

"Want me to fix you up before you go?"

"I don't know. Pa don't like it," Emily said.

"Well, your pa ain't here. He left you to pay all the bills, so I say you can wear a little makeup if you want to. I won't put on much, just enough to highlight those pretty blue eyes of yours. If you don't like it, you can always take it off."

"Really?"

She looked so excited that Stacy smiled. "Here, sit on the toilet and turn towards me. It'll be a surprise." Seeing her hesitate, she gently guided her into position. "Come on. Sit down and hold still. It'll only take a few minutes. Where did Jack say you were going?"

"He didn't. He said we'd figure something out. Where are you going?"

"We're going to Bravo, so whatever you do, don't go there. Look up. I just bought this eyeliner, so if you like how it looks, you can keep it. There we go, now the other side." After applying eyeliner, she dusted her lids a light shimmering brown and added a hint of light blue in the corners. "You have beautiful eyes. It's amazing what a bit of makeup can do." Stepping back to admire her handy work, she said, "Now, let's see if we can find another top for you to wear with those jeans."

"This is so fun!" Emily said, "It's been ages since I've had any girl-time."

Stacy opened the closet and began flipping through her clothes. She pulled out a red, formfitting, strapless blouse. "How about this?"

Emily's eyes widened. "I've never worn anything like that before. I don't think I have enough to hold it up if you know what I mean."

"It's small on me. Wanna try it on?"

Emily nodded.

Stacy went back into the bathroom to put things away. A few moments later, Emily opened the bedroom door.

"Wow. You look amazing. That shirt is perfect on you. Let me comb out your hair before you look in the mirror." Stacy grabbed a brush and ran it through Emily's hair, which was thick and shiny and fell halfway down her back. She had to admit, Emily was extremely attractive. "Take a look."

Emily stepped in front of the mirror and gasped. "Oh my gosh! I can't believe that's me. Look at my eyes. You have to teach me how to do this."

"Come on. I want to see Jack's face when he sees you. Do you have heels you can wear instead of tennis shoes?"

"With jeans?"

"Yes, honey. That's how you make jeans dressy," Stacy said.

"I've got some black ones. In fact, I've got some black jeans."

"Well, go put them on. You're gonna turn some heads tonight!"

* * *

The restaurant was busy, and Tyler was at the bar when Stacy arrived. She watched from a distance as he gulped down his drink as if it were water on a scalding hot day. He waved to the bartender, who nodded and set another drink down in its place.

Stacy made her way through the crowd, but Tyler didn't notice, so deep did he appear in his thoughts.

"Hey, Tyler."

He turned. "You look as amazing as I remember. I put our names in for a table. It's busy tonight, right?"

"Great food."

"Here, take my seat." He surrendered his stool, and she sat down. "What are you drinking?" he said.

"Wine, I think. You?"

"Oh, bourbon and coke." He picked up his glass. "This is my first."

Her eyes narrowed, but she let it slide. "How long did they say it would be before we get a table?"

"I'll go check."

She watched him push through the crowd.

"What can I get for you, miss?" the bartender said.

"Cabernet, thanks. How many drinks has my date had? I want to know if I should let him drive."

"That's his third."

"Thanks."

"Anytime. I wish more people would ask that question."

He poured her wine and set the glass in front of her.

Tyler motioned for her. She grabbed both drinks and joined him at the host stand.

"They're ready for us," he said, taking his drink from her hand. "After you."

"You like taking the rear position, don't you?" she said.

"Especially behind you."

She tossed him a pretend scowl and followed the host to a dimly lit booth. "How was your afternoon?" she said, once they had settled in.

"I had a hard time concentrating after you left. My life's been hell since Sarah died. Then I lost Pamela, and then Rachael. How much is one man supposed to take?"

"No wonder you've had three drinks already. Why did you lie and say that was your first? Didn't you think I would understand?"

He pushed his glass away. "I thought you'd judge me."

"I told you not to lie to me. I can accept the truth, Tyler, whatever it is, but don't lie to me again."

He nodded.

The waiter stopped by. "Good evening, folks. May I start you off with an appetizer?"

"No, thanks," Tyler said.

"We need a few more minutes," Stacy added.

"Very well. I'll check back with you."

"Thank you." Stacy could feel the darkness of Tyler's mood swirling around the table. "Do you want to order before we start talking?"

"No, you may as well ask your questions. It's not going to get any easier."

"All right. Where was Rachael the day you and Sarah took Cody on the boat trip?"

"With my mother. Mother adores Rachael, but I never connected with her. Cody's my favorite. In fact, Mother was arranging to adopt

Rachael. The kidnapping's been especially difficult for her."

"What did Pamela think of that idea?"

He shrugged. "Relieved, I guess. Three children are a lot to handle all at once. Besides, we planned to have our own children one day. The boys took to each other as brothers. It seemed only natural to keep them together, whereas Rachael…well, she seemed happy enough to be with my mother."

"Yet when Sarah died, she lost her mother, father, and her brother. Did you ever stop to think about that?"

Tyler's gaze turned hard. "Are you judging me?"

"Just askin'. If loss is difficult for you as an adult, can you imagine how confusing it must be for her? Tell me about your mother. What is she like?"

"Mother is a handful. She's independently wealthy, of course, and she uses that power to control everyone and everything she possibly can."

"What do you mean?"

The waiter stopped by again, and they placed their order.

"We were talking about your mother," Stacy said when the server left.

"Mother uses her money to get what she wants. She'll pay whatever it takes if she wants it badly enough. It's that simple. She even tried to buy my wife, and it was working, too. Sarah had never been around money before. She didn't even realize what was happening, yet mother knew if she gave Sarah money, and told her what to buy with it, she could get around my convictions to make it on my own."

"Why would she do that?"

"Mother doesn't think I provide well enough for my children. I can't afford private tutors or pay for the best schools. I don't buy them name-brand clothes. You get what I'm saying. I don't want her money or the strings that go with it, so she went after Sarah. I was about to get into the middle of that when Sarah died, and then it didn't matter."

"But you gave Rachael to your mother."

"What do I know about raising a girl? Mother was the one who wanted a daughter. She never wanted a son. I was a disappointment. Still am, I'm afraid. No, I won't sell out just to get my hands on her money. I've seen what money can do to people. No thanks!"

"Do you talk to her?"

"We talk, but I don't let her tell me what to do. I actually think she respects me for it, even though she doesn't like it."

"What did Pamela think of your mother?"

"She only met her twice, but she saw what mother is about, how everything is about money and negotiation. Mother makes a game out of making people sell themselves for the sake of money. It's not her best quality."

"What is her best quality?"

"She's intelligent. Though lately, I've seen signs that she's slipping a bit. She gets confused sometimes, ever since the stroke. Maybe it's just the stress."

"Your mother had a stroke?"

"It was minor. The doctor said there was no permanent damage, but I'm not so sure."

"What about your father?" Stacy said.

Tyler downed the rest of his drink. "Why don't you tell me about your parents."

"That's easy. A doctor screwed up and killed Daddy while he was on the operating table. Our attorney screwed up, so we lost the malpractice case. Momma was miserable without Daddy, so she started drinking. She soon lost her job so we couldn't pay our bills. We lost everything we had. We lost our house, the car, everything. Momma decided to take the easy way out; she hanged herself. I found her one day when I came home from school. The State came in and shipped me off to an aunt who didn't want me. Eventually, I graduated from high school and moved out of her house.

"I had to work two jobs, but I put myself through college. I was determined to make something of myself despite all that had happened. Now, here I am, a little screwed up, but mostly all right, thanks to Jack. He's my boss. He helps people when they've got nowhere else to turn."

"Sounds like someone I should meet," Tyler said.

"I agree, but he won't let you lie to him, either."

He took a few bites without saying anything. Then he said, "I guess I'm not the only one who's been through a lot, am I?"

"Life isn't easy for very many people. It's what we do with what happens that matters."

He nodded.

"Want to tell me about your dad?" she said.

"I was close to my father, as I am with Cody, I guess. When I was little, I went everywhere with him. He and my mother seemed happy together. He let her have her way a lot, but when something mattered enough, he stood his ground. I respected my father a great deal."

"Where is he now?"

"He died of a heart attack. It happened quite suddenly. We didn't even know he had heart trouble."

"I'm sorry."

He shrugged. "It's been six or seven years now. I'm used to it."

"It's been twelve years for me. A daughter never gets used to not having her father around. Remember that when we find Rachael."

"I need another drink."

"Not if you're driving, you don't. Where's your son?"

"The sitter lives just down the road from my house."

"They say most accidents occur within five miles of home."

"Don't start thinking you can run my life, Stacy. I've had my fill of pushy women."

"If you think someone caring about you is being pushy, then you better get used to it. I can't be your friend without caring about what happens to you, even if you obviously don't!"

He scowled fiercely, which made her laugh, which in turn made him smile, in spite of himself. "Fine. I'll drink water. Does that make you happy?"

"Yes. Now let's enjoy this meal and leave the negative stuff for another day."

"I'd drink to that, but you won't let me."

"Then I'll drink for us." She raised her glass. "Cheers!"

He rolled his eyes. "Whatever."

* * *

Jack liked the sound of Emily's laughter, though he had to work at getting her to do it. Emily had confessed to being nervous about eating in front of him. Eating in "fancy" restaurants wasn't something she did very often.

When he saw her confusion over having two forks, he explained and told her not to worry about impressing him; he just wanted them to enjoy their time together. That seemed to work, and she relaxed somewhat after that.

He had already learned that she and Sarah had been very close as sisters, though Emily was three years older than Sarah. Emily wasn't in a hurry to rush into marriage, having seen by her parent's example that matrimony wasn't all romance and happiness, but Sarah hadn't had a choice. When she had turned up pregnant, she had to get married or face being beaten and disowned by their father. Their mother had thought Sarah had hit the big-time, marrying into money as she did. It had come as a huge disappointment when Tyler wouldn't take his mother's help, and he and Sarah had struggled to get by on his salary. They pushed Sarah to ask for more, but she never would. Sarah, apparently, was the perfect example of a submissive wife.

After dinner, Emily ordered pineapple tiramisu for dessert, and they were waiting for it to arrive.

"If you had to guess," Jack said, "where do you think your mother and uncle are hiding?"

"If I tell you, what would keep you from tellin' the police?"

"I wonder if it wouldn't be worth it for them to turn themselves in. They could make a deal with the police, tell the truth, and open a formal investigation against the Chandlers. That way, we can search for Billy Ray and Rachael on Chandler property."

"What do you mean?" Emily said with a wrinkled brow.

"If Billy Ray didn't return to the car, we have to assume that something went amiss."

She gasped. "You think they killed him!"

Jack glanced around to see if anyone heard her. "We have to consider it. If what your mother says is true, how likely is it that your father would hide out without contacting your mother and uncle?"

"He adores my mother. He'd never abandon her."

"Well, if something has happened to him, there should be evidence of it somewhere on Chandler property. As for Rachael, the same holds true. If your mother and uncle don't have her, and Billy Ray never left the property, then something may have happened to her, too. Are you certain there's nowhere else your father might hide?"

"I've been wantin' to search his huntin' camp. It's a hundred and twenty miles south of Uncle—" Her eyes opened wide, and she looked afraid.

"Tommy Lee has a hunting camp?"

The waitress set the dessert on the table with two spoons. "Y'all enjoy it now."

Emily didn't even look at it.

"Thank you," Jack said.

"Tommy Lee and Pa share a camp." She picked up a spoon and looked at the dessert for the first time. "Wow, this looks amazin'."

Jack knew she was concealing something, but he didn't press her.

She took a bite and closed her eyes. "Truce, Jack. I want to enjoy this."

"Fair enough." He also took a bite. "You're not kidding; this is incredible."

"It is. There's blueberries, raspberries, *and* strawberries, and the tira whatever-you-call-it is delicious." She licked the back of her spoon. "I've never tasted nothin' like this before."

He watched her for a moment, debating if he should say what was on his mind. "You know, Emily, just because you have another uncle with a hunting camp, that doesn't mean I'm going to run to the police and tell them."

"Dang! How did you know that?"

"Detective, remember? Do you think we could get you up there to see your mom without anyone knowing about it?"

"I've been wantin' to go, but I've been afraid. What if the police are watchin' me?"

"Have you spoken to your other uncle?"

"No. Same reason."

"And you haven't heard from him either? He hasn't checked on you?" he said, suddenly annoyed.

"No. I just figured he was protecting Momma and Tommy Lee. Why are you mad?"

"Tell me about this *uncle*. Is he your mother's brother, or your father's?"

"He's one of Pa's cousins. They ain't never been that close, but Pa called him about adoptin' Rachael."

"He's the attorney?"

She nodded. "Over in Little Rock, but Pa says he's highfalutin'. They argued over how much the adoption was gonna cost. Uncle Hugh tried to get Pa to trade his huntin' camp, but Tommy Lee said no. Tommy

Lee said it was robbery, what he wanted. Maybe that's why they decided to kidnap Rachael instead."

"How much land does your family own?"

"Pa and Tommy Lee's camp is about a hundred acres. The two trailers sit on five more. Course, them trailers ain't nowhere near the huntin' camp."

"Who's taking care of Tommy Lee's trailer?"

"Nobody, I guess. I went and got his two hound dogs when nobody came back last spring, but they was old. They died last winter."

"Is your land paid for?" Jack asked.

"All but the taxes each year and the utilities each month. It was too much for me after I lost my job. That darn propane costs a fortune, not to mention the electricity, water, and trash pickup."

"Did you pay your taxes at the first of the year?" he said.

She looked down and shook her head.

"Have you been getting collection notices?" he added gently.

"Okay, so there's more than one reason I left, but them burnin' that cross was the last straw!"

"We'll go online tomorrow and have your mail forwarded to my house. We'll look at your bills and see what we can do. There's no point in you losing your land unless it's unavoidable. It'll be your inheritance one day."

Her spoon hit the side of the plate as her hand fell. "You'll help me keep our land?"

"I need to see what's involved, but I don't want to see you lose your home, Emily."

Tears filled her eyes. "I don't know what to say."

"You can start by eating the rest of this dessert. I'm stuffed."

"Me too, but it tastes too good to let it go to waste."

"We can take it with us, you know."

"Oh. I forgot."

"So what do you think about visiting your mom?" he said.

"I think I know just where to find 'em. Should I do it?" she said, excitement brightening her eyes.

"I don't know yet. Let's think it through a bit more. I'd like to talk it over with Stacy. You bring up a good point about people watching you. We'll have to be very careful."

"It's scary to think that someone might be watchin' everythin' I do," she said as her brow wrinkled.

"You're not alone anymore. We've got your back," Jack said.

She sighed. "I'm still getting used to that idea. It seems too good to be true."

"Nevertheless, it *is* true. We're going to help you get to the bottom of this, one way or the other." He flagged the waitress. "We're ready for our check now, and could you bring us a box for the tira-whatever-you-call-it?"

Emily finally laughed, which made Jack smile, too.

* * *

It was almost ten o'clock; Stacy was expecting Emily any minute. She picked up her cell phone and started to dial, but she hung up and tossed it on the bed. No, she had to trust that everything was going exactly as it should. She went into the bathroom to wash her face, but she hated to take her makeup off just yet. What if Jack wanted to pow-wow tonight? She heard the garage door open and grinned at herself in the mirror. "Just in time."

She walked through the kitchen, opened the door, and called down into the garage. "Hey, girl. Did you have a nice time?"

"I feel all sorts of things," Emily said as she climbed the stairs.

Stacy hit the garage door button and watched it close. "I'll put on some tea."

Emily nodded. "I've got dessert here if you want some."

"I've already made up your bed, so it's ready whenever you are."

"Thanks. I slept great last night. I think just knowing someone else is here makes a huge difference."

"I know the feeling." Stacy poured water into the coffee maker and dropped in two tea bags.

"Um, where did you get your jammie bottoms?" Emily said. "They're really cute. I'm embarrassed for you to see my old gown."

"I have some extras. Come see."

Emily followed Stacy into her bedroom. "I hate to keep borrowin' things."

"Nonsense. That's what girlfriends do. Here, what do you think of these?" She held up a pair of baby-blue and white flannel jammie bottoms and a blue T-shirt.

"Perfect! I'll go change," Emily said as she ducked into the bathroom and closed the door.

Stacy smiled as she was reminded what a little kindness could do for somebody. She went back to check on the tea. By the time she had poured two cups and dished up some leftover dessert, Emily joined her. "Those look cute on you."

"Thanks," Emily said. "I can't fill 'em out as well as you do, but they're very comfortable."

"That's what counts. Here's your tea." They settled onto the couch, and Stacy took a bite of tiramisu. "This is fantastic. It's a wonder there's any left knowing Jack was with you."

"Oh, he ate his share. You should have seen how big it was."

"Still, it's not like him to leave leftovers. So, tell me what's on your mind."

"Well, it was nice to go out to dinner with a man, for one thing. He treated me like such a lady."

"Jack's good about that, isn't he?"

"You were right about him bein' helpful and kind. He's gonna look at my bills and see if he can stop me from losin' my trailer and my land."

She looked into her teacup. "I couldn't pay the taxes when they came due in January and was startin' to get those mean collection letters."

Stacy was surprised. She kept the books; Jack didn't have any extra money. "That's nice of him. What else did he say?"

"We talked about what might have happened to Pa and little Rachael. I told him about my uncles' huntin' camps, where I think Momma and Tommy Lee may be hidin'. He plans to talk to you about whether it's a good idea for me to sneak in there to visit Momma. What do you think?"

Stacy set her tea down. "Wait. Whose hunting camps are we talking about?"

"There's two, but I think they're hidin' at Uncle Hugh's camp. He's Pa's cousin, the attorney over in Little Rock. Hugh tried to get Pa and Tommy Lee to give him their huntin' camp in exchange for arrangin' Rachael's adoption, but Tommy Lee wasn't havin' it. I think that's why they tried to kidnap her instead. Only, Jack seems to think that if Pa never met up with Momma and Tommy Lee, maybe somethin' bad happened to him and maybe Rachael, too. He says if Momma and Tommy Lee give themselves up and tell their story to the police, they'll search Mrs. Chandler's property." Her eyes clouded with tears. "I hate to think that somethin' bad might've happened to Pa and Rachael."

Stacy's eyebrows rose. "You and Jack were busy." Seeing she was upset, she added, "Listen, Emily, we don't know anything yet. We're just exploring the possibilities."

"Pa would never go into hidin' without gettin' in touch with Momma. Somethin' happened. I've thought this through, and I'm almost positive that Momma and Tommy Lee are hidin' out at Uncle Hugh's camp. The police raided it once, but there are caves on that land, lots of good places to hide, not to mention a lake to fish in and deer to hunt. They could easily live off the land up there, plus my uncle could bring stuff in. That's where they are. I just know it."

"Didn't you mention another camp?"

"Pa and Tommy Lee's camp, but it's way smaller, and it would be harder to live off the land. Hugh's camp is nearly three hundred acres."

"Why haven't you gone there already?" Stacy said.

"I've been afraid someone might be watchin' me. The last thing I want to do is lead 'em there."

"Ummm," Stacy said. "You might be right. We need to think this through. What else did you and Jack talk about?"

"He thinks my Pa and Rachael might be dead. Ain't that enough?"

* * *

Jack rolled onto his side and pulled the covers over his shoulders. What had possessed him to tell Emily he'd try to save her land? Hell, he could barely afford his own expenses. He rubbed his eyes. It was the Damsel-in-Distress Syndrome; he fell for it every time.

He turned again and stared at the ceiling. He hated to see females taken advantage of. None of this was Emily's fault, yet she was the one facing the bill collectors and burning crosses while her mother and uncle hid from their consequences. It wasn't right, and he didn't like it.

He knew what it was like to lose a home, to have it vandalized. Even after the repairs, it had taken several months for him to sleep soundly again, and he knew the same was true for Stacy. How Emily stayed alone in that trailer for as long as she did was a testament to her character. She did not deserve to have her inheritance stolen from her by a greedy, rich uncle! He smacked his pillow and turned onto his side again.

He had experienced generosity when he was in need. Teresa and Alan Lindsay had been so grateful for the work he had done on their case that they had remodeled his entire office and donated thirty thousand dollars to launch the "Find Missing Loved Ones" portion of his practice. Here was the perfect opportunity to repay that good deed, but he didn't have the money to do it.

He sighed and closed his eyes.

It would work itself out. It always did.

CHAPTER FOURTEEN

Jack let the phone ring and ring and ring.

"Why are you calling me at seven thirty on a Saturday morning?" Stacy grumbled when she finally answered.

"I have a lead on where Pamela Clarkston might be, and I want to discuss our plan of action before I head over to Christine's house to mow the grass. How 'bout a cup of coffee before I go?" She slammed the phone down, and he chuckled.

A few minutes later, Stacy wandered in still wearing her pajamas, which Jack greatly appreciated. "Good morning, sunshine," he said as he passed her a cup of coffee.

The kitchen door opened again, and Emily came in sporting a pair of jeans and a T-shirt. "You're not leaving me out of this. I drink mine black."

"Fair enough." He reached for another mug and poured her a cup. Everyone sat at the kitchen table. "I got an email from a friend of mine this morning. He was able to trace Pamela Clarkston's phone records to a townhouse on the outskirts of Atlanta. It's a six-hour drive from here. The weekend might be the best time to catch her since she likely works during the week."

"And what do you propose I say to her?" Stacy said.

"You, speechless?" She answered him with a dirty look. "I think you need to ask why she left," Jack said.

"Tyler already told me. She was afraid Billy Ray might come back for Jacob."

"Why would he do that?" Emily said. "When they realized they had kidnapped the boy instead of Rachael, they let him go. Right?"

"She's right, Stace. It's not likely they'd make that mistake again."

"So what?" Stacy said with a yawn and a stretch, which Jack also appreciated.

"Then why didn't Pamela come back after Rachael was kidnapped? The threat was over. It feels like there's more to it," Jack said.

"Unless she was worried he'd come back for Cody, too," Emily said.

"That still doesn't pose a threat to Jacob. We need to find out what made her leave, and more importantly, what made her stay away."

"Good idea. Why don't you find out and let us know," Stacy said. "It's too early to be thinking this hard."

"She's right," Emily said. "You should be the one to go. She'll be much more likely to talk to you, anyway."

"Why's that?" Stacy said with a scowl.

"Because you're too pretty. If she thinks you're talking to Tyler, she might be less likely to cooperate, especially if she still has feelings for him."

Jack tilted his head. "You got a knack for this, Emily. I think you're right again."

Stacy pushed from the table. "Fine. Y'all handle it. I'm going back to bed."

Emily's troubled eyes met Jack's, but he shook his head to tell her not to worry. Stacy had no sooner put her hand on the kitchen doorknob when she turned back. "Hey, Emily, what do you say we go check out your pa's hunting camp? We may as well check it off the list as a possible hiding place. Right?"

"Is it safe?" Emily said.

"I'll take my firearm," Stacy said.

"She's pretty darn intimidating with a gun in her hand," Jack said. "How sure are you that they're not at that camp?"

"There's a small shack out there, but it ain't nothin' you'd wanna live in. I brought Momma's .38, so I'll be packin', too."

"What is it about Mississippi women and guns?" Jack said.

"It ain't no big deal. I'm a real good shot."

"That's what worries me. All kidding aside, we still have to deal with the question of someone monitoring Emily. You could turn it into an overnight campout, I suppose, to make it look legit."

"Not without you, we're not," Stacy said. "Number one, I'm not that brave. Number two, I'm not stayin' anywhere there's no running water. A daytime visit is quite sufficient."

He chuckled. "I guess we'll all be taking road trips today."

"Wait a minute," Emily said. "We didn't settle what to do about someone watchin' me. I thought that was the problem with me goin' to the huntin' camps in the first place."

Stacy gave Jack a sideways look. "You thinkin' what I'm thinkin'?"

He nodded. "I'm afraid so."

Emily looked from one to the other. "What?"

* * *

Emily's sky-blue eyes went wide when she stepped in front of the mirror. Stacy had bleached her hair almost blonde and curled it into loose ringlets. Instead of combing them out, she let them fall gently around her face. She looked quite stunning.

"Wow," Emily said. "I always wanted to be a blonde. I can hardly believe that's me."

"You look amazing. You look like you *should* be blonde," Stacy said.

"I was when I was little, but it got darker as I got older. Can you take pictures? I never want to forget how this looks!"

Stacy laughed. "Yes, of course. Go put on something cute, and we'll take as many pictures as you like."

"Will you call Jack? I want him to see me before he leaves."

"Yes, I'll call him." While Emily went to change, Stacy dialed Jack. "Hey, you. I've got someone here I'd like you to meet. Come see."

"I was just about to head out the door. I'll be right over."

Stacy went into her room and changed into a pair of jeans and a long-sleeved shirt. Next, she dug around in the back of her closet for a pair of tennis shoes and then grabbed some socks from the dresser drawer. "Hey, Emily," she called. "Make sure you've got warm clothes. We'll be walking through who knows what out there. Right?"

Emily came around the corner wearing a simple sundress and sandals. Her hair bounced against the smooth skin of her shoulders, and her face shone with excitement. "Will this do for pictures?"

Stacy's eyebrows rose. "Damn, girl. I missed my calling."

Emily laughed.

"Knock, knock," Jack said from the kitchen.

"Go on," Stacy said. "I'm right behind you. I want to see the look on his face."

Emily giggled and turned towards the kitchen. "Hi, Jack."

"Hello. Where's—" He cocked his head to the side. "Emily?"

She nodded.

"Wow. You look stunning."

"She does, doesn't she?" Stacy said.

"Well done, ladies, mission accomplished."

Emily laughed. "Stacy's gonna take some pictures, then I gotta change so we can go."

"Keep your phone on, Stace. I want to know when you get there and when you leave."

"Back at you. Press Pamela about her thoughts on Joan Chandler. Tyler said she makes a game out of getting people to sell themselves out for the sake of money. It would be interesting to know if she ever tried anything like that with Pamela. He said they only met twice, so it's not likely, but you never know."

"I'll do that. You ladies be careful out there." He pulled out his phone. "Smile, Emily." She did, and he snapped a picture for himself.

* * *

Stacy grimaced as she stepped over a dead stump and her foot sunk into a pile of leaves. She was deathly afraid of snakes and would prefer being anywhere but here. She could hardly believe this was her idea. Emily tramped on ahead, seemingly at ease with her surroundings. "How far is the cabin?" Stacy called after her.

"It's a good ways yet. If we're quiet, we might see some deer. Besides, they won't recognize me. It's best if we see 'em first."

"Yeah, yeah. Watch out for snakes."

"I am," Emily said.

Stacy saw a broken branch and grabbed it. It was helpful for knocking down spider webs and checking the path as she pressed forward. The weather app on her phone had said there was a 30 percent chance of thundershowers, which for the South usually meant 100 percent. She hurried to keep up. The last thing she wanted was to get stuck out here in the rain.

It had been a long time since she'd been hunting. She'd forgotten how much she detested the raw outdoors. The worst part was knowing that she'd have to do it again when they checked the other camp. She should've kept her big mouth shut and gone back to bed when she had the chance.

About twenty minutes later, Emily dropped low to the ground and motioned for her to do the same. She pointed through the thicket to a rickety shack in the distance. Then she pointed upwards; there was smoke coming from the fireplace.

Stacy nodded and wondered if they'd found her missing

family members.

As Emily crept forward, Stacy drew her gun and continually glanced around behind them as they went. A twig snapped, making Emily turn back. Seeing the gun, she said, "Don't shoot my ma or Tommy Lee."

"Don't plan to."

They stopped at the edge of the woods, about ten feet from the cabin door. It seemed quiet inside. Stacy motioned to a window in the side wall. Emily nodded and moved through the woods in that direction. Once situated in front of the window, Stacy whispered, "Cover me."

Emily grabbed her arm. "Let me go. They're my kin." She trotted to the window and stood on tiptoe to peer in. She dodged to the other side of the window and looked again, and then she ran back to Stacy. "I don't see anyone. Let's go inside and see what it looks like. We should be able to tell somethin' by what's in there."

"You go. I'll keep watch. If someone comes, I'll throw a stone at the wall. Listen for it." Emily nodded. "Hurry, Emily. You don't need to get caught in there by some lonely hunter."

"Let's work our way back around to the front first," Emily said.

They made their way back through the woods to the front of the cabin, but there were no signs of anyone around. "I'm goin' in," she said.

Stacy could hardly stand the tension as she watched Emily approach the cabin door. It squeaked as she pulled it open. Emily stepped in, then stepped back out again, and shook her head. Relieved, Stacy checked the perimeter. Only a minute or two had passed, but it seemed like forever before Emily reappeared and jogged back to the woods.

"There's not much food there and only one sleeping bag. It don't look like they've been here long. Whoever it is, it ain't Momma and Tommy Lee. Let's go."

"Lead the way," Stacy said, but she kept her gun drawn for another ten minutes or so. Finally, she began to relax. "We were crazy to do this,

Emily. Anything could have happened back there."

"At least we know I was right about Momma and Tommy Lee not hidin' out here. They're at Uncle Hugh's. I'm sure of it now."

"Well, I'm not volunteering for that expedition. We need another plan."

"It was kinda scary. Thing is, whoever's stayin' at the cabin is huntin' on my land. I'd like to kick 'em out," Emily said.

"Do you think it could be your father?"

Emily's eyes flashed with hope, but it quickly faded. "It's not Pa. He would never keep the cabin in such a mess, and there's no sign of little Rachael. Reckon we should wait to see who comes back to the cabin?"

A rifle shot ricocheted off a branch not ten feet to their right.

"Holy crap!" Emily said. "Get down!"

Stacy was already down. "Should we yell? Maybe they think we're deer!"

"Don't shoot!" Emily yelled.

"Don't shoot!" they yelled at the same time.

Another shot hit in the same place.

"Emily, they're not shooting on accident. We'd better run!"

"Stay down! If we run, they'll hit us for sure. Let's stand our ground."

"Let's get behind some trees, at least," Stacy whispered.

"Let's go."

Crawling on their knees, they retreated about ten feet and then stood behind two oak trees, which were about two feet apart.

"You watch that way; I'll cover this direction," Emily said. "It might be Ma and Tommy Lee, so don't shoot if you can help it."

"Screw that! If they shoot at me again, I'm shootin' back," Stacy said. She held her breath as she listened for movement in the brush, but the wind picked up, so it was difficult to tell what was what. "Don't forget to watch behind us," Stacy whispered.

"I am," Emily said.

Ten minutes went by.

"Why don't they do something?"

"Look," Emily said. "There's something orange at three o'clock."

Stacy glanced between the two trees. "I see it. Is it moving?"

"Drop 'em, ladies," a young man said as he cocked a rifle directly behind them. "Right now, or I'll scatter you with this here shotgun."

"Do it, Emily," Stacy said as she dropped her gun.

"Emily?" the man said.

Emily dropped her gun and turned slowly around. "Clint? Is that you? What are you doin' out here?"

"This is our land now. What are you doin' here?" he said.

Stacy turned to see a young man about her age wearing blue jean overalls. He was toting a rifle over his shoulder and holding a shotgun, which he had lowered.

"This ain't your land! It belongs to Pa and Tommy Lee. How dare you say such a thing?"

"You ain't paid your taxes," Clint said, "but Pa did. He bought this land at auction, fair and square. It's ours now and yer tresspassin'."

"I oughta kick yer ass, Clint Richards," Emily said, stepping towards him.

Clint raised the shotgun.

"Stop, Emily!" Stacy said.

"You better listen to her, Emily *Richards*."

"Where's Ma and Tommy Lee?"

"They ain't here. That's for sure. Who's that with you?" Clint said, eyeing Stacy.

"I'm Emily's friend," Stacy said. "She's been worried sick about her ma. Where is she?"

"Even if I knew, I wouldn't tell you. Go on, Emily. Get on out of here, and don't come back neither. You don't own this land no more. Pa also paid the taxes on yer trailer, but if you can't pay 'em next year, he'll buy that land, too. Pa says I can keep yer trailer, and Rocky gets

Tommy Lee's place. So get off our land, and consider yerself lucky that you got kin that cares about you."

"Let's go, Emily," Stacy said as she bent to retrieve her gun.

"You can leave that right there," he said.

Stacy's eyes narrowed as she rose to face him. "If you want to murder me, go ahead, but my father gave me that gun, and I'm not leaving it here." She picked it up and headed back the way they came.

She heard Emily say, "Are they all right, Clint?"

"I ain't got nothin' more to say to you, Emily."

"Fine, but this gun belonged to Momma. You may have stolen Pa's land, but that's all of ours yer ever gonna get."

"Hey," Clint called after her a few seconds later.

"What?" Emily said without looking back.

"Ain't you gonna thank us for payin' yer taxes? If it weren't for us, you'd be out on the street already."

"Yeah, I'll thank you…when hell freezes over!"

* * *

When Jack pulled up across the street, he saw Jacob climbing on a swing set in the side yard. A moment later, he spotted his mother reclining in the shade beneath a dogwood tree; she had not left him alone, as he'd first thought. He'd have wondered about her if she had, considering that Jacob's safety was the reason she had left Jackson in the first place.

It was a quiet family scene. He almost hated to interrupt, but he patted his shirt pocket and stepped out of the truck. It was a quaint, modest neighborhood. Her garage door was down, so he couldn't tell if there was a second car to indicate a love interest who might interfere with his visit. He walked up the driveway, across the yard, and around the side of the house. "Hello. Excuse me for intruding."

"Oh, you startled me. Who are you looking for?" she said, coming to her feet.

"My name is Jack. I just drove in from Jackson. Are you Pamela Clarkston?"

She glanced back at her son and walked over. "What do you want?"

He handed her a business card. "As you can see, I'm a private investigator. We could talk out here, but you might prefer it if we talk inside."

"Jacob, sweetie, let's go in."

Jacob jumped to the ground and walked over to Jack. "Are you a good guy or a bad guy?"

He laughed. "I'm definitely one of the good guys. What about you?"

"I'm a caped crusader, but my cape is in the laundry," he said.

"Good to know. I'll bet you take good care of your mother, don't you?"

He nodded.

"Come on, Jacob. Get inside. What is this about Mr. Kendall?"

"Please, call me Jack. Do you mind if I have a glass of water? It was a very long drive."

They entered the kitchen through a sliding glass door, and she waved him to the table. "I have iced tea if you prefer."

"That sounds great." She joined him at the table, her back rigid and tense. He sipped the tea and took in the details of her home; no evidence of a male counterpart. "Thank you. I took a chance on catching you today. I'm glad it paid off."

"Can we get to the point, Mr. Kendall?"

"All right. There's been a breakthrough in Rachael Chandler's kidnapping case."

"Oh, thank heavens!" she said. "I've been praying for them to find her. How can I help?"

"I need to ask some difficult questions, and I need brutal honesty. Can you do that?"

"I'll try, but I don't know what I can add to the investigation. I was in Atlanta when she was taken."

"Yes, we know. I've come to ask your thoughts on Mrs. Joan Chandler. You met her, didn't you?"

Her brows knitted together. "Yes, we met."

"Did you have any private conversations with her?" She began tapping her foot; he could feel the vibration through the table.

"Yes. We spoke on a couple of occasions. Once after she and Tyler had an argument, and once when I went to see her before I left town."

Jack pulled out his notepad and his special spy recorder pen to make a few notes. He waited until she looked the other way to push the button. "Please, tell me about the argument she had with Tyler."

"We were visiting her home for dinner. There was a discussion about Joan adopting Rachael. Tyler made a snide comment, asking how much it was worth to her. I was deeply offended and wanted to break it off with Tyler right then and there. Joan asked to speak to me privately, so Tyler went outside. She offered to pay me to stay with Tyler."

"Why?"

"She was afraid that Tyler might follow me back to Atlanta and ruin her plans for adopting Rachael. Tyler had tried to tell me that everything came down to money with her, but I didn't believe him until this! I was outraged."

"How much did she offer you?"

"Two hundred and fifty thousand dollars."

Jack felt his eyebrows rise despite trying to control them. "Two hundred and fifty thousand dollars? For doing what, exactly?"

"To stay with Tyler until after the adoption was final. Then, she said, I could do whatever I pleased."

"How did you leave it with her?"

"I believe I said I would think about it. I was so stunned that I didn't know what else to say."

"Did you tell Tyler?"

"I told him I'd heard enough to realize that he was right about her using money to get what she wants. He didn't ask for details. All he cared about was me giving him another chance. That night Billy Ray kidnapped Jacob. The next day, I decided to leave Tyler and move back to Atlanta."

"What about the two hundred and fifty thousand dollars? You just forgot about that?"

An embarrassed smile appeared before she could hide it. "Not exactly."

"Do tell," he said with his most charming smile.

"I don't even know you. Why should I tell you anything more?"

"Because I care about finding Rachael Chandler. I think something bad may have happened to her, and I think Joan Chandler may be responsible."

"You can't be serious! She adores that child."

"If you answer my questions, I'll tell you what I know," he said.

"Jacob, go play in your room, please."

"Should I get my cape out of the laundry, Momma?"

"No, Mr. Kendall is on our side. I'll come and get you when he leaves. Go on. Do as I say."

"Yes, ma'am," Jacob said as he walked past them and headed down the hallway. They could hear his door close a few moments later.

"He certainly seems like a well-behaved young man."

She blushed. "He's always been that way. He's a very good little boy."

"You were about to tell me about the money," he said.

"Yes, well, since I decided I couldn't risk that Billy Ray might come back for Jacob, I went to see Mrs. Chandler before I left town. I offered to break off all communications with Tyler if she agreed to pay me a monthly fee."

"Why would she do that?"

"So that Tyler wouldn't change his mind about letting Joan adopt Rachael and follow me to Atlanta."

"Why would he change his mind?" Jack said.

She gave him a look.

"That's extortion. You know that, don't you?"

"That's what she said, but she agreed to pay it anyway—after she threatened Jacob."

"She threatened him? How?"

"She said there was nowhere I could hide my son where her private investigators couldn't find him if I failed to keep my end of the bargain. I was frightened, but the damage was already done. I took her money. Besides needing it to support myself and Jacob, it was the best incentive I could think of to make sure I stayed away from Tyler."

"How much is she paying you?"

"*Was* is the operative word. The deal was for the same amount she offered the first time, only in monthly installments over a two-year period, ten thousand dollars a month. She agreed to send checks monthly, so long as I avoided contact with Tyler."

"So, what happened?"

"She called a few days after Rachael disappeared and said the deal was off. I told her to give it more time. Surely, they'd find Rachael and bring her home. She said that Tyler would never have control over Rachael again, so there was no need to continue paying me."

"What does that mean?" he said.

"I didn't ask. There's something sinister about that woman when it comes to money. I recorded the entire conversation, which only lasted a minute or two at most. Wanna hear it?"

"Yes, I do. What made you think to record it?"

She shrugged. "She threatened my son. I thought it was the smart thing to do." She pressed the necessary buttons and handed her phone to Jack.

As Jack listened to the message, he noted a cold confidence and arrogance in Joan's voice that wasn't consistent with a grandmother in fear for her granddaughter's life. It was creepy. "Keep saving that. It may come in handy one of these days."

"Are you kidding me? I'll never testify against Joan Chandler in court! I'm saving it in case I need to share it with Tyler. I know he'll find me one of these days."

"You're afraid of her, aren't you?"

"Wouldn't you be?"

"I can certainly understand why you are. No mother feels comfortable when her child is threatened."

"You probably think I'm terrible for taking her money. I had planned to go back to school to get my master's degree. Of course, that's impossible now. At least I was able to stay at home with Jacob for a few months. He still has terrible nightmares."

"I'm not here to judge you, Pamela. You're obviously a good mother to Jacob."

Tears filled her eyes. "Thank you. I feel guilty, but Tyler deceived me. He should have told me he was married when we met. The whole relationship was wrong from the beginning."

"Tell me something, Pamela. Why would Tyler allow his mother to adopt Rachael in the first place? I can't imagine giving up one of my children—if I were ever blessed to have children, that is."

She shook her head. "I couldn't do it, but he never bonded with Rachael. Nobody wanted that child except Joan. What makes you think she's responsible for something bad happening?"

"There's talk that Billy Ray never met up with his accomplices after he allegedly kidnapped Rachael."

"Maybe they left another way," she said.

"Or maybe they never left at all," he said, watching her closely.

Pamela gasped. "You think she killed him?"

"I'd sure like to search her property to rule it out," he said.

"But what about Rachael? Surely, she wouldn't—"

"Do you think Joan is capable of killing Billy Ray?"

"I hate to say it, but yes. I think she'd kill anyone who got in her way. Does Tyler know about this?"

"Not yet. At this point, it's only supposition. We need a reason to search her property, probable cause, or evidence of a crime."

"Maybe Billy Ray took Rachael upriver," she said, wringing her hands in her lap. "Tyler told me once that they always keep a fishing boat tied at the dock. He wanted to show me the boathouse, but we never had the chance. If Billy Ray took the boat, then Mrs. Chandler would've had to buy a new one, right? Can't you check her bank records to see if she bought a new fishing boat since the kidnapping?"

"That's a great idea, but I'd need her banking information for that."

Her chair scraped against the floor as she pushed from the table. "I've got a copy of that first check."

"Do you have a copier?"

"On my printer." She paused. "I don't want to get into trouble for helping you."

"As far as I'm concerned, she offered to pay you, and you accepted. People make deals all the time."

"Can you leave me out of it?" she said.

"I'll try, but the main focus has to be about finding that little girl. If your name comes up, I'll let the police know how cooperative you've been."

She sighed. "I'm more afraid of Mrs. Chandler than I am of the police."

* * *

"It's about time you answered your phone," Stacy grumbled.

"I just got back to the truck. How did it go?" Jack said.

"Which part? Climbing through the snake-infested swamp, or getting shot at by Emily's kin?"

"Someone shot at you?" He tried to stick his keys in the ignition, but he dropped them. As Stacy described what had occurred, all he could think about was how incredibly thankful he was that they were safe. When she mentioned Emily's uncle's scheme to take over her land, his gratitude turned to anger. "How can that possibly be legal?"

"Ask him; he's the attorney, but I'll bet it has more to do with who he knows than what's legal. He knows Emily doesn't have the money to fight him. He stole that land from her family, pure and simple. He tried to get it from Billy Ray. When that failed, he took it from his daughter instead."

"I can't believe this! Who told you that?"

"The cousin who shot at us. I doubt they'll be any more hospitable when we go to check out the other hunting camp."

"I knew I shouldn't have let you two go alone," he grumbled.

"Oh? And you think it would've gone better if you were there?"

"That's not what I mean. I'm just upset that I wasn't there to protect you."

"I wanted to kick his teeth in, the scrappy little brat! It's embarrassing how easily he got the jump on us," Stacy said.

"Where are you now?"

"We're headed home," Stacy said. "How did it go on your end?"

"Pamela was quite pleasant, actually, and very helpful. She gave us an interesting lead to follow up. I don't want to talk about it over the phone, though. How far out are you?"

"It'll be ten o'clock before we get home."

"That's about the time I'll get there, too. Let's call each other on the hour to check in. Drive safe."

"You, too."

He hung up and exhaled. If anything had happened to them, he'd never have forgiven himself. Stacy was like a sister to him. Well, not a sister exactly, but not a girlfriend either. Stacy was, well, Stacy, and he wanted to keep her around for a very long time to come.

* * *

Stacy was relieved to cross the bridge over the Mississippi River at Vicksburg. She glanced at Emily, who had been silent for the last twenty minutes. "Penny for your thoughts?"

"Huh? Oh, I was just thinkin' on how to get my land back. I can't believe Uncle Hugh stole it out from under us like that. Pa will be so upset."

"I didn't like your cousin much, either," Stacy scoffed.

"Clint's a jerk. Always has been. What's he thinkin', shootin' at us like that? Think we should've called the police?"

"It's not too late to make a report. We'll see what Jack says," Stacy said. "At least we saw the cabin and can strike it off the list of possible hideouts. The problem is it'll be harder to sneak into the other camp after Clint tells your uncle that he saw us today."

"Just let him say somethin' 'cuz I'd like to tell my uncle a thing or two myself! Who the hell does he think he is, givin' our trailers away to my jackass cousins? They'll ruin 'em in six months. You should've seen how messy the cabin was—trash all over the place, beer cans everywhere. He ain't nothin' but a tee-total slob. I just *gotta* pay my taxes next year. That's all there is to it."

"Maybe your mom and uncle will be home by then, and everything will work itself out," Stacy said.

"Maybe Pa will be back by then, too."

Stacy's smile faded. "Yeah, maybe."

CHAPTER
FIFTEEN

J ack woke up early, which was rare. He had showered, made coffee, and was looking up the phone number for his banking contact when his cell phone rang. "Hello," he said without looking at the caller I.D.

"I'm making pancakes."

"Hey, you. Good morning, Christine." He turned from his desk and leaned back in his chair.

"The kids are upstairs getting dressed for yard work. You still coming over?"

He winced; he'd forgotten all about it. "Sure am. Twenty minutes?"

"See you then."

He sighed; he may as well do yard work. The banks weren't open anyway. He was anxious to find out if Mrs. Chandler had purchased a new boat. If she did, it would be time to call in the big guns, which meant telling Kevin he'd been working on the Chandler kidnapping case. Ever since Kevin had become a police captain, it seemed he always got in his way. Theirs was a like-hate relationship. Jack got away with doing things he wouldn't otherwise get away with, and Kevin solved cases that he wouldn't otherwise solve. There was no leaving him out of this one though. Search warrants were required for the type of investigation he had in mind. Any woman who'd pay someone a quarter of a million dollars not to break up with her son wasn't someone to take lightly. If she'd do that, what else might she pay someone to do?

After all this time, Jack didn't expect to find Rachael alive, but she deserved justice. And there was Emily to consider. Leaving her life to dangle in uncertainty was unacceptable, and he meant to put a stop to it if he could.

He thought about calling Stacy but decided against it. It was Sunday. If she could sleep in, why not let her? He, on the other hand, was looking forward to sharing pancakes with Daniel's wife, Christine, and their two children, Alexa and Jon. He just wished Daniel could be there. So many things change when a person dies.

* * *

Later that evening, when Jack stepped from his garage into the kitchen, he found a huge pot simmering on the stove. He lifted the lid and took a deep whiff, his lopsided smile appearing as the fragrant steam rose into his face. He loved Stacy's homemade spaghetti sauce. He dialed her number. When she answered, he said, "All right, when are you two coming over? It smells heavenly over here."

"You, however, probably stink, so call us when you get cleaned up. See ya."

Chuckling, he emptied his pockets and headed for his bathroom to take a shower. He did stink, but Christine's yard looked much improved, and he had enjoyed spending time with the kids. Alexa was eleven now, and Jon was nine. It was amazing to see how fast they grew. He turned on the shower and stepped in, sighing as the hot water pummeled his back and shoulders.

Christine had come a long way since Daniel's death. She'd begun to sell real estate again, and she was laughing more, too, which was wonderful to see. They had always been close, but they were even more so now. He thought back on the night she tried to get romantic with him because she thought the children needed a father. He'd set her straight on that score, telling her that if she ever were to marry again, it needed to be for the right reasons. That had happened mere weeks after Daniel's death. She was grieving and afraid. He would never take advantage of her vulnerability. Now, though …

He thought back on the day's activities. They had raked the leaves into huge piles only to engage in a family leaf fight. He had laughed so hard that he cried. He loved spending time with them. The kids called him Uncle Jack, and Christine was so sweet and pretty. Her naturally blonde hair was long now. It fell halfway down her back when she shook out her ponytail. She was smart, strong, and an excellent mother.

He turned towards the showerhead and forced himself to think about something else.

* * *

Jack was coming down the hallway when he heard Stacy say, "We're here."

"I'll set the table," Emily said.

"Jack, don't come out here naked!" Stacy yelled.

"I hear you," he said. "This is a nice surprise. I love your spaghetti."

"Good," Stacy said. "You can open the wine while we put everything on the table."

"Who's going first in our storytelling session tonight," he said.

"You," Emily said. "You know what happened to us."

After they settled at the table, Jack lifted his glass. "To us. To being together and staying safe. That's the most important thing."

"I'll drink to that," Stacy said.

"Me, too," Emily chimed in.

Jack heaped spaghetti onto his plate. "Apparently, Mrs. Chandler's reputation for manipulating people is well deserved. She agreed to pay Pamela Clarkston ten thousand dollars a month *not* to communicate with Tyler."

"Oh my word! Where do I sign up?" Emily said.

"Wait! She wanted to sever their relationship? I thought she wanted them to stay together," Stacy said as she covered her noodles with a steaming puddle of thick, meaty, sauce.

"It was Pamela who suggested a change in terms."

"I don't understand. Why would Joan pay Pamela anything at all?" Emily said.

"According to Pamela, Tyler was all too willing to move to Atlanta with her," Jack said.

A wide smile appeared on Stacy's face. "Now I get it. That's brilliant."

"I don't understand," Emily said, her brow wrinkling with confusion.

"Think, Emily," Stacy said. "If Pamela were to press Tyler into keeping Rachael with them—"

"That would destroy Joan's adoption plans," Emily said. "The very thing Mrs. Chandler fears. I'd be afraid to blackmail that woman! She's dangerous."

"Indeed," Jack said. "Joan threatened to harm her son if Pamela double-crossed her."

"Yikes. That woman plays for keeps," Stacy said.

Emily shook her head. "It's hard to believe that Sarah married into that family."

Jack glanced at Emily. It was easy to forget that her sister's death had precipitated all of this. "That's not all," he said, explaining how Joan had called to end the arrangement a few days later.

"How bizarre," Stacy said.

"Isn't it, though?"

Emily took another bite and pushed her plate away. "Pamela could be lying."

"She taped the entire conversation. I heard it myself. She also said that the family keeps a fishing boat tied to the dock behind the house. If Billy Ray left by river, then Mrs. Chandler should be the proud owner of a brand-new fishing boat." He pulled a folded piece of paper out of his pocket and waved it. "This is a copy of the first check Pamela received from Joan Chandler, which means we've got her checking account number, and it just so happens that I know someone who works at the bank this check is drawn on."

Stacy's eyes twinkled. "This is getting exciting, but I doubt you'll find that she purchased a new boat. I think Billy Ray's body is somewhere on that property."

"Ah!" Emily squawked as she pushed from the table and started crying. She ran for the back door, yanked it open, and rushed outside.

"Emily, wait!" Stacy called. Jack was on his feet with Stacy right behind him. "Dammit, Jack! I didn't mean—"

"I'll go," he said. He climbed the stairs to Stacy's apartment and knocked on the door. When Emily didn't answer, he opened the door. "Emily?" He could hear her crying in the living room. "Emily, I'd really like to talk with you. May I come in?"

"There's nothing to say!"

He walked into the living room. "May I sit with you for a moment?"

She kept her face buried in her hands.

He sat on the couch. "Emily, Stacy didn't mean to upset you. You know that, don't you?"

She cried even harder.

"We're detectives. Hunting down clues is what we do. Clues lead us closer to the truth. No one has heard from your father in over a year. Doesn't that tell you that something went wrong?"

Her cries slowed to a sniffle. "She doesn't have to make it sound like finding his body will be a happy day!"

"If your father died on Chandler property, wouldn't you like to find him and give him a proper burial?"

"Of course, but I want you to find him alive."

"We know you do, but that's not likely to happen. You have to accept that. You said yourself that your father wouldn't have stayed away all this time without contacting your mother. Isn't that right?"

"Yes, but I don't want him to be dead. I don't!"

When Jack reached out to squeeze her shoulder, she fell into his arms, crying like a child. He wrapped his arms around her as she shook with emotion. "You've been strong for so long, Emily. Let it out. You're safe." She wailed and cried as he patted her back and rocked her gently.

It was a long time before she pulled away. She hurried to the bathroom to wipe her face. When she came back out, she looked drained but resolved.

"I know in my heart that Pa is probably dead. I've known it for a while now, but I didn't want to face it. I *want* you to find every clue and follow every lead. I'm sorry I got so upset."

"Emily, you've been through more in the past two years than most people go through in a lifetime. We want to get this solved so that you, as much as anybody else, can move on with your life. We care about you. We really do."

Stacy came in from the garage and tiptoed through the kitchen. "Can I come in?"

Emily nodded.

"I'm sorry I upset you, Emily. I'm such an idiot sometimes. I was thinking about solving the case and forgot that it meant hurting you in the process. Please, forgive me."

"I know you didn't mean to hurt me. If Pa's out there, we need to find him."

"We'll find him," Stacy said.

Emily opened her arms, and they embraced.

CHAPTER SIXTEEN

"**R**eally? I can't thank you enough. Bye now." Jack leaned back in his chair, forgetting that Bonnie was lying behind him. Hearing her protest, he scooped her up and set her on his lap. "Hey, pretty kitty. What are you doing back there? I've got work to do." Bonnie Bella stood on his knees and yawned. He enjoyed having the cats around, but he was way too excited to be distracted for long. He dialed Stacy.

"Hey, Jack. What's up?"

"Bingo."

"Uh, can you be a bit more specific?"

"How does your afternoon look?" he said.

"Emily and I are grocery shopping. Then I thought we'd clean house and do some laundry. Got a better offer?"

"We need to go see Kevin."

"What did you find out?" she said.

"Mrs. Chandler's Visa bill was three times its normal size the month Rachael was kidnapped. Who goes shopping when their grandchild goes missing?"

"Did she buy a boat?"

"We won't know until we subpoena the credit card details. Want me to go alone?"

"Not a chance. Call me back when you know what time."

"Will do."

"Hey, Jack?" Stacy said. "If I continue to talk with Tyler, isn't that a conflict of interest issue?"

"He's not the one who's on the hot seat. At least, as far as we know," Jack said.

"He wants to know if I found Pamela. What do I tell him? He left me a message a little while ago."

"She can't have any contact with him or her son will be in danger."

"What would happen if he knew that?" she said.

"He'd confront his mother, and she'd know that Pamela told someone. No, we have to keep her confidence."

"Aren't you gonna tell Kevin?" she said.

"That's not the same thing as telling Tyler. Kevin will know how to proceed without endangering Pamela."

"You hope."

"Hmmm. Maybe we should make some deals before I give him her name."

"That's what I'm thinking," Stacy said.

"I knew I kept you around for some reason."

"And here I thought you just liked me for my cooking. One more question. We're helping Emily. Isn't that a conflict of interest with Tyler?"

"Tyler's not paying us. If he willingly gives us information, that's on him."

"I told him I'd help him find Rachael."

"You are, aren't you?"

"Yes, but I don't think he'll appreciate us accusing his mother," Stacy said. "What do I tell him?"

"Let's see what Kevin has to say first."

"Okay. Call me back," she said.

Jack hesitated for a moment before calling Kevin. He didn't want to endanger Pamela or her son. Maybe he could leave her out of it all together. He tapped his fingers on the desk and waited for him to answer.

"Captain Thomas here."

"Hey, Kev. How's it going?"

"Oh, no. What mess you into now, Kendall?"

He chuckled. "Suspicious, are we?"

"I know you, remember?"

"I'd like to see you about a case I'm working on; if that's what you mean," Jack said.

"Uh huh. Anyone dead?"

"Maybe."

"You bringin' Stacy with you?"

"Absolutely."

"Lord have mercy; it must be a doozy. Think you two can stay out of trouble until four thirty this afternoon?" Kevin said.

Jack leaned back in his chair and smiled. "It's a date."

* * *

Police Captain Kevin Thomas squeaked back in his chair, rubbed a hand over his black closely-shaven head and glanced from Jack to Stacy. "All right, you two, what are you in the middle of this time?"

Jack cleared his throat. "Have you made any progress on the Rachael Chandler kidnapping case lately?"

Kevin's eyes narrowed as he sat forward in his chair again. "If you know something, spit it out."

"There are people we need to protect—"

"Lord, here we go again. How is it you're always intimately involved with the people I need to investigate? That's not normal; you know that?"

"We assume you want to solve the case," Jack said.

"Who are you protecting?"

Jack glanced over at Stacy, who was fidgeting in her seat.

"What?" Kevin said as he glared at her.

"It's more that you've been protecting the wrong people," she said.

"What the hell is that supposed to mean? Talk to me, Jack."

"We have reason to believe that Billy Ray Richards didn't leave Chandler property the same way he went in."

"What are you talking about? The maid chased him down with a rifle and shot at the car as it drove off."

"So she said, but did you ever find the car?" Jack said.

"No, but we found the spent ammo shell."

"We *know* Billy Ray wasn't in the car when she shot at it. In fact, he never met back up with his accomplices at all. Not ever, in all these months."

"You've spoken to Leeann Richards?" Kevin said.

"Not directly, but we know someone who has. We also have a good idea where Leeann and Tommy Lee Richards are hiding. If what they say is true, then Billy Ray either left by boat, which is quite possible considering that Mrs. Chandler keeps a fishing boat tied to the dock, or he never left at all."

"What else?" Kevin said.

"Mrs. Chandler's Visa bill was three times its normal amount the month her granddaughter went missing. If she bought a new fishing boat, it was to replace the one Billy Ray Richards stole."

"I don't remember anything in the report about a missing fishing boat. Where are you getting your information?"

"Reliable sources who know the key players," Jack said.

Kevin sighed. "What do you want?"

"An order to subpoena Joan Chandler's credit card records and a warrant to search her property with a team of cadaver dogs."

"Shall I bring in Sherlock Holmes while I'm at it?" Kevin scoffed.

"All this is amusing, but you're barking up the wrong tree. Have you ever met Mrs. Chandler? She's worried sick about her granddaughter. She calls every week or so to check on our progress."

"Yeah, she's really sweet," Stacy said. "Did she tell you that she's party to blackmail and extortion? She may be worried about her own grandchild, but she has no problem threatening other people's children."

"Stacy—" Jack said.

"What the hell is she talking about?" Kevin said.

"Nothing we want to discuss at the moment. *Right*, Stacy?"

She scowled at them both. "Tell Captain Jerk, here, to listen to what we're saying. A little girl's life is at stake, not to mention the lives of several other people who have been caught in the crossfire."

Kevin scowled back. "Did she just call me a jerk?"

"I'm sitting right here, and, yes, I did. Your sweet little lady friend bribes people to say and do exactly what she wants them to and threatens them if they don't. I wouldn't be at all surprised if Billy Ray's body is buried somewhere on her property, and she bribed the maid to make up that story about chasing him back to the car."

"And what on God's green earth makes you say that?" Kevin scoffed.

"What woman in her right mind shoots at a car knowin' there's a child inside? I'm not saying she didn't shoot at the car, I'm just sayin' Billy Ray and Rachael weren't in it when she did. The only way we're gonna know if there's another possibility is to subpoena her credit card records to see if she bought a fishing boat after Rachael went missing."

"All right, Jack. I'm not following everything she said, but based on the fact that—as much as it pains me to admit it—you're usually right, I'll request her records. *If* there happens to be a boat purchase, then the three of us are gonna sit down and have a serious pow-wow, and you're gonna tell me everything you know. Agreed?"

"And if there isn't a boat purchase, you'll still search her property for Billy Ray *and* Rachael's remains?" Jack added.

"You think she killed them both?" Kevin said, amusement twitching at his lower lip.

Jack shrugged. "No one's seen or heard from either of them since the night of the kidnapping. Something happened," Jack said as he considered mentioning Pamela.

"And if we give you names, you'll protect our sources?" Stacy said.

"Did they break any laws?"

"It depends on how you look at it," Jack said, throwing a quick glance at Stacy.

"Why am I always dizzy by the time I get the two of you out of my office?" Kevin asked.

"How long will it take to get her records?" Jack said.

"Will she know that you're getting them?" Stacy said immediately after.

"It depends, and no. I'll request a non-disclosure directive."

"Nice," Stacy sighed.

"The next time the three of us meet," Kevin said, "I'll be driving the bus. So you two best smile now because the road is about to get bumpy."

* * *

Tyler Chandler was already at the bar when Stacy arrived, but she didn't intend to stay long enough to be bothered by how many drinks he'd had or if he lied about it. She wasn't feeling right about straddling the fence between Tyler and Emily, and she thought it best to distance herself before the investigation into Joan Chandler got underway. "Hey, Tyler," she said as she walked up behind him.

He raked his eyes down the front of her body, which was apparently his M.O. She was tempted to slap him.

"Hey, Stacy. You look delicious. I'll get us a table."

She forced a smile. "I can't stay for dinner. Wanna grab a table in the bar instead?"

"I'm disappointed. I don't often get nights out anymore. I'm usually stuck at home playing Daddy these days."

"Being a father is a privilege, as I'm sure you realize considering what's happened to Rachael."

His smile disappeared. "You're no fun. You know that?"

"PMS. It's been coming on all day."

He led the way to a small table near the window and dropped into a chair. "What would you like to drink?"

"Chardonnay, thanks."

He waved the waiter over and ordered a glass of their house Chardonnay. "So, how do I get you in a better mood?" he said.

"It could be difficult. I don't have the best of news to share."

"Pamela won't see me."

She frowned. "I'm investigating your daughter's kidnapping, and the first thing you ask about is your girlfriend? Why is that? Do you already know what happened to Rachael?"

"Don't start that suspicious crap with me. It's only been a few days. I'm assuming, after all these months, it'll take longer than that to solve the case. Nevertheless, I'll ask. Have you found Rachael?"

"What would you say if I have?" Stacy said.

"I'd say my mother will be very happy."

Anger pounded in her chest. "What about you, Tyler? Don't you care about Rachael at all?"

"Of course, I care, but she's not going to live with me. It'll change Mother's life more than mine."

"What about Rachael's life?"

"What do you mean? She'll be home; I'll see her. What do you want from me?" he snapped.

Realizing that his answers all had to do with seeing Rachael alive, she said, "I just wish you felt like being a daddy to her like you are to your son."

He swished the ice around in his glass. "So do I, but I can't make myself feel something I don't. If you'll just bring her home, I'll be happy. Now, what about Pamela?"

The waiter delivered her wine and a new drink for Tyler. She took a few sips. "She doesn't want to see you, Tyler. She's moved on with her life."

"You found her?"

"My partner met with her."

"She's fine? Jacob's fine?"

"She was clear about her decision."

Tyler threw back a healthy portion of his drink. "Well, then," he said, "I guess I need to move on, too. Wanna come back to my place after dinner?"

It shouldn't have surprised her, but it did. It felt like a slap in the face. "I think not. Are you driving?"

"Don't start that again," he said, sprawling back in his chair.

"Do you want your son to see you drunk?"

"It wouldn't be the first time," he scoffed.

"That's nice. I'll be sure to refer you to my girlfriends."

"You have a smart mouth; you know that?"

"I'm a smart girl." She took another swallow of her wine and stood up, "I'll do everything I can to find Rachael."

"I appreciate that. If you can talk Pamela into seeing me one more time, I'd appreciate that, too. We were happy together. She threw it all away like it was nothing."

"Not nothing, Tyler. Pamela just loves her son enough to put what's best for him ahead of what she might've wanted for herself. You have to respect that."

"Another dig about me not being a good parent?"

"Something to consider. Goodbye, Tyler."

"Wait, don't go. I know I'm being a jerk. It's just that I was hoping Pamela might see me after all this time. It hurts, you know?"

Stacy paused, and then sat back down. "Breakups always hurt when you care about the other person. I truly believe if you'll just do what you're supposed to do, and concentrate on being a good father, the perfect woman will come into your life. But if you start drinking and waste your time feeling sorry for yourself, you'll never attract the kind of woman you want for yourself and your son. I know it's hard to believe right now, but it's true."

"I know you're right, but it's awfully lonely right now."

She smiled. "Go home, Tyler. Make a full and happy life with your son. Something good will happen soon. Then your family will grow as it is meant to."

"Sure you won't come with me?"

"I'm not a second-choice kind of girl. Good night." She felt his eyes on her until she had pushed through the double doors and stepped out into the night.

CHAPTER SEVENTEEN

"Are you nervous?" Emily said as Stacy grabbed her suitcase from the trunk.

"Yes, but I'll keep him busy as long as I can. The last thing we need is for dear *Uncle Hugh* to take a drive out to his hunting camp this afternoon. Call me as soon as you head back into town."

"Cell phone reception ain't too good up there, so don't worry if it takes a while before you hear from us."

"How long will it take for you to get to the camp?"

Emily shrugged. "A half hour, maybe. Another hour to hike to the caves."

Stacy looked at her watch. "What's taking him so long?"

Jack stepped out of the hotel lobby and held up the keys. "Bottom floor, room 411."

Stacy snatched the room key from his hand. "Get out of here, and be careful! If I don't hear from you by late afternoon, I'm calling the cops."

Jack patted her arm. "Don't worry about us. You just concentrate on keeping your temper in check while you meet with Emily's uncle."

"Humph," Stacy said. "He's safe enough. After all, I'm leaving my gun at the hotel." She watched as Jack and Emily pulled out of the parking lot and turned towards the highway. She was happy to escape another hike through the woods, but she wasn't looking forward to meeting Hugh Richards, especially after knowing what he'd done to Emily. Jack was right about needing to keep her temper in check. If their diversion was going to work, she had to be at her best.

She yanked the handle of her suitcase and rolled it down the sidewalk towards room 411.

* * *

Stacy flipped her honey-blonde hair behind her back and waited for the elevator doors to open. When they did, she followed the signs until she arrived at the Law Offices of Hugh Dudley Richards. She opened the heavy glass door and stepped into a small lobby where a middle-aged receptionist glanced up and said, "You must be Twila Mason. I've got some paperwork for you to fill out before I let Mr. Richards know you're here."

Putting on her most Southern accent, she said, "You said on the phone that he'd give me a free consultation. I'm here for that."

"You still need to fill out the paperwork. He'll want to know a little bit about you and your case before he meets with you. You seem nervous, dear. Have you ever talked to an attorney before?"

"Never," she said. "I've always heard that attorneys charge you just for breathin', so I'm tryin' to be careful."

The woman laughed. "I haven't heard that one before. The form is straightforward. Don't answer anything you aren't comfortable with."

Stacy settled into a brown vinyl chair, read through the form, and deliberately took her time filling it out. When she was finished, she took the clipboard back to the desk. "Here ya go."

The woman picked it up and began reading. "Twila, how old are you, dear? You left that blank."

"What does that matter?"

"It doesn't, I guess," the woman said. "It says you just moved here from Jackson. Are you working here yet?"

"No, but I'll begin lookin' immediately. I don't have much money left in my savings account, thanks to my husband. How long does it usually take before I can expect to get some alimony comin' in?"

"Well, that depends. You'll have to ask Hugh that question. You didn't fill out your new address either. What is it?"

"I'm still lookin' for a place. I don't know which areas are safe and which ones to avoid. Besides, it seems best to find a job first and then an apartment."

"But where are you stayin'?"

Stacy stood. "I'm not comfortable giving out all my personal information just yet. I haven't even decided if I want him for my attorney. Maybe this was a bad idea."

"You're right. I shouldn't put the cart before the horse. Would you like something to drink? Some bottled water, maybe?"

Stacy nodded and sat back down. "That would be nice. Thank you."

"Good. I'll let Mr. Richards know that you're ready." She opened a door and disappeared behind it.

Stacy shrugged her shoulders and tried to remember the story she'd made up about her fictitious and unfaithful husband. A few minutes later, the door opened again.

"Mr. Richards will see you now."

"Thank you," Stacy said. "What was your name?"

"Oh, I'm Denise."

"Thank you, Denise."

"Right this way, dear." She led her through a door to their immediate right and motioned for her to sit at a small conference table.

Stacy had counted three closed doors in the short hallway; one she assumed was Hugh's office, another was presumably the bathroom, and the third might be another office or perhaps even a break room. Whatever it was, this wasn't a booming practice.

Hugh left her waiting about ten minutes before he finally came in. He was a tall, reasonably attractive man with broad shoulders. He was wearing a button-down shirt and dress slacks. He certainly looked the part of a small-town Southern lawyer.

"Good morning, Mrs. Mason, or would you prefer I call you Twila?"

"Twila will do. I'm lookin' to drop the Mason part."

"I'm not much for last names myself. Just call me Hugh. Mind if I join you?"

"That's why I'm here," Stacy said.

He gave her a half-smile and sat at the head of the table. "Denise tells me you're a bit nervous, but I want you to feel at ease. Think of me as an uncle. Someone who's looking out for your best interests."

"Forgive me for sayin' so, Hugh, but I've only got one uncle, and I can't say that I like him much." She bit back a smile at the surprised look on his face.

"All right then, think of me as a friend. What's the situation with you and your husband?"

"He's a no-good cheat, and I want a divorce."

"I see. Are you certain, or are you just suspicious?"

"I found her panties in my bed, and I've seen her X-rated texts on his cell phone. I'd call that pretty darn certain, wouldn't you?"

"Indeed. Is your husband well-to-do?"

"If you're asking if he's any good at it, I'd say no. He never did much for me, I'm afraid."

Hugh's face flushed. "What I mean is, does he have much money?"

"Oh, yes, but it's *my* money. I inherited it when Daddy died. When we married, he took over my checkin' and savings accounts. Now, I can't get a dime without his signature. He's probably spendin' it on that redheaded floozy as we speak!"

"How much money are we talking about, Miss Twila?"

"Pretty near three million dollars, I suppose, not counting stocks and gold."

"Gold?" he said, perking up.

"Oh, yes. Daddy collected gold bars, bless his heart. He had a whole safe full of them. We need to do something before you-know-who moves that safe out of our house."

"Does your husband know you're divorcing him?"

"Heavens no! I'm sure he's just cheatin' his little heart out while I'm here settin' up my new life. You practice law here *and* in Mississippi, don't you? That's why I picked you."

"Oh, yes. You've come to the right place," he said. "I just need to get your signature on a contract so that we can start framing your case."

"I want to know what your strategy is first, and more about you, while we're at it. Tell me, Hugh, how is it you came to be an attorney?"

"You don't want to hear about that, do you?" he said with a scowl.

"Oh, but I do. I couldn't possibly do business with someone I don't know anything about."

"I see."

She smiled and nodded in all the appropriate places as he detailed his long and boring journey into law.

* * *

"We just passed it," Emily said.

Jack drove another quarter mile before pulling off the road and putting the flashers on. Taking the note he'd already prepared, he taped it to the driver's side window.

"What's it say?" Emily said.

"Out of gas."

"Good idea."

"Not my first rodeo," he teased. "You ready?"

They got out of the car and hiked along the highway to the gated entrance of her uncle's property. She pointed to the chain around the gatepost. "It's locked."

"Wait till there's a break in the traffic, then we'll duck beneath the barbed wire fence."

"You see them no trespassing signs, don't you?"

"What no trespassing signs?" Jack said with a lopsided grin. Just that fast, his smile was gone. "After this car. Go!"

Emily quickly ducked through, and then held the wire up for him. Once he was through, they ran for cover.

"Where does the road lead?" Jack said.

"Straight to the cabin, and then to the dock, which is just behind the house."

"Let's walk along the roadside, but no talking. If we hear someone coming, duck into the woods. We'll circle behind the cabin and see what's going on back there before we approach the house. Agreed?"

"Agreed. There's a twisted tree before we get to the house. That's where we'll leave the road and circle around. I doubt they're stayin' in the cabin though. It'd be safer for 'em in the cave."

"Maybe, but caves are cold and damp. I know I'd rather stay in a cabin," he said.

"Especially this one. It's even nicer than your house, no offense."

"None taken. You've got your gun, right?" She patted her side. "Let's go."

As Jack followed Emily, he took a deep breath and sighed. Any other day, he'd have enjoyed an opportunity to be outside. He loved to roam through the woods, especially places like Arkansas with its rolling hills and rocky terrain. He counted a wide variety of trees including maples, oaks, redbuds, dogwoods, and magnolias, plus several others he didn't recognize. The undergrowth was thick, yet not so thick that they couldn't move through it. It was the perfect place to hunt deer, if he were a hunter, but he much preferred to see animals alive. To him, there was nothing more exciting than spotting a big proud buck strutting in the wild. About twenty minutes later, Emily pointed to a huge oak tree and veered off the road and into the woods.

The crunching leaves and snapping sticks seemed to echo in the stillness, but the birds ignored them and continued chatting away. He tapped her shoulder. "Watch out for snakes." She nodded and kept moving. About ten minutes later, she circled wide to the right and climbed a steep rocky hill. When they got near the top, she motioned for him to crouch low. They crawled to the summit and looked over. Below was a surprisingly large lake, the shoreline of which wasn't completely visible from their vantage point. The two-story cabin was like something you might see in a magazine, complete with a multi-tiered, wrap-around deck that connected to an outside staircase, which led down to the pier and a dual-bay boathouse. Next to the dock stood a small shack, which Jack assumed was a supply hut. "Wow, this place is incredible."

"I'll say. He's added on since I was here last. The deck is bigger now. It used to be one level, and you had to walk down a trail to get to the dock. Now, it's all connected. Those boathouses weren't there either. Guess Uncle Hugh's got himself some money now."

"If he's got all this, why does he want your father's hunting camp, too?"

She shrugged. "Pa says there's competition between the boys in the family: who's the best athlete; who's got the prettiest wife; who's got the best job; who makes the most money. All that stupid stuff. I guess Hugh wins. We ain't got nothin' that competes with this."

"I'm not so sure," Jack said.

"What do you mean?"

"When it comes to who has the finest daughter, your pa won."

Emily's eyes softened. "Thanks, Jack. You're awfully nice. What do we do now?"

"Well, I don't see any boats on the lake or tied at the dock. Can't tell about the boathouses. Let's see if we can get a closer look at the cabin. Can you get us down there without being seen?"

"There's a trail, but we'll have to go back the way we came. There ain't no trucks in the driveway, so I doubt anybody's here."

"That's good news. I'll follow you."

* * *

"So now that you know my life story, are you ready to sign the contracts?" Hugh said.

"May I see them?" Stacy said.

Hugh brightened. "Certainly." He picked up the desk phone and pressed the intercom button. "Denise, please bring in a new client contract."

A few moments later, Denise opened the door, handed him a folder, and then stepped out.

"Here you go, Twila. Just sign at the bottom."

"How long does it take for a divorce to become final?" Stacy said, disgusted to see him try to weasel his way into a contract without letting her read it first. She wondered how many women fell for such tactics.

"It depends on how your husband responds. Do you anticipate that he'll hire an attorney?"

"With my money, of course. We'll be able to recuperate all that, won't we?"

"We'll certainly do our best. Just sign there at the bottom."

"Oh, I couldn't possibly sign a contract without reading it first. I mean, you said you want me to be completely comfortable, right?"

"Yes, of course," he said with a strained smile. "Take your time."

"Thank you. I'll just start here at the beginning." She took a pen out of her purse and began to read. He waited a few moments, tapped on the desk, and then stood. "I'll have Denise check on you in a few minutes. Is that all right?"

"Perfectly fine with me," she said with a polite smile. "I'll just make a list of my questions."

"You do that," he said and walked out.

Stacy looked at her watch. She'd give anything to know what was going on with Jack and Emily right now.

* * *

Jack and Emily left the cover of the woods and stepped onto the lower level of the wooden deck. Emily peered through the windows and kept moving. When she came to the main section of the house, she peeked through the window and gasped.

"What is it?" Jack whispered.

"It's Momma! She's cookin' at the stove. Oh, Jack, can I knock on the door?"

"Do you see anyone else?"

She changed position and glanced around the room. "No, only Momma."

"We know Tommy Lee's around here somewhere. Try the doorknob. Quietly, Emily. We don't want to startle her. She won't recognize you as a blonde."

Emily tried the knob. "It's locked. Now what?"

"We can't stay out in the open like this."

"If I can just call to her," Emily pleaded.

Jack glanced around. About ten feet ahead was a series of open windows along the dining area. He motioned for her to stay low and move to the open windows. Meanwhile, he looked inside, but all he could see was the woman working at the stove with her back towards them. He nodded.

"Momma, it's me. It's Emily."

The woman spun around. Seeing Emily waving her arms, she looked afraid and then joyful. She ran to the door and unlocked it. "Emily, what on earth are you doing here?" They fell into each other's arms.

"Oh, Momma, I can hardly believe it," Emily said, choking on her tears.

"What did you do to your hair?" Leeann said, sobbing and laughing at the same time.

Jack smiled and stepped forward.

Leeann saw him and drew back. "It's okay, Momma. This is Jack. He's been helping me."

"Helping hisself is more like it," accused the booming voice of a big man as he entered the kitchen from the hallway.

"Tommy Lee!" Emily said as she ran to him for a hug. "I'm so happy to see you."

Tommy Lee hugged her with one arm but kept a suspicious eye on Jack.

Jack stepped forward and extended a hand for him to shake. "Hi, I'm Jack Kendall. I'm a—"

Tommy Lee's fist connected with his chin. Emily shrieked, and Jack crumpled to the floor.

* * *

Denise knocked once before she entered the conference room for the third time. "Are you ready yet? Mr. Richards has another appointment coming in."

"Oh, I didn't realize I was holdin' him up," Stacy said, coming to her feet. "You know what? I'll just take this with me. That way I can finish readin' it tonight and call you tomorrow."

"That's not what I meant," Denise said.

"But you just said he has someone comin' in, and I'm not ready to sign it yet. I think it's best if I do what I just said. Tell Hugh I appreciate his time today. I'll set another appointment once I have my list of questions ready." She brushed past Denise, who shamelessly stepped forward to block the way.

"Twila, perhaps he can meet with you after his appointment, or maybe I can push his next appointment back a bit."

"Oh, bless his heart, I don't want him changin' his schedule just for me. After all, I'm not even a client yet. I was almost finished, but no matter. It's all settled now." She opened the door to the lobby and looked back at Denise. "Thank you for being so kind and patient with me today. It's so important to choose the right attorney, don't you think?"

Denise sighed. "Of course, it is. I just wish you'd let me work something out for you today."

"Let's just sleep on it. Hugh might not even want me as a client. After all, five million dollars probably isn't much for someone like him."

"I thought you said three million," Denise said.

"Oh, didn't I mention what my grandparents left me the year before Daddy died? See what I mean about needin' to go over things? Have a good day, Denise. I'll call you tomorrow afternoon. Good night." She smiled and slipped out the door before Denise could say another word.

* * *

Jack was aware of the cold before he was aware of anything else. He was shivering, and his pants and shirt were wet because the floor was wet. He tried to stand, but he realized his hands and ankles were bound by thick rope. It was pitch black. He had been in several caves and recognized the musty smell and dank oppression. He wondered how deep it was, and how long he'd been unconscious. He flexed his jaw and winced. Surely, Emily wouldn't let them keep him here for long.

As the minutes passed and the chill permeated his bones, dread rose from within. He didn't really know Emily. He could hope that she'd feel some obligation to be kind to him, but these people were her family. Her loyalty would naturally fall to them. He should have thought of that before allowing himself to become vulnerable.

The minutes turned into hours.

Finally, he heard the sound of people coming. A light soon

illuminated the small cavern, which looked to be the end of a narrow passage. The walls and ceiling dripped with moisture, and the floor where he lay was dirt and puddles.

"Jack! Are you all right?" Emily cried as she ran to his side.

"I've been better. Untie me."

"I can't. Tommy Lee wants to talk to you first."

Jack glanced into the black hole from which she came. "Where is he?"

"He's comin'. I ran ahead. I couldn't stand to think of you in here. I brought you a blanket. She eased a bag from her shoulder and withdrew a blanket, which she wrapped around his back and shoulders. "Yer freezin'! We've got to get you out of here."

"I second that motion. Why'd he hit me?"

"He thinks we're foolin' around. I've spent the last three hours tellin' him otherwise. I think I've finally convinced him. Listen, I think they're comin'."

A few moments later, the cavern got brighter as Tommy Lee and Leeann squeezed through the entrance to the cramped, rounded space.

"My niece tells me you been helpin' her look for Billy Ray and Rachael. Is that right?"

"Yes. My partner and I have uncovered some information that refocuses the investigation on Joan Chandler. We believe that something went seriously wrong with Billy Ray's kidnapping attempt on Mrs. Chandler's property. We're in the process of getting a search warrant to look for his and Rachael's remains—which upsets Emily, I know—but we've got to get to the truth of the matter. If Joan Chandler is responsible for whatever happened, it isn't right that she escapes justice while you live in hiding for something you didn't do."

"We didn't think nobody'd believe us," Leeann said.

"Well, I believe you, and I'm searching for the truth. Will you untie me now?" Jack said.

"That depends," Tommy Lee said. "Emily says you want us to turn ourselves in. Why would we wanna do that?"

"We need your testimony so that we can move this investigation forward, which won't happen as long as Mrs. Chandler can conveniently blame Billy Ray for something you know he didn't do. I believe that she lied about Billy Ray getting into the car with Rachael, but we need to prove it."

"There's no way Billy Ray's still alive or he'd a been here lookin' for me, and you know it, Emily," Leeann said. Emily nodded and looked down. "We gotta know the truth! We done lost Sarah to them people already, and now Billy Ray and Rachael, too? I can't stand the thought of 'em walkin' around scot-free while I'm livin' like an animal, hiding out for somethin' I didn't do. I'm willin' to turn myself in if you'll fight for us. What about you, Tommy Lee?"

"You think you can find him after all this time? There can't be nothin' left of 'im by now," Tommy Lee said, wiping his nose with the back of his beefy hand.

"I've requested a special team of dogs that can detect even the smallest traces of blood. If they're there, we have a good chance of finding them. The sooner we start, the better, of course."

"What will happen to us?" Leeann said.

"I've already talked to a buddy of mine who's a police captain at the Jackson Police Department. I'll tell him how cooperative you're being, assuming you untie me and get me out of this blasted cave, that is. I'm freezing my ass off in here."

"Do it, Tommy Lee. Cut 'im loose."

"Let's think about this some more," he said.

"We've done nothin' but think about it for an entire year. We gotta find Billy Ray and Rachael, and this here man is willin' to help us. Now, cut 'im loose!"

Tommy Lee pulled out a pocketknife and jerked it through the rope between Jack's ankles and then his wrists.

Rising from the wet floor, Jack said, "Thank you. Now let's get out of here. I need to let my partner know that we're safe before she calls down the Arkansas police department on our heads."

"Lead the way, Leeann," Tommy Lee said. "Emily, you next."

When they emerged from the cave, Jack blinked several times as his eyes adjusted to the light. The wind cut through his wet clothes, making him tremble as they descended a steep and wooded hillside. Soon, the lake came into view. When they reached the shoreline, they walked along its rocky edge until they stopped at a fallen tree where a small fishing boat sat aground. After pulling the boat into the water, everyone climbed in, and Tommy Lee rowed back to the dock. It only took fifteen or twenty minutes to reach the pier, but Jack sat huddled beneath the blanket, miserably cold the entire time. All he could think about was getting warm. He was glad Stacy wasn't the one to accompany Emily on the journey. If she had received similar treatment, he'd never have forgiven himself.

When they reached the dock, they climbed the stairs and entered the cabin where embers still smoldered in the living room hearth. Jack stoked the fire and waited for the heat to penetrate the cold. Leeann made coffee while Emily and Tommy Lee sat quietly on the sofa.

"Where's my cell phone?" Jack said. "I need to see if I can get through to Stacy."

Tommy Lee nodded to Emily, who went into the kitchen to retrieve Jack's phone from her mother.

To Jack's relief, the call went through.

"Where have you been? I was just about to call the police!" Stacy said.

"Listen, Stace. Emily and I are fine, though we're going to be a bit longer getting back. I'll call you when we're headed your way. Are you at the hotel?"

"Why aren't you on your way right now?"

"We met up with some friends, and they might be joining us. We're making plans now."

"Well, isn't *that* good news?" Stacy said.

"Thought you'd like that. Keep your phone on you."

Pocketing his cell phone, he said, "I was right; she was just about to call in the troops. Let's decide how we want to do this."

Leeann looked at Tommy Lee, and Tommy Lee shrugged.

"All right, I have an idea," Jack said. "I need to make another call." This time he dialed Kevin and was extremely grateful when he answered. "Hey, Kev, how's it going?"

"That's Captain Thomas to you. I haven't had time to get the warrants yet, so why are you bothering me?"

"I have a favor to ask."

"Another one?" Kevin scoffed.

"You remember I told you that I might know where a certain couple was hanging out?"

"You have my attention," Kevin said.

"Well, I'm with them now. We'd like to know the best way for them to turn themselves in so that they can receive the best possible treatment. They're completely cooperative. They want to help us locate Billy Ray and Rachael, who, you'll remember, are kin to them. They love them very much and want this case solved as much as we do."

"How the hell did you do that so fast?"

"Should I bring them back to Mississippi, or should I call the authorities here?"

"You know damn well I want them in Mississippi," Kevin snapped.

"You'll remember that they released the Clarkston boy of their own accord. They were looking for their grandchild and took him by mistake. You'll also remember that, at the time, they had just lost their daughter, Sarah, in a tragic accident, and they were not in their normal state of mind. You will take that into consideration, won't you, Captain Thomas?"

"I hear you, Jack. If they cooperate, it will work in their favor, but I can't make any promises. It will depend on what happens with the investigation. You know that."

"That's all we ask. They want to help us. That's the reason they're willing to turn themselves in. You understand that, right?"

"I said yes. Where can we meet?"

"Hold on." He covered the receiver. "It's four o'clock. We could be in Jackson around nine or ten o'clock. Are you ready to do this thing?"

"What did he say about us working somethin' out?" Tommy Lee said.

"He says your willingness to cooperate will work in your favor, but no one can make any promises until we see how the investigation turns out. You and I know that Mrs. Chandler lied; the question is why? When we get the answer to that, this whole case will turn around. I believe the judge will look at the emotional circumstances of your case and grant leniency."

Tommy Lee and Leeann looked at each other. "What's leniency?" Leeann said.

"It means I believe you'll get off lightly if you cooperate. Look, you have to face this sometime. It's better to turn yourselves in while you've got people in your corner who are willing to help you. This is the best chance you're ever gonna get. The time is now."

"I wanna hear him say it," Leeann said. "Give me the phone."

"Captain, Leeann Richards wants to speak to you. Here she is."

"Captain, I wanna hear you say that you'll go easy on us if we cooperate. We didn't mean to take that boy. We thought we was gettin' Rachael on account of her daddy doesn't love her like he loves Cody. We wouldn't hurt nobody on purpose. Just promise that you'll work with us. That's all we ask."

"Mrs. Richards, first of all, anything you say to me can and will be used against you, so I suggest you don't say anything more until you have an attorney present. I have to say that to you because it is the law. I appreciate that you are willing to cooperate, and it will help things go easier on you and Tommy Lee, but I can't make any promises on how this will turn out. If what you say is true, I'll do my level best to see that you receive the lightest sentence possible. You have my word on that."

"Thank you, Captain. I reckon we'll be seein' ya soon," Leeann said.

"Let me talk to Jack," Kevin said.

Leeann handed the phone to Jack. "How are we gonna do this?" Jack said.

"I'll meet you on the Mississippi side of the Vicksburg Bridge at eight o'clock."

"Better make it nine. We've gotta pick up Stacy."

"And where was she during all this?"

"Doing what she does best," Jack said.

"Never mind; I don't wanna know. Keep me posted if you're running late."

"You coming?" Jack said.

"Wouldn't miss it for the world. I want to see you and Stacy in my office tomorrow afternoon at three o'clock. You got that?"

"Loud and clear, sir." He hung up and turned to Leeann and Tommy Lee. "Is there anything you need to do before we go?"

"I wanna freshen up," Leeann said.

"Fine. I'll finish drying my pants," Jack said as he turned towards the fire. Glancing over his shoulder, he said, "You've got a mean right jab, you know that?"

"I oughta. I'm twice yer size." Tommy Lee scratched his chin and glanced over at Emily. "Emily says she's been stayin' at yer house. Is that true?"

"I said I'm stayin' with Stacy in the apartment over the garage. There's a big difference, Tommy Lee."

"Hush up, girl. Let the man speak," Tommy Lee snapped.

"She's right. She's staying with my partner, Stacy, in her apartment above the garage. My only interest is in helping Emily, not that she isn't a perfectly lovely girl. I want to see your family set right, which includes getting your hunting camp back—if that's possible."

"What's he talkin' about, Emily?"

"I ran into Clint while Stacy and I was lookin' for you at your huntin' camp. He said Uncle Hugh paid the taxes I couldn't pay last January and bought your camp at auction. He said if we can't pay the taxes on our trailers next year, he'll buy that land, too, and give our trailers to Clint and Rocky."

Tommy Lee's face turned red as he rose to his feet. "Why, I oughta kill that lowdown snake, cousin or no! He's been after our land for as long as I remember."

"Calm down, Tommy Lee. We're gonna sort all that out. That's another reason for coming out of hiding. You can't fight for your land if you're living in a cave," Jack said.

"Maybe not, but I can kill the S.O.B. the next time he shows up here," Tommy Lee said as he clenched his hands into monstrous fists.

"That won't get your land back, and will only get you in more trouble. No, we're gonna beat him at his own game. He won't expect you to do what you're gonna do tonight. He thinks he can steal everything you own while you're hiding out on his property, but that's not gonna fly. We're on to him, but first things first."

Leeann came back into the room. "I'm ready."

"All right, then. I'll need my gun back, of course," Jack said.

"You ain't gettin' yer gun till we reach Mississippi," Tommy Lee said.

"I'm not taking you anywhere while you're packing my gun. Either you trust me, or you don't. What's it gonna be?" Jack said.

Emily rose to her feet and grabbed hold of her mother's arm. "Trust him, Momma. He's a good man."

Tommy Lee scowled.

"Give it to him, Tommy Lee. If he was gonna do somethin', he would've done it by now. He could've told the cops where we are, but he didn't," Leeann said.

Grumbling, Tommy Lee walked into the kitchen and came back with Jack's gun. "You screw us over, and you'll be sorry."

"Thanks for trusting me. Now hand over your pocketknife."

"Like hell, I will," Tommy Lee said, bucking up his shoulders in a way that reminded Jack of a chicken ruffling its feathers.

"They're gonna take it from you anyway. You can put it somewhere safe, but you can't take it with you." Tommy Lee took it out of his pocket and laid it on the mantel. "You carrying anything else?" Jack said.

"Naw, that's it."

"If they search you and find you armed, you'll lose your only chance at leniency. I'd hate to see you do something stupid like that."

"Who you callin' stupid?" he said.

"Give it to him, Tommy Lee," Leeann said.

"Oh, all right." He lifted his shirt and pulled a .38 from his waistband. Jack held out his hand.

"That's my gun," Emily said. "He took it from me earlier."

Tommy Lee slapped it into Emilie's hand with a scowl.

"Anything else?" Jack said.

"That's it," Tommy Lee said.

"Then let's get going so we can make our deadline."

"Wait," Tommy Lee said. He stepped to the fireplace and picked up the poker. Jack tensed, but relaxed again as Tommy Lee dispersed the logs to kill the fire. When he was satisfied, he closed the screen and said, "Let's go."

They exited through the front door and walked around the circular drive, which connected to the road. It was windy, and Jack's clothes were still damp, but he began to warm up as they kept moving. Emily and Leeann talked the entire way, discussing everything under the sun, which made the trek more bearable. When they reached the gate, they turned right and walked the last quarter mile along the highway. Once inside the car, Jack called Stacy to tell her they were on their way. "Hey," he added at the last second. "Have two large pizzas delivered to the room ASAP. We'll take them with us."

"Pizza? Don't that sound just heavenly?" Leeann sighed.

"I can eat a whole one by myself," Tommy Lee added.

"That's why I got two," Jack said with a grin that quickly turned into a grimace. His jaw ached something fierce.

* * *

The cavalcade of flashing red and blue lights on the other side of the bridge looked intimidating. Jack kept his foot steady on the gas and glanced in the rearview mirror. Leeann's eyes were wide with fear, and Tommy Lee looked none too comfortable either.

"Listen up, everybody. When we pull up beside them, stay put until they tell us what to do. They'll have to search you for weapons, so be prepared for that. Captain Thomas is my friend. I trust him to keep his word. Cooperate and let them do their jobs. Don't make any sudden moves. You got that?"

"You better be right about them workin' with us," Tommy Lee muttered.

"Telling the truth is the most important thing you can do. Don't hold anything back. If they catch you lying, your deal will be off the table."

"You trust him, don't you, Emily?" Leeann said.

"I do, Momma. Do as he says. I'll come see you as soon as they let me."

When they reached the middle of the bridge, Jack called Kevin on his cell phone. "We're here."

"We see you," Kevin said.

"Where do you want us to go?"

"We've got a place cleared for you. Pull in there. We'll surround the car, so don't be alarmed. Who's with you in the car?"

"It's Stacy and me in the front seat. Emily, Leeann, and Tommy Lee Richards are in the back."

"Who the hell is Emily?"

"She's Leeann's daughter. She's the one who helped us locate her mother and uncle. She's in my care, Captain. She's staying with Stacy above the garage."

"All right. When I give the signal, you, Stacy, and Emily get out of the car first. We'll call for Leeann and Tommy Lee one at a time," Kevin said.

"Got it. We're almost there. Emily, you and Leeann trade places. Emily, you'll be getting out when Stacy and I do." He watched in the mirror as the switch took place.

"Pull in slowly," Kevin said. "That's it. Take the car keys with you. Now you, Emily, and Stacy get out of the car."

"Okay, everybody, this is it. Stacy and Emily and I will get out first. They'll call for Leeann and Tommy Lee when they're ready."

"Look, Tommy Lee, they're everywhere," Leeann said as she glanced around at the men circling the vehicle with their weapons drawn.

"I told you they'd do that," Jack said. "It's standard procedure. Just do what I said so that everyone stays safe. Open the doors. Stacy and Emily stand up slowly. Hold your arms up where they can see them. Copy me."

They opened the doors and stepped slowly out of the car, holding their hands high in the air.

"All right, Jack, move this way," Kevin called to them from within the whirl of flashing lights. "Slowly, now."

They walked towards Kevin's voice and were soon encircled. A female officer took Emily by the arm and turned her towards a squad car.

"Jack?" Emily cried out, glancing over her shoulder.

"Spread your arms and legs. I've got to check you for weapons," the police officer said.

Jacked stepped in her direction, but another officer grabbed his arm. Scowling at him, Jack answered, "It's okay, Emily. It's standard procedure."

"I've got a .38 in my waistband," Emily said.

The officer quickly took her weapon. She ran her hands over the back of Emily's body and then turned her around to check the front. "She's clean."

Jack extended his hand and Emily came running. Glancing around, he saw Stacy pressed against a car as well.

"Captain Thomas, I'm armed, too! Get these people off me!" Stacy yelled.

"I've got my weapon, also," Jack said.

"Let them go," Kevin said. "I can vouch for those two."

Stacy yanked herself free and jogged over to where Jack and Emily were standing.

"That's Momma's gun, Jack. I want it back," Emily said.

"You hear that, Captain?" Jack said.

"I heard it, but it's stayin' with me for the time being." He reached into his car and picked up a megaphone. "All right, listen up," he said. "We're gonna do this one at a time. Tommy Lee, you step out of the car first. Keep your hands where we can see them."

Tommy Lee swung his heavy legs out of the car and shoved to his feet. When he had taken a few steps, Kevin yelled, "On your knees! We're gonna cuff and search you for weapons."

"I ain't packin' nothin'," Tommy Lee said as he dropped to his knees. Three officers moved in and, because of his size, used two pairs of cuffs to secure his arms behind his back. They helped him rise and checked him for weapons. "I thought you was gonna work with us," Tommy Lee called out.

Kevin stepped forward. "I'm Captain Thomas. This is standard procedure. Cooperate, and we'll get through this as quickly as possible. Everything we discussed on the phone still stands." To the officers, he said, "Read him his rights." Turning back towards the car, he spoke through the megaphone again. "Okay, Mrs. Richards, it's your turn. Step out of the car, please."

Leeann climbed out with her hands up. When the officers moved in, she doubled over and started to gag. "I'm gonna be sick," she said.

"I'm gonna be sick."

An officer placed his hand on her back as she dropped to her knees and emptied her stomach.

Emily looked to Jack with pleading eyes.

He wrapped his arm around her shoulders and squeezed. "She's fine. She's just scared."

After Leeann was sick, they gently led her a few feet away and cuffed her arms behind her back. As they searched her for weapons and read her rights, Jack said, "What happens now, Captain?"

"We'll take them in for questioning, and book them for attempted kidnapping. Do they have an attorney?"

"Do you trust Hugh to defend you?" Jack asked Tommy Lee.

"Hell no. He stole my land right out from under me. I want to press charges against *him*."

"Can you afford legal counsel, or do we need to appoint a public defender?" Captain Thomas said.

"We ain't got no money if that's what you mean," Tommy Lee said.

"I'll talk to someone I know and see if he can help," Jack said. "In the meantime, let them appoint an attorney for you. They'll take you through the process tonight, but I'll see you tomorrow morning."

"He ain't gonna forget his promise, is he?" Leeann called over her shoulder as they led her to a squad car.

"I won't forget," Kevin said. "Tell the truth, cooperate, and I'll do everything I can to make this as easy on you as possible."

"We will," Tommy Lee said. "Turning to Jack he added, "You won't forget about us, will you?"

"You have my word," Jack said.

Stacy grabbed Emily's arm to keep her from stepping forward as her mother ducked into the back of a police car. "I love you, Momma," she called out.

"I love you, too, baby girl. You make sure Jack gets us out of here."

"I will, Momma," Emily said as the car door slammed shut.

Two officers ushered Tommy Lee into the back of another car and closed the door.

"My office, three o'clock tomorrow afternoon," Kevin said as he pointed at Jack and Stacy, and then suddenly it was over. The police cars pulled away from the bridge, leaving the three of them silent and shaken as the lights faded from sight.

* * *

Jack took note when Emily lay down on the back seat, but he didn't say anything. They had been through a lot that day. It would take time to sort it all through. Even Stacy was quiet.

When they got home, Stacy said, "Anybody up for coffee?"

"Absolutely," Jack said.

"Good. I want to fill you in on my divorce case with *Uncle* Hugh."

"Not me; I'm going to bed," Emily said as she headed for the walkway beside the house.

Stacy caught Jack's eye, but he shrugged. "Do you want to talk first, Emily?" she said.

"No, I'm fine. I just want to be alone for a while."

"You know where to find us if you need anything. I'll be up soon," Stacy said. "I wish I knew what to say," she confessed to Jack once they were inside, "but what words can there be?"

"We'll just have to see where all this leads. Don't let me forget our meeting with Kevin tomorrow afternoon. He's going to want to know everything." He plopped into his recliner as Stacy settled on the couch. "Tell me about *your* day," he said.

Turning on her Southern drawl, she said, "You're speaking to a millionaire, I'll have you know. I'm Mrs. Twila Mason, and I'm fixin' to divorce my low-down, cheatin' husband and sue him for the money he stole from my estate after we married.

Hugh was practically drooling when I left his office, and cursing me out, too, I'll bet. I dragged out the paperwork process and didn't finish reading the contract in time to sign it today. Oh, darn!"

Jack chuckled. He knew firsthand how easy it was for Stacy to wrap men around her finger.

"Poor man, he didn't stand a chance," she said.

"Not so poor. You should see the cabin he has at the hunting camp. It sits on a lake and looks like something you'd see in a magazine."

"You wouldn't know it by looking at his office space. What happened with you and Emily?" she said.

Jack rubbed his jaw. "Let's just say that the introductions didn't go so well. Tommy Lee knocked me out with one punch. I woke up, bound hand and foot, in a freezing cold, pitch black cave. Let me tell you, your mind starts playing tricks on you, and you start wondering what's out there in the dark. I don't envy them, having to hide in there. Caves are cold, wet, and stinky. While I was unconscious, Emily spent the better part of three hours trying to convince Tommy Lee that I wasn't there for personal reasons."

"He thought you and Emily were an item?" she said with a smirk.

He chuckled. "I was waiting for him to pull out the shotgun and order another wedding right then and there. Thank goodness he finally saw reason."

"Do you believe them?" Stacy said, her eyes suddenly serious and searching.

He nodded. "I do."

CHAPTER
EIGHTEEN

J ack was still asleep when his cell phone rang the next morning. He grabbed it off the night table. "Jack here."

"Mr. Kendall, this is Valerie. At the bank? I shouldn't be doin' this, but I got some information that might be helpful to your case, only you can't tell anybody I told you this or I'll lose my job."

Jack blinked a few times and sat up in the bed. "What is it, Valerie?"

"It's just that you got me interested in Mrs. Chandler's account after you called the other day. I looked through her checking account records, which I got access to through someone in the online banking department. I searched to see if Mrs. Chandler had any unusual purchases after the kidnapping. Turns out she wrote a big check to Miskelly Furniture Company and spent thousands of dollars at Home Depot, all within a few days after Rachael disappeared. I don't know about you, but if I had that kind of money, I'd be spending it trying to find my grandchild. Ya know what I mean?"

"I do. Thank you, Valerie. You've been very helpful. Is there anything else you can tell me?"

"Her credit card companies are American Express and Bank of America. At least those are the ones she writes checks to every month. I gotta get back to work now. I hope this helps you find that little girl. Wouldn't it be awful if her grandmother had something to do with all this? I mean, what's happening to Christian family values, and us livin' in the Bible Belt and all?"

"It makes you wonder. Thanks again, Valerie. I'll let you know if this turns out to be a major break in the case. Good work."

"You're welcome, Mr. Kendall. I consider this a community crime-watch call. Though Mrs. Chandler hasn't done anything to me personally, she acts mighty uppity with the tellers when she comes in here. Bye-bye now."

Jack got out of bed. Why would Joan Chandler be buying new furniture and spending thousands of dollars at Home Depot after her granddaughter went missing? More intriguing than that was the question of whether Mrs. Chandler had hired a private detective. Valerie was right. Someone with that kind of money would certainly not rely on the police alone.

A shower and a hot cup of coffee would go a long way in helping him think things through. He kicked off the sheets and rose from the bed.

A knock sounded at the back door.

Pulling on yesterday's clothes, he went to the back door and looked through the blinds. Seeing that it was Emily, he unlocked the door and let her in. "Hey, Emily. What's up?"

"How much do I owe you so far?"

Noting that she was fully dressed and carrying her purse, he waved her inside and said, "Well, let me see. Since we're not finished with your case yet, why does it matter?"

"Cuz I'm going back to Arkansas to find a job. I can't keep stayin' in Stacy's living room, and I'm guessin' that my bill is getting' pretty darn high by now. It's costin' you money every single day for room and board, and that's gotta stop."

"Coffee?" he said. She nodded. He prepared the coffee maker and hit the button. "You're pretty upset about yesterday, aren't you?"

"I got my momma and uncle arrested. I should be upset." Tears filled her eyes.

"Emily, your mom and uncle needed to turn themselves in. They couldn't continue living the way they were. The stress of that takes a toll, you know. Couldn't you see how exhausted and scared your mother was?"

"Yes, but what if the police aren't as lenient as they said they'd be?"

"I trust Captain Thomas. Besides, we've got a case to figure out. You don't want them accused of kidnapping Rachael if they didn't do it, do you?"

"No," she said as she looked down.

"Well, that's what everyone thinks. Because of you, they have a chance to tell the truth and clear their names. I know it upset you to see them arrested, but it's one step closer to getting things resolved. Give the legal system a chance to work. It will take time to sort this through."

"It was horrible seeing 'em handcuffed like that. All they wanted was to take care of Rachael."

"I know, but you can't break into someone's house and take their child away by force," he said gently. "Are you unhappy here?"

"No, but stayin' here makes me think about it every single second. At home, at least, maybe I can forget about it while I'm busy living my life."

He nodded and got up to pour the coffee. "That makes sense. Why don't you go home, get a job, and we'll worry about the bill later? How's that?"

"Why are you so nice to me? My uncle thinks you want to marry me or somethin'."

He chuckled. "If I were ten years younger, maybe I would. As it is, though, all I want is to solve this case so that you and your family can get on with your lives. I want the innocent to go free and the guilty to face justice. I'm a detective; that's what I do."

"It's just business to you?"

"No. I care about my clients. I care about you. You held your momma in your arms yesterday. Did you stop to think about what a blessing that was?"

"It was wonderful to see her. I just wish she could come home now, and we could forget about all this, but I know that can't happen. I'm just scared, I guess."

Jack sipped his coffee. "There's a lot to face when you go home. Have you forgotten about the burning cross?"

"With everything going on, I guess I did. What am I gonna do? I can't stay here, and I can't go home."

"Why don't you find a job here in Jackson? Then you can find an apartment where you can live your life without thinking about this every day."

"There's an opening at a law firm. They're looking for a receptionist, someone who can file and do some basic paperwork. It pays ten dollars an hour."

"Are you going to apply?"

"I could, I guess."

"Good. They'd be crazy not to hire you. Whatever happens, you have Stacy and me to back you up. You know that, don't you?"

"Y'all are wonderful." She sipped her coffee and allowed the wrinkles to relax from her forehead. "I think I'll call that attorney's office today."

"Which attorney is it?"

"Some guy named Joshua Royce."

Jack choked on his coffee, spewing it on the table and down his shirt.

"Oh, are you all right? I'll get a napkin!"

He coughed several more times to catch his breath. As Emily set about wiping the table, he smiled. This was one job he could be sure she would get. After all, Josh owed him.

* * *

"Why are we leaving so early? You've never been in a hurry to meet with Kevin before," Stacy complained. "I wanted to run an errand before we left."

"Sorry for not filling you in in front of Emily, but we're following up a tip I got this morning."

"Oh? Do tell."

"Apparently, Joan Chandler made several unusual purchases right after the kidnapping, including spending thousands of dollars at Home Depot."

"What does that have to do with anything?"

"What do people usually buy at a hardware store?" he said.

"I don't know. Tools, items to repair what's broken, home improvement?"

"Something pretty darn big must have broken if she spent thousands of dollars. It seems curious, so I thought we'd play good detective, bad detective. You up for that?"

"Oooh, we haven't done that in a while. Which one am I?" she said, her eyes sparkling with delight.

"We'll ask for the manager. If it's a male, I'll be the bad guy. If it's female, you be the bad guy. How does that sound?"

"Much more fun than going to see Kevin," she said.

A few minutes later, he pulled into the parking lot. "Have your business card ready."

Stacy dug in her purse and pulled one out. "Got it."

"Let's roll." He strode up to the customer service desk where Stacy stood at his side. When the person ahead of them had finished his business, they approached the counter.

The associate smiled and said, "How can I help you?"

Jack held his business card in front of the young man's face. "We need some information."

With wide eyes, he said, "The manager ain't in."

"We're supporting an official police investigation and need the purchase history of one of your clients. Can you access that from this terminal?"

"Yes, but I don't think—" He stepped back and began glancing around.

Seeing his nametag, Jack said, "Look, Kirk, it's a simple question. Do we need to call the police in order to get this done?"

Stacy stepped forward. "We'd like to avoid causing a scene. Please, just call up Joan Chandler's account. We're trying to find her missing grandchild."

"Oh, I heard about that," Kirk said. "I feel so sorry for her."

"We do, too. Please help us," she said. "It should only take a few seconds."

Looking from Jack to Stacy, he said, "I'll do it, but don't tell my boss. I don't wanna get in any trouble."

"Thank you," Jack said. "By cooperating, you're keeping your company from receiving a court order where they'd have to provide the information anyway. This is much easier on everyone. We'll leave your name out of it."

Kirk punched several keys. "She hasn't been in for a while, but it looks like she did some major remodeling work about a year ago."

"What did she buy?" Stacy said.

"Kitchen cabinets, a sink, refrigerator, counter tops, an entire bathroom. There's also an electric sander, lumber, drywall, paint, primer. It's a pretty long list, and there are four other invoices besides."

"Can you print them out for us?" Stacy said.

"I guess so. Then I'll need to help the rest of my customers. There's a line behind you."

"Just print the invoices, and we'll be on our way," Jack said.

A few minutes later, he and Stacy walked out of the store with the invoice copies. When they got back in the car, Stacy said, "That was fun. It's amazing what a simple business card can do. Did you see the way he reacted?"

"Start reading. I want to hear what she bought," he said as he backed out of their parking space.

Stacy read through the list, though the abbreviations made it difficult to identify some of the items. Even so, one thing was clear; Joan had begun some major renovation work right after the kidnapping took place. Valerie was right; that in itself seemed strange.

Jack was still mulling over the possibilities as he followed Stacy through the police station, towards Kevin's office, greeting the people he knew along the way.

Stacy knocked on the door.

"Come in," Kevin said with a gruff voice.

Stacy glanced at Jack, and he nodded for her to go in.

"Well, if it isn't my two favorite detectives," Kevin said with unveiled sarcasm.

"Hello to you, too," Stacy said.

"Are you not amazed and astounded by our prowess and efficiency?" Jack said as he and Stacy settled into their usual chairs opposite his desk.

"You hit the jackpot this time, Kendall. Before we get into the details, tell me how the hell you talked those two into turning themselves in? Better yet, how did you get that woman's daughter to tell you where they were?"

Jack grinned. "When you're good, you're good."

"Hey, I had quite a bit to do with that; thank you very much," Stacy scowled. "After all, I'm the one who talked with Emily first."

"I'm not forgetting that," Jack said, "and you did an excellent job at Home Depot today, too. You've got quite a knack for this business."

"Thank you. Today was easy," Stacy said with a satisfied bow of her head.

"I hate to interrupt your mutual admiration party, but I'm not riding the merry-go-round today," Kevin said. "This is my meeting, and I'm in charge. Let me start by saying that the Richards have been extremely cooperative. In fact, they told us where they ditched their station wagon. We've dispatched a team to check it out. If it's there, we'll be able to determine whether Rachael was ever inside the car. If what they claim is true, you'll get your team of cadaver dogs."

"We've come across some interesting data ourselves today," Jack said. "It seems Mrs. Chandler spent thousands of dollars on building supplies just two days after the kidnapping. Here's a list of items."

Kevin took the invoices and scanned through them. "The timing seems odd. I wonder what she remodeled. There aren't enough cabinets here for a kitchen the size I'd expect in a house like hers unless it's for a guest unit. We'll make a point of matching it up when we do the search. Anything else?"

"She also purchased some new furniture, but we don't have an itemized list of that yet," Jack added.

"What's going to happen to Leeann and Tommy Lee?" Stacy said.

"It's too early to say, but we'll keep them here for now. They each met with a public defender this morning."

"Can we see them?" Jack said.

"Not yet. I'll let you know when," Kevin said. "Now, Miss Young, I haven't forgotten your comment from the last time you were here. Tell me about blackmail and extortion."

Stacy glanced at Jack.

"Don't look at him. You claim that Mrs. Chandler bribes people into saying and doing what she wants them to. Tell me why you said that."

"Are you going to protect our sources?" she said.

"That depends on the circumstances. Answer my question."

She glanced at Jack again, and he nodded. "I'll tell you what I know," she said.

After Stacy had filled Kevin in on her meetings with Tyler, Jack told him about his conversation with Pamela.

"Do you have proof of this?" Kevin said.

"Yes, but that's only half of the story," Jack said. "Apparently that was the same night Billy Ray Richards kidnapped and subsequently released Jacob Clarkston."

"With Leeann and Tommy Lee's help," Kevin added.

"Unwilling to risk that it might happen again, Pamela visited Joan Chandler the next day to accept her offer, but on different terms."

Kevin seemed to take it all in until Jack told him that Joan canceled their agreement.

"How could she know that Tyler wouldn't see Rachael again unless she knew where Rachael was?" Kevin said, his brows knitting together as he considered what they had said.

"Our point exactly, not to mention the threats, bribery, and extortion," Stacy said.

"Which both parties are guilty of," Kevin said. "What proof do you have?"

"Pamela taped her conversation with Joan Chandler. I heard it myself," Jack said. "Can we give her immunity in exchange for her testimony? After all, she was emotionally shaken by her son's kidnapping, and Joan approached her with the financial offer; she merely countered."

"I think we can make a case for that. Will she testify?"

"She's afraid to because Joan threatened Jacob."

"You're right; she's not the sweet little lady I took her for," Kevin scoffed. "We'll leave Pamela in our back pocket for now. I should hear something soon on Joan Chandler's credit card details, as well as what the station wagon reveals—*if* it's where the Richards say it is. If those things check out, then we'll move forward with search warrants. Good work, you two. We'll take it from here. You're officially off the case."

"You know that doesn't work with us," Jack said, "so you may as well not even try. When can we see the Richards?"

"When we feel like we've gotten everything out of them. I'll keep you informed."

"Can Emily visit her mother today?" Stacy asked.

"Everybody waits until I give the word. Why is she staying with you two anyway?" Kevin said.

"She called our office and spoke with Stacy. After they met, and we realized how difficult her circumstances were—"

"People threw bricks at her trailer," Stacy said. "She lost her job and couldn't pay her bills, let alone her taxes."

"Her entire life has turned upside down through no fault of her own," Jack added.

"Wouldn't you have helped her if she had come to you?" Stacy said.

Kevin nodded. "I understand how it happened, but having a suspect's daughter beneath your roof can cloud your judgment. Did either of you stop to think about that?"

Stacy gave him a dirty look. "We've been too busy tracking down the incredible leads she's been giving us to consider that."

Jack coughed to keep from chuckling. One thing about Stacy, she spoke her mind. She wasn't intimidated by anybody.

"You don't like me very much, do you, Miss Young?" Kevin said, his eyes narrowing as he leaned forward over the desk.

"Not when you imply that we should withhold help from someone who desperately needs it. It's easy to say we should've sent Emily on her way, but it's not so easy to do once you've looked across the table and watched her scarf down her food because she doesn't have any money, or you've seen her cry because she's scared. How would you feel if someone burned a cross in your yard? I'd be scared to death!"

"Stacy—"

Kevin raised a hand. "Let her finish."

"Oh!" Stacy said, the color draining from her face as she realized her faux pas. "I didn't mean it like that. It's just— Look, hate is hate, and it has no color. The point is that Emily came to us for help. We weren't about to send her back into that kind of situation, and because of that, it looks like we might be able to solve a kidnapping and murder case that you let grow cold. You might consider that the next time you withhold a gesture of human compassion."

"Jack, get her out of here."

Jack rose to his feet. "Come on, Stacy."

Stacy rose, also. "Look, Captain, I don't mean to annoy you, but God made me the way I am, just as he made you the way you are. Maybe we should recognize that our differences have worked out pretty darn well for us in the past, as I assume they will in this case, too. Because of Jack and me, you have Leeann and Tommy Lee Richards in custody. All I'm sayin' is when you think about Leeann, remember all that she's been through. She lost her daughter, Sarah. Her husband Billy Ray is likely dead. Her grandchild, Rachael, is still unaccounted for. She's been living in hiding for more than a year, and now she's in jail because she *willingly* turned herself in so that she could help with this investigation. All I ask is that you have some compassion when you deal with her. Even if you set her free today, she'll never hold her daughter, and maybe even her husband and grandchild, ever again. Have a good day, sir."

Jack opened the door and followed her out. He could see how stiff she was as they walked back to the car. Once they climbed in, he didn't start the engine right away. He looked over and waited for her to acknowledge him.

"You can yell at me now," she said, turning to face him.

"I'm not going to yell at you. In fact, I'm extremely proud of you. It's not easy to stand up to someone like Kevin. You gave him something to think about. Even I was speechless."

"Really?" She sank back in the seat with a sigh.

"Yes. Other than that...ah...difficult moment there, you reminded us that this isn't about solving a case. It's about repairing people's lives. Speaking of that, I need to call Josh."

"Josh? Whatever for?"

"You'll see." He pulled out his phone and placed the call.

"Law offices of Alister, Emerson & Maxwell. How may I help you?"

"Joshua Royce, please. Tell him Jack Kendall is calling."

A few moments later, Josh said, "Hey, Jack. Long time, no see. What's up?"

"Hey, yourself, Josh. I hear you're looking for a receptionist."

"You applying?"

"Very funny," Jack said.

Josh laughed. "Sorry, but it was right there. To answer your question, our group lost our receptionist last week, and I'm in charge of finding the replacement. Got somebody in mind? I'd love to steal Stacy back from you."

"Stacy's not available, but I do have someone in mind. Her name is Emily Richards."

"I met with Emily this morning. She's a nice girl, but unfortunately, her speech is too country casual for that position. We need someone a bit more professional."

"I understand. I forgot about that. She has a passion for filing and organizing paperwork. If you ever have a need for that—"

"We do, actually. We're looking for a file room manager. We generate mountains of paperwork over here, and we need someone to manage it."

"I think you found your girl," Jack said.

"Who is she, and why do you care?" Josh said.

"She's a person who deserves something good to happen in her life. If it doesn't work out, you can always let her go, but I think that you'll be extremely glad you hired her."

"I'll give her a call this afternoon," Josh said. "It would be nice to have that department organized for a change. I can't tell you how many times I've requested a file and have had to wait days for someone to find it."

"You can thank me over drinks sometime soon," Jack said.

"Sounds good. Say hey to Stacy for me."

"Will do," Jack said. "Oh, and don't tell Emily I called you. I'd like for her to believe that she did this on her own."

"You got it. Take care, Jack," Josh said and hung up.

"He's gonna hire her?" Stacy said.

"Sounds like it. The question is will she take it? She's been thinking about going back to Arkansas."

"Why would she do that?"

"She's feeling a bit overwhelmed and worried about being a burden to us. I think she wants to rent a place of her own," he said.

"Sleeping on someone's floor is never as good as having your own space. If they offer her the position, I'll warn her about Josh so that she'll be prepared in case he hits on her. She's so innocent that she'd likely be flattered instead of wary."

"Good idea," Jack said with a scowl. He'd forgotten that Josh had a tendency to flirt with the women he works with.

"Relax," Stacy said. "I'll warn her."

"It's probably good that I don't have daughters," he said.

"You'd survive."

"I would, but I'm not so sure about the young men who expressed interest in them. I'm already watching out for Christine's daughter, Alexa, and she's only eleven."

Stacy's phone rang. "Hello?" Her eyes widened, and she put a finger over her lips for him to stay quiet. "This is Twila."

Jack cracked a smile as he heard her exaggerated accent kick into gear.

"Yes, I read the contract. I'm sorry for not callin' sooner, but my husband and I decided to kiss and make up. He says he's sorry for cheatin', and he intends to do everything in his power to make it up to me. You should see the diamond necklace he bought me." She looked over at him and winked. "Well, yes. Technically, it is my money he bought it with, but Momma always said it's the thought that counts. Are you sayin' I should divorce him anyway?" She covered her mouth to keep from laughing. "Yes, I hear what yer sayin', but the Bible says we should forgive one another. Don't you believe in the Bible, Denise? I don't think I could work with an attorney that doesn't believe in the Bible."

Jack chuckled to himself. She was so much fun to be around. The people on the other end of the line had no idea how smart she was, or that she was playing them. In fact, they thought they were playing her.

"Yes, but I *want* to give him another chance. If he cheats again, *then* I'll divorce him. In the meantime, I plan to take money out of our account, so I don't leave empty-handed next time. That's a good idea, don't you think? After all, I'm nobody's dummy, you know." She looked over at him and rolled her eyes. "Oh, yes, I'm sure. Thanks so much for callin'. I'll be in touch when it's time to go further. At least, I've already read the contract. Have a good day, Denise. Send my regards to Mr. Richards. Bye-bye now."

Stacy dropped the phone into her purse and grinned. "How was that, Mr. Kendall? Do I pass?"

He laughed. "Indeed, you do, Miss Twila. Remind me never to make you angry. I don't want you playing for the other team."

"Good call," she said. "Let's go home. I'm hungry."

"I'm always hungry. Besides, maybe Emily will have heard something and have good news to report."

"That would make my day," Stacy said.

"Mine, too. Hey, what would you think if I asked Josh to handle the Richards case?" Jack said.

"Where are Tommy Lee and Leeann gonna get Alister, Emerson & Maxwell kind of money? Josh doesn't work for free, you know."

"No, but I bet he'd work to become famous."

Stacy raised a brow. "You better call him before he calls Emily."

"Humph," Jack grumbled as he dialed again. He didn't like having to cancel Emily's job opportunity. "Hey, Josh, how would you like to be famous?"

"I'm working on it, but it takes a long time in a huge firm like this."

"How would you like to land one of the biggest kidnapping cases Jackson, Mississippi has ever seen?"

"I already said I'd call Emily. What more do you want?" Josh said.

"For you not to call Emily."

"What the hell are you up to, Jack? I'm busy here," Josh said.

"Have you heard that they have two of the Rachael Chandler kidnappers in custody?" Jack said.

"It's a huge break in the case, but they're still looking for the third suspect."

"How would you like to represent those two?"

"Right," Josh smirked. "Like you can hand them to me on a silver platter."

"Who do you think arranged for them to turn themselves in?"

"You wish!"

"Did you notice that Emily just happens to have the same last name as the two *alleged* kidnappers, who are innocent, by the way?"

"All right. Where can we meet?" Josh said.

"Our old favorite will do. See you in an hour?"

"Are you about to make my life exciting again?" Josh said.

"I might."

"I have to admit, I've never experienced anything as nerve-racking or as exhilarating as working with you on Cedric's case. My life is boring now in comparison."

"Well, hold onto your hat because you're in for a doozie. Find someone else to hire Emily because a conflict of interest won't work. Can you do that for me?"

"I'll make a few calls. See you at Old Venice in an hour,"

Josh said.

Jack hung up and looked at Stacy. "His life is boring without us."

"If he married Elizabeth, of course his life is boring. They never were right for each other."

"Sour grapes?"

"Hell, no. If he can't see that what we had was far more valuable than Elizabeth's *connections*, then he doesn't deserve me. I'm over it already."

He noted her crossed arms and thought otherwise, but he knew better than to say so. "Let's call Emily and tell her we'll bring pizza home for dinner."

"You do it. I'm gonna walk around for a few minutes."

When she slammed the door and walked away, he chuckled. "You don't look over it."

* * *

Jack was watching for Stacy's reaction when Josh approached the table. As usual, Josh wore an expensive suit and tie, and his smooth brown hair was perfectly in place. Stacy managed to hide her feelings, but Jack felt a twinge of envy. Seeing Josh was a subtle reminder that due to his unruly mop of curls, even if he were to wear fancy clothes, he could never look as sophisticated as Josh. Though he knew that women considered him attractive in a Russell Crowe kind of way, a professional, polished look just wasn't in the cards for him.

"Hey, Josh," he said, extending his hand for him to shake. "How's it going, buddy?"

"Great to see you, Jack. Hey, pretty lady. Give me a hug."

Stacy stood and let Josh draw her into his arms, which made Jack uncomfortable. It had been over a year since Josh and Stacy had dated, but it still bothered him, even though he and Stacy were nothing more than friends.

Josh pulled up a chair and said, "So, tell me what's up and how it's going to make me famous."

"Spoken like a man who bills for every second of his time," Stacy said. "We're not on the clock now, are we?"

"Ouch. Do I detect animosity here?" Josh said.

"I see by your ring that you went through with the wedding," Stacy added. "How's married life treating you?"

"Ah, you're asking about Elizabeth. We may as well get the elephant out of the room, I suppose. We married last summer, and it's about what I expected. There are no fireworks, if that's what you mean, but we manage well enough. We're expecting our first child next month—a boy. We're going to name him Joshua Alan Royce."

Stacy blinked a few times. "Wow, a junior. It never occurred to me that there'd be children. Are you faithful?"

Jack cleared his throat. "Maybe we should talk about business."

"It's a fair question, considering," Josh said. "I haven't been involved with anyone since you. I learned the hard way that developing feelings for someone on the side only makes it more difficult to accept Elizabeth for what she is, and isn't. I gave up some things when I married her, but I gained other things in the bargain. I'm willing to honor my marriage vows to keep my family together, especially now that we'll have children.

"It took a long time to stop thinking about you, Stacy, and I don't intend to do that to myself or Elizabeth again. I feel better about myself when I'm faithful. Besides, we want to be one of those couples who stays married for fifty years and has tons of grand and great-grandchildren."

A tear fell down Stacy's cheek before she could wipe it away. "You've changed. I'm happy to hear that. I really am." She sniffed. "So, let's get down to business."

"Right," Jack said. "We have reason to suspect that something's amiss with the child's grandmother, Joan Chandler. At the very least, we know she's hiding something. I've requested warrants to look for

Billy Ray's remains."

He smiled. "You think she killed him?"

"Thanks for the vote of confidence."

"Come on, Jack. You have to admit it's a bit far-fetched. Why would she claim that he kidnapped the girl? Where's the kid?"

"We fear we might find her remains as well," Jack said.

"Didn't the maid say she chased them back to the car? Are you saying she committed perjury to cover for the old lady? I'm not buying it."

"We see that," Stacy said.

Jack's phone rang. "Sorry, let me turn this off." When he reached for it, he saw that it was Kevin. "Hold on; this is important. Yes, Captain?" He locked eyes with Stacy. "I see. Do you have the list?"

Stacy tugged on his arm, asking him to tilt the phone so that she could hear.

"Two twin beds and one queen. That's odd." He glanced over at Josh. "When did she buy the boat? Did she ever report one missing?"

Stacy leaned away and whispered, "Search warrants."

He nodded and tilted the phone again. "They did? How do you know?" He and Stacy looked at each other with surprise. "Doesn't that support their story?"

Josh scribbled a note on a napkin and slid it over to Jack. It read: "What?!"

"Yes, I understand," Jack said. "Call me back as soon as you know." He took the pen and wrote "Unbelievable!" and slid it back to Josh. "I will. Bye."

"What did he say?" Josh said.

"Oh my goodness," Stacy said. "I'll never sleep tonight."

"What!" Josh said.

"We have to know where you stand on being the Richards' attorney. They don't have any money. Will your firm do this pro bono?"

"I doubt it. I charge two hundred and fifty dollars an hour."

"If you represent these people and prove them innocent, you'll be able to write your own ticket from here on out. You'll get national media coverage. Are you happy at Alister, Emerson & Maxwell?"

"It's the most prestigious law firm in the state," Josh said.

"If you ask *them*. Are you happy?" Jack pressed.

"It pays the bills. It's secure. It gives me a career path."

"But are you selling out?" Stacy said.

"Why do you always ask me that?" Josh said. "Before today, I didn't think so."

"And now?" Stacy pressed.

"I'll talk to my boss and see if they'll let me represent them. If they say no, then I'll make my own decision. Tell me what Captain Thomas said."

"Can't do that, not unless we have attorney-client privilege," Jack said.

"Don't pull that crap with me. I need intel in order to coax them into doing something they're not inclined to do. Everyone thinks they're guilty. Tell me something to change their mind."

"We've already said too much," Jack said.

"All right, here's what I think. If the old lady's boat went missing and she bought a replacement, then it sounds like Billy Ray got away, which means your jailbirds are lying. I think they're covering for Billy Ray. Wherever they were hiding, how do you know Billy Ray isn't there? Maybe he and the kid have been there the entire time."

Jack and Stacy looked at each other. "That's a possibility," Jack said, "but then you don't have all the information." His phone rang again. "Humph. It's Kevin again." He answered, and Stacy leaned in.

"Right. Thanks for letting me know," Jack said.

"What now?" Josh said.

"Know an attorney named Hugh Richards?"

"I hate that guy," Josh scoffed. "I've come up against him a few times. He's smart, but he's sleazy. I can't quite put my finger on it."

"Well, he's about to steal your opportunity. He met with our jailbirds this morning."

"Is he related?"

"He's their cousin, but he's also guilty of aiding and abetting fugitives, stealing their property, and a few other things we probably haven't discovered yet. I'm sure they'd prefer an alternative. I've got another attorney who will jump at this chance, but we wanted to give you first grab at it."

"You're not right. You know that?" Josh said as he raked his fingers through his hair.

Jack was annoyed to see it fall perfectly back into place. "It's up to you, Josh, but I wouldn't wait or you'll miss your shot. Wanna call your boss?"

"Do you have anything else on the old lady?" Josh said.

"Let's just say that she's not the sweet little grandma the press has made her out to be. I've got a feeling that by tomorrow afternoon every attorney from here to Florida's gonna want to represent Leeann and Tommy Lee Richards. They did mistakenly take the Clarkston boy, but as soon as they discovered it, they let the child go. Rachael is their grandchild. They weren't out to harm her," Jack said.

"And they were grieving for their daughter, Sarah, who had died just days before," Stacy added.

"Joan Chandler is her grandmother, too. Why would she harm the girl? From what I hear, she was desperate to adopt her."

"You heard right," Jack said.

"So, what's going to happen tomorrow?" Josh pressed.

"You in, or are you out?" Stacy said.

"I can't do this on my own. I have to get permission," Josh said.

"Fine," Jack said. "When you get permission, we'll meet downtown, and I'll introduce you to Leeann and Tommy Lee. Let's order some pizza. Anybody else hungry?"

Josh nodded. "I'm hungry for more than pizza. You've got me thinking about being on my own again, dammit. Elizabeth would kill me."

"Maybe she'll encourage you," Stacy said. "After all, you'll be famous."

"I wouldn't count on that," Josh said.

Stacy wrinkled her nose. "Better you than Hugh Richards."

* * *

"Emily, we're home," Stacy called from the kitchen.

"I'm here."

Stacy set the pizza box on the counter. "Where are you?"

"In bed."

"It's only eight o'clock. I brought you some pizza," Stacy said as she settled onto the couch.

"They still won't let me see Momma. No one called me about a job today, and I'm tired of hangin' around here with nothin' to do. My bills must be sky high by now, and I'm thinkin' about selling our trailer to pay you off. Other than that, it's been a perfect day. How 'bout you?"

"Hmmm. I've had days like that. Don't worry; tomorrow will be much better. You won't be selling your trailer. In fact, you, your Mom, and even Tommy Lee will be going home to live in it one of these days very soon."

"You sound so positive. How come?" Emily raised herself up on the air mattress to sit cross-legged.

"Because things are progressing on your case, even if you can't see it. I wouldn't be at all surprised if someone doesn't call you about a job soon either. So hang in there a little bit longer. Things will turn around. You'll see."

"I wish I could be as optimistic as you are, but it seems mighty cloudy from where I'm sitting. I can't afford to keep waitin'."

"Have Jack or I ever mentioned anything about needing to get paid?"

"No," Emily said as she looked down.

"Have we ever even hinted that we're looking for money from you?"

"No."

"So stop worrying. We understand your situation. We're helping you because we want to see justice done. We want to see your life turn around, and we want to find Rachael and Billy Ray, wherever they are, and bring them home."

"It's just so hard to believe. Nobody's ever cared about me before, except my family, of course."

"Well, it's time that changed. Can't you smell that pizza?"

"It smells really good," Emily said with a half-smile.

"Well, come get some. It's too good to ignore."

"I'm glad you're home," Emily said.

"I'm glad you're here, too. It's been nice having you around. It's like having a kid sister. When all this is over, I hope we continue to be friends."

Emily smiled so genuinely that Stacy laughed and pulled her close for a hug.

CHAPTER NINETEEN

J oan Chandler lifted her head off the pillow and tried to shake free from her dream. She heard dogs barking. That was odd. It was at least two miles between her and the next house. She swung her feet onto the floor and went to the window. She blinked against the light, but after a moment, she could see clearly. The garden looked peaceful.

The doorbell rang, and someone knocked.

She glanced at the clock and scowled; it was 7:00 a.m. She pulled on her robe and stepped into her slippers.

The doorbell rang again, and the knocking continued.

Her heart raced as she hurried along the hallway and down the stairs. She could still hear barking and didn't know what to make of it. Had a neighbor's hunting dogs chased a deer onto her property again? If so, she was about to give him a piece of her mind for waking her up so rudely. She yanked the door open and gasped. A man, a woman, and several uniformed police officers stood on the other side of the screen door.

"What is the meaning of this?" she said.

"I'm Agent Madison, ma'am," the man said. "This is Agent Carson. We're with the FBI, and we'd like to ask you some questions. May we come in?"

Joan gripped her robe in a fist beneath her chin. "As you can see, I'm not properly dressed. Perhaps another time." She stepped back to close the door.

"We have a search warrant. You can make this easy on yourself, or we can do it the hard way," the agent said. "It's up to you."

"A search warrant? Whatever for?"

"We'll be happy to explain while the police conduct the search. Unlock the door and let these officers in."

"You want to search my home?" she said. "I want to call my lawyer."

"That's your prerogative, of course, but open the door, or we'll charge you with obstruction. Then you'll need that attorney. What's it gonna be?"

Joan unlocked the screen door and stepped back as two agents and six police officers poured through the door. She tried to watch where they were going, but the FBI agents guided her into the living room.

"Sit down, Mrs. Chandler," Agent Madison said.

"What is all that barking?" Joan said as she heard dogs running along the side of the house.

"Those are police dogs, ma'am. They're helping us search the grounds," Agent Carson said.

"What are you looking for?" Joan said as her mind raced in frantic circles. Could the dogs smell blood? Surely that was gone by now. Would the police find the attic entrance? Was everything in its proper place?

"We're looking for the remains of Billy Ray Richards and Rachael Chandler. What happened that night, Mrs. Chandler? We know it didn't happen the way you claim. We have Leeann and Tommy Lee Richards in custody. We found their abandoned station wagon. Billy Ray's jacket was still inside. DNA results reveal that Rachael was never inside that car, and that's just the beginning of what we know. This is your opportunity to tell the truth," Agent Madison said.

"I'm calling my lawyer. My telephone is in the kitchen. You're welcome to accompany me, but I'm not saying another word until I speak to my attorney."

She rose from the couch and headed for the kitchen. Though she kept her composure, her heart was thumping, and her mind was spinning. What else did they know? What should she say and not say?

Her hands were shaking as she looked up her attorney's number in her address book. She had to dial twice to get the number right. "Hello, this is Joan Chandler. Is Mr. Carrington in? This is an emergency." She turned her back to the agents. "Yes, I'll hold."

"I'm sorry Mrs. Chandler, but Mr. Carrington is tied up in court."

"I have two FBI agents and six police officers in my house with search warrants. What do I do now?" she said, clutching at her robe. She looked out the window and saw several officers roaming through the gardens.

"I'll get word to him right away."

"Thank you. Have him call me as soon as possible." She turned to the agents and said, "I want to see the warrant."

Agent Madison handed her a folded piece of paper. She opened it and tried to make sense of what she read, but it was difficult to concentrate. There was a paragraph in the middle, though, that caught her attention. It contained a list: receipts, financial records, correspondence, phone bills, and her cell phone along with a host of other items.

"You can't mean to take these things. This is my personal property."

The barking intensified. A few moments later, one of the police officers stepped into the kitchen. "Agent Madison, may I speak with you for a moment?"

Agent Madison nodded to Agent Carson and left the room.

"What's going on?" Joan demanded.

"Just stay calm, Mrs. Chandler. They'll inform us if it's important."

"I want to call my son," she said.

"It's probably best if you wait until we leave," Agent Carson said.

Two officers entered the kitchen with Agent Madison. One of them approached her and said, "Mrs. Chandler, I'm Officer Roberts. We're taking you in for questioning regarding the disappearance of Billy Ray Richards and Rachael Chandler."

"This is ridiculous! Billy Ray Richards kidnapped my granddaughter. You have his accomplices in custody. Why are you questioning me?"

"You have the right to remain silent. Anything you say…"

As the officer read her rights, she zoned out of the conversation. This couldn't be happening. She didn't murder Billy Ray. Should she tell them the truth? How much trouble would she be in? She didn't know what to do. When he finished, she said, "I am innocent, but I won't resist arrest. All I ask is that you allow me to go to the bathroom, and put on some decent clothes."

"Agent Carson will accompany you," Agent Madison said. "She's to remain in your presence every single second. Do you understand? If you do anything unwise, she'll use whatever force is necessary to protect her safety."

"Do I look like I'm going to challenge her?" She lifted her chin and walked towards the staircase. Agent Carson walked directly behind her, and two police officers followed. When she reached the stairs, the agent ascended on her left. She wanted to run, but she kept herself calm. She didn't dare glance to the left where the rocking chair sat in front of the hidden stairway. She turned to the right and upon entering the hallway, she said, "My room is the last door to the left." The police officers waited in the hallway as she and Agent Carson entered her room. Joan went straight to the bathroom, but the agent followed. "Is it too much to ask that I relieve myself in private?"

"I'm sorry, but I have to accompany you," she said. "No exceptions."

"Oh, very well." She lifted her gown and sat on the toilet. Afterwards, she stepped towards the closet.

"Stop," Agent Carson said. "Tell me what you want, and I'll hand it to you."

"This is ridiculous! Hand me those tan pants and that blue blouse." Taking the items from the agent, she stepped back. "I'll take those tan shoes there on the right. My bra and socks are in the bedroom."

When they reentered the bedroom, she pointed to the dresser. "My bra is in the top left-hand drawer." When she had it, she said, "Will you at least turn your back while I dress?"

"No, but you may turn yours."

"I've never been more humiliated in my entire life! Can a private citizen sue the FBI?"

"No, ma'am. Hurry along, please."

Joan thought about her gun, but she knew she didn't dare. Besides, the police might have found it already. She glanced at her desk and saw that the drawers were ajar and several items were missing from the top of it. It made her blood boil, but she didn't say anything. "I want to call my attorney's office to let them know you're taking me in."

"You can call them from the police station. Where are your socks?"

"Middle drawer on the right," she said. She yanked the socks from the agent's hand and sat in the chair to put them on.

A knock sounded at the door. The agent opened it. "She's putting on her shoes."

"When will I get the things you stole from my desk back?" she said, coming to her feet.

The officers came forward. "Let's go, Mrs. Chandler."

* * *

The day went by agonizingly slow. Jack and Stacy were working on an infidelity case, which made up the lion's share of their business. Neither of them enjoyed these types of cases, but someone needed to provide the service, and Jack was very good at getting the proof an innocent mate needed in order to make important decisions.

This particular case involved a young, female elementary school principal who had gotten involved with two male teachers, both of whom were married. Thus far, only one of the wives was aware of her husband's indiscretion. It went against Jack's nature to leave the other wife uninformed, but if the affairs became public knowledge, the school's reputation would suffer, dozens of children would lose their teachers, and the careers of three people would be destroyed. Jack groaned as he thought about it. Why didn't people consider the consequences of their actions?

Stacy's phone rang. She dug it out of her purse and raised a brow. "Hey, Tyler. What's up?" She snapped her fingers and put it on speakerphone.

"I need to see you. Can we meet?"

"What about?" Stacy said.

"Like you don't know? They arrested my mother this morning, and they won't let me near her. Did you have something to do with that?"

"I didn't even know it happened," Stacy said. "Let me make a few phone calls."

"Please, Stacy. I need to know what's going on."

"I'll call you back." She hung up and looked at Jack. "Did you know about this?"

Jack dialed Kevin. When Kevin answered, he said, "I thought you were gonna keep me informed. What the hell happened out there?"

"Good morning to you, too, Jack," Kevin snapped. "For your information, I don't know much yet. What I do know is that the dogs picked up Billy Ray's scent on the dock. They found traces of blood out there. They're combing the property and searching the house now."

"Are you sending divers into the river?" Jack said, his mind spinning with possibilities.

"That'll take some doing. They spotted several gators along the bank, and that's in the daytime. No telling how many there are. We're waiting on a team of dogs that specialize in finding decomposing bodies under water. If he's anywhere in that channel, they'll find him. We're searching the other buildings on the property also. So far, no match for the new kitchen, bath, or furniture she purchased. Nothing looks recently remodeled."

"Can Stacy and I go out and take a look?"

"No," Kevin said, "and that's final."

Jack rolled his eyes. "Have you seen Tyler Chandler?"

"He came down."

"And?"

"And he's not speaking to his mother until I'm damn good and ready," Kevin said. "We know she's lying. We want the truth, and we mean to get it."

"Maybe we can help," Jack said.

"You've already been a great help. You've split this case wide open."

"And I have another idea. I'll call you back," Jack said.

"Wait. I don't want—"

Jack turned to Stacy. "Call Tyler back and see if he'll meet with us. Now wouldn't be too soon."

"What are you doing?"

"I'll explain on the way. Set it up somewhere public, and don't tell him I'm coming."

When Stacy got Tyler on the phone, she said, "Hey, I've got some information to share with you. Where can we meet?"

"Wanna come by my house?"

"How about our usual? Say, thirty minutes?"

"I don't know if I can get a sitter," Tyler said.

"Then bring your son with you. We'll work around it, but I'm not comfortable going out to your house," she said.

"All right. Bravo in thirty minutes. See you there."

Stacy nodded to Jack.

"Good job," Jack said. "Now we'll see if he can shed some light on any of this."

* * *

Jack and Stacy got to the restaurant first. Stacy took a table near the bar, and Jack pulled up a stool. It was doubtful he'd be able to overhear very much, but at least he'd be nearby if the opportunity arose for him to enter the conversation.

"Hey, pretty lady," Tyler said as he swung himself into the chair across from her.

Stacy's breath caught as she was taken again by how attractive he was. "How are you, Tyler?"

"Worried. Why would they arrest my mother?"

"Are you hungry?" She picked up the menu and began glancing through it.

"I'm always hungry," Tyler said.

"You sound like Jack."

"Who's Jack?"

"My boss, remember?"

"You said I'd get to meet him one of these days, but that was before you dumped me."

"Still want to meet him?"

"I wanna know why they arrested my mother."

"Was that a yes or a no on meeting my boss?" she said.

"Let's see what you gotta say first, and then we'll see."

"Let's order an antipasto and some drinks; then we'll get down to business." After they had ordered, she cleared her throat and said, "Here's the thing—"

"Wait," Tyler said. "Before you say anything, have you heard any more from Pamela?"

"I really don't expect to. She made herself perfectly clear."

"I just wondered. Go ahead."

"I've got to ask you a question, Tyler. Did your mom buy a new fishing boat shortly after the kidnapping?"

His eyebrows shot up. "Why?"

She felt the table vibrate as his foot began to bounce. "Look, Tyler, your mom may be in trouble. If you want to help Rachael, you better tell me what you know about the boat."

"Whose side are you on?" he said, scowling darkly.

"Whose do you think?" she said.

"We're talking about my mother here."

"Does it come down to loyalty, Tyler? If it does, I've got news for you. Your mother doesn't give a damn about what matters to you. She's the reason Pamela won't talk to you anymore. She threatened to harm Jacob if she ever talks to you again."

He slammed his fist on the table. "You're lying!"

"Am I? Then how come I know about the argument you had at the dining room table when you and your mother were discussing her adopting Rachael, and you asked how much it was worth to her?"

"Pamela told you that?" he said, looking as if she'd struck him.

"She told my partner that and a whole lot more. If you want to know what she said, then you need to tell me everything you know about that boat."

"You're blackmailing me?" Tyler said.

"No, I'm bartering. You don't have to tell me anything you don't want to, and neither do I. So, decide. Do you want to tell me what you know about that boat, or not?"

"The day Rachael was kidnapped, I wandered around behind the house and down to the river. Our houseboat was tied at the dock, which was very unusual. I'm the only one who takes the houseboat out. The police were still there, so I didn't say anything, but a few days later, when I went back to check on Mom, I noticed that she had a new fishing boat. I was so preoccupied with losing Pamela and Rachael that I forgot to ask about it."

"Is it possible that Billy Ray and Rachael took the fishing boat, and that's why your mother had to replace it?" Stacy said.

"No. Someone had to row out to the boathouse in order to bring the houseboat back to the dock. There's no other way to get back to the dock once they returned the houseboat to the boathouse."

"You're saying there's no way to get to the boathouse except by boat?"

"That's right," Tyler said. "It's up around the bend. You can't see it from the house."

"Couldn't you swim to it?"

"Not with all those gators in the water. It'd be suicide," Tyler scoffed.

"Would Billy Ray know that?"

"He'd have no reason to know about the boathouse. And since the houseboat was still at the dock, he clearly didn't take it, which means the fishing boat had to be at the boathouse at the time of the kidnapping. Even if Billy Ray knew about the boathouse, he'd never swim for it, especially if he had Rachael. He was raised in the South. He's not that stupid."

"So what do you think happened to the original fishing boat?" Stacy said.

"I don't know."

"But you're saying the fishing boat wasn't at the dock the day Rachael was kidnapped because the houseboat was, and that in itself is unusual."

"Yes," Tyler said, though he looked uncomfortable about admitting it.

"Thank you. Now, I'll tell you about your mother and Pamela. I want you to remember that your mother threatened Jacob. If you tell her that you know what transpired between her and Pamela, you'll be putting Jacob's life in danger. Do you understand?"

"I wouldn't do anything to hurt Pamela or Jacob," he said.

"Pamela told my partner that your mother agreed to pay her two hundred and fifty thousand dollars if she broke off all communication with you. Ten thousand dollars a month for two years. I have a copy of the first check she wrote out to her. Wanna see it?"

"Pamela took the money?" Tyler said slouching lower in the chair. "Why would she do that? Why would either of them do that?"

"Your mother was afraid you'd move to Atlanta with Pamela, and that Pamela might talk you into keeping Rachael so that the two of you could provide a home for her, which would interfere with her adoption plans."

"No! Pamela wouldn't accept bribe money. I know she wouldn't."

"Your mother threatened Jacob, and Pamela is afraid of her. Besides, she's not collecting the money anymore. In fact, she only received one check. A few days after Rachael's alleged kidnapping, Joan called her to say that *you* would never have control over Rachael again, so there was no need to continue paying her."

"You're lying! All of this is a lie!"

"She has it all on tape, Tyler. Pamela taped their conversation. My partner heard every word of it."

He sat silent for several seconds and then sighed. "No wonder she won't talk to me."

"The dogs chased Billy Ray's scent to the dock this morning where the police found traces of blood, which they assume is Billy Ray's. Will you testify against your mother if it comes down to it?"

"Testify about what?" Tyler said.

"That you saw the houseboat tied to the dock the day of the alleged kidnapping. I'd never ask you to state anything other than the truth."

"I want to talk to Pamela. I need to know if any of this is true. What's going on, Stacy? What do you know?"

Jack slipped off his stool and stepped over to the table. "Hi, Tyler. I'm Jack Kendall. May I join you? I might be able to shed some light on all of this for you."

"Who the hell are you?" Tyler said.

"That's my boss. You said you wanted to meet him," Stacy said.

Jack held out his hand, "I'm Jack Kendall."

Tyler stared at him and then at Stacy. "Is this a setup?"

Jack withdrew his hand and sat next to Stacy. "No. We want the same things you do. We want to find your daughter and uncover the truth about what happened to her and Billy Ray Richards."

"What does any of this have to do with my mother?" Tyler said.

"We don't know, yet. Like you, we know she bought a new fishing boat shortly after the kidnapping. We have her credit card records to prove it. Who do you think rowed out to get the houseboat? Would your mother do that?"

"No, she'd send Gibbs."

"Who's Gibbs?" Jack said.

"The caretaker. Mr. Gibbs has been there forever, even before my parents bought the place thirty-something years ago. His sister, Regina, moved in about a year ago. She's done the cooking and cleaning ever since Gibbs' scatterbrained daughter, Dillia, ran off and got married. I don't know what that girl was thinking, leaving my mother to take care of that big house all by herself. Not to mention abandoning her son, Jayden. He'd be nearly eight by now."

"Where's Jayden now?"

"With Mr. Gibbs and Regina, I guess. He lives on the property."

"If you're the only one who takes the houseboat out, why would it be at the dock?" Stacy said.

"Mr. Gibbs does maintenance on it from time to time. Maybe that's why it was there. Like I said, I never asked. Is the blood they found the reason they arrested my mother?"

"We assume so," Jack said. "At the very least, they know she lied about what happened. It also seems that your mother made several unusual purchases right after the kidnapping. The police are trying to locate those items. They have warrants and are searching the entire property."

"What kind of items?" Tyler said.

"Did your mother do any major remodeling after the kidnapping?"

"Nothing major. They refinished the gallery floor, I think, and bought a new rug for up there. That's all I noticed. Why?"

"Call me stupid," Stacy said, "but what's a gallery?"

"It's the area at the top of the stairs. There's a seating area up there, a miniature art gallery with portraits of the family going back five generations. Mother is very proud of it," Tyler said.

"Well, apparently she remodeled something," Jack said. "She bought a small set of kitchen cabinets, counter tops, a sink, refrigerator, bathroom fixtures including a toilet, sink, vanity, shower, tile, and plumbing supplies. She also purchased paint, lumber, drywall, and electrical supplies. That sounds like something fairly major to me. She also bought three beds, but the police haven't located any of these items in the house. Do you have any idea where they might be?"

"There are two cabins on the property. Maybe that stuff was for them," Tyler said.

"Still, the timing is odd, don't you think?" Stacy said.

"Maybe she was trying to keep busy."

"But she's not the one who does the work, is she?" Jack said. "What do you think about her bribing Pamela?"

"I want to hear the recording for myself. If Mother did that, then—" Tyler took a deep breath and exhaled. "I don't know what to make of any of this. What's Billy Ray's blood doing on the dock? According to Mother, Billy Ray took Rachael from the garden and ran for the front gate. She never said anything about the dock. If they came by car, he'd have no reason to go down to the river at all."

"Those are good questions," Jack said. "I'll contact Pamela to see if she'll let you hear the recording. Remember though, you can't confront your mother about Pamela because of Jacob. She would never forgive you if you put Jacob in danger."

"I feel like I don't even know my mother right now. How could she do this to me? She knows how much I love Pamela, how broken up I've been. To think that she caused it—"

"Tyler, if she lied about Billy Ray and Pamela, she could have lied about Rachael, too," Stacy said.

"We've got to find my daughter."

"Yes," Stacy said. "That's where your loyalty must lie."

Tyler glanced from Stacy to Jack and nodded.

* * *

Jack waited until they got back in the car to say what was on his mind.

Stacy pulled her seatbelt across her lap and clicked it into place. "Can you believe it? He gave us a huge piece of information. It'll be interesting to hear what Joan says about why she bought that new boat."

"You bargained with Jacob's safety to get that information."

Her smile faded. "You don't think he'll tell his mother, do you? He knows she threatened Jacob."

"Chances are he *will* confront her. Wouldn't you? It's very difficult to be angry with someone and not confront them. What will you say to Pamela, who will worry every moment about what might happen to her son because she trusted me? You stepped out of line on this one, Stacy."

"But look how much he told us."

"Because you manipulated his feelings. You still aren't facing what you've done to Pamela and Jacob. Can you guarantee that Joan won't pay someone to harm Jacob? She can do that from behind bars, you know."

"How can I fix it?" Stacy said. "I didn't mean to put Jacob in danger."

"Yes, you did. You played that card knowing there was a chance he might tell Joan what Pamela said. All you can do is learn from this and not do it again, but I'm not going to let you deny what you did or excuse it away. Your decision could have serious consequences. As investigators, we often learn sensitive information, but we can't always use it. We have to protect the people we serve."

"Pamela wasn't exactly innocent," Stacy scoffed.

"But what about Jacob? Does he deserve to suffer?"

"No."

"Remember that when you inform Pamela that you told Tyler her secret."

Stacy's brows rose. "Me? But I don't even know her."

"Yet you broke my confidence with her and risked the safety of her son. You'll be the one to tell her."

Stacy looked down and bit her lip. "I guess I was bent on getting the information I wanted and didn't stop to think about the cost."

"That's incorrect. You didn't *care* about the consequences. We don't know what Tyler will do, and we certainly can't count on him to testify against his mother. Families have a way of sticking together, regardless of what they do to each other. Unless Joan killed Rachael, I doubt Tyler will turn on her."

"Even though she bribed Pamela to stay away from him?" Stacy said.

"That's a two-edged sword because Pamela took the money. It depends on whose story he believes most, I think, but Pamela holds a bargaining chip as well."

"If she chooses to use it," Stacy said with a nod. "I'm sorry for jumping ship on that one. I should have checked with you first."

"Yes, you should have. I must be able to trust you, Stacy, or I'll have to start hiding things from you, and that won't work."

"It won't happen again. I promise."

"Good. Just remember that we're a team. We're not Lone Rangers out here. Everything we do has consequences."

"I understand, and I'm sorry for blowing it with Tyler. What do we do next?"

"We tell Kevin that we have news, and then we call Pamela."

"Go ahead and call Kevin. I'd like to prepare myself before we call Pamela."

When Kevin answered, Jack said, "You busy right now?"

"Is it worth my time?" Captain Thomas said.

"Oh, yeah."

"Come on down, then. I've got some news for you also."

When Jack and Stacy reached the police station, Kevin ignored them for at least ten minutes while he listened to the person on the other end of the telephone. He grunted several times and took notes. Jack and Stacy glanced at each other and shifted anxiously in their seats. Whatever was going on, it had to do with the case, and it had to be big.

Finally, Kevin banged the receiver on its base and said, "It seems that Mrs. Chandler has been lying since day one. They found Billy Ray's blood in the house, as well as on the dock."

"Let me guess," Jack said. "They found it upstairs on the gallery floor."

Kevin's eyes nearly bugged out of their sockets. "How the *hell* do you know that?"

Jack chuckled. "We've been busy, too."

"I see," Kevin scoffed. "Did you get a confession while you were at it?"

"No, but we learned some interesting information," Jack said.

"Don't just sit there," Kevin snapped. "Spit it out."

Jack nodded towards Stacy. Her eyes widened as she realized he was turning it over to her. She said, "You'll find that they refinished the gallery floor soon after the kidnapping, and the rug up there is new. In fact, I wouldn't be surprised if it's not listed on one of the receipts we gave you from Home Depot. The biggest piece of news is that we're certain Billy Ray didn't leave by boat."

"How could you possibly know that? Mrs. Chandler now claims that her boat went missing at the time of the kidnapping."

"Not at the *time* of the kidnapping, it didn't," Stacy said. "Tyler Chandler, Joan's son, told us that the day of the kidnapping, while the police were still present, he walked down to the river and found the houseboat tied to the dock. They usually store the houseboat in the boathouse, which is up around the river bend. You can't see it from the dock. The only way to reach it is by boat, so if the houseboat was at the dock, the fishing boat was at the boathouse. End of story."

"He couldn't have swum for it with all those gators in the water," Kevin mused. "Especially if he had Rachael in tow. Will he testify to that? Will he testify against his mother?"

"That depends," Jack said. "We have a potential ace up our sleeve, but we have to be careful how we play it."

"What do you mean?" Kevin said.

"We told Tyler about his mother's arrangement with Pamela, and her subsequent claim that he would never have control over Rachael again," Jack said. "He wants to hear the recording for himself."

"So do I," Kevin said.

"Pamela is afraid of Joan," Stacy said, "but it might make the difference about whether or not Tyler will testify."

"What do you suggest?" Kevin asked.

"I don't know yet," Jack said. "We're planning to call Pamela later this afternoon. Where does Mrs. Chandler's case stand?"

Kevin scratched his chin. "It's early yet. If what you say is true, then it seems that Leeann and Tommy Lee are telling the truth about Billy Ray not returning to the car. So far, there's no DNA evidence to support that Rachael Chandler was ever in that car. We're searching for the maid and caretaker now. We haven't been able to locate them."

"You remember Joshua Royce," Jack said. "He's working for Alister, Emerson & Maxwell now. He may be interested in representing Leeann and Tommy Lee Richards. When can he get in to speak with them?" Jack said.

"I'll find out if they're willing to consider a new attorney," Kevin said. "As I said, their cousin was in to see them this morning."

"Their *cousin* is guilty of aiding and abetting fugitives, as well as stealing their property out from under them while they were in hiding on *his* land. I'll be happy to fill you in on Hugh Richards later, but there's a clear conflict of interest there," Jack said.

"Where do you get your information?" Kevin said, shaking his head. "Fine. I'll permit your attorney to see the prisoners, but I want proof of what you just alleged."

"We've got it," Stacy said. "Hugh Richards' son took pot shots at Emily and me with his rifle, so you can add that to the list of offenses if you like."

"I want to speak to Leeann and Tommy Lee before I have Josh go in," Jack said. "I'm sure they're suspicious, and I want them to know that they can trust Josh."

Kevin's eyes narrowed as he leaned back in his chair. "I should've seen that one coming."

As difficult as it was for Jack to keep silent, he waited for Kevin to sort it through.

"Come back in the morning," Kevin said. "I'll take you over."

Jack exhaled, though he hadn't realized he was holding his breath. "Did the dogs turn up anything else?"

"Boy, did they," Kevin said.

"Rachael?" Stacy said.

Kevin glanced from one to the other. "What I'm about to say doesn't leave this room. If I hear one word out there, we're done forever."

They nodded.

"We had one team of dogs on Billy Ray, another on Rachael. We expected them to catch her scent in the house, but they zeroed in on one corner of the gallery and barked their heads off. At first, they thought it was a corner where she'd been sent for "time out," but when they couldn't get the dogs to back away, they searched more carefully. They found a hidden entrance to a third-story attic behind one of the walls. Guess what they found upstairs?"

"Oh, no, don't tell me," Stacy said, covering her face.

Jack gripped the armrests and steeled himself for the gruesome news.

"Wow, for once I've got something you two don't already know. We found the new kitchen, all three beds, the new bathroom—the whole works. That's what she remodeled, or built is more like it. The *second*-floor bedroom that Mrs. Chandler identifies as Rachael's bedroom comes right out of a fairytale magazine, but all the scents in that room are cold. In the attic, however, and in the nursery, they found fresh prints everywhere. She has been keeping Rachael up in the attic, and, judging by the K9 reaction, it hasn't been long since she was there."

"But why would Joan keep her granddaughter in the attic and tell people she was kidnapped?" Stacy said.

"Perhaps she saw something she shouldn't have seen," Jack said.

Kevin nodded. "I want to know where she is now."

"We've got to find Mr. Gibbs," Jack said.

"Who?"

"The caretaker and his sister, Regina," Stacy added. "Tyler says there might be a young boy with them, too," Stacy said. "He's Mr. Gibbs' grandson."

Kevin nodded. "That would explain the other set of prints in the nursery and in the attic as well."

"You'd think they would've turned Mrs. Chandler in," Stacy said. "How could they go along with keeping a child in an attic?"

"It's amazing what people do to one another. Anything else?" Kevin said as if he were suddenly tired.

Jack stood up and motioned to Stacy.

"You two have done excellent work on this," Kevin said. "It's hard to believe that this was recently a cold case. We may not be far from finding that little girl."

"Do you think she's still alive?" Stacy said.

"The prints in the attic indicate she is, or she was until recently," Kevin said. "One thing is abundantly clear. Joan Chandler has a lot of explaining to do."

* * *

Emily greeted Jack and Stacy when they pulled into the driveway. "I got a job today," she said smiling brightly.

"You did? Where?" Stacy said as she stepped out of the car.

"That attorney. You know, Joshua Royce. He called me back today to work in their filing department, which sounds much more fun than being an assistant."

"We should celebrate," Jack said after catching a surprised look from Stacy. "Let's go out for dinner."

"Actually, I cooked for a change. I made fried chicken, black-eyed peas, mashed potatoes, and cornbread. I hope you're hungry."

"Starved," Jack said.

"Sounds good to me, too," Stacy agreed.

Emily beamed with pleasure. "Good. Give me about ten minutes, and I'll have everything on the table." She spun around and skipped back to the house.

Jack raised a brow. "I take it that means Josh decided not to represent the Richards. Too bad. Now I'll have to come up with plan B."

"He's missing out, especially after what happened today," Stacy said. "Wait till he finds out they picked up Joan Chandler."

Jack's cell phone rang. "Uh, I think he just found out. Hey, Josh. What's up?"

Stacy moved closer.

"Yes, we know," Jack said. "It happened this morning." He motioned for Stacy to get back in the car. Once they were inside, he put it on speakerphone. "Stacy's here with me."

"Hey, Josh," Stacy said.

"Hey, Stace. The firm wants to reconsider representing the Richards family. They think it'll produce good media coverage."

"What about Emily? She's pretty excited about her new job. I don't want her losing it," Jack said.

"It's a big firm. She doesn't have to report to me. When can I get in to see Leeann and Tommy Lee?"

"I want a guarantee on Emily first," Jack said.

"I'll do something; you have my word. Now when can I speak with the Richards?"

"I can get you in to see them tomorrow morning. I'll call you when I know what time. They're innocent, Josh. Tommy Lee and Leeann Richards didn't kidnap Rachael Chandler."

"I look forward to seeing proof of that," Josh said.

"Expect my call."

"You're not going to tell him what we know, are you?" Stacy said.

"You heard Kevin. We can't tell anyone what we just learned. It'll come out when it's supposed to. Now let's go celebrate Emily's new job."

* * *

After dinner, when Emily had gone back to the apartment, Jack said, "Now is as good a time as any. Let's call Pamela."

Stacy groaned and rolled her eyes. "I can't believe I did this. Now I have to tell a woman I don't even know that I've potentially ruined her life. Why don't you just shoot me and get it over with?"

Jack couldn't afford to let his emotions get in the way. Stacy created the situation; she had to experience what it cost to get out of it. "I'll get her on the phone and then hand it over to you." He scrolled through his contacts and pushed Pamela's number. A few moments later, she answered. "Hey, Pamela. This is Jack Kendall. I visited with you a while back about the Rachael Chandler kidnapping case."

"I remember," she said, her voice turning instantly cool.

"I'm sorry to bother you this evening, but there have been a few developments I think you should be aware of. Do you have a moment?"

"Jacob, honey, go to your room for a few minutes. I'll come for you when I'm off the phone."

"Yes, Mommy," Jack heard in the background.

"Thank you," she said. "I'm listening."

"First, they took Joan Chandler in for questioning today. I think they might file charges."

"You're kidding me! What for?" Pamela said.

"Suspicion of the murder of Billy Ray Richards. The police found his blood on the dock, which contradicts Joan's story about him taking Rachael from the garden."

"Oh my God. What about Rachael?"

"They're searching her property. It's early yet."

"Wow. She's more dangerous than I thought."

Jack looked up in time to see Stacy grimace. He could only imagine what she must be feeling. "Tyler met with my partner and me. He confirmed that his mother bought a new fishing boat just after the kidnapping."

"Did they leave by boat, then?"

"No. Tyler says the houseboat was at the dock the day of the kidnapping. The fishing boat was at the boathouse," Jack said.

"Oh. Then why did she buy a new boat? I don't get it," Pamela said.

"Neither do we, just yet. The other reason I called is, well, my partner, Stacy is here with me. I'm going to put her on speakerphone."

Stacy flashed pleading brown eyes towards him. When he nodded for her to take over, she made a face and looked away. "Hey, Pamela, this is Stacy."

"Hey," Pamela said, sounding a little wary.

"I'm the one who's been meeting with Tyler," Stacy continued. "We've become friends, so to speak. Well, comfortable enough to talk with one another openly."

"Are you dating?"

"No! No, it's just that I told him what happened between you and Joan, and he's pretty upset with her. He wants to hear the recording you have, so he can be sure that she really did bribe you into staying away."

Silence.

"Pamela?" Stacy said. "Are you there?"

"I trusted you, Jack! You know she threatened Jacob."

"Tyler knows that," Stacy said. "He's not going to do anything to put Jacob in danger."

"No? But you did! Jack, how could you? You gave me your word," Pamela said.

"It was my fault," Stacy said. "Jack told me not to tell him. He trusted me with the information because I'm his partner. I'm the one who blew it, not Jack. Tell me how to fix it, Pamela. I've never done anything like this before, and I want to make it right. I'm really sorry. Tell me what you want me to do."

Jack heard Pamela sigh. "I need to talk to Tyler. He can't confront his mother. If he does, she'll know I told someone, and she'll do something to hurt Jacob."

"He wants to hear the recording," Jack said. "When can we meet?"

"The sooner, the better. Tomorrow," Pamela said.

"We'll set it up," Jack said. "Bring the canceled check and anything else that will prove what Joan said and did. We've got to convince him to stay on your side."

"You've put me in a terrible position. Now, I'll have to move again," Pamela said. "I knew I shouldn't have trusted you."

"It wasn't Jack. It was me. We'll make this right, Pamela. We will," Stacy said.

"You put my child in danger. You can't *fix* it," Pamela said.

"Do you want me to bring Tyler to you?" Jack said. "Or do you want to come here? Tell us how you want to do this, and that's how it'll go down."

"I can't risk having someone Joan knows see us together. I want you to come here. We'll meet somewhere, and then you keep Tyler for a full thirty minutes after I leave, so I know he can't follow me. Agreed?"

"Agreed."

"I'm really sorry," Stacy said.

"You're sorry? Do you have children?"

"I'm not that fortunate," Stacy mumbled.

"Well, if you did, you'd know that sorry isn't enough. Jack, you come alone. That's the deal."

Jack cringed as Stacy hung her head. "You got it," he said.

"I want to hear you set this up. Get Tyler on the phone, but don't tell him I'm on the line."

"Good idea. That way you'll know that we've been honest about everything we've said."

"Exactly. Now get Tyler on the phone."

"Hang on." Jack dialed Tyler and prayed he would answer. After several rings, Tyler picked up, and Jack pointed to Stacy.

"Hey, Tyler. It's Stacy."

"Hey, pretty lady. What's happening?"

"I've got Jack on the line with us. You met him the other night. We're calling to tell you that Pamela is willing to meet with you so that you can hear the recording of her conversation with Joan. Her biggest concern, of course, is Jacob's safety. You haven't told your mother about any of this, have you?"

"I already told you, I wouldn't do anything to jeopardize Jacob's safety. I love that little boy as if he were my own. The fact that Mother threatened him makes me sick! This whole thing with Pamela has turned me inside out. I wish I could tell her how much I love and miss her. I'd do anything if we could be together again. I'd never let anyone near Jacob again, including my mother."

"I'm glad to hear that, Tyler. Can you get away tomorrow?" Stacy said.

"I'd drop everything this minute if she wanted me to."

"What if Jack picks you up at ten o'clock tomorrow morning, and then the two of you ride over together? You can meet with Pamela and drive back."

"No offense, but I'd rather drive over there with you. I don't know Jack," Tyler said.

Jack motioned for Stacy to indicate they both would go.

"We'll both come," Stacy said.

"All right. Can't we go any earlier?"

"I've got an appointment at eight o'clock," Jack said. "We'll come by as soon as it's over."

"Fine. Any news on my mother?"

"They're still trying to piece things together. We'll see you in the morning," Jack said.

"Can't wait," Tyler said and hung up.

"Pamela, are you still there?" Jack said.

"Yes. It's hard to believe he still cares so much. It makes me feel like I should've held on to what we had."

"It's not too late," Stacy said.

"Call me when you get into town, Jack," Pamela said.

After Pamela had hung up, Stacy headed for the door.

"Hey," Jack said. "How do you think that went?"

"I think I shouldn't have betrayed your trust. I think that Pamela has a right to be upset." She paused and then turned towards the refrigerator and pulled out a beer. "Want one?" He shook his head. "I also wonder what it would be like to have someone love me like that. I'm feeling lots of things, and none of them are making me feel very good right now."

"Would it help to know that I'm proud of the way you handled the call?"

"You mean I grovel well?"

"You didn't grovel. You owned up to making a bad judgment call, and you did what you could to make it right. Only people of quality and integrity are willing to do that. We all make mistakes. What matters is what we do once we've made them."

"How is it that you always make me feel better?" she said with watery eyes.

He opened his arms, and she stepped into them. It had been a long time since he'd hugged Stacy. He'd forgotten the scent of her strawberry shampoo and the feel of her firm, full body. He cared for her deeply. He hadn't enjoyed making her face the mistake she'd made, yet he knew it was the right thing to do. He felt sure she'd think twice about breaking his confidence in the future.

She pulled away with a sniff. "How do I find love like that?"

"I've been asking myself the same question," he said. "Let's just concentrate on finding Rachael right now."

"See you in the morning," she said. "I can't wait to meet Pamela so that she can hate me in person."

"Uh, she doesn't want to see you. Remember?"

"And Tyler's not hot on seeing you, either. We make a good team, don't we?" She slipped out the door before he could reply.

* * *

Jack and Stacy sat down on one side of the table and waited for them to bring in Tommy Lee. There were others in the room, talking low, and laughter rang out here and there. Stacy looked tense and rigid as she glanced around; it was her first time visiting a prisoner.

Jack watched as two officers led Tommy Lee through a door and to the table. His hands were cuffed, and his eyes looked weary.

"You got fifteen minutes," one of the guards said as he walked away.

"Hey, Tommy Lee," Jack said. "It's taken longer than I thought to get in to see you, but we've been working on your case non-stop. A lot of things are happening."

"I heard they arrested that Chandler woman. Is that true?" Tommy Lee said.

"Yes."

"They find Billy Ray yet?"

"They're in the process of searching her property," Jack said. "I hear your cousin, Hugh Richards, has been in to see you. You've also met with a public defender. Is that right?"

"Yep. Don't trust neither of 'em. Hugh's more worried about me tellin' the police that he let me stay on his land than he is about gettin' me out of jail. He wants me to say that he didn't know we was there, which makes us guilty of trespassin' and who knows what else."

"Breaking and entering, and perjury for starters," Jack said. "If you follow his advice, you're more likely to stay *in* jail than get out."

"I knew it! I oughta wring his scrawny neck," Tommy Lee said. "I should've known he was lookin' out for hisself!"

"That's all right. He'll have his hands full defending himself soon enough."

Tommy Lee chuckled. "Ya know, if I'm not careful, I might just like you."

"Well, I sure as hell don't like being on your bad side," he said, rubbing his jaw.

"Sorry about that."

Jack saw the twitch of Tommy Lee's lip and doubted he was sorry at all. "We may have another legal option for you. Stacy and I have a friend who works for a big law firm in town. His firm is interested in the media exposure your case is generating, and they may agree to represent you for free. Are you willing to talk with them?"

"Everybody's in it for somethin'."

"There's one thing you can count on with Alister, Emerson & Maxwell; they won't take your case unless they think they can win it," Stacy added.

"You talk to Leeann yet?" Tommy Lee said.

"Not yet," Jack said.

"I don't trust none of them people, but I'm gonna trust you, Jack. If it weren't for you, we'd still be sleepin' in that cold, dark cave, and Mrs. Chandler would still be prancin' around in that big fancy house of hers. I want the truth. I wanna know what happened to my brother and my niece. I want justice! If you think this highfalutin' lawyer friend of yers can make that happen, then I'm willin' to cooperate."

Jack nodded. "I'll let him know. I'll give you the same advice I gave you last time. Tell the truth, Tommy Lee. Tell it all. Hold nothing back."

"Even about Hugh knowin' we was on his land?" Tommy Lee said.

"Do you want to stay in jail for breaking and entering? Because Hugh is clearly willing to pin that on you," Jack said.

"What penalty is he facin'?"

"He'll probably lose his license to practice law."

Tommy Lee winced. "Sounds like a hefty price to pay for helpin' us."

"Who was he helping when he stole your huntin' camp out from under you?" Stacy said with a raised brow. "And if I remember right, he has plans to take your homes next January and hand them over to Clint and Rocky."

Tommy Lee's nostrils flared. "I forgot about that. If me and Leeann gotta face what we done, then Hugh's gotta face what he done, too."

"If you need reinforcement," Stacy said, "just think of Clint Richards taking pot shots at me and Emily with his rifle, and then ordering her to get off *his* land while he pointed a shotgun in her face. That ought to keep you hot enough to tell the truth. It makes me mad as hell every time I think of it."

"That boy needs to be turned over someone's knee. That's what he needs," Tommy Lee said. "As for his father, we Richards got our own ways of dealin' with each other. No matter what the law does, I'll get my licks in. Don't you worry about that."

"He's an attorney. Hugh knew full well what he was doing," Jack said.

"Me, Leeann, and Billy Ray ain't done nothin' but try to give our Rachael a home where she feels loved. Her daddy don't want her. You should see the way he treats her. Tyler went off and left her the day her momma died, and didn't even speak to her at the funeral. Not only that, he had the nerve to bring hisself a new woman to his own wife's funeral. That boy's lucky Billy Ray didn't take him out right then and there. That Chandler family don't know nothin' about treatin' folks right. All we wanted was to get Sarah's baby away from them people and love her like she deserves."

"Tell the attorney every bit of this Tommy Lee, but make sure you tell the truth. All this will be over before you know it. I'll let Josh know that you'll meet with him. If you feel comfortable, then let them represent you. They'll do a much better job than Hugh or any public defender; I promise you that. After all, their reputation is on the line. These attorneys normally charge somewhere between two hundred and fifty to five hundred dollars an hour, so if they're willing to represent you for free, jump on it."

Tommy Lee whistled. "Lord have mercy. Who can afford that kind of money?"

"Mrs. Chandler, for one. You'll need that kind of firepower to go up against her team of lawyers. I'm telling you what they charge because

I want you to value what they're offering you. The charges against you are no joke."

"Why you helpin' us?" Tommy Lee said, his eyes squinting into narrow slits. "We ain't yer kin."

"Because Emily won our hearts and because we want to find Rachael and Billy Ray. We want you and Leeann to return to a normal life and see justice done. All those reasons and more," Jack said as he stood up. "It may not all have a happy ending, but we'll do the best we can."

"If yer referring to Billy Ray, I done accepted that he ain't comin' home. I just wanna find 'im," Tommy Lee said. "Tell Leeann I said to hang tough."

"Will do."

"I mean it. You tell 'er I said to hang tough."

Stacy nodded and followed Jack out of the visitation room.

* * *

The meeting with Leeann Richards had been brief, and though she had said she understood what to expect, Jack wasn't sure that she did. He could see that she hadn't been sleeping well. The year she'd spent in hiding had left dark shadows beneath her eyes. He doubted she'd had any real sleep since the night Billy Ray went missing. He felt sorry for her and hoped that her ordeal would soon be over. Stacy had been a huge comfort to Leeann. Her soothing words seemed to calm her in a way his logic and reason could not.

When they had risen to leave, Leeann grabbed onto Stacy's hand and pleaded for them to look after Emily. Again, Stacy reassured her, but it was when she remembered to add Tommy Lee's encouragement to hang tough that Leeann's countenance changed. She dropped Stacy's hand, straightened her shoulders, and said, "I will. I won't give up." It was odd. Perhaps it was some form of family code, but whatever it was, it had helped to strengthen Leeann, and he was glad to see it.

Jack turned his attention to Stacy as she played a verbal "what if" game with Tyler, which proved to be incredibly revealing indeed. She asked question after question, which Jack would have never gotten away with, but Tyler gave her every bit of the information she requested. It was amazing. From what he gathered, if Tyler was convinced that Joan really did bribe Pamela into breaking off their relationship, he wouldn't be very forgiving, not when Joan had known how badly he missed her, and how hard it had been on him to lose Sarah, Rachael, *and* Pamela, all within a few short weeks of each other. Stacy asked what he would do if they learned that Joan had killed Billy Ray. Tyler laughed and said she might be mean, but it wasn't in her to commit murder. She was certainly capable of hiring someone else to do it, but she wouldn't kill anyone herself. When she asked what he'd do if they found out that someone had killed Rachael, he said he'd make the guilty pay, no matter who they were.

Jack took all of this in and decided that Tyler was levelheaded, but he had a vindictive streak that deserved cautious attention. Stacy needed to be wary of telling him too much. He meant to tell her that at the first opportunity.

Sometime later, while Tyler filled up the gas tank, Jack warned her to be careful not to push too far or reveal too much, and then he called Pamela. After getting directions about where to meet, he asked where he should leave Stacy.

Pamela sighed loudly in his ear. "You can bring her. I believe she's sorry for what she did. We all make mistakes."

"Thanks, Pamela. Stacy is a good one to have on your side; believe me," Jack said.

A few minutes later, they pulled through the entrance of the Atlanta Botanical Gardens and followed the narrow road up to the visitor's center. Once they had parked, they walked together into the visitor's center and climbed the stairs to the second-floor balcony. Jack caught

Stacy's eye as Tyler bounded up the stairs and then waited impatiently for them to catch up.

The balcony was lovely, though no one took any time to look out the windows, which overlooked the fabulous gardens. Instead, Jack led them to the left, to the last quiet grouping of tables where Pamela stood waiting. Jack didn't know what type of greeting they'd receive, but it wasn't the one that occurred. Pamela ran forward and fell into Tyler's arms and a kiss that lasted several seconds.

Stacy looked as surprised as Jack felt. After a few moments, they pulled apart, both of them smiling the silly smile of someone madly in love. Jack gestured towards the chairs. "Shall we?"

Tyler and Pamela held hands and couldn't take their eyes off each other.

"I see that you're happy to be reunited," Jack said. "Perhaps we can conclude our business quickly, and then the two of you can talk privately. Agreed?" They nodded. "All right then. Pamela, did you bring a copy of the check?"

That sobered the group.

"I did."

"Why didn't you tell me?" Tyler said as the light in his eyes darkened with pain.

"You knew she talked to me privately. I told you I understood what you meant about her using money to get what she wants. You never asked for details. I assumed you didn't want to know," Pamela said.

"It wasn't that. I was just so relieved that you were giving me another chance, I didn't think to ask," Tyler said. "Why did you take the money?"

"I was afraid for Jacob. Once she threatened him, I knew that taking the money would keep me from giving in to what *I* wanted for myself. If he was in danger, I knew I wouldn't give in."

"What about now?" Tyler said.

"Joan said that you'd never have control over Rachael again. It was creepy, Tyler. Like she *knew* what had happened to her. Like she wasn't coming back. I'm afraid of your mother. I don't want her knowing that I saw you today. She might hurt Jacob."

"She won't touch Jacob. I'll testify against her if it comes down to that. Let me hear the recording."

Pamela played the recording.

Tyler stiffened, as did Stacy, at the smug tone in Joan's voice. She didn't sound like a grieving grandmother; she sounded cold and calculating. There was little doubt that she knew *something*.

"Did you mean what you said, Tyler?" Jack said. "Are you willing to testify against your mother if it becomes necessary in order to protect Pamela and Jacob, and to get to the truth about what happened to Rachael?"

"What do you mean? What do you think happened to Rachael?" he said.

"I don't know yet, but we need to know where you stand."

Tyler glanced at Pamela whose eyes asked the same question. "If mother is lying, I won't protect her. I love you, Pamela. I want a future with you and Jacob and my kids."

"Both of them?" Pamela asked.

"Yes, God willing, if Rachael is still alive."

"Your words are nice, but I'm not making any promises. Joan is your mother. I don't want her anywhere near Jacob. I'll never trust her. Swear to me you won't tell her you've seen me today, or that I've let you hear that conversation. Swear it!"

"I won't tell her, Pamela. I swear it! Tell me there's still a chance for us. Just tell me there's a chance."

"I'm not going to give you false hope, Tyler. I obviously still have feelings for you, but I have to put what's best for Jacob first. He can't protect himself. That's my job, and come hell or high water, I intend to do it. This is the last time I ever intend to see you. My mind is made up. You need to accept that and move on."

Tyler sighed. "As much as I don't want to hear that, you being a good mother is one of the things I love about you."

Jack rose from his chair. "Why don't Stacy and I take a walk and give you a few minutes alone?"

The silly smiles returned.

"We'll be back in fifteen or twenty minutes. Do you care if I leave my jacket and notepad here, or are you going to be walking around?"

"We'll stay here," Pamela said. "I can't risk being seen by anyone we know."

"Will you go already?" Tyler said, pulling Pamela onto his lap for a kiss.

"Don't forget that you're in public over here," Jack said with a chuckle.

As he and Stacy walked away, she said, "I'd be feeling like a complete idiot right now if I had gone to Tyler's house like he wanted me to."

He wrapped his arm around her shoulder and squeezed. "But you, my dear, are no idiot."

* * *

Tyler stared out the window, resisting Stacy's attempts to draw him into conversation. He revealed only that Pamela hadn't changed her mind; this was a one-time visit.

Jack was grateful when his cell phone rang because the tension in the silence was palpable. "Hey, you. What's cookin'?"

"It's Captain Thomas to you on this call. We found the remains of what we believe is Billy Ray's body this morning."

"Hold on a second." He pulled to the side of the interstate, slowed, and came to a stop.

"What's wrong?" Stacy said.

"Be right back." He stepped out of the truck and shut the door just as a semi-truck whizzed by. Once it passed, he crossed in front of the vehicle and climbed up the embankment to escape the noise.

"Where the hell are you, Kendall?"

"On the interstate. I had to get out of the truck in order to talk. "Tell me what you found."

"It can wait until you come in."

"Tell me now," Jack said. "My heart is beating a thousand times a minute."

"It's hard to hear you, so I'll make this quick. The dogs went crazy when they checked out the boathouse. It took some doing, but they recovered the missing fishing boat and partial human remains. The gators got most of him, but there were bits of clothing wrapped around what looks to be an arm and a section of torso."

"I'm not looking forward to telling Emily that," Jack said. "When will they know for sure if it's Billy Ray?"

"The material matches the description Leeann gave of what Billy Ray was wearing the night he went missing."

Jack plugged his ear to block out the din of the traffic. "None of this makes sense. Why would Joan claim that Billy Ray kidnapped Rachael?"

"I can't hear you, Kendall. Call me back when you can talk."

"I—" He scowled at his phone. How was he supposed to pretend that everything was fine? He skidded down the hill and stepped back onto the road. When the traffic cleared, he got back in the truck.

"What was that about?" Stacy said.

"News on one of our cases. We can talk about it later."

Stacy's eyes narrowed. "Which case?"

"We only have two." He kept his eyes on the road and refused to make eye contact. "So, how did it go with you and Pamela?" he said.

"I just want this thing over with so we can be together," Tyler said. "She wouldn't say it, but I think she wants that, too. You saw how she was with me, but that won't happen as long as I can't confront Mother and get to the bottom of whatever happened between them.

I promised Pamela I wouldn't tell her about the recording. She'd just deny it anyway. So where does that leave me?"

"Let's see how everything plays out. If it's meant to be, love will find a way," Jack said.

"That's the most romantic thing I've ever heard you say," Stacy said. "Can I borrow your phone?"

"No," he said, knowing she wanted to see his call log. "Yours is in your purse."

She rolled her eyes. "Thanks. I forgot."

Jack was grateful when everyone grew silent once more.

* * *

"Well?" Stacy said as soon as Tyler stepped out of the truck.

Jack backed up his truck and headed down Tyler's long driveway, superficially aware of the gravel beneath his tires and the bumps in the ground. "They found Billy Ray, or at least part of him."

Stacy wrinkled her nose. "Where?"

"Submerged in the missing fishing boat."

"How can that be? Tyler said the houseboat was tied up at the dock."

"Kevin said the fishing boat sank in front of the boathouse."

"Wait, we gotta work this out. If Billy Ray took the fishing boat, how did they get the houseboat?"

"It's pretty clear to me," Jack said.

"Tyler's lying," they said at the same time.

"Billy Ray took the fishing boat, so Joan bought a new one," Jack said.

"But why make up the lie about him running back to the car with Rachael and say that she was kidnapped?"

Jack scratched his jaw, which was now dark with stubble. "Maybe Joan decided to skip the adoption process all together."

"But what kind of life would that be for Rachael? She couldn't take her out in public or put her in school. When would she play with other children? That's so screwed up."

"Let me call Kevin back. Maybe he has more information." He tapped the steering wheel and waited for Kevin to answer.

"Captain Thomas here."

"It's Jack. I can talk now. I've got Stacy with me."

"I don't have any more to tell you, except that there will be a hearing for Joan Chandler tomorrow. Now that they've found Billy Ray, her attorney is clamoring for us to release her."

"Why would they let her go?" Jack said.

"They're arguing that if Billy Ray rowed out to the boathouse, then, obviously, Joan didn't kill him."

"Have you talked to Mr. Gibbs and his sister yet?" Jack said, his mind grasping for something—anything—he had missed.

"There's no sign of anyone else staying on the property."

"I wonder if Tyler knows where Mr. Gibbs went," Stacy said.

"If you think he'll tell you, it's worth asking," Kevin said.

"Tyler tells Stacy anything she asks," Jack scoffed. "It's disgusting."

"You're just jealous," Stacy teased.

"Anything else?" Kevin said, his tone signaling his impatience.

"Can't you charge Joan with kidnapping? You have proof that she kept Rachael in the attic and lied about Billy Ray," Jack said.

"We're working on that, but Tyler would have to press charges. Think you can accomplish that little miracle before tomorrow's hearing?"

"What time's the hearing?"

"Come on, Kendall. You said yourself it's unlikely he'd testify against his own mother."

"What time's the hearing?" Jack pressed.

"Nine o'clock."

"Can I tell him about the attic?"

Silence.

"If you want him to press charges, he has to know the truth," Jack said.

"All right. You can tell him. Any woman who could do what she's done isn't safe out in society. I want to keep her locked up as much as you do."

"All right then," Jack said. "Start praying for a miracle."

* * *

The porch light burned brightly when Jack and Stacy pulled up to Tyler's trailer. He immediately came outside, picked up a duffle bag, and walked over to the truck. "I got the flashlights," he said as he climbed into the passenger's seat next to Stacy. When they got on the main road, he said, "You gonna tell me where we're going?"

"We've got a lot of information to share with you. You ready for it?" Jack said.

"Rachael isn't dead, is she?"

"We don't know yet, but the police found evidence that she was being held somewhere against her will. At least, until recently. We want to take you there. We're hoping you can tell us something the police might have overlooked."

"I *knew* Billy Ray had her. I'm gonna kill that son of a bitch!"

"It wasn't Billy Ray. He's dead, Tyler. The police found his body submerged inside your mother's missing fishing boat, which sank in front of the boathouse."

"But that's impossible. The houseboat was at the dock the day Billy Ray took Rachael. He *couldn't* have taken the fishing boat. That's a physical impossibility. You can't get to the boathouse without a boat."

"They found his body, Tyler, or what's left of it."

"But Mother said Regina saw him take Rachael back to the car. She shot at them. None of this makes sense!"

Jack was watching Tyler's reactions. He seemed genuinely confused, and he was sticking to his story about the houseboat. "The police found the abandoned station wagon, and it had a bullet hole in the fender. According to Leeann and Tommy Lee, someone shot at them while they were waiting for Billy Ray, which is why they drove off. They waited down the road, but he never came back to join them."

"Doesn't the bullet hole prove that Mother is telling the truth?"

"Only that someone shot at the car; not that Billy Ray and Rachael got in it. The police found Billy Ray's jacket inside the car, but there's no DNA evidence to show that Rachael was ever inside that car."

"Why would Regina lie?" Tyler said.

"You've said yourself that your mother pays people to do and say exactly what she wants them to," Stacy said. "Besides, what woman in her right mind would shoot at a car with a child inside it?"

"You have a point there," Tyler said, "but it's gonna take a lot more than a bullet hole to convince me that Mother's lying."

"Tyler, do you know where Mr. Gibbs and his sister went?" Jack said.

"What do you mean? You can find Mr. Gibbs in his cabin. His sister lives in the one nearby."

"The police searched the cabins. They're both empty."

"Mr. Gibbs has lived in that cabin his entire life. He wouldn't leave." Jack turned onto the Trace Parkway.

Tyler gripped the door handle. "We're headed to Mother's house, aren't we?"

"You can show us Mr. Gibbs' cabin. Maybe the police searched the wrong one."

"There are only two cabins, Jack. Didn't the police question him when they arrested Mother?"

"No," Jack said.

"What about Regina?"

"They haven't been able to locate either one of them," Stacy said.

"Maybe they're afraid. Maybe they went away for a while.

I know where Mr. Gibbs keeps his important paperwork. Maybe we can figure out where they went and get them to come back to testify on Mother's behalf."

"Maybe so," Stacy said. "Let's hope for the best."

It was quiet but tense inside the confines of the truck. When they had driven down the tree-lined driveway, Tyler told them to park outside the gate.

"Wow, it's some kind of dark out here," Stacy said as Tyler fished the flashlights out of his duffle bag.

"Especially when it's overcast like this," Tyler said. "Watch where you walk. The path is uneven in places."

Yellow crime tape barred the gate, but they easily maneuvered around it and headed towards the house, which loomed large in the distance. Jack felt his skin crawl. He was glad to have Tyler to guide them. They turned towards the left, away from the house, and followed a path through the gardens and into the woods. Stacy stayed close. They had to move quickly to keep up with Tyler.

When they came to the cabin, Tyler trotted up the stairs and knocked on the door. "Mr. Gibbs, open up. It's me, Tyler." He knocked again. "Mr. Gibbs, open up." When no one answered, he slid his fingers along the top of the doorframe. When he located the key, he unlocked the door and turned on the lights. "Mr. Gibbs?" He ducked into the kitchen and then the bedroom. The bookshelves were bare. The cabin was vacant.

"I can't believe it. He's gone," Tyler said. "Let's check Regina's cabin." He switched off the light, returned the key, and then jogged along the path through the woods to another cabin. He was already inside when Jack and Stacy caught up. It, too, was vacant.

"I wonder if they had a family emergency," Tyler said. Has anyone checked the hospitals?"

"They wouldn't move out for a medical emergency unless it was for a family member out of state," Jack said.

"What does my mother say?"

"We don't know. Let's go to the house," Jack said. "There's something there I want to check."

"Follow me," Tyler said.

Jack patted his waistband to be sure that his gun was secure, and then he grabbed Stacy's hand. He didn't trust Tyler, but he didn't distrust him either. He seemed genuinely distressed that the cabins were empty.

Stacy gripped the back of Jack's shirt as they climbed the porch steps and stood at the front door of the house. "You grew up here?"

"Huge, isn't it? I always liked the yard more than the house. I had the best time building tree houses and forts and playing on the river."

Crime tape barred the front door.

"Let's go around to the servant's entrance." Tyler trotted down the stairs, through the gardens, and around the house to another entrance. Jack and Stacy followed him through the butler's pantry and into the kitchen.

"Wow," Stacy said as she flashed her light around. "Your house is beautiful."

"It's not my house," Tyler said. "What do you want to check?"

"Take us to the gallery, but keep the lights off," Jack said. "I don't want to announce our presence, just in case the police decide to show up."

"This way," Tyler said as he headed down the hall.

"This staircase reminds me of *Gone with the Wind*," Stacy whispered as she followed Jack up the stairs.

When they got to the top, Jack flashed his light around, looking for the most likely corner. He noticed the rug and wondered if it would be wise to mention finding Billy Ray's blood up here, but he decided to wait until after they checked the attic.

"What are you looking for?" Tyler said.

"Just a second." He flashed the light along the walls. Spotting the rocking chair in the corner, he walked over to it. "Stacy, come hold your light." He pulled the chair away from the wall and felt along the crack.

"What are you doing?" Tyler said.

Jack found the latch and slid the panel back, revealing the staircase.

"What the hell? I never knew that was there!" Tyler said.

"How did you?" Tyler said. Pushing ahead, he located the light switch, flipped it on, and climbed the steps. He opened the door at the top of the stairs and walked in. Jack and Stacy followed. "Oh my God. There's a whole apartment up here. Someone's been living up here."

"Let's check the bedrooms," Jack said.

Tyler stepped into the first room, a bedroom with a twin bed and a small dresser. "Nothing here."

Jack and Stacy entered the next room and reported the same. They joined Tyler in the third bedroom, arriving as he reached for something from under the bed.

A choked cry came from his throat. "This is Rachael's teddy bear. Find the light. Turn on the damn lights!"

Jack and Stacy shined their flashlights at the ceiling, and then Jack looked for a lamp, but there wasn't one. "Tyler, there aren't any lights in here."

"What do you mean? This is Rachael's teddy bear!" Tyler flashed his lights along the wall and then stepped back into the hallway. "Check for lights, everybody. There have to be lights in here somewhere."

Jack and Stacy split up. She checked the bathroom. "Jack, there's a nightlight in here but no overhead lights at all."

"Check for nightlights, Tyler." Jack went back into Rachael's room. "There's a nightlight in Rachael's room."

"There's one in the living room, too," Tyler said.

"There's one in the kitchen," Stacy said, "but no overhead lights in here either. Oh my God, Jack! They made that child live in the dark, and it's freezing in here! Check for heating vents."

"What's going on, Jack? What do you know?" Tyler said.

A quick walkthrough revealed no heating or air-conditioning vents.

"I can't even imagine how hot it must have been in the summertime," Jack said, "or how cold it must have gotten in the winter. It gets down into the teens!"

"At least she had a fireplace," Stacy said, "but there'd be no way to keep cool in the heat."

"What are you saying, Jack? That mother kept Rachael up here? I don't believe it! Rachael may have played up here, but there's no way she lived up here. That's not possible!"

"The police found Rachael's prints all over the place—fresh prints, Tyler. Rachael wasn't kidnapped by Billy Ray; Joan was keeping her here until recently."

"But why would she lie? Why make me worry like this?"

"It explains why she told Pamela that you would never have control over Rachael again. She knew because she was keeping her away from you," Stacy said.

Tyler pressed his hands to the side of his head as if it might explode. "How could Mother do this to me? How could she do it to Rachael? Where is Rachael now?"

"We don't know. Let's go back downstairs," Jack said.

They closed the attic door and descended the stairs. When they reached the gallery, Jack closed the sliding door and pushed the chair back into place. "There's more, Tyler."

His eyes looked haunted, and he stiffened. "Tell me everything."

"They found traces of Billy Ray's blood up here in the gallery."

His shoulder slumped downward as if he'd been struck with a cane. "She killed him?"

"We don't know, but something nefarious happened up here, and it wasn't what she told the police. We're still trying to piece it together, but we need to talk to Mr. Gibbs and his sister. Do you have any idea where they might have gone?"

"I think Regina moved here from Chicago. That's all I know."

Tyler sank to his knees, holding the teddy bear against his chest. "I can't believe she's been here the whole time! How could she do this to me?" His shoulders began to shake as he choked back tears.

"I'm so sorry, Tyler," Stacy said, dropping to the floor beside him. He clung to her and buried his face against her shoulder, crying for several seconds before he pulled away.

"I'm sorry," he sniffed. "It's just that I feel so betrayed. How could she see me struggle day after day and keep Rachael locked in that attic? What kind of person does that?" He rose to his feet, sniffed, and wiped his eyes with the back of his arm. "What's next?"

"Can we go out to the river?" Jack said.

"Is it safe?" Stacy said. "What about the alligators?"

"It's safe on the dock," Tyler said.

"Jack, why don't we come back in the daytime?" she said.

"You can wait in the car if you want," Jack said. He knew she was frightened, but he wanted to see the layout for himself. Kevin would be none too happy about them coming out here, so he had to make it worth it.

"Like I'm really gonna do that," she scoffed.

Tyler started down the stairs. "I've been out at night a million times. I've never seen a gator on the dock."

"Come on," Jack said, urging her after Tyler.

They left the house through the same entrance and wound their way around the back of the house and down to the river.

Stacy clung to Jack's arm. "I don't like this, Jack."

He patted her hand. "Don't worry. We'll be fine."

When they got to the dock, Tyler shined his light into the water. "Here's the new fishing boat. This is where she always keeps it." Stacy stayed back, but Jack stepped forward. Tyler aimed his light along the water's edge. "See those red dots? Those are gators. The boathouse is up that way, around that thick mass of trees. As you can see, there's no way anyone could swim from here with all those gators in the water."

"Let's go, Jack," Stacy said, her voice rising with anxiety.

"I've seen enough," he said.

Tyler nodded. "If Billy Ray was bleeding before he got down here, it's a wonder he made it as far as the boathouse. Those gators can smell blood a mile away."

Jack froze for a second and then looked back at the fishing boat.

"What is it?" Tyler said.

"Nothing. Let's go."

They followed Tyler up to the garden and along the path towards the gate. Jack helped Stacy maneuver through the crime tape, handed her his flashlight, and crawled through after her. Once they were back inside the truck, Jack turned to Tyler. "There's a good chance they'll release your mother tomorrow based on the fact that they found Billy Ray's body. The defense will claim that since he rowed out to the boathouse, she clearly didn't kill him." Tyler looked away. "The Feds want to charge her with kidnapping," he added, "but we need your support to make it stick. You're the one who has to charge her, Tyler. Are you willing?"

"There's no excuse for what she's done!"

"Do you think it had anything to do with avoiding the adoption proceedings?" Jack pressed.

"But why do that? I was gonna let her adopt Rachael," Tyler said.

"Clearly, she thought Pamela was a threat. Maybe she thought you might keep Rachael and make a family together," Stacy said.

"We might have, but she destroyed that possibility, too. Didn't she?"

"Let's go back to Billy Ray," Jack said. "I don't believe he rowed out to the boathouse. I think it went down another way."

"I know. I've already thought it through."

"What do you mean?" Stacy said.

"If there was blood in the house and on the dock, they probably killed

Billy Ray inside and then rowed him out to the boathouse."

"Right," Tyler said, "and then they sank the fishing boat, and Mr. Gibbs brought the houseboat back to the dock. That's the only scenario that works."

Stacy nodded. "So that's why they refinished the upstairs floor and bought the new rug."

"Exactly," Jack said. "Now, what about your mother? Are you willing to press kidnapping charges and help us find your daughter?"

"What time is the hearing?"

"Nine o'clock, but we want you to meet with Captain Thomas before the hearing. Besides pressing kidnapping charges, we need you to tell him about the houseboat being at the dock the day of the alleged kidnapping, and your theory about how it got there."

"Like I said, there's only one way it could have gone down," Tyler said.

"Besides," Stacy said, "if Billy Ray had taken her fishing boat, wouldn't she have reported it to the police?"

Tyler stared at Jack for several seconds. "Mother will never forgive me."

Stacy took hold of his hand. "Tyler, do you care if she forgives you?"

Tyler opened the truck door and got out. He looked down at Rachael's teddy bear, which he still gripped in his left hand. "Where do you want me to meet you tomorrow morning?"

"I'll pick you up at seven o'clock," Jack said.

"I don't know what I'll say, but I'll say something," Tyler said.

* * *

"You did what?" Kevin yelled into the phone.

"You got your miracle and more. I'd say the end justifies the means," Jack said.

"I'm going to pretend you didn't just say that. I'm tempted to throw your ass in jail. Don't you ever listen?"

"You said you wanted Tyler to press kidnapping charges. Well, he is, and we figured out how to prove the murder charge, too. I'm bringing Tyler to meet with you at seven thirty tomorrow morning. See if you can calm your temper enough to listen to what he has to say."

He disconnected the call and started pacing. In all the years Jack had known and enjoyed pestering Kevin, this was the first time he had hung up on him in anger. There was too much on the line to play silly games. He just hoped Tyler carried through on what he said he'd do.

He grabbed a cold beer out of the fridge and headed for his bedroom. It was going to be a long night, and he still had to figure out how to tell Emily they'd found her father, or pieces of him, in the river outside Joan Chandler's mansion where she likely had her caretaker dump him. What words could he possibly speak to break that kind of news to Emily? How would Leeann feel about learning what had happened to her husband, and what about Tommy Lee? And they had yet to find Rachael. It appeared that Joan Chandler had a hell of a lot to answer for.

CHAPTER TWENTY

Tyler had called and said he would meet Jack at the police station. He was already ten minutes late, and Jack was beginning to think he wasn't coming. Just when he was about to call, he saw Tyler's pickup truck turn into the parking lot. Relieved, he walked out to meet him. "I thought you weren't coming," he said as he extended his hand for Tyler to shake.

"I almost didn't, but I kept seeing Rachael banging on the attic door, crying for someone to let her out. I didn't sleep at all last night. When I was a kid, Mother used to shut me in the closet when I was bad. I can't even tell you how many times I went to bed without supper. I was afraid of the dark until I graduated from college. I guess I blocked that out somehow, but I remembered it all last night. It kills me to think that Rachael went through that."

"You're doing the right thing, Tyler. We can't afford to let your mother go back to the house. She might destroy whatever clues are left that will help us find Rachael."

"If she's still alive," Tyler said.

"Don't give up hope." Jack led the way up the stairs and around the maze of cluttered desks to Kevin's office. The door was open. "Kevin, this is Tyler Chandler. Tyler, Captain Thomas."

Kevin nodded for them to take their seats. "Jack tells me you have information that may help us with your daughter's case. Tell me what you saw the day your daughter went missing."

"Well," Tyler said, "the house was crawling with cops. I needed some fresh air, so I wandered down to the river and saw the houseboat tied to the dock. I thought it strange because I'm the only one who takes the houseboat out. I thought maybe Mr. Gibbs was doing maintenance, but he'd just done that, just before Sarah and I—"

Kevin nodded. "Go on."

"With everything going on, I forgot to ask her about it. Then last night, when Jack told me they found Billy Ray's blood in the gallery, as well as on the dock, it became clear that Mother lied about Billy Ray taking Rachael from the garden. The fact that they found his body in the submerged fishing boat in front of the boathouse made it easy to figure out. Jack and I both figured it out."

Kevin raised a brow. "By all means, enlighten me."

"First of all," Tyler said, "you can't get to the boathouse by land."

"Who do you think rowed out there?" Kevin said.

"It had to be Mr. Gibbs. Mother wouldn't step foot in a fishing boat. She hates boats. Mr. Gibbs must've rowed Billy Ray out to the boathouse, sank the fishing boat, and then brought the houseboat back. There's no other way it could've gone down. None."

Kevin threw another look at Jack.

Jack cleared his throat. "Billy Ray had to have been severely wounded or already dead when Mr. Gibbs rowed him out there."

"Where are Mr. Gibbs and his sister now?" Kevin said, watching Tyler closely.

"I don't know, but Mr. Gibbs has lived in that cabin his whole life. It makes no sense that he'd move out. He and Regina probably know what happened to Rachael."

"You saw the attic?" Kevin said.

Tyler nodded. "I grew up in that house, and I never knew there was an attic."

Kevin's eyes narrowed as he leaned forward in his chair. "I'm going to ask you an important question, son. Did you know that your mother was keeping Rachael out at her place?"

"As God is my witness, I thought she'd been kidnapped by Billy Ray Richards. I've been going through hell worrying about what he might be doing to her. It makes me sick to know she let me think it!"

"Are you willing to press kidnapping charges?"

"I am. We need to find my daughter, Captain. Whatever Mr. Gibbs did that night, I'm convinced he did it because she threatened, bribed, or browbeat him into doing it. I know how she works. Mother always gets her way. Where do I sign?"

CHAPTER TWENTY-ONE

I t had taken nearly a week to accomplish what Jack had known was a foregone conclusion. Still, when Josh called, he held his breath.

"It's done," Josh said. "The judge dismissed the charges against Leeann and Tommy Lee in connection with Rachael Chandler, and Pamela Clarkston has agreed to drop her charges as well. All that's left is for the Richards pair to walk free, which is scheduled to take place tomorrow morning."

"Thank God. It took long enough," Jack said.

"Are you kidding me? We got this done in record time. Of course, the media attention helps. You've seen the coverage. People are outraged! They're ready to string Joan Chandler up right now."

"Well, let's just hope they keep the pressure up until she tells us what happened to Rachael."

"I doubt they'll get anything out of her," Josh said. "Her attorneys are top notch. Everyone thinks she knocked off the old man and his sister and buried them wherever Rachael is."

"I can't think that way. I've got to believe there's still hope."

"Be realistic, Jack. Nobody's heard from them in all this time. If they are alive, someone would've seen them by now. Two black people traveling with a white child aren't exactly inconspicuous, you know."

"I'm not giving up. I'm not ready to declare them all dead."

"All right. We got good news today. Let's just celebrate that."

"Thanks. Call me back when we can pick up Leeann and Tommy Lee."

"Will do, Jack."

Jack grimaced as he climbed the steps to Stacy's apartment. He'd been dreading this day because it meant telling Emily the truth about her father. He'd kept it from her until now, but with Leeann and Tommy Lee due for release, he couldn't put if off any longer. He wasn't sure how much Tommy Lee and Leeann knew yet, but he thought Emily should hear it from him. He knocked on Stacy's door.

"Come in," Stacy called from the other side of the door.

"Hey, Jack. You're just in time. I'm just now straining the spaghetti. Doesn't Stacy's sauce smell heavenly?" Emily said.

"Indeed." He closed the door behind him and gave each girl a hug. Dinner preparations continued, so he sat at the table, out of the way.

"Any news?" Emily said as she poured the pasta into a bowl.

"Yes, but it can wait till after dinner. I'm starved."

"Me, too," Stacy said. "Emily, can you take the bread out of the oven while I put the salad on the table?"

"Sure."

"How's work going?" Jack said.

"Good. I like being off in an area by myself, only I've never seen so much paperwork in my entire life. I barely have time to work on getting anything organized because I keep getting requests to look stuff up, and piles of new stuff arrive all the time. It's a mess in there. Whoever was there before me didn't know what they were doin'." She set a basket of bread on the table and then sat in her chair.

Stacy sat down, too. "Dig in."

Dinner was pleasant, but the pasta sat heavy in Jack's stomach. He tried to figure out the best way to break the news, but he couldn't think of any words that would make what he had to say any easier. He wished he were someplace else. When they had cleared the dishes from the table, he and Stacy exchanged glances; the moment had come. "Hey, Emily, let's talk," he said.

"Just a second. I'm almost finished helping Stacy."

Stacy turned off the water and nodded towards the living room. "Come on. Let's get it over with."

Emily's smile disappeared. "It's bad news, isn't it? They found Pa?"

Stacy nodded.

Emily's eyes clouded with tears.

"Come on, sweetie," Stacy said. "There are several things to talk about."

Emily and Stacy sat on the couch facing Jack.

"Where did they find him?" Emily said.

Jack sighed. "In Joan Chandler's fishing boat, submerged in the river. It looks like someone killed him and then sank the boat."

"My God! He's been there this whole time? Does Momma know?"

"If she doesn't, she soon will," Jack said.

Emily started crying. As Stacy wrapped her arms around her, Jack looked away. He hated to see her hurt. He wanted to tell her the good news right away, but he knew it was proper to give her space in between. When she finally pulled away from Stacy, he handed her some tissue from the box on the end table and let her pull herself together.

"I already knew it in my heart," she said. "If he was alive, he would've found Momma months ago. It's just that hearing it is more difficult than I thought."

"I know," he said. "We're sorry it happened, but at least he can be laid to rest now." She nodded. "Would you like some good news?"

"Is there any?" she said, rubbing her eyes.

"There is. Because they found your father, and for other reasons, the police know that Joan Chandler lied. The kidnapping charges against your mother and uncle have been dropped."

Emily looked up. "What?"

"I spoke to Joshua Royce earlier. The judge dismissed the charges against your mom and Tommy Lee, and Pamela Clarkston has agreed to drop her charges also, which means your mother and uncle are free to go home—with you if you like."

Emily blinked tears from her eyes. "Momma and Tommy Lee can come home?"

"It's over, Emily. They are releasing them maybe as soon as tomorrow," he said.

Tears filled Stacy's eyes, too.

Emily launched herself into Jack's arms. "Thank you! This would have never happened without you and Stacy."

Jack hugged her and then set her back into place.

"Oh, Stacy, can you believe it? Momma is comin' home! They're free! I can hardly believe it."

Stacy hugged her. "We're so happy for you, Emily."

"Hey, Em?" Jack said.

She turned, still smiling brightly.

"I hate to bring this up, but we still need to find Rachael."

She sobered immediately. "Yes, we must find Rachael."

* * *

Two months passed. Jack and Stacy could barely keep up with the phone calls, interviews, and new clients, who were coming through the doors in droves. It seemed that after twenty-five years, Jack's investigative practice had finally arrived, and yet it was a hollow victory. The police had turned up no new clues as to the whereabouts of Rachael, Mr. Gibbs, or his sister. It was as if they had vanished from the planet. The police had conducted a thorough search of the river channel between the boathouse and the dock, but they found nothing unusual.

Though Joan Chandler denied all charges, the judge refused to grant bail. She faced charges of kidnapping, murder, lying to the FBI, obstruction, interfering with a police investigation, and a host of other charges. Her attorneys continued to work feverishly in her defense.

Emily had returned to Arkansas with her mother and uncle. That, at least, made his failure to find Rachael a little easier to take. Nevertheless, Rachael was never far from Jack's mind. He was staring out the window when Clyde jumped up from the floor and lay across his desk. "Hey, you," Jack said. "Where have you been? I was looking for you earlier." He scratched Clyde's ears and smiled when he rolled onto his side and began to purr. Clyde's sister, Bonnie, jumped up for her share of attention. He rubbed his hand down her back and then laughed when the two black and white cats hissed at each other, licked one another, and then bounded off the desk to play. He looked at his hands, which were covered with fur.

"If you didn't pet them so hard, that wouldn't happen," Stacy said.

"But they like it."

"They like it when I pet them, too, but they keep more of their fur."

He went into the bathroom to wash his hands. "What did you think of the meeting we had this morning?"

She shrugged. "It sounds like we'll get to try out some of our new super-duper spy monitoring equipment on this new case, but I hate to hear about another family torn apart by infidelity. Why do people get married if they don't plan to stay faithful?"

He reached for a paper towel. "Hey, hold on, there. You're far too young to be cynical. Wait till you've been doing this as long as I have, *then* you can get cynical."

"No, thanks. I think we should concentrate on reuniting missing loved ones. I've been working on a marketing campaign. I'll let you know when it's ready. Prepare to be impressed."

"You always impress me."

She shot him a dazzling smile. "Thanks, Jack. I needed that." Her cell phone buzzed. "Oh my gosh, it's Tyler. I haven't heard from him in weeks. Hey, Tyler, what's up?" Her eyes widened as she snapped her fingers and hit the speakerphone button. "Where is he? What did he say?"

"I don't know if I'm doing the right thing by calling you guys, but I don't want to mess this up. I know the police are looking for him. What do I do?"

"What did he say, Tyler?" Stacy said again.

"He said he wants to tell me what happened that night. He wants to tell me what happened to Rachael."

"Who?" Jack said.

She covered the phone. "Gibbs."

A sick feeling shot through Jack's heart. What little hope he'd held that Rachael might still be alive died with Tyler's statement. He saw it on Stacy's face, too. "Where, Tyler? When?" she said.

"He wants me to meet him out at the cabin," Tyler said. " I don't think I can face this by myself."

"We have to call the police. You know that, don't you?" Jack said.

"I figured, but Mr. Gibbs has been good to me my whole life. Can you ask your police captain friend to take it easy on him? He's seventy-five years old."

"Yes. I'll call as soon as we hang up. When does he want to meet?"

"Tonight at seven o'clock."

"Can Stacy and I ride out with you?"

"I'm leaving here at six thirty."

"We'll see you at six. I'll call you back after I talk to Kevin. Stay by your phone."

"I hope I'm doing the right thing," Tyler said.

"You are. Maybe this thing can finally come to an end,"

Jack said.

"Finally. If Mother killed her—"

"Let's not jump to conclusions," he said, though he was thinking the same thing. "We'll call you back in a few minutes." He motioned for Stacy to hang up.

"Wow. That changed the focus of the day," Stacy said.

Jack dialed Kevin.

"Captain Thomas, here."

"We got Gibbs."

"Okay, everybody out of my office," Kevin said. "I've gotta take this call."

* * *

A trail of police cars followed Tyler's truck down the long tree-lined driveway. Jack and Stacy, both of them armed, got out of the truck and walked to the gate with Tyler. Someone had removed the crime tape, so Tyler swung the gate wide and headed down the path towards the cabin. The plan was for the police to surround the cabin and wait for Jack's signal. Jack could hear the sound of many feet moving behind them. His heart was pounding. Tonight they would learn the fate of little Rachael Chandler.

When they reached the cabin, Tyler climbed the porch steps and knocked on the door. "It's me, Mr. Gibbs. Open up."

The door squeaked open and an old black man, withered and weary, stood framed within the light. "I wondered if you'd bring somebody. Guess you had to."

"Mr. Gibbs, this is Jack and Stacy. They've been working to help me find Rachael. I'd like them to hear what you've got to say."

"Fine by me. I can't run no more, no how. It's time the truth be told." He stepped back into the room, and Tyler stepped inside.

Jack felt for his gun and then pushed the mini digital recorder in his pocket. Pausing in the doorway, he glanced around the room and then moved aside so that Stacy could enter first.

"Sit down. Sit down," Mr. Gibbs said. "I ain't got nothin' to offer but water."

"No thanks," Tyler said as he sat on the couch. "Tell us, Mr. Gibbs. Tell us what happened."

Jack and Stacy settled onto rustic wooden chairs, which Mr. Gibbs carried in from the small kitchen table. Stacy flashed him a quick smile, but her eyes betrayed the tension she was feeling. As he surveyed the room, he noted the clinched set to Tyler's jaw and the way he gripped the arm of the couch. Everyone was on edge.

"I ain't lookin' forward to the tellin', Mr. Tyler, but like I said, Regina and me can't keep it to ourselves no more. The night Mr. Billy Ray tried to take Rachael from your place, Mrs. Chandler came knockin' at my door. She wanted me to stay at the big house to watch after her and Miss Rachael in case Billy Ray came callin'. That night was all quiet-like, but the next night, Billy Ray broke in through the back door while I was checkin' the front part of the house. When I came back through the kitchen, he knocked me upside the head, drug me into the back room, and then he went upstairs lookin' for Miss Rachael.

"Mrs. Chandler must've heard him cuz she went and fetched her gun. She was waitin' for him in the dark when Miss Rachael came running across the gallery from her room. Billy Ray called out for her, but Miss Rachael said she weren't goin' nowhere with him."

"Where were you?" Tyler asked.

"Unconscious near the back door."

"Then how do you know what happened?" Tyler said.

"Cuz Regina done snuck up behind Billy Ray with my rifle. When he stepped towards Mrs. Chandler, Regina called 'im out. He lunged at her, and my rifle went off. Regina shot Billy Ray, but it were an accident."

"No! That's not true!" The bedroom door burst open, and

a little girl rushed into the room. "Gramma killed Billy Ray. I saw it!"

"Rachael, come back here!" a black woman called from the doorway.

"I saw him bleeding on the floor! Grandma told me not to look, but I did."

"Rachael!" Tyler said, coming to his feet.

Jack and Stacy rose also.

Rachael looked suddenly wary and turned back to the black woman, who opened her arms as she ran into them.

Tyler dropped to his knees. "Come here, Rachael. It's me. It's Daddy."

"No! You don't want me. I'm staying with Regina and Mr. G!"

"Rachael, go back to the bedroom now," Mr. Gibbs said. "We ain't finished talkin' yet."

"Yes, sir," Rachael said as Regina guided her back into the bedroom and shut the door.

"Please, everyone, sit down. There's more of this story yet to tell."

Jack's heart was thumping. Rachael was alive!

"Why do you have Rachael?" Tyler demanded.

"I'm getting to that, Mr. Tyler."

Regina opened the bedroom door and joined them in the living room. "Jayden and Rachael are fine in there, but I want to be in on this here discussion since it's me Mrs. Chandler blamed for Billy Ray's death."

"What?" Tyler and Jack said simultaneously.

"That child knows what she saw. It ain't never done no good to try to convince her otherwise. We may as well tell the truth, G, and let the chips fall where they may."

"But you—"

"I was willin' to go along with her plan because she threatened to tell the police I done it and have me arrested if I didn't. She said they'd take Jayden, and we couldn't let that happen."

"Is that true, Mr. Gibbs?" Jack said.

"We gotta tell 'em what we done with Billy Ray," he said. "I ain't meetin' my maker without helpin' that man get a decent burial. I just ain't."

Regina nodded. "G and I wanted to call the police that night, but Mrs. Chandler was afraid they wouldn't let her adopt Miss Rachael if they knew she killed Billy Ray. She told us to throw him in the river and claim that he kidnapped Miss Rachael."

"But why claim that he took Rachael?" Tyler said.

"Miss Rachael saw what she done, so she decided to hide her from the police. We told her that she couldn't hide Miss Rachael forever, but she said she'd claim that somebody dropped her off one day, only that day never came, and we began to see that it never would."

"Tell us about Billy Ray," Jack said.

"The plan was for G to row him out to the deepest part of the river and dump him there, but them gators attacked the boat and G barely got to the boathouse in time."

Mr. Gibbs nodded. "That's God's honest truth. Them gators sunk that boat. I had to take the houseboat back to the dock."

Stacy grimaced, as did Jack. It was a gruesome picture, but it matched what they had already figured out, only worse. In fact, the whole story was in line with what they knew to be true about Joan Chandler. She used money, threats, lies, and intimidation to get what she wanted.

"After that," Regina said, "we scaredt that station wagon away and stayed up half the night cleaning up the blood from Billy Ray. Lordy, but we must've gone over our story three dozen times before she finally called the police."

"How long after Billy Ray died did she wait to call the police?" Jack said.

"Two days," Regina said.

Mr. Gibbs nodded.

"We did everythin' we could to help Miss Rachael, but it weren't easy 'cuz Mrs. Chandler became a totally different person—cold and mean. She kept Rachael in that attic sometimes without fire, and often without supper. We wanted to go to the police, but we couldn't on account of Jayden."

"Did she threaten him?" Jack said.

Regina cast a startled look at Mr. Gibbs. "Tell 'em, G. We done gone this far."

Jack watched the wrinkles shift on the old man's face as he wrestled with his emotions.

"I done worked for Mrs. Chandler nigh on thirty-five years now. In all of that time, I never once told her private business, not even to Regina, but when I saw that Mason man creepin' around my cabin, I knew that if we survived till mornin', we wouldn't see another night in these here cabins. So we ran. We took Miss Rachael, and we got ourselves away."

"What man?" Jack said. "Who did you see creeping around your cabin?"

"Mr. Tyler knows. Don't you, son?"

Tyler's head snapped upwards, breaking his gaze from the floor. "You want me to believe that mother planned to have you executed?"

"The Mason man don't make no social calls, do he, Mr. Tyler? If Mrs. Chandler called him in, it was time to go."

Jack watched Tyler's face as he struggled to accept Mr. Gibbs story. "Did your mother tell you when Mr. G and Regina left?"

"Hell, no," Tyler scoffed. "I didn't even know they were gone until you told me."

"We been hidin' out ever since," Mr. Gibbs said, "but that's no life for a child to live. We can't put her in school or take her out in public.

We stay on a farm where she can play outside, but it still ain't right. And we never know when that Mason man might find us."

"Mason man. A Freemason, you mean?" Jack said glancing from Mr. G to Tyler, but neither answered. "Why take the risk by speaking out now?"

"When we heard that Mrs. Chandler got arrested, we thought she'd get herself out right away, so we waited. But they ain't let her out, and the TV people say that she's in a heap of trouble, so we thought it might be safe to come out of hiding." He turned to Tyler. "What your momma done to you and Miss Rachael ain't nothin' but meanness, and we couldn't let you worry about her even one more day. Now, we's trustin' you, Mr. Tyler, to protect us. You can call that Mason man off of us. I know you can."

Tyler cast a quick glance at Jack and cleared his throat. "I can't thank you enough for taking care of Rachael. I can see that she trusts you. Will you bring her out here, please?"

"What about the Mason man?" Mr. Gibbs said, locking eyes with him—man to man.

"I'll take care of it. You have my word."

Stacy bumped her leg against him, but Jack didn't need the nudge; he had caught the exchange.

Mr. Gibbs nodded. "Regina, bring Jayden out here, too, please."

Regina opened the bedroom door. "Come out, you two. It's all right."

Rachael grabbed the side of Regina's dress, and Jayden walked across the floor to stand next to his grandfather. Mr. Gibbs wrapped an arm around his waist.

"You two shouldn't have been listening at the door. You know that ain't polite."

"Did those gators really eat Billy Ray?" Jayden said.

"Never mind that," Mr. Gibbs said. "Rachael, pay respects to your Pa."

Rachael buried her face into Regina's skirts.

Tyler dropped to his knees again. "Rachael, I'm very sorry for what happened to you. I didn't know your grandmother was keeping you in the attic."

"It was cold and dark and scary up there, but you never came for me!"

Jack wanted to take the little girl into his arms. How could any man neglect such a beautiful child? How could Tyler ever have thought to allow Joan Chandler to adopt her?

"Rachael, Daddy made a big mistake by letting you stay with Grandma. I should've kept you home with Cody and me. I'm very sorry. I want to make it up to you. Please, let me take you home with me."

"No! I wanna stay with Jayden!" She looked up at Regina. "I don't want to go with Daddy. He gave me away so he and Pamela would have room for more babies."

Jack felt like someone punched him in the stomach. Had someone actually told her that?

"Rachael, I'm sorry I said that. I didn't know you were listening," Tyler said. "I'm here to take you home."

Jack glanced at Stacy, whose eyes flashed daggers as she focused on Tyler.

"No! I'm staying with Jayden!"

"Give her time, Mr. Tyler. She's been through a powerful lot already." Regina petted the top of Rachael's head. "We done become a family, G, Jayden, Rachael, and me. We been lookin' out for her nearly a year now."

"But she's my daughter, and I'm not leaving here without her. Come here, Rachael. You're going home with me whether you like it or not." He reached out and took hold of Rachael's arm.

"No!" She kicked him in the shin, ran into the bedroom, and slammed the door.

Tyler moved to go after her, but Regina stepped in front of the door. "No, Mr. Tyler. You ain't forcin' that child to do nothin' she don't wanna do."

"Get out of my way, Regina. Tell her, Mr. Gibbs."

Mr. Gibbs crossed the floor and put his hand on Tyler's shoulder. "She's right, son. Rachael needs a gentle touch just now. She's mighty scared. She's afraid you'll give her back to Mrs. Chandler. Remember how scared you was when she used to lock you up in that closet? Well, Miss Rachael's been scared for a long time. We been slowly mendin' what Mrs. Chandler broke, but these kind of hurts don't heal overnight. She needs love right now, not discipline."

"He's right, Tyler. You can force her to go with you, but you can't make her want to," Jack said. "Listen to them. They're the ones who have been looking out for her. They know her best."

Tyler exhaled, and the fight seemed to leave him. He dropped back onto the couch and covered his face with his hands. "How could she do this to me?"

Stacy's brows shot up. She was about to say something, but Jack put a hand on her arm, which she heeded by biting her lip.

"All right, everyone," Jack said. "As Tyler knows, there are a lot of men outside waiting to hear from me about what's going on in here. None of us expected this happy turn of events. It's wonderful to see Rachael alive, but the police need to know what's going on so they can decide what happens next. Regina, please bring Rachael back out here. We should all be together when they come in."

"We done told you what happened. Don't let 'em take Miss Rachael away."

"I'm going to recommend that she stay in your care for the time being, but it isn't up to me. Please do as I ask. Bring Rachael in here with us."

Regina opened the bedroom door and went inside. A moment later, she reappeared with Rachael clinging to her hand. She sat on one end of the couch and pulled Rachael up onto her lap.

"All right. I'm going to make a phone call. Everyone, stay put." He dialed Kevin. "Hey, Captain. I've got wonderful news."

"It took you long enough. We were just about to break through the door," Kevin snapped.

"Rachael Chandler is here with us, along with Mr. Gibbs, Regina, and little Jayden. They have given us a first-hand account of what has taken place. Rachael doesn't want to go home with her father. She wants to stay with Regina and Mr. Gibbs. You'll need to determine that once you hear their story. How should I proceed?"

"Is anyone armed?" Kevin said.

"Hold on."

"Mr. Gibbs, are you or Regina armed? The police will search you, and it won't go well for you if they find any weapons."

"No, sir. We ain't got no weapons. Ain't that right, Regina?"

"We ain't got nothin'," she said.

"Tyler?" Jack said.

"Just my .44, but that's out in the truck."

"Captain, only Stacy and I are armed."

"Have Stacy open the door, and we'll come in real gentle-like because of the kids," Kevin said.

"Very good, and what about Rachael and Jayden?" Jack said.

"What's your call?"

"Stacy and I could take them home with us for the night. That would give you the opportunity to talk with Regina and Mr. Gibbs. No one wants to see them go into foster care, and Rachael is dead-set against going anywhere with Tyler right now."

"See if everyone is agreeable and call me back."

Jack looked at Stacy. She nodded and went over and knelt on the floor in front of Rachael. "Hey, Rachael. I'm Stacy. You don't know me, but I've been working very hard to find you. I've been praying every day that you were safe, and I'm so happy you are! You and Jayden are really good friends, aren't you?"

Rachael nodded.

Stacy pointed at Jack. "I'm friends with Jack the way you are friends with Jayden. It's nice to have a best friend, isn't it?" Rachael nodded again. "The police are here, and they need to talk to Regina and Mr. Gibbs about what happened to Billy Ray. In fact, they might even want to talk to you, but not tonight. It's getting late, and it's almost time for bed. I was wondering if you and Jayden might like to spend the night with Jack and me. We could have a little slumber party in Jack's living room. We can build a fire in the fireplace and pop some popcorn. We've even got four sleeping bags, so we can all sleep on the floor in front of the fire." Stacy glanced over at Jayden. "Doesn't that sound like fun?"

Jayden looked to his grandfather. "Can I, Papa?"

"Do you know this man, Tyler?" Mr. Gibbs said.

"I trust them."

Mr. Gibbs shook his head. "I don't know."

"You don't want the children to go to the police station, or into foster care, do you?" Jack said. "Because that, or forcing Rachael to go with Tyler tonight, is the only other alternative. It will only be for a day or two, and it will allow Rachael and Jayden to stay together."

"What do you think, Rachael?" Stacy said. "Would you like to have a slumber party with Jayden, Jack and me, or would you rather go home with your Daddy?"

Rachael pointed to Stacy.

"Mr. Gibbs?" Stacy said.

"If it's only for a day or two, but I want to know how to reach my boy. And I want him and Miss Rachael to be able to call me anytime they want."

"Agreed," Jack said. He pulled out his wallet and handed cards to Regina and Mr. Gibbs. "You can call them anytime. I'm gonna call Captain Thomas back now." He dialed and updated Kevin.

"All right, Kendall. Let the men in. We'll do everything as nonchalantly as possible. Let Regina and Mr. Gibbs know that we'll be taking them in for questioning, once the children leave with you."

"Got it, Captain. Call me later to let me know what to do tomorrow."

"Don't worry; I will. Oh, and Jack?"

"Yes?"

"Don't ask the children any questions about what happened. Let us do that. We don't want the defense claiming someone coached them. You got me?"

"I understand."

"You never cease to amaze me. I never thought we'd see that little girl again," Kevin said.

Jack sighed. Finding Rachael alive made facing all the ugliness that had come to light worth it. He glanced over and saw that she was watching him intently. He winked at her and was rewarded with a shy but heartwarming smile.

He wished that reuniting Rachael with Tyler was the end of the matter, but clearly it wasn't. There were issues he hadn't anticipated. Finding her was one thing, getting her safely settled was another.

Aware that everyone was watching him, he smiled at Rachael. "There are some men outside who want to talk to Mr. Gibbs and Regina, sweetheart, so we're gonna let them in. Then you, Jayden, Stacy, and I are going to ride with your daddy back to his house to drop him off. Then the four of us are going to my house for the sleepover."

Jayden looked at his grandfather.

"You call me before you go to sleep tonight, and you mind Mr. Jack and Miss Stacy."

"I will, Papa," Jayden said.

"You, too, Miss Rachael," Regina added. "I don't wanna hear of no tee-tee in your bed."

"I'll be a good girl for Miss Stacy."

"Come give me a hug then. I'll miss ya," Regina said. "You too, Jayden."

After hugging Regina, Rachael ran over to Mr. Gibbs. "Bye Mr. G. I'm gonna sleep in a sleeping bag and pop some popcorn."

"That's real fine. We'll see ya soon," he said. "Run back to Regina, now, while these men come in."

Stacy opened the door, and three uniformed policemen walked into the room.

"Hello," Stacy said. "This is Mr. Gibbs and his sister Regina, and this is Tyler Chandler."

"Good evening," one of the officers said.

"That handsome young man over there is Mr. Gibbs' grandson, Jayden, and that pretty little girl is Rachael Chandler," she added. "Jack, Tyler, and the kids and I are going to leave now. Have a good night." She smiled and walked over to Rachael. "You ready, sweetie?" Rachael nodded and accepted Stacy's hand. "Let's go."

"Have fun tonight," the officer said.

"Thank you," Rachael said. "I've never had a sleepover before."

Jack and Jayden led the way. Once they were outside, Tyler moved to the front and led the way down the path, back to the truck. Jack couldn't see anyone, but he knew there were officers watching them. It felt amazing, after fifteen months, to lead Rachael Chandler to safety.

* * *

"Can we leave the lights on?" Rachael said as she wiggled into her sleeping bag.

"What if I leave the kitchen light on?" Jack said as he switched off the main overhead light. "Can you see well enough?"

"Can you leave the bathroom light on, too, and close the doors in the hallway so I won't be scared?"

"You can wake me up if you have to go to the bathroom," Stacy said. "I'll go with you."

"That way nobody can get me?"

"Nobody's gonna get you, Rachael," Jack said. "You and Jayden are safe here with us."

"He's right," Stacy said. "How did you like cooking over the fire?"

Rachael giggled. "I never knew you could make popcorn like that. It was fun. Huh, Jayden?"

"Yes, but I miss Papa," Jayden said.

"Oh, I almost forgot. We're supposed to call him before you go to sleep tonight. Let's do that right now," Jack said as he dialed.

"I was expecting you to call," Kevin said.

"I've got Jayden here. He promised to call his Papa before he goes to sleep tonight. Can you put him on the phone?"

"This is highly irregular, you know. Hang on."

"Is he getting him?" Jayden said.

"Yep. We just have to wait a few minutes."

"Jack, they're in the middle of taking his statement. Make it quick."

"He's pretty busy, Jayden, so don't take too long. Here you go."

"Hi, Papa!"

Jack chuckled as Jayden's face lit up.

"I'm good," Jayden said. "We're gonna sleep in sleeping bags in front of the fire, just like when we go hunting. I miss you, Papa." Jayden listened for a few moments and then nodded his head. "I will, Papa. I love you, too. Good night." He handed the phone to Jack. "When will I get to see him?"

"If not tomorrow, then maybe the next day. The police will call to let us know."

"Why do the police want to talk to him?" Jayden said, tilting his face so that the light caught his thick curly hair and shone onto his smooth, dark complexion. He was adorably cute, Jack thought, and extremely intelligent.

"Mrs. Chandler did a very bad thing by keeping Rachael locked in the attic. She also did a bad thing to Billy Ray," Jack said. "They want to find out more about it."

"She kept me locked in the attic sometimes, too," Jayden said.

"She did?" Jack said, unable to hide his surprise.

"Whatever for?" Stacy said.

"Whenever anybody came to the house, she made me hide in the attic with Rachael. If we were in school, we'd have to run to the attic quick, and she'd shut us in. Rachael wasn't allowed to go downstairs at all. Mrs. Chandler didn't want anybody knowing she lived with us. It was a secret."

"I see," Jack said. "Thankfully, all of that is over now. Once we talk to the police tomorrow, we'll find out what to do next. In the meantime, Stacy and I will take good care of you. Would you like to put up a tent in the backyard tomorrow? You can play in it and pretend like we're camping."

"I never played in a tent before," Jayden said.

"Me, either," Rachael said.

"It will be lots of fun. Do you two like spaghetti? Miss Stacy makes the best spaghetti in Mississippi. Maybe she'll make some tomorrow."

"Will you, Miss Stacy? Please?" Rachael said, her brown eyes pleading.

"I will, and you can help me if you want to."

"We can count to a hundred in French. Want to hear us?" Jayden said.

"In French?" Stacy repeated. "Wow. That's impressive."

"Come on, Rachael. Ready, set, go!"

After they had counted together in perfect unison, they took turns telling them other things they had learned on the computer. From what Jack could gather, they studied in a room called the nursery, which was on the second floor of the mansion. They apparently had a private online tutor, or rather, Jayden did. Rachael wasn't allowed to talk in class, but she did the same study work. When she did accidentally speak, she was forced back into the attic for the rest of the day, sometimes without dinner. Jack whispered for Stacy to remind him to pass that information along to Kevin. They knew a lot considering how young they were, but he hated to think of the restrictions and intimidations that had gone along with it.

"Miss Stacy?" Rachael said. "Will you hold my hand while I go to sleep?"

"Of course, I will," Stacy said as she moved her sleeping bag closer to Rachael. She reached out her hand, and Rachael took it.

"Want me to hold your hand, Jayden?" Jack said.

"You better not. I'm dirty," he said.

"No, you're not. You just took a bath, remember?"

"No, I mean *dirty*," Jayden said.

"What does that mean, Jayden?" Stacy asked.

"You know, white people shouldn't touch me because I'm black."

"Who told you that?" Jack said, anger rising in his chest.

"Mrs. Chandler. She doesn't let me touch Rachael. She says I'll make her dirty, like me."

"You know what, Jayden? Mrs. Chandler was wrong about a whole lot of things. You are *not* dirty, unless, of course, you play in the dirt, and we all do that sometimes. Otherwise, you're as clean as everybody else on this planet. I promise you that. Here, take my hand."

Jayden hesitated. "Papa will wear me out."

"Your papa works for Mrs. Chandler, and he has to do what she says when he's on her property, but you're at my house now, and I say you can hold my hand if you want to, but only if you want to. You can hold Stacy's other hand if you'd rather or no one's hand at all. It is entirely up to you."

Jack felt Jayden reach for his hand. "That a boy. You can let go whenever you want. Do you feel safe?"

Jayden nodded.

"Jayden, do you and Rachael ever touch each other?" Jack said.

"No, sir. Our feet touched once on accident, but we didn't tell Mrs. Chandler because she said she'd whip us until the cows come home. She says I'm not good enough to touch Miss Rachael."

Jack flipped on his flashlight. "Okay, everybody up on our knees. Let's go," he said.

Jayden's eyes grew wide. "Are you gonna whip me, Mr. Jack? I didn't mean to touch her feet."

"No, Jayden, of course not. You haven't done anything wrong. Come here, Rachael. Crawl over here to me."

"Are you gonna whip *me*, Mr. Jack?"

"No, silly rabbit. Everybody sit in a circle. You, too, Stacy. We're going to do something fun before we go to sleep, and we're going to learn something very important while we're at it."

When everybody sat in a circle, Jack leaned forward and put his hand down in the center of the circle. "Rachael, put your hand on top of mine."

Rachael put her hand on top of Jack's. "Like that?"

"Yep. You're next, Stacy. Put your hand on top of Rachael's." Jack nodded with approval. "Okay, Jayden. You're next. You put your hand on top of Stacy's, and then I'll add my second hand, and we'll keep going until we have a whole mountain of silly hands."

"Are you sure?" Jayden said.

"Do it, Jayden. It's fun!" Rachael said.

"Put yours on top," Jack said.

Jayden put his hand on the top of the pile, and Rachael giggled.

"I'm next," Jack said as he added his other hand, and this time, Jayden giggled.

"Me, next," Rachael said.

"My turn," Stacy said.

"You get to be at the very top. Go ahead, Jayden," Jack said.

Jayden laid his hand on top of Stacy's with a huge smile on his face.

"Everybody's hands have five fingers, right?" Jack said.

Everyone said, "Yes."

"Now look at all of our hands. See the fingers sticking out? They are all a slightly different color, aren't they? That's because God made us that way. He made the flowers different colors, and he made us different colors, too, yet he loves us all just the same. All right, let's take them off, one at a time, as fast as we can. Jayden first, then Stacy, then Rachael, and we'll keep going. Ready, set, go!"

When all the hands were gone, the kids were laughing. "Let's do it again," Rachael said.

"I've got a better idea," Jack said. "Give Jayden a high-five, and let's get some sleep." He watched them high-five each other with a tear in his eye, but he blinked it away. This was one wrong he meant to correct. "Way to go, you two. Back in the sleeping bags." Once everyone was settled, and the chatter had quieted down, he said, "Good night, everybody."

"Good night," everyone said more or less at the same time.

A few moments later, he felt Jayden reach out for his hand. He took it and gave it a light squeeze.

CHAPTER
TWENTY-TWO

Tyler stayed home from work, but he was in no condition to concentrate. Cody was still at preschool, and he was anxiously waiting for the telephone call that would tell him if Rachael would be returning home today—alive—no thanks to his mother. Rising from the couch, he headed out the back door to chop some firewood, hoping that the physical activity would take his mind off of everything else.

The rusted hinges creaked as he opened the heavy workshop door. It was a cloudy day, but there was enough mote-filled light to see his ax hanging on the peg board on the opposite wall. The plywood floor sagged beneath his weight, and the air smelled musty from the rain. He sighed. Everywhere he looked there was work to do, but even as he calculated what needed to be done, he decided to ignore it.

Reaching for the ax, he recoiled as something moved near his feet. Grabbing a rake instead, he poked and jabbed at some boxes until a snake slithered along the wall and took cover between some paint cans.

"Yeah, I see you. You're going down!"

When he reached for the ax again, his cell phone vibrated in his pocket, making him jump. Heart pounding, he yanked the ax from the wall and stepped out of the workshop to take the call. "Tyler, here," he said, his eyes never leaving the workshop floor.

"Don't bother looking for me," a deep voice said. "When I learned that Rachael is Roger's granddaughter, I returned your mother's money. Now that Rachael has resurfaced, she'll try again if she gets the chance." The call dropped.

"Wait! Dammit!" So his mother *had* ordered their murders. He hurled the ax towards the cutting block, taking perverse satisfaction at seeing the head lodged deep into the stump. Retrieving it, eyes ablaze, he charged into the workshop and began kicking paint cans and jabbing at them with the ax. "Come out of there, you sneaky, slithering, viper!" He yanked a can out of the way and retreated. "You think you're so cleaver, but you've been found out, and there's nowhere to hide!"

The four-foot water moccasin slid across the floor towards the other corner. Spotting it, Tyler threw his ax, beheading it cleanly. As the lower half continued to flail, Tyler took out his frustrations until all that remained were bloody pieces strewn across the plywood floor.

* * *

Hours later, Tyler glanced round Rachael's bedroom. It didn't look much like a little girl's room anymore. Cody had most of his toys in here, and the bed was unmade. He opened the closet and took out one of Rachael's old dresses. It certainly wouldn't fit her now. If she did come home, he didn't want her to find her room looking like this. He bent to pick up a handful of Cody's Tonka trucks and carried them into his bedroom.

Cody's room looked very different from Rachael's. The furniture was nicer, the bedspread more expensive, and the walls freshly painted. Pictures of zoo animals decorated the walls, a striking contrast to Rachael's drab room and bare walls. Anyone comparing the two could easily see where his affections lie. He shook his head. Had he not allowed his feelings to show, would things have turned out differently?

When he told Cody they had found his sister, he wasn't happy about it. In fact, Cody had said he wished they had found Jacob instead. He realized that Cody was mimicking his own disinterest towards

Rachael, disdain he had learned from *him*. Was there a way to make up for what Rachael had suffered? Would he feel differently once she came home? More importantly, could he *act* differently?

He returned to Rachael's room for another load of Cody's toys. Once he had it cleaned out, he stripped the bed and threw the sheets into the wash. Next, he dusted the furniture and saw how filthy everything was. He hadn't cleaned in here since he'd dropped her off at his mother's house over a year ago. It was as if he'd written her out of his life and didn't expect to see her ever again. Now, he had to make room in his heart for her return. It had to be different this time. *He* had to be different. He could no longer let Cody run roughshod over his sister. He could no longer ignore her or make her cry on purpose. He had to be a real father to her. He had to win her trust and love.

It had been a real eye-opener when she had refused to come home with him. She had preferred to go with strangers, and he deserved it.

He opened her dresser drawers to see what was in there. He'd likely have to buy her an entire wardrobe unless there were clothes at the mansion that fit. He sighed. He was about to be faced with raising an angry little girl.

He sat on her bare mattress and dialed Pamela. It went straight to voicemail, of course. "Hey, it's me. I just wanted to let you know that we found Rachael. I'm hoping she'll come home to live with me today or tomorrow, although she doesn't want to. I'm waiting for the call now. Uh, it seems that Mother is the one who killed Billy Ray. She told the police he kidnapped Rachael, but she was keeping her locked up in her attic because she saw her kill Billy Ray. Can you believe it?" He paused. "She bribed and threatened Mr. Gibbs and Regina the same way she bribed and threatened you. She even threatened to kill Jayden if they didn't help cover up what she had done. It looks like she'll be in jail for a very long time. Anyways, I miss you, and I'd give anything if you were here beside me." He hung up the phone, covered his face with both hands, and cried.

"Jack, Kevin's on the line," Stacy called from the patio doors.

Jack stuck his head outside the tent just as Jayden climbed onto his back and growled like a lion. "I'll be right there," he called. He shook him loose and then tickled the kids until they were squealing with delight. "Okay, you two, I'll be right back." He crawled out of the tent and took the phone from Stacy. "Keep an eye on them, will you? Watch out, though. The lions are restless!"

"I see that," Stacy chuckled as she turned to join the children in the tent.

"Hey, Kev, what's going on?" Jack said.

"You mean besides the fact that someone leaked to the press that we found Rachael Chandler alive? We just got a call for backup because of the crush of reporters outside your door. Seems the officer on duty there is overwhelmed."

"Oh, no!" Jack hurried through the kitchen and to the front door. He glanced out the window and saw the crowd pressing towards his door, just waiting to get a photo or catch a headlines quote. "They're out there all right."

"We'll do our job. You just keep Rachael out of sight."

"She's out in the backyard now. I hope those clowns don't hop the fence."

"If they do, we'll arrest them for trespassing," Kevin said.

"Little good that will do Rachael."

"Listen, Jack. They had to rush Joan Chandler to the Emergency Room about an hour ago."

"Why? What happened?"

"Apparently, she was so distressed by the news that Mr. Gibbs and Regina had turned themselves in, and that they claim she killed Billy Ray, she went into some sort of seizure and into a coma. They say this happened once before, about a year ago, but this time is much worse.

We're waiting to hear the prognosis. In the meantime, her attorney states that Joan denies shooting Billy Ray. She says Regina killed him."

"That's what Regina said she threatened to say if they didn't help her cover up the murder. It's also her way of threatening Jayden," Jack said. "If Regina was the one who shot Billy Ray, why would Joan risk so much to cover it up? Why claim Billy Ray kidnapped her grandchild; why keep Rachael hidden in the attic? Nope, I'm not buying it."

"Neither is the district attorney. He's adding first-degree murder, bribery, kidnapping, endangering the life of a child, and a whole host of other crimes to her existing list of charges. Assuming she wakes up, she's going away for a very long time."

"What about Mr. Gibbs and Regina?"

"They certainly broke their share of laws, but it speaks volumes that they came forward. They've met with a public defender and have agreed to testify against Mrs. Chandler in exchange for lesser charges. My guess is they'll walk with probation. They're being released on bail this afternoon."

"Where did they get the money for bail?" Jack said.

"Apparently, Mr. Gibbs has saved most of what he's earned over the last sixty-five years. For the time being, at least, they plan to return to the cabin on Mrs. Chandler's property. According to Mr. Gibbs, he's lived there his entire life. Until we sort this out, or the property is sold, I see no reason he can't continue living there. Jayden will, of course, remain in their custody. As for Rachael, she'll need to go through some physical and psychological evaluations. A judge will have to decide what's in her best interest as regards to custody."

"She says she saw her grandmother shoot Billy Ray," Jack said.

"You got that recorded?"

"Yes, and about custody, she's particularly close to Jayden. She wants to stay with Regina and Mr. G—that's what she calls Mr. Gibbs."

"They aren't her legal guardians. If her father won't take her, she'll probably end up in foster care," Kevin said.

"Foster care? Do you have any idea what that child's been through? Why can't she stay with Mr. Gibbs and Regina?"

"I hear you, Jack, but it's very unlikely that the court will award the custody of a white child to a black family, and you know it. Nevertheless, I'll make a few calls and see what I can do."

Jack groaned. Now she would lose her only friends? It made him want to adopt her himself, just to keep her from being hurt.

"Jack?"

"I'm here."

"Look, I know you're emotionally wrapped up in this, but let's give the system a chance to work. I'll see if I can call in some favors. I don't want her going through any more trauma, either, but who's to say that living on that property is emotionally good for her?"

"She's made it very clear who she wants to live with, which reminds me—I recorded everything that went down last night. Rachael speaks her mind plainly enough. Perhaps that will persuade a judge."

"It certainly won't hurt. Are you sure her father won't take her?" Kevin said.

"Rachael doesn't want to go with him. She heard him say that he doesn't want her."

"Wow, that has to be rough on a kid," Kevin said.

"That would be rough on an adult. Listen, I need to fill you in on a bit more information. Apparently, Joan Chandler also kept Jayden locked in the attic sometimes, too."

"I thought I told you not to talk about what happened," Kevin snapped.

"I changed the subject immediately, but he spoke a few sentences here and there. I didn't want to make him afraid to talk or feel self-conscious. He'll repeat it, I'm sure."

"What else did he say?"

"Just that he isn't allowed to touch Rachael because he's dirty—because he's black. I straightened him out on that one, but there's no telling what else that woman's put into his head. He may need some counseling, too."

"Stupid, ignorant woman," Kevin muttered.

"I knew you'd appreciate that."

"Anything else?"

"I'd say that's enough. Wouldn't you?" Jack said.

"I'll call you when it's time to return Jayden to Mr. Gibbs and his sister."

"Kevin, I can't stress this enough; for Rachael's sake, the best place for her, until all of this gets sorted out, is with Jayden, Mr. Gibbs, and Regina."

"Later, Jack."

Jack looked at his phone and made a face. If he had to tear Rachael away from Jayden and turn her over to complete strangers, he didn't know what he would do. He didn't want to betray her like all the rest. He looked up and said a quick prayer. Someone needed to help this little girl, and it was beyond what he could do on his own.

His phone rang in his hand.

"Jack, I just got a call from the hospital," Tyler said. "They say Mother might not make it. I tried to leave the house, but there's a forest of people outside my door. What's going on?"

"They know we found Rachael."

"I need to get to the hospital. Oh my God, Jack. What if she dies?"

"Let's hope for the best. Do you want me to meet you there?"

"Could you?"

"Yes. Stacy can stay with the kids," Jack said.

"What about all these people? How do I get through them?"

He could hear them pounding on Tyler's door and the doorbell ringing in the background. "You can call the police and wait for them to get there, or you can muscle your way through. Don't hurt anybody, though, or they'll charge you with assault. I've got them outside my door, too."

"What do I say?" Tyler said.

"Something like, 'Rachael is safe. I have no other comment at this time.'"

"Right. See you at the hospital. I'm leaving now," Tyler said.

"Which hospital?" Jack said.

"Dixie Medical Center."

"I'm on the way." He walked back through the house and stepped onto the back patio. He heard giggling coming from inside the tent. "Hey, Stacy, can you come out here for a minute?"

"Be right there." She crawled out of the tent, laughing and smiling like he'd never seen her do before. He hated to change the mood.

"What is it? What did Kevin say?"

"Plenty. First of all, there's a mob of reporters on the front lawn. Second, Joan Chandler is in some type of coma. I'm leaving to meet Tyler at Dixie Medical. Keep the kids inside the house and away from the windows. It might even be best to sneak them up to your apartment. I doubt the reporters would climb the fence, but you never know. Some of these guys will do anything to get a photograph."

She cast a worried glance towards the tent. "How long will you be gone?"

"I don't know. They're not even sure Mrs. Chandler's gonna make it."

"How's Tyler?"

"Upset. He's got a pack of wolves outside his door, too."

"How am I supposed to get the kids upstairs without them seeing us?"

"I'll distract them." He took a few steps and paused.

"What?" she said, giving him a wary look.

"Stay with the kids. I'll be right back." He went into the garage, reached behind the front seat of his truck, and pulled out his spy kit, which he took into the house and into his private bathroom. Using his trusty hair gel, he slicked down his curls and combed them flat against his head. Next, he affixed a goatee mustache, a beard, and put on a pair of black-rimmed glasses. When he had completed his disguise, which he relished having the opportunity to effect, he went back out onto the porch. Everyone was inside the tent.

Changing his voice, he said, "Is anybody home?"

Stacy came roaring out of the tent. "Hey, you have no right to be back here. I'm calling the police!" She pulled out her cell phone and dialed 911.

"Stacy, it's me. Calm down or you'll upset the kids."

Rachael and Jayden crawled to the door of the tent and looked out.

She stared at him and then put the phone back into her pocket. "You should warn me before you do that, you know."

Jack pointed to the kids.

"It's all right everybody. I'll be back in a minute. You guys hide under the blankets, and I'll come find you on the count of twenty. Go!"

The kids squealed and crawled back inside.

"Jack, I looked out the front window. There must be fifty people out there. This is crazy!"

"I'm going out through the garage. That should distract them long enough for you to hurry through the gate and into your own garage. Lock yourselves in and then get them upstairs. You'll be fine once you're up there. I'll call you when I have news."

"Be careful, and remember to tell Tyler who you are. If you don't, he's likely to punch you out before he realizes it's you."

"Thanks," he chuckled. "I'll do that. Get the kids ready. I'll beep my horn when it's time for you to move." He went into the garage and climbed into his truck. He waited for two full minutes and then hit the garage door opener. Reporters swarmed the opening before he could back out onto the driveway. He rolled his window halfway down and continued to back out of the garage.

"Excuse me! Excuse me! What can you tell us about Rachael Chandler? We understand that Jack Kendall played a role in her recovery. Where is Jack Kendall now?" said one of the reporters as cameras flashed all around.

Jack tapped the horn hoping that Stacy heard it and that people had the good sense to move out of the way.

"We understand that another child was discovered with Rachael Chandler. What can you tell us about him?" a man said as he shoved his microphone towards the window.

"Is it true that the second child is African American?" a man shouted.

"Is it true that Mrs. Chandler's son cheated on his wife, and this child is the product of that affair?" a woman called from somewhere in the crowd. Someone else banged on the side of his truck with the palms of his hands.

Jack rolled his window the rest of the way down as the cameras continued to flash. "I *can* tell you that Mr. Kendall will not be pleased if you scratch his truck. As for the children, you'll have to wait until the family releases a statement."

"Where is Mr. Kendall now?" a reporter repeated. "Why are you driving his truck?"

"Mr. Kendall is on assignment. As for me, I have some errands to run, so if you'll kindly move out of my way."

"Can't you tell us anything?" a male reporter shouted. "What about Stacy Young?"

"What Rachael Chandler needs is an opportunity to return to a normal life. If you care anything about her, give her the space she needs to do that. Seeing people gang around the house would be frightening for any child. Respect her privacy and give her time to adjust. That's all I have to say. Thank you." He rolled up the window, lowered the garage door, and backed into the street.

* * *

When Jack arrived at the intensive care unit, Tyler was in the room with his mother. He took a seat in the waiting room, wondering what it would mean to the case if she didn't pull through. The nurses wouldn't give him any information, even when he presented his private investigator card. He considered dropping his disguise, but he figured he might need it to get back into the house later. If he hadn't left his spy kit at home, he'd be tempted to retrieve his lab coat and impersonate a doctor, as he'd done on many occasions, so that he could review her medical records, but he figured Tyler would tell him what was going on as soon as he came out. He just had to be patient, which wasn't his strong suit.

"Excuse me," a nurse said as she stepped out from behind the nursing station. "Are you Jack Kendall?"

"Yes."

"I just received a call from the administration department. Because the patient is a suspect in an ongoing federal and police investigation, it seems you may be present to monitor anything she might say if she wakes up. Follow me, please." Jack followed her down the hallway. "She's in there," she said.

"Thank you." He nodded to the police guard at the door and walked into the room. When he saw Tyler's mother, he hesitated. Whatever he had expected, it wasn't this frail, older woman who lay deathly still, hooked up to several machines, many of which were buzzing and beeping. This was completely incongruent with the image he'd created in his mind of a strong, obsessively controlling, domineering woman, who would say and do anything to get her way. It was unsettling, shocking even. "Hey, Tyler."

"Who are you?"

"It's me, Jack. I had to disguise myself to get past the paparazzi. How did you manage it?"

"I asked if they knew it was legal for me to shoot them for ignoring my no trespassing sign. I walked right past them."

"Clever."

"I'm glad you're here," Tyler said, his voice breaking. "I'm… she…"

"I understand."

"There's another chair over there," Tyler said pointing to a plastic chair.

"Have they given you any updates?" Jack said. Tyler shook his head. "Has she said anything?"

"No. She hasn't moved. I don't know if she can hear us or not. This is much worse than the last time this happened."

"When was that?" Jack said.

"Oddly enough, it happened right after Billy Ray came to my house threatening to adopt Rachael. He told Mother that he and Leeann had a better chance of getting her because they were younger. It really upset her."

The heart monitor beeped, and the lines rose sharply on the graph.

"Hey, did you see that?" Jack said. "I think she heard what you just said, and the monitor registered her reaction. I'll go get the nurse." He stepped into the hall and flagged down an elderly nurse as she stepped out from another room. "Hey, we think she can hear us. Her heart rate went up in response to something we said."

The nurse came in and checked her pulse, and then made notes about the readings on the monitors. "Can you hear me, Mrs. Chandler?" The graph remained steady. The nurse smiled. "It may have seemed like she heard you, but there doesn't appear to be any change. Let me know if it happens again."

"Wait. Let me say it again," Tyler said. "Mother, did it upset you when Billy Ray said he was going to take Rachael away from you because he and Leeann would make better parents?"

The monitor spiked again.

The nurse's eyebrows rose. "Perhaps she *can* hear you. Say

something else."

"Mother, did you shoot Billy Ray?"

The monitor spiked, and an alarm went off.

Tyler jumped to his feet. "What does that mean?"

"Step back," the nurse said. She reached to turn off the alarm, but another one sounded, and then another. She pushed several buttons.

Jack hurried out of the room and called for a doctor.

Two nurses and a doctor rushed past him. "Step outside, please," one of them said.

Tyler stepped back. "I didn't mean to—"

"Come on," Jack said. "Let them do their jobs."

"But—" A nurse pushed them out of the room and yanked the curtains closed. Tyler started pacing. "What did I do? I didn't mean for her to go into distress."

"Take it easy. You couldn't have known this would happen. Let's stay calm and hope for the best. They know what they're doing."

Tyler continued to pace.

"Let's go back to the waiting room," Jack said. "They'll come and get us as soon as she's stable."

Tyler allowed Jack to lead him away. Jack waved him towards the chairs and approached the nursing station. "Please let us know as soon as there's word on Mrs. Chandler's condition."

"We'll send someone out as soon as we know something."

"Thank you." He went to where Tyler sat with his head buried in his hands.

"Her monitor spiked the second I asked if she shot Billy Ray. I wonder if that means she did it," Tyler said.

"We can't know that for sure," Jack said.

"Well, it had to mean *something*."

About an hour later, a man stepped off the elevator and approached the nursing desk. Jack noticed him because he was sharply dressed in a designer suit and appeared too focused to be visiting a loved one.

"Tyler, I'm Mr. Carrington, your mother's attorney. How is she doing?"

Tyler grasped his outstretched hand. "I don't know. They haven't told us anything. She had a relapse about an hour ago."

"I'm sorry to hear that," the man said. "Can we talk somewhere private?"

"You can say whatever you've got right here. I don't have anything to hide from Jack."

The man half-suppressed a frown and handed Tyler a business card. "In addition to handling your mother's defense, I am also the executor of her estate. Call me if you have any questions. Good day."

After he had stepped into the elevator, Jack said, "Do guys like that ever laugh?"

"Like I really want to see *him* right now," Tyler said.

A man in a white lab coat came striding towards them.

"Tyler—" Jack said.

They stood up.

"Mr. Chandler, I'm Doctor Ruben, head of the neurology department. I regret to inform you that your mother passed away about twenty minutes ago. We tried diligently to revive her but were unsuccessful. I'm sorry."

Jack put a hand on Tyler's shoulder. "What was the official cause of death?" he said.

"It's too early to be certain, but we believe she died from a blood clot in the brain. An autopsy will be necessary to know for certain."

"Is an autopsy required?" Tyler said.

"No, but it's the only way to know for certain what caused her death."

"I don't think she'd want me to let you do that. What's done is done. I'd rather let her rest in peace," Tyler said.

"You don't have to decide right now," the doctor said. "Would you like a few minutes to say goodbye?"

Tyler's eyes glazed over, and he looked dazed. "Oh, I…Not by myself. Not after losing Sarah. I can't keep losing the people I love!" He dropped back into his chair.

"Is there anything I can do?" the doctor said.

"Do you have a card? He may have some questions later," Jack said.

"The nurse will let you know how to reach my office. I'm sorry about your mother, Mr. Chandler." He nodded to Jack and walked away.

"Tyler, do you want me to go with you?" Jack said. He didn't answer. "Tyler?"

He sniffed and stood up. "By all means, let's go say goodbye. It's not like I can put it off. It's now or never."

"It's gonna work out. It might not seem like it right now, but it is."

Tyler walked to his mother's room and paused at the door. He took a few deep breaths and stepped inside. It was quiet now. All the machines were off, and Joan lay peacefully on the bed. A nurse stepped away to allow Tyler room to approach. Once he walked up to the bed, she quietly made her way out of the room.

Tyler looked down at his mother for several seconds before taking hold of her hand. "Hey, Mother, it's me. Can you believe it? There's no more work for you to do. It's all over. You can rest now." He wiped his eyes and sniffed.

"There's nothing left for you to worry about. No trial. No jail. Nothing. There are so many things I wanted to say to you, but they don't matter now, do they? You managed to avoid it all. It's so like you, Mother, to do something awful, and then turn it all around so that you don't have to deal with it. Why should I be surprised?" He dropped her hand and took a few steps away, and then turned back towards the bed.

"How could you! How could you lock Rachael up in that attic? How could you keep that child in the dark? Do you know how frightening that is? You did that to *me*, Mother! You did it to me, too! How could you let me believe that Billy Ray had kidnapped her when you had her the entire time? Why would you do that? Did you hate me so much that you had to destroy everything in my life that was good? Is that why you drove Pamela away? Is that why you bribed her not to see me? Is that why you threatened Jacob? You're good at threatening little children. You threatened Rachael; you threaten Jacob; you even threatened Jayden. After all that Mr. Gibbs has done for you, all these years, how could you threaten his grandson? And then you blame Regina for what *you* did? What's wrong with you? Can't you let anyone live in peace? Must everyone bow to what you want them to say and do?"

Raising his voice still higher, he stepped back and pointed his finger at her. "I pity you! Wherever you are, your lies can't save you now. You have been found out. At last, you will answer for the damage you've done! You could have saved Dad, but you didn't. You could've called for help, but you didn't. You let him die when you could have saved him, and for what? So that you could rule your stupid castle all by yourself? Look, Mother, look where it got you! You're famous all right, famous for lying, kidnapping, and murder. May God have mercy on your soul. I hope He makes you relive every wicked deed so that you *see* the damage you have done. I pray He forgives you, Mother, because it will be a long damn time before I do!"

He stalked past Jack, whose brows stayed raised several seconds after Tyler left the room. He looked at Joan Chandler, as she lay deceptively peaceful, and found it difficult to imagine that she had done all the things he knew she had done. After hearing what Tyler said to his mother, he wondered at her fate. Surely, all the evil wasn't worth it. Surely, she'd change it if she could, but that was the problem. By the time someone got to where Joan Chandler likely was, there was no changing anything.

He shuddered.

"May God have more mercy on you than you had for Rachael or Tyler, or the dead body of Billy Ray Richards."

He turned away with a heavy heart and went to find Tyler.

* * *

Jack had just parted from Tyler in the hospital parking lot when Kevin called.

"Your recording last night proved very beneficial to our investigation," Kevin said. "They took black lights out to the mansion. We found traces of blood on the banister, the legs of the furniture, and on the stairs, which corroborates Regina's account of what happened that night. We're running DNA samples to see if they match Billy Ray's remains, but there's little doubt that they will. We've already confirmed that the blood on the dock belonged to Billy Ray."

"This case is wrapping itself up quite nicely for you. Isn't it, Captain?"

"Do I detect sarcasm, Kendall? I would've thought you'd be pleased."

"I am. It's just that I see first-hand all the hurt that woman caused. She did a lot of damage during her time on earth. It makes me wonder why a woman who had so much in the way of material possessions couldn't be content with her blessings. What makes a person seek to control the lives of everyone around them, even to the point of threats and violence? I pity her. In the end, she gained nothing from the people she sought to control but their enmity."

"Ah, I heard that Mrs. Chandler passed. How's Tyler holding up?" Kevin said.

"He's been through a lot the past year or so. I'm not sure how well he's doing."

"Keep an eye on him then. We don't want him going off the deep end. Can you keep the kids another night?"

"Yes, but what about Regina and Mr. Gibbs?"

"We're checking the rest of the house for blood tonight. The crime scene should be clear again tomorrow. Jayden can return home once that's complete. As far as Rachael's custody goes, I haven't gotten an answer. She's been assigned a caseworker, and they've arranged for her to speak with a child psychiatrist tomorrow so that the judge can make a ruling. I'll have someone call you with the information."

"Who's representing Rachael's best interest?"

"The State, since her father hasn't stepped forward on her behalf," Kevin said.

"I doubt he knows he's supposed to. Should I talk to him about it?"

"Let's see what the psychiatrist says tomorrow and make a determination from there. We'd hate to have him fight for her if she'll only suffer more abuse under his care."

"Mrs. Chandler's attorney stopped by the hospital before she died. It'll be interesting to see what she's arranged in her will. My guess is that Tyler will inherit the mansion. I wonder if he'll sell it," Jack said.

"I wouldn't encourage him to get his hopes up. There's no telling what a woman like that might do. She could've left it all to charity."

"With everything going on, I doubt he's even thought about it yet."

"Oh, I'll bet he has," Kevin said. "But just in case, remind him to contact that attorney. He's going to need him."

"He probably needs his own attorney," Jack said.

"You may be right about that. When you call to check on him later, why don't you suggest it?"

"Yes, sir."

"Why do I get the impression that you're mocking me?" Kevin said.

"I just watched someone die. Whether she was evil or not, it was still upsetting. I'll be adding another file to the Dropbox folder tonight. For all of Joan's money, she couldn't buy what matters most, and I pity her."

CHAPTER TWENTY-THREE

Rachael licked her fingers. "Can I have more syrup for my toast, Miss Stacy?"

"You most certainly may. I figured since you and Jayden can count so high in French, you might like French toast."

"I like it," Jayden said. "You cook almost as good as Auntie Regina."

"Thanks a lot!" Stacy laughed. "Eat up, Rachael. You have to leave in a few minutes."

"I gotta go to the doctor."

"That's right, and later today we're going to visit Mr. G and Auntie Regina."

"I'm ready to go home," Jayden said. "Our garden is probably covered in weeds by now."

"I like to work in the garden, too," Rachael said as her forehead creased. "But Gramma doesn't let me play outside anymore. If I go home, will I have to go back to the attic?"

"No, Rachael. You don't ever have to go back to the attic again," Stacy said.

"Can I sleep in my princess room?" she said, her face brightening with hope.

"What princess room?"

"My bedroom! I have a castle bed with steps that lead up to it. I have bookshelves and a white dresser. I have two lamps, and it's not dark in there at all. All my toys are in there, and all my pretty dresses. It's the most beautiful room in the whole wide world. Can I sleep in my princess bed tonight?"

"I don't know, Rachael. The police will have to tell us where you'll sleep tonight."

"But I wanna go home with Jayden."

"Jack! Are you ready?" Stacy called.

Jack came rushing down the hall and into the kitchen. "Sorry. I got caught on the phone. You ready, Rachael?"

"Yes, but my hands are sticky."

Jack scooped her up and took her to the kitchen sink. "Stick 'em in. We gotta go!"

Once her hands were clean, Jack ruffled Jayden's thick, curly hair. "Bye, Jayden. See you soon."

"Bye, Rachael. Can I eat the rest of your French toast?" Jayden said.

"Sure," Rachael said as Jack led her out the door.

"I'll be right back, Jayden. I'm going to walk them out," Stacy said as she followed them into the garage.

Jack opened the truck door and waited for Rachael to climb inside. "We're gonna play a game."

"What game?" Rachael said.

"I want you to crawl under the blanket, count to fifty in French, and then guess where we're going. If you guess right, I'll take you to get some ice cream later."

"I want chocolate ice cream."

"Chocolate it is. Cover up and start counting!" Jack said.

"Call me," Stacy said and stepped back.

Jack hit the garage door opener. Fortunately, there were police officers on either side to ensure that the crowd stayed out of the way. Once he had backed out into the driveway, Stacy hit the garage door button, pausing to make sure that no one ducked beneath the door before she went into the house.

*　*　*

Jack sat in the waiting room for nearly two hours before the door leading into the interior offices opened. "Mr. Kendall?" said an older woman in a white lab coat.

"Yes," he said, rising to his feet.

"I'm Dr. Crimshaw. Come with me, please."

Jack followed the tall, gray-haired woman down the long hallway and into a small office. As she sat behind the desk, she pointed to a chair and said, "Have a seat." She slipped on a pair of glasses and opened a manila folder. "I understand that you're serving as Rachael's temporary caregiver. Is that correct?"

"She's been staying with me since we recovered her. I'm recommending that she remain in the custody of Mr. Gibbs until matters are settled with her father. What conclusions have you drawn from your session today?"

"Frankly, this child will need a great deal of counseling. She's exceptionally bright, but she has suffered a tremendous amount of trauma. We always hope, of course, that she can be reunited with her birth family. I'll have to meet with her father to see if that's possible."

"What did Rachael tell you about that situation?" he said.

"Her father doesn't want her. She says he loves her brother, Cody, but he doesn't love her. Many children believe that, of course, but it isn't usually true."

Jack cocked his head.

"You think it's true?" she said.

"I've heard Tyler say as much, and so has Rachael. I hope that he may change, of course, but Tyler needs counseling every bit as much as Rachael does."

"What makes you say that?"

"Apparently, Tyler's mother used to lock him in the closet when he was young. He said he's just now remembering that. He has recently lost his wife, and now his mother, on top of learning of her deceit regarding the fate of his daughter and the breakup between him and the woman he currently loves. He's got a lot to sort through. When it comes to Rachael, I think he genuinely wants to do right by her. Perhaps, in time, the entire family can heal, but for the moment…"

"This is a complicated case, but it is very unlikely that the courts will award custody to Mr. Gibbs. Are you willing to continue caring for Rachael?"

He felt his eyebrows rise. "I haven't considered that."

"Rachael wants to stay with Mr. Gibbs because of Jayden, but she says she trusts you and Stacy, whoever Stacy is."

"Stacy is my friend and assistant. There's no romantic connection between us."

"I will be meeting with Rachael's caseworker to present my recommendations later this afternoon. I need to know if you are willing to care for Rachael a while longer. If not, we'll need to look for another family to take her in."

"What about Tyler?"

"As you said, there are issues. It is something to work toward, but not something I'm willing to recommend immediately. Will you or won't you keep Rachael?"

"What time frame are we talking about?"

"I can't say. Anywhere from a few weeks to a few months. It depends on how fast everyone makes progress."

"What if Tyler doesn't make progress?"

"Then we'll search for a family to adopt Rachael on a permanent basis. There aren't any other options."

He sighed. "Yes. I'll keep Rachael a while longer. Are her father and brother allowed to see her? Can she visit with Mr. Gibbs, Regina, and Jayden?"

"You'll be her foster father for the time being. You'll have to determine what is good for her and what isn't, depending on how she responds to things. We'll be counseling with her once a week, so we'll be monitoring her progress closely. Again, the goal is for her to be restored to her birth family if at all possible."

"Have you talked with Tyler?" Jack said.

"Not yet." She slid two business cards across the desk. "Keep one of these and give the other one to Tyler. Ask him to contact us as soon as possible. The sooner we get these issues dealt with, the better off everyone will be."

"I haven't told Rachael about her grandmother's death yet. What do you recommend as far as the funeral goes?"

"Considering what she's been through, it might be good for her to go. It's important for her to understand that her grandmother won't reappear and push her into the attic again. I wouldn't force her to see the body if she doesn't want to."

Jack shook his head. "That poor child has been through so much; it breaks my heart."

"How are you connected to this little girl?"

"Through her Aunt Emily and through Tyler. More importantly, I guess, because I seem to be the best one for the job right now. Nothing else matters."

"True enough, Mr. Kendall. Right now, what's best for Rachael has to be what matters most. You mentioned an aunt. Is it possible that Rachael could stay with her?"

Jack grimaced. "Emily is wonderful, but she lives out of state, and the connection with her family might cause some serious complications, I'm afraid. It was her parents who were falsely accused of kidnapping Rachael, and it was Emily's father, Billy Ray, that Mrs. Chandler is accused of killing."

"I see. All the more reason for Rachael to stay with you." Dr. Crimshaw rose and extended her hand. "Thank you, Mr. Kendall. I'll draw up my recommendations and submit them to her caseworker this afternoon." She picked up the phone on her desk. "Anita, please bring Rachael into my office."

A few moments later, someone tapped on the door. "Come in," Dr. Crimshaw said without glancing up from her notepad.

"Hi, Mr. Jack!" Rachael said.

"Hey, you. Where did you get that lollipop?"

"Miss Anita gave it to me for being a good girl."

"Are you ready to go?" he said. "Because I have a surprise for you on the way home."

Her smile lit up the room. "We get to stop for ice cream!"

He held out his hand for her to take, which she readily did. "That's right, but I have another surprise for you, too. Goodbye Dr. Crimshaw. I'll be in touch."

"See you back here next Friday," she said.

He gave her a salute and held Rachael's hand as she skipped down the hall.

"Tell me about your meeting," he said when they had stepped outside.

"Dr. Crimshaw asked me lots of questions, and I drew pictures and sang songs."

"Was it fun?"

She shrugged. "She wanted to know about Gramma and Billy Ray. Why does everybody want to talk about Billy Ray? I don't like him."

"Do you know what a lie is, Rachael?"

She nodded and looked down. "I get a spankin' when I tell a lie."

He had to keep himself from smiling. "That's because telling a lie is very bad. Your Gramma told the police some lies about Billy Ray, and they're trying to find out the truth about what happened. You were there. That's why they want to talk to you about it. Does that make sense?"

She nodded.

"Once they know what happened, they'll stop talking about it.

Won't that be nice?"

"Yes. I'd rather talk about Jayden, and the garden, and counting in French. I counted in French for Dr. Crimshaw. She liked it."

"I bet she did. Do you want to know about your other surprise?"

"Tell me!"

"I'm going to take you and Jayden to visit Mr. Gibbs and Auntie Regina today."

"Yay! I can't wait to see them."

"That's not all. How would you like to go into your princess room and get some of your books and toys to bring back with you to my house?"

"I get to go into my princess room?" she said, her eyes wide with wonder.

"You do."

"But why am I going back to your house? Why can't I stay with Mr. G. and Regina?"

"The doctor says she wants you to stay with Stacy and me a little longer, but we'll go visit Mr. Gibbs, Jayden, and Auntie Regina lots and lots."

"Isn't Jayden going to live at your house, too?" she said, drawing her brows together.

"He's welcome to stay if Mr. Gibbs will let him, but I think he'll want Jayden to live in the cabin with him. Don't you?"

"How long will I stay at your house?" Rachael said.

"I don't know yet. The doctors are trying to figure out the best place for you to live."

"I want to live in my princess room," Rachael said.

"I know you do, but we'll have to wait and see what the judge decides."

"Why do people always tell us what to do? Why can't we decide for ourselves?"

"Even grownups have to listen to judges."

* * *

"Do you think she told him?" Regina said as she smoothed her dress down into place.

"I don't know," Mr. Gibbs said.

"What caused her to tell such a lie in the first place? Regina said. "That child ain't in the habit of tellin' lies."

"We done been over this. It must be what she remembers," Mr. Gibbs said. "I just hope them doctors don't get her to rememberin' somethin' different."

"I can hardly sleep at night, worryin' about it."

"That's what we get for not telling the truth," Mr. Gibbs said, shifting his weight to lean against the gate.

They were expecting Jack to pull up any minute.

"How can you be so calm about this? Ain't you worried?" Regina said with a wrinkled brow.

"It don't do no good to fret over it. If she tells 'em the truth, we goin' to jail. If she don't, we stay here and keep raisin' Jayden. Either way, we gotta face our Maker. There ain't no lie gonna save us from that."

"I know it," Regina said as she bit down on a fingernail, "but I don't see how me sittin' in some jail cell is gonna help nobody. I ain't gonna shoot nobody else, and yer so old, I can't count on you stayin' around to raise that young'un yer daughter abandoned."

He chuckled. "Stop yer frettin'. I ain't plannin' to die today."

"It ain't like Mrs. Chandler's an angel herself," Regina said. "It wasn't right for her to keep that child locked up the way she did, and deny her supper for every little thing. She'll be answerin' for that one day, and her money won't do her one bit of good then. God don't care how much money she's got."

"Until then, though, her money has a good chance at buyin' her freedom," Mr. Gibbs said. "It works like that for rich folks. As for me, I'm more o'feared of God than I am of the police."

"Me, too, but we'll have to face the police sooner than we'll have to face God if Miss Rachael admits she lied."

"Speak for yerself," Mr. Gibbs said. "My heart might not survive another trip to the police station. I don't like to lie, especially with 'em sittin' across the table starin' at me like that. No, sir. I don't like it one little bit. If it weren't for Jayden, I'd be tellin' 'em everythin' we done."

Regina gave him a sympathetic look and bit another fingernail. "Thank God for Jayden. This not knowin' business is about to *kill* me, so I might be dead right along with ya. Then where'd we be? Lord have mercy; I hope that child don't remember the truth."

* * *

Mr. Gibbs and Regina were waiting at the gate when Jack pulled up. Regina rushed around to the passenger's side and opened the door. "Well, if it ain't my two most favorite children! Come on down here and give me some love."

Jack chuckled as he listened to Jayden tell them about the tent and how they had camped out in the back yard.

Mr. Gibbs stretched out his hand for him to shake. "We sure is grateful for you takin' such good care of these young'uns. We had us quite a trip downtown, we did. Now, I expects it's up to Mrs. Chandler to tell her side of the story."

"You don't need to concern yourself with that anymore," Jack said.

"Can we go check on the garden, Papa? I just know it's covered with weeds," Jayden said.

"You go on and check, boy. We'll wander that way in a minute," Mr. Gibbs said.

Rachael squealed with delight and chased after Jayden.

"What are you trying to say, Mr. Kendall?" Regina said.

"Please, call me Jack. Mrs. Chandler passed away yesterday afternoon. Tyler will be making the funeral arrangements. I'll ask him to let you know when the service is."

"Lordy," Regina said as she put a hand over her heart and turned to Mr. Gibbs. "You hear that, G? It's over."

"Well, it's almost over. They haven't read the will yet," Jack said.

"Surely, she left everything to Mr. Tyler," Mr. Gibbs said. "So, I can take care of the place like I always done."

"I hope so, Mr. Gibbs, but there's always the possibility that he may sell it. I'm not trying to alarm you. I only want to remind you that it could go either way. All will be disclosed soon enough." Mr. Gibbs and Regina looked at each other, and Jack saw the worry in their eyes. "I've told the doctors and police that I think Rachael would be happiest staying with you folks until Tyler is ready to love her as she deserves. For the time being, however, they want her to stay with me."

"Does Rachael know that?" Regina asked.

"Yes. I've promised to bring her to visit as often as I can," Jack said.

"We love Rachael," Mr. Gibbs said, "and we'd keep her if they'd let us, but we know they ain't gonna give no white child to a black family, so we'll make do with your visits. We're mighty thankful."

"Rachael made me promise to ask if Jayden could stay with us at my house, too."

"No, sir. I ain't givin' my grandson to nobody."

Jack raised his hands to stop him from going on. "I expected you to say that, but I told her I'd ask. She loves Jayden, you know."

Mr. Gibbs chuckled. "They love each other. They sure 'nuff do."

"They's a mess is what they is," Regina said with a smile and a shake of her head.

"Well, let's go see this garden they talk so much about. I've heard it grows peas, butter beans, carrots, strawberries, cucumbers, tomatoes, and I forgot what else," Jack said.

"Oh, we gots more than one garden," Mr. Gibbs said, "but they'll be in the vegetable garden. That's where they'll be. It's this way."

Jack followed them down the path and was amazed to see how beautiful the grounds were in the daytime. The mansion in the distance looked elegant and inviting. He found himself wanting to explore the winding pathway that intersected the main path at various points. "This is an amazing piece of property. How big is it?"

"Four hundred and fifty acres, but the house and gardens, they's only forty," Mr. Gibbs said. "There's twenty kinds of trees, including nearly every fruit you can name, and countless plants and flowers. You should see it in the spring, Mr. Jack. These gardens are a sight to behold, especially them fancy gazebos over the creek. I picture little Rachael marrin' some fine beau there someday. And the cliff over the river? That's another prime spot. Can't stay sad up there. No, sir. It's too pretty to stay sad up there." He sighed and shook his head. "I hope we get to stay. There ain't no place I'd rather be."

Jack smiled. How nice to feel so perfectly content. Then again, Pearl River Mansion was a wonderful place to be—but it hadn't been for Rachael. His cell phone rang. He reached to turn it off but saw that it was Tyler. Turning to Mr. Gibbs and Regina, he said, "I need to take this call. Sorry." He walked down a side path. "Hey, Tyler. What's up?"

"Why the hell are you keeping my daughter?"

"It's temporary. It was either that or let her go to a foster family. This way, at least, you can see her, and she can visit Mr. Gibbs, Regina, and Jayden."

"You talk like they're family. I'm her father. Everyone seems to forget that. I'm coming to get my daughter, Jack, and don't you try to stop me."

"If you pull something stupid like that, you can kiss your chances of getting Rachael back anytime soon goodbye. The FBI is involved, for God's sake. You can't call the shots. I've been on your side this entire time. You need to listen to me. You need to be patient."

Tyler exhaled loudly. "Fine. You're right. What do I need to do?"

"Breathe. We'll get through this one step at a time. We need to get through the funeral first. Have you made the arrangements?"

"Some of them, I guess. I don't really know what to do. The funeral director called. He wants me to go down there."

"You have to go, Tyler. They'll walk you through everything you need to do. You need to make a list of people to call. You'll have to choose a casket, a headstone, and all that stuff. I'm sure your mother has made some of these arrangements herself. Have you called her attorney?"

"No. I haven't felt like talking to anybody."

"Where's your son? How is Cody doing?" Jack said as he stopped to pluck a daisy.

"I've been taking him to the sitter. I keep telling you; I'm not up for dealing with this right now. I've reached my limit. It's too much. I know it'zzz important, but...I..."

Jack scowled as Tyler's words came out a bit slurred. "Have you been drinking?"

"Hell, yes, I've been drinking. Wouldn't you?"

"Tyler, you've got to pull yourself together. I thought maybe you and Cody could come by to visit Rachael this evening, but I see that's not a good idea."

"I can't do this, Jack. I can't lose anything else."

"If you don't pull yourself together, not only might you lose Rachael for real, but you might lose Cody also. People are watching you right now. You have to man up, Tyler, whether you feel like it or not. Take advantage of the counseling you're being offered. It can do wonders to talk with someone who knows how to deal with what you're going through. You don't have to handle this on your own, but you need to handle it the right way. Drinking only makes things worse. Surely, you can see that. Do you want me to come over there? Do you want me to go to the funeral home with you?"

"What do you know about losing someone you love? I bet your life is picture perfect."

Dropping the daisy, Jack closed his eyes as a sharp, unexpected pain shot through his heart. "You bet wrong. I lost my mother when I was eight, my father when I was in my early twenties, and my best friend, who was like a brother to me, last year. So don't tell me I don't know what it's like to lose someone, because I do. When Daniel died, I wanted to check out, too, but I couldn't because his wife and children were depending on me to help keep them together. It didn't matter how I felt. I had to stay strong for *them.* That's what you have to do. You have to stay strong for Cody and Rachael. You have to, whether you like it or not."

"You're right. I need to man up," he said bitterly. "Nobody cares what *I'm* going through. I'm expected to perform. I get it. I'll call you back when I get it all together. Goodbye, Jack."

The line went dead.

Jack sighed. Had he said the wrong things? Should he go over there? He stood for several seconds thinking about their conversation. He'd had no idea when he took this case how much would be required in order to see it through. He walked back to where Mr. Gibbs and Regina were waiting. "Shall we go find the children?"

"Is everything all right?" Mr. Gibbs said.

"That was Tyler. He's having a difficult time dealing with all of this, as you might imagine. He wants to take Rachael home with him, but the judge hasn't determined what's best for her yet."

Mr. Gibbs nodded and exchanged a worried glance with Regina.

Jack would have liked to reassure them, but he couldn't. "I'd like to take some of Rachael's things home with us this evening. I think she'd feel more comfortable if she has some of her books and toys."

"She's got a few things in the attic, but Mrs. Chandler kept most of her toys locked up in her bedroom," Regina said. "That poor child wasn't allowed to touch nothin' after what happened. Mrs. Chandler said she had to keep her room just as it was, in case the police came back." She shook her head. "It was like Rachael was the criminal. It weren't right, Mr. Jack. It weren't right at all."

"No, but at least it's over." He gestured down the path. "Shall we?" He was silent as he followed them towards the vegetable garden. He couldn't blame them for being nervous. Their futures were as tenuous as everyone else's. He could hear the children laughing before they came into view, and it reminded him of how wonderful it was to be a child. Children had the most amazing ability to live in the moment.

Rachael was sitting on the ground next to a pile of carrots. "Pull harder, Jayden! You can get it," she said.

Jayden groaned with effort, loosening the soil as he tugged. When it finally came free, rich, dark dirt showered them both as he fell squarely on his backside.

"Yay, we got another one!" Rachael cried. "It's my turn."

"Are you two having fun?" Jack said as he stood next to the two-foot-high picket fence that ran the perimeter of the garden.

"Oh, yes, but look at our poor garden. We have lots of work to do," Rachael said. "Look, Auntie Regina. We found carrots!"

"You done real good. Now come here, Miss Rachael, and let me dust you off so Mr. Jack can take you inside to get some of your things from yer bedroom. You ain't goin' in the house with all that dirt on you."

"I get to see my princess room! Wanna come with me, Jayden?"

"Naw, I'm gonna keep pullin' carrots," he said.

"Okay. I'll come back when I'm done." She jumped up and ran to Regina, dusting herself as she went. "Am I good yet?"

"Not yet," Regina said. "Turn around." She dusted her from head to foot. She even had her flip her head forward so she could shake out her brown shoulder-length hair. "Okay, you's about as good as we can make you. You ready, Mr. Jack?"

"Indeed, I am. We'll need to get some clothes while we're at it."

"While she's in her room, I'll go up to the attic and get what she's got up there. That's where most of what fits her is," Regina said.

Rachael gasped and grabbed Jack's arm. "I don't wanna go up to the attic. Please don't make me go up there."

"Don't worry, sweetie. You're not going to the attic. I promise," Jack said.

Regina knelt in front of Rachael. "You listen to me, Miss Rachael. I never wanted you in that attic. You remember all those nights I stayed up there with you?" Rachael nodded as her lip began to tremble and tears fell down her cheeks. "I held you tight and kept you warm. Didn't I?"

"Uh huh," she whimpered.

"When your Grandma made Jayden and me move back to the cabins, I told her it was too dark and too cold up there for you all by yerself, but she wouldn't listen to me. That's why I waited until she went to bed, and then I'd sneak back upstairs to stay with you, even though she'd throw herself all kinds of fits when she'd catch me. Do you remember that?"

Rachael nodded and wiped her eyes.

"That's why we went away, remember? But yer safe now. You don't have to be scaredt no more."

"But where's Gramma? If she sees me, she'll make me go to the attic. I know she will."

Regina looked to Jack.

"Rachael," Jack said as he knelt also. "Your Grandma isn't here anymore. She got sick and went to the hospital. Do you know what a hospital is?" She nodded. "Sometimes people get so sick that they don't come back from the hospital. They die and go to heaven. Your grandmother died, Rachael. She's never coming back again."

"You mean she's gone like Mommy is gone?" Rachael said.

"Yes. Your grandmother can't hurt you ever again."

Rachael wrinkled her forehead. "But Mommy's coming back to find me someday. Daddy said so."

Jack smiled. "Your grandmother is never coming back. I promise. Now let's go to your room and get some of your toys and stuffed animals, and anything else you want to bring to my house."

Regina sniffed, wiped her eyes, and said, "Come, now, child. Let's not keep Mr. Jack awaitin."

"Okay," Rachael said as she turned and ran down the path towards the back of the house.

"Kids," Regina said. "They's something, ain't they?"

"I've only just met them, but it's easy to see that these kids are special."

"They is, but they's *all* special, Mr. Jack. They's all special."

* * *

Stacy paced back and forth across the office floor, oblivious to the fact that Bonnie was up on her desk, walking across the keyboard, which under normal circumstances would never go unchallenged. She was trying to decide if she should call Pamela. Finally, she concluded that Pamela deserved to know that Jacob was no longer in danger. Catching sight of Bonnie from the corner of her eye, she scowled. "Hey, you, get down from there."

Bonnie meowed and lay down right where she was.

Stacy scooped her up and set her on the floor. "You know I don't like that. What's with you today?" Clyde jumped up onto Jack's desk and promptly knocked his penholder on to the floor. "Oh," Stacy said, "I forgot to feed you, didn't I? No wonder you're having issues." She went to retrieve the cat food from beneath the bathroom sink, both cats fast on her heels, and found the cabinet door already open. "I see. I should teach you how to open the container, too." She sprinkled food into their bowls and refreshed their water dish. "There you go."

Her mind made up, she went back to her desk and picked up the phone. She expected to get voicemail, but Pamela answered. "Hey, Pamela. This is Stacy, from Jackson."

"Oh. I—If you're calling to tell me you found Rachael, Tyler already left a message. I'm thrilled to hear it, of course. I really am, but I haven't changed my mind about Tyler."

"I understand. I'm calling to tell you that Joan Chandler passed away yesterday. Jacob is safe now."

"What?"

"She died from some kind of blood clot in the brain, I think. The funeral will be held sometime later this week."

"I don't know what to say. Tyler must be very upset, but I'm…"

"Relieved?" Stacy said.

"Yes. I've been scared to death for Jacob, especially since I shared that recording with Tyler. Did she ever find out about that?"

"As far as I know, Tyler never told her. He was very angry with her for threatening you and Jacob."

"Well, that makes two of us," Pamela said. "Wow. It's hard to believe it's finally over. Does that mean I can breathe?"

"You and Jacob are safe. Jack and I wish you the very best. Thank you for helping us solve this case. Without you, we might not have found Rachael."

"I appreciate you calling about Mrs. Chandler. Have a good day. Goodbye."

Stacy exhaled. Her screw-up in telling Tyler about the recording didn't end up causing any damage, yet the mere fact that it could have still bothered her. It was a mistake she was determined never to repeat. She closed her eyes and whispered, "Thank you."

* * *

Rachael jumped up and down as she waited for Jack to open her bedroom door.

"I don't know where she keeps that key, Mr. Jack," Regina said. "She locked it when we started keepin' Miss Rachael in the attic, and it ain't never been opened since."

Jack ran his fingers along the top of the doorframe to no avail. "Not to worry," he said as he pulled his favorite gadget out of his wallet. He inserted a tension wrench into the lock, and then the pick, and began feeling for pins.

"Hurry, Mr. Jack. Hurry!" Rachael said.

"Why don't you call me Uncle Jack? Would you like that?" The cylinder was clear.

"Okay. Are you almost done, Uncle Jack?"

"I don't feel any pins. The police must have opened it when they searched the house." He withdrew the pick and turned the doorknob.

Rachael gasped and a huge smile spread across her face.

He chuckled; it was like seeing a child step into Disneyland, and then he looked into the room, and his own eyes widened. He'd never seen anything like it. No wonder she talked about it the way she did.

Rachael ran to the bed, scampered up the steps, and then threw the decorative pillows onto the floor. She yanked the bedspread down and tugged on the sheets.

"Miss Rachael, child, what are you doin'?" Regina cried.

"My locket. I have to find it." She reached beneath her bed pillow and squealed. "I found it, Uncle Jack! I found it. Look!" She sat on the bed, her legs hanging off the side, and opened the locket. "Mommy! I'm back. Now you can find me!"

"I'll go upstairs and get her clothes," Regina said.

Jack sat on the bed next to Rachael. "Can I see?" Rachael handed him the necklace. "Your mommy is beautiful, isn't she?"

"Yes."

"You look like your mommy. Do you know that?"

Her face brightened. "I do?"

"Except you're even prettier. Want me to fasten it around your neck so you can wear it?"

"No, Gramma won't let me wear it."

"Gramma is gone now. I say you can wear it if you want to. Would you like that?"

She nodded. As he started to fasten it, she said, "Wait!" She took the locket from his hands and kissed her mother's face. "I love you, Mommy." She closed it and handed it back to him. "You can put it on me now."

He fastened the delicate chain around her neck and set her on the floor. "Gather whatever you want."

"Oh, I don't know where to start!" She collected some of her books, stuffed animals, a few toys, and laid them in a pile on the floor. Suddenly, her lips puckered and she looked like she might cry. "My teddy bear is in the attic."

"No, it isn't. Your daddy has it. We'll ask him to bring it the next time he sees you."

"But I left Bo in the attic. I know I did."

"Yes, you did, but your daddy went up to the attic, and he saw it there. He's keeping it for you."

Rachael cocked her head. "If Daddy knows about the attic, why didn't he save me?"

"Because he didn't know about the attic until after you were already gone. Otherwise, he would have saved you. Your daddy was very upset with your grandmother for keeping you up there."

"How do you know?" she said.

He knelt down and took hold of her hands. "Can I tell you a secret?" She nodded.

"I'm only going to tell you this because I want you to know that I'm telling you the truth about your daddy. He would never have let you stay in the attic because he knows how dark and scary it is up there for you."

"He does?"

"Yes. He knows because your grandmother used to lock him in a very dark closet when he was a little boy. It used to scare him, too."

Rachael blinked a few times as she took that in. "It's scary in the dark."

"Would you have let your daddy out of the closet if you knew he was locked inside?"

She nodded her head. "I wouldn't want him to be scared."

"Well, your daddy wouldn't want you to be scared either. That's how I know he would've let you out."

"I want to get my toys now."

"Great. We need something to carry them in."

"I gots somethin' right here," Regina said as she returned with her clothes. She reached into the closet and pulled out a canvas beach bag. "Will this do?"

"Perfect." Jack filled the bag while Regina packed a small suitcase with her clothes.

"Uncle Jack?"

"Yes?"

"I'm glad you found me in the cabin."

"Me, too. Are you about ready? Stacy is waiting on us. You're supposed to help her make spaghetti for dinner tonight, remember?"

"Yummy! I like Miss Stacy."

"I like her, too, and I love her spaghetti."

* * *

"There will be no way to keep the media at bay once they see Rachael at the funeral, so be prepared to protect her the best you can," Captain Thomas said. "We bought her some time to adjust, but they'll be taking a slew of photographs today."

"Today will be stressful for her all the way around. It will be the first time she's seen her father since the night we found her. It will also be the first time she's seen her brother, Cody, not to mention the funeral itself. That's a lot to take in for a little girl," Jack said.

"What about the Gibbs family. I assume they'll be in attendance?"

Captain Thomas said.

"Yes, as far as I know. Can you have officers watch for them when they drive up?"

"Will do, plus we've got uniformed police stationed at all the doors. Restricting the service to close friends and relatives should keep out curious onlookers, but be prepared for a crush outside, and you can forget about going to the graveside."

"I wouldn't take Rachael there anyway," Jack said. "Thanks for the heads up. I'll go get Rachael."

* * *

Jack and Stacy looked at each other as they buckled their seatbelts.

"Ready, sweetie?" Stacy said.

"Are you going to cover me now?" Rachael said.

"Yep, duck down," Stacy said as she lifted the blanket and pulled it over her. "It will only be for a few minutes. Just until we get out of the driveway and down the street a little way."

"Don't tickle me!"

"I might," Stacy said, and Rachael giggled.

Reporters stormed the truck as soon as they backed out, but Jack continued to move slowly backward, ignoring their waving arms, microphones, and cameras. When he backed into the street, he pressed the remote again and waited for the garage to close before proceeding down the street, leaving twenty or thirty frustrated reporters behind.

"I'm gonna tickle you now," Stacy said.

"No!" Rachael giggled.

Stacy tickled her through the blanket as Rachael shrieked and pulled the blanket from her head.

"Do you remember where we're going, Rachael?" Jack said.

"We're going to say goodbye to Gramma before they bury her in a box like they did my mommy."

"That's right. There might be some people there who want to take your picture. Do you know why?"

"Because I'm pretty?"

Jack and Stacy laughed. "You are pretty, but that's not why they want to take your picture. This is very important, so I want you to listen," Jack said. "Do you remember what happened to Billy Ray?"

"Gramma shot him with her gun."

"After that, your Gramma started keeping you in the attic, didn't she?"

"Yes."

"Why did she do that?"

"Because she didn't want me to tell anyone what she did to Billy Ray. She said it was our secret," Rachael said.

"That's right. Your Gramma didn't even tell your daddy what happened to Billy Ray. She told him that Billy Ray took you away, so your daddy and the police have been looking for you all this time."

"Gramma lied?"

"Yes, she did. There are lots of people who have been worried about you, including Stacy and me. Everyone is happy we found you in the cabin. That's why they want to take your picture, and that's why they've been outside my house, but there are also some people who aren't very nice. We haven't let anyone take your picture because it's hard to tell which people are nice and which ones are mean. I'm telling you this because you may see a lot of people today, and some of them might try to take your picture."

"Will any of the mean people be there?" she said wrinkling her brow.

"We don't know, but we hope not."

"Jack and I will be with you," Stacy said. "So there's nothing to worry about."

"Will Mr. G, Auntie Regina, and Jayden be there?" Rachael said.

"Maybe," Jack said. "If they are, Jayden can sit next to you if that's okay with Mr. Gibbs. We're almost there now, so we're gonna keep you covered up until we get inside the building. I'll carry you in."

Stacy pulled the blanket over Rachael. "Under you go."

Jack turned into the parking lot and cringed as reporters surrounded the truck. He pulled slowly towards the back of the mortuary, just as Kevin had instructed. Four uniformed police officers stepped forward to keep the reporters away. "Rachael, I'm going to get out and then scoop you up. Here we go." Stacy was right behind them. Once they were inside, he set Rachael on her feet. "There. That wasn't so bad, was it?"

"Nobody got me," Rachael said.

"Here, let me fix your hair." Stacy pulled a comb from her purse and ran it through Rachael's hair. "There you go. You look very nice."

A distinguished-looking elderly gentleman approached and extended his hand. "Welcome. I'm Mr. Foley. I'll show you to the chapel. Follow me, please."

Rachael reached for Stacy's hand as they walked down the hallway. When they entered through the double doors, Rachael cried, "Look! There's Jayden." She pulled her hand free and ran to the pew where Mr. Gibbs and Regina sat, some ten rows back from the open casket.

Jack and Stacy followed. There were quite a few people gathered, but Jack didn't see Tyler.

Mr. Gibbs rose and extended his hand. "Good to see you, Mr. Jack."

"Have you seen Tyler?"

"No, sir. We ain't seen him yet."

"I'm going to take a look out in the hall. Would you mind keeping an eye on Rachael?"

"She'll be right here," Mr. Gibbs said with a nod.

"I'll go with you," Stacy said. As they walked up the center aisle, she whispered, "I hate funerals. If it weren't for Rachael, I wouldn't be here."

Jack chuckled. "If Tyler asked you, you would."

"Oh, shut up. I forget how well you know me. Hey, look. There's

Tyler," Stacy said. "The little boy must be Cody. He looks a lot like Rachael."

"And that's Joan Chandler's attorney. I wonder if he goes to all his clients' funerals. If so, that's a high price to pay for being an attorney. I wouldn't want to do it."

"No kidding," Stacy agreed.

Tyler shook hands with the attorney and headed towards the chapel. He saw them immediately and waved.

"Thanks for coming," Tyler said as he and Cody drew near. "I'm sure there are lots of places you'd rather be. You've been a great help through all of this."

"Hello, Cody. I'm Stacy, and this is my best friend, Jack."

"Nice to meet you, Cody," Jack said as he extended his hand for Cody to shake.

"I have to go to the bathroom," Cody said, ignoring Jack's hand.

"Again? Go ahead, but come right back here. You hear me?" Cody took off at a run and Tyler shook his head. "That boy's got more energy than the Energizer bunny."

"Was that Mr. Carrington I just saw?" Jack said.

"He wants to meet with me about the will, right after the service. Where's Rachael?"

"She's in the chapel with Mr. Gibbs," Jack said.

"Good. The attorney wants the children present for the meeting."

"They are probably beneficiaries in some way, perhaps with a college fund or something," Jack said. "How are you holding up?"

"I haven't been drinking, if that's what you mean," Tyler sneered.

"Glad to hear it. Hopefully, this will all be over soon, and you can settle into a normal routine again."

"Have you heard anything about when Rachael can come home?"

"No, but I take Rachael back to the psychologist next week. I think we'll hear the results of her evaluation soon."

"I've got an appointment to speak with one of those people myself next week," Tyler said. "If they can help me deal with all this, I would be stupid not to let them. I'm not committing to anything, but I'll talk with them at least once."

Jack nodded. "Good for you."

"Where is that boy? Excuse me while I go hunt down my son. The service is about to start."

Jack glanced at his watch. "So it is. See you soon. Oh, Tyler, is it possible for Rachael and Cody to have a few minutes together after the meeting? They haven't seen each other in over a year."

"Why not? See you in there," he said and headed off to look for his son.

Jack looked at Stacy. "Don't say it."

"All right," she said, "but I'm thinking it."

The small chapel was nearly full. The director came forward and escorted them to the front row. Rachael fixed her eyes on the casket for the first time. "Is Gramma in there?" she said.

"Yes," Jack said. "You don't have to see her if you don't want to."

Rachael stood up, but she couldn't see inside. "Can she hear us?"

"Your Gramma is gone, Rachael. Only her body is in the box," Jack said.

"Oh." She sat down, but her eyes stayed on the casket.

The minister walked up to the pulpit. "If anyone else would like to approach the casket, please do so now. We will be closing it for the service, which will begin in about five minutes."

Rachael glanced up at Jack as if she were startled.

"That's what always happens," he said.

Tyler walked by with Cody, who pulled back on his hand as they got close to the casket.

"I don't want to," Cody said.

Jack rose. "Tyler, Cody can wait with us."

"Go wait with your sister. I'll come get you in a minute," Tyler said.

Jack took hold of Cody's hand. "Come sit with us. Rachael is right over here."

"I don't want to sit with Rachael," Cody said and pulled his hand free. "I hate Rachael!"

Tyler turned from the casket and scooped up his son, just as a camera flashed.

Jack turned towards the door in time to see two plainclothes policemen usher the reporter out of the chapel.

Tyler set Cody on the pew, on the opposite side of the aisle. "I'm going to say my respects to your grandmother. You sit here and don't move. If you do, I'll wear out your backside when we get home."

"Yes, sir," Cody said with a pout.

Jack got up and sat next to Cody.

"Thanks," Tyler said. He approached the casket for the second time and looked upon his mother.

Jack wondered what he was thinking. After all the things Tyler said to her in the hospital room, had his anger worn off? Was he remembering the good times they shared? Had he forgiven her? Would he ever forgive her?

Tyler took the sunglasses from his head and put them on. He sat next to his son and looked straight ahead.

Jack went back to his seat.

"Why is Daddy wearing sunglasses?" Rachael whispered.

"Do you want to sit by him, Rachael?"

She shook her head and grabbed hold of Stacy's hand.

Two attendants closed the casket and slid the flower arrangement to the center. It was a lovely arrangement of cascading orchids. Jack wondered if Tyler had chosen it or if Joan herself had chosen them in advance. He suspected that Joan had prearranged all the details, down to the font they used on her headstone.

The service was brief and unemotional. No one spoke eulogies on her behalf. No one sang songs. Those in attendance cleared out quickly, and only a few stopped to offer condolences to Tyler. Cody was nowhere in sight. Jack remained in the hallway, just outside the chapel doorway, so that he would have Rachael available for the meeting with Joan's attorney. When Tyler wandered out, Rachael grasped Jack's hand, which drew his attention.

"Hi, Rachael. Come give Daddy a hug."

Rachael shook her head.

Tyler knelt in front of her. "Still mad at me, huh? That's okay, I understand. I'm still mad at Grandma, too. Can I tell you a secret?" When she nodded, he leaned forward and whispered something in her ear.

"I forgive you, Daddy." She opened her arms and gave him a hug.

Tyler wrapped his arms around her and kissed her cheek. "Thank you, Rachael. Guess what I have for you out in my truck?"

"My teddy bear!"

"How did you know?"

"Uncle Jack told me you had it. I was hoping you'd bring it today. Where's Cody?"

Tyler glanced around, apparently just realizing that Cody was missing. "I don't know. I'd better look for him. Want to come with me?"

"I'll wait with Uncle Jack and Stacy," she said as she took hold of Jack's hand again.

"Jack isn't your uncle. Stop calling him that."

"She's got to call me something," Jack said.

Tyler scoffed as he turned once again to look for his son. "I'll bring the bear back with me."

Jack saw Mr. Carrington approach Tyler and point to a closed door about halfway down the hall. Tyler nodded and headed back towards Jack. Jack met him in the middle. "Rachael, you need to go to a meeting with your Daddy. I'll be right outside the door."

"I'm afraid not. Apparently, since you are serving as her *foster* father, you're required to stay with her during the meeting. I've got to find Cody."

"Have you checked outside?" Jack said. "Oh, there he is. He just came out of that room down there."

Tyler turned just as his son ducked into yet another room. He shook his head and strode down the hall to retrieve his son.

When they returned, Jack said, "Sorry to leave you here, Stace. See you in a bit."

"No worries. I'll be over there catching up on email or something," she said, pointing to a small grouping of chairs."

"Hi, Cody!" Rachael said.

"Daddy made me take my toys out of your room. It looks like a *girl's* room now. I wish you'd go away and never come back!"

Rachael looked up at Jack.

"You take after your father, I see." He took hold of Rachael's hand and led the way into the meeting room. It was just him, Tyler, Cody, Rachael, and the attorney.

"Please, folks, sit down. I won't take much of your time. Tyler, I just want to make you aware of a few things. You'll receive copies of the will and trust documents so you can read them yourself. We can meet again once you've had the chance to review them. Were you aware that your mother filed a new will a little over a year ago?"

"No. Mother and I didn't discuss her finances."

"Very well. I'll outline the main provisions. She has a sister to which she left fifty thousand dollars. She is the only heir outside your immediate family."

"That much I knew," Tyler said.

Mr. Carrington, who remained standing, pressed his lips together. "In the original will, all of your mother's holdings went directly to you, save for what she put in trust for Cody and Rachael. Joan's holdings include not only the Pearl River Mansion estate, but large holdings of stocks, bonds, and mutual funds, as well as cash holdings and a few additional pieces of real estate. When she changed her will, however, she transferred the bulk of her holdings directly to Rachael. She now inherits Pearl River Mansion, along with an immediate monthly income of fifteen thousand dollars per month, which will increase when she reaches age eighteen, and again when she reaches age twenty-one."

"What?" Tyler said coming to his feet. "How can a six-year-old inherit property and a ridiculous income like that? What the hell was she thinking?"

"I'm not six yet, Daddy. I'm five."

"Shut up, Rachael. No one's talking to you."

"Stay quiet, Rachael," Jack whispered.

"Sit down, Tyler," Mr. Carrington said as his graying eyebrows drew together. "There's more."

"But that's my house. How could she do that to me? I grew up there."

Rachael climbed into Jack's lap. "It's okay, sweetie," Jack whispered as he wrapped his arms around her.

Mr. Carrington waited until Tyler sat down before continuing. "Mr. George Gibbs shall remain on the estate for the remainder of his natural life, and his final expenses shall be paid by the estate. His sister, Regina, may remain as long as Rachael approves of her service."

"That's ridiculous!" Tyler said.

"Clearly, your mother had no intention of dying as soon as she did. I'm sure she expected Rachael to be much older when she inherited. Be that as it may, Rachael is the main beneficiary. Mr. Kendall, as her legal guardian, you will manage her estate until she reaches her eighteenth birthday, or until other arrangements for Rachael's care are forthcoming from the state."

"But I'm not her legal guardian. He is," Jack said, pointing to Tyler. "I'm just helping out temporarily."

"That's right. I'm Rachael's father, and I'll manage her estate!"

"I understand that you're upset, but until a judge is prepared to place Rachael back into your care, temporary management falls to her foster father, Jack Kendall."

"This is outrageous!"

"Tyler," Mr. Carrington said, "your mother didn't leave you out of the will. You are to inherit a respectable portion of her holdings. Cody will have money also. You'll be well provided for. It's just that, for whatever reason, your mother decided to make large concessions to Rachael."

"Can I fight it?" Tyler said.

"You can, but it won't do you any good. My firm drafted the documents. She was in her right mind, and well within her legal rights to do what she did. You'd be much better served to be satisfied with what you're receiving, which is quite a lot of money, Tyler."

"How much?"

Mr. Carrington looked at Jack. "Wouldn't you like to discuss that at a later time, in private?"

"Tell me now. Jack already knows everything else. It makes no difference. He's not getting any of it."

"Nor do I want it," Jack said. "My entire goal, here, has only been to help you, Tyler. I certainly didn't know that your mother did this."

"Why is Daddy yelling?"

"He's not mad at you, sweetie. He's mad at your Grandma again. Tell her, Tyler. Tell her that you're not mad at her."

Tyler yanked Cody out of his seat and stormed out of the room.

"I'm sorry, Mr. Carrington. I don't know what to say," Jack said.

"There's no easy way to break that kind of news. I can't blame him for being upset, but if he plays his cards right, he'll be living in the mansion *and* managing Rachael's fortune until she turns eighteen."

"I think his mother has betrayed him once too often," Jack said. "Let me know if there's anything I should do."

"Here's my card."

Jack pulled out his card also.

"A private investigator?"

"Yes, that's how I came to know Tyler. I was involved in

finding Rachael."

"Well, we owe you a great debt of gratitude, don't we?" Mr. Carrington said.

Jack gave him a sideways look. "Do you know where Rachael has been the past twelve months?"

"Only that when the caretaker returned with her, he and his sister blamed my client for killing Billy Ray Richards. I have no knowledge as to where they have held her."

"Come here, Rachael." Rachael stood next to him. "Can you tell Mr. Carrington why you went away with Mr. G and Regina?"

"Grandma used to keep me locked in the attic. She wouldn't let me go outside or talk to anybody because I saw her shoot Billy Ray. She told me not to look, but I saw him fall on the floor, and I saw blood all over him. She didn't want me to tell anybody, so she made me stay in the attic. Then one day, I ran away with Mr. Gibbs, Auntie Regina, and Jayden. We lived on a farm, but now I live with Uncle Jack."

Mr. Carrington looked stunned. He started to speak, but Jack held up his hand. "What was it like up in the attic, Rachael?"

"It was very cold and dark at night. I was scared, but Gramma said there couldn't be any lights up there or someone might know there was an attic, and then they'd get me."

"Thank you, sweetheart."

"You promised that I'd never have to go to the attic again. Isn't that right, Uncle Jack?"

"That's right, sweetie. You never have to go to that attic again. Your grandmother is gone, and you are safe now."

"But I can go to my princess room?"

"Yes, you can." Jack opened the door and spotted Stacy. "Go wait with Stacy now. I'll be right out."

Rachael glanced back at Mr. Carrington and ducked out the door.

"Do you mean to tell me that story is true?" Mr. Carrington said.

"Every word. I saw the attic myself. Your *client* lied to the police, and she lied to her son. If Joan Chandler changed her will and gave the estate to Rachael, I say the girl deserves it. Tyler should have never given up his child in the first place."

"I'd like to talk to Joan about this, but that's not possible now, is it?"

"She may have escaped justice in this life, but I doubt she'll escape it in the next," Jack said.

"That's a sobering thought."

"Yes, it is. If Tyler fights this thing, I hope you'll remember what Rachael just told you."

"Thank you, Mr. Kendall. I'll keep that in mind."

They shook hands, and Jack went to find Stacy and Rachael.

* * *

Tyler was so angry that he had difficulty driving anywhere near the speed limit. He swerved hard left to avoid the ditch. It was just like her to do something like this on her way out, one more vicious twist of the knife, one more way to insult him, one more confirmation that she didn't love him and had never loved him.

Cody sat quietly, for once, as if he sensed that this wasn't the time to test his father's patience. Tyler glanced over. She cheated his son, too, but not Rachael, not the granddaughter, not the *girl* he could never be. He was furious with Rachael, and it wasn't even her fault.

His mother had to know that he'd feel this way. Of course, she did, but she did it anyway. She was some piece of work. Did she think he'd mourn her? Ha! She'd made his entire life a living hell. Nothing he did was ever good enough! He was a disappointment, a failure in her eyes. Well, she was a failure in his! Always bribing people, lying, and scheming to get her way. And Rachael, the one she supposedly loves, she locks up, and then leaves her a bloody fortune! He struck the steering wheel with the palm of his hand. "What was she thinking?"

"What's wrong, Daddy?" Cody said, shrinking towards the window.

"Nothing, son. Daddy is just mad at Grandma."

"We don't like Grandma, do we?" Cody said with a crinkled nose.

"Not today, we don't."

"We don't like Rachael either, do we?"

Tyler pulled the truck to the side of the road. "What did you just say?"

Cody looked unsure.

"Rachael is your sister. It's not her fault that Gramma hid her from us, and gave her more money than she gave us. None of this is Rachael's fault!" he yelled. "Do you hear me, boy?"

"Yes, Daddy," he whimpered.

"Don't you forget it, either." He pulled the truck back onto the road and hit the gas. He didn't want to admit it, but he needed to heed his own counsel.

* * *

"What are you thinking so hard about?" Jack said as he glanced at Rachael, who sat quietly beside Stacy on the front seat of the truck.

"Daddy."

Jack glanced at Stacy. "What about Daddy?"

"Why is he so angry all the time?"

"I think your daddy has a lot of things to work out in his mind."

"Why do *you* think he's angry, Rachael?" Stacy said.

"I think he misses Mommy. I miss Mommy, too, but I'm not angry. I'm just sad."

"Would ice cream make you feel better?" Jack said.

"Chocolate ice cream might help."

Jack chuckled. "Chocolate ice cream it is, then."

Rachael smiled, her sunny personality brightening her face. "I'd rather eat ice cream than be sad," she said.

"Me, too," Stacy said.

"Me, three," Jack agreed. "Only I want whipped cream and a cherry on top."

"Yummy," Rachael said.

"After we eat our ice cream, I have another idea," Jack said.

"What?"

"How about we pick out a brand-new teddy bear for you?"

"Because Daddy didn't give Bo back to me like he promised?"

"I just think there's a cute little bear out there that needs a pretty little princess to take care of it."

"I love stuffed animals," Stacy said. "Maybe I'll pick one out for me, too. I could use something to hold onto at night."

Jack gave her a reproachful look, but she just winked at him and smiled.

* * *

When Tyler pulled into the driveway, he could hardly believe his eyes. At first, he thought it was another reporter—until he got close enough to see that it was Pamela sitting on the front porch steps, reading a book to Jacob. She stood up and grabbed hold of Jacob's hand.

"Look, Cody, it's Pamela and Jacob."

"Cool! Can Jacob play with me in my room?"

"It's up to Pamela. You can ask her." Tyler ran a hand through his hair and got out of the truck with Cody right behind him.

"Hi, Miss Pamela. Can Jacob play with me in my room?"

"Sure, Cody. Hello, Tyler."

"I'm surprised to see you. Hi, Jacob. Come on in." He unlocked the door and held it open. The boys ran in first and disappeared down the hall with thundering footsteps. Pamela laughed as she entered the living room. "Your maid is on vacation, I see."

"Oh. I'm…uh…" Tyler glanced around helplessly, but there was no quick fix for the condition of his house. The laundry basket was upside down in the middle of the living room floor next to huge piles of dirty clothes, which he'd been digging through only that morning to find the least dirty socks to wear. Cody's toys were scattered everywhere, and dirty dishes covered the kitchen counters, as well as the coffee table and end tables. "Maybe I should have kept you outside," he said. "I've had a lot going on, and I, I—" He lifted his hands and gave her a sheepish smile. "I don't have a good excuse."

She pushed some toys out of the way and sat down on the couch. "I didn't come here to see your house."

"Have you been waiting long?" he said. "Outside, I mean."

"About thirty minutes. I knew the funeral time. I thought about going, but that didn't work out so well the last time."

He chuckled. "Different cast of characters; you would've been safe." He cleared off the recliner and sat across from her. He wanted to sit on the couch, but he didn't trust himself to be that close. "I'm glad to see you."

"How did it go?" she said.

He gave her the *how do you think it went* look.

"Well, you know what I mean," she said.

"None of that matters at the moment. The only thing that matters is that you're here. Why did you come?"

"I know that losing your mother must be difficult for you, but because she's gone, I don't feel threatened anymore." She looked down. "I wanted to be here for you."

Her voice came out so softly that he leaned forward to hear it. He dropped to his knees in front of her. "Pamela, I've missed you so much; my life is empty without you. Not a minute goes by that I don't long to have you with me."

"Oh, Tyler. I've missed you, too. It's hard to believe that we might actually have a chance now. I never thought we would, but now that your mother is gone—"

"I'm sorry for what she did to you and Jacob. She did so many horrible things. All this time I thought I knew her, but I didn't. I never knew her at all. Can you believe that she kept Rachael locked in an attic? What kind of person does that?"

"Hush. Don't think about that now. It's over. Rachael is safe, and we can start over."

"All of us? Because I can't give Rachael up again. I'm still praying they'll give her back to me. How could I have let her go in the first place?" Tears filled his eyes. "What the hell is wrong with me?"

"You were grieving for your wife. You weren't thinking straight, and neither was I. I was jealous of the woman you once loved, and of the daughter who looks so much like her. We were both wrong, but we have a chance to make things right."

"Are you saying you'll give me another chance?"

"Yes, Tyler. Yes!" Tears spilled down her cheeks.

He took her in his arms and kissed her.

CHAPTER TWENTY-FOUR

Jack's cell phone woke him just before he kissed the woman with long honey-blonde hair. She disappeared entirely with the second ring. Annoyed, he grabbed the phone from the nightstand. "Yeah, this is Jack."

"Mr. Kendall, this is John Carrington—Joan Chandler's attorney."

Jack sat up and tried to blink the day into place. "Yes, sir. How can I help you?"

"I have some business to discuss with you. May I stop by this morning?"

"There's no need for you to come here. I can stop by your office," Jack said.

"No, I prefer to meet there. Would nine o'clock work for you?"

Jack looked at the clock; it was a quarter past seven. "Sure, that's fine. Let me give you the address."

"I have it. See you then."

Jack scowled. It would be easy to find his address, but it annoyed him all the same. He got out of bed and went straight to the shower.

The hot water served to wake him up, but it did little to improve his mood. He wondered what the attorney could possibly want to discuss, and it worried him. What if he wanted to take Rachael home today? There was no doubt she ultimately belonged with Tyler, but he seemed too volatile, and he didn't want her subjected to her father's fits of anger. He wondered if Kevin had heard anything from the court.

Showering quickly, he stepped out and grabbed a towel. Without even drying himself, he moved into the bedroom and grabbed his phone from the dresser. "Don't you ever go home?" he said when Kevin answered.

"I'm busy, Jack."

"Have you heard anything about Rachael's custody decision?"

"Last I heard, they were waiting to review the psychological evaluations. Have they done that?"

"That's scheduled for next week."

"Then why are you calling?" Kevin pressed.

"It's just that Joan Chandler's attorney wants to meet with me this morning. I'm a little concerned that he might try to pull something in regards to Rachael's custody. I don't have any rights, do I?"

"No, but neither does anybody else, except Tyler, and he's the one the judge put a hold on. I think she's safe for the time being. If anything out of the ordinary comes up, call me back. Otherwise, let me get some work done."

"Okay. Sorry. I guess I'm just feeling protective."

"Deal with it, Jack. I'll talk to you when there's something concrete."

Jack hung his head for a few moments and then dialed Stacy's apartment. "Hey, you. Good morning."

"It was until you woke us up," she grumbled.

"We're having a visitor come by at nine—Joan Chandler's attorney. I hate to say it, but it makes me nervous."

"What did he say?" Stacy said.

"Nothing. I offered to meet at his office, but he wants to come here. Please make sure Rachael looks nice. We can eat breakfast here if you like."

"Let's do that. It'll be nice and homey-looking. May as well make a good impression, right?"

"I'll make the coffee," Jack said.

"Save some for me," Stacy said as she hung up.

* * *

Tyler tapped lightly on Rachael's bedroom door.

"Come in."

As he opened the door, his breath caught at the sight of Pamela lying in Rachael's bed.

She stretched and smiled. "Good morning. Did you sleep well?"

"You look beautiful."

She wrinkled her nose. "I'll bet. Are the boys up?"

"They've already had breakfast and are playing outside. I'm surprised you haven't heard them. They seem happy to be together again."

"Jacob was looking forward to seeing Cody and Rachael. Is there any coffee left?" she said as she sat up in the bed.

"I just brewed a fresh pot."

"Perfect. Give me a few minutes, and I'll join you." When he didn't respond right away, she gestured for him to leave.

"Oh, right." He chuckled as he closed the door and headed for the kitchen. Having Pamela in the house again was like receiving a present. Every glance was a gift. He could hardly wait until they had another intimate moment, another kiss, yet he knew he needed to take his time. He wanted to do this right.

"Good morning," she said as she came walking through the living room wrapped in a soft-looking purple robe. Her long, layered hair was loose and mussed from sleep.

Tyler handed her a steaming mug of coffee.

"You've been busy," she said.

"Nothing like motivation," he said, pleased that she had noticed. He had worked hard to put the house back in order. "Want some breakfast?"

"I didn't know you could cook."

"It's debatable. We could go out," he said.

She laughed. "I'll make us something. What did the boys eat?"

"Cereal, but I'm sure they could eat again."

"Do you have eggs and bread?"

"Yes."

"Syrup?"

"Ooh, that sounds like French toast," Tyler said.

"Would you rather have something else?" He smiled and let his eyes drop slowly down her body. "Tyler!" She brushed by him and entered the kitchen.

He chuckled. "Pamela?"

"Yes?"

"I think the last time I laughed was when I was with you. I'm so glad you're here."

She turned and let him wrap his arms around her. "It feels right, doesn't it?"

He kissed her gently and let her pull away. As she began taking items out of the refrigerator, he set the frying pan on the stove and began to set the table.

Pamela cracked the eggs into a bowl and began to beat them vigorously. "Have you thought about what it will be like to live in that giant house again?"

Tyler's hand froze as he reached for the glasses. "Who said I was moving there?" Suspicion settled over him, and he didn't like it. He set the glasses on the table and then concentrated on the silverware.

"Oh. I just assumed you would. Will you sell it, then?"

"It's not mine to sell. Can we talk about something else, please?"

Turning from the bowl, she said, "Don't tell me she left it all to charity? Although it wouldn't surprise me if she did. She was so incredibly contrary."

"Why do you care?" he said watching her closely.

"I don't, except that after all she's put you through, it would be nice if you got something out of it in the end."

"I get Rachael," he said, surprising himself by saying it.

Pamela turned back to the stove, dipped a piece of bread into the batter, and dropped it onto the hot pan. It immediately began to sizzle. She added a second piece next to it. "She's the only thing that matters, of course, but I know what it's like to be cheated out of an inheritance. My father's attorney ended up with mine. I'd rather have my father back than any amount of money, of course, but knowing that the property he intended for *me* went to his greedy attorney isn't an easy pill to swallow. I hate to think of you going through what I did. It takes a long time to get over being angry. I'm still not over it."

"Really, can we talk about something else?" Tyler said.

"Can you at least tell me what your plans are? Will you stay in Jackson? Do you plan to stay in the trailer? It's a bit small for the five of us, don't you think?"

He banged the plates onto the counter, grabbed her arm, and turned her around to face him. "Is that why you came here? To see if I'm rich now?"

She yanked her arm free. "Is that what you think?"

"I don't know. You seem awfully interested in my finances all of a sudden."

"You finish breakfast; I'm leaving." She ran through the living room, down the hall, and into Rachael's bedroom.

When the door slammed, Tyler winced. He didn't know what to think. If she would've left the topic alone, but she kept pushing. What did that mean? Was she here because of him, or because of the money? This was what had kept him isolated in high school and college. He never knew who his true friends were. Everyone wanted to be friends with the *rich boy*. It wasn't until he shunned his mother and her money that he had found out who his true friends were, and there weren't many of them. He wanted Pamela, but not if she only wanted him for his money.

He took the pan off the fire and tossed it on the back burner. "Dammit!" He didn't want her to leave, especially until he got to the truth of the matter. He stalked down the hallway and knocked on the door. "Pamela, please open the door."

* * *

"You like scrambled eggs, don't you?" Jack said.

Rachael nodded and took another bite. "Auntie Regina makes eggs, too. Jayden can eat three, but I can only eat two."

The doorbell rang.

Jack looked at his watch and frowned. "He's a half hour early."

"Maybe he's hungry," Stacy said.

Jack went to the door and glanced out the side window. Emily spotted him and waved. He opened the door and held out his arms. "Emily, I'm so glad to see you!"

Emily stepped into his embrace. "I would've called, but I was afraid you wouldn't let me come."

"Why on earth would you think that?" He held the door open and motioned for her to come in.

"You haven't called me about Rachael. I thought, maybe, because of Momma and Tommy Lee, you didn't want me to see her."

"Oh, Emily, I'm so sorry we haven't called. Rachael is in the kitchen."

"She is?" She tossed her purse onto the floor and ran for the kitchen. When she reached the doorway, she stepped shyly into the room. "Hi, Stacy. Hello, Rachael."

Rachael's eyes grew wide. "Mommy!" She ran to Emily. "I knew you'd come for me. I knew it!" She threw her arms around Emily's neck as she dropped to her knees for a hug.

"Rachael, sweetie, it's me. It's Auntie Emily."

Rachael pulled back and wrinkled her brow, and then looked at Jack. He picked her up. "Let's go into the den where we can talk."

Rachael reached out for Emily. "I want my mommy!"

Jack set her down, and Emily took hold of Rachael's hand, but her eyes met his. When they had settled in the den, Jack said, "Rachael, show Emily your special locket."

"Look, Mommy, I have your picture. I've been waiting and waiting for you to come back for me." She pulled at it, but the chain was too short for her to see it. "Take it off me, please."

Emily unhooked the necklace and handed it to Rachael.

Rachael opened the locket and said, "Look!" She looked at Emily, then the locket, and back to Emily again. She was clearly confused.

"Rachael, your mommy was my sister. Her name is Sarah. My name is Emily. Your mommy and I are sisters. I'm your Auntie Emily, and I love you very much. I came a long way to see you today."

"Emily looks a lot like your mommy, doesn't she?" Jack said.

"You're not my mommy?" Rachael said.

"No, sweetie. I'm your Auntie Emily."

Rachael looked down. "You look like my mommy."

"So do you," Emily said with a smile. "You are very pretty. Do you remember me, Rachael?"

"You came to Daddy's house with Billy Ray, didn't you?" Rachael said. "You read me a book in Cody's room."

"Yes, I'm glad you remember," Emily said. "I've been waiting a very long time to see you."

"You have?" Rachael said cocking her head.

"Yes, but I live far away. But you know what?"

"What?" Rachael said.

"I'm moving to Jackson so I can see you lots and lots. Would you like that?"

Rachael turned to look at Jack again.

"Stacy and I have missed you," Jack said.

"What great news!" Stacy said.

"I'm glad you feel that way because everything I own is in the back of my car. I'm going apartment hunting today. I've saved up some money, and Alister, Emerson & Maxwell gave me my job back. I start next Monday."

"Do you hear that, Rachael? Your Auntie Emily will be living nearby so she can visit. Isn't that wonderful?"

"And we can read more books, and I can teach you how to count in French?"

"That sounds amazing," Emily said with her trademark smile. "Let me put your locket on you."

"Okay," Rachael said and climbed back into her lap.

Jack felt unaccountably happy. He wished he had thought of the idea himself. Stacy caught his eye and winked at him; she, too, was pleased. The only question was what Tyler would say about it. Would he hold what Leeann and Tommy Lee did against Emily? He hoped not. Without Emily, they might never have found Rachael. He needed to make sure Tyler understood that.

The doorbell rang again.

"Oops, forgot about him," Jack said. "Mrs. Chandler's attorney is stopping by. After introductions, maybe you ladies could take Rachael back to Stacy's apartment." He got up and headed for the door. He scooped up Emily's purse, set it on the table in the foyer, and opened the door. "Good morning, Mr. Carrington. Come on in."

"Nice to see you again, Mr. Kendall."

"Please, call me Jack." The two men shook hands. "Rachael is in the den with Stacy and her Aunt Emily. Would you like to meet in there, or would you prefer to speak in the kitchen?"

"The den will do nicely."

Jack felt his skin crawl as he watched the attorney openly assess *the environment.* He was grateful to Stacy, who kept his household organized. Without her, Mr. Carrington might have taken one look and yanked Rachael out of there. "Excuse the kitchen; we had just finished breakfast when Emily arrived. Hello, everybody. This is Mr. Carrington, Joan Chandler's attorney."

"Greetings everyone. Hello, Rachael," Mr. Carrington said.

"This is my Auntie Emily. She looks like my mommy."

"How nice," he said.

"Would you care for something to drink? Some coffee?" Stacy said, rising to her feet.

"No, thank you. I won't take up much of your time, Mr. Kendall, but it might be best if we chat in private."

"Emily and Rachael, let's go back to my place," Stacy said. "I've got some lemonade up there."

"Yummy!" Rachael said. "I love lemonade."

"Nice to meet you, Mr. Carrington," Stacy said.

"Likewise," he replied. When the girls had gone, he added, "So that was Stacy."

"She rents the apartment above the second garage."

"Yes, I know. A pity there's no romantic attachment between you."

"Excuse me?"

"She's a lovely girl. How are you enjoying having Rachael underfoot?"

"Rachael is a pleasure. I love children," Jack said.

"None of your own?"

"No, but you already know that," he said, pressing his lips together.

Mr. Carrington chuckled. "I like you, Jack. I've spoken with Rachael's psychologist. She thinks that despite Rachael's confinement, she's reasonably well adjusted. She also says that Rachael feels quite comfortable with you, so the court finds no reason to seek alternate housing for the child at this time. It is our intent, of course, to restore Rachael to her birth family, but Tyler has yet to complete his own set of evaluations, and I have some reservations, especially now that Pamela Clarkston is back in the picture. That being the case—"

"What do you mean, Pamela's back in the picture? Are they back together?"

"I wouldn't look so happy about it; she's nothing but a gold digger. At least, Joan thought so."

"I would hardly trust Joan Chandler's assessment. I may know more about that situation than you do."

Mr. Carrington raised a brow.

Jack knew he should stay quiet, but he couldn't. "Joan offered Pamela two hundred and fifty thousand dollars to leave Jackson and break off communications with Tyler. I have a copy of the first ten-thousand-dollar check. She also threatened Pamela's five-year-old son with harm if she didn't stay away."

Mr. Carrington cleared his throat. "As Rachael's temporary guardian, you will be entrusted with her monthly maintenance account. It was Joan's wish that her grandchild have the finest clothes, the best education, first-class vacations—all the advantages money can buy. You'll keep records of your expenditures on her behalf, and turn them in to me on a monthly basis. You'll receive reasonable compensation for your time, of course. Say, five thousand dollars a month?"

Jack bristled, but he bit his tongue. He needed to hear him out before voicing objections or calling him the snob he thought him to be.

"Now I am aware that you are unable to live in a manner equal to that which I have described. That being the case, when you dine out, in order for Rachael to enjoy the lifestyle that Joan intends, her account will pick up the tab. The same holds true for all reasonable ventures."

"What about Cody? How does he figure into this equation?" Jack said.

"When and if the family reunites, Tyler will be responsible for supplying Cody's needs out of his own monthly maintenance account. No special provisions were made for Cody except in trust, which he will inherit at the age of twenty-one. This will no doubt create resentment and friction between the twins, but that can't be helped. It's up to Tyler to make up the difference, if he so chooses, to whatever degree he decides. As you know, his inheritance in no way matches what Joan left to Rachael, but he will inherit a sizeable sum. Rachael is a *fortunate* little girl; forgive the pun."

"If you call being locked in a cold, dark attic for a year fortunate," Jack scoffed.

"Your feelings about my client are irrelevant, so please refrain from making any more comments about Joan. They are not helpful here."

"Look, I'm not thrilled to be in the middle of this," Jack said, "and Tyler resents it."

"You can refuse, and the court will appoint another foster parent if you wish. That is the only option available for Rachael at the moment."

Jack scowled. "I can't do that to Rachael. How long do you suppose it might be before she can be reunited with Tyler and her brother?"

"Under the best of circumstances, a matter of weeks."

He nodded. "Very well. Let's hope for the best."

Mr. Carrington's eyes narrowed. "Most people in your circumstance would hope for the opposite."

"I'm not most people, Mr. Carrington. I am only interested in what's best for Rachael."

"Believe it or not, so am I. I'll admit that Joan wasn't the easiest woman to deal with. I don't agree with every decision she made, but I will tell you this; she loved Rachael. Despite how everything turned out, there was a time when her greatest desire was to adopt that child and give her every happiness under the sun."

"Well, something went seriously wrong. This is one case that I will be happy to leave behind me, though I hope to stay in contact with Rachael from here on out. She calls me Uncle Jack, you know."

"Yes, I know," Mr. Carrington said.

"Of course, you do."

* * *

Tyler could hear Pamela crying through the door. He knocked again. "Please, Pamela, let me in." He heard the lock turn, and he opened the door.

Pamela plopped down on the bed, her face streaked with tears. "What?" she sniffed. "What do you want me to say? I can't tell you that money has absolutely nothing to do with it because it does, but it's only one piece of the puzzle, Tyler. I would never be with someone for the sake of money alone, but I'm like everyone else. I want to be safe. I long to feel secure. I need to know that my son will be able to attend college. What woman doesn't consider those things when she looks for a husband?"

Tyler sat down on the floor and sighed. He didn't know what he was expecting, but it wasn't that. And yet, what she said was reasonable. Had he not looked down on Sarah and her family because they didn't have money? Hadn't he felt they were inferior, less educated, and less worthy? He couldn't deny it; he *had* felt that way. Isn't that the reverse of what Pamela was saying? Would he rather she lied?

"You forget that I wanted to be with you before I knew about your mother's fancy house. I care about *you*, Tyler, but I come from money, too, you know, and I have a responsibility towards my son. I have a responsibility towards myself, too. I have to consider everything. It's not as if having money was something new to me. It makes me sad that you're treating me like this." She sniffed and wiped her eyes. "I can't be with someone who doesn't trust me." She stood up, reached for a pile of clothes, and threw it into her already full suitcase. "It's a shame. We had an opportunity to have it all, but we can't because, even from the grave, your mother interferes. Her money divides us yet again." She closed the suitcase and struggled to zip it.

"Don't go," he said. "It's my fault. Please forgive me."

Pamela shook her head. "It's no use. You're not ready for a lasting relationship. You've got way too many issues to work through. I shouldn't have come." Having zipped the suitcase, she added, "Will you please leave so I can change?"

"Please, Pamela, I don't want you to go. Can't you forgive me?"

"I forgive you, but where does that leave us? You still don't trust me."

Tyler gently took hold of her shoulders. "There's nothing more important to me than you. I'd marry you today if you'd let me."

"Yeah, right," she scoffed.

"I would."

"I'm important to you, but you won't even tell me your plans. I don't want a relationship like that. You forget how it was when I was your boss. You respected me. Do you think I'll settle for less now?"

He motioned for her to sit on the side of the bed. "Mother changed the will. The mansion and most of the money now goes to Rachael. I'll still inherit, but not nearly as much as she does. There you have it. Can you believe it?"

Pamela's eyes widened. "Wow. That's a slap in the face. No wonder you're resentful."

"When it comes to Mother, I've come to expect it."

"Is that why you want Rachael back?"

"Now I'm insulted."

"Good. That means it's not true," she said.

"I want Rachael back because I've got a lot to make up for. She deserves to feel loved, and I haven't done a very good job of that. I've treated her like Mother treated me. I don't want to do that to her anymore. I don't want her resenting me like I resent my mother. I want to be as good a father to her as I am to Cody."

"That's nice to hear."

"Easier said than done, though." He gave her a sly smile. "Would the mansion be big enough for you, me, and the kids? We'll have Mr. Gibbs and Regina to help take care of it."

"I'm not going to live with you before we get married, Tyler, but yes, it would serve quite nicely."

"You could live in the trailer or one of the cabins until the wedding. For that matter, there's an entire apartment in the mansion attic. You and Jacob could live up there, though I'd have to put some lighting and some heat up there first."

"Do you mean to tell me she kept Rachael up there in the dark?"

Tyler lifted his hands as if to block her line of questioning. "Look, I can't think about that right now. Will you, at least, consider it?"

"One of those options might be acceptable. I know Jacob would love it, and it would give us a chance to see if it would work between us before we get married, especially if we live in the mansion. We can live together without actually living together, if you know what I mean."

He gently lifted her chin and looked into her eyes. "Does that mean you'll stay?"

"I don't know. Kiss me while I think about it."

He kissed her softly. As she pulled him closer, their kiss deepened. He felt as if all their negative emotions melded together and then shattered. They loved each other; he could feel it.

She pulled away and sighed. "We'll stay, but only if you love us and treat us like we matter more than everything else in the world, except for Cody and Rachael, of course. Family is the most important thing, Tyler. If we stay, it's so that we can become a family."

"As God is my witness, I want that more than anything! I love you, Pamela. I always have, and I always will."

They smiled at each other and kissed again.

* * *

Rachael ran into Regina's open arms. "I missed you, Auntie Regina.

Where's Jayden?"

"He's in the garden pickin' roses."

Jack shook hands with Mr. Gibbs. "Good to see you, sir."

"It's mighty good of you to bring this young'un out here to see us. Does our heart good, it does." He nodded after Rachael, who took off running down one of the trails.

"Ummm hmmm," Regina said. "Jayden's been drivin' us crazy, askin' after her. They's been two peas in a pod this past year or so. Let's go up to the porch, and I'll bring us out some sweet tea."

"I'd like to see the flower garden first if you don't mind. In fact, Stacy and I would enjoy a tour of the grounds if you've got the time for it, Mr. Gibbs."

"Well, now, I think I can put off my chores a bit," he said, his eyes twinkling as he grinned.

"You been lookin' for an excuse all mornin'," Regina said. "You may as well enjoy it 'cuz the back lawn needs cuttin', and I ain't acceptin' no excuses for it tomorrow. Y'all go on while I make up a nice picnic lunch. I'll have the tea awaitin'."

"That sounds wonderful," Stacy said.

Regina nodded. "We's real glad to be back here, Miss Stacy, and we know it's because of you two. We's real appreciative. We sure is."

"Thanks, Regina," Jack said. "So, Mr. Gibbs, where are those roses?"

"There are lots of roses, Mr. Jack, but the ones Jayden is after are this way." He chuckled. "I know 'cuz it'll give 'im an excuse to visit the creek."

Jack glanced back at Stacy, who was smiling as she basked in the beautiful day. As he followed Mr. Gibbs, he was aware of the birds singing, the flowers blooming, and the branches swaying in the cool summer breeze. This was an amazing place, so close to town and yet seemingly set back in time a hundred years. A lovely rock border framed the path and formed beds for countless varieties of flowers, trees, and shrubs. He didn't know the names of all of them, but they were colorful and made him smile. They took the left fork in the path and entered beneath an ivy-covered archway. Roses of various colors lined either side of the flagstone walkway.

"Wow. This is what I call a rose garden," Stacy said as she paused to smell an orange colored rose. "I could stay here all day."

"Glad you like it," Mr. Gibbs said with a nod. "Roses are my favorite flower. Pick whatever you like."

"Is there another way out other than the way we came?" Jack said.

"Oh, yes, at the far end, but like I said, I suspect them young'uns went to the creek." He chuckled. "Can't blame 'em none. I like that spot, too, what with those pavilions like they is. It's nice and shady this time of year."

"Pavilions?" Stacy said.

"Two of 'em, one on either side of the creek. Jayden likes to jump from the bridge when he's swimmin'."

"Surely, they're not swimming without supervision," Jack said with alarm.

"He knows better, but let's go on up, just in case," Mr. Gibbs said. He turned to lead the way.

"May I pick this white one?" Stacy said.

Mr. Gibbs pulled a knife from his pocket. "I'll get it." After cutting it, he quickly sheared off the thorns. "Here ya go."

"Thank you," Stacy said. "It's lovely."

"So are you, if you don't mind me sayin' so."

"How could I mind?" She threw a smile at Jack as they followed their guide out of the rose garden and along another path towards the creek.

"This place is incredibly beautiful," Jack said. "You keep the grounds up all by yourself?"

"Jayden helps me some. It's a pleasure, mostly, and the work keeps me young. Truly, there's no place else I'd rather be."

"I can understand that," Jack said.

"Me, too," Stacy agreed.

A squeal of delight carried on the air.

"I think we've found our kids," Jack said with a smile.

As they rounded the bend, a picturesque creek spanned by a wooden bridge came into view. On either side of the bridge was a white gazebo, surrounded with plants and hanging flowerpots.

"Oh my," Stacy said.

"Uncle Jack! Jayden is splashing me!" Rachael giggled as she kicked water back at him, Jayden every bit as soaked as she was.

"You young'uns get on up here," Mr. Gibbs said.

Rachael kicked at Jayden one last time, squealed as he retaliated, and then ran towards them with a huge grin on her face.

"Hi, Mr. G," she said. Jayden was right behind her, water glistening in his black, curly ringlets.

"You know better than to come down here without me. What if you fell in?"

"We stayed out of the swimmin' hole, Papa. We just got our feet wet," Jayden said.

"More than yer feet, I reckon. Regina is makin' us a picnic lunch. Are you hungry?"

"Yes!" They said together.

"Can we run, Papa?"

"Get on with ya, then," he said.

"Come on, Rachael. I'll race you."

"Wait! I have to get my roses," Rachael said.

"I'll bring them," Jack said.

She looked at Jayden and smiled. "Ready, set, go!"

They took off running and disappeared from sight.

Mr. Gibbs shook his head. "They got more energy in one hour than I gots for a whole month."

"They do, don't they?" Jack chuckled. "Don't worry; we'll be content with a leisurely walk back. Won't we, Stace?"

"Yes. Is there another trail we can take back? I'm enjoying this tour more than I can say."

"We'll cross the creek and go back the other way. It's a bit longer, but it won't make much difference. There's an Italian fountain on that side I think you'll fancy."

"Lead the way," Jack said as he picked up a bouquet of roses, which was lying in the grass. He waited for Stacy to go ahead of him, and when she did, he stepped into the river and splashed her.

"No, you didn't!" she exclaimed. She climbed down into the water and splashed him back.

He laughed and splashed her again, which launched the same type of water fight Jayden and Rachael were having, complete with shrieks of outrage and delight. It was the most fun he'd had in ages.

* * *

Tyler was surprised to see Jack's truck parked in his spot. He considered leaving, but curiosity got the better of him. He turned to Pamela. "Jack's here with Rachael. This should be interesting."

"It'll be fine. It'll give us a chance to see Rachael," Pamela said.

"All right. Everybody out," Tyler ordered.

Cody and Jacob climbed out of the back seat. "Can we go play in my room, Daddy?"

"I don't know, son. Let's see what everybody's doing, then we'll decide."

"Can we look for croc-a-gators?" Cody said.

"We'll walk down to the river, but you wait on me."

"I will, Daddy."

"Jacob, you make sure he remembers."

"Yes, sir."

Tyler held the gate, and the boys ran down the path towards the house. "Think you could get used to this?" Tyler said.

"It's beautiful. I love how the oak trees form an arch over the driveway. It reminds me of my grandparent's old house down in Georgia."

"The hanging moss looks spooky at night," Tyler said.

"You think so?" Pamela said, hooking her arm in his. "I like it."

"Me, too," Tyler said.

"Now that your mother is gone, will you keep the gate, or open up the driveway to the front of the house?"

"I guess I agree with her about the view. Come and see for yourself."

* * *

Jack and Stacy sat at the front porch table drinking iced tea, waiting for Regina to finish with the final preparations for their picnic lunch. It was a warm, sunny day, and a breeze kept the air cool and fresh. Jack smiled as he listened to Rachael and Jayden chat about their water fight as they sat cross-legged, facing each other in the swing. It was good that she felt comfortable here.

"Hi, Daddy," Rachael said.

Jack's head turned as the two boys came thundering up the steps. "Tyler, what a nice surprise." He and Stacy stood to greet them with handshakes and hugs. "You're just in time," Jack said. "We're just about to have a picnic. Are you hungry?"

"Can we, Daddy?" Cody said.

"I don't see why not."

"I'll let Regina know you're here," Stacy said as she stepped through the front door.

"Making yourself at home here, aren't you, Jack?" Tyler said.

"Just bringing Rachael for a visit. What brings you by?"

"I wanted to show Pamela and Jacob around."

"Hi, Cody," Rachael said with a big smile.

Cody lifted his hand in a weak wave.

"Jacob, do you know Jayden?" Jack said. "Jayden, come say hello to Cody and Jacob."

Jayden climbed down from the swing and stood shyly next to Jack.

"Jayden lives in one of the cabins near the creek. He knows every inch of this place. Don't you, Jayden?"

Jayden nodded.

"He and Rachael know how to count to a hundred in French."

"You do?" Jacob said. "I can only count to ten in French."

"Let's do it at the same time," Rachael said.

"On the count of three," Jack said. "One, two, three."

The three children counted together to ten, and then Rachael and Jayden continued on to twenty.

"Will you teach me to do that?" Jacob said.

"It's easy," Jayden said.

"Will you teach me, too?" Cody asked.

"Sure, we will. Wanna see our garden? We grow all kinds of fruits and vegetables. We might have some more carrots ready."

"Don't go anywhere else, now. We're gonna have our picnic soon, and I want to be able to find you," Tyler said with a scowl.

"We'll stay in the garden," Rachael promised as she turned to chase after the boys.

"Have fun," Jack called after them as they scampered off.

"Do you think it's a good idea to let Rachael play with Jayden like that?" Tyler said as he and Pamela sat down in the swing.

"Why wouldn't it be?" Jack said, trying not to take offense.

"It's just that Mother kept us separate from the help."

"I don't consider her to be the best example of parenting," Jack said.

Tyler laughed. "You've got a point there. Still, I am Rachael's parent."

"Jayden is polite and exceptionally bright. You can't help but like that child. You'll see," Jack said.

The screen door squeaked as Stacy joined them again. "Regina says she's got plenty of food. Pamela, would you mind helping us with a few things?"

"Let Regina do that," Tyler said.

"She could," Stacy said, "but a picnic for nine is a lot easier if everyone helps."

"Nine?" Tyler said.

"I'm happy to help," Pamela said as she pushed from the swing and followed Stacy into the house.

"Who else is here?" Tyler said.

"Mr. G and Regina will be joining us."

"Apparently, I've got some attitude changing to do," Tyler grumbled.

"Regina is a hired professional," Jack said. "When we treat people with the respect they deserve, life is more pleasant for everyone. You don't want your children growing up with the same attitude your mother had, do you?"

"Until today, I didn't realize I had an attitude."

"It all starts with seeing people as our equals, as they truly are. Some people have more possessions than others do, but we're all equal before our creator, and that's what counts."

"I expect to be living here with my children in the near future. I want to treat Mr. Gibbs and Regina properly."

"They're charming people, and they've done an amazing job with Rachael. There's no telling what might have happened to her if it weren't for them. Did you know that Regina used to sneak up to the attic to stay with Rachael after your mother went to sleep? She helped keep her warm, and kept her from being scared."

"No, I hadn't heard that. Pamela and I are going to work on becoming a family."

"A family of five?" Jack said.

"Absolutely. At least until there's six."

"I'm glad to hear that. Rachael deserves a family that loves her. She's not a second-class citizen. She deserves every bit as much love as those two boys."

"I know. Pamela and I have talked about that. We're going to do our best to see that she feels loved and wanted."

"I'd like to go on being her Uncle Jack if you don't mind. I've grown rather fond of Rachael."

"I owe you a tremendous debt, Jack. We'd be honored to have you as part of the family."

"Do what the State asks of you, Tyler. Do your counseling. They're waiting on that. Then, when the courts are ready, they'll reunite Rachael with your family. Until then, I'll take good care of her."

"I can hardly believe how much my life has changed in such a short time. I've got Rachael back, and now I have Pamela and Jacob back, too."

"You've definitely got it goin' on. Now, don't mess it up."

"You don't have to tell me twice!"

Pamela, Stacy, and Regina filed through the door, their arms loaded with items. Jack jumped up to hold the door. "What can I do?"

"The food basket is on the counter, and so is the jug of iced tea," Regina said. "That's the last of it."

"I'm right behind you," Jack said.

The women had made their way onto the front lawn by the time Jack caught up with them. Regina, having set her pile beneath a huge oak tree, was in the process of spreading blankets for them to sit on. Jack spotted Tyler leaning against the porch railing watching them work. So much for their heart-to-heart discussion, he thought. "Tyler, why don't you help Regina with the blankets while I go find the children?"

"That's woman's work. I'll go find the kids." All three women turned around.

"What?" he said. "It is, isn't it? Men are hunters and gatherers."

"You better change your attitude, Tyler Chandler, or you can hunt and gather yourself a new girlfriend," Pamela said.

"What's with everybody today? I can't say anything right." He stomped down the stairs and headed along the side of the house.

Pamela glanced at Stacy.

"Don't look at me, I would've slapped him," Stacy said.

"That could be why you're still single," Jack teased.

"That could be why I'm still happy," she shot back. "I don't put up with that crap."

"I wonder how Sarah put up with it," Pamela said.

"You're best not to go down that road," Jack cautioned. "You and Tyler need to make your own way. Train him early, though, or you'll wish you had."

Soon, a delicious lunch of tuna sandwiches, potato salad, pickles, fresh tomatoes, carrots, celery, cake, and cookies lay before them. The children came racing across the yard and plopped down on the blankets.

"Did you wash your hands?" Pamela said.

"Yes, ma'am," Jacob and Rachael said.

Smiling, she handed them each a plate. "Wait until we say grace, now. Tyler, do you want to do the honors?" she said as he sat down.

Tyler cleared his throat. "Father, thank you for this food and our time together. Amen."

Everyone began eating and talking amiably.

A few minutes later, Tyler said, "You never gave me my hug, Rachael. Come give Daddy a hug."

"I don't want to," she said and looked down.

"I don't care what you want. I'm your father, and you'll do what I say!"

"Tyler!" Pamela exclaimed.

Rachael scooted closer to Jack. He offered his hand, and she grabbed it. "Don't worry, sweetie. Your Daddy's not going to hurt you. Are you, Tyler?"

"I'm not going to hurt her. All I want is a hug."

"I don't want to go home with Daddy," Rachael said. "He yells at me and pulls my hair, and he pinches me, too."

"I'm not yelling at you, Rachael, and I haven't pulled your hair or pinched you in a very long time. All I want is to hug you and tell you how happy I am to see you," Tyler said.

Rachael climbed into Jack's lap. Jack wrapped his arms around her. "Don't force her, Tyler. She'll come around when she's ready."

"What did you do to make her trust you like that?"

"I'm nice to her, and we have fun together. Don't we, Rachael?"

"We have lots of fun! We play in the tent. I ride on your back like a horsey, and you tickle me and Jayden! We eat ice cream, you tell me stories, and you talk to me when I'm scared."

"He does all those things?" Tyler said.

"And he bought me a new teddy bear because you never gave Bo back to me like you said you would."

Tyler hung his head for a moment, and then pushed to his feet and strode away.

"Tyler," Pamela called after him.

Glancing over his shoulder, Tyler called for his son. "Come on, Cody, let's go look for alligators."

"Oh, boy! Come on, Jacob!" Cody said as he bounded after Tyler.

"Can I, Momma?" Jacob said, his face alight with anticipation.

"Stay away from the water's edge," Pamela said.

"Yes, ma'am."

Jack glanced at Pamela, but she looked away. He knew she was embarrassed, but he didn't know what to say to her. Instead, he spoke to Rachael. "Your Daddy isn't used to having a little girl around. You'll have to teach him how to take care of you. Think you can do that?"

"I'll help you," Pamela said.

"But you and Daddy don't want me," Rachael said, her lips rising to a pout.

"Yes, we do. We want to become one big family: you, me, your daddy, Cody, and Jacob. Would you like that?"

"Jacob is nice, but Cody is mean like Daddy is mean. He kicks me, hits me, and he throws things at me, too."

Pamela reached out and gently touched Rachael's cheek. "I'm sorry Cody hurts you, Rachael. I'll do my best to protect you. I want to be like a second mommy to you. I want to love you and take care of you. I want to tuck you in at night and read you bedtime stories, too. I used to do that, remember?"

"Yes, but you told Daddy to let me live with Grandma because you'd rather have your own baby girl."

"I'm very sorry I said that. I do want to have a baby girl someday, but if that happens, she'll be your little sister, and I'll love and take care of you both. Do you remember when I used to hug you and tell you how pretty you are?"

Rachael nodded.

"Can I give you a little hug right now?"

Rachael climbed from Jack's lap and into Pamela's arms. As Pamela glanced at him, Jack smiled. For the first time, he felt like there might be some hope for Rachael to find love in Tyler's home.

CHAPTER TWENTY-FIVE

Stacy came running into the den where Jack sat at his desk concentrating on his computer screen. "It's here!"

Jack took the envelope. "As much as I'm ashamed to admit it, I've been waiting for that money. It's been hard to concentrate on business since Rachael came to stay, and my checking account is looking mighty lean. I was getting used to staying busy."

"Tell me about it. I can't keep going like this either," Stacy said. "We had that huge rush of business after first finding Rachael. Maybe we shouldn't have been so quick to turn cases away. Besides, Bonny and Clyde are running amuck in the office. They keep knocking things off your desk. I think they're sending you a message."

"They tend to do that when they feel neglected. Maybe we should bring them home for a while."

"We could," Stacy said. "Rachael would like that."

He opened the envelope and removed two checks: one for fifteen thousand dollars, the other for five thousand. "I opened a separate account for Rachael's money so that I can keep them separate. It's amazing how much money you can go through when you have a child around. I wonder how Christine does it. She has two."

"Kids are expensive," Stacy said. "What are you gonna do with Rachael's money?"

Jack bit back a smile. "You really want to know?"

"Yes." She plopped down on the couch.

"I've got a surprise planned for her. Something I think she'll love more than anything else I can think of."

"Now, I'm really curious."

"Where in the world does every little girl want to go?"

"Tiffany's?"

"Tiffany's?" he scoffed. "No. I'm taking her to Cinderella's Castle."

"Disney World? What a fabulous idea! She'll love that. I've never been there myself, but I've always wanted to go."

"Me, too," Jack said. "I've always thought it would be a great place to take a kid. Can you just imagine the look on her face when she sees Snow White or Sleeping Beauty walking around? I've been reading up on it all week. I want to do it before the courts turn her back over to Tyler and I lose my chance."

"It's a great idea, Jack. Take lots of pictures."

"You'll be in charge of that."

"Me?"

"You thought I'd leave you behind?" he said, pleased to have caught her off guard.

She squealed, flew across the room, and landed in his lap. "Thank you! I've always wanted to go to Disney World. You have no idea."

"Wow, if I had known I'd get this response, I'd have done it sooner."

She cuffed him on the arm and went back to the couch, but her face was aglow with excitement. "There are so many rides I want to see," she said. "The Pirates of the Caribbean, The Matterhorn, Space Mountain, Thunder Mountain; I can't wait!"

"I have a feeling we'll be doing a lot of Tea Cup, and Peter Pan rides, too," he said. "I'm just as excited to see what Jayden thinks."

"Oh, how fun! What a wonderful gift you're giving them."

He grinned. "She'll enjoy it more if Jayden is there, don't you think? I've already talked to Mr. Gibbs."

"I'm so excited. When are we going?"

"This weekend. I'll make the room reservations if you'll book our flights. And don't tell Rachael," he added. "I want this to be a surprise."

Stacy pretended to zip her lips. "You going to tell Tyler?"

"Should I?"

"What if he doesn't want you to take her?"

"I don't want to chance it."

"I wouldn't. The way he's been acting lately, he might say no just to spite you," she said.

"I'm not trying to take his place. I just want to give her the best possible care while I have her."

"Don't worry about Tyler. He'll grow up one of these days. It takes a long time for men."

Jack wrinkled his brow. "Should I take comfort in an insult?"

She laughed, but she didn't take it back.

* * *

Tyler exhaled and leaned back in his chair. "It's difficult to talk about this stuff."

Dr. Myers took off her glasses and tossed them on the desk. "I know, but it's important that you let it out. If you keep your emotions bottled up, it can cause problems in your future relationships. How did you feel when you saw Sarah dying on the river bank?"

"How do you think I felt? It was terrible. I couldn't help her. There was nothing I could do!" He covered his eyes and sank lower in the chair. Why was this woman pestering him with these questions?

"You're right; there was nothing you could do. It was a terrible tragedy; it's no one's fault. Do you feel like it's your fault?"

"No. Yes. I don't know. Maybe if I had jumped into the river, I could have pulled her back to the boat."

"Didn't you say you saw an alligator slide into the water?"

"Yes, but I had already pulled Cody into the boat."

"And when you looked up, where was Sarah?"

"Paddling towards shore."

"Why, though? Why didn't she swim towards the boat?"

"The boat had drifted too far away. I should've pulled them in together, but it was too late. It was too late!" His shoulders shook as he began to cry. He didn't want to cry, but he couldn't help himself. "Sarah!"

Several seconds went by. When he finally looked up, he saw that Dr. Myers had moved into the chair next to him. She offered him a tissue. "Excellent work, Tyler. We just recounted what happened. Sarah didn't know there were snakes in the water. You didn't want it to happen. It just happened. You don't have to feel guilty anymore. You wanted to save Sarah, but there was nothing you could do. Even if Sarah was still in the river, there were alligators in the water. You couldn't leave Cody alone in the boat. What if something had happened to both of you? There was nothing you could have done differently. There was nothing you could do to save Sarah."

He sniffed and wiped his eyes. "I felt helpless."

"But it wasn't your fault. Sarah rests in peace. Do you believe that?"

"Yes."

"Good. Now you must live your life in peace."

"But how can I do that?" he said lifting his hands helplessly.

"We'll talk about that on Friday. Same time."

He sniffed. "I guess I needed this more than I realized."

She smiled kindly. "We all need people to talk to, especially when we've been through something difficult. You've been through quite a lot in your young life. You've suffered a tremendous amount of loss."

He looked up, unable to hide his pain. "You're the first person who seems to grasp that. I've lost my father, my wife, my daughter for a time, my girlfriend, and now my mother. It's an awful lot to bear."

"You need more counseling, but you're a good man, Tyler. You'll come through this, and you'll soon enjoy a happy, healthy, and productive future."

"Thank you, Dr. Myers. I'm glad I came," Tyler said.

"I'm glad you did, too."

He offered his hand with a mixture of respect and appreciation, and she shook it.

* * *

"Are you going to tell Rachael that she owns that house?" Stacy said as she stirred the simmering gravy on Jack's stove.

"Don't you think that's Tyler's job?" Jack said.

"If he does it," she scoffed.

"But what's a five-year-old going to do with that kind of information?"

"You said that Mr. Carrington said it right in front of her," Stacy said as she dipped her finger into the gravy and tasted it. "Needs more salt."

"Well, I don't think she grasped it. I can call Mr. Carrington, I guess, and see what he says, but I think it'll end up causing fights down the road. She's bound to throw it in somebody's face during an argument." The doorbell rang. "I'll get it," he said.

"*Yeah,*" Stacy muttered as he went.

He glanced out the window and opened the door. "Hey, Tyler. What's up?"

"Can I see Rachael for a minute?" Tyler said.

"She's not here, but you're welcome to come in."

"What do you mean, she's not here?" Tyler said.

"She's with Emily. They went to get some ice cream."

"You let that woman take my daughter? You have no right to make that kind of decision!"

"Tyler, lower your voice. Would you care to come in so we can discuss this privately? I don't want the neighbors knowing my business."

"I don't give a damn about the neighbors. Why the hell would you let *anyone* in that family touch my daughter?"

"Emily is her aunt. We found Rachael largely because of Emily. Did you know that?" Jack said.

"What are you talking about?"

He gestured for Tyler to come inside.

Tyler stomped past him into the foyer, and Jack closed the door.

"What's going on, Jack?" Stacy said as she entered from the kitchen. "Oh. Hi, Tyler."

"Are you two shacking up?" Tyler said.

"What is your problem?" Jack said. "For your information, Emily contacted Stacy at my detective agency, seeking help in locating her mother and uncle, as well as Billy Ray and Rachael, whom she had learned were in two separate locations after her mother had finally contacted her. Because of Emily, we learned that your mother lied to the police. She's responsible for helping us break this case. You owe her your gratitude, not your enmity."

"She hired you to find Rachael?"

"Yes."

"Where did the likes of her get that kind of money?"

"Not that it's any of your business, but she got a job here in Jackson to help pay for it. You never thought of hiring a detective, did you? And your mother certainly didn't, but that's because she had Rachael all along."

Tyler swallowed hard. "She did all that? Why didn't you tell me about Emily?"

"Because she was afraid that you would respond like this," Stacy said. "Emily moved here from Arkansas so that she could be near Rachael. She loves her and wants to be part of her life. When Rachael first saw Emily, she thought she was Sarah, but Emily reminded her that they had played together in your trailer, and then Rachael remembered.

They get along wonderfully well together. Rachael needs as many loving people in her life as she can get."

"Pamela is loving to Rachael," Tyler said.

"Yes, she is," Jack agreed, "and that's encouraging to see. I've always liked Pamela. What do you want to see Rachael about?"

"I've got her teddy bear out in my truck. I may as well give it to you since Rachael's not here." He opened the door, and Jack followed him out.

Just as they reached Tyler's truck, Emily pulled into the driveway.

Once Emily helped her from her car seat, Rachael said, "Hi, Daddy! Auntie Emily and I went out for ice cream."

Tyler glanced back at Jack. "Hey, Rachael. I brought you something."

"A surprise?"

"Sort of." He reached into the truck and pulled out a worn and beaten teddy bear.

"Bo!" Rachael exclaimed as she reached for her old friend. She hugged the bear close to her chest and kissed it several times. "I missed you, Bo!"

"I wish you'd hug me like that," Tyler scoffed.

"I'll hug you, Daddy. You finally kept your promise."

Tyler opened his arms and Rachael gave him a quick hug. "Thank you for bringing my bear."

"You're welcome, Rachael."

"Did you two have fun?" Jack said to Emily.

Emily, who had stayed in the shadows, nodded, but she didn't step forward.

Tyler turned. "Emily, I understand you're partly responsible for helping us find Rachael. Thank you for that. You're welcome to spend time with Rachael. Like Jack says, she needs as many loving people around her as possible."

Emily's eyebrows rose. "Thank you, Tyler. Does that mean Momma can see her, too?"

"No, now that's asking too much. I don't want her laying eyes on Rachael ever again!"

"We get it, Tyler," Jack said. "She had to ask, you know."

Tyler nodded. "Yes, well, I'll go. Goodbye, Rachael. See you again soon."

"Bye, Daddy."

Everyone seemed to heave a sigh of relief as Tyler backed down the driveway.

And this was Tyler making progress? Jack shook off the thought and offered Rachael his hand. "So, this is Bo. You'll have to introduce him to your new bear. Do you think they'll be friends?"

"Of course," Rachael said. "Bears need friends, too."

* * *

Dr. Myers pushed her glasses back on her nose. "And why do you think that is?"

Tyler shrugged. "I don't know. Maybe it's because I didn't want any of them to begin with. Sarah got pregnant the first night I met her. When she called me about five months later, I just thought she wanted to hook up again. She didn't tell me that her daddy was waiting with his shotgun to make me marry her right there on the spot."

"He had a shotgun?" Dr. Myers said, her eyebrows rising with genuine surprise.

"Hell, yes, he had a shotgun, and the justice of the peace was waiting there, too."

"What happened?"

"We said our vows. We didn't pass go or collect two hundred dollars either. My mother didn't know anything about Sarah until after the wedding. She was supposed to be a one-night stand at the county fair, not my wife! When Mother found out, she was furious. She threatened to have the marriage annulled, but we knew Sarah was carrying twins."

"You could have refused to marry her, of course. He wouldn't have shot you in front of the justice of the peace."

"I know, but I figured I could get a divorce if it didn't work out, and I knew it would irritate my mother. I think I did it for that reason more than any other. Stupid, huh?"

"Are you sure they're your children?"

"Sarah was a virgin. Besides, if you saw pictures of me when I was a baby, you wouldn't be able to tell Cody and me apart. He's mine all right."

"I'm surprised your mother didn't insist on a paternity test."

"Oh, she did, and she got one, too, but nothing ever came of it. I assume that's because it proved that they were mine. Sarah wasn't the type to go sleeping around."

"You just said she was a one-night stand."

"For me, it was, but not for her. I told her all kinds of lies to get her to give in. She was upset that I never called after that. In fact, we never talked until the day she tracked me down, saying she wanted to meet again."

"Well, since they are your children, it wasn't a bad thing that you married their mother, although I thought shotgun weddings were a thing of the past."

"Not in Sarah's family, they're not."

"That doesn't explain why you're so distant with Rachael."

"It's simple," Tyler said. "I wanted sons."

"You have Cody. Dig deeper."

"You mean like my mother never wanted me because she wanted a daughter?"

"Is that true?"

"Yes."

Dr. Myers made a few notes. "How do you feel about that?"

"It makes me angry. I couldn't help being a boy."

"And Rachael can't help being a girl," Dr. Myers countered.

"So, that gets us nowhere," Tyler said. "Can we move on?"

"Did you resent your mother for telling you that she only wanted a girl?"

"Wouldn't you?"

"Have you ever told Rachael you didn't want her?"

"No, but she overheard me tell someone else that, and she definitely resents it."

"That's not good. How can you overcome your feelings about Rachael and care for her as she deserves?"

"I don't know; you're the doc."

"That's not exactly the answer I was hoping for," Dr. Myers said. "What do you think about when you look at your daughter?"

"That she stole my inheritance. She's getting a ridiculous amount of money, more than I'm getting, and she owns *my* house. I think that's incredibly unfair. And then I look into her pretty little face, and I know it's not her fault. It's my mother's fault, every bit of it. Rachael is quiet and sweet. She didn't ask to be born. She didn't ask to be a girl. I need to learn how to be a good father to her, as I am for my son, Cody. I want to love Rachael, but I don't know how."

"At least, you know what you need to do. Next time, we'll talk about how to do it."

"I'm glad that's over. It's not easy talking to you."

Dr. Myers laughed. "Maybe not, but you're making progress. See you tomorrow, Tyler."

CHAPTER
TWENTY-SIX

Jack got the biggest kick out of seeing the children take in the sights and sounds of Disney World. Jayden especially loved the Swiss Family Tree House. He climbed it three times before Jack could get him to move on. Stacy liked the Pirates of the Caribbean, and he liked Splash Mountain. They met Mickey Mouse, Goofy, and Donald Duck, but they had yet to see any of the Disney princesses. They were heading towards the center of the park when Rachael saw the castle. Her eyes grew so big that Jack laughed.

"Look, Uncle Jack, a castle!" She took off running through the crowd. Jack glanced back at Stacy, who had just grabbed Jayden's hand and was fast after them. Rachael dodged people left and right and circled to the front of the castle. She stopped on the drawbridge.

Jack caught up to her and grabbed her hand.

"Look, Uncle Jack! It's a real castle. It's so beautiful!"

"That's Cinderella's castle. Let's go in." They walked across the drawbridge, under the archway, and into the castle courtyard. He followed her wherever she wanted to explore. One gift shop had princess costumes for sale, and she wanted to try them on. He began to worry about losing Stacy and Jayden, but Stacy called to him from the doorway. "We'll be out here," she said.

He waved her in. "Can you help Rachael try on a princess dress?"

"I'd love to," Stacy said. "Do they have any my size?"

Rachael laughed. "No, silly. *I'm* the princess!"

"I'll keep Jayden busy," Jack said. "We'll be right here."

The clerk showed Stacy and Rachael to the dressing room while Jack and Jayden amused themselves with pirate swords. When Rachael stepped out of the dressing room, she was smiling so brightly that her face was the only thing Jack saw, and then she twirled around. "Can I try on Sleeping Beauty's dress, too? I don't know which one I like best."

"You certainly may," Jack said. "What do you think of Jayden's sword?"

"Wow, Jayden. Now you can protect me."

"I could always protect you," Jayden said, "only now I can do it with my sword instead of my fists."

As Rachael and Stacy went to try on the other gown, Jack and Jayden loaded up on pirate accessories.

It was quite fun spending Joan's money.

* * *

"Now I know this ain't none of my business," Regina said, "but I thought you should know that Tyler's got workers all up in that attic. I don't know what they's doin' up there, but there sure is a lot of 'em."

Jack stepped outside the hotel room. "Are there any work trucks outside? Vans with names on them?"

"I didn't think to look. I'll go find out and call you back."

"Thanks, Regina."

"I hope I'm doin' the right thing by callin' you, Mr. Jack. I know it's his house and all, but I don't want him thinkin' he can put Miss Rachael up in that attic again, even if he do put lights up there."

"It's not his house, Regina. It's Rachael's house. Joan left the mansion to her. If anyone's going to stay in that attic, it won't be Rachael, so help me God!"

"Glory be, Mr. Jack. But Mr. Tyler don't know that 'cuz he done told me to clear out all of Mrs. Chandler's things from her room. Course, that was after he went through all her belongings and took what he wanted for hisself. He's moving into her room today. He told me to get Cody's room ready for him, too. They's movin' into the mansion to stay."

"I'll call Joan's attorney to see what he has to say about all this. Do what Tyler says for now. Call me back when you know about the vans."

"So, if Miss Rachael owns Pearl River Mansion, does that mean she owns all Mrs. Chandler's jewelry, too? Mr. Tyler took it all out of her jewelry box this mornin'. I think he means to give it to Miss Pamela."

"I don't know, but I'll find out about that, too," Jack said as outrage thumped in his temples.

"I'm glad I called you, Mr. Jack. I don't want him stealin' what belongs to Miss Rachael."

"Thank you for calling, Regina. Feel free to call anytime you like."

"Sure will. Bye now."

Stacy stepped outside the room just as he hung up. "What is it?"

"Tyler's doing some pilfering and remodeling. He's moving into the mansion as we speak. He's way out of line on this. He didn't even discuss it with me first." He hit his forehead with the palm of his hand. "I can't believe I just said that. I'm calling Mr. Carrington."

"I doubt you'll reach him till Monday," Stacy said.

"Maybe not, but I can sure as hell leave him a message." He dialed and waited for voicemail.

"Mr. Kendall, I didn't expect to hear from you this weekend."

"I didn't expect you to answer," Jack said.

"Then why did you call?"

"Tyler is moving into the mansion. He's doing some remodeling, moving into the master suite, and he's taken possession of Joan's jewelry. Do you have a problem with any of that?"

"Did you approve any of this in advance?"

"No. I just got a call from Regina, whom Tyler is ordering about at will. What do you suggest?"

"The jewelry is specifically mentioned in the will as belonging to Rachael. Each piece is photo documented, so it won't be difficult to recover. Apparently, I need to arrange for a safety deposit box until she's of age. As for the mansion, he'll be within his rights once he assumes custody. You can put a stop to his moving in now if you choose, but I would consider the rift it will cause in your relationship and the one you hope to continue having with Rachael in the future."

"Are you saying I should let him do whatever he wants?"

"Not when it comes to property like the jewelry. I'll intervene so that you're not involved. I'll call to arrange an inventory of Joan's personal items on Monday. If he doesn't return the jewelry, that will become a legal matter. As for sleeping quarters, I've seen pictures of Rachael's bedroom. No one can complain about her accommodations. Tyler will be managing her estate once the family is reunited. As her father, it's appropriate that he reside in the master suite. At this point, whatever remodeling he's doing will come out of his personal allowance, so I doubt he'll go too far. Keep an eye on it, if you can, and I'll do what I'm able as well. How is Rachael enjoying her vacation?"

"She's having a wonderful time. It's so much fun to see the excitement on her face."

"I'm pleased that you arranged this trip so quickly," Mr. Carrington said. "Perhaps these happy memories will help to replace her unhappy ones."

"I hope so, Mr. Carrington. I truly hope so."

* * *

There were three work vans present when Jack parked near the gate, a handyman truck, an electrician's van, and a home appliance delivery truck. According to Mr. Carrington, Tyler had begrudgingly accounted for all the jewelry items during their inventory meeting earlier that afternoon. That, at least, was settled. He decided not to interfere with Tyler's move into the house. As the attorney had said, it was only a matter of time before he would be living in the mansion anyway. Still, it didn't sit well that Tyler had taken the jewelry when he had known it belonged to Rachael. Money did strange things to people. You'd think that his upgrade in status would be sufficient, but no, he had to grasp for more.

Jack looked over at Rachael and Jayden. "Did you have a good time?"

"The best ever, Uncle Jack. I never dreamed there was such a place."

Jack, Jayden, and Rachel, laden with Disney gifts, made their way up to the house, up the front steps, and rang the bell.

Regina came to the door immediately. "Oh, you're home! I wish I'd known; I'da waited at the gate. Come on in. There's lemonade in the kitchen. I'll go fetch G."

The trio filed into the kitchen and took seats around the table. A few moments later, Tyler strolled in. "Hey, what are y'all doin' here?"

"Hi, Daddy! We brought you a present. We brought Cody, Pamela, and Jacob presents, too."

Jack stood and extended his hand. "Hey, Tyler. What's up, man?"

"You could've called first."

"Considering this is Rachael's house, I didn't think we needed to call first. What are you doing here?" Jack knew he shouldn't have let Tyler goad him, but his cold and detached treatment of Rachael never ceased to annoy him.

"I live here now. Cody and I moved in this weekend."

"I saw the work vans. Are you remodeling already?"

"Just the attic. I'm putting electricity up there, as well as a stove. I'm going to run heat and AC up there, too. Pamela and Jacob will be living there until we get married."

"I see. Rachael's afraid of the attic, you know."

"Yes, well, it won't be dark anymore. I'm going to open up the sliding wall panel so that the staircase isn't hidden. I'll build it to match the quality of the rest of the house, and make the attic an official third floor. Rachael won't ever have to go up there if she doesn't want to. The boys will like that."

Jack swallowed what came to mind. "Where's Cody? We've got a present for him. We just got back from Disney World."

"You what?"

"We spent the weekend at Disney World. I thought Rachael and Jayden would enjoy it, so we went."

"Oh, and I suppose her monthly maintenance check picked up the tab, did it?" Tyler took a threatening step closer.

"I cleared it with Mr. Carrington before we went. His instructions were that Joan wanted Rachael to enjoy a first-class lifestyle with first-class vacations. I hope this is only the first of many vacations she'll enjoy, and you and your family will share many wonderful times together."

"I'll bet you do." Tyler went to the fridge and took out a beer.

"Perhaps we can discuss this at a later time. Is Cody here?" Jack asked again.

"He's up in his room. I'll get him." He took a few swallows of his beer. "Did it ever occur to you to take Cody with you instead of that—"

"Jayden is Rachael's best friend; he was the perfect choice. Besides, you know as well as I do that you wouldn't have let me take Cody."

"You got that right." He walked into the hallway. "Cody, come down here! Your sister has a present for you."

Jack heard feet thundering down the steps. A few seconds later, Cody skidded into the kitchen.

"What kind of present?" Cody said.

"Hi, Cody," Rachael said, her face lighting up with pleasure.

"Hi."

"Hello, Cody," Jack said. "You remember Jayden, don't you?"

Cody ignored Jayden and turned back to Rachael. "Well? What did you bring me?"

She pulled a stuffed Winnie the Pooh bear out of the bag and offered it to him.

"Winnie the Pooh?" Cody said with a curled lip.

Rachael nodded. "He's famous."

Cody took the bear and looked at him from several angles.

"You can be like Christopher Robin. Look, I got the book for you, too." She handed him the book. "Christopher Robin gets lost in the woods, and Winnie the Pooh becomes his best friend. Winnie the Pooh likes honey, just like you do."

Finally, he smiled. "Thanks, Rachael. He's a good bear."

Rachael pulled out the large Mickey Mouse mug and handed it to Tyler. "Here, Daddy. Pamela has one just like it except hers has Minnie Mouse on it."

Tyler took the cup. "Thank you, Rachael."

"I have a present for Jacob, too. I'll give them their presents next time I see them."

"Did you have a good time at Disney World?"

"Oh, Daddy, I saw Cinderella's castle and got three princess dresses. We went on rides and climbed around in caves. We even took a jungle cruise. It was the most fun ever!"

"I wanna go to Disney World," Cody whined.

Tyler mussed Cody's hair. "We'll go someday."

"We'll be going, now," Jack said, "but we've got presents for Mr. Gibbs and Regina first."

"I'm right here, Mr. Jack," Regina said from the kitchen entrance. "G is waitin' on the porch to see Jayden. We'll be out there whenever yer ready. Take yer time." She turned and walked back down the hall.

"That woman knows everything that goes on around here," Tyler said.

"That's because she's good at what she does. You're blessed to have her," Jack said. "Say goodbye to your daddy, Rachael. We've got to go."

"What did you get?" Cody asked Jayden.

Jayden glanced at Jack, and he nodded. "I got a pirate sword."

"A pirate sword? Let me see."

Jayden reluctantly pulled it out of his sack.

"Wow, that's cool! Why didn't you get me a pirate sword, Rachael? I want a pirate sword. Can I hold it?"

Jack leaned in and took the sword. "Not in the house. Come on, guys. We have to go."

Rachael and Jayden got down from the table and trailed Jack onto the porch. Regina and Mr. Gibbs were waiting outside.

Cody followed them out. "I wanna see the sword. Let me hold it."

"This is Jayden's sword," Jack said. "But your daddy can order one for you if he wants to. Why don't you go ask him?"

Cody turned immediately and went running down the hall. "I want a pirate sword, Daddy!"

"Sorry," Jayden said. "I only showed him one present."

"You didn't know he'd act like that," Jack said. "Go ahead and give them their presents."

Jayden's eyes widened, but he accepted the bag with a smile. "Here's a big Tigger coffee cup for you, Papa. Do you like it?"

"It's the finest mug I ever did see. Thank you kindly, Jayden."

"Here's something for you, Auntie Regina. This is for when you rest your feet." He handed her the tea set, which was made of beautifully painted china.

She gasped. "Mercy, child. I ain't never had nothin' this fancy in my whole life. Thank you. I'll treasure it always."

Jayden grinned as each of them hugged him close.

"Show them what you brought home, Jayden, and then Rachael and I have to go."

Jayden showed them his bag of goodies and then placed it all back in the bag.

"You done somethin' we couldn't have done for our boy," Mr. Gibbs said. "I don't know how to thank you."

"In a roundabout way, Joan did it. She just doesn't know it," Jack said, and they all laughed.

"Oooie, but she'd turn over in her grave if she knew her money sent that boy to Disney World with her grandchild," Regina said.

"Wouldn't she though?" Jack grinned.

"Yer bad, Mr. Jack. Yer bad, and I like it!" Regina said with a belly laugh.

"We'll walk you out, won't we Jayden?"

"Yes, Papa."

The sun was beginning to set, and its light stretched in every direction across the garden. For one brief moment, Jack wished this was his home and Rachael was his daughter, but the reality was he could only protect her a short while longer. Eventually, she'd come back here to live with Tyler and her brother. He dreaded that day, and he prayed that Pamela would be here to soften the blow.

CHAPTER
TWENTY-SEVEN

"They don't pay me enough to clean up no piss off the floor, and I ain't never seen so much laundry in all my life. He's got me waitin' on him and Cody hand and foot. They don't do nothin' for themselves no more. I'm sorry Mister Jack, but I won't be treated like no Negro slave. Tyler acts like he owns me, and I ain't puttin' up with it no more. I hate to leave G and Jayden, not to mention Miss Rachael, but I'm headin' back to Chicago at the end of the month."

"Calm down, Regina. I'll talk to him. You're right about your agreement not covering those services. You were hired to take care of one older lady and a little girl, not a man and his spoiled brat son. If they want those kinds of services, they can hire a maid, and she can work under your supervision. Technically, you work for Rachael, not Tyler anyway. Her money pays your salary, not his. He has no right to order you around. You're there to take care of Rachael, and she isn't even there yet."

"Is that right? What about G?"

"He works for Rachael, too."

"You mean Tyler can't fire him?"

"No, he can't. Has he threatened to?" Jack tugged on his collar as his anger began to rise.

"Only about a hundred times. He's working him so hard; I'm afraid he'll fall down dead."

"I'll be there in thirty minutes."

Stacy walked into the den, took one look at his face, and said, "Tyler?"

"How'd you guess?"

"I'll go with you."

"Why not? I'll let Emily know to keep Rachael out a bit longer. Remind me to hit the button on my pocket recorder when we get there. I don't want him lying to Mr. Carrington, whom I'm calling right now," Jack said as he dialed.

"Good afternoon, Mr. Kendall. How may I help you today?"

Jack briefly described the problem and was pleased to hear that he had the authority to say what he wanted to say. He felt better after hanging up, but his blood was still pounding through his veins.

"Good news?"

"Not for Tyler," he smirked.

"What would Rachael do without you?"

"That's a scary thought."

"Yeah, Jack. It really is."

* * *

A rail-thin black woman wearing a tan, fitted dress stepped to the side of the driveway as they passed by. Stacy turned around in her seat for a second look. The woman set the suitcase down for a few seconds, shook out her hands, and then picked it up again.

"Stop, Jack. Let's offer her a ride. I'll jump in the back."

"I was thinking the same thing."

When Stacy opened the door and got out, the woman dropped her suitcase and ran for the woods.

"Wait!" Stacy yelled. "We just want to give you a ride." The woman stepped out into the open, and Stacy saw that she wore large dark sunglasses.

"I'd rightly appreciate it," the woman said. "I come to see my boy, and I needs me a job."

"I might know of some work you can do. I'll put your suitcase in the back of the truck. Come on. You can sit up front."

"No, ma'am. I'll sit in the back. Go on, now. I'll tend to my own bag."

"All right," Stacy said as she got back into the truck. Jack glanced over, and she shrugged.

Once the woman was in the truck, Jack drove slowly down the driveway towards the gate.

* * *

Regina didn't wait for them to get out of the truck. She threw open the gate and hurried over.

"I'm so glad you're here, Mr. Jack. That man's about to drive me insane."

"Hey, Auntie Regina."

Regina shrieked and drew back. "Who's that?"

The woman stepped down from the back of the truck. "It's me, Dillia. Jayden's momma."

"Lordy, girl, but you gave me a fright. What are you doin' in the back of Mr. Jack's truck?"

"We found her walking along the driveway." Jack reached into the back for her suitcase and set it on the ground. "Hello, Dillia. I'm Jack."

"Thank you kindly for the ride."

Regina snatched off Dillia's sunglasses. "Why you wearin' these stupid—" She gasped. "Dillia, baby, what happened to your face?" Dillia grabbed the glasses out of Regina's hand and put them back on.

"Now that you done showed everybody, there ain't no use in me lyin' about it. Lyin's what got me in trouble in the first place. I been missin' my boy, so I told my husband about Jayden, but he don't like me havin' no young'un, so he beat me for not tellin' 'im in the beginnin', and then he beat me for wanting to see 'im. He was so angry that he beat me again a few days later. I couldn't take no more beatin's, so I left."

"Is that the first time he hit you," Stacy asked, "when he found out about Jayden?"

"Think I'da left if it was? I don't blame 'im for bein' upset. I should've told 'im the truth afore we got married."

"Do you need to see a doctor?" Stacy said.

"I'm almost well now. You should've seen me after he first done it, though I still got bruises all over my back and shoulders where he hit me with his belt buckle."

Jack could see that for all her brave words she was shaking. "We're sorry you went through that. No one has the right to beat another person."

"Bad thing is he'll probably come after me, but I got no place else to go. He says the next time he beats me, he'll kill me." A sob escaped her as she turned into Regina's comforting embrace.

"Don't worry, child. He won't beat you no more," Regina said. "Not while I'm around, he won't."

"I've got friends at the police station," Jack said. "You can press assault charges and file a restraining order."

"If I get the police after 'im, he'll kill me twice!"

"Dillia, we trust Mr. Jack. He's got some mighty powerful friends. They can tell the mister to stay away from you, or they'll put him in jail. They sure 'nuff will."

Dillia shook her head. "He'll just send someone else to do his dirty work. You don't know how mean he is."

"He'll think twice about having someone do something if he knows he'll have to go to jail for it," Jack said.

"Look, I didn't mean to cause no trouble. If there ain't no work here for me to do, I'll have to find me somethin' else."

"Mrs. Chandler is dead," Regina said. "Mr. Tyler's livin' in the big house now."

"And it just so happens he needs someone to look after him and his new family. Isn't that right, Regina?"

Regina's eyes widened. "So he do, Mr. Jack. So he do."

"You would be working under Regina's supervision, of course, and I'd have to run the idea by Tyler first, which is why I'm here this morning, though I had no idea about you, Dillia. I thought we'd need to look for someone in the newspaper."

"Oh, no need for that. I'd be happy to work for Mr. Tyler," Dillia said.

"Under Regina's supervision," Jack repeated. "You will report to her."

"Yes, sir."

"Very well, I'll talk to Tyler and let you know."

"Thank you kindly," Dillia said. "Is there a place I can rest up a bit? It was a frightful long trip."

"You can go to my cabin, for now," Regina said patting Dillia's shoulder, but she stopped when she saw her grimace. "We'll work out the details about where you'll stay once Mr. Jack talks to Mr. Tyler. I'll be along with yer suitcase in a few minutes."

Once she was out of earshot, Regina shook her head. "That girl ain't nothin' but trouble. She done ran off and left Jayden with no warnin', and that ain't the first time neither. Now she's lookin' for a job? How's Jayden supposed to take that? What good's a mother that comes and goes like the wind?"

"I think we should give her a chance," Jack said. "She's probably safer here than anywhere else, and maybe she's learned her lesson. If Tyler agrees to hire her on a trial basis, where do you suggest she live?"

"I ain't givin' up my cabin, and there ain't no room for her in G's cabin neither. As it is, Jayden sleeps on the couch. I don't want her movin' in there and makin' Jayden sleep on the floor like she done before. Besides, Mr. Tyler's wantin' me to move into the maid's quarters so he can yell for me to fetch and do for him all hours of the day. Let *her* stay in the house since she's the one who's supposed to wait on him and his young'un anyway."

"I'm going to remind Tyler that you're not servants, but it may take some time for him to get it through that thick head of his. He is, after all, his mother's son. I'll carry Dillia's suitcase to your cabin. Then I'll talk to Tyler."

"What would we do without you, Mr. Jack?"

"I don't know, but I've been wondering lately what my life would be like without all of you. Certainly, it would be empty."

"I'll second that," Stacy said as they headed down the trail towards Regina's cabin.

* * *

Tyler tossed his empty beer can into the trash and opened another. "And who's gonna pay for another maid?"

"It'll come out of your budget. Regina and Mr. Gibbs' wages come out of Rachael's account," Jack said.

"If Regina isn't willing to take care of me and my family, then let's fire her and hire someone to take her place. Then Rachael can pay for it."

"No, Tyler, that's not how it works."

Tyler slammed his beer can on the granite counter top. "Oh, and I suppose you're here to tell me how to run my household?"

"I spoke with Mr. Carrington this afternoon. These are his instructions. If you want to hire someone to do the extra chores that are required to take care of you and your new family, then you may, but she'll work under Regina's direct supervision. Regina will continue caring for her current responsibilities, which include overseeing the general operations of Pearl River Mansion, such as meal planning, shopping, and keeping track of expenses. She is also responsible for caring for Rachael directly. That is what she was hired to do in the first place. Your maid will help with the cooking, laundry, and general cleaning. Mr. Carrington said to remind you that they are paid professionals and are to be treated as such. They work a set number of hours each day and are not to be prevailed upon outside of those hours.

They are not available at your beck and call, Tyler. You are encouraged to do ordinary things for yourselves, and give the children normal chores to do, to prevent them from becoming spoiled. Since Dillia has conveniently returned today, she may be the perfect person to step into this position because she's already familiar with your household. If you agree to hire her, she can live in the maid's quarters, but normal workday hours still apply. Does this meet with your approval?"

"Dillia's back? I thought she got married."

"Apparently, that didn't work out. You should know that her husband was abusive; he could show up here at any time."

"Humph," Tyler said. "He'll only show up here once."

"I'm not going to ask what you mean by that," Jack said.

"What's Dillia's salary?"

"I can find out what she was paid before and let you know."

"Don't bother. You've done quite enough. Having Dillia around will be quite handy. She's much more pliable than Regina ever thought about being."

"Don't forget that Regina is responsible for overseeing her schedule."

He smirked. "Yeah, I'll remember that."

"Just curious," Jack said. "Did you quit your job? I've noticed that you're around a lot more during the daytime."

"Not that it's any of your business, any more than the rest of this is, but yes, I quit my job. It's not like I need to spend all those hours working for that little bit of pay anymore. I can concentrate on being a man of leisure now."

"That means you can concentrate on being a good father and a good person, a worthy goal for any man. We'll see ourselves out. Have a good afternoon."

"Bye, Tyler," Stacy said, her first words since the discussion began.

"I'd have my maid walk you out, but she hasn't started yet. Ha!" He lifted his beer and took a long drink as he watched them leave.

* * *

Rachael screamed and bolted upright on the couch.

Stacy ran from her room and was at her side in an instant. "What is it, sweetie? Did you have a bad dream?" She grabbed a tissue and wiped the sweat from Rachael's brow.

"Jayden. They took Jayden!"

Stacy wrapped her arms around Rachael and patted her back. "No, sweetie. He's safe. He's with his Papa. They're sleeping in their cabin right now. We can call them in the morning if you like."

"No, they took him. They took him because I told the secret," Rachael whimpered, her eyes still closed.

"What secret, baby?"

"I can't tell you or they'll take Jayden. Gramma said so."

"Did Gramma tell you to keep a secret?"

"Uh huh."

"You keep Gramma's secret and go back to sleep now. We'll talk to Jayden in the morning."

"Can we talk to Jayden now?"

"Jayden is sleeping, but we can talk to him tomorrow." Rachael nodded and then yawned. "Lie back down, and I'll cover you up," Stacy said. Rachael turned onto her side, and fell asleep again within moments.

"Humph," Stacy grumbled as she rose from Rachael's side. She'd never had cause to be angry with a dead person before, but Joan Chandler's poison lived on. The fact that she had threatened Rachael was inexcusable, a terrible burden to lay upon a child. If she were hiding more than the murder of Billy Ray Richards, then she and Jack would damn sure find out about it.

CHAPTER TWENTY-EIGHT

"I can't help it, Jack. I think there's more to this than we know," Stacy said.

"What more could there be? She said it was Joan's secret. We already know that." He reached down and scooped up Clyde, who was rubbing against his legs. "Hey, boy. I'll bet you've been thinking, 'Now why don't he write?'"

"Really, Jack, *Dances with Wolves*?" Stacy scoffed.

"I love that line."

"This is serious, Jack. What are we going to do?"

"*We* aren't going to do anything. I'll talk to Rachael if the opportunity presents itself, but I want to talk to Dr. Crimshaw first. Rachael has been upset after the last couple of sessions, and I'd like to know why."

"Fine. Since you don't need *me*, I'll butt out." She grabbed her purse and headed for the door. "I'm nobody, apparently."

"Wait. That's not what I meant."

"Well, that's not how you've been treating me lately. You get the big checks coming to you, so that makes you more important than the rest of us, is that it? We spent the same amount of time and effort searching for Rachael as you did. If you're not careful, the day will come when you have to give Rachael back, and you'll turn around to find that there's no one there because you treated us all like underlings during your fifteen minutes of fame."

He cringed as the office door slammed. Was he letting his parental authority go to his head, or was she jealous? Either way, he didn't want her upset. He sighed. None of this was easy. When his phone rang, he expected it to be Stacy calling to apologize, but it was Tyler.

"Hey, Jack. I'd like to have Rachael out for a visit tomorrow. She can spend the night, and I'll drop her off at your place Sunday afternoon."

Jack's heart began thumping. He wanted to say no, but he knew that wasn't wise. It was a reasonable request, especially if they were working towards that end, but he didn't want to let her go. "I don't see why not," he said through his teeth, "but I'd like to ask Rachael how she feels about it first. She's been upset by her last two therapy sessions, and she woke up with a nightmare last night. I was about to call her doctor to discuss it. I'll ask her what she thinks about a visit and call you back."

"She's got to start visiting sometime," Tyler said.

"Yes, she does. I'll call you back as soon as I speak with the doctor."

"Thanks, Jack. I don't know why, but I thought you'd give me a hard time about this. Maybe I'm reading you wrong."

"I just want what's best for Rachael. Talk to you soon." He hung up and rolled his eyes. He grabbed his notepad and flipped through it until he found Dr. Crimshaw's number. She was in session, of course, but he left a message.

He was feeling bad about Stacy and decided to pick up some flowers on the way home. None of this would have happened without Stacy or Emily, or even Tyler for that matter. It was a group effort that had resulted in recovering Rachael; he certainly couldn't take the credit. He needed to remember that and not let his protective instincts damage the important relationships he had with other people, but recognizing what he needed to do was one thing, doing it was quite another.

"She sticks to her story every time she tells it, so I feel confident that we've gotten to the bottom of what happened," Dr. Crimshaw said. "I'm ready to move on to her time in the attic. If she's having nightmares, it's because it was so horribly traumatic, as it would be for anyone. Expect a few more difficult sessions, and counter them with positive reinforcement at home. Then we'll begin building her hopes for a positive future. It's a slow process, but it's important that she works through these difficult memories so that they don't come back to haunt her when she's older."

"Is that possible? Can she really forget all that's happened?" Jack said.

"I don't know that she'll forget, but when she remembers, it can be far less painful and damaging than it otherwise might have been. The more happy memories she makes along the way, the less often she will dwell on the past."

"I best get busy, then," Jack said.

"She told me about Disney World," Dr. Crimshaw said. "It sounds like she had a fabulous time.

Jack chuckled as he remembered the wonder on her face when she realized she could have three princess dresses. She was quite fun to spoil. "By the way," he said, "Tyler just called. He wants to have Rachael out for an overnight visit tomorrow night."

"Well, it has to begin sometime," Dr. Crimshaw said as she made a note on her chart. "I've spoken to Dr. Myers, and she says he's making acceptable progress."

"You don't think it's too soon?"

"There's only one way to find out," Dr. Crimshaw said.

* * *

The kitchen smelled of rosemary and thyme when Jack stepped in from the garage. "Hey, everybody. I'm home." He set his briefcase on the counter and then thought better of it. He carried it into the den and set it on his desk, which was now organized, thanks to Emily. Hiding the flowers behind his back, he walked through the sliding doors and onto the back patio. Seeing that the gate was ajar, he walked up to the side door of Stacy's garage and rang the bell.

"It's open," Stacy said through the speaker.

He entered the garage, climbed the steps, and knocked on the door. Rachael opened it. "Surprise! We're baking cookies."

"You're cookin' dinner at my place, too. Aren't you?"

"Yep."

"I've got a surprise, too, but this one's for Stacy."

"For me?" Stacy closed the oven. "That *is* a surprise."

He brought the flowers from behind his back. "I'm sorry for being a jerk today. I'll do much better. I promise."

"Flowers! That's what I love about you, Jack. You listen when I've got something to say, and you care about my feelings."

Jack chuckled. "I think our business neighbors heard the door slam halfway around the block."

Stacy took the bouquet and pressed her lips into a sheepish smile. "It's been building." She took a vase from the cabinet, added water, and carefully arranged the daisies, carnations, and lavender asters. "Thank you. These will look lovely on our dinner table tonight, won't they, Rachael?"

"They're pretty! Jayden brings me flowers, too."

Jack took a seat at the bar. "So, what's the special fuss with dinner tonight?"

"My way of apologizing, too."

"That's what I love about us," Jack said with a lopsided smile. "We make a great team."

"Am I part of the team?" Rachael said.

"Of course, you are," Jack and Stacy said at the same time.

"Hey, Rachael, how would you like to wear your princess dress tomorrow night?"

"I can't. I can only wear it in my castle."

"Well, your daddy called a little while ago. He wants you to spend the night with him tomorrow night, which means you can sleep in your princess bed and wear your princess dress. What do you think about that?"

Stacy glanced at Jack.

"It's okay," Jack said quietly. "I cleared it with Dr. Crimshaw."

"Will you be there?" Rachael asked.

"No, sweetie. He only invited you."

Her brows drew together. "What if Daddy and Cody are mean to me?"

"They won't be mean to you. Besides, Regina and Mr. G will be there."

Rachael seemed to think about that as she plopped onto the couch.

"Do you want to go?" Jack said as he sat next to her.

"What if Daddy makes me go to the attic?"

"He won't make you go up there. I'll make him promise."

"Is that big house really mine?" she said.

Jack glanced at Stacy. "Yes. Your grandmother left it to you when she died."

"Then why can't you, me, Jayden, and Miss Stacy live there? Jayden can live in Cody's room, and we can all be happy."

Jack laughed. "That would be nice, but it doesn't work that way."

"Why not?" she said with a wrinkled brow.

"Because even though the house is yours, you can't take care of it by yourself until you're eighteen years old, and you are only five."

"I'm almost six."

"Yes, but until you're eighteen, your daddy gets to live in the house with you. Stacy and I have to live in our own houses, but we can visit, and you can visit us."

"I like my plan better. Will I get to see Jayden?"

"I imagine so."

"If I don't like it, will you come and get me?"

"Yes. Now, let's practice saying my phone number so you can call if you need me."

It only took a few tries for Rachael to have it memorized.

"Good girl. Decide which princess dress you want to take, but take some regular clothes, too. You can't play in the garden in your princess dress."

"I'll just wear my dress inside the castle."

"You do that, little one. You do that."

CHAPTER
TWENTY-NINE

"How do I look?" Tyler said as he held the screen door open for Pamela.

Pamela raised a brow. "Why are you nervous?"

"There's a lot riding on Rachael being happy here. People are watching me."

Pamela sat on the swing and patted the cushion. Tyler joined her and wrapped his arm around her shoulders. "I'm glad you're here," he said. "That will make it a lot easier."

"The apartment is wonderful. The way it looks now, you'd never know anything bad happened up there. I had no idea it would be so big. I can't believe it has three bedrooms. It's bigger than your trailer."

"Well, it *is* the third floor of the house. I wonder what Rachael will think when she sees what I've done with the staircase, how open it is after I removed the sliding panel. I hope it doesn't frighten her."

"We'll need to tell her about the changes before she goes upstairs. The main thing is not to force her to go up there. You're not planning on it, are you?"

"I thought she might like to see that it has lights now."

"You can tell her, but you can't force her. Tell me you won't," Pamela pleaded.

"I won't force her. If someone had told me that they put lights in the closet my mother used to lock me in, it wouldn't have made me want to see the closet, so I hear what you're saying. I won't force her. I'm just glad you like it, and Jacob seems happy as well."

Pamela chuckled. "Are you kidding? He likes all the stairs he has to climb to get to it."

Tyler looked at his watch. "They should be here any minute." Just as he said it, Rachael and Jack appeared on the path. He and Pamela went out to meet them. "Hey, Rachael. I'm so glad you're here. Welcome home."

"Hi, Daddy."

Jack and Tyler shook hands, and Jack handed him Rachael's bag.

"Hi, Rachael. It's nice to see you," Pamela said. "I can't wait to see you in your princess dress."

"I brought my Snow White dress. She has dark hair just like me."

"We'll all dress up for dinner, so that will be the perfect time to change," Pamela said.

"Where's Jayden?"

"I don't know, but Cody and Jacob are in Cody's room. Would you like to go up there?" Tyler said.

"I want to see my princess room."

Pamela linked arms with Tyler. "Your daddy has something to tell you before we go inside. Don't you, Tyler?"

Tyler threw a quick glance at Jack before answering. "I did a lot of work in the attic since you were here. It's not like it used to be. I broke down the secret panel and made a brand new staircase. There are lights in the attic now. It's not dark and scary up there anymore. Daddy fixed it."

Rachael stepped back. "I don't want to go up to the attic, Daddy."

"You don't have to. I just wanted you to know that it isn't dark up there anymore. I fixed it," Tyler said.

"Uncle Jack said he'll come get me if I want to go home."

"I did say that," Jack said, "but you're going to have a wonderful time with your family, and you'll see Jayden, Mr. G, and Auntie Regina, too. You'll have lots of fun. Now give me a hug; I've got to go."

Rachael hugged him tightly. "Don't forget me."

"I'll never forget you. Bye, everybody. See you tomorrow."

"Thanks, Jack," Tyler said as he reached for his daughter's hand. "Let's go put your things in your room, and then we can come down and get some lemonade."

"Can Pamela come, too?"

"I'm right here, sweetie. We'll go up together."

Tyler glanced over his shoulder, but Jack was already out of sight. He could see that Jack was reluctant to leave Rachael. Considering everything that had happened, he could understand that, but he was determined to prove that he was ready to be a father to his daughter. When they got to the top of the stairs, he said, "Come look at the staircase."

Rachael grabbed hold of Pamela's hand. "I don't wanna go up to the attic, Daddy."

"Come and see what the new stairs look like. You don't have to climb them."

Pamela led Rachael to the bottom of the stairs. "Jacob and I live up there now."

"You do? Why do you live up there?" Rachael said as she clung tightly to Pamela's hand.

"Your daddy and I aren't married yet, so I live in my own place until we get married. It's very nice up there now. It's been painted, there's a new stove, and big lights in the ceiling."

"It's cold up there," she said making a face.

"Not anymore. It stays the same temperature as the rest of the house," Pamela said.

"It has its own heating and cooling unit," Tyler said, "but that doesn't matter. The main thing is it's not scary up there anymore."

Rachael craned her neck to look up the stairs. "It looks different."

"Let's go put your bag in your room," Tyler said, "then we can go down and get some lemonade."

"Okay." Rachael ran down the hall towards her room.

Tyler smiled at Pamela. "That wasn't so bad. Maybe I'm getting the hang of this."

* * *

Rachael stood on a stool in front of the bathroom mirror combing her hair. She had tried to fasten the buttons on the back of her dress, but she couldn't reach them, so the sleeves were falling off her shoulders. Her necklace caught her eye in the mirror. She laid down her brush and touched the locket. "I wish you were here, Mommy."

A knock sounded at her door making her flinch. She stepped off the stool and ran to the door. "Who is it?"

"It's Pamela."

"Oh." She unlocked and opened the door.

"I came to see if you needed any help with your dress."

"I can't reach the buttons."

"Turn around." Pamela fastened all six buttons and then tied the ribbon into a bow. "There now. Let me see." Rachael turned around. "You look beautiful, Rachael. Shall we do something special with your hair?"

"Like what?"

"I can braid it and wrap it into a bun if you like? Let's go into the bathroom, and I'll show you."

Rachael stepped up onto the stool and watched as Pamela divided her hair into three parts and intertwined them into a braid. "Oh, so that's a braid. I like it."

"Are you ready for dinner?"

"Will Daddy think I'm pretty?"

"Your daddy will think you're beautiful," Pamela said.

Rachael smiled and followed her out the door. "Wait," she said when they got to the top of the stairs. "Go get Daddy so he can see me come down the stairs in my dress."

"Good idea. We'll be right back." Pamela hurried down the stairs and turned towards the kitchen. A few moments later, she and her father appeared at the bottom of the stairs.

"Are you ready, Daddy?"

"You better hurry. Dillia's got dinner ready."

She giggled as she walked slowly down the stairs, letting her skirts bounce against her legs. She was so glad she had waited to wear the dress. Daddy even took out his phone and snapped some pictures. When she reached the bottom of the stairs, he scooped her up into his arms.

"You are the prettiest little princess I ever saw."

"Do I look like Snow White?"

"Even prettier," he said.

She beamed in her happiness. Her father offered Pamela one arm, and she took the other as they walked into the dining room. Cody and Jacob were already at the table.

"Wow, Rachael, that sure is a pretty dress," Jacob said.

"Thank you. I have three princess dresses."

Dillia filled everyone's water glass. "Are you ready for me to bring in supper now?"

"It's called dinner, Dillia, and yes, we're ready."

"Yes, sir, Mr. Tyler."

Cody made ugly faces at her, but Rachael ignored him. "Daddy, how come Jayden isn't here?"

"Because Jayden isn't part of our family. Jayden is part of Mr. Gibbs and Regina's family. They're all having dinner together, just like we are."

"But Dillia's here."

"That's because she's taking care of us. That's her job. She'll eat later."

"All by herself?"

"I don't know. Don't worry about Dillia. You're supposed to be having fun."

Dillia delivered their dinner and went back to the kitchen.

"Uncle Jack lets Jayden eat with us."

"Jayden isn't here, Rachael," Tyler said, his voice growing louder and sharper. "He's at home."

"We'll have to visit him tomorrow. Won't we, Tyler?" Pamela said with a tight smile.

"You'll get to see him" Tyler smirked. "Is that what you wanted to hear?"

Rachael nodded and sampled her food.

The boys talked about catching worms so that they could go fishing. She didn't care about worms. Daddy and Pamela were all cuddly together. No one spoke to her for the rest of dinner. It wasn't at all like Uncle Jack's house. Here, she was on the outside. There, she was in the middle. She kept waiting to see if anyone would include her in something they were talking about, but they didn't. It was just like when she was younger. When dinner was over, she slipped off her chair and went up to her room. She locked herself in, climbed into her princess bed, and cried herself to sleep.

* * *

"Rummy, again. You just threw away two kings," Stacy said. "Are you having that much trouble concentrating?"

"I didn't want to leave her, Stace. I have no right to feel that way, but I do. I wish she were mine. I want to protect her, but I can't."

"They'll learn how to be a family again. It might not be as good for her as it is here. That's unfortunate, but there's nothing we can do about it. She's Tyler's daughter."

"I never expected to get so involved," he said. "Every time he raises his voice to her, I could just—"

"But you can't," Stacy said softly.

"No, I have to encourage him to be a good father. I have to coax him into loving her when that should be so natural, so easy. I don't understand why it isn't!" His cell phone buzzed; he had a text message.

"It's from Tyler. Hey look, it's Rachael. Oh, isn't she adorable?" He leaned over so Stacy could see the pictures of Rachael as she came down the stairs in her Snow White dress. She had a huge smile on her face.

"There, you see? She's doing just fine."

He nodded and texted back, "Thanks. I needed that."

* * *

Tyler knocked on Rachael's door.

"Who is it?"

"It's Daddy."

A few moments later Rachael unlocked the door.

"Hey, why are you in bed already?"

"I don't know."

"Aren't you having a good time?"

"No. You have Pamela, Cody has Jacob, and I'm all by myself."

"I see. How does it work at Jack's house?"

"I sleep at Stacy's house, so it's just us girls at night."

"I thought you lived with Jack," Tyler said.

"I do, but I sleep over at Stacy's house. She lives above the garage behind Jack's house. It works well for us."

"You know, Rachael, it's gonna take some time for all of us to get used to living together again. There will be five of us, so none of us should be lonely, and you'll have Jayden nearby. You and Jayden are pretty good friends, aren't you?"

"He's my best friend."

"You and Cody will be starting school soon. You'll make lots of new friends then."

"Are you going to marry Pamela?" she asked as she climbed back into bed.

"I am."

"Are you going to give me away again?"

"Nope. We're gonna keep you forever and ever. I shouldn't have given you to your grandmother. I'm very sorry I did that, Rachael. I'd take it back if I could, but I can't. All I can do is be a good daddy to you from here on out."

"Do you want me?" she said.

"I do, and I want to tickle you, too." He reached between her arms and tickled her until she shrieked and squirmed with laughter. She twisted around until her feet were against his chest.

Grabbing her pillow, Tyler growled like an animal and used the pillow to push her legs away. Rachael squealed, laughed, and struggled to push him away. Tyler leaned over the bed, trapping her legs, and shoved the pillow over her face, growling all the while. "I've got you, you squirmy little goose. Gerrrr, gerrrr," he growled.

She kicked and tried to shove the pillow away. "Stop, Daddy! I can't breathe!"

"Gerrr, gerrr." For the briefest moment, he thought about the money, the house, the estate, the stocks, bonds, and other investments. He could undo all of his mother's schemes and reclaim what was rightfully his, all in a matter of seconds. Rachael began to struggle in earnest. Her arms flailed against him, striking his arms with her fists as he pushed down a little harder. "I've got you now. Gerrr, gerrr," he growled. All that money, the money he had refused to sell out for, was his for the taking. The time had come. It was his turn to control the family fortune.

Is this what she thought, is this how she felt, when she watched his father struggling to stay alive when she could have saved him, but didn't? Was he like her? A horrified groan escaped him as he yanked the pillow away from Rachael's face.

She sucked in air and choked on it, sputtering saliva and tears as she struggled to breathe.

Tyler threw the pillow on the floor and gathered Rachael into his arms. "Are you all right, Rachael? Daddy didn't mean to hurt you."

She pushed away from him. "Don't touch me! You always hurt me when you touch me!"

Tyler shot to his feet. "Fine. I won't touch you. You're fine. You're gonna be fine. We were just playing a little rough; that's all. Daddy has to remember that you're a girl. You aren't as tough and strong as Cody is. You get hurt easier. I won't tickle you anymore."

Her eyes were watering, but she was breathing, and the color was draining from her face.

"I want to call Uncle Jack. I wanna go home!"

"Dammit, Rachael, this is home, and you're not calling anyone! Lie down, now, and go to sleep. It's past your bedtime."

"Stop yelling at me! I don't like it when you yell at me!"

"I'm your father. I'm gonna yell at you, but that doesn't mean I don't…*care* about you. Fathers yell at their kids. That's the way it is."

"Uncle Jack doesn't yell at me."

"Jack isn't your father. He isn't even your uncle. He's a stranger who somehow got his nose in the middle of our business. It's after nine o'clock. What time do you normally go to bed?"

"Around nine," she sniffed.

"Why are you locking your bedroom door?"

"Stacy locks the door whenever she goes into her apartment. That way, no one can come into her house without her knowing it."

"We lock the doors downstairs at night. You don't have to lock your bedroom door. It's just *us* in the house."

"What if Cody comes in to scare me?"

He sighed. "I can't promise that he won't."

"If I lock my door, then nobody can sneak in and hurt me!"

"Fine. Come and lock your door."

She followed him to the door.

He leaned over and kissed the top of her head. "Good night, Rachael. You looked beautiful when you came down those stairs tonight. I sent Jack a picture of you."

"You did?"

"I did."

"Good night, Daddy."

He heard the door lock and shook his head. Why had he ever let her leave?

* * *

Rachael jerked violently in her sleep as Billy Ray reached out to grab her away from her grandmother. Regina stood behind Billy Ray with Mr. G's rifle. Billy Ray tried to take it from her, but the gun went off, and Billy Ray and Regina fell to the floor. Rachael screamed and shot upright in the bed.

Her heart was pounding. She switched on her lamp and glanced around the room, but no one was there. Thank goodness she had locked her door! She climbed down from the bed and went to the bathroom. Afterward, she got back into bed, but she was afraid to go back to sleep. She thought about calling Uncle Jack, but the only phone she knew about was in the kitchen. She was afraid to go downstairs. The last time she left her room in the middle of the night, Gramma had grabbed her as she ran by the stairs, and Billy Ray was in the house. She didn't want to stay, but she was afraid to leave. She'd call Uncle Jack in the morning.

She left the lamp on, but every little noise made her jump. At one point, she thought she heard someone trying to turn her doorknob. She stared at it for at least thirty minutes before she decided that they had given up. She missed knowing that Stacy was in the next room. She yawned and wondered how long it would be until morning, when she could see Jayden and play in the garden. She thought about Dr. Crimshaw and how she kept asking what had happened to Billy Ray. She didn't want to lie, but Gramma said if she didn't keep her secret, the police would take Jayden away. She couldn't let that happen. She couldn't! She didn't want to see Dr. Crimshaw anymore.

She grabbed hold of her locket. "Please, Mommy. Please find me!"

CHAPTER
THIRTY

The knock on her door startled her, but she was glad to see that it was daylight. She climbed down from the bed. "Who is it?"

"It's Pamela. Can I come in?"

She unlocked the door and brushed the hair back from her face.

"Good morning, Rachael. Can I have a hug?" Rachael allowed her a brief hug. "How did you sleep?"

"I had bad dreams again."

"Oh, I'm sorry. Did you wake anybody up?"

She shook her head. "I was afraid to leave my room."

"You poor baby. Next time, we'll have to leave a phone in here, so you can call one of us. Would you like that?"

She nodded.

"Are you hungry? Dillia's cooking something good downstairs. The boys ate already, but guess who's here to see you?"

"Jayden?" she said with a smile.

"Yep."

"I'll get dressed." She ran into the bathroom and pulled off her nightgown, changed into her clothes, and pulled on her tennis shoes.

Pamela was waiting by the door. "Let's go," she said as she held out her hand for Rachael to take.

Rachael smiled. She liked Pamela.

When they got to the stairs, Rachael held the handrail and hurried down. "Where is he?"

Pamela was right behind her. "He's in the kitchen. You can eat breakfast in there if you like."

She ran down the hallway, into the kitchen, and nearly collided with Dillia.

"Watch it, Miss Rachael. I got me a hot pan in my hands."

"Sorry. Hi, Jayden!" She ran forward to hug him, but Jayden's eyes widened, and he shook his head. "Momma says you're about to have breakfast. I'll wait for you outside."

"Wait. Aren't you hungry?"

"Yes, but Momma says Mr. Tyler doesn't want me eating here anymore."

"Why not?"

"He says I need to eat at home."

"But why? We always eat together."

"That's enough. Do like your daddy says and eat your breakfast, Miss Rachael." Dillia set a plate of eggs, grits, and toast on the table in front of her.

"No, thank you. If I can't eat with Jayden, I don't want it." She slipped off her chair. "Let's go pick something from the garden and eat it."

Jayden looked over at his momma.

"Now see what you done?" She smacked him on the head. "You gonna get me in trouble with Mr. Tyler."

Jayden winced and drew back. "I didn't do anything wrong, Momma. I just told the truth."

"Well, the truth's gonna get me in trouble," Dillia mumbled as she turned back to the stove.

"Why did you hit Jayden?" Rachael said.

"Don't you go sassin' me, too. I didn't come here to get sassed by no childrens."

"What's going on in here?" Tyler said as he entered through the butler's pantry.

"Dillia hit Jayden on the head for telling the truth, and I wanna know why I can't share my breakfast with Jayden."

"Got some coffee over there, Dillia?"

"Yes, sir." She poured him a cup and handed it over.

"First of all," Tyler said, "I don't want anybody hitting anyone else. Is that clear, Dillia?"

"Yes, sir."

"As for breakfast, young lady, you can share it with Jayden if you want to. I just told Dillia that I thought it best if Jayden eats his meals at home from now on. We're trying to become a family here. Having extra people around doesn't make it any easier."

"You can have my breakfast, Daddy. If Jayden can't eat here, then I'd rather eat at his house." She started for the door.

"Wait a minute. Didn't I just say that you can share your breakfast?"

"Yes."

"Then why are you leaving?"

"Jayden is big enough to eat his own breakfast. We'll just go to his house. Auntie Regina doesn't mind sharing *her* food. She says that even if there's only a little, it tastes better when you share."

He sighed. "Dillia, make up a plate for Jayden."

"No, sir. He can go without. I don't want no deductions comin' out of my paycheck."

"Did I say I was going to deduct anything from your wages?"

"No, sir."

"Then do as I say. Rachael can pay for it." He got up from the table and stormed out the door.

Rachael looked over at Jayden and smiled. Jayden glanced at his momma, but she was busy at the stove. He smiled, too.

"Let's eat breakfast," Rachael said.

* * *

Tyler sat on the edge of Pamela's bed watching her fold a basket of clothes and put them away. "You shouldn't be doing that. Things will be different when Dillia moves into the house. I can't get Regina to do anything I ask her to."

"She says it's not her job to fetch and do for Jacob and me," Pamela said, her lips pressed tight with disapproval.

"I'd fire her if I could, but I can't. She's paid from Rachael's account. I have no say in the matter."

"That's ridiculous. How can your mother control the purse strings from the grave? There must be something you can do about it."

"Mother may control the money, but she doesn't control me," he sneered. "I make my own decisions."

"No, you don't," she scoffed. "You had to ask Jack's permission to have your own daughter spend the night with you, for God's sake! I don't know what he's been telling her, but Rachael's becoming quite precocious. This morning, I heard Dillia tell her to leave her muddy shoes at the back door. She told Dillia that this is her house, and she doesn't have to do what she says. Fortunately, I was there and explained that muddy shoes make a lot more work for Dillia, so she gave in and took her shoes off, but I can tell we're gonna have our hands full with that one."

Tyler shook his head. "She's in desperate need of discipline. Jack's got her thinking she's a fairytale princess or something."

"Ah, I think that is your mother's doing; just look at her bedroom. Besides, every little girl dreams of becoming a princess. It's more important that she finds her place within the family and learns how to behave properly. I'm also concerned about her getting along with Cody. She and Jacob do well together, but she and Cody don't get along at all. Cody wants nothing to do with her."

"That's nothing new," Tyler scoffed. "He's never liked his sister. Becoming a family is going to be an adjustment for all of us. Did you know she locks her bedroom door at night because she's afraid Cody might come in and scare her?"

"Being locked in the attic must have had a terrible effect on her," Pamela said.

"Humph. I just think she's spoiled. She may have Jack wrapped around her finger, but that won't work around here. Speaking of Jack, he'll be coming to pick her up later this afternoon. I need to do as much father-daughter bonding as possible while she's here. I don't want her telling the judge she'd rather stay with Jack."

"She did look precious coming down the stairs last night," Pamela said. "I can't wait till we have a little girl of our own. I fear she'll be quite spoiled, too."

"Maybe, but that's not the same. There won't be all these other people up in the middle of it. Nevertheless, if Rachael's gonna live here, I need to have a relationship with her. It may as well start today."

Pamela turned from the dresser and stepped into his arms. "I'm so glad to hear you say that. You could easily be resentful about the will, and what she's inherited, but you aren't. I can't say I'd be as gracious. I respect you for that."

He pulled her close and breathed in the lavender scent of her hair. "I love you, Pamela. As long as you're with me, I can handle anything."

* * *

"Think you can climb it?"

"Easy!" Rachael said as she scrambled up the chiseled steps, leaning forward into the rock face.

She was fearless, and Tyler had to push himself to keep up. The trail was steeper than he remembered. "I'm right behind you," he called to her. "Be careful. It's a long ways down, and the cliff is very steep on the other side."

"Don't worry, Daddy. I'm a good climber."

"I see that." His breath became ragged as he neared the top of the ridge. "Wait for me. Stay where I can see you."

"I will, Daddy. It's pretty up here!"

When Tyler caught up with her, he pointed to the left. "That way." They walked along the rim, winding their way through the trees and shrubs until they came to a rocky peak. Here they ducked into a shallow cave, which gave them shade from the heat and an amazing view of the Pearl River Valley.

"What is this place?" Rachael said.

"It's just a place. I used to come here when I was a boy. If we're very quiet and still, we might see some wild animals."

Rachael's eyes grew wide. "What kind of wild animals?"

"Deer, squirrels, possums, we'll just have to see."

"I hope we see a deer. If we do, I'll name him Bambi."

Tyler wiped his forehead with the back of his shirtsleeve and hung his legs over the edge of the cliff. "There are lots of deer in these woods, but we'll have to be very quiet if we hope to see any. Think you can do that?"

Rachael nodded and took her place beside him, dangling her legs over the edge, just like he did.

The birds soon resumed their chirping, and the forest came to life. Rachael leaned forward and pointed to a lizard as it scampered across the rocks below. Tyler nodded. He pointed to the treetops where two squirrels chased each other from tree to tree. Rachael put her hands over her mouth and giggled. In spite of himself, he smiled, but her gesture reminded him of the night before, when he could have easily ended her life. A few more seconds and everything she owned would've been his. Why hadn't he pressed just a little bit harder?

He had thought about it for a long time last night, when sleep wouldn't come. It wasn't a newfound appreciation for his daughter. It had simply been too risky. He wouldn't have gotten away with it; it was that simple.

He responded to her discoveries as she excitedly pointed to the wildlife as it stirred around them: a bird, a butterfly, a rabbit, but his heart was beating so loudly that he could barely hear himself think. "Look, Rachael, a deer. He's got big, huge antlers."

"Where, Daddy?"

He pointed into the ravine beneath their feet. "Down there. See? He's behind that boulder." Rachael leaned out over the edge, and Tyler pushed.

* * *

Jayden heard Tyler whistling and ducked into the bushes. He was surprised that Rachael wasn't with him. Once Tyler had disappeared down the trail, he grabbed hold of his sword and ran along the rim until he came to the look out. "Rachael? Where are you?"

"Jayden, help me!"

"Hold on, Rachael, I'm coming." Jayden pushed through the bushes, past the overlook to a dry gulch, and began scurrying down towards Rachael. He climbed over roots, slid on loose gravel, and grabbed at the tall, dry grass as he hurried to help his friend. "Where are you?" he cried, fearing that she might fall before he got there.

"Down here. Hurry!"

Jayden spotted her about ten feet below him where she clung to the exposed roots of a tree. "How did you get down there? I just saw your pa. Does he know that you fell?"

"Help me! I can't hold on much longer."

Jayden maneuvered downward, lowering himself into dangerous positions as he made his way to Rachael. Finally, he perched on a small, flat piece of ground to the left of her and reached out his hand. "Grab on. I'll pull you over."

"I can't! If I let go, I'll fall."

"You've got to try. It's only a short jump."

"I'm scared, Jayden. What if I fall?"

"Do you want me to find your pa?"

"No! Don't leave me."

Jayden sat on the ground and wrapped his legs around a dry stump. He held the sword out with both hands. "Come on. You can do it."

Rachael looked down. "There are alligators down there. Look, on the bank."

"There are always alligators down there. Papa says not to look down when you're climbing on something high. Just keep your eyes on me. You're not gonna fall. On the count of three, I'll yank my sword back this way. One, two, three!"

Rachael grabbed the sword just as he yanked. It was all she needed to make the short leap. She fell forward onto her hands, but her feet held firm.

"You did it, Jayden. You saved me!"

Jayden smiled and slid his sword back into its casing. "We can climb up the way I came. It's easy."

The two of them climbed to the top of the ridge and sat in the cave to rest.

"What happened? How did you fall?" Jayden said as a cool breeze flowed over the ridge.

Tears gathered in her eyes, and she looked down. "Daddy said there was a deer down there, but there wasn't."

He knew she was hiding something, but folks had a right to keep their peace. At least, that's what his papa said. "We best get back. Your pa will be lookin' for you."

"Hopefully, it's Uncle Jack who finds me. He should be here soon to take me home."

* * *

Jack rang the front bell, but no one answered. Thinking that they might be around back, he took the trail along the side of the house, past the vegetable and herb gardens and onto the back lawn, where he came upon Cody and Jacob sword fighting with sticks. Rachael, dressed in her princess dress, sat on a small, pink blanket watching the match. The boys were fighting harder than he thought was safe, but he didn't interfere.

"May I join you, Princess?"

"They're sword fighting, Uncle Jack. Cody stabbed me in the stomach, and Jacob is defending me."

"I see," Jack said as his brows drew together. "Are you all right? Did he hurt you?"

"I cried, but only for a little while. I'm okay now," she said.

"Who's winning?"

"I don't know, but it sure is exciting."

"Where's Tyler and Pamela?" he said, wondering if they were aware of what was happening.

"Jacob said he took the fishing boat out on the river."

"Ouch!" Cody cried. "You hit my hand again."

"I didn't mean to. Do you promise not to hurt Rachael again?"

"No," Cody said, "but I'm tired. Can we rest a while?"

"Yes," Jacob said. "I'm tired, too."

The boys lowered their sticks, and then Cody took one more vicious jab at Jacob.

"Ouch! That's not fair," Jacob cried.

"Can I help it if you're stupid? You should never let your guard down," Cody scoffed.

Jack came to his feet, reached for Cody's stick, and snapped it over his knee. "There's such a thing as fighting fair, Cody. What you just did to Jacob isn't right. You boys need to be careful. You can really hurt each other with these sticks."

"I had to fight. I'm defending Rachael," Jacob said.

"I heard. Thank you for protecting her. It's not right for boys to hit girls. You apologize for hurting your sister."

"I don't want to apologize," Cody said. "I meant to stab her."

"But why?" Jack said, stunned by the vehemence in his tone. "Why do you want to hurt Rachael?"

"Because I want her to go away again. I want her to die!"

"Those are very ugly, hateful words. If I had some soap, I'd wash your mouth out. Come on, Rachael. Let's go get your things."

"I can't wait until we get our real swords," Cody said, "then we can fight Jayden."

"I've been practicing with him already," Jacob said. "He's quite good. I like Jayden. He's smart."

"Well, I don't play with the help," Cody said. "If I fight him, it'll be to show him who's boss."

Jack rolled his eyes. He hoped Rachael, Jayden, and Jacob influenced Cody and not the other way around.

"Jayden says you're teaching him to fight, Mr. Jack. When I get my sword, will you teach me, too?" Jacob said.

"I'll teach you, too, Cody, as long as you agree to play by the rules."

"Naw. My dad can teach me."

"Don't mind him," Jacob said. "He's not very polite."

"I'm glad you recognize that, Jacob. Keep up the good work. Good manners will take you far in this world."

"Good manners are for sissies," Cody said.

"How would you know? You haven't learned any," Jack said. Cody wrinkled his brow, but didn't respond. "Ready, Rachael?"

She reached out and took his hand. "I missed you, Uncle Jack. Especially last night. I wanted to call you, but the phone was downstairs, and I was afraid to leave my room."

They walked up the flagstone walkway, up the back steps, and into the house. "Why were you afraid?"

"I had another bad dream."

"Good afternoon, Dillia," he said as they walked through the kitchen. "Want to tell me about it?"

"Yes," she said. When they had climbed the stairs, she pointed to the new staircase. "Look what Daddy did to the stairs."

"I see. Did you go up there?"

Rachael shook her head. "Pamela and Jacob live up there now."

"How is it going with you and your daddy?" he said.

When they went into her room, she closed the door and locked it.

"Why are you locking the door?" he said.

"So nobody can come in."

"All right, then. Where's your bag? I'll help you pack."

"Uncle Jack? Can I tell you something?"

"Yes, sweetie. You can tell me anything."

"What if I am doing something wrong because somebody told me to, and if I don't do it, something bad will happen to someone I love?"

"Whoa, this sounds important. Come. Let's sit by the window for a few minutes." Jack sat on the left side of the window seat and patted the cushion next to him. When he looked past her, he couldn't help noticing how vast the gardens were.

"There's no one here but you and me, and I'll do everything I can to help you. You know that, don't you?" When she nodded, he added, "So, tell me, who told you to do something wrong?"

"Gramma."

"What did she tell you to do?"

"She told me to keep a secret."

"What secret?"

"She said if I tell anyone, the police will take Jayden away. I can't let them take Jayden. Promise me you won't let that happen. Promise me, Uncle Jack!"

"I won't let anyone take Jayden. Not if I can help it. What secret are you talking about? The secret about your Gramma keeping you in the attic?" She shook her head. "There's another secret?"

She nodded and looked down. "The one about Billy Ray."

He had often wondered if she knew that they had dumped his

body in the river, but he didn't want to ask her. It would only fuel her nightmares.

"Do you want to tell me the secret?" he asked.

Her eyes brimmed with tears. "I'm afraid Dr. Crimshaw will make me tell her, and then the police will take Jayden. I don't want to talk to Dr. Crimshaw anymore."

"Jayden's mommy is here now. She'll take care of him."

Just as quickly as her tears had come, they vanished. "No, she won't. She hits Jayden. I saw her. I don't like her at all."

"She hits him?" Jack said calmly, though he felt like exploding. "Does Mr. Gibbs know that Dillia hits Jayden?" Rachael shrugged. "I can't imagine that Mr. G will tolerate anyone mistreating Jayden."

"Dillia didn't even want him to have breakfast this morning. She was afraid Daddy was going to take it out of her paycheck."

"What did your daddy say?"

"Daddy said he doesn't want Jayden eating with us anymore. He wants him to eat at home. When I said I didn't want my breakfast if Jayden couldn't eat, Daddy got mad and told Dillia to make him a plate. He said I could pay for it."

"I see. You've had a busy morning, haven't you? What about your secret?"

"Gramma didn't shoot Billy Ray. She was going to, but Auntie Regina came up the stairs behind Billy Ray. Billy Ray turned on her and tried to take her gun, but Auntie Regina shot him."

Jack was so surprised his mouth fell open. "Are you sure, Rachael?"

"I saw it. Regina wanted to call the police, but Gramma said if they told the police they'd put Regina in jail and take Jayden away. So, we can't tell the truth. We can't!" Tears filled her eyes as her whole body shook with emotion.

He gathered her in his arms and let her cry. If this was true, it shifted all kinds of things, but he couldn't deal with that right now. He had to take care of Rachael. What a terrible burden she'd been carrying.

"It's all right, sweetie. This is not something we want to tell your daddy or Dr. Crimshaw right now. You did the right thing by telling me. You keep Grandma's secret, and I'll take care of everything else."

She sniffed and sucked in a breath. "I love Jayden. He saved me."

"Because he stayed with you in the attic?"

"No, he saved me today. Daddy wanted me to fall into the river."

"What are you talking about? When were you by the river?" Jack said, tensing at the thought of her getting into a boat with Tyler.

"I wasn't by the river. Daddy took me up on the cliff. We were looking for wild animals. I saw butterflies and squirrels, but Daddy saw a deer. When I leaned over the cliff to see where he was pointing, Daddy pushed me."

A searing light flashed in Jack's eyes. He couldn't be hearing right. "Rachael, honey, surely your daddy didn't push you. Did you fall?"

"I did fall, but I hit a tree and then landed between some rocks. I called to Daddy, but it was Jayden who saved me."

"Where was your daddy? How did you get back to the house?" Jack was so stunned that he didn't know what to say. He wanted to believe that she was making the story up, but he feared she was telling the truth.

"Look at my knee. I scraped it when I fell, and my elbow, too, and there's a big black bruise on my bottom where I hit the tree." She showed him her elbow and then lifted her princess dress to show him her knee. "And this is where Cody stabbed me in the stomach."

Jack reached out to soothe the terrible bruises and gathered her into his arms. He could barely process what she was saying. How could he accuse Tyler of pushing his daughter off a cliff so that he could claim her inheritance?

"Where's Jayden?" he asked.

"He went back to the cabin. He's afraid Daddy will be mad at him for saving me, and he's worried Mr. G will be angry because he followed us up the mountain."

"If your daddy pushed you, sweetie, we're going to have to tell the judge. You know that don't you?"

"We can't! Jayden made me promise. We have to protect Jayden. We have to! He's like me, Uncle Jack. My Daddy doesn't want me, and his momma doesn't want him. She left him when she got married without even saying goodbye. She hits him, and she doesn't give him enough food to eat. We can't let the police take him. We have to protect him like he protected me when Gramma locked me in the attic, and when Daddy pushed me off the cliff."

Jack pulled her close again. If this story was true, it had huge implications. Jayden was in more danger from Tyler than the police or his papa. "We'll protect him, Rachael. I promise we'll protect him."

"You won't let them take him?"

"No, sweetie. Not if I can help it."

"Don't make me see Daddy. I'm afraid of Daddy! He pushed my pillow into my face last night, and I couldn't breathe. I thought Daddy wanted me, but all he does is hurt me." She turned into his shoulder and cried for several minutes.

Jack didn't ask about the pillow incident. He was so angry that he was having a difficult time deciding what to do next. "Are you ready to go home?" he said as softly as he could manage.

She nodded.

"Let's go wash your face, and then we'll go."

She ran to the bathroom. He took a washcloth from the shelf, gently washed her face, and then wiped the dirt from her scrapes. "You're a brave little girl."

"Not as brave as Jayden," she sniffed.

"I'm glad he was there for you today. Let's go home."

* * *

"Wait a minute. Are you telling me that Joan was actually protecting Regina?" Stacy said as they continued the discussion they had started once Rachael had fallen asleep on Stacy's couch. "You seriously want me to believe that she locked up her own grandchild in order to protect a person she referred to as 'the help'? I'm sorry, but I don't believe that for one minute. Something's not right."

"I understand your hesitation, but why would Rachael make that up? She was terrified that the police might take Jayden away. Joan threatened him to keep her quiet."

When they entered the den, Stacy sat on the couch and Jack began pacing.

"Jack, none of this makes sense. Why would Joan put her entire existence at risk by lying to the police? If Regina shot him, it was clearly a case of self-defense. Why lie? This was Rachael's grandfather, for God's sake. Not only did they kill him, they dumped him in the river for the alligators to eat."

"It sounds so ghastly when you put it like that," Jack said. He wanted to tell her what Rachael had said about Tyler pushing her off the cliff, but…

"If Regina was the one who pulled the trigger," Stacy said, "I can see why she might have been frightened, but why would Mrs. Chandler cover for her? It sure as hell wasn't for Jayden's sake. No, we're missing something here. How could she go from desperately wanting to adopt Rachael, to locking her in the attic? If she had changed her mind about wanting her, she could've sent her back to Tyler. I think Rachael saw something they didn't want her to see."

Jack was trying to stay focused, but it was hard to care about who killed Billy Ray when Rachael and Jayden were in danger. "If Regina was the one who shot Billy Ray, why didn't Joan say that when she got arrested?"

"She did, but no one believed her," Stacy said.

Jack plopped into his recliner. "But she didn't accuse her until after we recovered Rachael. She kept silent until then."

Stacy tapped her chin. Clearly, she didn't want the police to know what they had done with Billy Ray's body. I mean, this is a woman who let her own son believe that Billy Ray had kidnapped his daughter while she had her in the attic the entire time."

Jack nodded. "There's no reasoning that one away, assuming Tyler didn't know the truth."

"Are you questioning that?" Stacy said.

"At this point, I'm questioning everything. Let's say Tyler is telling the truth, and he didn't know anything about the murder. Did he truly believe that Rachael was missing?"

"I believe him, Jack. Everything points to that. No one is *that* convincing."

"Okay, If Regina killed Billy Ray, like she said she did at first, why did she tell the police where to find Billy Ray's body?" Jack said.

"Doesn't that point back to Joan? At the very least, she went along with throwing Billy Ray's body in the river. For all we know, she's the one who suggested it."

They sat for a few moments, thinking through the possibilities.

Finally, Jack said, "If Regina is guilty, I'm sure she's afraid that Rachael will tell somebody. That could potentially put Rachael in danger."

Stacy grimaced. "That's a terrible thought."

Jack eyes narrowed. "Does it really matter who killed Billy Ray? I mean, we could exonerate Joan of murder, but not kidnapping; both of which are federal offenses. We could hold Regina responsible for Billy Ray's murder, but what happens to Jayden when Mr. Gibbs dies?"

"Wouldn't he stay with his mother?"

"I hope not," Jack said. "According to Rachael, his mother hits him and doesn't give him enough food to eat. She abandoned him once already. Who's to say she wouldn't do it again? I promised Rachael I'd do everything in my power to protect Jayden."

Stacy's lip twitched with disgust. "And I was happy his mother came back. Some people have no business having children. My mother never wanted me either."

"Hey, hold on there. Just because your mothers didn't have the sense to appreciate you, that doesn't make you any less valuable. Come here." He gave her a hug and then set her back from him. "Help me figure this out. Does Tyler have a right to know that his mother didn't kill Billy Ray?"

"If you tell him, he'll turn Regina in. He doesn't care what happens to Jayden. He wouldn't hesitate five seconds."

He nodded. "I agree. So, what do we do?"

"I think we need to tell Regina that we know. That way, there's no need to silence Rachael. Not that she would, of course, but it's best to take any incentive away."

"I can't imagine Regina ever hurting Rachael, but you're right," Jack said. "It's never a good idea to give somebody a reason to want you dead. If she knows we know, then Rachael isn't the only threat. If we tell her we understand that it was self-defense, and we aren't going to report it, then perhaps that will relieve her of the fear that it will one day be discovered."

"Isn't that what the Bible calls mercy?" Stacy said.

"I don't know, but I don't see how punishing the only people who have ever protected Rachael is going to help anyone—least of all, Rachael. Can you imagine her life with Tyler if Regina wasn't there to watch over her?"

"Regina is Jayden's best hope also," Stacy said. "Mr. G is the best Papa anyone could hope for, but he won't be around forever. You can see it in his eyes. He knows his days are numbered."

Jack nodded. "Rachael and Jayden both need Regina. We'll talk to her and Mr. Gibbs as soon as the opportunity presents itself."

"I think it's ironic that we're keeping Joan's secret, not for her sake, but for Rachael and Jayden's sake. Her lie, instead of protecting her reputation, has served to make her look guilty instead."

Jack chuckled. "She'd be fit to be tied over that one."

Stacy chuckled, too. "Who says there's no justice?"

* * *

"Stand still," Stacy said as she smiled at Rachael in the mirror. "I have two more buttons to go. Hey, what did you do to your elbow?"

"I fell."

"Does it hurt?"

"Only a little. I hurt my knee, too."

"Let me see," Stacy said. Rachael lifted her skirt. "Ouch. Want me to put a Band-Aid on it?"

"No, thank you. Can I go downstairs now? I can't wait for Steve and Auntie Emily to see my dress," Rachael said as she squirmed with excitement.

"Turn around. I need to tie your ribbon first." Stacy tied a huge pink bow at her waist and spun her back around. "Who's Steve?"

"Emily's boyfriend. He's nice. He has a big house, and we're going swimming there one day soon."

"I didn't know Emily had a boyfriend," Stacy said with a smile. "Does Jack know?"

"I don't know."

"Well, let's go tell him," Stacy said.

Rachael pushed from the sink and ran for the back door.

"Wait! Don't forget your shoes!"

"Oh." She quickly slipped on her shiny pink shoes and opened the door.

Stacy was right behind her. If Emily had a boyfriend, she definitely wanted to meet him.

* * *

When the doorbell rang, Jack scowled at his computer—not that he could concentrate on what he was working on anyway—and went to answer the door. His eyebrows rose when he saw a well-dressed, handsome young man standing next to Emily.

"Hi, Jack. This is Steve Barlow. He's an attorney at Alister, Emerson & Maxwell. He's taking Rachael and me to the *Sleeping Beauty Musical* tonight."

Jack extended his hand. "Hi, Steve, I'm Jack." He turned to hug Emily. "This is a nice surprise. Come on in."

She blushed as they stepped into the foyer. "Steve and I started seeing each other when I was here before. We kept in contact while I was away, and…"

"I missed her terribly and begged her to come back," Steve said with a laugh as he finished her sentence.

"Can't say as I blame you," Jack said. "She's a wonderful girl."

Emily's face turned even redder. "Stop it, you two. Where's Rachael?"

"Stacy's helping her get dressed. They'll be here any minute now."

"Emily tells me you have helped her through some very difficult times. I want to thank you for that," Steve said.

"It has been a pleasure to help Emily, but many share the credit for the outcome. In fact, Emily, if you hadn't come forward, your mother and Tommy Lee might still be in hiding, and the fate of your father and Rachael might still be a mystery. You deserve a great deal of the credit yourself."

"I'm glad everything worked out the way it did, except for what happened to Pa, of course."

"Hi, Emily," Stacy said as she came around the corner and opened her arms for a hug.

"Hey, Stacy." Turning to Steve, she said, "Steve, this is Stacy. She's the one who got me wearing fun, sexy clothes."

Stacy laughed. "If you've got it, flaunt it. Right?"

"It's nice to meet you," Steve said. "Emily speaks very fondly of you."

"Where's Rachael?" Emily said.

"Oh," Stacy said, "allow me to introduce Sleeping Beauty."

Rachael giggled as she stepped from around the corner to make her grand entrance into the foyer.

"Wow," Emily said. "Don't you look pretty? I ain't…I mean, *I have never* seen a more beautiful dress in all my life."

Jack caught a quick glance from Stacy, who was smiling like a Cheshire cat.

"I have three beautiful dresses," Rachael said, "so we'll have to go to two more musicals."

Steve laughed and glanced at his watch. "We'll just have to do that, but we better be going, or we'll miss the opening scene of this one."

"Have a wonderful time," Stacy said.

Emily lingered a moment to let Steve and Rachael go out first, and then she smiled at Jack and Stacy. "I may not be Sleeping Beauty, but I've definitely found my Prince Charming."

* * *

Jack glanced at the clock; it was 10:00 p.m. He had turned in early, but sleep was impossible. He was at a complete loss as to what to do with what Rachael told him that afternoon. He had hoped to run into Tyler before they left the mansion, but that didn't happen. He and Pamela were nowhere around, which, from a parental standpoint, was frustrating in itself. Did he know that Jayden had saved Rachael?

Tyler had issues, but it was hard to believe that he would actually kill Rachael. It was too awful even to contemplate, yet the scrapes on Rachael's arm and knee were real. Did she make the story up because she didn't want to stay with her father? He'd never known her to lie, especially if the truth was something that might endanger Jayden. That fact alone made him believe she was telling the truth. She had promised Jayden not to tell so that *he* wouldn't get in trouble. She wasn't even thinking of herself. What was he supposed to do with the information? If what she said was true, both she and Jayden were in danger. How could he stay silent? And he hadn't even questioned her about Tyler holding a pillow over her face!

He shot out of bed and pulled on his sweatpants. A few seconds later, he was knocking on Stacy's door. He heard the lock turn, and she opened the door.

"Hey, Jack, what's up?" she said, wrapping her robe tighter around herself.

"We need to talk." She stepped back as he walked by. "Want some coffee?" she said.

"Yes. No. I don't know."

She joined him at the kitchen table. "What is it, Jack? I've never seen you like this."

"It's Rachael. Did you see her arm and her knee today?"

"Yes. She told me she fell."

"Well, she told me that Tyler pushed her from the top of a cliff. She fell and hit a tree, which bounced her onto some rocks where she held on until Jayden found her and helped her to safety."

"What the hell? Did you call the police?"

"No. Jayden made her promise not to tell anyone."

"Screw that! You have to call the police," Stacy said heading for her phone.

"Wait. Jayden is afraid his Papa will be angry because he followed Rachael and Tyler up the hill. If we reveal this, Tyler may suspect that Jayden saw what he did."

"This is crazy. Are you telling me Rachael and Jayden may both be in danger? Does Mr. G know what Tyler did? What did Tyler say when he saw that Rachael had come back safe?"

"I don't know; I didn't see him. When I got there, Cody and Jacob were stick fighting because Cody stabbed Rachael in the stomach and told her he wanted her to die. I heard him say it myself."

"Oh my God," Stacy said. "What is wrong with that family? Poor Rachael. No wonder she locks her door at night."

"She told me about Regina killing Billy Ray when I took her upstairs to get her things. That's also when she told me about Tyler pushing her off the cliff. I didn't know what to say or even think. It's incredibly hard to believe that Tyler would do such a thing."

"He has a lot to gain by her death, but still," Stacy said. "Could he really be that cold-hearted?"

"I don't know, Stace. I don't know what to do or whom to tell. There are huge consequences, no matter which way we turn."

"Get dressed," she said. "We're going out to see Mr. G tonight!"

"What about Rachael? They should be home any minute," Jack said.

"I'll text Emily and ask her to keep Rachael overnight. This can't wait till morning."

* * *

The windows were dark in the mansion, which made Jack heave a sigh of relief.

"Do you think we're on the right path?" Stacy whispered.

"I think so," Jack said. "We should be coming upon the cabin any minute."

"What are you going to say?" Stacy said.

"I'm hoping it will come to me."

"Look, there's the cabin," Stacy said as she pointed to the dim light between the trees.

They jogged the rest of the way, and Jack tapped on the door.

"Who's there?" Mr. Gibbs said from inside the cabin.

"Mr. G, it's Jack and Stacy. Can we come in?"

"Mr. Jack?" he mumbled. The door creaked open. "Come

in, come in."

"We need to talk with you and Jayden for a minute. It's important," Jack said.

"Jayden? Did he do somethin' wrong?" He shuffled to the couch and gently shook Jayden. "Wake up, boy. Mr. Jack is here to see you."

Jayden's eyes grew wide as he sat up.

Stacy followed Jack inside and closed the door.

"Hi, Jayden. Sorry to wake you," Jack said. "We need to ask you about Rachael's visit this weekend."

"What's this about?" Mr. G said.

"Did either of you see Tyler this evening?" Jack said.

"I did," Mr. Gibbs said. "He spent all afternoon in his fishing boat down on the river. He didn't come back till almost dark."

"How was he? Did he say anything?" Jack said.

"I stayed out of his way, but Dillia said he seemed mighty upset about somethin'. She done fed the boys afore he came in, but Mr. Tyler wanted nothin' for himself. Dillia said he went straight upstairs. She didn't hear nothin' else from him all evenin', and that's not normal, accordin' to her. She said Miss Pamela came down to put the boys to bed, and then she knocked on Tyler's door, but he didn't answer. Dillia knows because she was upstairs cleanin' up after the boys. She seen Miss Pamela go back up to the attic. When Dillia finished with her duties, she told Regina what she seen. She always *was* one to tell other folks' business."

"I think I know why Tyler was upset," Jack said. "Mr. G, if you knew Rachael was in danger, would you help her even if it might upset Tyler?"

"You know I would. Regina and I made Mrs. Chandler upset plenty of times for that very reason. We'd do the same with Mr. Tyler if it came down to it. Why are you askin'? Why are you here?"

"Would you want Jayden to help Rachael if she was in trouble, and he was the only one able to help her?"

"I raised him, didn't I?"

"Indeed. I need to ask Jayden some questions, and I don't want him to be afraid to answer."

"Tell Mr. Jack the truth, boy, even if you done somethin' wrong. Ya hear?"

"Yes, Papa."

Jack sat on the floor in front of Jayden. "Hey, buddy. Rachael has a nasty scrape on her knee and another one on her elbow. Do you know how she got those today?"

Jayden glanced up at his papa.

"If you know, tell him," Mr. Gibbs said.

"She fell."

"Where did she fall?"

"She fell from the top of the ridge above the river," he said.

"Lord have mercy," Mr. Gibbs said as he dropped into his rocking chair.

"Do you know how she fell?"

Jayden shook his head.

Jack cocked a brow and exchanged a glance with Stacy. "Was she up on the ridge by herself?"

"No."

"Who was with her?"

"She was with her pa. I saw them go up there together."

"Did you see Tyler come back down?" Jack said.

"Yes, sir. I hid myself in the bushes and watched him go back down the trail without Rachael."

"Did he look upset?"

"No, sir. He was whistling."

Jack felt his chest tighten with rage. The S.O.B. was guilty. He pushed her off the cliff so that he could get her money. "Did he see you?" he said, swallowing hard.

Jayden threw another glance at his papa. "No, sir. I didn't want him to know I was following them."

"Then what did you do?"

"I went looking for Rachael."

"Where was she?" he said, suddenly aware of Stacy's supporting hand on the back of his shoulder.

"I found her hanging onto some dry roots about halfway down the ravine. I was afraid she was going to fall."

"What happened when you got back to the mansion?"

"I went back to the cabin, and Rachael went to her room. I didn't see her after that."

"Did you see Tyler after you came back?"

Jayden shook his head. "I had chores to do. I didn't go back to the big house."

"Thank you, Jayden. You've been very helpful. You're a brave little boy. You saved Rachael's life today. You know that?"

"There were alligators on the bank below. We saw them."

Mr. Gibbs walked over to the couch and motioned for Jayden to get up. When Jayden got to his feet, he wrapped him in a hug. "God bless you, Jayden. You make your papa proud. You're a real fine boy."

"Mr. Gibbs," Jack said, "will you walk Stacy and I out?"

"Yes, sir."

"Good night, Jayden," Stacy said. "Thank you for being there for Rachael today."

"I'm glad I'm not in trouble," Jayden said. "Y'all had me worried."

"Keep this quiet, Jayden," Jack said. "Tyler doesn't need to hear about any of this from you."

"Yes, sir. I'm not happy with Mr. Tyler just now."

"And don't tell your momma about it neither," Mr. G added.

"Don't worry, I won't. I'm not happy with her either," Jayden said.

Jack ruffled his hair and led the way outside. After Mr. G shut the door, he said, "I've gotta think about how to handle this. Are you willing to testify to seeing Tyler in his boat on the river?"

"If I testify, Mr. Tyler will be powerful mad. I know he can't fire Regina and me, but he can sure 'nuff make life miserable. What I don't get is why, after Miss Rachael slipped, he wasn't running his fool head off, tryin' to get down there before them alligators could get 'er."

"Because Rachael didn't slip," Jack said.

Mr. G took a step back, and his knees buckled.

Stacy put her arm around his waist. "Are you alright, Mr. G?"

"I can't believe it." He righted himself, and Stacy moved away. "What's we gonna do, Mr. Jack?"

"I don't know yet, but keep an eye on Jayden. If Tyler knows that Jayden saved Rachael, he may think Jayden saw him push her."

"Take Jayden with you. I won't let Tyler hurt my boy. I won't."

Jack looked to Stacy; she nodded.

"Wait, I've got an idea. I think I know how to defuse this whole situation. Don't say a word; I'm calling Tyler." Jack pulled out his phone and placed the call. "Hey, Tyler. I'm calling to thank you for taking such good care of Rachael this weekend. Thanks for the picture, by the way. Seeing her big smile put me at ease." He glanced at Stacy and shrugged. "Yes, she was out in the yard with the boys when I came home. Sorry we didn't have the chance to chat, but I was running late. We'll have to do it again sometime." He nodded. "It's great to see Rachael feeling more comfortable at home with you and Cody. She likes Pamela and Jacob, too. You've got a great family, Tyler. I'm happy for you." He rolled his eyes. "Talk to you later." He made sure that the call disconnected. "Well, what do you think?"

"Brilliant," Stacy said. "Do you think he bought it?"

"We'll see," Jack said. "If he did, it will calm everything down. He'll be much less likely to do anything rash if he thinks Rachael didn't realize what actually happened. My guess is he'll pretend it never happened. For everyone's sake, when we're dealing with Tyler, we must pretend the same. Can you do that Mr. G, and make sure Jayden doesn't tell anyone what happened?"

"So Mr. Tyler don't know that Jayden helped Rachael?"

"That's my guess," Jack said. "What do you think, Stacy?"

"That's what it sounds like to me. If Tyler went down to the river to look for Rachael, he didn't see them come down from the ridge. He'd have no way to know about Jayden unless Cody and Jacob know. Maybe we should ask Jayden if they told the boys."

Mr. G opened the door. "Jayden, come here, boy." Within moments, Jayden stood in the doorway. "Did anyone see you and Rachael come back down the hill together?"

"No, sir. I had her go first, and then I went back a different way. Nobody knows unless Rachael told them, but I don't think she did because she promised me she wouldn't."

"Go back to bed now, Jayden. I'll be in directly," Mr. G said and closed the door.

"That's good news," Jack said. "I'd keep Jayden away from the big house for a while, just to be safe."

"I'll keep him away and make sure he's quiet about it, too. What are you gonna do now, Mr. Jack?"

"We'll let you know when we figure it out."

CHAPTER THIRTY-ONE

"**H**ow was your overnight visit with Rachael?" Dr. Myers said.

"Great. Rachael feels right at home. She loves sleeping in her princess room. That's what she calls her bedroom at the mansion. It's all dolled up like some fairytale or something. Here, take a look." Tyler pulled out his cell phone and showed pictures of Rachael's bedroom and of her coming down the stairs in her dress.

"She certainly looks happy."

"Oh, she is. I am her father, after all. She belongs at home with me." He forced a smile. Jack's call had taken him by surprise. He was certain Rachael had fallen in the river; he had heard the splash after she fell. How she had gotten from the water and back to the house without him seeing her, he didn't know, but she did. She was safe and, apparently, unaware that he had pushed her. If it came up, he could always say she slipped.

"Tyler?"

"Oh, sorry. I was somewhere else, I guess."

"I asked how she is getting along with Cody," Dr. Myers said.

"They didn't interact much. Cody usually plays with Jacob."

"Jacob is your girlfriend's son?"

"Pamela is my fiancée. She and Jacob live in the attic

apartment now."

"How does Rachael feel about that?"

"She doesn't go up there if that's what you mean."

"That's exactly what I mean. The attic holds difficult memories for Rachael," Dr. Myers said.

"I know, but it looks very different now. Even the staircase looks different. She'll forget, in time." He watched as Dr. Myers made some notes and wondered if he had said the wrong thing. "You know, Dr. Myers, in the beginning, I thought you were trying to help me work through some issues, but the last few sessions have felt like you've been interviewing me to see if I'm an acceptable parent. Whose side are you on?"

"I'm not on anyone's side, Tyler. We are working through your issues, but I'm also trying to determine if you're ready to have Rachael back in your household. You want me to be honest about that, don't you?"

"What I want is to live my life without people looking over my shoulder all the time. Rachael is my daughter. She belongs with me. Maybe it's time I got an attorney."

"You can certainly do that, of course, but it would be a clear indication that you are resisting the process."

"Resisting the process? My daughter is living with a complete stranger, who is managing her financial affairs. How does that make sense? I should be taking care of her, not Jack Kendall. I want full custody, and I want it now!"

Dr. Myers pressed her lips together with what he had learned was disapproval. "Tyler, this isn't about what you want. Rachael has endured several major traumas over the past two years. If we are taking longer than you like to return her to the home you so easily cast her out of, get over it. Rachael's needs in this matter are more important than your *wants*. If you aren't willing to put her welfare above your personal desires, then I assure you, we'll do it for you." She got up from her desk, walked to the door, and opened it. "We're ending this session early. I've got nothing more to say to you today."

Stunned, Tyler got to his feet. He wasn't sure what had made her so upset, but he was angry, too. "I got news for you, Dr. Myers. I've got nothing more to say to you, *ever*." He strode past her, down the hall, and struck the elevator button with the bottom of his fist. Once the elevator doors closed, he clenched his fists and yelled, "Ahhhh!" To hell with counseling, he thought. I'd rather stay screwed up than deal with her!

* * *

"What do you think about your daddy's girlfriend?" Dr. Crimshaw said.

"Good."

"What about Jacob?"

"He's nicer than Cody is."

"Was Cody glad to see you?"

"No. Cody is mean like Daddy is mean. He wants me to die. Wanna see where he stabbed me?" Rachael lifted her shirt.

"That's a nasty bruise you've got there. Does it hurt?"

"It's not as bad as my other bruises." Rachael showed her the other bruises.

"Did Cody give you those bruises?"

"No."

"You said that Cody is mean like Daddy is mean. Is your daddy mean to you?"

She nodded. "He used to pinch me and pull my hair."

"Your daddy did that to you?" Dr. Crimshaw said with a raised eyebrow.

"Uh huh. When I was little."

"Does he still do that?"

"Not yet, but he pushed me. That's how I got my bruises."
"Surely, he didn't push you on purpose. What else did your daddy do this weekend?"

"He took pictures of me in my dress, and he came to tuck me in."

"That sounds nice. Did you see Jayden this weekend?"

"Yes, and we got to work in the garden, too! You should see our carrots, Dr. Crimshaw. We've got a whole bunch of them this year."

"It's nice to see you smile, Rachael. You like working in the garden, don't you?"

"It's my very favorite place. We're growing all kinds of yummy things. My favorite is strawberries, but it isn't time for strawberries right now."

"Did you see Mr. G and Auntie Regina while you were there?"

"Uh huh."

"Are they good to you?"

"Oh, yes. They share their food whenever I'm hungry."

"That's good. Do you want to spend more time with your daddy and his girlfriend?" Rachael shook her head. "Why not?" Rachael looked down and didn't answer. "Did you play with Cody and Jacob?" she asked again.

"Cody won't play with me. The only time I have somebody to play with is when I see Jayden, but Daddy doesn't want Jayden to eat our food anymore unless I pay for it, but I don't have any money."

Dr. Crimshaw pursed her lips and pushed her reading glasses further back on her nose. "Well, we'll just have to talk to him about that, won't we?"

* * *

"Tomorrow? Isn't that a bit sudden?" Jack said, raking a hand through his tousled curls.

"He's hired himself a high-powered attorney," Dr. Crimshaw said. "Unless we can prove he's an unfit parent, I'm afraid there's nothing we can do. Trust me, Mr. Kendall; I don't like it any more than you do. I've been on the phone all morning."

"I'll call John Carrington," Jack said.

"I've already spoken to him. There's nothing we can do."

Stacy tugged on his sleeve. "What is it?"

He shook his head, unable to speak the words.

"Mr. Kendall?"

"I'm here. I don't know what to say."

"I understand that this is upsetting, but we'll continue to monitor Tyler's progress, as long as he continues his sessions, that is."

"And if he discontinues?"

"We'll have to hope for the best, Mr. Kendall."

"Thanks for calling. I'll tell Rachael." He set his phone on the desk.

"Jack, what is it?"

"Tyler hired an attorney. They want me to deliver Rachael back to him tomorrow."

"Oh, no," Stacy said. "We have to fight it."

"I can't without telling them what happened this weekend."

"Then tell them. Will they take the word of children so young?"

"I don't know. Until we talked to Jayden last night, I wasn't sure I believed it myself."

"Oh, Jack, we can't let Tyler have Rachael. It's not safe! He only wants her money."

"He can have her money. I just want her. If the police won't help us, maybe I need to threaten Tyler myself."

"What do you mean?"

"What if I tell him that we know he pushed her off the cliff? I can tell him if anything else happens to her, we'll know he did it. Maybe that'll be enough to keep her safe."

"Can't you call Kevin and see what he says?"

"I'll try." He picked up his phone and punched in the number.

"Hey, Jack. What is it this time?" Captain Thomas said into the phone.

"It's Rachael. Tyler hired an attorney. They're demanding I turn her over to him tomorrow."

"And you have a problem with that?"

"Rachael spent the night over there the night before last. She came back with scrapes and bruises. She said that Tyler took her up to the cliff overlooking the river and pushed her off. Jayden was hiding in the bushes and saw Tyler coming back down the trail without Rachael, and the SOB was whistling! Jayden saved Rachael all by himself."

"Hold on there, Jack. Did Jayden see Tyler push Rachael?"

"No."

"If this is true, it is extremely serious, but without witnesses—"

"What about the bruise on Rachael's backside where she bounced off a tree? Doesn't that count for anything?"

"Hold your temper, Kendall. Let me make a few phone calls. Maybe we can delay this thing. Did you take Rachael to the hospital to get her checked out?"

Jack exhaled as he realized his error. "No."

"Have you told anyone else about this?"

"Stacy, Mr. Gibbs, and Jayden know."

"Without witnesses, we can't prove that he pushed her, so keep your accusations to yourself until I get back to you."

Jack set the phone on his desk and looked over at Stacy. "He's right, you know. We can't prove it."

Stacy shook her head as she took this in. "It's not going to be the same around here without her."

Jack hung his head. "We knew this day would come. I just didn't expect it so soon. I'll never forgive myself if he hurts her."

"If he gets custody, he'll get her money. Maybe that'll be enough for him. Maybe she'll be safe," Stacy said.

"What if he won't let us see her? What if he tries something again?"

"He won't, Jack. He has to know someone would figure it out."

"If I threaten him, he won't let us see her. I'm dreading this, Stace. I can't even imagine not hearing her laugh anymore."

Stacy's lips rose to a pout. "You love her, don't you?"

"Hell, yes, I love her, but I don't have any say in what happens."

Stacy walked over and sat in his lap. "It's really sweet though. Why don't we all sleep in the tent tonight? She loves that."

He didn't trust himself to speak. She stared at him for so long that he wondered what she was thinking. He thought about kissing her.

"I'll go get the sleeping bags," she said.

"I'll call Emily and ask her to bring Rachael home early."

CHAPTER
THIRTY-TWO

Regina was careful not to let the screen door bang as she slipped out of the house. She hurried down the steps and towards G's cabin, though she doubted she'd find him there this early in the day. She was halfway down the path when she heard the weed eater buzz into action. Taking a left, she followed the trail away from the cabin and soon found her brother working near the greenhouse. He didn't see her, so she waited for him to turn in her direction.

He cut the power immediately and wiped his brow with his shirtsleeve. "Somethin' must be powerful wrong for you to search me out like this."

"Mr. Tyler's done hired him an attorney. Miss Rachael's comin' home tomorrow to stay."

"Glory be, that's good news," he said, but then he wrinkled his brow. "You sure about that?"

"I heard Mr. Tyler say so on the phone just now. I'm wondering, though, what happens if Rachael tells him it was me who shot Billy Ray? He'll throw us out faster than we can run."

Mr. Gibbs put the weed eater down and took a big swig from his water bottle, which he kept strapped to his belt. "We can't live our lives afraid of that. If she tells, we can deny it or admit the truth. What's it gonna be?"

Regina wrung her hands. "I hate lyin', but I don't wanna go to jail neither, and I don't wanna leave Jayden with Dillia. She's too hard on that boy. Can't you see how unhappy he is when he's with her? She's done boxed his ears in front of me twice already."

"That man o' hers was no good," he said. "She's doin' the same kind of meanness to Jayden, and I'll not stand for it. I'll talk to her, but we can't be with 'em every minute."

"That's what I mean. What happens when yer gone? What happens to Jayden?"

"Maybe you should adopt him," Mr. Gibbs said.

"Over Dillia's dead body," Regina scoffed. "She's done applied for state money already. She's not givin' that up for nobody."

"Maybe Mr. Jack can help," he said.

"Maybe. I'm wonderin' about somethin' else, too. I don't wanna give up my cabin, but I can't watch out for Rachael if I ain't there to see what's goin' on. Maybe I should let Dillia stay in my cabin, and I should move up to the big house."

"What if Mr. Tyler objects?" he said. "After all, he calls on Dillia day and night."

"Maybe Mr. Jack can help with that, too," Regina said. "He says it's Miss Rachael's house now. It's her money what pays us."

"All right. We'll talk to him when he brings Miss Rachael tomorrow."

"Don't forget to talk to Dillia about whoopin' up on Jayden," Regina said. "If I see it again, I might just box *her* ears so she can see how it feels."

"Box 'em once for me, too. There ain't nobody gonna hurt that boy, and that includes his momma."

* * *

"I love sleeping in the tent!"

"Good," Jack said. "Why don't you and Stacy go upstairs and get changed."

"Bye, Auntie Emily." She gave Emily a sweet little kiss and followed Stacy through the gate.

Once they were gone, Emily said, "What is it, Jack? What's happened?"

Jack pounded the last tent peg into the ground and got to his feet. "Tyler's assuming full custody tomorrow."

"Oh, no. What if he won't let me see her?"

"I'll speak to Tyler on your behalf. If you get the chance, maybe you can do the same for me."

"You'll miss her. Won't you, Jack?"

"Humph," he groaned as he turned away.

Emily placed a comforting hand on his shoulder.

"I can't stand the thought of him taking her back," Jack said.

"Does Rachael know?"

"We just found out," he said. "I'll tell her tonight."

Tears welled in Emily's eyes. "It's not right, Jack. He doesn't even want her. Why can't she live with me?"

"We'd have to prove that he's an unfit parent. Even if we could do that, it can't happen before tomorrow." He wanted to say more, but he knew he shouldn't.

"But she doesn't want to live with him," Emily said. "She told me that."

"Tyler is her father. She has to go back."

Emily started crying.

Jack put his arms around her and patted her back. She had been through so much already. It would be incredibly unfair if Tyler kept her from seeing Rachael, especially now that they were so close.

"I'm going to talk to Steve. Maybe one of the attorneys where we work can help."

"You like him a lot, don't you?"

She nodded and smiled through her tears. "We talk about having a family of our own someday."

"Wow. I didn't know it was that serious. He's a smart guy for choosing you."

She smiled and wiped her eyes.

"That child has many people who love and want to take care of her. Let's just hope Tyler becomes one of them."

"I'm goin' home," Emily said. "I don't want Rachael to see me cry. Keep me posted?"

"I will. You know you're welcome here anytime. Would you and Steve come over for dinner one of these nights?"

"Yes, of course. Thanks for everything, Jack. Talk to you soon." She gave him a quick hug and let herself out through the gate.

Jack turned back to secure the rain fly. Half of him wanted to come up with a solution; the other half knew this had to happen. He had always been a temporary caregiver; Rachael was never his. Any time he spent with her was a gift. He had no right to interfere, but that didn't mean it didn't hurt. He tried to tell himself that once Tyler had control of her money, Rachael would be safe, but he didn't believe it.

"We're ready, Uncle Jack," Rachael said from the other side of the tent.

"Crawl on in. I'll be right there."

"I've got the sleeping bags," Stacy said. "Here, Rachael, spread these out while I grab the pillows."

"I get to sleep in the middle," she said.

Jack secured the last line and then crawled into the tent. "Hey, you."

"Hey, you," Rachael said back.

Stacy appeared and tossed the pillows into the tent. Rachael giggled and put them into place.

"I'm coming in," Stacy said.

When they had settled into their sleeping bags, Jack said, "Do you know how much we love having you here?"

"Nope."

"Yes, you do. It makes us very happy. Isn't that right, Stacy?"

"Absolutely. We love you bunches and bunches!"

"I love you, too," Rachael said.

"It has been a good place for you to be while your daddy got your house ready for you to move into," Jack said. "He called today and said he's ready for you to come home now. He wants you to move back to the mansion tomorrow."

"Naw, that's okay. I wanna stay here with you and Miss Stacy."

"We want you to stay, but the judge says you have to go live with your daddy." Rachael sat up, so Jack did, too. "I don't like it either. I'd keep you here forever if I could, but the judge won't let me."

"But I'm afraid of Daddy. What if he pushes me again?"

"I'm going to talk to him, Rachael. It won't happen again. Besides, shouldn't a princess live in her castle?"

"Why can't I visit the castle but live here?" she said with a furrowed brow.

Jack met her troubled gaze, which he could see even in the shadows.

She heaved a heavy sigh. "Will you visit me?"

"If your daddy lets me, I will."

"What do I do if Daddy is mean to me?"

"You can call me anytime, day or night. Do you still remember my phone number?" She nodded and repeated it by rote. "I'll always be your Uncle Jack," he said.

"Will Jayden, Mr. G, and Auntie Regina be there?"

"Yes. Your daddy can't fire them. They work for you, remember? Don't forget that. He can fire Dillia, but he can't fire the others."

"I don't like Dillia anyway. She's mean to Jayden." She sighed and lay back down. "You'll come see me, won't you, Miss Stacy?"

"Yes, sweetie, I'll come," Stacy said.

Jack lay back and waited to see if she would say more, but she didn't. "Good night, Rachael. We love you."

"Good night," Rachael said.

Jack heard Stacy sniffle and knew that she was crying.

CHAPTER THIRTY-THREE

"**C**an I have more syrup, please?"

"Sure, sweetie." Stacy handed her the bottle and then flipped the two pieces of bread that were browning in the pan. "Ready for two more, Jack?"

"Just about." The doorbell rang. "I wonder who that could be."

"Well, deal with them quickly. This toast is just about ready," Stacy said.

Jack looked out the window and was surprised to see Tyler standing there. He opened the door. "Hey, buddy. What are you doing here?"

"I had a few errands to run and decided to save you a trip out to the house. I figured I'd take Rachael back with me."

"We're having breakfast. Care to join us?" He gestured towards the kitchen. As Tyler made his way into the kitchen, Jack did his best to control his emotions. He didn't want his time with Rachael cut short. "You hungry?"

"No, I ate earlier. Hey, pumpkin. How ya doin'?"

"I'm not a pumpkin. I'm a princess," Rachael said as she licked the syrup from her fingers.

"Well, excuse *me*," Tyler said.

"Want some coffee, Tyler?" Stacy said.

"Black is fine."

Stacy poured him a cup and set it on the table. Returning to the stove, she placed the remaining two pieces of toast onto her plate and joined them at the table.

Jack took a bite and said, "We really don't mind taking her out there. We've still got to pack her things."

"I'll wait," Tyler said. "It's not like she's got that much stuff."

"So, when's the big day for you and Pamela?" Stacy said.

"We haven't set a date yet, but before the first of the year, I think. The sooner, the better as far as I'm concerned. Having her near but not in my bed is making me crazy."

"Tyler," Jack scolded.

"What?" he sneered. "She doesn't know anything."

"Yes, I do. I know that you and Pamela sneak off to kiss."

Tyler laughed. "Maybe you're not as stupid as I thought."

"Rachael's not stupid at all," Jack said. "In fact, she's very bright."

"Jacob told Cody and me that you kiss a lot!"

"Did he now? That Jacob is a smart boy."

Jack cleared his throat. "You about finished, Rachael?"

"Yes. I'm full."

"You'll finish what's on your plate, young lady," Tyler said.

"Not at my house, she won't. If she's full, she can stop eating. Come on, Rachael. Let's go pack your things. Your daddy's going to take you out to the house with him."

"But I don't wanna go with Daddy. I wanna stay here with you and Stacy."

"Go get your stuff, Rachael. I haven't got all day."

"I don't want to, Daddy. I wanna stay with Uncle Jack and Stacy."

Tyler stood up and pointed his finger in her face. "I'm tired of you telling me what you do and don't want to do. Go get your things, or I'll give you a whippin' you won't soon forget."

Rachael started crying and turned to Jack for comfort. He picked her up. "That's not the best way to start things off, Tyler. We've had Rachael all this time and never once had to spank her. All you need to do is talk to her and be reasonable."

"I'm her father. It's reasonable that she obeys me. Now, go get her things so we can leave."

"Come on, sweetie. Let's go pack your things," Jack said.

"They're in a box near the hallway," Stacy said.

"Thanks." He let the back door close a little louder than he intended.

"Don't let him take me, Uncle Jack. He's gonna spank me."

"Hold on, baby. Let me make a quick call."

He pressed Kevin's number and waited.

"Kevin! Thank God, you're in. Tyler's here to take Rachael. What do I do?"

"I got nothin' for you, Jack. If you want to press charges, we can investigate, but even then, it's his word against hers. And since the boy didn't see her fall, as awful as it is, you're gonna have to let this one slide. She'll have to go with him for now."

"It's not right, and you know it!" he said and hung up. He set her down and nudged her up the garage steps. "I don't like it either, Rachael, but we have to do what the judge says. Mind your daddy when he tells you to do something. Don't give him any reason to spank you."

"But he scares me!"

"I know, baby. Just do what he says unless he tells you to do something wrong."

"Okay," she said in a pitiful voice. She opened the apartment door and they went in.

"You can call me anytime you want." When she turned back, he saw her bottom lip quiver. He knelt and took her in his arms as she began to cry. Closing his eyes, he smelled her hair and tried to imprint the feel of her tiny body into his memory. She was the daughter he never had, and he loved her dearly. He so longed to protect her from the pain, sorrow, and neglect that she would surely suffer at Tyler's hands that he felt sick at the thought of it.

"I don't wanna go with Daddy. I wanna stay with you!"

He choked back tears. "I want you to stay, but we have to do what the judge says." After a few moments, he gently set her down and wiped the tears from her face. "I love you, Rachael. Don't ever forget that. Stacy loves you, too, and so does Emily, Mr. G, Auntie Regina, and Jayden. Lots of people love you. Pamela and Jacob are going to be there, and so will your daddy and Cody. You'll all become a family. It's going to be all right."

"I don't want to go," she whimpered.

He picked up her box. "Look, here's your new teddy bear. Whenever you hold him, you can think of Stacy and me, and remember how much we love you."

She took the bear and hugged it to her chest. "Please let me stay!"

He set the box down and knelt on one knee. "I want you to stay, baby. Truly I do, but the judge says you have to go with your daddy, and we have to do what the judge says. I'll come out to see you as soon as I can. I promise. You be a good little girl and do what your daddy says. We have to go." As they headed down the stairs, he hiked his shoulder to wipe his cheek.

"Got everything?" Tyler said as he reached for the box.

"Nope. She's got to give me a great big hug," Stacy said. "I'll miss you so much, but we'll come out to see you very soon."

"Don't promise her that," Tyler said. "I think it's best that we bond as a family for a while. It could be quite some time before you see her again."

Stacy tossed down her drying towel and turned from the sink. "Tyler, how can you say that after all that we've been through?"

"She's been shuffled around enough. She needs to settle in. She needs to learn who she has to obey."

"We just need to hear that you won't keep us away forever," Jack said. "We love Rachael, you know."

"Look, I appreciate what you've done for my family and me, but it is *my* family. I decide what happens when and where. You've forgotten that a time or two."

"Daddy, I want Uncle Jack and Stacy to visit me."

"Not until I'm damn good and ready. Now, go get in the truck."

"But, Daddy—"

"Now, Rachael."

She started to cry again. Jack stepped forward, but Tyler stretched out his arm to block the way. "Your days of interfering in my business are over, Jack. Say goodbye to Rachael, and I do mean goodbye."

Stacy started crying, also. "We love you, Rachael!"

Rachael trudged to the front door, and through gasping tears, she said, "I love you, too!"

"Thanks again for all you've done. We'll just end it at that." Tyler followed Rachael out the door, climbed into his truck, and drove away.

"If this is what it feels like when you get a divorce and your ex takes your child away, it sucks," Stacy said, tears still wet on her cheeks.

"At least *then* you have rights," Jack sighed. "In this situation, we've got nothing."

* * *

Tyler listened to Rachael cry for nearly ten minutes. Finally, he struck his fist against the steering wheel. "That's enough! Stop your crying, or I'll give you something to cry about." He glanced back at the road and then scowled at her again. "Where did you get that bear? I see your old one in the box. You made such a big deal about me bringing it to you; why aren't you holding that one?"

"Uncle Jack gave me this bear," she sniffed.

Tyler clinched his teeth. He rolled down the window, yanked the bear out of her arms, and threw it into the woods.

"Daddy, no!" she screamed. "My bear! I want my bear!" She twisted in her seat to look through the rear window.

"Jack isn't part of your life anymore. Get used to it."

Rachael kicked her feet against the dashboard. "I hate you, Daddy. I hate you!"

"All right, that's it." Tyler screeched the truck to a stop at the side of the road, yanked her out of the cab, and pulled her up the embankment towards the trees. He broke off a limb and proceeded to whip her with it.

"I'm sorry, Daddy! I'm sorry!"

"You're…gonna…learn…not…to…back-talk…me," he said as he struck her between words.

"Stop, Daddy! Stop!" she screamed as he continued to beat her.

"I…am…your…father…and…you…damn…well…better… remember…that."

"Drop that switch, or I swear I'll pull this trigger," Jack said.

"And if he doesn't, I swear to God I'll pull mine," Stacy added.

Tyler let go of Rachael and dropped the switch. Rachael ran to Jack and Stacy. Stacy stuffed her gun into her waistband and gathered Rachael in her arms as she cried in pain. Just a few seconds later, a police siren heralded the imminent arrival of a squad car. Tyler knew he couldn't run. Even if Jack and Stacy didn't shoot him, there were too many patrol cars on this highway; something he knew from bitter experience. He turned towards Jack and Stacy and saw that several drivers had pulled to the side of the road to watch.

When a police car arrived seconds later, two police officers approached with weapons drawn.

"What's going on here, Kendall?" a heavyset officer demanded as he huffed his way up the embankment.

"Charlie, is that you?" Jack said without looking back.

"It is. We've had several calls about a man beating a child on the side of the road."

"This is Rachael Chandler's father," Jack said. "She's the little girl who went missing over a year ago and was recently recovered. I'm her temporary foster father. Tyler, here, came to take custody of her today. She wasn't in his care a full fifteen minutes, and you see what he does to her."

"I'm her father," Tyler said. "I have a right to discipline my child any way I see fit."

"Not in Mississippi, you don't," Charlie replied. "Lower your weapon, Kendall. We'll take it from here."

"All right, but I'm taking Rachael with me until we see a judge and speak to her psychologist. Dr. Crimshaw will want to know what Tyler did to her today." He lowered his gun. "I'm filing charges for aggravated child abuse."

"Child abuse?" Tyler scoffed. "Since when is it illegal for a man to discipline his own daughter?"

"You call that discipline!" Jack yelled.

"All right, Jack. As I said, we'll take it from here," Charlie said.

"What did you throw out the window before you pulled over?"

"That's none of your damn business, Jack," Tyler spat.

"He threw my teddy bear out the window. He threw my new bear away!" Rachael cried.

"Charlie," Stacy said, "look at her legs. Here, sweetie, let the policeman see what your daddy did to you." Tyler watched as Stacy pulled up her dress to show the ugly red welts that crisscrossed the back of her legs. She was scratched and bleeding in several places.

"Lord have mercy," Charlie said. "I'm gonna call the paramedics. We need a record of this." He nodded to his partner to make the call.

"Come on! I didn't hit her that hard," Tyler said. "She's not hurt. It looks worse than it is."

"Did you see her legs?" Jack said. "If you needed to discipline her, you don't pull to the side of the road and beat her half to death. How many times were you going to hit her, Tyler? What the hell's wrong with you? You're nowhere near ready to be a father to Rachael."

"Oh, and I suppose you are? Well, we'll just see what my attorney has to say about that!"

"We'll see what Rachael's attorney has to say about it, too. While I'm at it, I'll ask him what he wants to do about the scrapes on her elbow and her knee, and the bruise she got on her bottom over the weekend."

Tyler's stomach muscles cramped like he'd been punched in the gut. Did Jack know? That was a terrifying thought.

"All right, that's enough," Charlie said. "We're gonna read you your rights and take you in, so I wouldn't resist if I were you. You'll only make things worse for yourself. Tommy, handcuff this man."

"What?" Tyler scoffed. "Can't I press charges on Jack because he pulled a weapon on me?"

"Not today, you can't," Charlie said.

"Once I get Rachael back, you'll never see her again, Jack. Never!" Tyler swore as the officer turned him around and cuffed his wrists.

"Thanks, Charlie," Jack said. "I owe you one."

"You owe me more than one, but who's counting?"

* * *

The paramedics arrived and gently treated Rachael's wounds. Jack was amazed at how good they were with her, doing everything possible to make her feel safe and comfortable. He held her hand and took pictures of the welts, some of which were bleeding and already bruising.

"That is a nasty bruise, young lady. How did you bruise your bottom?" one of the paramedics asked as he gently pulled her underpants up and turned her around to face him.

"I fell."

"You did? Where did you fall?"

"Now is not the best time to discuss this," Jack said. "I've given Captain Thomas all the details. Please make note of it in the report, but that's all that needs to be said at this moment."

"Are you the girl's father?" he said, eyeing him with suspicion.

"No, I'm her foster caregiver. She got the bruise, the scratches on her knee and elbow, plus the one on her stomach, while she was staying with her father over the weekend. It is a cause of great concern, as is what happened here today."

"Is that true, sweetie?" he said, turning back to Rachael.

"Daddy is mean to me. He pushed me, and I fell. I wanna stay with Uncle Jack and Stacy, but the judge won't let me. Please don't make me live with Daddy. I'm scared of Daddy!"

"Come here, sweetie," Jack said. Rachael went willingly. "You're going home with us now. I'm going to do everything I can to make the judge change his mind. I promise."

Stacy moved in to put a supporting hand on Rachael's back. "We're here, Rachael. You're safe, now."

"Do you want us to take her to the hospital and have her checked out there?" the medic said.

"If you think she needs to go, take her. Either way, I want this event well documented."

"You say you've reported the abuse?" he said.

"Yes, and, of course, we'll report what happened today," Jack said. "I just want to be sure that it's officially recorded for the courts. Do I need to take her to the hospital for that to happen?"

"No," the paramedic said. "We have to file a full report on any suspected child abuse, and we have the photo evidence as well. Keep Neosporin on those scratches. Physically, she should be fine, but she should probably see a psychiatrist if she's being abused."

"She's already under a doctor's care. I want you to document what she said about where she got those scratches and that bruise. If you remember, she said her father pushed her, and she fell. We'll take her to her doctor for a follow-up tomorrow."

"I guess we're finished here. You take care now," the medic said to

Rachael. He and Jack watched as she and Stacy walked back to Jack's truck and climbed in. "I got a little one that age. The guy who did this is a real jerk."

"There's something not right about that man. He needs help," Jack said. "Thanks for being so gentle with her." He could see that the medic might say more, but he simply nodded. As he and his partner drove away, a cold chill ran up Jack's back. He shouldn't have taunted Tyler about Rachael's fall over the weekend.

CHAPTER THIRTY-FOUR

"What was I supposed to do, let him beat her?" Jack said.

"Calm down, Mr. Kendall. I'm just saying, this isn't the way we would've liked this transition to go," Dr. Crimshaw said.

"I'm not the problem. Clearly, Tyler was out of line. Did you see the pictures?"

"Not just the pictures; it was all over the news last night. It is quite unfortunate. I fear Rachael will have even more difficulty integrating into her family now because of it. Tyler has canceled his sessions altogether, although he had done so before this happened," Dr. Crimshaw said. "I'm afraid he's being rather difficult."

"Difficult? That man needs help. He didn't have Rachael even fifteen minutes before he was beating her. I want to know what can be done to ensure that he doesn't get the chance to do it again."

"Are you prepared to adopt Rachael on a permanent basis?"

"Yes, if needs be." There, he said it, though he hadn't thought it through.

"Look, Mr. Kendall, there's a lot to consider here. I'll get back to you. In the meantime, just do what you do best: keep Rachael happy."

"Thank you. I'll wait to hear from you." Jack disconnected the call and dialed Mr. Carrington.

"I was expecting a call from you," the attorney said.

"Have you heard the latest?"

"If you're referring to the abuse charges against Tyler Chandler, yes. I've already heard from Tyler's attorney. How's Rachael?"

"She's calming down, but she's in a fair amount of pain. She took an awful beating. On top of that, she's worried that the judge will make her go back to live with Tyler. She's afraid of him."

"Understandably so."

"Are his actions bad enough to make him lose his custody rights?"

"The child has to go somewhere. Are you willing to adopt her?"

"I am."

"There are some challenges with your bid, but it's not impossible. Tyler's attorney is trying to freeze Rachael's assets until this is settled. He thinks you're trying to hold on to her for the money."

"I don't give a damn about her money. I just want to keep her safe. She's not even six years old, for God's sake, and I doubt she's ever felt entirely safe in her whole life. She deserves better than that."

"Indeed, she does. One question, Mr. Kendall. Why were you following Tyler in the first place?"

"Rachael forgot her locket. It's incredibly special to her. It's the only picture she has of her mother. I tried to call Tyler's cell phone, but he wouldn't answer. He'd already said he wouldn't let us see Rachael for quite some time, so I followed them to give it back to her."

"I see. There may be an alternative to you adopting Rachael. I understand that she's been spending time with her aunt Emily. What do you think of the girl?"

"Emily is wonderful. You couldn't ask for a more sincere, upright young woman."

"Have you told her that Rachael has inherited a great deal of money?"

"No. The only person I've told is Stacy," Jack said.

"Has Stacy told Emily?"

"Not to my knowledge. Why?"

"An attorney from Alister, Emerson & Maxwell inquired about the possibility of Emily adopting Rachael. What do you think of that idea?"

"I think the idea has possibilities. I'd like to see Emily's life more stable first, but Emily would be an excellent choice. Rachael adores Emily."

"You impress me, Mr. Kendall. If you were after Rachael's money, you would've found a reason to object to Emily Richards as a possible candidate for adopting Rachael."

Jack smiled. "Tell me, was the attorney's name Steve?"

"Yes, Steve Barlow. He's a bright young man," Mr. Carrington said. "I've known his father, Senator Barlow, for years."

"I rather liked Steve myself. He's dating Emily."

"Correction, he's Emily's fiancé. They plan to marry in the near future."

"Wow. That's wonderful news."

"As for Tyler, my firm is drafting a motion that he forfeit his custody rights, and recommend that the courts require supervised visitation. I'll keep you informed. Guard yourselves. It takes time for these things to work themselves out, and there's no telling how Tyler will respond. While I suspect he cares very little for Rachael herself, his interest in her finances is another matter. His attorney inquired only yesterday as to when Rachael's next maintenance check is due. He insisted it go directly to Tyler."

"Like I said, I don't care what you do with her money. You're welcome to keep her checks. I'll take care of her out of what you pay me. I'd tell you to keep that, too, only I haven't been able to do my job with all of this going on. I'm behind in paying my bills."

"I'm well aware of that, Mr. Kendall."

Jack grimaced. "I don't mind telling you that it's very disconcerting to have you so familiar with the inner workings of my life."

Mr. Carrington laughed. "At least it's working in your favor, Mr. Kendall. Keep up the good work."

Jack scowled at the phone and then dropped it into his pocket. Without hesitation, he walked out onto the patio, through the gate, and up the stairs to Stacy's apartment. Before he could knock, Stacy opened the door and put a finger to her lips. He nodded and stepped inside. "I want to see her." Stacy gestured towards the living room where he looked down upon Rachael, who lay sleeping with her arms wrapped around her teddy bear. It had taken nearly an hour to find that bear. It had landed in a bush, and Rachael was the one who had spotted it.

His heart ached for her. Every child deserves to feel safe and loved, but she had been betrayed by those who should have loved her. He wondered how long it would be before the courts took her away again.

He thought back on what Mr. Carrington had said; Emily was getting married. He smiled at the thought. He certainly hoped she remained as happy as she looked the other night. If so, perhaps Rachael might finally have the home and love she so desperately deserved. He glanced over at Stacy. "Want some coffee?"

"My place or yours?"

"Let's stay here. I don't want her to wake up and find us gone."

Stacy went into the kitchen and put on a fresh pot.

He pulled up a stool at the bar. "Got a question for you. Have you told Emily anything about how much money Rachael inherited?"

"I haven't told anybody anything. After blowing it with Pamela, I've been extremely careful about what I say. Why do you ask?"

"I talked with Mr. Carrington today. He asked if you'd said anything to Emily. I told him I didn't think so, so I'm just checking. He told me something very interesting."

"Yes?" she said as a brow raised and her eyes began to sparkle.

"It concerns someone else's business," he teased.

"That doesn't count between you and me. We're partners. What matters most is that you trust me. I'll never blow it again like I did with Pamela."

"I do trust you, which is why I'm telling you that Emily and Steve are engaged."

"Oh my gosh! That's great news. That's wonderful, that's…that's sudden, isn't it?" she said, biting her lower lip.

"Well, they saw each other when she lived here before."

"Jack?" she said with a sideways look.

"Mr. Carrington said Steve called to ask about them adopting Rachael."

Stacy's eyes narrowed. "No wonder you asked if I mentioned Rachael's money. Surely he—"

"He'd certainly know how to access the details of the will if it can be done."

"Jack, I don't like what we're thinking," Stacy said.

"Neither do I. I want nothing more than for Emily to be happy. Mr. Carrington says he's known Steve's father for years. Still, it seems a little convenient. Let's invite them to dinner."

"How about tomorrow night?" Stacy said. "I'll make chicken fettuccini."

"Perfect."

* * *

It was early when the doorbell rang the next morning.

"Oh, no," Stacy said as she looked up from the omelet she was cooking. "Don't answer it."

"I'll go see," Jack said.

"Wait!" She turned the fire on low and followed him to the front door.

He carefully pulled the curtain aside. "Huh."

"Be careful, Jack. He probably put her up to it," Stacy said.

"My gun's on the dresser," he said.

"I'm on it." She spun around and headed down the hallway.

The doorbell rang again.

"Got it," Stacy said as she patted the bump at her waistband.

He cracked the door open. "Hello, Pamela. Are you alone?"

"Jacob's out in the car. Can we come in? Maybe Jacob can play with Rachael while we chat."

She looked nervous, which made Jack nervous. "Sure. Go get him." He watched as Pamela walked back to the car and opened the front passenger's side door for Jacob. When they approached again, he said, "Where's Tyler?"

"He had a meeting with his attorney this morning. He doesn't know we're here. I'm a little worried he might see my car, though."

"Stacy has room in her garage. It's off the street."

"That would be great. Can Jacob wait with you?"

"Hi, Jacob," Jack said and extended his hand for a high-five.

Jacob obliged. "Can I play with Rachael?"

"I think she's still sleeping, but we'll find out once your momma comes in."

"I'll go out and meet her," Stacy said.

Jack watched Pamela as she got back in the car and saw no indication that Tyler was anywhere around. "How was your evening, Jacob?"

"Not very good, sir. Momma and Tyler argued a lot."

"Do you know why?"

"It had to do with you and Rachael. That's all I know. Mr. Tyler sent us to Cody's room right after dinner, but we snuck out to the top of the stairs to listen. I don't know what you did, but he's very upset with you."

"Well, I'm upset with him, too. When you see Rachael, ask her to show you where Tyler hit her with a switch yesterday. No one should beat a child like that."

"Is she all right?"

"She will be, but I don't want it to happen again."

Stacy and Pamela came in through the kitchen. "Come on, Jacob. I'll take you to my place so you can visit with Rachael," Stacy said.

Jacob threw a glance towards his mother. "Go on, Jacob. I'll join you shortly."

Jack gestured towards the kitchen. "Coffee?"

"Thanks," Pamela said.

Jack poured the coffee and waited for her to say something, but she didn't. "What's on your mind, Pamela?"

"Did you see the news last night?" she said.

"The news? No."

"The top news story was about Tyler whipping Rachael on the side of the interstate. I could hardly believe my eyes. It was awful!"

"Wait till you see the bruises," he scoffed.

"Tyler blames you. Tell me what happened, Jack. I need to know."

"According to Rachael, she was hugging the teddy bear I gave her when Tyler yanked it out of her arms and threw it out the window. When she complained, he pulled over and proceeded to beat the living daylights out of her. We saw him throw the bear out the window, so I know she's telling the truth. Several cars pulled over when he started whipping her. I pulled my gun to make him stop."

"I know. Someone filmed it on their cell phone."

"Wow. That will play well for the judge. Here are the results." He took out his phone and showed her the pictures of Rachael's legs. He had taken a few more this morning while she lay sleeping, her legs striped with black and blue bruises.

Pamela gasped. "Oh my God, Jack! How could he do such a thing?"

"How can you marry someone like that?"

"That's just it," she said. "I can't. I can't trust that he won't do something like that to Jacob."

"Or to you," Jack said.

"I can't take that chance. Jacob and I are leaving Jackson from here. I'm finished with Tyler Chandler!"

"I wish it were that easy for Rachael," Jack said. "As much as I hate to say it, for her sake, I think you're making the right decision. He clearly can't control his emotions. I've heard him threaten to spank Rachael before, but I thought it was a manipulative, parental threat. Clearly, I was wrong."

"You won't hear me threaten my son like that," Pamela said. "A child shouldn't fear his parent. That's not to say I've never spanked him. I have, but only when it's necessary, and never out of anger."

"Anyone can see what a fine job you're doing with Jacob. He's a pleasure to be around."

"Thank you. I'd like to say goodbye to Rachael if you don't mind. I wanted to be a second mommy for her, but that's clearly not going to happen. I want her to know that it's not her fault. There's no telling what Tyler might tell her."

"Fair enough. Let's go." He led the way to Stacy's apartment and knocked on the door.

"Jack?"

"Yes. It's me."

Stacy opened the door and let them in. Jack and Pamela joined the children, who were coloring in Disney books on the coffee table.

"Hi, Rachael," Pamela said.

"I don't want to live with you and Daddy," she said.

Jack sat on the floor beside her.

"I know," Pamela said. "I came to say goodbye."

Rachael stopped coloring and was silent for a moment, then she stood up, lifted her dress, and turned around. "Look what Daddy did to me."

Tears welled in Pamela's eyes. "I know, sweetie. I'm very sorry. Your daddy shouldn't have hit you like that. You're a good little girl."

"Are you going to marry Daddy?"

"No. Jacob and I are going away, so we probably won't see each other again, but I want you to know something very important. No matter what anybody says to you, the fact that Jacob and I are leaving is not your fault. We are leaving because Tyler shouldn't have hit you.

It's his fault I'm leaving, not yours. Do you understand?"

"Uh huh."

"Even if he says it's your fault, he's wrong. It's his fault and no one else's." Pamela looked towards Jack. "I guess we'll go now. You remember what I said, Rachael."

"Goodbye, Jacob," Rachael said.

"Goodbye, Rachael. I'll miss having you for my sister. You are much nicer than Cody is."

"That's because Cody is mean like Daddy is mean."

Jack walked Pamela and Jacob down to their car and opened the door. Jacob crawled in first. "You be careful," Jack said. "He's not going to like this one little bit."

"I know," Pamela said. "I'm not going to Georgia this time. Jacob and I are starting completely over."

"I'm glad to hear it. Drop us a line sometime, if you're ever curious."

"Thanks for the offer, but I'm leaving everything that has to do with Tyler Chandler behind me."

"Can't say I blame you." As he watched her pull out of the driveway, he knew things were about to get even more unpredictable.

* * *

"What is there to investigate? It's all on tape."

"Calm down, Jack. These things take time," Captain Thomas said.

"How the hell am I supposed to tell her that she has to go back with him? She hasn't even healed yet. No, Kevin, I can't do it. Has the judge seen the photos?"

"There's a court date for early next week. That's as fast as I can make it happen."

"That's not good enough. Pamela left him today, and he's going to take it out on Rachael. I'm not letting him take her back to that place all by herself."

"You have no choice," Kevin said.

"Like hell, I don't. We're out of town, and we won't be back until right before our court date."

"Nice try, but Officer Jenkins is parked outside your house. "You have to give her up, Jack. I don't like it either, but that's how it is."

"This isn't about giving her up. It's about protecting her from abuse. How can you even think about returning her to his care? What's wrong with you people?"

"Hey, *we people* are charged with enforcing the law, and the law says Tyler is her biological parent. He has legal custody."

"Well, I haven't seen any paperwork to that effect. Last I heard, I had temporary custody. I'm calling my attorney." He hung up and took a few deep breaths. He couldn't imagine giving Rachael back to Tyler. There had to be another way.

Rachael came running into the den with Stacy following behind her. "I don't wanna go with Daddy!"

"I know, sweetie. I'm doing everything I can to keep that from happening."

A knock sounded at the door.

"Don't answer that," he said. "Stacy, why don't you call the news station? Let's make this very uncomfortable for the justice department. I seriously doubt that the public will want to see Rachael returned to her father today."

"I know just who to call," Stacy said. "Come on, Rachael. Let's go to the back bedroom."

The knock sounded again, along with the ringing of the doorbell.

"And keep her out of sight!" Jack called after them as he took out his cell phone and dialed Mr. Carrington. His assistant answered. "This is Jack Kendall. Is Mr. Carrington in? I've got an emergency on my hands."

"He's out right now, but he said to tell you that he filed a motion to stall Tyler's bid for custody until an investigation can be made into yesterday's beating. The judge granted his petition. Rachael is to remain under the current foster care arrangement until further notice."

"You mean I don't have to let her go?" Jack said closing his eyes as relief washed over him.

"That's what he told me," the young woman replied.

"Is there something you can fax me as proof of that? The police are telling me I have to give her up."

"What's your fax number? I'll see if he has anything and call you back."

He gave her the number. "Can I hold while you get ahold of him?"

"I'll call you back, Mr. Kendall. Hang tight."

"Please hurry. I've got people banging on my door." He went to the front door and looked outside. Tyler's truck sat in the driveway next to a car he didn't recognize. He called Kevin. "My attorney says the judge suspended Tyler's custody rights until an investigation can be made into yesterday's beating. She's faxing proof as we speak. Tyler's pounding at my door. Can you send someone out here?"

"Hold on."

Jack went back into the den to check the fax machine. Still nothing.

The knocking persisted.

"Come on, Kevin," he muttered into the phone.

"Jack, are you there?" Captain Thomas said.

"Yes, I'm here."

"I've got two black and whites on the way. Don't open your door until they get there."

"I want that jerk off my property!"

"That jerk is Rachael's father," Kevin said. "We don't want this escalating out of control. Now fax me a copy of that court order. I want to see it for myself."

"Thanks, Kevin. Will do."

Jack hung up and called the attorney's office again. "Did you reach him?"

"Yes, but I won't have access to the documents until he returns. You can have the police call our office if you like."

"When do you expect him?" Jack said as the pounding on his door continued.

"He's on his way to another meeting. It will likely be after lunch," she said.

"Can you just write something on letterhead to the effect that he has the order, and you'll fax it to me later this afternoon? I'm going to need it when the police get here."

"I don't feel comfortable doing that, Mr. Kendall, but you're welcome to have them call me."

Jack clenched his jaw. "Call me the second he gets in."

"Will do, Mr. Kendall. Goodbye."

Sirens. He could hear them coming up the street. He went back to the front door and peeked out. Two police cars pulled into the driveway.

"Jack, the police are here!" Stacy shouted as she and Rachael came running down the hall.

"I know. I talked to Mr. Carrington's assistant. She says the judge put a stay on Tyler's custody order. He can't take her."

"Try telling *him* that," Stacy said. "Tyler's about to break the door down."

Another knock came. "Open up, Mr. Kendall. This is the police."

Jack waved Stacy and Rachael back down the hall and then cracked the door open. "Finally."

"Give me back my daughter, Jack. You have no right to keep her," Tyler yelled as two uniformed officers forcefully held him from the door.

"My attorney says the judge suspended your custody rights until they can investigate the beating you gave Rachael yesterday. She's to stay in my care for the time being."

"Do you have proof of that?" the police officer said.

"My attorney just left the courthouse. He's going to fax me a copy of the motion as soon as he returns to the office. His assistant says you're welcome to call her, and she'll confirm it."

"That's not good enough," a stout woman in a brown suit said as she stepped forward. "Mr. Chandler is the biological father. Return Rachael to him immediately."

Jack hadn't seen her in all the commotion. "Who the hell are you?" he said.

"I'm Louise Blackwell with Child Services. I'm here to ensure that Rachael is reunited with her birth family."

"If you're here to protect Rachael, you're on the wrong side. Didn't you see the news last night? Tyler beat Rachael on the side of the road for the whole world to see. She's not going anywhere with him."

"I'm sorry, Mr. Kendall, but unless you have proof of a court order, you'll have to hand the child over," the officer said.

"I'm calling Captain Thomas," Jack said. "We just spoke about this not ten minutes ago."

"He's wasting our time," Mrs. Blackwell said. "Tell him to bring Rachael out. We haven't got all day."

"What do you mean, he's out?" Jack said. "I just spoke to him. Can you page him? This is an emergency." He was so frustrated he could barely control his temper. "Yes, have him call me immediately. Thanks."

"Well?" Mrs. Blackwell said. "Go get Rachael."

"Do you have any proof, Mr. Kendall?" the officer said.

"Not at this exact moment, but I will."

"Then you'll have to turn Rachael over to Mr. Chandler. I'm sorry. You folks wait out here while I accompany Mr. Kendall as he brings out the girl."

Tyler smirked, and Jack could have punched him. He wished he hadn't opened the door, but there was nothing he could do about that now. He motioned for the officer to come inside.

"Where is she?" the officer said.

"She was here just a moment ago. Let's check the den." He led the way into the den and checked the fax machine. Still nothing. He glanced around. "She must be hiding. She doesn't want to go with Tyler. She's afraid of him." He pulled out his phone and quickly brought up the pictures of Rachael. "Did you see what he did to her?"

The officer made a move to push the phone away, but one glance was enough. He winced. Jack saw it and flipped through the rest of the photos. "I'm telling the truth about the judge's order. I'm just waiting for them to fax it. The judge doesn't want her in any more danger. If she goes back to him, he might kill her, especially when he learns that his fiancée has left him because of this incident. He's bound to take it out on Rachael. Do you want to be responsible for making me return her just because I don't have that fax?"

The officer clenched his jaw. "I have a daughter her age. There's no excuse for this kind of abuse, but I see it all the time. I hate it, but I have my orders."

"I'm gonna call the attorney's office again." He pushed redial. "Hey, have you heard from Mr. Carrington?"

"Yes, I told him about your predicament. He's postponed his meeting. He should be here any minute with the court order. I'll fax it immediately."

"Thank God. I've got Officer—what's your name again?"

"Officer Patrick."

"I've got Officer Patrick here. Please tell him what you just told me." He handed the phone to the officer.

Someone pounded on the door, and a voice came through the officer's radio.

"Yes, ma'am. Thank you." He handed the phone back to Jack and pushed the radio button. "Unit Nine, over."

"Where the hell are you? There's news media all over the place," a voice said through the radio.

"It's my partner," he told Jack.

"I'll be right there. Over." He moved through the house and opened the front door. Cameras flashed wildly. Jack stepped back, out of sight.

"Where's my daughter?" Tyler demanded.

"I'm sorry, Mr. Chandler, but the court has ordered that your daughter remain in the temporary custody of Jack Kendall. You'll have to wait for your court date to pursue custody."

"I wanna see that court order!" Tyler yelled.

The moment the officer stepped past the threshold, Jack closed the door and locked it.

His phone rang. "Jack, here."

"I'm faxing the order right now."

A knock sounded again. He ignored it and rushed towards the den just as the fax came through. "Got it, and not a moment too soon."

"I hope everything turns out all right, Mr. Kendall. We're pulling for you."

"Thanks, I'll let you know what happens." He threw the order on the copier as the pounding continued. While he was at it, he grabbed photocopies of the pictures he had taken of Rachael's bruises and returned to the front door.

"Open the door, Mr. Kendall."

"I've got a copy of the court order in my hand. If I present it, do I have your word that Rachael stays with me?" he said through the door.

"Let's see the order," Officer Patrick said.

Jack scanned it quickly and then opened the door. He handed the order to the officer, and he then shoved the pictures of Rachael towards Tyler. "See what your stupid temper did to your daughter? Tell me that she's safe with you. Tell me you're ready to be a loving father to Rachael!"

Tyler grabbed the pictures from the woman in the suit, who had stepped in to intercede. He looked at them and choked. "I did this? There must be some mistake. I only hit her a few times."

Cameras continued to flash as reporters grabbed at the photocopies of Rachael.

"Don't you remember?" Jack said. "You struck her at least a dozen times before I could get to you. I had to stop you, Tyler, because you weren't going to stop."

The woman gasped and drew back when she saw the pictures, and everyone grew quiet.

Tyler was clearly stunned. He stared at the pictures and then at Jack. Finally, he turned and headed for his truck.

"How did you feel when you saw those pictures, Mr. Chandler?" shouted one reporter.

"What will you do now, Mr. Chandler? Will you continue to fight for custody?" another reporter said as he shoved a microphone towards Tyler's face.

"Didn't you realize how badly you were hurting your daughter?" a woman said.

Jack almost felt sorry for him. It was obvious he hadn't realized how badly he had hurt Rachael. Still, what might happen when he learned that Pamela had left him? Tyler was quickly losing everything he had recently regained. He was his own worst enemy.

Officer Patrick's partner waved the people back from the door. "All right, folks, show's over. Clear out."

"Are you just going to let him go?" Jack said.

"What do you suggest? His attorney arranged to have the charges against him dismissed," Officer Patrick said.

"It's amazing what money will buy," Jack scoffed.

"If it makes any difference," Officer Patrick said, "I'm glad you got that fax."

"Me, too." Jack shut the door and locked it. He watched from the window until every last car had pulled away, and then he headed for his bedroom. He opened the closet and knocked on the back wall. A moment later, a panel slid to the side, and Rachael and Stacy came out.

"We were hiding, Uncle Jack."

"I see that. You can come out now. Everybody's gone." He reached in, pulled the light chain, and shut the secret panel. It was a small space. He kept a safe in there, but it was the perfect hiding place for Stacy and Rachael. "Good thinking, Stacy."

"It was looking a bit dicey out there."

"Yes, it was. It's been quite a morning. Shall we finish breakfast?"

"Oh, I forgot all about the omelet. It's trashed by now," she said.

"Anything will work. Won't it, Rachael?"

"I could just eat toast."

Stacy laughed. "We'll come up with something."

Jack followed them down the hallway with the strangest sense of belonging, as if Stacy and Rachael were his family. He knew he shouldn't feel that way. He had no real claim on either of them, and he could lose them at a moment's notice. He pushed the thought aside. "Did you call Emily about dinner tonight?"

"Ah, no. I've been a little busy this morning," Stacy said.

"What? And here I thought you were the queen of multitasking."

"One order of burnt toast coming up," she said.

"But I don't like burnt toast," Rachael said, her brow wrinkling with distaste.

"Oh, yours won't be burnt. Just Jack's."

"Hey," he said.

"Well, you can't expect me to cook breakfast, call Emily, *and* protect Rachael all at the same time, can you? Something's gotta give."

"Stacy, I was just—"

She winked at him.

He chuckled as he sat down at the table. "All right. What's Emily's number?"

* * *

"Jack had just stepped out of the shower when his phone rang. Immediately tense, he wrapped a towel around his hips and stepped into the bedroom to grab his phone. "Jack, here."

"I hope I'm not disturbin' you none, but Regina saw the news, and we's mighty worried for Miss Rachael. Is she all right?"

Jack sat on the edge of the bed and pushed the dripping hair from his forehead. "She's recovering, Mr. G. I should've thought to get word to you. I don't know how long I'll get to keep her, but she's safe for the moment."

"Mr. Tyler's been yellin' at everybody who gets close enough to hear him. Poor Dillia can hardly do her work."

"I hate to say it, but that might get worse. Don't tell Tyler, but Pamela is gone, and she's not coming back. There's no telling what he'll do when he finds out, so stay out of his way till he cools off."

"He's been pacing like a caged tiger, just waitin' for her to come home. I'll let Regina know, and tell her to stay clear."

"Mr. G, there's somethin' I need to talk to you about. It's very important."

"How can I help you, Mr. Jack?"

"When Rachael first came to stay with me, she was having terrible nightmares. She'd wake up crying, worried that the police would come and take Jayden away if she didn't keep Mrs. Chandler's secret. She finally confided in me, and now the nightmares have stopped.

"Stacy and I know that Regina shot Billy Ray. Rachael told us that Regina wanted to call the police, but Joan wouldn't let her. She also told us that Joan threatened to harm Jayden if any of you told the truth. It's been a terrible burden for her to bear, but she doesn't have to carry it alone anymore.

"Stacy and I can't imagine what would've happened if you and Regina hadn't been there to help Rachael during that terrible time, and it's obvious that she adores you. As far as we're concerned, history has been written, and we see no reason to change it. Joan's secret is safe with us. I rather appreciate the irony myself. The very lie that Joan thought would protect her has actually served to make her look guilty instead." He heard a heavy sigh come through the phone. "Mr. G?"

"I'm here, Mr. Jack. I'm relieved; that's all. Regina and I both wanted to confess. Truly, we did, but Mrs. Chandler was sure them courts wouldn't let her adopt Miss Rachael if'n they knew she'd seen her grandfather die. We'd confess now, but we's worried what would happen to Jayden if'n Regina and I went to jail. We don't want him livin' with his momma 'cuz she's not good to him like he deserves. We's been mighty worried about you findin' out, Mr. Jack, but to tell the truth, I'm glad it's out in the open. Now, I can make peace with my Maker and ask His forgiveness. That's the part that's worried me most, wonderin' how God can forgive somethin' as terrible as what we done to Billy Ray. I'll never forget that night as long as I live."

"I hope that, now, you and Regina can find peace," Jack said.

"Do you think Miss Rachael will tell anyone else?"

"She knows that she's protecting Jayden by keeping the secret. The difference is she's not carrying the weight of it all by herself anymore. She's free to become a carefree and happy child again, once we get past all this difficulty with her father, that is."

"Yer a good man, Mr. Jack. Thank you doesn't begin to cover all that you done for us."

"I can say the same to you, Mr. Gibbs. Knowing that you, Regina, and Jayden will be there to look after Rachael as she grows up gives me great comfort. Please pass this on to Regina for us. We want her to be at peace."

"Will do, Mr. Jack, and God bless you."

Jack tossed the phone on the bed and nodded. It was done. Mr. G and Regina could rest easy knowing that he and Stacy would keep their secret. Rachael was safe, at least from that quarter.

* * *

"Where is she?" Tyler roared as he paced back and forth across the breakfast room floor. His outburst startled Dillia so much that she splashed soup from the pot she was stirring onto the floor.

"I'm sorry, Mr. Tyler. I didn't mean to make a mess." She reached for a towel and quickly wiped it up.

"Did Pamela say anything to you before she left? Anything at all?'

"No, sir. Only—"

"Only what? Tell me!"

Dillia flinched in the face of his anger. She backed herself into the corner where the two counters met as he advanced. "They was carryin' suitcases. One for her and one for the boy. I thought you knew."

"Oh, no!" He ran down the hallway and took the stairs two at a time. When he reached the gallery, he climbed the attic steps and entered Pamela's apartment. He went straight to her closet and threw the doors open. Groaning, he stepped back into the bedroom and yanked open drawer after empty dresser drawer. Then he saw it, the folded note on the bed. "No!" he cried as he snatched it up. He read it, wadded it up, and tossed it away like she was doing to him.

He sank onto the bed and buried his face into her pillow. He could smell her, the light scent of her perfume. He loved the sight of her waking in the morning, her skin so soft and inviting, her hair tousled by sleep. How could he live without her? How could he face even one day knowing there was no one to blame but himself?

"Where's Jacob?" Cody said as he entered the room. "I want him to help me build a space ship."

"He's gone, Cody. Pamela and Jacob are gone."

"Does that mean it's just you and me again? I like it when it's just us."

"It won't be just us, Cody. Rachael's coming back."

"I don't want her to come back. I want her to die!"

Tyler didn't correct him. If it weren't for Rachael, Pamela would be downstairs right now, telling Dillia what to make for dinner.

"Is this really Rachael's house?" Cody said. "Jacob says that Rachael can fire us any time she wants. Did Rachael fire Pamela and Jacob? Is that why they left?"

"Rachael isn't the boss around here."

"I want to play, Daddy. Will you play with me?"

"Play?" Tyler pushed to his feet and tossed the pillow onto the bed. "Sure, I'll play. In fact, let's celebrate. Let's have a giant party that everyone will remember. Maybe they'll think twice about destroying a man's life the next time they get the chance."

"We're gonna have a party?" Cody said.

"Fireworks and everything," Tyler mumbled.

"Oh, boy! I like parties."

"Go get your jacket and meet me down by my truck." Tyler followed Cody down the attic stairs and then stopped to enter his bedroom. He took his gun from the dresser drawer, tucked it into his waistband, and grabbed his favorite Winchester rifle from the closet.

Why did everyone think they could trample upon his rights and he wouldn't fight back?

The facts, as he saw them, swirled in his mind like the darkest clouds of an approaching storm.

He yanked a knapsack from the shelf and loaded it with ammunition.

Pamela wasn't coming back, and Rachael preferred to live with strangers. He and Cody couldn't afford to live in the mansion without Rachael's money, and the attic renovations had put him into debt. What was he to do, go begging for his newspaper job and live in the trailer with Cody? He groaned as he slung the knapsack over his shoulder and headed for the stairs.

It might well come down to that, but he'd be damned if he'd stand quietly by while Jack Kendall robbed him of what was rightfully his!

CHAPTER THIRTY-FIVE

"Want to help me set the table for your aunt Emily and Steve?" Stacy said.

"I can't wait to see them!" Rachael said. "We had so much fun when we went to see Sleeping Beauty. She sure can sing pretty."

Stacy handed her the napkins. "I bet you were the most beautiful girl there."

"No, I wasn't. I saw lots of girls in pretty dresses. Some were just like mine. I didn't know that there were so many princesses in the world. Do you think they all have castles like I do?" She began placing the napkins next to the plates.

"You never know," Stacy said. "Do you like Steve?"

"Oh, yes! If I didn't already love Jayden, I might want to marry him."

Stacy laughed. "Wow, he must be wonderful, indeed. He certainly seems to make Emily happy."

"I think they love each other. I saw him kiss her on the cheek."

"Maybe Steve is Emily's Prince Charming."

Rachael giggled. "I want to visit Jayden. I miss him."

"Well, that might be difficult with your daddy upset with us right now. Maybe Jayden, Mr. G, and Regina could come here for a visit. Would you like that?"

"Can they come tonight?" Rachael said. "I have enough napkins."

"Not tonight, but we'll ask Jack if we can work that out

pretty soon."

The doorbell rang.

"Jack, they're here," Stacy called out. Rachael ran towards the door. "Wait! Don't open it, just in case it's not them." She caught up with Rachael and whisked her back into the hallway just as Jack approached the window and looked out.

"It's Steve and Emily," he said as he opened the door. "Welcome. Come on in."

Rachael ran into Emily's arms, and then Steve picked her up to receive a kiss on the cheek. Once they had exchanged greetings, everyone made their way into the den.

"Dinner is almost ready," Stacy said, "but let's settle in for a few minutes before we eat."

"How are you doing, Rachael? Can I see the back of your legs?" Emily said.

Rachael lifted her dress. "Daddy tried to make me go with him today, but Stacy and I hid in the closet."

"Today?" Emily said with surprise.

Jack cleared his throat. "Thankfully, we got a court order granting a delay on Tyler's custody suit. We don't know how long Rachael can stay, but we get to keep her a bit longer anyway."

"I don't want to live with Daddy. He's mean to me, and he threw my teddy bear out the window."

"Your teddy bear?" Emily said. "That is so sad. We'll have to get you another one."

"No, we won't. Uncle Jack and Stacy took me to look for him. We found him in a tree. Wanna see him?"

"Yes, I do. He sounds like a very important bear," Emily said as she stroked Rachael's cheek.

"I saw the news," Steve said, "but Emily missed it. We're happy to have a chance to come over tonight."

"Can I go get my bear, Uncle Jack? I want him to meet Auntie

Emily and Uncle Steve."

"Do you want me to go with you?"

"No, I can go. He's taking a nap on Stacy's couch." She spun on her toes and trotted towards the kitchen as everyone chuckled.

"She's so adorable," Steve said.

Emily glanced at him and blushed. "We have some news to share."

"Tell us," Stacy said.

Steve reached for Emily's hand and gave it a squeeze. "I've asked Emily to be my wife, and she's agreed."

"Oh, Emily," Stacy cried, "that's wonderful news!"

"You're just glowing with happiness," Jack said, and it was true.

Emily giggled. "That glow might be for another reason. We're expecting."

"Wow. Congratulations," Jack said. "You are just full of surprises tonight."

"We were already discussing our wedding plans when we found out," Steve said. "We're moving the wedding date up, of course, but there was never any question that we wanted a family together. In fact, we're hoping that Rachael will become part of our family, as well. I know Mr. Carrington has mentioned that to you."

"Yes, but I haven't discussed it with Rachael yet," Jack said. "Right now, it's all I can do just to keep her safe."

"Of course," Steve said.

Jack's phone rang. "Sorry, gotta take it. Excuse me a moment." He rose from his recliner and moved towards the kitchen.

Stacy hugged Emily. "I'm so happy for you. You're going to have your very own family. Is your momma pleased?"

"I haven't told her yet. We're going to drive over for a visit next weekend. I hate to say it, but it will be easier without Daddy there. He would've had a fit about the baby."

"I think he'd be at peace with it because I'm going to marry you and make you very, very happy."

Emily blushed. "I know Mama will be delighted to have another grandbaby."

"Well, let me see your ring," Stacy said.

Emily held up her hand, which sparkled with a one-karat, princess-cut diamond.

"Emily, that's gorgeous!"

"It is, isn't it? I never thought I'd have nothin' like…I mean, *anything* like this in my whole life."

"You're becoming quite the proper lady, I see. I'm very happy for you!"

"Steve is so good to me; I can hardly believe this is happening."

"I'm the lucky one," Steve said. "I've never met a more sweet or genuine person."

"See what I mean?" Emily said with a radiant smile. "We want to get married the last day of November, which means we only have a few weeks to get ready. Will you be my maid of honor?"

"Me?"

"Of course. If you hadn't taken me in, who knows what would've become of me? You saved my life."

"Oh, Emily, you've been such a blessing to us. I'd be delighted to be your maid of honor."

They laughed and embraced each other again.

"Excuse me," Jack said as he stepped in from the kitchen. "Stacy, can I talk to you for a second?"

"I'll be right back," she said, realizing that for Jack to call her out like this, something must be wrong.

"Stace, that was Regina. Tyler took Jayden and Cody someplace in his truck."

"Jayden? Why would she let Jayden go anywhere with Tyler? Did Tyler find out that Jayden followed him and Rachael up on the ridge?"

"It was Dillia who let him go. She told Regina that Tyler was taking the boys to a party. Regina isn't buying it," Jack said, "and neither am I. She and Mr. G are worried sick."

"I don't blame them. The way Tyler is, I'm surprised he even let Jayden inside his truck. He's up to something. What should we do?" Stacy said as she furrowed her brow and bit her lip.

"Let's ask Rachael if she knows anything about a party."

"I'll go ask her," Stacy said as she opened the back door.

* * *

Moments earlier...

Rachael ran down the concrete pathway that connected Stacy's apartment with Jack's house. She opened the gate and ran the last few steps to the side door of the garage and stepped inside.

"Hello, Rachael. I've been waiting for you."

"Daddy," she gasped as he stepped from behind Stacy's car.

"Jayden and Cody are waiting in the truck. We're going to a party."

Rachael glanced at the open door. "What party?"

Tyler inched forward. "It's a family party with fireworks and everything."

"I can't go; we have company."

Tyler lunged for her, scooping her up and covering her mouth as she screamed. He ran down the driveway and across the street where he had left the truck parked in the shadow of a huge magnolia tree. "Ouch! Stop kicking me or I'll beat you within an inch of your life!"

He shoved her into the truck and climbed in after her.

"Get out, Jayden. Run!"

When Jayden didn't move, Rachael looked back at her father who was pointing a gun in their direction.

"I kept him here, Daddy, just like you said. I had to hit 'em a time or two, but he's learnin' who's boss."

"Good job, Cody."

"Let me out, Daddy. I—"

"Be quiet, Rachael, I need to think!" He pushed her hard against the seat. "Now buckle up or I'll shoot your little friend." He hit the gas and roared off down the street.

Rachael reached for Jayden's hand and realized it was tied behind his back. "Where are you taking us?"

"Daddy says we're goin' to a party," Cody said, "but because of you, Jacob went away again, so he's not comin'."

"I didn't make Jacob go away; Daddy did. Pamela said so."

"Shut up, Rachael. Everybody be quiet and let me think!"

Rachael scooted as close to Jayden as she could.

"If you're gonna shoot Jayden, can I have his sword?" Cody said as he slid his hand along the leather scabbard at Jayden's right side. "Why not? He's not gonna need it."

"Uncle Jack gave me that sword," Jayden said. "I'm not giving it up without a fight."

"I said shut up! The next one who talks gets a whipping, and you know what that's like, don't you?"

Rachael's eyes widened, and the boys nodded.

* * *

"Jack!" Stacy said as she came running through the kitchen clutching Rachael's bear.

"What is it?" Jack said as he rose from the couch.

"Rachael's not upstairs. She's gone!"

"All right, everybody spread out. Look everywhere." Jack searched the back of the house, even his closet hiding place, but when they met in the kitchen a short time later, Rachael was not among them. "It has to be Tyler," he said. "He's taken Jayden, and now Rachael, too. I'm calling Kevin."

"What can we do?" Emily said as she wrung her hands.

Steve put his arm around her. "We'll find her, sweetheart. Don't worry."

A multitude of scenarios ran through Jack's mind as he waited for his call to go through. What if it wasn't Tyler? What if someone else had taken Rachael? If it was Tyler—

"Kevin! Rachael is missing." As Jack filled Kevin in on the details, the words turned sour in his mouth. Why had he allowed her to fetch the bear on her own? Her disappearance was his fault. If anything happened to her, he would never forgive himself.

"Where do you think he'll take them?" Kevin said.

"Where better than the mansion? There are lots of places to hide on that property."

"Stay put, Kendall. Keep everybody away from where the abduction occurred. If there's evidence there, we want to find it."

Jack winced as he realized that they might have already spoiled the crime scene. "We'll be here," he said. "Let me know if you hear anything at all. Promise me, Captain."

"I'll keep you posted."

"She means the world to me, Kevin. She really does." He turned to the small group. "We don't know where Tyler grabbed her, so we need to stay away from Stacy's apartment until they check out the area. It could be a long night."

"I think I'll take Emily home," Steve said. "It's not good for the baby for her to be upset. There's nothing we can do here but wait."

"Good idea," Jack said, "but you'll need to wait until after the police clear the crime scene. If you back over tire tracks, it could make them difficult to identify."

"Yes, of course. I should've thought of that," Steve said.

They settled into the den to wait.

The minutes ticked by so slowly that Jack glared at the clock. "If he hurts her, I'll kill him."

"Don't even think that," Stacy said. "He's got all three kids with him. Surely, he won't do anything terrible in front of Cody."

Jack rubbed his eyes, suddenly feeling as if he'd been awake for days. "You've got more faith in him than I do."

Car doors slammed.

They jumped to their feet and hurried to the front door. Two police cars with flashing lights sat in the driveway. Jack grimaced and opened the door.

An hour later, when everything that could be done had been done, the foursome stood on the porch and watched the last policeman drive away.

"Oh, Jack, are you sure?" Emily said. "I don't mind waiting."

"No, Steve is right," Stacy said. "Go home and get some rest. We'll call you as soon as we find her."

"But—"

"Go," Stacy said gently.

After waving goodbye to Steve and Emily, Jack said, "I'm done waiting. Let's ride out to the mansion and talk to Dillia. Maybe she can tell us something she didn't tell Regina, something that might give us a hint as to where he might have taken them."

"Let me grab my gun." She jogged along the sidewalk and faded into the shadows.

Jack wasn't thinking charitable thoughts towards Dillia as he retrieved his weapon and climbed into his truck.

Stacy joined him a few minutes later. "Let's go talk to Dillia."

* * *

Jack and Stacy were heading north on the Natchez Trace when Kevin called. "Yeah," Jack said, "we're here." He pressed the speaker button so Stacy could hear.

"Where are you?" Kevin said.

"Halfway to the mansion. What's going on?"

"Tyler's asking for you. He's holed up in his trailer out on Holly Bush Road. For some damn reason, he thinks you can get his girlfriend to answer her phone. He says if she won't talk to him, he's blowing himself and the children into a million pieces. The news media is all over it."

"Oh my God," Stacy said. "Do you really think he'll do it?"

"He's totally ruined his life," Jack said. "He's blown his chance to get Rachael back, and he might even lose Cody after this. If he realizes what he's done—"

"Think you can get ahold of his girlfriend?" Kevin said.

"I can try. What are you doing to get the kids out of there? Surely, we can work this out so that nobody gets hurt."

"Try to reach Pamela and call me back," Kevin said.

"Will do."

The call to Pamela went to voicemail. "Pamela, this is Jack. Tyler is holding Cody, Rachael, and Jayden hostage in his trailer. He's threatening to kill himself and the children if you don't talk to him. Call me back. It's a matter of life and death. Please, Pamela, call me." He ended the call and slammed his fist on the steering wheel. "Dammit! What is Tyler thinking?"

"He's not thinking; he's reacting. He's desperate."

"Why didn't I go with Rachael to get her teddy bear? If I had, she wouldn't be inside that trailer!"

"Why didn't I go with her? It does no good to blame ourselves! Rachael goes back and forth between our houses all the time. We didn't know Tyler was going to take her. He's so stupid to pull this kind of stunt! Pamela will never come back now. He must realize that. I'm so afraid he might go through with it," Stacy said.

Jack took hold of Stacy's hand just as his phone rang. He glanced at the ID and pushed the button.

"Oh my God, Jack! What can I do? I'll talk to him, but you know I can't come back, especially after this."

"Let me get the captain on the call with us. He'll know what to do. Hold on." He handed the phone to Stacy. "See if you can three-way us in."

Stacy dialed Kevin. "Hey, we've got Pamela on the line. She wants to know what she should say to Tyler."

"I'll commend you for this miracle later. Patch me in," Kevin said.

"Pamela, it's Stacy. I've got Captain Thomas on the line."

"Ms. Clarkston, we need your help. We need you to calm Tyler down so that he'll let the children come out of the trailer. If possible, we'd like him to lay down his weapons and come out, too. Think you can talk some sense into him?"

"I broke off our engagement over him beating Rachael. Should I lie and give him hope? Because, truthfully, there's no way in hell I'll ever go near him again."

"Say whatever you have to say to save their lives. You can't control the outcome. All we ask is that you try."

"I'll do my best."

"We're almost there," Jack said. "How do you want to handle this?"

"Since Tyler asked us to call you, I'll hang up and you can three-way him in. Wait until you get here, though, so I can listen in. I'll meet you in the driveway. We've got a spot cleared for you. Thank you, Ms. Clarkston. I don't have to tell you how important this is."

"Tyler has a lot of issues to work out, but underneath it all, I believe he's a good person."

"That's good to hear. Over and out," Kevin said.

"Pamela, you still there?" Jack said.

"What if I say the wrong thing, Jack? What if I push him over the edge?"

"It won't be your fault. Tyler is responsible for his own decisions."

"I know, but—"

"You did the right thing," Stacy said. "How could you stay with a man who beats a child like that? You have to protect Jacob."

Jack turned into the driveway, which glowed from the barrage of red and blue flashing lights.

Spotlights lit up the entire front side. Dozens of armed men surrounded the trailer. "Pamela, we're here. Hold on while I find Captain Thomas." He parked between two police vans and glanced over at Stacy. "This is it."

"I pray to God he's reasonable," Stacy said as they got out of the truck.

Jack spotted Captain Thomas as he made his way through the men. "Hey, Kevin. Have you talked to Tyler?"

"We told him you have Pamela on the phone. He's waiting to talk to her."

"Has he agreed to release the kids?" Stacy said.

"No, but we'll make that a condition of the connection and see what he says. Let's go over here, away from the commotion, so I can hear through the speakerphone."

Jack and Stacy followed him to the edge of the yard where the woods bordered the property.

"Get Tyler on the line," Kevin said.

* * *

Rachael and Jayden sat on the floor beneath the living room window where Tyler had commanded them to wait. As Tyler rustled about, Rachael loosened the knots behind Jayden's back.

"Daddy, there are police cars everywhere," Cody said, his eyes round with fright. "Are they going to arrest us?"

"You kids go to Cody's room. Go on, now. I want that door closed, and it had better stay closed until I come and get you! You got that, Cody?"

"Yes, sir."

"Go!" he yelled.

Rachael gasped and scurried after the boys down the hall.

Cody closed the door behind them. "This is my room, so don't touch anything unless I say so." He reached for Jayden's sword.

Jayden pulled his hands free from the rope and raised his fists.

"That's not how it works. This is my house, and I make the rules."

"I don't agree," Jayden said.

"Me either!"

"Shut up, Rachael. Nobody asked you." Cody opened the closet door and took out his stick sword, complete with cross bar handle. "I'll fight you, Jayden, with this! You're nothing but the help anyway."

"And Papa says you're ignorant," Jayden said. "Get somewhere safe, Rachael."

Rachael jumped up onto the bed and looked out the window. "The police have the trailer surrounded. Why are they here, Jayden? Are they going to arrest us?"

"Yeah, they're gonna arrest you for being stupid," Cody sneered as he struck Jayden's sword so hard that he dropped it. "Ha! Told you, you were stupid."

"You don't fight fair," Jayden cried as he reached for his sword, but Cody stabbed him in the stomach. "Ouch!" Jayden grimaced as he backed away.

"Jayden!" Rachael cried.

Cody laughed. "Pa says if you fight fair, you give your opponent a better chance of beating you, and I want to win!" He hit Jayden hard across the back as he bent again to retrieve his sword.

Jayden raised his sword with an upward swing that caught Cody unaware, and the fight was on. Rachael cheered for Jayden as he abandoned the formal technique that Jack had been teaching him and began defending himself as Cody did everything he could to stab and wound him with his stick.

"Stop, Cody, you're going to hurt him! This is supposed to be a game," Rachael said.

"This ain't no game, Rachael."

Their swords knocked against each other again and again.

"I don't want to hurt you, Cody. I think we should stop," Jayden said.

"You can't hurt me. I'm a great fighter," Cody shouted as he jabbed him in the shoulder.

"Ahhhh!" Jayden cried out in pain. "Okay, I've tried to warn you." He raised his sword as he jumped to the side and brought it down hard on Cody's head, knocking him to the floor.

"Did you kill him?" Rachael said as she jumped from the bed.

"I don't know. I just wanted him to stop fighting me." He slid his sword back into his scabbard. "Let's get out of here. Your pa could come back any minute!" He climbed onto the bed, opened the window, and pushed the screen out onto the ground. "Come on, climb through. We'll have to drop to the ground and run to the police."

"The police? Do you think they'll arrest us?" Rachael said.

"They helped us last time. Who do you trust more, the police or your pa?"

"The police," Rachael said.

Jayden stretched out his hand to pull her back onto the bed. "Hurry then."

Rachael climbed through the window, hung by her hands, and then dropped to the ground with Jayden right behind her. They grabbed for each other's hand and ran towards the lights.

"Come on, kids. We've got ya!" someone yelled from behind the lights.

Tears streamed down Rachael's cheeks as she and Jayden ran. When they ran past the lights, a group of men surrounded them. She glanced about, but she didn't know any of them.

"Uncle Jack!" Jayden cried.

She whirled around and saw Uncle Jack and Stacy racing towards them.

"How did you get out?" Jack said as he drew Rachael into his arms.

"It was Jayden," Rachael said. "He had to sword fight with Cody. He hit him on the head, and Cody fell down and didn't get up. That's when we climbed out the window."

"I didn't mean to make him fall down, but he kept stabbing me, and he hit me hard across my back. He wouldn't fight fair, so I had to do something to make him stop," Jayden said.

"He was wonderful, Uncle Jack. Jayden's my hero."

"He's my hero, too," Jack said, hugging them both one more time.

"Come on, I'm taking you back to the truck," Stacy said.

"Jack," Kevin called from twenty feet away.

"You guys go with Stacy. I'll see you in a bit," Jack said. "I'm so proud of you, Jayden! That's twice you've saved Rachael's life. You're an amazing young man; you know that?"

"Bye, Uncle Jack," they said at the same time, which made them giggle.

* * *

"You might want to have someone check on Jayden," Jack told Kevin. "He said Cody stabbed him with the stick and hit him over the back."

"I've already arranged for the medics to check them out, and I've assigned someone to watch over them afterwards. Right now, though, I need you *and* Stacy."

"Cody may be unconscious. Are you going to try to get him out?"

"Negative," Kevin said. "If his injuries need tending, that may be the leverage we need."

"Jack! Shouldn't I stay with the kids?" Stacy said as she came running from the ambulance, which sat parked at the far end of the driveway. "They said you needed me."

"We've still got an explosive situation, here, Miss Young," Captain Thomas said, his formal address reminding them of the seriousness of the situation. "Tyler seems to respond to you better than anyone else."

Jack handed the phone to Stacy. "Pamela, are you still there?" she said, closing her eyes as if to concentrate on where they left off.

"Yes. I'm here."

"Jayden and Rachael are safe. They escaped out a back window, but Cody is still inside."

"Thank heavens. Maybe Tyler will be more reasonable now that it's just him and Cody. He'd never do anything to hurt that boy."

"That's what we're hoping," Stacy said. "I'm going to get Tyler on the line now. See if you can get him to give up peacefully and come out."

"I'll try," Pamela said.

Stacy dialed and waited for Tyler to answer.

"It's about damn time," Tyler said.

Kevin motioned for Stacy to hand him the phone. "Tyler, this is Captain Thomas. We've got Pamela on the line. If you want to talk to her, we need an act of good faith on your part. We've got two of the children. Release Cody and we'll let you talk to Pamela."

"What? How the hell did they get out? Hold on."

A few uncomfortable minutes passed before he finally picked up the phone again.

"I found my son unconscious. He's awake now, but he has a huge knot on top of his head. It's lucky those little brats got out."

"Is that a threat?" Captain Thomas said.

"Let me talk to Pamela, or I'll blow this thing sky high!"

"If you want to talk to your girlfriend, set the boy free."

"How do I know you have her? Maybe you're lying," Tyler said.

Jack leaned in. "Tyler, it's Jack. He's telling you the truth. Pamela is waiting on the other line."

"Like I'm really gonna believe *you*?"

Stacy motioned for them to let her try. Jack handed her the phone. "Tyler, this is Stacy. How are you doing in there?"

"Stacy? Why do you work with that dude? He's trying to steal my daughter."

Jack glanced at Kevin. There was an edge to Tyler's voice, a vulnerability that hadn't been there the moment before.

"He's not trying to steal Rachael. He just wants to be sure that you're ready for her; that's all. Really, how are you doing in there? Do you need anything?"

"Cody's hungry, and I'm a little worried about the knot on his head. The last thing he remembers is sword fighting with Jayden."

"We can have the paramedics check him out," Stacy said.

"No. I'm not letting Jack anywhere near my son."

"Jack is pretty busy right now. I'll take care of him myself. You have my word on that," she said. "I've always kept my word to you, haven't I?"

"Yeah, but you're the only one," Tyler said.

Kevin motioned for her to keep going.

"Ask Cody if he wants some pizza," Stacy said.

"If you got pizza out there, bring it to the door. I'll give it to him in here," Tyler said.

Kevin shook his head.

"I can't do that, Tyler. The captain says if you want to talk to Pamela, Cody has to come out. I'll take good care of him until you're ready to come out, too."

"I ain't coming out and neither is Cody. To hell with you and your pizza!" He hung up.

"Wait!" Stacy said, but it was too late. She looked up at Kevin. "Did I say something wrong?"

Kevin shook his head. "You sounded like a pro. For a second there,

I thought he might do it."

"Now what?" Jack said.

His phone rang. "It's Tyler," Stacy said. "If I answer it, I'll lose Pamela."

"Answer it," Kevin said.

"Hey, Tyler."

"If you let me talk to Pamela, I'll let Cody come out. That's my final offer." He hung up again.

"It's a chance we have to take," Kevin said. "Get Pamela on the line."

Stacy dialed. "Hey, Pamela, sorry we lost you. Tyler said he'd let Cody go if you'll talk to him, so I'm going to get Tyler on the phone now. Are you ready?"

"I don't know what to say," she said.

"Just do your best. Hold on." She dialed Tyler again.

"Well?" Tyler said.

"I've got Pamela on the line. Are you going to keep your promise about releasing Cody?"

"I'll set him free. Put her on."

Stacy connected the calls. "Pamela, are you there?"

"I'm here," Pamela said.

"Pamela, why did you leave without talking to me first? We could've worked it out. The news is only telling one side of the story, and they're not telling it right," Tyler said.

"It was a mistake, Tyler. I should've talked to you first. I realized that after I left. I'm willing to hear what you have to say. I miss you."

"That's the second time you've left. How can I trust you? How do I know you won't do it again?"

"I know it wasn't right. I was upset over the news report. I was afraid you might hit Jacob."

"Have I ever even yelled at Jacob?"

"No, you are wonderful with the boys."

"That's right. I'm a damn good father, no matter what anybody says."

"I know you are. It was wrong of me to leave like that. Will you forgive me?"

"I can't trust you, Pamela. I can't trust anyone," he said, his voice breaking. "I thought Jack wanted to help me, but all he wants is Rachael's money."

"That's not true, Tyler. Jack is the reason you have Rachael back. He and Stacy helped you find her."

"And he ruined my mother's reputation in the process!"

"Tyler, please come out so we can go home. It's late, and the boys need to go to bed."

"Where are you? Are you nearby?"

"Close enough to be in your arms tonight. Come out of there. Nobody needs to get hurt."

"How do I know you're not lying?" Tyler said. "How do I know that this is not some stupid trick to make me come out?"

"You know me better than that," Pamela said. "I speak my mind. Don't you want to marry me?"

He choked off a sob. "Of course, I do, but my life is a mess now. I can't undo what I've done. The police are here. They'll take me to jail if I come out."

"Make a deal with them. Show them you're willing to be reasonable by letting Cody go free."

"That's what I thought. You're just like them! I'm blowin' this damn thing up. Nobody cares anyway."

"I care, Tyler. I want to help you make this right, but I can't do that if you keep threatening to blow yourself up. You've got to make some concessions."

"I said I'd set Cody free, and I'll keep my word. This is my mess; I'll deal with it myself. He's innocent, though he's the only one who is. You hear that, Jack? I know you're listening. You're partly to blame for this. You and your damn greed. Get married and have your own damn kids. You have no right to steal mine!"

"So, what are you going to do, Tyler?" Pamela said. "Will you lay down your weapons and come out? That's the only way we can get back together and move on with our lives. We've got a wedding to plan, remember?"

He sighed. "That seems impossible now. I need to think this through. I love you, Pamela. I've loved you from the first day we met."

"Tyler?" Pamela said. "Tyler? He's gone."

"Hold on," Stacy said. "I'll try to call him back." She dialed his number, but he didn't answer.

"Text him," Jack said. "Tell him he needs to keep his end of the bargain and let Cody go free."

Kevin nodded.

Stacy clicked over to Pamela. "Stay near your phone. We'll call you back." Switching to the texting window, she typed the message and hit the send button.

"Let's get into position," Kevin said.

Jack and Stacy followed him back to the center of the command group and stayed out of the way while he talked with the SWAT team, the FBI, and the local police units. Jack felt sick with dread. He didn't see this ending well and wondered what move Tyler would make next.

The front door opened, and Tyler shoved Cody onto the porch.

"Don't make me go, Daddy. I wanna stay with you!" Cody cried.

"It's all right, son. They aren't gonna hurt you; I promise."

"But I don't wanna go."

"You heard him," Tyler yelled. "He doesn't wanna go." He pulled Cody back inside and slammed the door.

"Dammit!" Kevin said. He picked up a megaphone. "Tyler, let the boy go as you agreed. We kept our end of the deal; now you keep yours. We've got you surrounded. Don't make us come in after him."

Jack's phone vibrated in his hand. It was a text from Tyler. "He wants to know if he's going to jail."

"Ask him if he's going to send Cody out," Captain Thomas said.

Stacy took the phone and typed the message. A text came back. "He wants you to answer his question."

"All right," Kevin said. "Tell him we have to take him in, but if he sends Cody out now, it'll go a lot easier on him."

A few moments later, the front door opened and Cody appeared in the doorway, but he looked back into the house. He was crying. He took a few hesitant steps and shielded his eyes from the lights.

Jack knelt beside one of the police officers and called to him. "Come on, Cody. Come on."

Cody took a few more steps and looked back at the house.

"Go on, son. Remember what I told you," Tyler yelled from the house.

Cody took several more steps and stopped again.

"Come on, Cody. You're almost here," Jack said, which got him moving again. When Cody was about five yards from the firing line, Jack stepped forward to greet him. "Come on, Cody. It's me, Jack. You're safe. I've got you." He held out his arms and Cody ran towards him.

A shot rang out.

Jack grabbed Cody and fell back.

"Jack!" Stacy screamed.

A barrage of high-powered rifle fire answered the attack, and then a massive explosion lit up the sky and shook the ground beneath them. Jack was aware of Cody's weight on top of him; he heard men yelling; he saw falling debris and fire; and then everything faded and there was peace.

CHAPTER THIRTY-SIX

Beep. Beep. Beep.

Jack opened his eyes and glanced around. He didn't like what he saw, so he shut them again. He was in a hospital. He tried to remember why.

Fire, trees, burning.

"Jack, can you hear me? It's me, Stacy."

Jack opened his eyes as Stacy took hold of his left hand. "Tyler?" he said, but his mouth was so dry that he barely heard it himself.

"You certainly gave us a scare. You've been out of it for two days."

"Water."

"I can only wet your lips." She dipped a Q-tip into a cup and rubbed it over his lips. "Better?"

He gave a slight nod. "Where's Cody?"

"Can I get you anything? Do you want me to call the nurse?"

She was distressed. He could see it. "What aren't you telling me?" His tongue felt thick and heavy.

She turned to fold the blanket at the foot of the bed. "There'll be plenty of time to talk about this once you're well."

"Tell me."

Tears filled her eyes. "Tyler shot Cody in the back. The bullet went straight through his heart and hit you. Another quarter inch and it would've pierced your lung."

Her words ricocheted through his brain. "Are you sure? Why would he do that?"

She sniffed and wiped her eyes. "We don't know. Maybe he was aiming for you. Maybe he didn't want Cody to live in the world without him. Who knows what Tyler was thinking?"

"Does Rachael know?"

"She saw the explosion, of course, but we didn't tell her the outcome. She keeps asking if the police arrested her daddy and Cody. I've been telling her that I'll find out and let her know. I'm afraid she'll see something on the news, so we don't let her watch television. Emily is staying at the house with her until you come home. We think it's best if you tell her."

He tried to choke back tears, but he couldn't stop them. "Tyler had his whole life ahead of him. He had Rachael and Pamela. He was wealthy. He was living at the mansion. What did he want that he didn't already have? And why would he kill Cody?"

Stacy started crying, too. "I've tried to figure it out, but there's no way to know. Did we say the wrong thing? Was there more we could have done? It's such a horrible, tragic waste. Emily is the only family Rachael has left." She cried so hard that she gasped for breath.

Jack wanted to comfort her, but he couldn't contain his own grief. He cried for Tyler, he cried for Cody, but most of all, he cried for Rachael. Stacy turned her face away and rested her head on his chest. Gradually, as their tears subsided, the only sound in the room was the steady beeping of the medical monitors.

CHAPTER THIRTY-SEVEN

Stacy stared straight ahead, numb as she slowed to a stop at a busy intersection. It had been an incredibly difficult afternoon, and she was glad it was over.

A car honked; the light was green.

She had helped Emily plan the quiet memorial service for Tyler and Cody, since Cody was her nephew, but her mother and uncle had thought it best not to come. Several people attended from the newspaper where Tyler had worked, but he didn't seem to have any close friends. It was sad in the sense that there wasn't anyone there to celebrate Tyler's life. She had thought Pamela might come, but she didn't, not that she blamed her. It would've been terribly upsetting for Jacob to see Cody in a casket. Of course, there was no open casket for Tyler. They had found very little of his remains.

She wiped fresh tears from her cheek. She would never forget the sight of little Cody lying there. He was so young, and though he was cruel to Rachael and Jayden, she had to believe that even that was Tyler's doing. Cody's future had been stolen from him, and for what? A broken love affair? She certainly couldn't imagine Tyler killing himself over losing Rachael. She was angry, but what good did it do? The brightest spot in the entire day was seeing how supportive Steve had been for Emily. He was clearly her rock, and she was happy for Emily.

Rachael had stayed at the hospital with Jack, which was where she was headed now. Everyone had agreed that it wouldn't be good for Rachael to attend the funeral. Jack would tell her what happened when the time was right, or at least some version of what had happened. She was far too young to know that Tyler had killed Cody, whether by accident or on purpose, and then had killed himself, too. Poor Rachael. She desperately wanted to believe that the troubles in her life were over.

She turned into the hospital parking lot and gave herself a mental shake. She didn't want Jack and Rachael to see how upset she was. She was still worried about Jack, though he was mending well enough. He would soon come home, but it would take several more weeks for him to recover completely. She needed to get busy on casework; their unpaid bills were piling up. Her stomach knotted at the thought of it, but she pushed it out of her mind. It was too much to think about on an already stressful day.

When she reached Jack's room, she peeked inside and saw Rachael sleeping on the bed beside Jack, curled at his side, under a blanket. They looked so sweet that she took out her cell phone and took a picture.

Jack opened his eyes. "Hey, when did you get here?"

"Just now. Is she okay right there?"

"She's fine. How did it go? Are you all right?"

She dropped into a chair and despite her determination not to burden him with her feelings, she told him everything she could think of, including how sad it was to see Cody lying there, and how angry she was at Tyler.

"I'm sorry I wasn't there for you," he said. "You've been so incredibly brave through all of this. I'm very proud of you."

"Don't say that. You'll make me cry," she said, swiping at a tear as it formed.

"I'm happy to hear that Steve is so supportive of Emily," he added.

"They're cute together. He's so attentive. It almost makes me believe in romance again."

Jack chuckled. "Glad you're not a complete cynic. It would be criminal to waste all those gorgeous curves."

Stacy gave him a dirty look, but she didn't mean it. Jack always made her feel better, and she loved him for that. "I agree," she teased. "In fact, I'm thinking about asking Emily if Steve has a brother."

He chuckled again. "You do that."

Rachael stirred and opened her eyes. "Hi, Stacy. Can we go home now?"

"Pretty soon. Did you have a good nap?"

She looked up at Jack. "Did we sleep, Uncle Jack?"

"We did. You've been out for over an hour."

"Oh." She climbed off the bed and went around to where Stacy was sitting. "I'm hungry."

"Let's go home and make some dinner," Stacy said as she reached to smooth Rachael's hair.

"When can you come home, Uncle Jack?"

"They haven't told me yet, but the sooner, the better. I miss Stacy's cooking."

"I'll bet you do," Stacy said. "Hospital food is a major incentive to get well soon. Let's go, little one. Put your shoes on." Stacy leaned over and kissed Jack's cheek. "I miss you."

He lifted his chin and glanced down her blouse as she pulled away. "Wanna kiss me again?" he teased.

"You are incorrigible."

"I'm going stir crazy in here. Glad you miss me, though. You mean the world to me."

"Yeah? You're pretty special to me, too. Ready, Rachael?"

"Bye, Uncle Jack. I love you."

"Bye, sweetie."

Stacy winked at him as she stepped out into the hall.

CHAPTER
THIRTY-EIGHT

Jack checked his watch again; the ceremony was in little more than an hour. Stacy had promised to arrive early; she was Emily's maid of honor. As he sorted through the mail at his desk, waiting for Stacy and Rachael to appear, a jumble of emotions distracted him. He was pleased for Emily and Steve, of course, but it meant that his time with Rachael would soon come to an end. They planned to begin the adoption process soon after the wedding so that Rachael could settle into the family before the baby was born. He hadn't told Rachael yet, nor had he told her about Tyler and Cody; he'd only been home a few days. Rachael was excited about being Emily's flower girl, and he didn't want to do anything to take away from Emily's special day.

He opened another medical bill and winced. His finances were a huge concern. He'd been ordered to take it easy for another six to eight weeks, but he doubted he'd be able to wait that long, not with the stack of bills he had on his desk. He had received another of Rachael's fifteen-thousand-dollar maintenance checks, but he'd already deposited it into her personal account. It didn't belong to him. He'd have to get by some other way. He was thinking, however, about taking Rachael somewhere special before she went to live with Steve and Emily, but he hadn't decided where.

"We're ready," Stacy said as she sailed into the room wearing a pink satin dress that draped off both shoulders and dipped low in the front to display the full swell of her breasts.

"Wow. Are you the bride?"

"Very funny."

Rachael twirled in a circle to allow the full skirt of her ivory-colored dress to swirl around her legs. "What about me, Uncle Jack?"

"Oh, *you* must be the bride."

"No, silly. I'm the flower girl. Auntie Emily is the bride!"

"Well, you both look fabulous. Shall we go?" He offered his arms. Stacy took one and Rachael giggled as she took the other. Rachael chatted happily all the way to the church where she and Stacy rushed off to help Emily with her last-minute preparations. Jack lingered outside for a few minutes, admiring the intricately carved moldings and stained glass windows. It was a picturesque little church, situated on a hillside, bordered on three sides by thick woods. He could see the overgrown entrance to a cemetery off in the distance and thought of Cody and Tyler. Marshaling his emotions, he stepped into the chapel and paused to sign the guest book and pick up a memento basket for the girls.

It was a small sanctuary, yet comfortable and beautifully appointed. The seats were filling quickly, and judging by the suits, a contingent of Steve's friends from Alister, Emerson & Maxwell made up nearly half the crowd. He looked towards the altar and smiled. Emily had been excited for him to see the ivory roses and white and pink Calla Lilies she had chosen. She had made him repeat the names until he remembered. He spotted them around the podium. They were lovely.

"Ain't this the prettiest church you ever did see?"

Jack turned. "Hello, Leeann. It's good to see you. Hey, Tommy Lee." He extended his hand towards the big man, but Tommy Lee drew him into a bear hug and patted him on the back.

Jack held his breath and grimaced with pain.

"We're right proud of our girl," Tommy Lee said with a grin. "She done real good, catchin' herself a man like Steve. He'll take real good care of our Emily."

"They make a wonderful couple. Wait till you see Rachael. She looks adorable."

Leeann's face brightened. "I'm so excited to see my grandbaby. It's hard to believe there ain't nobody to keep us apart no more."

"It's time that this family had some joy for a change," Jack said. "I hear you'll soon have another grandchild to love as well."

Tommy Lee grinned. "I'm hopin' for a boy since we lost little Cody, but we'll love us a girl all the same."

"How are you doing in Arkansas? Have the townspeople been accepting?" Jack said.

"They really have," Leeann said with a nod. "Once they knew we didn't kidnap Rachael, everyone's gone out of their way to be kind. We've had neighbors droppin' off groceries and stoppin' by to mow the yard. It's been real nice."

"I'm glad to hear it," Jack said.

"We been meanin' to thank you for all you done. You turned our whole world around. We're real appreciative."

"You're welcome."

"Well, I guess we should take our seats. We get to sit up front," Leeann said with a smile.

"She's excited on account of it's her first child to have a proper wedding and all, what with how Sarah and Tyler got hitched by the Justice of the Peace."

Jack rubbed his jaw. "May it be the first in a long line of happy events to come."

Tommy Lee reached into the pocket of his rented suit jacket and pulled out a flask. "I'll drink to that." After taking several gulps, he offered it to Jack, who eyed it with a twist of his lips.

"Gotta pass on that, Tommy Lee. Your moonshine is more than I can handle."

"Then I'll drink it for ya."

"You do that."

Jack spent the next several minutes meeting people and scouting out the attractive women. To his disappointment, he tired easily, which reminded him that complete recuperation was still a long way off. He took a seat and continued to watch the people. He wondered if he might see Mr. Carrington.

A few minutes later, Josh and his wife, Elizabeth, entered the church. It was interesting to watch them together. Josh took on a sophisticated arrogance when he was with Elizabeth, so different from the timid young man he'd been when he had helped him and Stacy solve Daniel's murder a little more than a year or so before. He caught Josh's eye and waved.

The organ music began, and a hush fell over the sanctuary as the minister made his way to the front. Steve entered the chapel through a side door and took his place before the minister. He was a handsome groom in his light gray tux. As he gazed towards the back of the church, the music changed, and everyone turned to see the bridal procession. Rachael came out first, walking like the regal young princess she was, tossing rose petals to the left, and then to the right with each measured step. She was happy and smiling, caught up in the excitement of Emily's big day.

Stacy followed, more sexy than regal, but that was Stacy, and he liked her just the way she was. He winked at her as she passed by, and her smile got bigger.

Next came Emily, gorgeous in her elegant gown of satin and lace. An exquisite train of four or five feet trailed behind her as she walked down the aisle. Since her father couldn't be with her, Emily had decided to forego the custom of having someone give her away, in honor of Billy Ray. When she reached the front of the church, Stacy handed her bouquet to Rachael and moved to spread Emily's train, which made for beautiful pictures as the bride and groom exchanged their vows.

It was perfect.

After the ceremony, Jack's first order of business was to make sure Leeann saw her granddaughter. Rachael didn't remember her, but she warmed up soon enough, especially when she learned that Mammaw Leeann had given her the locket with her mother's picture in it. Tommy Lee was another story. Though he tried everything he could to charm her, Rachael kept her distance. Jack suspected that he might remind her of Billy Ray. They did resemble one another, especially in size. He stayed nearby in case she needed him.

After dinner, sometime after the dancing began, Jack decided to take Rachael home. Stacy, of course, decided to stay. She had danced with several of Steve's friends from the law firm, and it was difficult to watch. He didn't want to feel jealous, but he did.

He put Rachael to sleep on his couch for the night and went to bed wishing he were ten years younger.

* * *

Jack sat working at his desk early the next morning.

"You hungry?" Stacy said as she entered from the kitchen.

"I didn't expect you to be up for hours yet," he said without looking up.

"Neither did I, but I couldn't sleep in for some reason."

"Hmmm," he said.

"Hmmm," she said.

"You looked like you were having fun when I left."

"I *do* love to dance. There was one guy there I really wanted to dance with, but he didn't ask me."

"I'm surprised you didn't ask him. You're not exactly shy."

"I guess I wanted him to ask me."

She sat on the couch, but he resisted looking over. "Maybe he has a girlfriend."

"Maybe he's not interested."

"The man would have to be an idiot not to be interested," he scoffed.

"Is that supposed to be a compliment?"

He finally glanced over, and, just as he suspected, the smile on her face told him that she was enjoying herself at his expense. Still, he said it anyway. "Stacy, you looked irresistibly gorgeous last night, but that's nothing new. You light up every room you enter. What's surprising is that the more time someone spends with you, the more beautiful you become, inside and out. Any man would be beyond fortunate to have you at his side."

"Then why didn't you ask me to dance?"

"Me? You were talking about me?"

"Of course, silly. Every other man there couldn't wait to get his hands on me, which I found quite unfulfilling, actually. I know what they wanted, and it wasn't to hear what I think, or understand how I feel about things. You're the one who cares about that. Nope, I wanted to dance with you. So, the next time we're at a wedding, ask me to dance before you leave me to the wolves, okay?" She got up from the couch and headed for the kitchen.

He stared after her completely unsure about what had just happened, which, he figured, was exactly what she intended. He just loved how women's minds worked. He turned back to his desk but found it impossible to concentrate. Why didn't he ask her to dance? He was a great dancer.

He sliced open another envelope and pulled out a check. "Holy crap!"

"What's wrong?" Stacy said from the kitchen.

"Come look at this."

Stacy came in and whisked the check out of his hand. "Holy crap! What's this for?"

"If that's my monthly maintenance check, it's a mistake! There are two extra zeros in that number. I'm calling Mr. Carrington right now." His receptionist answered. "Good morning. This is Jack Kendall. Is Mr. Carrington in?"

"Can't we just deposit it without asking?" Stacy said.

"Are you kidding? The last thing I need is for them to discover the mistake and come looking for the money. I don't even want to be tempted. Yes. Good morning, Mr. Carrington. I'm calling because there seems to have been a mistake in your accounting department. I just received a check for—" He nodded. "Yes, that's the amount. Do you want me to shred it, or send it back in the mail?"

Stacy made a face and dropped onto the couch.

"You can't be serious. Whatever for?" He glanced over at Stacy. "I don't know, maybe six to eight more weeks, but—"

Stacy got up and motioned for him to let her listen.

"I appreciate that, but Stacy was in every bit as much danger as I was. In fact, she's been at my side throughout this entire process. She helped me find Rachael. She helps take care of her. In fact, she and Emily have looked after her the whole time I was in the hosp—" He rolled his eyes. "Yes, of course, you're aware of that."

"What? You sent her a check also?" He met Stacy's eyes as hers widened. She ran for the kitchen. "That's very kind of you, but that's not why we do what we do for Rachael."

She reappeared with her own stack of mail and began shuffling through the envelopes.

"No, but I plan to tell her today. How long do you think the adoption process will take? We would like to take Rachael somewhere special before she moves into her new home."

Stacy pulled an envelope out of the stack and tossed the others aside. She ripped it open. "Oh my gosh, Jack! Oh my gosh! Between us, we have a million dollars!"

Jack nodded. "Stacy just opened her check. We're incredibly

grateful. Do you realize what would have happened if your fax hadn't come through when it did, or if Jayden hadn't knocked Cody unconscious and gotten Rachael out of that trailer?"

Jack threw his eraser into Stacy's lap to catch her attention. "You've sent a check for Jayden and his family, too? I'm so pleased. Jayden is such a bright boy. He deserves every happiness this life can bring... Yes, we've all played our parts, haven't we? It's incredibly rewarding to think that from here on out Rachael's life will be happy."

"I'm sorry, what was that?" Jack glanced at Stacy as his lopsided smile appeared. "Yes, sir. We'd love to play an active role in Rachael's life after the adoption. You have no idea how much that means to us."

He laughed. "Yes, of course, you do. Thanks again, Mr. Carrington. Have a truly wonderful day."

COMING SOON

Operation Commander in Chief
The third installment in the
Underdog Detective Series

In an era of unprecedented disrespect towards the President of the United States, Mississippi President Hunter Logan fights to stop the rising number of domestic terrorist attacks. Stalwart in his determination, nothing rattles him until treason strikes at the very heart of his family. Suddenly, the President isn't sure whom he can trust.

Capitalizing on perceived vulnerability, pressure intensifies, even from those he had counted on as allies. President Logan turns to his rich Southern connections, who are as diverse and perverse as they are powerful, and he means to use them to conduct his own investigation. In Washington, betrayal is expected, but this has become personal, and he'll be damned if he'll allow anyone to destroy his legacy.

Detective Jack Kendall receives a call to duty from the President of the United States, and he has no choice but to accept. As the investigation unfolds, the stakes rise to staggering heights. Millions of lives are at risk, including that of the President, who has already survived two assassination attempts.

When Jack and his assistant, Stacy Young, uncover an international web of deception, they face the ultimate penalty. With nothing left to lose, they fight for freedom, country, and good old Southern values, which they are determined to champion, even in the face of death...

...which turns out to be infinitely more horrifying than they expected.

ACKNOWLEDGMENTS

As a busy attorney, it is a challenge to find time to write, and I couldn't do it without the support of those around me. Many thanks to my ever-supportive friends and family, who are unceasingly patient as I write my stories. I appreciate your encouragement more than you know. Thanks also to Wendy Carter, whose writing assistance, hard work, and dedication help me tell my stories.